ROSAMUNDE PILCHER

SEPTEMBER
ANOTHER VIEW
THE EMPTY HOUSE

Rosamunde Pilcher

Hodder & Stoughton

September copyright 1990 by Robin Pilcher, Fiona Pilcher, Mark Pilcher
and Philippa Imrie
Another View copyright 1968 by Rosamunde Pilcher
The Empty House copyright 1973 by Rosamunde Pilcher

September first published in Great Britain in 1990 by
New English Library

Another View first published in Great Britain in 1990 by
Hodder and Stoughton Ltd

The Empty House first published in Great Britain in 1990 by
Hodder and Stoughton Ltd

This collected volume first published in Great Britain in 1996 by
Hodder and Stoughton
A division of Hodder Headline PLC

ISBN 0 340 68026 1

Printed and bound in Great Britain by
Mackays of Chatham PLC, Chatham, Kent

Hodder and Stoughton Ltd
A Division of Hodder Headline PLC
338 Euston Road
London NW1 3BH

SEPTEMBER

Contents

MAY

1

Tuesday the Third

In early May, the summer came, at last, to Scotland.
Winter had clung, with steely fingers, for far too long,
refusing to relinquish its cruel grip. All through April,
bitter winds had blown from the north-west, tearing the
first blossom from the wild geynes, and burning brown
the yellow trumpets of the early daffodils. Snow frosted
the hilltops and lay deep in corries, and the farmers,
despairing of fresh grazing, tractored the last of their
feed out to the barren fields where lowing stock huddled
in the shelter of the drystone walls.

Even the wild geese, usually gone by the end of March,
were late in returning to their arctic habitats. The last of
the skeins had disappeared around the middle of April,
honking away north into the unknown skies, flying so
high that the arrowhead formations looked no more
substantial than cobwebs drifting in the wind.

And then, overnight, the fickle Highland climate relented. The wind veered around to the south, bringing
with it the balmy breezes and the soft weather that the
rest of the country had been enjoying for weeks, along
with the scent of damp earth and growing things. The
countryside turned a sweet and verdant green, the wild
white cherry trees recovered from their battering, took
heart, and spread their branches in a mist of snowflake
petals. All at once, cottage gardens burgeoned into
colour – yellow winter-flowering jasmine, purple crocus,

11

and the deep blue of grape hyacinths. Birds sang, and the sun, for the first time since last autumn, brought a real warmth with it.

Every morning of her life, rain or shine, Violet Aird walked to the village to collect, from Mrs Ishak's super-market, two pints of milk, *The Times*, and any other small groceries and supplies needed for the sustenance of one elderly lady living on her own. Only sometimes, in the depths of winter, when the snow piled in deep drifts, and the ice became treacherous, did she eschew this exercise, on the principle that discretion was the better part of valour.

It was not an easy walk. Half a mile down the steep road, between fields which had once been the parkland of Croy, Archie Balmerino's estate, and then the stiff half-mile climb home again. She had a car, and could perfectly well have made the journey in that, but it was one of her convictions that, as old age crept up on you, once you started to use the car for short journeys, then you were in dire danger of losing the use of your legs.

For all the long months of winter, she had had to bundle up in layers of clothing for this expedition. Thick boots, sweaters, waterproof jacket, scarf, gloves, a wool-len hat pulled well down over her ears. This morning, she wore a tweed skirt and a cardigan and her head was bare. The sun lifted her spirits and made her feel energetic and young again, and being uncluttered by extraneous garments reminded her of childhood satisfac-tion when black woollen stockings were abandoned and one felt the pleasant, draughty sensation of cool air on bare legs.

The village shop, this morning, was busy, and she had to wait for a little to be served. She did not mind, because it meant that there was time to chat with other customers, all of whom were familiar faces; marvel at the weather; ask after somebody's mother; watch a small boy choose, with painful deliberation, a packet of Dolly Mixtures, which he proceeded to pay for with his own money. He was not hurried. Mrs Ishak stood with gentle patience, while he made up his mind. When he had finally done this, she put the Dolly Mixtures into a little paper bag and took the money from him.

"You must not eat them all at once, or you will lose all your teeth," she warned him. "Good morning, Mrs Aird."

"Good morning, Mrs Ishak. And what a lovely day it is!"

"I could not believe it when I saw the sun shining." Usually Mrs Ishak, exiled to these northern climes from the relentless sunshine of Malawi, was bundled in cardigans and kept a paraffin heater behind the counter, over which she huddled whenever there was a moment of quiet. This morning, however, she looked much happier. "I hope it will not become cold again."

"I don't think so. Summer is here. Oh, thank you, my milk and my paper. And Edie wants some furniture polish and a roll of paper towel. And I think I'd better take half a dozen eggs."

"If your basket is too heavy, I can send Mr Ishak up to your house in his motorcar."

"No, I can manage, thank you very much."

"It is a lot of walking you are doing."

Violet smiled. "But just think how good it is for me."

Laden, she set off once more for home, for Pennyburn. Down the pavement, past the rows of low cottages, with windows blinking reflected sunlight, and doors standing open to the fresh warm air; then through the gates of Croy and up the hill again. This was a private road, the back driveway of the big house, and Pennyburn stood halfway up it, to one side and surrounded by steep fields. It was approached by a neat lane bordered by clipped beech hedges, and it was always something of

13

a relief to reach the turning and to know that one did not have to climb any further.

Violet changed her basket, which was becoming heavy, from one hand to the other, and made plans as to how she would spend the rest of her day. This was one of Edie's mornings for helping Violet, which meant that Violet could abandon her house and instead get busy in the garden. Lately, it had been too cold for even Violet to garden, and things had become neglected. The lawn was looking tired and mossy after the long winter. Perhaps she should run her spiker over it and give it a bit of air. After that, a huge pit of carefully nurtured compost needed to be barrowed and spread over her new rose-bed. The prospect filled her with satisfying joy. She could not wait to get down to work.

Her step quickened. But then, almost at once, she saw the unfamiliar car parked outside her front door, and knew that the garden, for the moment, would have to wait. A visitor. Such irritation. Who had come to call? Who was Violet going to have to sit with and talk to, instead of being allowed to get on with her digging?

The car was a neat little Renault and betrayed no clue as to its owner. Violet went into the house through the kitchen door, and there found Edie at the tap and filling the kettle.

She dumped the basket on the table. "Who is it?" she mouthed, making pointing gestures with her forefinger.

Edie, too, kept her voice down. "Mrs Steynton. From Corriehill."

"How long has she been here?"

"Only a moment. I told her to wait. She's in the sitting room. She wants a wee word." Edie resumed her normal voice. "I'm just making you both a cup of coffee. I'll bring it in when it's ready."

With no excuse or possible escape route, Violet went to find her visitor. Verena Steynton stood at the window of the sun-filled sitting room, gazing out at Violet's garden. As Violet came through the door, she turned.

14

"Oh, Violet, I am sorry. I feel embarrassed. I told Edie I'd come back another time, but she swore you'd be home from the village in a moment or two."

She was a tall and slender woman around forty, and invariably immaculately and elegantly turned out. Which instantly set her apart from the other local ladies, who were, for the most part, busy country women, with neither the time nor the inclination to bother too much about their personal appearance. Verena and her husband Angus were newcomers to the neighbourhood, having lived at Corriehill for a mere ten years. Before that, Angus had worked as a stockbroker in London, but having made his pile, and tiring of the rat race, he had bought Corriehill, ten miles distant from Strathcroy, moved north with his wife and his daughter Katy, and cast about, locally, for some other, and hopefully less demanding, occupation. He had ended up taking over a run-down timber business in Relkirk, and over the years had built this up into a lucrative and thriving concern.

As for Verena, she too was something of a career woman, being heavily involved with an organisation called Scottish Country Tours. During the summer months, this company shuttled busloads of American visitors hither and yon, and arranged for them to stay, as paying guests, in a selection of well-vetted private houses. Isobel Balmerino had been roped into this exercise, and hard labour it was, too. Violet could not think of a more exhausting way of making a bit of money.

However, from the social point of view, the Steynton family had proved themselves a true asset to the community, being both friendly and unassuming, generous with their hospitality, and always willing to give time and effort to the running of fêtes, gymkhanas, and various other fund-raising events.

Even so, Violet could not begin to imagine why Verena was here.

"I'm glad you stayed. I would have been sorry to miss you. Edie's just making us a cup of coffee."

"I should have telephoned, but I was on my way to Relkirk and suddenly thought, much better to drop in and take my chance. On the spur of the moment. You don't mind?"

"Not in the least," Violet fibbed robustly. "Come and sit down. I'm afraid the fire's not been lighted yet, but . . ."

"Oh, heavens, who needs a fire on a day like this? Isn't it blissful to see the sun?"

She settled herself on the sofa and crossed her long and elegant legs. Violet, less gracefully, lowered herself into her own wide-lapped chair.

She decided to come straight to the point. "Edie said you wanted a word with me."

"I just suddenly thought . . . you'd be the very person to help."

Violet's heart sank, envisaging some bazaar, garden-opening, or charity concert, which she was about to be asked to knit tea-cosies or sell tickets for, or to declare open.

"Help?" she said faintly.

"No. Not so much help, as give advice. You see, I'm thinking of throwing a dance."

"A *dance*?"

"Yes. For Katy. She's going to be twenty-one."

"But how can *I* advise you? I haven't done such a thing for longer than I can remember. Surely, you'd be better to ask somebody a little more up to date. Peggy Ferguson-Crombie, or Isobel, for instance?"

"It's just that I thought . . . you're so experienced. You've lived here longer than anybody I know. I wanted to get your reactions to the idea."

Violet was nonplussed. Casting about for something to say, she welcomed the appearance of Edie with the coffee tray. Edie set this down on the fireside stool. "Are you wanting biscuits?" she asked.

16

"No, Edie, I think that will do very nicely. Thank you so much."

Edie departed. In a moment, the vacuum cleaner could be heard roaring away upstairs.

Violet poured the coffee. "What sort of an affair did you have in mind?"

"Oh, you know. Reels, and country dances."

Violet thought that she did know. "You mean tapes on the stereo, and eightsomes in the hall?"

"No. Not like that. A really *big* dance. We'd do it in style. With a marquee on the lawn . . ."

"I hope Angus is feeling rich."

Verena ignored this interruption. ". . . and a proper band for the music. We'll use the hall, of course, but for sitting out. And the drawing room. And I'm sure Katy will want a disco for all her London friends, it seems to be the thing to do. Perhaps the dining room. We could turn it into a cave, or a grotto . . ."

Caves and grottoes, thought Violet. Verena had clearly been doing her homework. But then, she was an excellent organiser. Violet said mildly, "You *have* been laying plans."

"And Katy can ask all her friends from the south . . . we'll have to find beds for them, of course . . ."

"Have you spoken to Katy about your idea?"

"No, I told you. You're the first person to know."

"Perhaps she won't want a dance."

"But of course she will. She's always loved parties."

Violet, knowing Katy, decided that this was probably true. "And when is it to be?"

"I thought September. That's the obvious time. Lots of people up for the shooting, and everybody still on holiday. The sixteenth might be a good date, because by then most of the younger children will have gone back to boarding school."

"This is only May. September's a long way off."

"I know, but it's never too early to fix a date and start making arrangements. I'll have to book the marquee,

17

and the caterer, and get invitations printed . . ." She came up with another pleasurable idea. "And, Violet, wouldn't fairy lights be pretty, all the way up the drive to the house?"

It all sounded dreadfully ambitious. "It's going to be a lot of work for you."

"Not really. The American Invasion will be over by then, because the paying guests stop coming at the end of August. I shall be able to concentrate my mind. Do admit, Violet, it is a good idea. And just think of all the people I'll be able to cross off my social-conscience list. We can get everybody off in one fell swoop. Including," she added, "the Barwells."

"I don't think I know the Barwells."

"No, you wouldn't. They're business colleagues of Angus's. We've been to dinner with them twice. Two evenings of jaw-aching boredom. And never asked them back, simply because we couldn't think of anybody who could be asked to endure an evening in such excruciatingly dull company. And there are lots of others," she remembered comfortably. "When I remind Angus about *them*, he's not going to raise any difficulties about signing a few cheques."

Violet felt a little sorry for Angus. "Who else will you ask?"

"Oh, everybody. The Millburns and the Ferguson-Crombies and the Buchanan-Wrights and old Lady Westerdale, and the Brandons. And the Staffords. All their children have grown up now, so they can be invited, too. And the Middletons should be up from Hampshire, and the Luards from Gloucestershire. We'll make a list. I'll pin a sheet of paper to the kitchen noticeboard, and every time I think of a new name, I'll write it down. And you, of course, Violet. And Edmund, and Virginia, and Alexa. And the Balmerinos. Isobel will give a dinner party for me, I'm sure . . ."

Suddenly, it all began to sound rather fun. Violet's concentration drifted back to the past, to forgotten

18

occasions now remembered. One memory led to another. She said without thinking, "You should send Pandora an invitation," and then could not imagine why she had come up with the impulsive suggestion.

"Pandora?"

"Archie Balmerino's sister. One thinks of parties, and one automatically thinks of Pandora. But of course you never knew her."

"But I know *about* her. For some reason, her name always seems to come up at dinner-party conversations. You think she would come? Surely she hasn't been home for over twenty years?"

"That's true. Just a silly thought. But why not give it a try? What a shot in the arm it would be for poor Archie. And if anything would bring that errant creature back to Croy, it would be the lure of a full-blown dance."

"So you're on my side, Violet? You think I should go ahead and do it?"

"Yes, I do. If you have the energy and the where-withal, I think it's a wonderful and generous idea. It will give us all something splendid to look forward to."

"Don't say anything until I've bearded Angus."

"Not a word."

Verena smiled with satisfaction. And then another happy thought occurred to her. "I shall have a good excuse," she said, "to go and find myself a new dress."

But Violet had no such problem. "I," she told Verena, "shall wear my black velvet."

2

Thursday the Twelfth

The night was short and he did not sleep. Soon it would be dawn.

He had imagined that, for once, he might sleep, since he was tired, exhausted. Drained by three days of an unseasonably hot New York; days filled to the brim with breakfast meetings, business lunches, long afternoons of argument and discussion; too much Coca-Cola and black coffee, too many receptions and late nights, and a miserable dearth of either exercise or fresh air.

Finally, successfully, it had been achieved, though not easily. Harvey Klein was a tough nut, and some persuasion was necessary to convince him that this was the very best, and indeed the only, way to hook the English market. The creative campaign that Noel had brought with him to New York, complete with a time-schedule, layouts and photographs, had been approved and agreed upon. With the contract under his belt, Noel could return to London. Pack his bag, make a last-minute telephone call, stuff his briefcase with documents and calculator, take another telephone call (Harvey Klein to say safe journey), get himself downstairs, check out, flag down a yellow cab and head for Kennedy.

In the evening light Manhattan, as always, looked miraculous – towers of light thrusting upwards into the suffused glow of the sky, and the freeways moving rivers of headlights. Here was a city that offered, in its brash and open-handed way, every conceivable form of delight.

Before, on previous visits, he had taken full advantage of all the fun, but there had been no opportunity, this time, to accept any of the offered hospitality, and he knew a pang of regret at leaving unfulfilled, as though he were being hustled away from a stupendous party long before he had even started to enjoy it.

At Kennedy the cab dropped him at the BA terminal. He duly queued, checked in, rid himself of his holdall, queued again for Security, and at last made his way to the departure lounge. He bought a bottle of Scotch in the duty-free, a *Newsweek* and *Advertising Age* from the newsstand. Finding a chair he sat, slumped with tiredness, waiting for his flight to be called.

By courtesy of Wenborn & Weinburg, he was travelling Club Class, so at least there was space for his long legs, and he had asked for a seat by the window. He took off his jacket, settled himself, longed for a drink. It occurred to him that it would be fortuitous if no one came to sit beside him, but this faint hope died almost at once as a well-upholstered individual in a navy-blue chalk-stripe suit claimed the seat, stowed various bags and bundles in the overhead locker, and at last collapsed, in an overflowing fashion, alongside.

The man took up a great deal of space. The interior of the aircraft was cool, but this man was hot. He pulled out a silk handkerchief and dabbed his brow, heaved and humped, searched for his seat belt, and managed to jab Noel, quite painfully, with his elbow.

"Sorry about that. Seems we're a full load this evening."

Noel did not wish to talk. He smiled and nodded, and pointedly opened his *Newsweek*.

They took off. Cocktails were served, and then dinner. He was not hungry, but ate it, because it passed the time and there was nothing else to do. The huge 747 droned on, out over the Atlantic. Dinner was cleared and the

21

movie came on. Noel had already seen it in London, so he asked the flight attendant to bring him a whisky and soda and drank it slowly, cradling it in his hand, making it last. Cabin lights were extinguished and passengers reached for pillows and blankets. The fat man folded his hands over his stomach and snored momentously. Noel closed his eyes, but this made them feel as though they were filled with grit, so he opened them again. His mind raced; it had been working full throttle for three days and refused to slow down. The possibility of oblivion faded.

He wondered why he was not feeling triumphant, because he had won the precious account and was returning home with the whole thing safely sewn up. A suitable metaphor for Saddlebags. Saddlebags. It was one of those words which, the more times you said it, the more ridiculous it sounded. But it wasn't ridiculous. It was immensely important not only to Noel Keeling, but to Wenborn & Weinburg as well.

Saddlebags. A company with its roots in Colorado, where the business had started up some years ago, manufacturing high-class leather goods for the ranching fraternity. Saddles, bridles, straps, reins, and riding boots, all branded with the prestigious trademark of a hoof-print enclosing the letter S.

From this modest beginning, the company's reputation and sales had grown nationwide, outstripping all rivals. They moved into the manufacture of other commodities. Luggage, handbags, fashion accessories, shoes and boots. All constructed from the finest of hide, hand-stitched and hand-finished. The Saddlebag logo became a status symbol, vying with Gucci or Ferragamo, and with a price-tag to match. Their reputation spread, so that visitors to the United States, wishing to return home with a truly impressive piece of loot, chose a Saddlebag satchel, or a hand-tooled, gold-buckled belt.

And then came the rumour that Saddlebags were moving into the British market, retailing through one or two carefully chosen London stores. Charles Weinburg, Noel's chairman, got wind of this by means of a chance remark dropped at a London dinner party. The next morning Noel, as Senior Vice-President and Creative Director, was called for his briefing.

"I want this account, Noel. At the moment only a handful of people in this country have ever heard of Saddlebags, and they're going to need a top-gear campaign. We've got the headstart and if we land it we can handle it, so I put through a call to New York late last night, and spoke to Saddlebag's president, Harvey Klein. He's agreeable to a meeting but he wants a total presentation . . . layouts, media coverage, slogans, the lot. Top-level stuff, full-page colour spreads. You've got two weeks. Get busy with the Art Department and try to work something out. And for God's sake find a photographer who can make a male model look like a man, not like a shop-window dummy. If necessary, get hold of a genuine polo-player. If he'll do the job, I don't care what we have to pay him . . ."

It was nine years since Noel Keeling had gone to work for Wenborn & Weinburg. Nine years is a long time in the advertising business for a man to stay with the same firm, and from time to time he found himself astonished by his own uninterrupted progress. Others, his own contemporaries, who had started with him, had moved on – to other companies, or even to set up their own agencies. But Noel had stayed.

The reasons for Noel's constancy were basically rooted in his personal life. Indeed, after a year or two with the firm, he had considered quite seriously the possibility of leaving. He was restless, unsatisfied, and not even particularly interested in the job. He dreamed of greener fields: setting up on his own, abandoning advertising altogether and moving into property or commodities. With plans for making a million, he knew that it was simply lack of the necessary capital that was holding him back. But he had no capital, and the frustration of lost opportunities and missed chances drove him nearly to distraction.

And then, four years ago, things had changed dramatically. He was thirty, a bachelor, and still resolutely working his way through a string of girlfriends, with no inkling that this irresponsible state of affairs would not last for ever. But his mother quite suddenly died, and for the first time in his life Noel had found himself a man of some means.

Her death had been so totally unexpected that for a little while he was shocked into a state where he found it almost impossible to come to terms with the cold fact that she had gone for ever. He had always been fond of her, in a detached and unsentimental manner, but basically he'd thought of her as his constant source of food, drink, clean clothes, warm beds, and, when he asked for it, moral support. As well, he had respected both her independence of spirit and the fact that she had never interfered, in any way, with Noel's own adult and private life. At the same time, much of her dotty behaviour had maddened him. Worst was her habit of surrounding herself by the most down-at-heel and needy of hangers-on. Everybody was her friend. She called them all her friends. Noel called them a lot of bloody spongers. She disregarded his cynical attitude, and bereaved spinsters, lonely widows, penniless artists, and unemployed actors were drawn to her side as moths seek a candle flame. Her generosity to all and sundry he had considered both mindless and selfish, for there never seemed to be any money to spare for the things in life that Noel believed to be of primary importance.

When she died, her will reflected this thoughtless bounty. A hefty bequest was left to a young man . . . nothing to do with the family . . . whom she had taken

24

under her sheltering wing, and whom, for some reason, she wished to help.

For Noel, it was a bitter blow. His feelings – and pocket – deeply hurt, he was consumed by a resentment that was totally impotent. It was no use raging, because she was gone. He could not have it out with her, accuse her of disloyalty and demand to know what the bloody hell she thought she was doing. His mother had moved beyond his reach. He imagined her, safe from his wrath, across some chasm or uncrossable river, surrounded by sunshine, fields, trees, whatever constituted her own personal conception of Heaven. She was probably, in her mild way, laughing at her son, her dark eyes bright with mischievous amusement, unperturbed as always by his demands and reproaches.

With only his two sisters to make miserable, he turned his back on his family and concentrated instead on the one stable element left in his life – his job. Somewhat to his surprise, and to the astonishment of his superiors, he discovered, just in time, that he was not only interested in advertising but extremely good at it. By the time his mother's estate was cleared, and his share of the loot was safely deposited in the bank, youthful fantasies of enormous gambles and fast profits had faded for ever. Noel had come to realise that making money with some other person's hypothetical fortune was actually very different from parting with your own. He felt protective about his bank balance, as though it were a child, and was not about to risk its safety. Instead, in modest fashion, he bought himself a new car and began, tentatively, to put out feelers for some place new to live . . .

Life moved on. But youth was over, and it was a difficult life. Gradually Noel came to terms with this and, at the same time, discovered that he was incapable of sustaining his final grievance against his mother. Nourishing useless resentment was far too exhausting. And at the end of the day he had to admit that he hadn't

25

come out of it all too badly. Besides, he missed her. During the last years he had seen little of her, closeted as she was in the depths of Gloucestershire, but still she was always *there* – at the end of a telephone, or at the end of a long drive when you felt you couldn't stand the hot summer streets of London a moment longer. It didn't matter if you went alone or took half a dozen friends for the weekend. There was always space, a relaxed welcome, delicious food, everything or nothing to do. Fires flickering, fragrant flowers, hot baths; warm comfortable beds, fine wines and easy conversation.

All gone. The house and garden sold to strangers. The warm smell of her kitchen and the good feeling that somebody else was in charge and you didn't have to make a single decision. And gone was the only person in the world with whom you never had to put on an act or pretend. Life without her, maddening and capricious as she had been, was like living a life with a ragged hole in the middle of it, and had taken, he recalled wryly, some getting used to.

He sighed. It all seemed a long time ago. Another world. He had finished his whisky and sat staring out into the darkness. He remembered being four years old and having measles and how the nights of illness had seemed long as a lifetime, each minute lasting an hour, and the dawn an eternity away.

Now, thirty years later, he watched the dawn. The sky lightened and the sun slid up from beneath the false horizon of cloud, and everything turned pink and the light was dazzling to the eye. He watched the dawn through the aircraft window and was grateful, because it had chased away the night, and now it was the next day and he did not have to try to sleep. Around him, people stirred. The cabin crew came round with orange juice and scalding face towels. He wiped his face and felt the stubble on his chin. Others collected themselves, found wash-bags, went to the lavatory for a shave. Noel

26

stayed where he was. He could shave when he reached home.

Which, three hours later, he did. Weary, dirty, and dishevelled, he clambered out of the taxi and paid the driver off. The morning air was cool, blessedly cool after New York, and it was raining lightly, a dampening drizzle. In Pembroke Gardens the trees were greening, the pavements wet. He smelled the freshness and, as the taxi drove away, stood for a moment and thought of spending this day on his own, recovering. Having a nap, taking a long walk. But this was not to be. There was work to be done. The office and his chairman waited. Noel picked up his bag and his briefcase, went down the area steps and opened his own front door.

It was called a garden flat because, at the back of it, french windows opened out on to a tiny patio, his share of the larger garden of the tall house. In the evening the sun fell upon it, but at this early hour it lay in shadow, and the upstairs cat was comfortably ensconced in one of his canvas chairs, having apparently spent the night there.

It was not a large flat but the rooms were spacious. A living room and a bedroom, a small kitchen and a bathroom. Overnight guests had to sleep on the sofa, a tricky piece of equipment which, if resolutely approached, folded down into a second double bed. Mrs Muspratt, who did for him, had been in while he was away and so all was neat and clean, but airless and stuffy.

He opened the french windows and chased the cat away. In his bedroom, he unzipped his suitcase and took out his wash-bag. He undressed and dropped his soiled and crumpled clothes on to the floor. In the bathroom he cleaned his teeth, took a scalding shower, shaved. By now he needed, more than anything, black coffee. In his towel robe and barefooted, he padded into the kitchen, filled the kettle and switched it on, spooned coffee into his French coffee-pot. The smell of this was heartening and delicious. While the coffee filtered, he collected his mail, sat at the kitchen table and leafed through the envelopes. Nothing looked too urgent. There was, however, a garish picture postcard of Gibraltar. He turned it over. It had been posted in London and was from the wife of Hugh Pennington, an old school friend of Noel's, who lived in Chelsea.

Noel, I've been trying to ring you, but no reply. Unless we hear to the contrary, we'll expect you for dinner the thirteenth. Seven-thirty for eight. No black tie. Love, Delia.

He sighed. This evening. Unless we hear to the contrary. Oh well, by then he'd probably have got his second wind. And it would be more amusing than watching television. He dropped the postcard on to the table, heaved himself to his feet, and went to pour his coffee.

Shut in the office, in conference for most of the day, Noel lost track and sight of what was happening out of doors. Finally emerging and driving home through rush-hour traffic that did not rush but moved at the pace of an arthritic snail, he saw that the rain of the morning had been blown away by the breeze and it was a perfect May evening. By now he had reached that state beyond exhaustion when all is light and clear and strangely disembodied, and the prospect of sleep seemed as far away as death. Instead, another shower, a change of clothes, and a drink. And then he would not take his car but walk to Chelsea. The fresh air and exercise would whet his appetite for the excellent meal that he hoped was waiting for him. He could scarcely remember when he had last sat at a table and eaten something that was not a sandwich.

The walk was a good idea. He went by leafy back-streets, residential terraces, and gardens where magnolias opened and wistaria clung to the faces of expensive London houses. Coming out into the Brompton Road, he crossed over by the Michelin Building and turned down into Walton Street. Here his steps slowed as he paused to look in at the delectable shop windows, the interior decorators and the art gallery that sold sporting prints, hunting scenes, and oil paintings of faithful Labradors bounding through the snow with pheasants in their mouths. There was a Thorburn that he craved. He stood longer than he intended, simply looking at it. Perhaps tomorrow he would ring the gallery and discover its price. After a little, he walked on.

By the time he reached Ovington Street, it was twenty-five to eight. The pavements were lined with the cars of the residents, and some older children were riding their bicycles up and down the middle of the road. The Penningtons' house was halfway down the terrace. As he approached it, a girl came along the pavement towards him. She had with her, on a lead, a small white Highland terrier and was apparently on her way to the post box, for she carried a letter in her hand. He looked at her. She wore jeans and a grey sweatshirt and had hair the colour of the very best sort of marmalade, and she was neither tall nor particularly slender. In fact, not Noel's type at all. And yet, as she passed him, he gave her a second glance because there was something vaguely familiar about her, and it was difficult to think where they might once have met. Some party, perhaps. The hair was distinctive . . .

The walk had tired him and he found himself sorely in need of a drink. With better things to think about, he put the girl out of his mind, went up the steps and gave the bell a token push. He turned the handle to open the door, with a greeting ready and waiting. Hi. Delia, it's me. I've arrived.

But nothing happened. The door remained firmly closed, which was odd and out of character. Knowing that he was on his way, Delia should surely have left it on the latch. He rang the bell again. And waited.

More silence. He told himself that they had to be there, but already knew with hideous certainty that nobody was going to answer the bell and the Penningtons, damn their bloody eyes, were not at home.

"Hello."

He turned from the inhospitable door. Below, on the pavement, stood the dumpy girl and her dog, back from posting the letter.

"Hi."

"Did you want the Penningtons?"

"They're meant to be giving me dinner."

"They've gone out. I saw them going off in their car."

Noel digested, in gloomy silence, this unwelcome confirmation of what he already knew. Disappointed and let down, he felt very much ill-disposed towards the girl, as one usually does when told something perfectly horrible by another person. It occurred to him that it couldn't have been much fun being a medieval messenger. There was every chance you'd end up without a head, or else employed as a human cannonball for some monstrous catapult.

He waited for her to go away. She didn't. He thought, shit. And then, resigned, put his hands in his pockets and descended the steps to join her.

She bit her lip. "What a shame. It's miserable when something like this happens."

30

"I can't think what's gone wrong."

"What's worse," she told him, in the tones of one determined to look on the bright side, "is when you arrive on the wrong night, and they're not expecting you. I did that once, and it was dreadfully embarrassing. I'd got the dates mixed up."

This did not help. "I suppose you think I've got the dates mixed up."

"It's easily done."

"Not this time. I only got the postcard this morning. The thirteenth."

She said, "But this is the twelfth."

"No, it isn't." He was quite firm. "It's the thirteenth."

"I'm terribly sorry, but it's the twelfth. Thursday, the twelfth of May." She sounded deeply apologetic, as though the mix-up were all her fault. "Tomorrow's the thirteenth."

Slowly, his punch-drunk brain worked this out. Tuesday, Wednesday . . . damn her eyes, she was right. The days had run into each other, and somewhere he had lost track of them. He felt shamefully foolish, and because of this he instantly began to come up with excuses for his own stupidity.

"I've been working. Flying. I've been in New York. Got back this morning. Jet lag does ghastly things to your brain."

She made a sympathetic face. Her dog smelled at his trousers and he moved aside, not wishing to be peed upon. Her hair in the evening sunlight was astonishing. She had grey eyes flecked with green and milkmaid skin, bloomy as a peach.

Somewhere. But where?

He frowned. "Have we met before?"

She smiled. "Well, yes, actually. About six months ago. At the Hathaways' cocktail party, in Lincoln Street. But there were about a million people there, so there's no reason why you should remember."

No, he wouldn't remember. Because she was not the

31

sort of girl that he would register, would want to stay with, or even talk to. Besides, he had gone to that party with Vanessa, and spent most of his time trying to keep track of her, and stop her from finding some other man to have dinner with.

He said, "How extraordinary. I am sorry. And how clever of you to remember me."

"Actually, there was another time." His heart sank, fearing to be faced with yet another social gaffe. "You're with Wenborn & Weinburg, aren't you? I cooked a directors' lunch for them about six weeks ago. But you wouldn't even have noticed, because I was wearing a white overall, and handing round plates. Nobody ever looks at cooks and waitresses. It's a funny feeling, as though you are invisible."

He realised that this was true. By now feeling more friendly towards her, he asked her name.

"Alexa Aird."

"I'm Noel Keeling."

"I know. I remembered from the Hathaways' party, and then for the lunch, I had to do a placement, and write names on cards."

Noel cast his mind back to that particular day and recalled in satisfying detail the meal she had produced. Smoked salmon, a perfectly grilled fillet steak, watercress salad, and a lemon sorbet. The very thought of these delights caused his mouth to water. Which reminded him that he was ravenously hungry.

"Who do you work for?"

"Myself. I'm freelance." She said this quite proudly. Noel hoped that she was not about to embark upon the history of her career. He did not feel strong enough to stand and listen. He needed food, but, more importantly, he needed a drink. He must make some excuse, take his leave, and be rid of her. He opened his mouth to do this, but she spoke first.

"I suppose you wouldn't like to come and have a drink with me?"

The invitation was so unexpected that he did not immediately reply. He looked at her and met her anxious gaze, and realised that she was, in fact, extremely shy, and to come out with such a suggestion had caused her some courageous effort. As well, he found himself uncertain as to whether she was inviting him to the nearest pub or to some grotty attic pad filled with co-habiting colleagues, one of whom would doubtless just have finished washing her hair.

No point in committing himself. He was cautious. "Where?"

"I live two doors down from the Penningtons. And you look as though you could do with a drink."

He stopped being cautious. "I could."

"There's nothing worse than arriving in the wrong place at the wrong time, and knowing that it's all your own fault."

Which could have been more tactfully put. But she was kind. "You're very kind." He made up his mind. "I'd like that very much."

3

The house was identical to the Penningtons', except that the front door was not black, but dark blue, and a bay tree stood in a tub beside it. She went ahead of him, opened it with her key, and he followed her indoors. She shut the door behind them and then stooped to unfasten the little dog's lead. The dog instantly went to drink copiously from a round dish that stood, handily, near the foot of the stairs. The dish had DOG written on it.

She said, "He always does that when he comes in. He seems to think that he's been for a long, long walk."

"What's his name?"

"Larry."

The dog lapped noisily, filling the silence, because, for once in his life, Noel Keeling found himself at a loss for words. He had been caught on the hop. He was not certain what he had expected, but certainly not this – an instant impression of warm opulence, loaded with evidence of wealth and good taste. This was a grand London residence, but on a miniature scale. He saw the narrow hallway, the steep staircase, the polished banister rail. Honey-coloured carpeting, thick to the wall; an antique console table upon which stood a pink-flowering azalea; an ornately framed oval mirror. But what really threw him was the smell. It was poignantly familiar. Wax polish, apples, a suggestion of fresh coffee. Pot-pourri, perhaps, and summery flowers. The smell of nostalgia, of youth. The smell of the homes that his mother had created for her children.

Who was responsible for this assault of memory? And who was Alexa Aird? It was an occasion to fall back on small talk, but Noel couldn't think of a mortal thing to say. Perhaps that was best. He stood waiting for what was going to happen next, fully expecting to be led upstairs to some rented bedsitter or tiny attic apartment. But she laid the dog's lead on the table and said in hostessy fashion, "Do come in," and led him into the room that lay beyond the open door.

The house was a twin of the Penningtons' but about a thousand times more impressive. Narrow and long, this room stretched from the front of the house to the back. The street end was the drawing room – too grand to be called a sitting room – and the other end was furnished as a dining room. Here, french windows led out on to a wrought-iron balcony, bright with pansies in terracotta pots.

All was gold and pink. Curtains, padded thick as eiderdowns, hung in swags and folds. Sofas and chairs were loose-covered in the best sort of country chintz, and scattered haphazardly with needlepoint cushions. Recessed alcoves were filled with blue-and-white porcelain, and a bulging *bombé* bureau stood open, stacked with the letters and paperwork of an industrious owner.

It was all very elegant and grown-up, and did not match up in the very least with this quite ordinary and not particularly attractive girl in her jeans and sweatshirt.

Noel cleared his throat.

"What a charming room."

"Yes, it is pretty, isn't it? You must be exhausted." Now that she was safe, in her own territory, she did not seem so diffident. "Jet lag's a killer. When my father flies in from New York he comes by Concorde because he hates those night flights."

"I'll be all right."

"What would you like to drink?"

35

"Have you any whisky?"

"Of course. Grouse or Haig's?"

He could scarcely believe his luck. "Grouse?"

"Ice?"

"If you have some."

"I'll go down to the kitchen and get it. If you'd like to help yourself . . . there are glasses . . . everything's there. I won't be a moment . . ."

She left him. He heard her talking to the little dog, and then light footsteps as she ran down the stairs to the basement. All quiet. Presumably the dog had gone with her. A drink. He moved to the far end of the room, where stood an enviable sideboard, satisfactorily loaded with bottles and decanters.

Here hung charming oil paintings, still lifes and country scenes. His eyes, roaming, assessing, took in the silver pheasant in the centre of the oval table, the beautiful Georgian coasters. He went to the window and looked down into the garden – a small paved courtyard, with roses climbing the brick wall and a raised bed of late wallflowers. There was a white wrought-iron table with four matching chairs, conjuring up visions of al-fresco meals, summer supper parties, cool wine.

A drink. On the sideboard were six heavy tumblers, neatly lined up. He reached for the bottle of Grouse, poured himself a slug, added soda, and then returned to the other end of the room. Alone, and still curious as a cat, he prowled. He lifted the fine net curtain and glanced down into the street, then moved to shelves of books, glancing at the titles, endeavouring to find some clue as to the personality of the owner of this delectable house. Novels, biographies, a book on gardens, another on growing roses.

He paused to mull things over. Putting two and two together, he came to the obvious conclusion. Ovington Street belonged to Alexa's parents. Father in some sort of business, sufficiently prestigious to fly Concorde as a matter of course and, moreover, to take his wife with him. He decided that they were, at this moment, in New York. In all probability, once the hard work was over and the conferences finished with, they would fly down to Barbados or the Virgin Islands for a restorative week in the sun. It all clicked logically into place.

As for Alexa, she was house-sitting for them, keeping bandits at bay. This explained why she was on her own, and able to be generous with her father's whisky. When they returned, sun-tanned and bearing gifts, she would go back to her own abode. A shared flat or terraced cottage in Wandsworth or Clapham.

With all this tidily settled in his mind Noel felt better, and strong enough to continue his investigative circuit. The blue-and-white porcelain was Dresden. By one of the armchairs a basket stood on the floor, brimming with bright wools and a half-worked tapestry. On top of the bureau were a number of photographs. People getting married, holding babies, having a picnic with thermos flasks and dogs. Nobody recognisable. One photograph caught his attention, and he picked it up the better to inspect it. A large Edwardian mansion of some bulk, smothered in Virginia creeper. A conservatory bulged from one side, and there were sash windows and a row of dormer windows in the roof. Steps led up to an open front door, and on top of these sat two stately springer spaniels, obediently posed. In the background were winter trees, a church tower, and a rising hill.

The family's country house.

She was coming back. He heard her soft footsteps ascending the stair, carefully replaced the photograph, and turned to meet her. She came through the door, carrying a tray loaded with an ice-bucket, a wineglass, an opened bottle of white wine, and a dish of cashew nuts.

"Oh, good, you've got a drink." She set the tray down on the table behind the sofa, edging some magazines aside to make space for it. The little terrier, apparently

37

devoted, dogged her heels. "I'm afraid I could only find a few nuts . . ."

"At the moment" – he raised his glass – "this is really all I need."

"Poor man." She fished for a handful of ice-cubes and dropped them into his drink.

He said, "I've been standing here coming to terms with the fact that I've made a complete fool of myself."

"Oh, don't be stupid." She poured herself a glass of wine. "It could happen to anybody. And just think, now you've got a lovely party to look forward to tomorrow evening. And you'll have had a good night's rest, and be the life and soul. Why don't you sit down? This chair's the best, it's large and comfortable . . ."

It was. And bliss, at last, to be off his aching feet, buffered by soft cushions, and with a drink in his hand. Alexa settled herself in the other chair, opposite him, and with her back to the window. The dog instantly jumped into her lap, made a nest and went to sleep.

"How long were you in New York?"

"Three days."

"Do you like going?"

"Usually. It's getting back that's so exhausting."

"What were you doing there?"

He told her. He explained about Saddlebags and Harvey Klein. She was impressed. "I've got a Saddlebag belt. My father brought it back for me last year. It's beautiful. Very thick and soft and handsome."

"Well, soon you'll be able to buy one in London. If you don't mind paying an arm and a leg."

"Who plans an advertising campaign?"

"I do. That's my job. I'm Creative Director."

"It sounds frightfully important. You must be very good at it. Do you enjoy it?"

Noel thought about this. "If I didn't enjoy it, I wouldn't be good at it."

"That's absolutely true. I can't think of anything worse than having to do a job one hates."

"Do you like cooking?"

"Yes, I love it. Just as well, because it's about the only thing I can do. I was dreadfully thick at school. I only got three O-levels. My father made noises about me going to do a secretarial training, or a design course, but in the end he agreed it would be a total waste of time and money, and let me be a cook."

"Did you do a training?"

"Oh, yes. I can produce all sorts of exotic dishes."

"Have you always worked on your own?"

"No, I started with an agency. Then, we worked in pairs. But it's more fun on my own. I've built up quite a good little business. Not just directors' lunches, but private dinner parties, and wedding receptions, or just filling people's deep-freezes. I've got a little Mini van. I cart everything about in that."

"You do the cooking here?"

"Most of it. Private dinner parties are a bit more complicated, because you have to work in other people's kitchens. And other people's kitchens are always a total enigma. I always take my own sharp knives."

"Sounds bloodthirsty."

She laughed. "For chopping vegetables, not for murdering the hostess. Your glass is empty. Would you like another drink?"

Noel realised that it was, and said that he would, but before he could shift himself, Alexa was on her feet, spilling the little dog gently on to the floor. She took his glass from his hand and disappeared behind him. Comforting clinking sounds reached his ears. A splash of soda. It was all very peaceful. The evening breeze, stirring through the open window, moved the filmy net curtains. Outside, a car started up and drove away, but the children who played on their bicycles had apparently been called indoors and sent to bed. The abortive dinner party had ceased to be of åny importance, and Noel felt a little like a man who, trudging across a barren desert,

39

had inadvertently stumbled upon a lush, palm-fringed oasis.

The cold glass was slipped back into his hand. He said, "I always thought that this was one of the nicest streets in London."

Alexa returned to her chair, curling up with her feet tucked beneath her.

"Where do you live?"

"Pembroke Gardens."

"Oh, but that's lovely, too. Do you live alone?"

He found himself taken off-guard, but, as well, amused by her directness. She was probably remembering the Hathaways' party, and his dogged pursuit of the sensational Vanessa. He smiled. "Most of the time."

His oblique reply went over the top of her head. "Have you got a flat there?"

"Yes. A basement, so it doesn't get much sun. However, I don't spend much time there, so it doesn't really matter. And I usually manage to avoid London weekends."

"Do you go home?"

"No. But I have convenient friends."

"What about brothers and sisters?"

"Two sisters. One lives in London and one in Gloucestershire."

"I expect you go and stay with her."

"Not if I can help it." Enough. He had answered enough questions. It was time to turn the tables. "And you? Do you go home for weekends?"

"No. I'm very often working. People tend to throw dinner parties on Saturday evenings, or Sunday lunches. Besides, it's hardly worth going to Scotland just for a weekend."

Scotland.

"You mean . . . you live in Scotland?"

"No. I live here. But my family home is in Relkirkshire."

I live here.

"But I thought your father – " He stopped, because what he had thought had been pure conjecture. Was it possible that he had been barking up entirely the wrong tree? ". . . I'm sorry, but I got the impression . . ."

"He works in Edinburgh. With Sanford Cubben. He's the head of their Scottish office."

Sanford Cubben, the vast international trust company. Noel made a few mental adjustments. "I see. How stupid of me. I imagined him in London."

"Oh, you mean the New York bit. That's nothing. He flies all over the world. Tokyo, Hong Kong. He's not in this country very much."

"So you don't see much of him?"

"Sometimes when he's passing through London. He doesn't stay here, because he goes to the company flat, but he usually rings, and if there's time, he takes me out for dinner at the Connaught or Claridge's. It's a great treat. I pick up all sorts of cooking ideas."

"I suppose that's as good a reason as any to go to Claridge's. But . . ." *He doesn't stay here.* ". . . who owns this house?"

Alexa smiled with total innocence. "I do," she told him.

"Oh . . ." It was impossible to keep the disbelief from his voice. The dog was back in her lap. She stroked his head, played with the furry, pricked ears.

"How long have you lived here?"

"About five years. It was my grandmother's house. My mother's mother. We were always very close. I used to spend some part of all my school holidays with her. By the time I came to London to do my cooking course, she was a widow and on her own. So I came to stay with her. And then, last year, she died, and she left the house to me."

"She must have been very fond of you."

"I was terribly fond of her. It all caused a bit of family ill-feeling. My living with her, I mean. My father didn't think it was a good idea at all. He was quite fond of her, but he thought I should be more independent. Make friends of my own age, move into a flat with some other girl. But I didn't really want to. I'm dreadfully lazy about things like that, and Granny Cheriton . . ." Abruptly she stopped. Across the space that divided them, their eyes met. Noel said nothing, and after a pause she continued, speaking casually, as though it were of no importance. ". . . she was getting old. It wouldn't have been kind to leave her."

Another silence. Then Noel said, "Cheriton?"

Alexa sighed. "Yes." She sounded as though she were admitting to some heinous crime.

"An unusual name."

"Yes."

"Also well-known."

"Yes."

"Sir Rodney Cheriton?"

"He was my grandfather. I didn't mean to tell you. The name just slipped out."

So that was it. The puzzle solved. That explained the money, the opulence, the precious possessions. Sir Rodney Cheriton, now deceased, founder of a financial empire that stretched world-wide, who, during the sixties and the seventies, had been associated with so many takeover bids and conglomerates that his name was scarcely ever out of the *Financial Times*. This house had been the home of Lady Cheriton, and the sweet-faced, unsophisticated little cook who sat, curled in her chair like a schoolgirl, was her granddaughter.

He was flabbergasted. "Well, who'd have thought it?"

"I don't usually tell people, because I'm not all that proud of it."

"You should be proud. He was a great man."

"It isn't that I didn't like him. He was always very sweet to me. It's just that I don't really approve of huge takeovers and companies getting bigger and bigger. I'd like them to get smaller and smaller. I like corner shops and butchers where the nice man knows your name. I

42

don't like the thought of people getting swallowed up, or lost, or made redundant.''

''We can scarcely move backwards.''

''I know. That's what my father keeps telling me. But it breaks my heart when a little row of houses gets demolished, and all that goes up in their place is another horrible office block with black windows, like a hen battery. That's what I love about Scotland. Strathcroy, the village we live in, never seems to change. Except that Mrs McTaggart, who ran the newsagent's, decided that her legs couldn't take the standing any longer and retired, and her shop was bought by Pakistanis. They're called Ishak, and they're terribly nice, and the women wear lovely bright silky clothes. Have you ever been to Scotland?''

''I've been to Sutherland, to fish on the Oykel.''

''Would you like to see a picture of our house?''

He did not let on that he had already taken a good look. ''I'd love to.''

Once more, Alexa set the dog on the floor and got to her feet. The dog, bored by all this activity, sat on the hearthrug and looked fed up. She fetched the photograph and handed it to Noel.

After an appropriate pause he said, ''It looks very comfortable.''

''It's lovely. Those are my father's dogs.''

''What's your father's name?''

''Edmund. Edmund Aird.'' She went to replace the photograph. Turning, she caught sight of the gold carriage clock which stood in the middle of the mantelpiece. She said, ''It's nearly half past eight.''

''Good heavens.'' He checked the time with his watch. ''So it is. I must go.''

''You don't have to. I mean, I could cook you something, give you supper.''

The suggestion was so splendid and so tempting that Noel felt bound to make some small noises of refusal. ''You're too kind, but . . .''

43

"I'm sure you haven't got any food at Pembroke Gardens. Not if you've just come home from New York. And it's no trouble. I'd like it." He could tell from her expression that she was yearning for him to stay. As well, he was painfully hungry. "I've got some lamb chops."

That did it. "I can't think of anything I'd like more."

Alexa's face lit up. She was as transparent as clear spring water. "Oh, good. I'd have felt really inhospitable letting you go without something inside you. Do you want to stay here, or do you want to come down to the kitchen and watch me?"

If he stayed in this chair, he would fall asleep. Besides, he wanted to see more of the house. He heaved himself out of the chair. "I'll come and watch you."

Alexa's kitchen was predictable, not modern at all, but quite homely and haphazard, as though it had not been planned, but simply come together over the years. It had a stone-tiled floor with a rush mat or two, and pine cupboards. A deep clay sink stood beneath the window, through which could be seen the little area with its steps leading up into the street. The sink was backed with blue-and-white Dutch tiles and the same tiles lined the walls between the cupboards. The tools of her trade were very evident: a thick chopping board, a line of copper saucepans, a marble slab for rolling pastry. There were racks of herbs and bunches of onions and fresh parsley in a mug.

She reached for a blue-and-white butcher's apron and tied it around her waist. Over the thick sweatshirt this made her look more shapeless than ever and accentuated her rounded, blue-jeaned bottom.

Noel asked if there was anything he could do to help.

"No, not really." She was already busy, turning on

the grill, opening drawers. "Unless you'd like to open a bottle of wine. Would you like some?"

"Where would I find a bottle of wine?"

"There's a rack through there . . ." She indicated with her head, her hands being occupied. "On the floor. I haven't got a cellar, and that's the coolest spot there is."

Noel went to look. At the back of the kitchen an archway led into what had probably once been a small scullery. This too was stone-floored, and here stood a number of shining white electrical appliances. A dish-washer, a clothes washer, a tall refrigerator, and a huge chest deep-freeze. At the far end, a half-glassed door led directly out into the little garden. By the door, in country fashion, stood a pair of rubber boots and a wooden tub of gardening tools. An ancient raincoat and a battered felt hat hung from a hook.

He found the wine-rack beyond the deep-freeze. Crouching, he inspected a few bottles. She had an excellent selection. He chose a Beaujolais, went back to the kitchen.

"How about this?"

She glanced at it. "Perfect. That was a good year. There's a corkscrew in that drawer. If you open it now, that'll give it time to breathe."

He found the corkscrew and drew the cork. It came, sweetly and cleanly, and he set the open bottle on the table. With nothing more to be done, he drew back a chair and settled himself at the table to enjoy the last of his whisky.

She had taken the chops from the refrigerator, assembled the makings of a salad, found a stick of French bread. Now she was arranging the chops on the grill-pan, reaching for a jar of rosemary. All this was accomplished deftly and with the greatest economy of effort, and it occurred to Noel that, working, she had become quite assured and confident, probably because she was engaged in doing the one thing she knew that she was really good at.

45

He said, "You look very professional."

"I am."

"Do you garden as well?"

"Why do you ask that?"

"All the clobber by the back door."

"I see. Yes, I do garden, but it's so tiny that it's not *really* gardening. At Balnaid, the garden's enormous, and there's always something needing to be done."

"Balnaid?"

"That's the name of our house in Scotland."

"My mother was a manic gardener." Having said this, Noel could not think why he had mentioned the fact. He did not usually talk about his mother unless somebody asked him a direct question. "Perpetually digging, or barrowing great loads of manure."

"Doesn't she garden any longer?"

"She's dead. She died four years ago."

"Oh, I am sorry. Where did she do her gardening?"

"In Gloucestershire. She bought a house with a couple of acres of wilderness. By the time she died, she'd transformed it into something very special. You know . . . the sort of garden people walk around in after lunch parties."

Alexa smiled. "She sounds rather like my other grand-mother, Vi. She lives in Strathcroy. Her name's Violet Aird, but we all call her Vi." The chops were grilling, the bread put to warm, the plates to heat. "My mother's dead, too. She was killed in a car accident when I was six."

"It's my turn to be sorry."

"I remember her, of course, but not really very well. I remember her mostly coming to say goodnight before she went out for a dinner party. Lovely airy dresses, and furs, and smelling of scent."

"Six is very young to lose your mother."

"It wasn't as bad as it might have been. I had a darling nanny called Edie Findhorn. And after Mummy died we

46

went back to Scotland and lived with Vi at Balnaid. So I was luckier than most."

"Did your father marry again?"

"Yes. Ten years ago. She's called Virginia. She's much younger than him."

"A wicked stepmother?"

"No. She's sweet. A bit like a sister. She's terribly pretty. And I've got a half-brother called Henry. He's nearly eight."

Now she was making the salad. With a sharp knife she chopped and shredded. Tomatoes and celery, tiny fresh mushrooms. Her hands were brown and capable, the nails short and unvarnished. There was something very satisfactory about them. He tried to recall the last time he had sat thus, slightly woozy with hunger and drink, and peacefully watched while a woman prepared a meal for him. He couldn't.

The trouble was that he had never gone for domesticated females. His girlfriends were usually models, or young, aspiring actresses with immense ambition and little brain. All they had in common was their general appearance, for he liked them very young and very thin with tiny breasts and long, attenuated legs. Which was great for his own personal amusement and satisfaction, but not much use when it came to being good about the house. Besides, they were nearly all . . . however skinny . . . on some sort of diet, and while able to down enormous and expensive restaurant meals, were not interested in producing even the simplest of snacks in the privacy of either their own flats, or Noel's.

"Oh, darling, it's such a bore. Besides, I'm not hungry. Have an apple."

From time to time there had come into Noel's life a girl so besotted that she wished only to spend the rest of her days with him. Then much effort – perhaps too much – had been made. Intimate dinners by gas-fired logs, and invitations to the country and doggy weekends. But Noel, wary of commitment, had backed away,

47

and the girls in question, after a painful period of abortive telephone calls and tearful accusations, had found other men and married them. So he had reached thirty-four and was still a bachelor. Brooding over his empty whisky glass, Noel could not decide whether this left him feeling triumphant or defeated.

"There." The salad was ready. Now she began to mix a dressing with beautiful green olive oil and pale wine vinegar. Various herbs and seasonings were added, and the smell of these made his mouth water. With this done, she started to lay the table. A red-and-white-checked cloth, wineglasses, wooden mills for pepper and salt, a pottery butter dish. She took forks and knives from a drawer and handed them to Noel and he set the two places. It seemed an appropriate moment to pour the wine, so he did, and handed Alexa her glass.

She took it from him. In her apron and bulky sweatshirt, and with her cheeks glowing from the heat of the grill, she said, "Here's to Saddlebags."

He found himself, for some reason, much touched. "And here's to you, Alexa. And thank you."

It was a simple but splendid meal, living up to all Noel's greedy expectations. The chops were tender, the salad crisp; warm bread to mop up juices and dressings, and all washed down by fine wine. After a bit, his stomach stopped groaning, and he felt infinitely better.

"I can't remember food ever tasting so good."

"It's not anything very special."

"But perfect." He took more salad. "Any time you need a recommendation, let me know."

"Don't you ever cook for yourself?"

"No. I can fry bacon and eggs, but if pushed I buy gourmet dishes from Marks and Spencer and heat them up. Every now and then, if I'm desperate, I go and spend an evening with Olivia, my London sister, but she's as useless in the kitchen as I am, and we usually finish up eating something exotic, like quails' eggs or caviare. A treat, but not very filling."

"Is she married?"

"No. She's a career lady."

"What does she do?"

"She's Editor-in-Chief of *Venus*."

"Goodness." She smiled. "What illustrious relations we both seem to have."

Having devoured everything on the table, Noel found himself still peckish, and so Alexa produced cheese and a bunch of pale-green seedless grapes. With these, they finished the last of the wine. Alexa suggested coffee.

By now it was growing dark. Outside, in the dusky blue street, the lights had come on. Their glow penetrated the basement kitchen, but mostly all was shadowy. Noel was, all at once, overcome by a mammoth yawn. When he had dealt with this, he apologised. "I'm sorry. I really must get home."

"Have some coffee first. It'll keep you awake until you reach your bed. I tell you what – why don't you go upstairs and relax, and I'll bring your coffee up to you. And then I'll phone for a taxi."

Which sounded an eminently sensible idea.

"Right."

But even saying the word took much conscious effort. He was aware of arranging his tongue and his lips in the correct position to make the appropriate sound, and knew that he was either drunk or on the point of flaking out from lack of sleep. Coffee was an excellent idea. He put his hands on the table and levered himself to his feet. Going up the basement stairs, headed for the drawing room, was even more of a trial. Halfway up he stumbled but somehow managed to keep his balance and not to fall flat on his face.

Upstairs, the empty room waited, quiet in the bloomy twilight. The only illumination came from the street-

49

lights, and these were reflected from the brass fender and the facets of the crystal chandelier that hung from the middle of the ceiling. It seemed a pity to dispel the peaceful dusk by turning on switches, so he didn't. The dog was asleep on the chair that Noel had previously occupied, so he sank down in a corner of the sofa. The dog, disturbed, awoke and raised his head, and stared at Noel. Noel stared back. The dog turned into two dogs. He was drunk. He had not slept for ever. He would not sleep now. He was not sleeping.

He was dozing. Sleeping and waking at the same time. He was in the 747, droning back over the Atlantic, with his fat neighbour snoring alongside. His chairman was telling him to go to Edinburgh, to sell Saddlebags to a man called Edmund Aird. There were voices, calling and shouting; the children playing in the street on their bicycles. No, they were not in the street, they were outside, in some garden. He was in a cramped and steeply ceilinged room, peering from the peephole of a window. Honeysuckle fronds tapped on the glass. His old room, in his mother's house in Gloucestershire. Outside on the lawn, a game was in progress. Children and adults played cricket. Or was it rounders? Or baseball? They looked up and saw his face through the glass. "Come down," they told him. "Come down and play." He was pleased that they wanted him. It was good to be home. He went out of the room and downstairs; stepped out into the garden, but the cricket game was over, and they had all disappeared. He did not mind. He lay on the grass and stared at the bright sky, and everything was all right. None of the bad things had happened after all, and nothing had changed. He was alone, but soon somebody would come. He could wait.

Another sound. A clock ticking. He opened his eyes. The street-lamps no longer shone, and the darkness had gone. It was not his mother's garden, not his mother's house, but some strange room. He had no idea where he was. He lay flat on his back on a sofa, with a rug over

50

him. The fringe of the rug tickled his chin, and he pushed it away. Staring upwards, he saw the glittering droplets of the chandelier, and then remembered. Moving his head, he saw the armchair, with its back to the window; a girl sat there, her bright hair silhouetted against the morning light beyond the uncurtained window. He stirred. She stayed silent. He said her name. "Alexa?"

"Yes." She was awake.

"What time is it?"

"Just after seven."

"Seven in the morning?"

"Yes."

"I've been here all night." He stretched, easing his long legs. "I fell asleep."

"You were asleep by the time I came up with the coffee. I thought about waking you, but then I decided against it."

He blinked, clearing the sleep from his eyes. He saw that she was no longer wearing her jeans and sweatshirt, but a white towelling robe, wrapped closely about her. She had bundled herself up in a blanket, but her legs and feet, protruding, were bare.

"Have you been there all night?"

"Yes."

"You should have gone to bed."

"I didn't like to leave you. I didn't want you to wake up and feel you had to go, and not be able to find a taxi in the middle of the night. I made up my spare bed, but then I thought, what's the point? So I just left you to sleep."

He caught the tail end of his dream before it faded into oblivion. He had lain in his mother's garden in Gloucestershire, and known that someone was coming. Not his mother. Penelope was dead. Somebody else. Then the dream was gone for good, leaving him with Alexa.

He felt, surprisingly, enormously well, energetic and refreshed. Decisive. "I must go home."

51

"Shall I call you a taxi?"

"No. I'll walk. It'll do me good."

"It's a lovely morning. Do you want something to eat before you go?"

"No, I'm fine." He pushed aside the rug and sat up, smoothing back his hair and running his hand over his stubbly chin. "I must go." He got to his feet.

Alexa made no effort to persuade him to stay, but simply came with him into the hall, opened her front door on to the pearly, pristine May morning. The distant rumble of traffic was already audible, though a bird was singing from some tree, and the air was fresh. He imagined that he could smell lilac.

"Goodbye, Noel."

He turned to her. "I'll ring you."

"You don't need to."

"Don't I?"

"You don't owe me anything."

"You're very sweet." He stooped and kissed her peachy cheek. "Thank you."

"I've liked it."

He left her. Went down the steps and set off, at a brisk clip, down the pavement. At the end of the street he turned and looked back. She was gone, and the blue front door stood closed. But it seemed to Noel that the house with the bay tree had a special look about it.

He smiled to himself and went on his way.

❦ JUNE ❦

4

Tuesday the Seventh

Isobel Balmerino, at the wheel of her minibus, drove the
ten miles to Corriehill. It was nearly four o'clock in the
afternoon and the beginning of June, but although the
trees were heavy with leaf and the fields green with
growing crops, there had, so far, been no summer at all.
It was not exactly cold, but it was dank and drizzling,
and all the way from Croy her windscreen wipers had
been working. Clouds hung low over the hills and all
was drowned in greyness. She felt sorry for the foreign
visitors, come so far to see the glories of Scotland, only
to find them shrouded in murk and almost invisible.

Not that this troubled her. She had made the complicated journey, cross-country and by back roads, so many
times before that she sometimes thought that if she were
to dispatch the minibus on its own it would manage
very nicely, getting itself to Corriehill and back with no
human assistance, reliable as a faithful horse.

Now she had come to the familiar junction and was
nearly there. She changed down and swung the minibus
into a single-track lane hedged with hawthorn. This lane
led up and on to the hill, and as she climbed, the mist
grew thicker; prudently she switched on the headlights.
To her right appeared the tall stone wall, the march
boundary of the Corriehill estate. Another quarter of a
mile, and she had reached the great entrance gates, the
two lodges. She turned between these and bumped her

way up the rutted drive lined with historic beeches and deep verges of rough grass which, in spring, were gold with daffodils. The daffodils had long since died back, and their withered heads and dying leaves were all that remained of their former glory. Some time, some day, Verena's handyman would cut the verges with his garden tractor, and that would be the end of the daffodils. Until next spring.

It occurred to her, sadly, and not for the first time, that as you grew older you became busier, and time went faster and faster, the months pushing each other rudely out of the way, and the years slipping off the calendar and into the past. Once, there had been time. Time to stand, or sit, and just *look* at daffodils. Or to abandon housekeeping, on the spur of the moment, walk out of the back door and up the hill, into the lark-song emptiness of a summer morning. Or to take off for a self-indulgent day in Relkirk, shopping for frivolities, meeting a girlfriend for lunch, the wine bar warm with humanity and conversation, smelling of coffee and the sort of food that one never cooked for oneself.

All treats that for a number of reasons didn't seem to happen any longer.

The driveway levelled off. Beneath the wheels of the minibus, gravel scrunched. The house loomed up at her through the mist. There were no other cars, which meant that probably all the other hostesses had been, collected their guests, and gone. So Verena would be waiting for her. Isobel hoped that she would not have become impatient.

She drew up, switched off her engine and got out into the soft, drizzly air. The main door stood open, giving on to a large paved porch, with an inner glass door beyond. This porch was stacked with an enormous amount of expensive luggage. Isobel quailed, because it seemed to be even more lavish than usual. Suitcases (hugely big), garment bags, small grips, golf bags, boxes and parcels and carriers, emblazoned with the familiar names of large stores. (They'd obviously been shopping.) All of these were tagged with distinctive yellow labels: SCOTTISH COUNTRY TOURS.

Diverted, she paused to read the names on the labels. Mr Joe Hardwicke. Mr Arnold Franco. Mrs Myra Hardwicke. Mrs Susan Franco. The suitcases were heavily monogrammed, and the golf bags had prestigious club labels hanging from their handles.

She sighed. Here we go again. She opened the inner door.

"Verena!"

The hallway at Corriehill was immense, with a carved oak stairway rising to the upper floors, and much panelling. The floor was scattered with rugs, some quite ordinary and others probably priceless, and in the middle stood a table bearing a varied collection of objects: a potted geranium, a dog's lead, a brass tray for letters, and a massive leather-bound visitors' book.

"Verena?"

A door, distantly, shut. Footsteps came up the passage from the direction of the kitchen. Verena Steynton presently appeared, looking, as always, tall, slender, unfussed, and perfectly turned out. She was one of those women who, maddeningly, always appeared co-ordinated, as though she spent much time each day selecting and matching her various garments. This skirt, this shirt; that cashmere cardigan, these shoes. Even the damp and muggy weather, which ruined the hairdos of most right-minded women, didn't stand a chance with Verena's coiffure, which never wilted under the most adverse of circumstances, and always appeared as neat and glamorous as if she had just come out from under the drier. Isobel had no illusions about her own appearance. Stocky and sturdy as a Highland pony, her complexion rosy and shining, her hands roughened by work, she had long stopped bothering about the way she looked. But, seeing Verena, she all at once wished that she had taken the time to change out of her corduroy trousers

57

and the quilted sludge-coloured waistcoat that was her oldest friend.

"Isobel."

"I hope I'm not late."

"No. You're the last but you're not late. Your guests are ready and waiting for you in the drawing room. Mr and Mrs Hardwicke, and Mr and Mrs Franco. From the look of them, slightly more robust than our usual run of clients." Isobel knew some relief. Perhaps the men would be able to hump their own golf bags. "Where's Archie? Are you on your own?"

"He had to go to a church meeting at Balnaid."

"Will you manage?"

"Of course."

"Well, look, before you whisk them away, there's been a slight change of plan. I'll explain. We'd better go into the library."

Obediently, Isobel followed her, prepared to take orders. The library at Corriehill was a pleasant room, smaller than most of the other rooms, and smelled comfortably masculine – of pipe smoke and wood-smoke, of old books and old dogs. The old-dog smell emanated from an elderly Labrador snoozing on its cushion by the ashy remains of a fire. It raised its head, saw the two ladies, blinked in a superior fashion and went back to sleep.

"The thing is . . ." Verena started, and at once the telephone on the desk began to ring. She said, "Damn. Sorry, I won't be a moment," and went to answer it. "Hello, Verena Steynton . . . Yes." Her voice changed. "Mr Abberley. Thank you for calling back." She pulled the chair from the desk and sat down, reaching for her ballpoint pen and a pad of paper. She looked as though she was settling in for a long session and Isobel's heart sank, because she wanted to get home.

"Yes. Oh, splendid. Now, we shall need your largest marquee, and I think the pale-yellow-and-white lining. And a dance floor." Isobel pricked up her ears, stopped

58

feeling impatient and eavesdropped shamelessly. "The date? We thought the sixteenth of September. That's a Friday. Yes, I think you'd better come and see me, and we'll talk it over. Next week would be fine. Wednesday morning. Right. I'll see you then. Goodbye, Mr Abberley." She rang off and leaned back in her chair, wearing the satisfied expression of one with a job well done. "Well, that's the first thing settled."

"What on earth are you planning now?"

"Well, Angus and I have been talking about it for ages, and we've finally decided to take the plunge. Katy's twenty-one this year, and we're going to have a dance for her."

"Heavens above, you must be feeling rich."

"No, not particularly, but it is something of an event, and we owe about a million people hospitality, so we'll get them all off in one smashing do."

"But September's ages away, and it's only the beginning of June."

"I know, but one can't start too early. You know what September's like." Isobel did know. The Scottish season, with a mass exodus from the south to the north for the grouse-shooting. Every large house filled with house parties, dances, cricket matches, Highland games, and every sort of social activity, all finally culminating in an exhausting week of hunt balls.

"We have to have a marquee because there's really not space for dancing indoors, but Katy insists we must fix up some corner as a nightclub so that all her yuppie friends from London can have their little smooch. Then I'll have to find a really good country dance band, and a competent caterer. But at least I've got the tent organised. You'll all get invitations, of course." She gave Isobel a stern look. "I hope Lucilla will be here."

It was hard not to feel a little envious of Verena, sitting there planning a dance for her daughter, knowing that that daughter would be helpful and co-operative and enjoy every moment of her party. Her own Lucilla and

59

Katy Steynton had been at school together, and friends in the lacklustre fashion of children thrown together by their parents. For Lucilla was two years younger than Katy, and had a very different personality, and as soon as school was behind them, their ways had parted.

Katy, any mother's dream, had dutifully conformed. A year in Switzerland, and then a secretarial course in London. Graduated, she'd found herself a worthwhile job . . . something to do with funding for charity . . . and shared a small house in Wandsworth with three eminently suitable friends. Before long, she would doubtless become engaged to an excellent young man called either Nigel, Jeremy, or Christopher, her blameless face would appear on the front page of *Country Life*, and the wedding would be predictably traditional with a white dress, a great number of small bridesmaids, and 'Praise My Soul the King of Heaven'.

Isobel did not want Lucilla to be like Katy, but sometimes, as at this moment, she could not help wishing that her darling, dreamy daughter had turned out to be just a little more ordinary. But even as a child, Lucilla had shown signs of individuality and gentle rebellion. Her political tendencies were strongly left-wing, and at the drop of a hat she would involve herself, with much passion, in any cause that caught her attention. She was against nuclear power, fox-hunting, the culling of baby seals, the cutting of student grants, and the planting of tracts of horrible conifers in order to provide pop stars with tax-deductible incomes. At the same time, she voiced much concern over the plight of the homeless, the down-and-outs, the drug addicts, and the poor unfortunates who found themselves dying of AIDS.

From an early age, she had always been intensely creative and artistic, and after six months in Paris working as an au pair, she was accepted at the College of Art in Edinburgh. Here, she made friends with the most extraordinary people, whom, from time to time, she brought to Croy to stay. They were a funny-looking lot, but no funnier than Lucilla, who dressed from the Oxfam shop and thought nothing of wearing a lace evening dress and a man's tweed jacket and Edwardian lace-up boots.

With art school behind her, she stayed in Edinburgh but had failed entirely to find any sort of way in which to earn her keep. No person seemed inclined to buy her incomprehensible paintings, and no gallery wished to exhibit them. Living in an attic in India Street, she had kept herself by going out to clean other people's houses. This had proved strangely lucrative, and as soon as she had saved up enough to pay her fare across the Channel, she had taken off for France with a back pack and her painting gear. Last heard of, she was in Paris, staying with some couple she had met on the road. It was all very worrying.

Would she come home? Isobel could write, of course, to the poste restante address her daughter had given her. *Darling Lucilla, be here in September because you have been asked to Katy Steynton's dance.* But it was unlikely that Lucilla would pay much attention. She had never enjoyed formal parties, and could think of nothing to say to the well-connected young men she met at them. *Mummy, they're quite gruesomely square. And they've all got hair like tweed.*

She was impossible. She was also sweet, kind, funny, and overflowing with love. Isobel missed her quite dreadfully.

She sighed and said, "I don't know. I don't suppose so."

"Oh dear." Verena was sympathetic, which didn't make it any better. "Well, never mind, I'll send her an invitation. Katy would so love to see her again."

Privately, Isobel doubted this. She said, "Is your dance a secret, or can I talk about it?"

"No, of course it's not a secret. The more people who know, the better. Perhaps they'll offer to have dinner parties."

"I'll have a dinner party."

"You are a saint." They might have sat there making plans for ever had not Verena, all at once, remembered the business in hand. "Heavens above, I've forgotten those poor Americans. They'll be wondering what's happened to us. Now, look . . . the thing is" – she rummaged on her desk and produced some sheets of typed instructions – "that the two men have spent most of their time playing golf, and they want to play tomorrow, so they're going to give the trip to Glamis a miss. Instead, I've fixed for a car to come and fetch them from Croy at nine o'clock tomorrow morning and take them to Gleneagles. And the same car will bring them back some time during the afternoon when they've finished their game. But the ladies want to go to Glamis, so if you could have them back here at about ten o'clock, they can join the others in the coach."

Isobel nodded, hoping that she would forget none of this. Verena was so efficient and, to all intents and purposes, Isobel's boss. Scottish Country Tours was run from a central office in Edinburgh, but Verena was the local co-ordinating agent. It was Verena who telephoned Isobel each week to let her know how many guests she could expect (six was the limit, as she had no room for more) as well as to fill her in with any small idiosyncrasies or personality problems of her guests.

The tours started in May and continued until the end of August. Each one lasted a week and followed a regular pattern. The group, arriving from New York, began their stay in Edinburgh, where they spent two days sightseeing in the Borders and the city itself. On Tuesday their coach brought them to Relkirk, where they dutifully plodded around the Auld Kirk, the local castle, and a National Trust garden. They were then transported to Corriehill, to be welcomed and sorted out by Verena. From Corriehill they were collected by the various hostesses. Wednesday was the day for Glamis Castle and a scenic drive to Pitlochry, and on Thursday they set off yet again in the coach to view the Highlands and to visit Deeside and Inverness. On Friday they returned to Edinburgh, and on Saturday they flew home, back to Kennedy and all points west.

Isobel was certain that by then they must all be in a state of total exhaustion.

It was Verena who, five years ago, had roped Isobel into the business. She explained what was involved and gave Isobel the firm's handout to read. It was effusive.

Stay as a guest in a private house. Experience for yourself the hospitality and historic grandeur of some of Scotland's loveliest homes, and meet, as friends, the ancient families who live in them. . . .

Such hyperbole took a bit of living up to.

"We're not an ancient family," she'd pointed out to Verena.

"Ancient enough."

"And Croy's not exactly historic."

"Bits of it are. And you've got lots of bedrooms. That's what really counts. And think of all that lovely lolly . . ."

It was this that had finally decided Isobel. Verena's proposition came at a time when the Balmerino fortunes, in every sense of the word, were at a low ebb. Archie's father, the second Lord Balmerino, and the most charming and impractical of men, had died leaving the estate in some disarray. His unexpected demise took him, and most other people, quite by surprise, and because of this, stupendous death duties creamed off most of the inherited family wealth. With the two children, Lucilla and Hamish, in the throes of their education, the large and inconvenient house to keep going, and the lands to be maintained in some sort of order, the young Balmerinos found themselves faced with certain problems. Archie, at that time, was still a regular soldier. But he had joined the Queen's Loyal Highlanders at the age of nineteen simply because he could think of nothing else

63

he particularly wanted to do, and although he had thoroughly enjoyed his years with the regiment, he was not blessed with a driving ambition to succeed and knew that he would never make Major General.

Keeping Croy, living there, come hell or high water, became their first priority. Optimistically, they laid plans. Archie would retire from the Army, and while he was young enough to do so, find himself some sort of a job. But before this could happen he was committed to a last tour of duty with his regiment, and went with them to Northern Ireland.

The regiment returned home four months later, but it was eight months before Archie came back to Croy, and it took Isobel about eight days to realise that in spite of his rehabilitation any sort of a job was, for the time being, out of the question. In some desperation, through long and sleepless nights, she reviewed their plight.

But they had friends. In particular Edmund Aird. Realising the gravity of the situation, Edmund moved in and took control. It was Edmund who found a tenant for the home farm, and Edmund who assumed responsibility for the grouse moor. Together with Gordon Gillock, the keeper, he saw to the burning of the heather and the maintenance of the butts, and then let the entire concern out to a syndicate of businessmen from the south, retaining a gun for himself and a half-gun for Archie.

For Isobel, to be shed of at least some of her anxieties was an enormous relief, but income remained a vexing problem. There was still some inherited capital, but this was tied up in stocks and bonds, and was all that Archie had to leave to his children. Isobel had a little money of her own, but this, even added to Archie's army pension and his sixty-per-cent disability pension, did not amount to very much. The day-to-day expenses of simply running the house and keeping the family fed and clothed remained a constant source of worry, so that Verena's suggestion, initially daunting, was in fact the answer to a prayer.

"Oh, come on, Isobel. You can do it standing on your head."

And Isobel realised that she could. After all, she was well used to managing the big house, and accustomed to having people to stay. When Archie's father was alive there were always house parties to be arranged for the shooting, and the dances in September. During the school holidays, Croy filled up with the children's friends, and Christmas and Easter never passed without entire families coming to share the festivities.

Compared to all this, Verena's proposition did not sound at all arduous. It would only take up two days a week throughout the four months of summer. Surely that could not be too demanding. And . . . cheering thought . . . it would be stimulation for Archie, people coming and going. Helping to entertain them would give him an interest and bolster his morale, sadly in need of a boost.

What she hadn't realised, and what she had painfully learned, was that entertaining paying guests was a very different kettle of fish to having one's own friends about the place. You couldn't argue with them, any more than you could sit about in a companionable silence. Nor could you allow them to slope into the kitchen to peel a pot of potatoes or concoct a salad. The real rub was that they were paying. This put hospitality on a totally different level because it meant that everything had to be perfect. The tour was not cheap and, as Verena forthrightly insisted, the clients must be given value for their dollars.

There were certain guidelines printed out on a special instruction sheet for hostesses. Every bedroom must have its own bathroom, preferably adjoining. Beds must have electric blankets, and the rooms must be centrally heated. Also, if possible, there should be supplementary heating . . . preferably a real fire but, failing this, then an electric or gas fire. Fresh flowers must be arranged in the bedrooms.

(Reading this, Isobel had known some annoyance. Who did they think they were? She had never in her life put a guest in a room without seeing that there were fresh flowers on the dressing-table.)

Then there were more rules about breakfast and dinner. Breakfast must be robust and hearty; orange juice, coffee, and tea, all available. In the evenings, a cocktail must be offered, and wine at dinner-time. This meal had to be formally served, with candles, crystal, and silver on the table, and consist of at least three courses, to be followed by coffee and conversation. Other diversions, however unlikely, could be offered. A little music . . . perhaps bagpipe-playing . . .?

The overseas visitors awaited them in Verena's drawing room. Verena flung open the door. "I am sorry we've been so long. Just one or two ends that needed to be tied up," she told them in her best committee-meeting voice, which brooked no question nor argument. "Here we are, and here is your hostess, come to take you to Croy."

The drawing room at Corriehill was large and light, palely decorated and little used. Today, however, because of the inclement weather, a small fire flickered in the grate, and around this, disposed on armchairs and sofas, sat the four Americans. To while away the time, they had switched on the television and were watching, in a bemused fashion, cricket. Disturbed, they rose to their feet, turning smiling faces, and one of the men stooped and politely switched the television off.

"Now, introductions. Mr and Mrs Hardwicke, and Mr and Mrs Franco. This is your hostess for the next two days. Lady Balmerino."

Shaking hands, Isobel understood what Verena had meant when she described this week's guests as being slightly more robust than usual. Scottish Country Tours seemed, for some reason, to attract clients of an extremely advanced age, and sometimes they were not only geriatric but in a dickey state of health – short of breath and uncertain about the legs. These two couples, however, were scarcely beyond middle age. Grey-haired, certainly, but apparently bursting with energy, and all of them enviably tanned. The Francos were small of stature, and Mr Franco very bald, and the Hardwickes were tall and muscled and slim, and looked as though they spent their lives out of doors and took a great deal of exercise.

"I'm afraid I'm a little late," Isobel found herself saying, although she knew perfectly well that she was not. "But we can go whenever you're ready."

They were ready right now. The ladies collected their handbags and their beautiful new Burberry raincoats, and the little party trooped through the hall and out into the porch. Isobel went to open the back doors of the minibus, and by the time she had done this, the men were humping and heaving the big suitcases across the gravel, and helped her to load them. (This, too, was novel. She and Verena usually had to do the job by themselves.) When all were safely aboard, she shut the doors and fastened them. The Hardwickes and the Francos were saying goodbye to Verena. "But," Verena said, "I'll see you ladies tomorrow. And I hope the golf's a great success. You'll love Gleneagles."

Doors were opened and they all climbed in. Isobel took her place behind the wheel, fastened her seat belt, turned on the ignition and they were away.

"I do apologise for the weather. We've had no summer at all yet."

"Oh, it hasn't bothered us in the least. We're just sorry you had to come out on such a day to come and collect us. Hope it wasn't too much trouble."

"No, not at all. That's my job."

"Have we far to go to your home, Lady Balmerino?"

"About ten miles. And I wish you'd call me Isobel."

"Why, thank you, we will. And I am Susan and my husband is Arnold, and the Hardwickes are Joe and Myra."

"Ten miles," said one of the men. "That's quite a distance."

"Yes. Actually my husband usually comes with me on these trips. But he had to go to a meeting. He'll be home for tea, though, so you'll meet him then."

"Is Lord Balmerino in business?"

"No. No, it's not a business meeting. It's a church meeting. Our village church. We have to raise some money. It's rather a shoestring affair. But my husband's grandfather built it, so he feels a sort of family responsibility."

It was raining again. The windscreen wipers swung to and fro. Perhaps conversation would divert their attention from the misery of it all.

"Is this your first visit to Scotland?"

The two ladies, chipping in on each other like a close-harmony duo, told her. The men had been here before, to play golf, but this was the first time their wives had accompanied them. And they just loved every inch of the place, and had gone crazy in the shops in Edinburrow. It had rained, of course, but that hadn't bothered them. They had their new Burberrys to wear, and both decided that the rain made Edinburrow look just so historic and romantic that they had been able to picture Mary and Bothwell riding together up the Royal Mile.

When they had finished, Isobel asked them what part of the States they came from.

"New York State. Rye."

"Are you by the sea there?'

"Oh, sure. Our kids sail every weekend."

Isobel could imagine it. Could imagine those kids, tanned and wind-blown, bursting with vitamins and fresh orange juice and health, scudding over starch-blue seas beneath the curving wing of a snow-white mainsail. And sunshine. Blue skies and sunshine. Day after day of it, so that you could plan tennis matches and picnics and evening barbecues and know that it wasn't going to rain.

That was how summers, in memory, used to be. The endless, aimless summers of childhood. What had happened to those long, light days, sweet with the scent of roses, when one had to come indoors only to eat, and sometimes not even then? Swimming in the river, lazing in the garden, playing tennis, having tea in the shade of some tree because it was too hot anywhere else. She remembered picnics on moors that shimmered in the sunlight, the heather too dry to light a campfire, and the larks flying high. What had happened to her world? What cosmic disaster had transformed those bright days into week after week of dark and soggy gloom?

It wasn't just the weather, it was the fact that the weather made everything so much worse. Like Archie getting his leg shot off, and having to be nice to people you didn't know because they were paying you money to sleep in your spare bedrooms. And being tired all the time, and never buying new clothes, and worrying about Hamish's school fees, and missing Lucilla.

She heard herself saying, with some force, "It's the one horrible thing about living in Scotland."

For a moment, perhaps surprised by her outburst, nobody commented on this announcement. Then one of the ladies spoke. "I beg your pardon?"

"I'm sorry. I meant the rain. We get so tired of the rain. I meant these horrible summers."

5

The Presbyterian church in Strathcroy, the established Church of Scotland, stood, impressive, ancient and venerable, on the south bank of the River Croy. It was reached from the main road that ran through the village by a curved stone bridge, and its setting was pastoral. Glebelands sloped to the water's edge, a grassy pasture where, each September, the Strathcroy Games were held. The churchyard, shaded by a mammoth beech, was filled with time-worn, leaning gravestones, and a grassy path led between these to the gates of the Manse. This too was solid and imposing, built to contain the large families of bygone ministers and boasting an enviable garden burgeoning with gnarled but productive fruit trees and old-fashioned roses, for these flourished behind the protection of a high stone wall. All of this, so charmingly disposed, exuded an ambience of timelessness, domestic security, and god-fearing piety.

In contrast, the little Episcopal church, like a poor relation, crouched directly across the bridge, totally overshadowed, both literally and metaphorically, by its rival. The main road ran close by, and between the church and the road was a strip of grass which the rector, the Reverend Julian Gloxby, himself cut each week. A small lane led up a slope to the back of the church and to the rectory that stood behind it. Both were modest in size and whitewashed. The church had a little tower with a single bell, and a wooden porchway enclosed its main door. Inside, it was equally unassuming. No handsome pews, no flagged floors, no historic relics. A worn drugget led to the altar, and a breathless harmonium did duty as an organ. There was always a faint smell of damp.

Both church and rectory had been erected at the turn of the century by the first Lord Balmerino and handed over to the Diocese with a small endowment for maintenance. The income this produced had long since trickled to nothing, the congregation was tiny, and the Vestry, endeavouring to make ends meet, found themselves perpetually strapped for cash.

When the electric wiring was discovered to be not only faulty but downright dangerous, it was very nearly the last straw. But Archie Balmerino rallied his meagre troops, chaired committees, visited the Bishop and wangled a grant. Even so, some fund-raising was going to be necessary. Various suggestions were put forward, discussed, and eventually turned down. In the end, it was decided to fall back on that old dependable, a church sale. This would take place in July, in the village hall. There would be a jumble stall, a plant and vegetable stall, a white elephant and handwork stall, and, of course, teas.

A committee was duly appointed and met, on that grey and damp June afternoon, around the dining-room table at Balnaid, home of Virginia and Edmund Aird. By half past four the meeting was over, with business satisfactorily concluded and modest plans laid. These included the printing of eye-catching posters, the borrowing of a number of trestle-tables, and the organising of a raffle.

The rector and Mrs Gloxby, and Toddy Buchanan, who ran the Strathcroy Arms, had already taken their leave and driven away in their cars. Dermot Honeycombe, busy with his antique shop, had been unable to attend. In his absence, he had been given the job of running the white elephant stall.

Now only three people remained. Virginia and Violet, her mother-in-law, sat at one end of the long mahogany

71

table and Archie Balmerino at the other. As soon as the others had gone, Virginia had disappeared into the kitchen to make tea, and brought it to them on a tray, without ceremony. Three mugs, a brown teapot, a jug of milk, and a bowl of sugar. It was both refreshing and welcome, and it was pleasant to relax after the concentrated discussions of the afternoon and to be able to chat without restriction, enjoying the easy closeness of family and old friends.

They were still mulling over the church sale.

"I just hope Dermot won't mind being told he has to run the white elephant stall. Perhaps I should ring him and give him the opportunity to say he doesn't want to do it." Archie was always cautious about other people's feelings, terrified of it being thought that he was throwing his weight about.

Violet pooh-poohed the very idea. "Of course he won't. Dear man, he never minds pitching in. He'd probably be far more hurt if we gave the job to somebody else. After all, he knows the value of everything . . ."

She was a tall lady in her late seventies and very large, dressed in a much-worn coat and skirt and shod in sensible brogues. Her hair was grey and wispy, skewered to the back of her head in a small bun, and her face, with its long upper lip and wide-set eyes, resembled that of a kindly sheep. And yet she was neither plain nor dowdy. Wonderfully upright, she had presence, and those eyes were both merry and intelligent, dispelling any suggestion of haughtiness. Now they twinkled with amusement. ". . . Even pottery doggies with bones in their mouths, and table-lamps made out of old whisky bottles plastered in shells."

Virginia laughed. "He'll probably pick up some wonderful bargain for twenty-five pence and sell it for some incredible price in his shop next day."

She leaned back in her chair and stretched, like a lazy girl. In her early thirties, Virginia Aird was a blonde and as slender as the day she had married Edmund. Today,

72

making no concession to the formality of the occasion, she wore her usual uniform of jeans, a navy-blue Guernsey sweater, and polished leather loafers. She was pretty in a pert and catlike way, but this prettiness was elevated to beauty by her eyes, which were enormous and of a glittering sapphire blueness. Her skin was fine, innocent of make-up, and the colour of a delectable brown egg. A fine tracing of lines fanned out from the corners of those eyes, and these alone betrayed her age.

Now she flexed her long fingers and circled her wrists, as though performing some prescribed exercise.

"And Isobel will be the tea-lady." She stopped stretching. "Why didn't Isobel come today, Archie?"

"I told you . . . or perhaps you were out of the room. She had to go to Corriehill to pick up this week's batch of visitors."

"Yes, of course, how stupid of me. Sorry . . ."

"That reminds me." Violet held out her mug. "Pour me a little more tea, would you, dear? I can drink it till it comes out of my ears . . . I met Verena Steynton in Relkirk yesterday, and she told me that I didn't have to keep it a secret any longer. She and Angus are going to throw a party for Katy in September."

Virginia frowned. "What do you mean, keep it a secret?"

"Well, she confided in me a few weeks ago, but she said I wasn't to say anything until she'd spoken to Angus about it. It seems that he has finally been persuaded."

"Goodness, how enterprising! A little hop, or a full-blown affair?"

"Oh, full-blown. Marquees and fairy lights and copperplate invitations and everybody dressed to the nines."

"What *fun*." Virginia was filled with enthusiasm as Violet had known she would be. "It's lovely when people throw private parties, because then you don't have to pay for your ticket. Instead I'll have a good excuse to go and buy myself a new dress. We'll all have to rally

73

round and have people to stay. I'll have to be certain that Edmund's not planning to go to Tokyo that week."

"Where is he now?" asked Edmund's mother.

"Oh, in Edinburgh. He'll be back about six."

"And Henry? What's happened to Henry? Shouldn't he be back from school?"

"No. He's stopped off to have his tea with Edie."

"That'll cheer her up."

Virginia frowned, puzzled, as well she might be. The boot was usually on the other foot, and Edie the person who did the cheering. "What's happened?"

Violet looked at Archie. "Do you remember that cousin of Edie's, Lottie Carstairs? She was housemaid at Strathcroy the year you married Isobel?"

"Do I *remember* her?" His expression was one of horror. "Dreadful female. Nutty as a fruit-cake. She broke most of the Rockingham tea-set, and she was always creeping around the place, just where you least expected to find her. I never knew what induced my mother to employ her."

"I think it was a case of any port in a storm. It was a busy summer and she was desperate for help. Anyway, Lottie only lasted about four months, and then she went back home to Tullochard to live with her aged parents. She never married . . ."

"That's no surprise . . ."

". . . and now, of course, they're dead, and she's been on her own. Becoming, apparently, odder by the day. Finally, she went over the top and was wheeled off to the nearest mental hospital. Edie's her next-of-kin. She's been visiting the poor creature every week. And now the doctors say that she's well enough to be discharged, but of course she can't live alone again. At least, not just yet."

"Don't tell me Edie's going to have her?"

"She says she has to. There's nobody else. And you know how kind Edie is . . . she's always had a great

74

sense of family responsibility. Blood is thicker than water and all that nonsense.''

''And a great deal nastier,'' Archie commented dryly. ''Lottie Carstairs. I can't think of anything worse. When is all this going to happen?''

Violet shrugged. ''I don't know. Next month maybe. Or August.''

Virginia was horrified. ''She's surely not going to *live* with Edie?''

''Let's hope not. Let's hope it's just a temporary measure.''

''And where on earth will Edie put her? She's only got two rooms in that little cottage of hers.''

''I didn't ask.''

''When did she tell you this?''

''This morning. When she was hoovering my dining-room carpet. I thought she was looking a bit down in the mouth, so I asked her what was the matter. I heard all about it over a cup of coffee.''

''Oh, poor Edie. I can't bear it for her . . .''

Archie said, ''Edie is a saint.''

''She certainly is.'' Violet finished her tea, glanced at her watch, and began to gather her belongings: her large handbag, her papers, her spectacles. ''That was very nice, dear. Most refreshing. And now I must take myself home.''

''Me too,'' said Archie. ''Back to Croy to drink more tea with the Americans.''

''You'll be awash. Who have you got this week?''

''No idea. Just hope they're not too elderly. Last week I thought one old boy was going to die of angina right there, in the middle of the soup. Mercifully, however, he survived.''

''It's such a responsibility.''

''Not really. The worst are the ones who've signed a pledge and take no drink. Bible-Belt Baptists. Orange juice makes for sticky conversation. Have you got your car, Vi, or do you want a lift home?''

75

"I walked down, but I'd like a lift back up the hill."

"I'll take you then."

He too gathered together his papers and heaved himself to his feet. For an instant he paused and then, when certain of his balance, made his way towards them down the length of the thickly carpeted room. He limped only slightly, which was a miracle because his right leg, from a stump of thigh downwards, was made of aluminium.

He had come to the meeting today straight from his garden and apologised for his attire, but nobody took much notice because this was the way he looked most of the time. Shapeless corduroy trousers, a checked shirt with a patched collar, and a threadbare tweed jacket that he called his gardening coat, though in truth no self-respecting gardener would be seen dead in it.

Virginia pushed back her chair and stood up and Violet did the same, but much more slowly, matching her movements to Archie's painful gait. She was in no way impatient to be gone but, even if she were, would never show it, for her feelings towards him were sympathetic and fiercely protective. She had, after all, known him all his life. Remembered him as a boy, as a wild young man, as a soldier. Always laughing, and an enthusiasm – almost a lust for life – that was as catching as the measles. She remembered him endlessly active. Playing tennis; dancing at the Regimental Ball, swinging his partners nearly off their feet; leading a line of guns up the hill behind Croy, his long legs covering the heather with an easy stride that left all the others behind.

Then, he had been Archie Blair. Now, he was Lord Balmerino. The Lord and the Laird. Fine titles for a man thin as a stick, with a tin leg to boot. The black hair was now flecked with white, the skin of his face netted with lines, his dark eyes deep-set and shadowed by the jutting brows.

He reached her side and smiled. "Ready, Vi?"

"All set."

"In that case, we'll go . . ." And then, in mid-step, he stopped again. "Oh, God, I've just remembered. Virginia, did Edmund give you an envelope to give me? I called him last night. It's rather urgent. Some document from the Forestry Commission?"

Violet was instantly suspicious. "You're not going to start planting conifers, are you?"

"No, it's about some access road they're wanting to build at the edge of the moor."

Virginia shook her head. "He didn't say anything about it. Perhaps he forgot. Let's go and look on his desk in the library. It's probably there . . ."

"Right. I'd like to take it with me if I can."

They moved at a leisurely pace out of the dining room and into the hall. This was even larger, panelled in pine with a massive staircase, heavily balustraded, rising in three short flights to the upstairs landing. Various items of undistinguished furniture stood about. A carved oak chest, a gate-leg table, and a chaise longue that had seen better days. This was quite often occupied by dogs, but at the moment was empty.

"I shall not come and look for Forestry Commission documents," Violet announced. "I shall sit here until you have found them." And she settled herself majestically on the dogs' bed to wait.

They left her. "We shan't be a moment." She watched them go down the wide passage that led to the library and on to the drawing room, and on again through glassed doors to the soaring conservatory.

Alone, Violet savoured her momentary solitude, with the old house around her. She knew it so well, had known it for almost as long as she could remember. Its every mood was comfortably familiar. Every creak of the stair, every evocative smell. The hall was draughty, but the draughts did not bother her. No longer Violet's home, but Virginia's. And yet it felt much the same as it ever had, as though, over the years, it had assumed a strength of character all its own. Perhaps because so

77

much had happened here. Because it had been the haven and the touchstone of a single family.

Not that Balnaid was a very old house. In fact, it was younger than Violet by a few years, and built by her father, then Sir Hector Akenside, and a man of considerable means. She always thought that Balnaid was a little like Sir Hector. Large, kindly, and lavish, and yet totally unassuming. At a time when men of newly acquired wealth were constructing for themselves huge monuments to their pride of startling hideousness, castellated and turreted, Sir Hector had concentrated his able mind on less glamorous but infinitely more important features.

Central heating, efficient plumbing, plenty of bathrooms, and kitchens filled with sunlight, so that servants (and there were plenty of them) would work in pleasant surroundings. And from the day it was finally completed, Balnaid never looked out of place. Built from local stone on the south side of the Croy, with its back to the village and the river, the face of the house smiled out over a view both domestic and magnificent.

The garden was large, rich with shrubs and mature trees. Sir Hector's passion, he had planned and landscaped it himself, so that formal lawns flowed into drifts of unknown grass, daffodils, and bluebells. Azaleas, coral and yellow, grew in fragrant masses, and mown paths twisted away invitingly out of sight between tall stands of pink- and scarlet-blossomed rhododendrons.

Beyond the garden, and separated from it by a steep ha-ha wall, was an acre or so of parkland, grazing for the hill ponies; and, beyond again, the stone-dyked fields of the neighbouring sheep farmer. Then, in the distance, the hills. They swelled to meet the sky, dramatic as a stage-drop. Constant, and yet continually changing, as the seasons and the light changed: snow-clad, purple with heather, green with spring bracken, swept by gales . . . whatever. They were always beautiful.

Had always been beautiful.

Violet knew all this because Balnaid had been her childhood home, and so her world. She had grown up within these walls, played solitary games in that magic garden, guddled for trout in the river, ridden her stubby Shetland pony through the village and up on to the lonely hills of Croy. At the age of twenty-two, she had been married from Balnaid.

She remembered driving the little distance to the Episcopalian church in the back of her father's stately Rolls-Royce, with Sir Hector, top-hatted, beside her. The Rolls had been decked out for the occasion with white silk ribbons. These somehow lessened its dignity, and it looked almost as incongruous as Violet felt, with her ample frame laced into a white satin dress of quite hideous uncomfortableness and a mist of inherited Limerick lace veiling her homely features. She remembered returning to Balnaid in the same opulent vehicle, but on that journey even the agonising tightness of her stays had ceased to matter, because she was, at long last, the triumphant wife of Geordie Aird.

She had lived at Balnaid, on and off, ever since, and had not finally moved out until ten years ago, when Edmund married Virginia. He brought Virginia back to Balnaid to live, and Violet knew then that the time had come for her to bow out and allow the old place to welcome its new young mistress. She made the property over to Edmund and bought a gardener's derelict cottage from Archie Balmerino. This house was called Pennyburn, and there, within the estate walls of Croy, she had made a new home for herself. The restoration and refurbishment of the little house had kept her happy for a year, and she was still not finished with the garden.

I am, she told herself, a fortunate woman.

Sitting there, on the dog-smelling chaise longue, Violet looked about her. Saw the worn Turkey rug, the old bits of furniture that she had known all her life. It was pleasant when things did not change too much. When she said goodbye to Balnaid, Violet had never imagined that so

79

little would change. Edmund's new wife, she decided, would be the new broom, come to sweep away all the dusty old traditions, and she was indeed quite interested to see what Virginia – as young and vital as a breath of fresh air – would achieve. But, apart from completely revamping the big bedroom, freshening up the drawing room with a lick of paint, and turning an old pantry into a utility room that fairly hummed with deep-freezes, washing machines, drying machines, and attendant luxuries, Virginia did nothing. Violet accepted this, but found it puzzling. There was, after all, no lack of money, and to her it seemed strange that Virginia should be content to live with the worn rugs and the faded velvet curtains and the old Edwardian wallpapers.

Perhaps it had something to do with the arrival of Henry. Because after Henry was born, Virginia abandoned all other interests and immersed herself in her baby son. This was very nice, but came as something of a shock to Violet. She had no idea that her daughter-in-law would prove so deeply maternal. With Edmund away so much, and mother and child left on their own, Violet had secret reservations about this overwhelming devotion, and it was a constant source of astonishment to her that despite his upbringing, Henry had grown into such a delightful little boy. A bit too dependent on his mother, perhaps, but still, not spoiled, and a charming child. Perhaps . . .

"Sorry, Vi, to keep you waiting."

Surprise made her start. She turned and saw Archie and Virginia coming towards her, Archie holding up the long buff envelope as though it were a hard-won banner. " . . . took a bit of searching for. Come along now, and I'll drive you home."

6

Henry Aird, eight years old, banged with some importance at Edie Findhorn's front door, using her brass
knocker shaped like a pixie. The house was one of a row
of single-storey cottages that lined the main street of
Strathcroy, but Edie's was nicer than anybody else's
because it had a mossy thatched roof and forget-me-nots
grew in the little strip of earth between the pavement
and the wall. Standing there, he heard her footsteps; she
unsnibbed the door and threw it open.

"Well, here you are, turned up like a bad penny."

She was always laughing. He loved her, and when
people asked him who his best friends were, Edie came
on top of the list. She was not only jolly, but fat, white-
haired and rosy-cheeked, and appetising as a fresh and
floury scone.

"Did you have a good day?"

She always asked this, despite the fact that she saw
him every lunch-time, because she was the school
dinner-lady and served out the midday meal. It was
handy having Edie doing this because it meant that she
stinted on helpings of things he hated, like curried mince
and stodgy custard, and was lavish with the mashed
potatoes and chocolate shape.

"Yes, it was all right." He went into her sitting room,
dumped his anorak and his school-bag on the couch.
"We had drawing. We had to draw something."

"What did you have to draw?"

"We had to draw a *song*." He began to undo the

buckles of his satchel. He had a problem and thought that probably Edie could help to solve it for him. "We sang 'Speed Bonnie Boat Like a Bird on the Wing over the Sea to Skye', and we had to draw a picture of it. And everybody else drew rowing boats and islands, and I drew *this*." He produced it, slightly crumpled from contact with his gym shoes and his pencil box. "And Mr McLintock *laughed*, and I don't know why."

"He laughed?" She took the drawing from him, went to find her spectacles and put them on. "And did he not tell you why he laughed?"

"No. The bell rang and it was the end of class."

Edie sat on the couch and he sat beside her. Together they gazed in silence at his work. He thought it was one of his best pictures. A beautiful speedboat slicing through blue waters, with white water pouring up at its bow and a snowy wake at the stern. There were seagulls in the sky and, on the front of the boat, a baby wrapped in a shawl. The baby had been difficult to draw, because babies have such funny faces. No noses or chins. Also, this baby looked a bit precarious and as though at any moment it might slip off the boat and into the sea. But still, it was there.

Edie did not say anything. Henry explained to her, "It's a speedboat. And that's the lad that's been born."

"Yes, I can see that."

"But why did Mr McLintock laugh? It's not funny."

"No, it's not funny. It's a lovely picture. It's just that . . . well . . . speed doesn't mean a speedboat in the song. It means that the boat's going very fast over the water, but it's not a speedboat. And the lad that was born to be king was Bonnie Prince Charlie, and he was grown up by then."

All was now explained. "Oh," said Henry, "I see."

She gave him back the drawing. "But it's still a good picture, and I think it was very rude of Mr McLintock to laugh. Put it in your bag and take it home for your mother to see, and Edie will go and start getting your tea."

While he did this, she heaved herself to her feet, put her spectacles back on the mantelpiece and went out of the room through a door at the back that led to her kitchen and bathroom. These were modern additions, for when Edie was a little girl, the cottage had consisted solely of two rooms: the living room, which was the kitchen as well, and the bedroom. A but and ben it was called. No running water, and a wooden lavatory at the end of the garden. What was more astonishing was that Edie had been one of five children, and so seven people had once lived in these rooms. Her parents had slept in a box-bed in the kitchen, with a shelf over their heads for the baby, and the rest of the children had been crowded into the other room. For water, Mrs Findhorn had made the long walk each day to the village pump, and baths were a weekly affair, taken in a tin tub in front of the kitchen fire.

"But however did five of you get into the bedroom, Edie?" Henry would ask, fascinated by the logistics of sheer space. Even with just Edie's bed and her wardrobe, it still seemed dreadfully small.

"Oh, mind, we weren't all in there at the same time. By the time the youngest was born, my eldest brother was out working on the land, and living in a bothy with the other farm hands. And then, when the girls were old enough, they went into service in some big house or other. It was a sore wrench when we had to leave, tears all over the place, but there was no space for us all here, and too many mouths to feed, and my mother needed the extra money."

She told him other things too. How, on winter evenings, they would bank up the fire with potato peelings and sit around it, listening to their father reading aloud the stories of Rudyard Kipling, or *Pilgrim's Progress*. The little girls would work at their knitting, making socks for the menfolk. And when it came to turning the heels, the

83

sock was given to an older sister or their mother because that bit of the knitting was too complicated for them to do.

It all sounded very poor, but somehow quite cosy too. Looking about him, Henry found it hard to imagine Edie's cottage the way it had been in olden days. For now it was as bright and cheerful as it could be, the box-bed gone and lovely swirly carpets on the floor. The old kitchen fire had gone too, and a beautiful green-tiled fireplace stood in its place, and there were flowery curtains and a television set and lots of nice china ornaments.

With his drawing safely stowed, he buckled up his satchel once more. Speed Bonnie Boat. He had got it wrong. He often got things wrong. There was another song they had learned at school. "Ho ro my Nut Brown Maiden." Henry, singing lustily with the rest of the class, could just imagine the maiden. A little Pakistani, like Kedejah Ishak, with her dark skin and her shining pigtail, rowing like mad across a windy loch.

His mother had had to explain that one to him.

As well, ordinary words could be confusing. People said things to him, and he heard them, but heard them just the way they sounded. And the word, or the image conjured up by the word, stuck in his mind. Grown-ups went on holiday to 'My Yorker' or 'Portjiggal'. Or 'Grease'. Grease sounded a horrid place. Edie once told him about a lady who was very cut up because her daughter had married some fly-by-night who was not good enough for her. The poor lady, all cut up, had haunted his nightmares for weeks.

But the worst was the misunderstanding that had happened with his grandmother, and which might have come between them for ever and caused a lasting rift, had not Henry's mother finally found out what was bothering him and put it right.

He had gone to Pennyburn one day after school to have tea with his grandmother, Vi. A gale was blowing and the wind howled around the little house. Sitting by the fire, Vi had suddenly made an exclamation of annoyance, got to her feet and fetched from somewhere a folding screen, which she set up in front of the glass door that led out into the garden. Henry asked her why she was doing this, and when she told him he was so horrified that he scarcely spoke for the rest of the afternoon. When his mother came to fetch him, he had never been so glad to see her and could not wait to scramble into his anorak and be out of the house, almost forgetting to thank Vi for his tea.

It was horrible. He felt that he never wanted to go back to Pennyburn, and yet knew that he ought to, if only to protect Vi. Every time his mother suggested another visit, he made some excuse or said he would rather go to Edie's. Finally, one night while he was having his bath, she came and sat on the lavatory and talked to him . . . she brought the conversation gently around to the touchy subject and at last asked him straight if there was any reason why he no longer wanted to go to Vi's.

"You always used to love it so. Did something happen?"

It was a relief at last to talk about it.

"It's frightening."

"Darling, what's frightening?"

"It comes in, out of the garden, and it comes into the sitting room. Vi put a screen up but it could easily knock the screen over. It might hurt her. I don't think she should live there any more."

"For heaven's sake! What comes in?"

He could see it. With great tall spotted legs, and a long thin spotted neck, and great big yellow teeth with its lips curled back, ready to pounce, or bite.

"A horrible *giraffe*."

His mother was confounded. "Henry, have you gone out of your mind? Giraffes live in Africa, or zoos. There aren't any giraffes in Strathcroy."

"There are!" He shouted at her stupidity. "She said so. She said there was a horrible giraffe that came out of the garden, and through the door and into her sitting room. She *told* me so."

There was a long silence. He stared at his mother and she stared back at him with her bright blue eyes, but she never smiled.

At last she said, "She wasn't telling you that there was a giraffe, Henry. She was telling you that there was a draught. You know, a horrid, shivery draught."

A draught. Not a giraffe but a draught. All that fuss about a stupid draught. He had made a fool of himself, but was so relieved that his grandmother was safe from monsters that it didn't matter.

"Don't tell anybody," he pleaded.

"I'll have to explain to Vi. But she won't say a word."

"All right. You can tell Vi. But not anybody else."

And his mother had promised, and he had jumped out of the bath, all dripping wet, and been gathered up into a great fluffy towel and his mother's arms, and she had hugged him and told him that she was going to eat him alive she loved him so, and they had sung 'Camptown Races', and there was macaroni cheese for supper.

Edie had cooked sausages for his tea and made potato scones, and opened a tin of baked beans. While he ploughed his way through this, sitting at her kitchen table, Edie sat opposite him, drinking a cup of tea. Her own meal she would eat later.

Munching, he realised that she was quieter than usual. Normally on such occasions they never stopped talking, and he was the willing recipient of all the gossip in the glen. Who had died and how much they had left; who had abandoned his father on the farm and hightailed it

86

off to Relkirk to work in a garage; who had started a baby and was no better than she should be. But today no such snippets of information came his way. Instead Edie sat with her dimpled elbows on the table and gazed out of the window at her long, thin back garden.

He said, "Penny for your thoughts, Edie," which was what she always said to him when he had something on his mind.

She sighed deeply. "Oh, Henry, I don't know, and that's for certain."

Which told him nothing. However, when pressed, she explained her predicament. She had a cousin who had lived in Tullochard. She was called Lottie Carstairs and had never been bright. Never married. Gone into domestic service, but had proved useless even at that. She had lived with her mother and father until the old folks had died, and then turned very strange and had had to go to hospital. Edie said it was a nervous breakdown. But she was recovering. One day she would come out of hospital, and she was coming to stay with Edie because there was no other place for the poor soul to go.

Henry thought this a rotten idea. He liked having Edie to himself. "But you haven't got a spare room."

"She'll have to have my bedroom."

He was indignant. "But where will *you* sleep?"

"On the Put-U-Up in the sitting room."

She was far too fat for the Put-U-Up. "Why can't Dotty sleep there?"

"Because she will be the guest, and her name's Lottie."

"Will she stay for long?"

"We'll have to see."

Henry thought about this. "Will you go on being dinner-lady, and helping Mummy, and helping Vi at Pennyburn?"

"For heaven's sake, Henry, Lottie's not bedridden."

"Will I like her?" This was important.

Edie found herself at a loss for words. "Oh, Henry, I don't know. She's a sad creature. Nineteen shillings in

87

the pound, my father always called her. Screamed like a wet hen if a man showed his face around the door, and *clumsy*! Years ago, she worked for a wee while for old Lady Balmerino at Croy, but she smashed so much china that they had to give her the sack. She never worked again after that."

Henry was horrified. "You mustn't let her do the washing-up or she'll break all your pretty things."

"It's not just my china she'll be breaking . . ." Edie prophesied gloomily, but before Henry could follow up this interesting line of conversation she took a hold of herself, put a more cheerful expression on her face, and pointedly changed the subject. "Do you want another potato scone, or are you ready for your Choc Bar?"

7

Emerging with Archie and Virginia from the front door of Balnaid, and descending the steps to the gravel sweep, Violet saw the rain had stopped. It was still damp but now much warmer, and lifting her head she felt the breeze on her cheek, blowing freshly from the west. Low clouds were slowly being rolled aside, revealing here and there a patch of blue sky and a piercing, biblical, ray of sunshine. It would turn into a beautiful summer evening – too late to be of much use to anybody.

Archie's old Land-Rover stood waiting for them. They said goodbye to Virginia, Violet with a peck on her daughter-in-law's cheek.

"Love to Edmund."

"I'll tell him."

They clambered up into the Land-Rover, both with some effort, Violet because she was elderly, and Archie because of his tin leg. Doors were slammed shut, Archie started up the engine, and they were off. Down the curving driveway to the gate, out on to the narrow lane that led past the Presbyterian church, and so across the bridge. At the main road Archie paused, but there was no traffic, and he swung out and into the street which ran through Strathcroy from end to end.

The little Episcopal church squatted humbly. Mr Gloxby was out in front of it, cutting the grass.

"He works so hard," Archie observed. "I do hope we can raise a decent bit of cash with a church sale. It was good of you to come today, Vi. I'm sure you'd much rather have been gardening."

"It was such disheartening weather, I had no desire to get at my weeds," Vi said. "So one might as well spend the day doing something worthy." She thought about this. "Rather like when one is worried sick about a child or a grandchild, but you can't do anything, so you go and scrub the scullery floor. At the end of the day you're still worried sick, but at least you've got a clean scullery."

"You're not worried about your family, are you, Vi? What could you possibly have to worry about?"

"All women worry about their families," Violet told him flatly.

The Land-Rover trundled down the road, past the petrol station, which had once been a carpenter's workshop, and the Ishaks' supermarket. Beyond this stood the open gates that led to the back drive of Croy. Archie changed down and drove through these, and at once they were climbing steeply. Once, and not so long ago, the surrounding lands had all been park, smooth green pastures grazed by pedigree cattle, but now these had been ploughed for crops, barley, and turnips. Only a few broad-leaved trees still stood, witness to the splendour of former years.

"Why do you worry?"

Violet hesitated. She knew that she could talk to Archie. She was as close to him as if he had been her own son, for although he was five years younger than Edmund, the two boys had been brought up together, spent all their time together, and become the closest of friends.

If Edmund was not at Croy, then Archie was at Balnaid; and if they were at neither house, then they were walking the hills with guns and dogs, potting at hares and rabbits, helping Gordon Gillock burn the heather and repair the butts. Or else they were out in the boat on the loch, or casting for trout in the brown pools of the Croy, or playing tennis, or skating on frozen floodwater. Inseparable, everybody had said. Like brothers.

But they were not brothers, and they had parted. Edmund was bright. Twice as bright as either of his not unintelligent parents. Archie, on the other hand, was totally unacademic.

Edmund, sailing through university, emerged from Cambridge with an Honours Degree in Economics, and was instantly employed by a prestigious merchant bank in the City.

Archie, fearing the boredom of a City job, decided to try for the Army. He duly appeared before a Regular Commission Board and somehow managed to bluff his way through the interview, for the four senior officers had apparently felt that a modest scholastic record was outweighed by Archie's outgoing and friendly personality and his enormous enthusiasm for life.

He went through Sandhurst, joined the Queen's Loyal Highlanders, and was posted to Germany. Edmund stayed in London. He became, to no person's surprise, enormously successful, and within five years had been head-hunted by Sanford Cubben. In the fullness of time he married, and even this romantic event added glitter to his image. Violet recalled pacing up the long aisle of St Margaret's, Westminster, arm in arm with Sir Rodney Cheriton, and finding time to hope in her heart that Edmund was marrying Caroline because he truly loved her, and not because he had been seduced by the aura of riches that surrounded her.

And now the wheel had gone full circle, and both men were back in Strathcroy, Archie at Croy, and Edmund at Balnaid. Grown men in their middle years, still friends, but no longer intimate. Too much had happened to both of them, and not all of it good. Too many years had slipped by, like water under a bridge. They were different people: one a very wealthy man of business, the other strapped for cash and perpetually struggling to

91

make ends meet. But it was not because of this that a certain formality, a politeness, lay between them.

They were no longer close as brothers.

Violet sighed gustily. Archie smiled. "Oh, come on, Vi, it can't be as bad as that."

"Of course not." He had troubles enough of his own. She would make light of hers. "But I do worry about Alexa, because she seems so alone. I know she's doing a job she enjoys, and that she has that charming little house in which to live, and Lady Cheriton left her enough to give her security for the rest of her life. But I am afraid that her social life is a disaster. I think she truly believes that she's plain and dull and unattractive to men. She has no confidence in herself. When she went to London, I so hoped that she would make a life for herself, make friends of her own age. But she just stayed at Ovington Street with her grandmother, like a sort of companion. If only she could meet some dear kind man who would marry her. She should have a husband to take care of, and children. Alexa was born to have children."

Archie listened sympathetically to all this. He was as fond of Alexa as any of them. He said, "Losing her mother when she was so little . . . perhaps that was a more traumatic experience than any of us realised. Perhaps it made her feel different from other girls. Incomplete in some way."

Violet thought about this. "Yes. Perhaps. Except that Caroline was never a very demonstrative or loving mother. She never spent much time with Alexa. It was Edie who provided all Alexa's security and affection. And Edie was always there."

"But you liked Caroline."

"Oh yes, I liked her. There was nothing to dislike. We had a good relationship, and I think she was a good wife to Edmund. But she was a strangely reserved girl. Sometimes I went south, to stay for a few days with them all in London. Caroline would invite me, very

92

charmingly, knowing that I would enjoy being with Alexa and Edie. And of course I did, but I never felt totally at home. I hate cities, anyway. Streets and houses and traffic make me feel beleaguered. Claustrophobic. But, quite apart from that, Caroline was never a relaxed hostess. I always felt a bit in the way, and she was an impossible girl to chat with. Left alone with her I had to struggle, sometimes, to make conversation, and you know perfectly well that, if pressed, I can talk the hind-legs off a donkey. But pauses would fall, and they were silences that were not companionable. And I would try to fill those silences in, stitching furiously at my tapestry." She looked across at Archie. "Does that sound ridiculous, or do you understand what I'm trying to say?"

"Yes, I do understand. I hardly knew Caroline, but the few times I met her I always felt my hands and my feet were too big."

But even this mild attempt at levity did not raise a smile with Violet, preoccupied as she was with Alexa's problems. She fell silent, brooding about her grand-daughter.

By now they had climbed halfway up the hill that led to Croy and were approaching the turning for Pennyburn. There were no gates, simply an opening that broke the fence to the left of the road. The Land-Rover turned into this, and Archie drove the hundred yards or so along a neatly tarmacked lane bordered on either side by mown grass verges and a trimly clipped beech hedge. At the end of this the lane opened up into a sizeable yard, with the small white house on one side and a double garage on the other. The doors of this were open, revealing Violet's car, and, as well, her wheelbarrow and lawn-mower and a plethora of garden tools. Between the garage and the beech hedge was her drying-green. She had done a wash this morning, and a line of laundry stirred in the rising breeze. Wooden tubs, planted with hydrangeas the colour of pink blotting paper, flanked the entrance to the house, and a hedge of lavender grew close to its walls.

Archie drew up and switched off the engine, but Violet made no move to alight. Having started this discussion, she had no wish to end it before it was finished.

"So I don't really believe that losing her mother in that tragic way is the root cause of Alexa's lack of confidence. Nor the fact that Edmund married again and presented her with a stepmother. Nobody could have been sweeter or more understanding than Virginia, and the arrival of Henry brought nothing but joy. Not a hint of sibling rivalry." The mention of Henry's name reminded Violet of yet another tiresome worry. "And now I'm fretting about Henry. Because I'm afraid that Edmund is going to insist on sending him to Templehall as a boarder. And I think he's not ready for that yet. And if he does go, I'm anxious for Virginia, because her life *is* Henry, and if he is torn away from her against her will, I'm afraid that she and Edmund might drift apart. He is away so much. Sometimes in Edinburgh for the entire week, sometimes on the other side of the world. It's not good for a marriage."

"But when Virginia married Edmund, she knew how it would be. Don't get too worked up about it, Vi. Templehall's a good school, and Colin Henderson's a sympathetic headmaster. I've got great faith in the place. Hamish has loved it there, enjoyed every moment."

"Yes, but your Hamish is very different from Henry. At eight years old, Hamish was quite capable of taking care of himself."

"Yes." Archie, not without pride, had to admit this. "He's a tough little bugger."

Violet was visited by another dreadful thought. "Archie, they don't hit the little boys, do they? They don't beat them?"

"Heavens, no. The worst punishment is to be sent to sit on the wooden chair in the hall. For some reason this puts the fear of God into the most recalcitrant infant."

94

"Well, I suppose that's something to be thankful for. So barbaric to beat little children. And so stupid. Getting hit by someone you dislike can only fill you with hatred and fear. Being sent to sit on a hard chair by a man you respect, and even like, is infinitely more sensible."

"Hamish spent most of his first year sitting on it."

"Wicked boy. Oh dear, it doesn't bear thinking about. And Lottie doesn't bear thinking about either. Now I've got Edie to worry over, saddling herself with that dreadful lunatic cousin. We've all depended on Edie for so long, we forget that she's no longer young. I just hope it's not all going to be too much for her."

"Well, it hasn't happened yet. Maybe it'll never happen."

"We can scarcely wish poor Lottie Carstairs dead, which seems the only alternative."

She looked at Archie and saw, somewhat to her surprise, that he was near to laughter. "You know something, Vi? You're depressing me."

"Oh, I am sorry." She struck him a companionable blow on the knee. "What a miserable old gasbag I am. Take no notice. Tell me, what news of Lucilla?"

"Last heard of, roosting in some Paris garret."

"They always say that children are a joy. But at times they can be the most appalling headaches. Now, I must let you get home and not keep you chattering. Isobel will be waiting for you."

"You wouldn't like to come back to Croy and have more tea?" He sounded wistful. "Help amuse the Americans?"

Violet's heart sank at the prospect. "Archie, I don't think I feel quite up to doing that. Am I being selfish?"

"Not a bit. Just a thought. Sometimes I find all this barking and wagging tails daunting. But it's nothing compared with what poor Isobel has to do."

"It must be the most dreadfully hard work. All that fetching and carrying and cooking and table-laying and bed-making. And then having to make conversation. I

95

know it's only for two nights each week, but couldn't you chuck your hands in and think of some other way to make money?"

"Can you?"

"Not immediately. But I wish things could be different for you both. I know one can't put the clock back, but sometimes I think how nice it would be if nothing had changed at Croy. If your precious parents could still be alive, and all of you young again. Coming and going, and cars buzzing up and down the drive, and voices. And laughter."

She turned to Archie, but his face was averted. He gazed out over her washing-green, as though Violet's tea-towels and pillowcases and her sturdy brassiere and silk knickers were the most absorbing sight in the world.

She thought, *And you and Edmund the closest of friends*, but she did not say this.

"And Pandora there. That naughty, darling child. I always felt that when she left she took so much of the laughter with her."

Archie stayed silent. And then he said "Yes," and nothing more.

A small constraint lay between them. To fill it, Violet busied herself, gathering up her belongings. "I mustn't keep you any longer." She opened the door and clambered down from the bulky old vehicle.

"Thank you for the ride, Archie."

"A pleasure, Vi."

"Love to Isobel."

"Of course. See you soon."

She waited while he turned the Land-Rover, and watched him drive away, along the lane, and on up the hill. She felt guilty, because she should have gone with him, and drunk tea with Isobel, and made polite chat to the unknown Americans. But too late now, because he was gone. She searched in her handbag for her key and let herself into her house.

Alone, Archie continued on his way. The road grew
steeper. Now there were trees ahead, Scots pine and tall
beeches. Beyond and above these, the face of the hillside
thrust skywards, cliffs of rock and scree, sprouting tufts
of whin and bracken and determined saplings of silver
birch. He reached the trees; and the road, having climbed
as high as it could, swept around to the left and levelled
out. Ahead, the beech avenue led the way to the house.
A burn tumbled down from the hilltops in a series of
pools and waterfalls and flowed on down the hill under
an arched stone bridge. This stream was Pennyburn,
and lower down the slope it made its way through the
garden of Violet Aird's house.

Beneath the beeches all was shaded, the light diffused,
limpid and greenish. The leafy branches arched thickly
overhead, and it felt a little like driving down the centre
aisle of some enormous cathedral. And then, abruptly,
the avenue fell behind him and the house came into
view, set four-square on the brow of the hill, with the
whole panoramic vista of the glen spread out at its feet.
The evening breeze had done its work, tearing the clouds
to tatters, lifting the mist. The distant hills, the peaceful
acres of farmland, were washed in golden sunlight.

All at once, it became essential to have a moment or
two to himself. This was selfish. He was already late,
and Isobel was waiting for him, in need of his moral
support. But he pushed guilt out of his mind, drew up
out of earshot of the house, and switched off the engine.

It was very quiet, just the sough of the wind in the
trees, the cry of curlews. He listened to the silence, from
some distant field heard the bleat of sheep. And Violet's
voice: *All of you young again. Coming and going . . . And
Pandora there . . .*

She shouldn't have said that. He did not want his

memories stirred. He did not wish to be consumed by this yearning nostalgia.

All of you young again.

He thought about Croy the way it had once been. He thought about coming home as a schoolboy, as a young soldier on leave. Roaring up the hill in his supercharged sports car with the roof down and the wind burning his cheeks. Knowing, with all the confidence of youth, that all would be just as he had left it. Drawing up with a screech of brakes at the front of the house; the family dogs spilling out of the open door, barking, coming to greet him, and their clamour alerting the household, so that by the time he was indoors, they were all converging. His mother and father, Harris the butler, and Mrs Harris the cook, and any other housemaid or daily lady who happened to be helping out at the time.

"Archie. Oh, darling, welcome home."

And then, Pandora. *I always felt that when she left she took so much of the laughter with her.* His young sister. In memory, she was about thirteen and already beautiful. He saw her flying, long-legged, down the stairs, to leap into his waiting embrace. He saw her, with her full, curving mouth and her woman's provocative, slanting eyes. He felt the lightness of her body as he swung her around, off her feet. He heard her voice.

"You're back, you brute, and you've got a new car. I saw it out of the nursery window. Take me for a ride, Archie. Let's go a hundred miles an hour."

Pandora. He found himself smiling. Always, even as a child, she had been a life-enhancer, an injector of vitality and laughter to the most stuffy of occasions. Where she had sprung from he had never quite worked out. She was a Blair born and bred, yet so different in every way from the rest of them that she might have been a changeling.

He remembered her as a baby, as a little girl, as that delicious leggy teenager, for she had never suffered from puppy fat, spots, or lack of confidence. At sixteen, she

98

looked twenty. Every friend he brought to the house had been, if not in love with her, then certainly mesmerised.

Life had hummed with activity for the young Blairs. House parties, shooting parties, tennis in the summer, August picnics on the sunlit, purple-heathered hills. He recalled one picnic when Pandora, complaining of the heat, had stripped off all her clothes and plunged naked, with no thought for astonished spectators, into the loch. He remembered dances, and Pandora in a white chiffon dress, with her brown shoulders bare, whirling from man to man through Strip the Willow and the Duke of Perth.

She was gone. Had been gone for over twenty years. At eighteen, a few months after Archie's wedding, she had eloped with an American, some other woman's husband, whom she had met in Scotland during the summer. With this man she flew to California, and in the fullness of time, became his wife. Waves of shock and horror reverberated around the county, but the Balmerinos were so loved and respected that they were treated with much sympathy and understanding. Perhaps, people said hopefully, she will come back. But Pandora did not come back. She did not return even for her parents' funerals. Instead, as though engaged in an endless Strip the Willow, she flung herself, wayward as always, from one disastrous love affair to another. Divorced from her American husband, she moved to New York, and later to France, where she lived for some years in Paris. She kept in touch with Archie by means of rare and sporadic postcards, sending a scrawled address, a scrap of information, and a huge straggling cross for a kiss. Now she seemed to have ended up in a villa in Majorca. God knew who was her current companion.

Long since, Archie and Isobel had despaired of her, and yet, from time to time, he found himself missing her more than anybody else. For youth was over, and his father's household dispersed. Harris and Mrs Harris had long retired, and domestic help was reduced to

Agnes Cooper who, two days a week, climbed the hill from the village to give Isobel a hand in the kitchen.

As for the estate, matters were hardly better. Gordon Gillock, the keeper, was still in situ in his small stone house with the kennels at the back, but the grouse moor was let to a syndicate, and Edmund Aird paid the keeper's salary. The farm, as well, had gone, and the parkland was ploughed for crops. The old gardener – a weathered stick of a man and an important part of Archie's childhood – had finally died, and not been replaced. His precious walled garden was put down to grass; unpruned, the rhododendrons grew massive, and the hard tennis court was green with moss. Archie now was officially the gardener, with the sporadic assistance of Willy Snoddy, who lived in a grubby cottage at the end of the village, trapped rabbits and poached salmon, and was pleased from time to time to earn a little drinking money.

And he himself? Archie took stock. An ex-Lieutenant Colonel in the Queen's Loyal Highlanders, invalided out with a tin leg, a sixty-per-cent disability pension, and too many nightmares. But still, thanks to Isobel, in possession of his inheritance. Croy was still his and would, God willing, belong to Hamish. Crippled, struggling to make ends meet, he was still Balmerino of Croy.

Suddenly, it was funny. Balmerino of Croy. Such a fine-sounding title, and such a ludicrous situation. It was no good trying to work out why everything had gone so wrong because there was nothing much he could do about it anyway. No more harking back. Duty called and the Lady Balmerino waited.

For some obscure reason he felt more cheerful. He started up the engine and drove the short distance across the gravel to the front of the house.

8

It had drizzled most of the day but now it was fine, so after his tea Henry went out into Edie's garden with her. This ran down to the river, and her washing-line was strung between two apple trees. He helped her to unpeg the washing and put it into the wicker basket, and they folded the sheets together with a snap and a crack to get all the creases out of them. With this accomplished, they went back into the house and Edie set up the ironing board and began ironing her pillowcases and the table-cloth and a blouse. Henry watched, liking the smell and the way the hot iron made the crunchy damp linen all smooth and shiny and crisp.

He said, "You're very good at ironing."

"I'd need to be after all these years at it."

"How many years, Edie?"

"Well . . ." She dumped the iron down on its end and folded the pillowcase with her dimpled red hands. "I'm sixty-eight now, and I was eighteen when I first went to work for Mrs Aird. Work that one out."

Even Henry could do that sum. "Fifty years."

"Fifty years is a long way to look ahead, but looking back it doesn't seem any time at all. Makes you wonder what life's all about."

"Tell me about Alexa and London." Henry had never been to London, but Edie had lived there once.

"Oh, Henry, I've told you these stories a thousand times."

"I like to hear them *again*."

"Well . . ." She pressed a crease, sharp as a knife edge. "When your daddy was much younger, he was married to a lady called Caroline. They were married in London, at St Margaret's, Westminster, and we all went down for the occasion, and stayed at a hotel called the Berkeley. And what a wedding that was! Ten lovely bridesmaids, all in white dresses, like a flock of swans. And after the wedding we all went to another very grand hotel called the Ritz, and there were waiters in tailcoats and so grand you'd have thought they were wedding guests themselves. And there was champagne and such a spread of food you didn't know where to start."

"Were there jellies?"

"Jellies in every colour. Yellow and red and green. And there was cold salmon and wee sandwiches you could eat with your fingers, and frosted grapes all sparkling with sugar. And Caroline wore a dress of wild silk and a great long train, and on her head was a diamond tiara that her father had given her for a wedding present, and she looked like a queen."

"Was she pretty?"

"Oh, Henry, all brides are beautiful."

"Was she as pretty as my mother?"

But Edie was not to be drawn. "She was good-looking in a different sort of way. Very tall, she was, with lovely black hair."

"Did you like her?"

"Of course I liked her. I wouldn't have gone to London to look after Alexa if I hadn't liked her."

"Tell me about that bit."

Edie set aside her pillowcases and started in on the blue-and-white-checked tablecloth.

"Well, it was just after your Grandfather Geordie died. I was still living at Balnaid, and working for your Granny Vi. It was just the two of us in the house, keeping each other company. We knew that Alexa was on the way, because Edmund had come up for his father's funeral and he told us then. 'Caroline is having a baby,' he told us, and it was a wonderful comfort to your Granny Vi to know that even if Geordie was with her no longer, there was a new wee life on the way. And then we heard that Caroline was looking for a nanny to take care of the bairn. Your Granny Vi was up to high doh. The truth of the matter was that she couldn't bide the thought of some uninformed bisom having the care of her grand-child, filling her wee head with all the wrong ideas, and not taking the time to talk to the child, nor read to her. I never thought about going until your Granny Vi asked me to. I didn't want to leave Balnaid and Strathcroy. But . . . we talked it over and in the end decided that there was nothing else to be done. So I went to London . . ."

"I bet Daddy was pleased to see you."

"Och, yes, he was pleased enough. And at the end of the day, it was a mercy I went. Alexa was born safe and sound, but after the baby arrived, Caroline became very, very ill."

"Did she have measles?"

"No, it wasn't measles."

"Whooping cough?"

"No. It wasn't that sort of illness. It was more nervous. Post-natal depression they call it, and it's a horrible thing to see. She had to go to hospital for treatment, and when she was allowed home she was really not able for anything, let alone taking care of a baby. But eventually she recovered a wee bit and her mother Lady Cheriton took her off on a cruise to a lovely island called Madeira. And after a month or two there, she was better again."

"Were you left all alone in London?"

"Not *all* alone. There was a nice lady who came in every day to clean the house, and then your father was in and out."

"Why didn't you come back to Scotland and stay with Vi?"

"There was a time when we thought we might. Just for a visit. It was the week of Lord and Lady Balmerino's wedding . . . only then of course he was Archie Blair,

103

and such a handsome young officer. Caroline was still in Madeira and Edmund said we'd all come north together for the occasion and stay at Balnaid. Your Granny Vi was so excited when she heard the news that we were coming to visit. She got the cot down from the attic and washed the baby blankets and dusted up the old pram. And then Alexa started teething . . . she was only a wee thing and what a time she had of it. Crying all night and not a mortal thing I could do to quieten her. I think I went two weeks without a proper night's sleep, and in the end Edmund said he thought the long journey north would be too much for the pair of us. He was right, of course, but I could have cried from disappointment.''

''And Vi must have been disappointed too.''

''Yes, I think she was.''

''Did Daddy come to the wedding?''

''Oh, yes, he came. He and Archie were old, old friends. He had to be there. But he came on his own.''

She had finished the tablecloth. Now she was on to her best blouse, easing the point of the iron into the gathered bit on the shoulder. That looked even more difficult than ironing pillowcases.

''Tell me about the house in London.''

''Oh, Henry, do you not weary of all these old tales?''

''I like hearing about the house.''

''All right. It was in Kensington, in a row. Very tall and thin, and what a work. The kitchens in the basement and the nurseries right up at the top of the house. It seemed to me that I never stopped climbing stairs. But it was a beautiful house, filled with precious things. And there was always something going on – people calling, or dinner parties, and guests arriving through the front door in their fine clothes. Alexa and I used to sit on the turn of the stairs and watch it all through the banisters.''

''But nobody saw you.''

''No. Nobody saw us. It was like playing hide-and-seek.''

104

"And you used to go to Buckingham Palace . . ."

"Yes, to watch the Changing of the Guard. And sometimes we took a taxi to Regent's Park Zoo and looked at the lions. And when Alexa was old enough, I walked her to school and dancing class. Some of the other children were little Lords and Ladies, and what a toffee-nosed lot *their* nannies were!"

Little Lords and Ladies and a house filled with precious things. Edie, Henry decided, had had some marvellous experiences. "Were you sad to leave London?"

"Oh, Henry, I was sad because it was a sad time, and the reason for leaving was so sad. A terrible tragedy. Just think, one man driving his car far too fast and without thinking of any other body on the road, and in a single instant Edmund had lost his wife and Alexa her mother. And poor Lady Cheriton her only child, her only daughter. Dead."

Dead. It was a terrible word. Like the snap of a pair of scissors cutting a piece of string in two and knowing that you could never, ever put the piece of string together again.

"Did Alexa mind?"

" 'Mind' is not the word for such a time of bereavement."

"But it meant that you could come back to Scotland."

"Yes." Edie sighed and folded her blouse. "Yes, we came back. We all did. Your father to work in Edinburgh and Alexa and I to live at Balnaid. And things gradually got better. Grief is a funny thing because you don't have to carry it with you for the rest of your life. After a bit you set it down by the roadside and walk on and leave it resting there. As for Alexa, it was a new life. She went to Strathcroy Primary, just as you do, and made friends with all the village children. And your Granny Vi gave her a bicycle and a wee Shetland pony. Before very long you'd never have known she ever lived in London. And yet every holidays, when she was old enough to travel

105

on her own, back she went to stay a little while with Lady Cheriton. It was the least we could do for the poor lady."

Her ironing was finished. She turned off the iron and set it in the grate to cool, and then folded up her ironing board. But Henry did not want to stop this fascinating conversation.

"Before Alexa, you looked after Daddy, didn't you?"

"That's what I did. Right up to the day when he was eight years old and went away to boarding school."

Henry said, "I don't want to go to boarding school."

"Oh, come away." Edie's voice turned brisk. She was not about to have any teary nonsense. "And why not? Lots of other boys your own age, and football and cricket and high jinks."

"I won't know anybody. I won't have a friend. And I shan't be able to take Moo with me."

Edie knew all about Moo. Moo was a piece of satin and wool, remains of Henry's cot blanket. It lived under his pillow and helped him to get to sleep at nights. Without Moo he would not sleep. Moo was very important to him.

"No," she admitted. "You won't be able to take Moo, that's for certain. But nobody would object if you took a teddy."

"Teddies don't work. And Hamish Blair says only babies take teddies."

"Hamish Blair talks a lot of nonsense."

"And you won't be there to give me my dinner."

Edie stopped being brisk. She put out a hand and ruffled his hair. "Wee man. We all have to grow up, move on. The world would come to a standstill if we all stayed in the same place. Now" – she looked at her clock – "it's time you were away home. I promised your mother you'd be back by six. Will you be all right on your own, or do you want me to come a bit of the way with you?"

"No," he told her. "I'll be all right on my own."

106

9

Edmund Aird was nearly forty when he married for the second time, and his new wife Virginia was twenty-three. She hailed not from Scotland but from Devon, the daughter of an officer in the Devon and Dorset Regiment who had retired from the Army in order to run an inherited farm, a considerable spread of land between Dartmoor and the sea. She had been brought up in Devon, but her mother was American, and every summer she and Virginia crossed the Atlantic in order to spend the hot months of July and August in her old family home. This was in Leesport on the south shore of Long Island, a village facing out over the blue waters of the Great South Bay to the dunes of Fire Island.

The grandparents' house was old, clapboard, large and airy. Sea breezes blew through it, stirring filmy curtains and bringing indoors the scents of the garden. This garden was spacious and separated from the quiet, tree-shaded street by a white picket fence. There were decks furnished for outdoor living, and wide porches screened for coolness and sanctuary from bugs. But its greatest charm was that it adjoined the country club, that hub of social activity with its restaurants and bars, golf course, tennis courts, and enormous turquoise swimming pool.

It was a world away from damp and misty Devon, and the annual experience gave the young Virginia a polish and sophistication that set her apart from her English contemporaries. Her clothes, purchased during mammoth Fifth Avenue shopping sprees, were both sleek and trendy. Her voice held a trace of her mother's charming drawl, and returning to school with her groomed blonde head and her long, slender American legs, she was a source of much wonder and admiration and, inevitably, on the receiving end of a good deal of malicious envy.

Early on she learned to cope with this.

Not particularly scholastic, her passion was the open air and any sort of outdoor activity. In Long Island she played tennis, sailed and swam. In Devon she rode, hunting every winter with the local foxhounds. As she grew up, young men flocked to her side, poleaxed by the sight of her in hunting gear astride some enviable horse, or flying expertly about the tennis court in a white skirt that barely covered her bottom. At Christmas dances they clustered like bees around the proverbial honey-pot. When she was home, the telephone constantly rang, was constantly for her. Her father complained but secretly he was proud. In time, he stopped complaining, and installed a second telephone.

Leaving school, she went to London and learned to work an electric typewriter. This was extremely dull, but as she had no particular talent nor ambition, seemed to be the only thing to do. She shared a flat in Fulham and did temporary jobs, because that way she was free to come and go whenever a pleasant invitation came her way. The men were still there but now they were different men: older, richer, and sometimes married to other women. She allowed them to spend enormous sums of money on her, take her out to dinner and give her expensive presents. And then, when they were at their wits' end with unrequited lust and devotion, she would without warning disappear from London – to spend another blissful summer with her grandparents, or head for a house party in Ibiza, or a yacht on the west coast of Scotland, or Christmas in Devon.

On one of these impetuous jaunts she had met

Edmund Aird. It was September and at a house party in Relkirkshire for the hunt ball, where she was staying with the family of a girl with whom she had been at school. Before the ball, there was a lavish dinner party and all the guests – those staying in the house and others who had been invited – foregathered in the great library.

Virginia was the last to make her entrance. She wore a dress of so pale a green that it was almost white, strapless but caught over one shoulder by a spray of ivy, the dark leaves fashioned of gleaming satin.

She saw him instantly. He was standing with his back to the fireplace, and he was tall. Across the room their eyes met and held. He had black hair streaked with white, like silver-fox fur. She was accustomed to men in all the peacock glory of Highland dress but she had never seen one who looked so easy and so well in his finery, the diced hose and the kilt, and the sombre bottle-green jacket sparked with silver buttons.

". . . Virginia dear, there you are." This was her hostess. "Now who do you know and who do you not know?" Unknown faces, new names. She scarcely heard them spoken. Finally, ". . . and this is Edmund Aird. Edmund, this is Virginia, who is staying with us. All the way from Devon. And you mustn't talk to her now because I've put you next to each other at dinner, and you can talk to her then . . ."

She had never before fallen so instantly and totally in love. There had, of course, been affairs, mad infatuations in the high old days of the Leesport Country Club, but never anything that lasted longer than a few weeks. That evening was very different, and Virginia knew, without question, that she had met the only man with whom she had ever wanted to share the rest of her life. It did not take very long to realise that the incredible miracle was actually happening and that Edmund felt exactly the same way about her.

The world became brilliant and beautiful. Nothing could go wrong. Dazzled by happiness, she was ready to throw in her lot with Edmund, abandon all common sense and any tiresome principle. Give him her life. Live in the back of beyond if necessary; on the top of a mountain; in blatant sin. It didn't matter. Nothing mattered.

But Edmund, having lost his heart, kept a tight rein on his head. He went to some lengths to explain his position. He was, after all, head of the Scottish branch of Sanford Cubben, a man of some prominence and very much in the eye of the media. Edinburgh was a small city, and he had many friends and business colleagues, and their respect and trust he valued. To step too blatantly out of line and end up with his name plastered over the gossip columns of the tabloid newspapers would be not only foolish but possibly disastrous.

As well, he had to consider his family.

"Family?"

"Yes, family. I have been married before."

"I should think it very strange if you hadn't been."

"My wife was killed in a car accident. But I have Alexa. She's ten. She lives with my mother in Strathcroy."

"I like little girls. I would be very careful of her."

But there were still other hurdles to be faced.

"Virginia, I'm seventeen years older than you. Does forty seem so very decrepit?"

"Years don't matter."

"It would mean your living in the wilds of Relkirkshire."

"I shall drape myself in tartan and wear a hat with a feather."

He laughed, but wryly. "Unfortunately, it's not September all the year round. All our friends live miles apart and the winters are long and dark. Everybody hibernates. I am so afraid that you would find it very dull."

"Edmund, it sounds a little as though you're having second thoughts and are trying to put me off."

"It's not that. Never that. But you have to know

110

all the truths. No illusions. You are so young, and so beautiful, and so vital, and you have all of life in front of you . . .''

"To be with you."

"That's another thing. My job. It's demanding. I'm away so much. Abroad so often, sometimes for two or three weeks at a time."

"But you'll come back to me."

She was adamant, and he adored her. He sighed. "I wish for both our sakes that it could be different. I wish that I were young again, and without responsibilities. Free to behave any way I wanted. Then we could live together and have time to get to know each other. And be totally sure."

"I am totally sure."

She was. Undeviating. He took her in his arms and said, "Then there's nothing for it. I shall have to marry you."

"You poor man."

"You will be happy? I want so much to make you happy."

"Oh, Edmund. Darling Edmund. How could I be anything else?"

They were married two months later, at the end of November, in Devon. It was a quiet wedding in the tiny church where Virginia had been christened.

The end of the beginning. No regrets. The casual, indiscriminate affairs were over and she let them go without a backward glance. She was Mrs Edmund Aird.

After their honeymoon they travelled north to Balnaid, Virginia's new home, and her new and ready-made family: Violet, Edie, and Alexa. Life in Scotland was a very different experience from anything that Virginia had previously known, but she made every effort to adjust, if only because others, very obviously, were doing the same thing. Violet had already moved firmly out and gone to live at Pennyburn. She proved a model of non-interference. Edie was equally tactful. The time

111

had come, she announced, for her to leave as well and settle herself in the cottage in the village where she had been brought up and which she had inherited from her mother. She was retiring from resident work but instead would continue on a daily basis, sharing her time between Virginia and Violet.

Edie was, in those early days, a tower of strength, a source of excellent advice, and a fund of cosy gossip. It was she who, for Alexa's sake, filled in for Virginia some details of Edmund's previous marriage, but once this was done, she never mentioned it again. It was over, finished. Water under the bridge. Virginia was grateful. Edie, the old servant who had seen and heard everything, could well have proved to be the fly in the ointment. Instead she became one of Virginia's closest friends.

Alexa took a little longer. Sweet-natured and self-contained, she was inclined to be shy and withdrawn. She was not a beautiful child, with a dumpy shape and pale-red hair and the white skin that goes with this colouring, and was at first uncertain of her position in the family, yet almost touchingly anxious to please. Virginia responded to the best of her ability. This little girl was, after all, Edmund's child and an important part of their marriage. She could never be a mother, but she could be a sister. Unobtrusively, she eased Alexa out of her shell, speaking to her as though they were the same age, taking much care not to tread on any tender toes. She showed interest in Alexa's ploys, her drawing and her dolls, and included her in every possible activity and occasion. This was not always convenient, but the most important thing was that Alexa should never feel abandoned.

It took about six months, but it was worth it. She was

rewarded by Alexa's spontaneous confidences, and a touching admiration and devotion.

So there was family, but there were friends too. Liking her for her youth, for their affection for Edmund, for the fact that Edmund had chosen to marry her, they made her welcome. The Balmerinos, of course, but others too. Virginia was a gregarious girl who did not relish solitude and found herself surrounded by people who seemed to want her. When Edmund was away on business, which he was more often than not, right from the start, everybody was enormously kind and attentive, asking her out on her own, constantly phoning to be certain that she was neither lonely nor unhappy.

Which she was not. Secretly she almost relished Edmund's absences because, in some strange way, they enhanced everything; he was gone but she knew that he was coming back to her, and each time he came back, being married to him was even better than before. Occupied with Alexa, with her new house, and her new friends, she filled in the empty days and counted the hours until Edmund should return to her. From Hong Kong. From Frankfurt. Once he had taken her with him to New York, and afterwards had indulged in a week's leave. They had spent it at Leesport, and she remembered that time as one of the best in the whole of her life.

And then, Henry.

Henry changed everything, not for the worse, but for the better, if that was possible. After Henry, she didn't want to go away any more. She had never imagined herself capable of such selfless love. It was different from loving Edmund, but all the more precious because it was utterly unexpected. She had never thought of herself as maternal, had never analysed the true meaning of the word. But this tiny human being, this little life, reduced her to wordless wonder.

They all teased her, but she didn't mind. She shared him with Violet and Edie and Alexa, and relished in the sharing because, at the end of the day, Henry belonged to her. She watched him grow and savoured every moment of his progress. He stumbled and walked and spoke words, and she was enchanted. She played with him, drew pictures, watched Alexa push him in her old doll's pram across the lawn. They lay in the grass and watched ants, walked down to the river and threw pebbles into the swift-flowing brown stream. They sat by winter fires and read picture books.

He was two. He was three. He was five years old. She took him for his first day at the Strathcroy Primary School and stood at the gate watching him walk away from her up the path to the schoolhouse door. There were children everywhere but none of them took any notice of him. He seemed, at that moment, especially small and very vulnerable, and she could scarcely bear to see him go.

Three years later, he was still small and vulnerable, and she felt more protective of him than ever. And this was the cause of the cloud that had gathered and now lay on the edge of her own personal horizon. She was afraid of it.

From time to time the subject of Henry's future had come up, but she had shied from discussing it through with Edmund. He knew, however, her opinion. Lately, nothing had been said. She was happy to leave it this way, on the principle that it was best to leave a sleeping tiger to lie. She did not want to have to fight Edmund. She had never stood up to him before because she had always been happy to leave important decisions to him. He was, after all, older, wiser, and infinitely more competent. But this was different. This was Henry.

Perhaps, if she did not look, if she paid no attention, the problem would go away.

When Archie and Violet had left, trundling away down the drive in the battered old Land-Rover, Virginia stayed where she was, in front of the house, feeling unsatisfactorily aimless and at a loss for something to do. The church meeting had broken the day in half, and yet it was too early to go indoors and start thinking about dinner. The weather was improving by the moment, and the sun was about to appear. Perhaps she should attempt a little gardening. She considered this idea and then rejected it. In the end she went into the house, gathered up the tea-mugs from the dining-room table and carried them through to the kitchen. Edmund's spaniels were dozing in their baskets under the table. As soon as they heard her footsteps, however, they were awake, on their feet and anxious for exercise.

"I'll just put these in the dishwasher," she told them, "and then we'll go out for a bit." She always talked aloud to the dogs, and sometimes, like right now, it was comforting to hear the sound of her own voice. Mad old people talked to themselves. At times it was not difficult to understand why.

In the back kitchen, with the dogs milling around her, she took an old jacket off a hook and pushed her feet into rubber boots. Then they set off, the dogs racing ahead, down the wooded lane that ran along the south bank of the river. Two miles upstream another bridge crossed the water, leading back to the main road, and so to the village. But she left this behind her and walked on to where the trees stopped and the moor began, untrammelled miles of heather and grass and bracken, leaning up into the hills. Far away, the sheep grazed. There was only the sound of flowing water.

She came to the dam, the river sliding over its rim, the deep pool beyond. This was Henry's favourite swimming place. She sat on the bank where, in summer, they brought picnics. The dogs loved the river. They stood now knee-deep, and drank as though they had not seen water for months. When they had done this, they came

115

out and shook themselves lustily all over her. The afternoon sun felt warm. She pulled off her jacket and would have sat on, revelling in the sun's warmth, but inevitably the midges appeared in droves and started biting, so she got to her feet, whistled the dogs, and went home.

She was in the kitchen preparing dinner when Edmund returned. They were having roast chicken and she was grating breadcrumbs for bread sauce. She heard the car, looked with surprise at the clock, and saw that it was only half past five. He was very early. Driving from Edinburgh, he did not usually arrive back at Balnaid until seven or even later. What could have happened?

Speculating, hoping there was nothing wrong, she finished the breadcrumbs and dumped them into the saucepan with the milk and the onion and the cloves. She stirred. She heard his footsteps coming down the long passage from the hall. The door opened and she turned smiling, but faintly anxious.

"I'm back," he announced unnecessarily.

Her husband's masculine appearance, as always, filled Virginia with satisfaction. He wore a navy-blue chalk-striped suit, a light-blue shirt with a white collar, and a Christian Dior silk tie that she had given him for Christmas. He carried his briefcase and looked a bit creased, as well he might after a day's work and a long drive, but not in the least weary. He never looked weary and he never complained of feeling tired. His mother swore he had never been tired in his life.

He was tall, his figure youthful as it had ever been, and his handsome face, with the quiet, hooded eyes, hardly lined. Only his hair had changed. Once so black, it was now silvery-white but thick and smooth as ever. For some reason the ageless face, in juxtaposition to that white hair, rendered him more distinguished and attractive than ever.

She said, "Why so early?"

"Reasons. I'll explain." He came to kiss her; looked at

116

the saucepan. "Good smells. Bread sauce. Roast chicken?"

"Of course."

He dumped his briefcase on the kitchen table. "Where's Henry?"

"With Edie. He won't be back till after six. She's giving him his tea."

"Good."

She frowned. "Why good?"

"I want to talk to you. Let's go into the library. Leave the sauce, you can cook it later . . ."

He was already on his way out of the kitchen. Puzzled and apprehensive, Virginia put the saucepan aside and replaced the big lid on the hob. Then she followed him. She found him in the library, crouched by the fireplace, setting a match to the newspaper and kindling.

She felt faintly defensive, as though this were some sort of criticism. "Edmund, I was going to light the fire when I'd got the sauce made and the potatoes peeled. But it's a funny sort of day. We spent all afternoon in the dining room, having the church meeting. We never came in here . . ."

"Doesn't matter."

The paper had caught, the kindling snapped and crackled. He straightened, dusting his hands, and stood watching the rising flames. His profile gave nothing away.

"We're going to have this sale in July." She sat on the arm of one of the chairs. "I've got the worst job of all, collecting jumble. And Archie wanted some envelope from the Forestry Commission . . . he said you knew about it. We found it on your desk."

"Yes. That's right. I meant to give it to you."

". . . oh, and something frightfully exciting. The Steyntons are going to have a dance, for Katy, in September . . ."

"I know."

"You know?"

117

"I had lunch with Angus Steynton in the New Club today. He told me then."

"They're going the whole hog. Marquees and bands and caterers and everything. I'm going to get a really sensational dress . . ."

He turned his head and looked at her, and her chatter died. She wondered if he had even been listening. After a little, she asked, "What is it?"

He said, "I'm home early because I haven't been in the office this afternoon. I drove down to Templehall. I've been with Colin Henderson."

Templehall. Colin Henderson. She felt her heart drop into her stomach and her mouth was suddenly dry. "Why, Edmund?"

"I wanted to talk things over. I hadn't made up my mind about Henry, but now I feel sure it's the right thing to do."

"What is the right thing to do?"

"To send him there in September."

"As a boarder?"

"He could scarcely attend as a day boy."

Apprehension by now had gone, overwhelmed by a slow, consuming anger. She had never experienced anger like this against Edmund. As well, she was shocked. She had known him to be overbearing, even dictatorial, but never underhand. Now, behind her back, it seemed that he had betrayed her. She felt betrayed, without defences, destroyed before she had even had time to fire a single gun.

"You had no right." Her own voice, but it did not sound like Virginia. "Edmund. You had *no* right."

He raised his eyebrows. "No right?"

"No right to go without me. No right to go without telling me. I should have been there, to talk things over, as you put it. Henry is my child just as much as he is yours. How dare you sneak off and organise everything behind my back, without saying a single word!"

"I didn't sneak off and I'm telling you now."

118

"Yes. As a fait accompli. I don't like being treated as a person who doesn't matter, someone who has no say. Why should *you* always make all the decisions?"

"I suppose because I always have."

"You were underhand." She rose to her feet, her arms folded tightly across her breast, as though the only way to stop herself from actually striking her husband was to keep her hands under control. Always so compliant, she was a tigress now, fighting for her cub. "You know, you've always known, that I don't want Henry to go to Templehall. He's too little. He's too young. I know you went when you were eight to boarding school, and I know that Hamish Blair is there, but why should it have to be a rigid tradition that we all have to follow? It's archaic, Victorian, out of date, to send little children away from home. And what is worse is that it doesn't have to happen. Henry can perfectly well stay at Strathcroy until he's twelve. And then he can go to boarding school. That's reasonable. But not before, Edmund. *Not now.*"

He gazed at her in genuine perplexity. "Why do you want to make Henry different from other boys? Why should he be marked out as an oddity, staying at home until he's twelve? Perhaps you're confusing him with American children who seem to rule the family household until they're practically adult . . ."

Virginia was incensed. "It's nothing to do with America. How can you say such a thing? It's to do with what any sensible, normal mother feels about her children. It's you who are on the wrong track, Edmund. But you won't ever consider the possibility that you might be wrong. You're behaving like a Victorian. Old-fashioned and pig-headed and chauvinistic."

She got no reaction from this outburst. Edmund's expression did not change. On such occasions, his was a poker-face, with sleepy eyes and an unsmiling mouth. She found herself longing for him to behave naturally, let himself go, lose his temper, raise his voice. But that

119

was not Edmund Aird's way. In business, he was known as a cold fish. He stayed unmoved, controlled, unprovoked.

He said, "You are thinking only of yourself."

"I'm thinking of *Henry*."

"No. You want to keep him. And you want your own way. Life has been kind to you. You've always had your own way; spoiled and indulged by your parents. And perhaps I continued where they left off. But there comes a time when we all have to grow up. I suggest that you grow up now. Henry is not your possession and you must let him go."

She could scarcely believe that he was saying these things to her.

"I *don't* think of Henry as a possession. That is the most insulting accusation. He's a person in his own right, and I've made him that person. But he's eight years old. Scarcely out of the nursery. He needs his home. He needs *us*. He needs the security of surroundings he's known all his life, and he needs his Moo under the pillow. He *can't* be just sent away. I don't want him to be sent away."

"I know."

"He's too little."

"So he needs to grow."

"He'll grow away from me."

Edmund made no comment on this. Her bracing anger had dissolved and she was left hurt and defeated, and near to tears. To hide these, she turned away from her husband and walked to the window, and stood there with her forehead against the cool glass. She stared, hot-eyed, unseeing, at the garden.

There was a long silence. And then, reasonable as ever, Edmund began to speak again. "Templehall's a good school, Virginia, and Colin Henderson's a good headmaster. The boys are never pushed, but they're taught to work. Life is going to be hard for Henry. It's going to be hard for all these youngsters. Competitive

120

and tough. The sooner they face up to this, and learn to take the rough with the smooth, the better. Accept the situation. For my sake. See it my way. Henry is too dependent on you."

"I'm his mother."

"You smother him." With that, he walked calmly from the room.

10

In the golden evening, Henry walked home. There were few people about because it was nearly six o'clock and they were all indoors eating their tea. He imagined this comforting meal. Soup perhaps, and then haddock or chops and then cakes and biscuits, all washed down with strong and scalding tea. He himself felt pleasantly full of sausages. But perhaps before he went to bed there would be space for a mug of cocoa.

He crossed the curving bridge that spanned the Croy between the two churches. At the top of the curve he stopped and leaned over the ancient stone parapet to gaze down at the river. There had been much rain, too much for the farmers, and it was running deeply, carrying on its spate stray scraps of flotsam gathered on its journey. Branches of trees and bits of straw. Once he had seen a poor little dead lamb swept away beneath the bridge. Further down the glen the land flattened out and there the river changed character, to widen and wind through pastureland, between fields where the peaceful cattle came down at evening-time to drink at the water's edge. But here it flowed steeply downhill, leaping and sliding over the rocks in a series of miniature waterfalls and deep pools.

The sound of the Croy was one of Henry's earliest memories. At night he could hear it from the open window of his bedroom, and he awoke to its voice every morning. Upstream was the pool where Alexa had taught him to swim. With his friends from school he played many wet muddy games on its banks, building dams and making camps.

Behind him, the big clock on the Presbyterian church tower struck the hour with six solemn donging tolls. Reluctantly he drew back from the parapet and went on his way, down the lane that bordered the south bank of the river. Tall elms towered overhead, their topmost branches noisy with a colony of cawing rooks.

Reaching the open gates of Balnaid and anxious all at once to be home, he began to run, his satchel bumping at his side. As he came around the house he saw his father's dark-blue BMW parked on the gravel. Which was splendid, and an unexpected treat. His father did not usually get home until after Henry was in bed. But now he would find them in the kitchen, comfortably chatting and exchanging news of the day, while his mother prepared dinner and his father had a cup of tea.

But they were not in the kitchen. He knew this the moment he went through the front door because he could hear voices from behind the closed library door. Just voices and the closed door, so why did he have this feeling that it was wrong; that nothing was as it should be?

His mouth had gone dry. He tiptoed down the wide passage and stood outside the door. He had truly meant to go in and surprise them, but instead he found himself listening.

". . . scarcely out of the nursery. He needs his home. He needs *us.*" His mother, speaking in a voice he had never heard before, high-pitched and sounding as though she was about to burst into tears. ". . . he *can't* be just sent away. I don't want him to be sent away."

"I know." That was his father.

"He's too little."

"So he needs to grow."

"He'll grow away from me."

They were quarrelling. They were having a row. The unbelievable had happened: his mother and father were

123

fighting. Cold with horror, Henry waited for what was going to happen next. After a bit, his father spoke again.

"Templehall's a good school, Virginia, and Colin Henderson's a good headmaster. The boys are never pushed, but they're taught to work. Life is going to be hard for Henry . . ."

So that was what the row was about. They were going to send him to Templehall. To boarding school.

". . . and learn to take the rough with the smooth, the better."

Away from his friends, from Strathcroy, from Balnaid, from Edie and Vi. He thought of Hamish Blair, so much older, so superior, so cruel. *Only babies have teddies.*

". . . Henry is too dependent on you."

He could not bear to listen any more. Every fear that he had ever known crowded in on Henry. He backed away from the library door and then, reaching the safety of the hall, turned and ran. Across the floor, up the stairs and down the passage to his bedroom. Slamming the door shut behind him, he tore off his satchel and threw himself on to his bed, bundling the duvet around him. He reached under his pillow for Moo.

Henry is too dependent on you.

And so he was going to be sent away.

Plugging his mouth with his thumb, pressing Moo to his cheek, he was, for the moment, safe. Comforted, he would not cry. He closed his eyes.

11

The drawing room at Croy, used only for formal occasions, was of enormous size. The high ceiling and scrolled cornices were white, the walls lined with faded red damask, the carpet a vast Turkey rug, threadbare in places but still warm with colour. There were sofas and chairs, some loose-covered, some in their original velvet upholstery. None of them matched. Small tables stood about, littered with Battersea boxes, silver-framed photographs, stacks of back numbers of *Country Life*. There were a great many dark oil paintings, portraits and flower arrangements, and on the table behind the sofa stood a Chinese porcelain jar containing a flowering and scented rhododendron.

Behind the leather-seated club fender, a log fire burned brightly. The hearthrug was shaggy and white, and if wet dogs sat about upon it, smelled strongly of sheep. The fireplace was marble with an impressive mantelpiece, and on this stood a pair of gilt-and-enamel candelabra, two Dresden figures, and a florid Victorian clock.

This clock, chiming sweetly, now struck eleven o'clock.

It surprised everybody. Mrs Franco, sleek in black silk trousers and creamy crêpe blouse, announced that she could not believe it was so late. They had all been talking so much that the evening had just flown by. She must get to bed, and her husband as well, if he was to be fit and ready for his golf game at Gleneagles. With that, the

125

Francos gathered themselves and rose to their feet. So did Mrs Hardwicke.

"It's been perfect, and such an elegant dinner . . . Thank you both for your hospitality . . ."

Goodnights were said. Isobel, in the two-year-old green silk dress that was her best, led them from the drawing room to see them safely on their way upstairs. She closed the door behind her and did not return. Archie was left with Joe Hardwicke, apparently disinclined to retire so early. He had settled back in his chair again and looked good for at least another couple of hours.

Archie did not mind, and was content to be left in his company. Joe Hardwicke was one of their better guests, an intelligent man with liberal views and a dry sense of humour. Over dinner . . . often a sticky session . . . he had done his bit to keep the easy conversation going; he told, against himself, one or two extremely funny stories, and proved to be unexpectedly knowledgeable about wine. Discussing Archie's inherited cellar had taken up most of the second course.

Now Archie poured him a nightcap, which the American gratefully accepted. He then filled a tumbler for himself, threw a log or two on the fire, and sank deep into his own chair, his feet on the sheepskin rug. Joe Hardwicke began to question him about Croy. He found these old places fascinating. How long had his family lived here? From where had the title come? What was the history of the house?

He was not curious but interested, and Archie happily answered his questions. His grandfather, the first Lord Balmerino, had been an industrialist of some renown, who had made his fortune in heavy textiles. His elevation to the peerage had followed on from this, and he had bought Croy and its lands at the end of the nineteenth century.

"There wasn't a dwelling-house here then. Just a fortified tower dating back to the sixteenth century. My

126

grandfather built the house, incorporating the original tower. So, although bits at the back are ancient, it's basically Victorian."

"It seems large."

"Yes. They lived on a grand scale in those days . . ."

"And the estate . . .?"

"Mostly let out. The moor's gone to a syndicate for the grouse shooting. I have a friend, Edmund Aird, and he runs it, but I have a half-gun in the syndicate and I join them on days when they're driving. I've kept some stalking, but that's just for my friends. The farm is tenanted." He smiled. "So you see, I have no responsibilities."

"So what do you do?"

"I help Isobel. I feed the dogs and exercise them when I can. Deal with all the fallen timber, keep the house supplied with logs. We've got a circular saw in one of the outbuildings and an old villain comes up from the village every now and then and gives me a hand. I cut the grass." He stopped. It wasn't much of an answer but he couldn't think of anything more to tell.

"Do you fish?"

"Yes. I have a beat on the Croy, about two miles upstream from the village, and there's a loch up in the hills. It's good to go up there for the evening rise. Take the boat out. It's very peaceful. And when it's winter and dark at four, I have a workshop down in the basement. There's always something that needs repairing. I mend gates, renew skirtings, build cupboards for Isobel, put up shelves. And other things. I like to work with wood. It's basic, very therapeutic. Perhaps instead of joining the Army I should have been a joiner."

"Were you with a Scottish regiment?"

"I was a Queen's Loyal Highlander for fifteen years. We spent two of those in Berlin with the American forces . . ."

The conversation moved on, from Berlin to the Eastern Bloc, and so to politics and international affairs. They

127

had another nightcap, lost track of time. When they finally decided to call it a day, it was past one o'clock in the morning.

"I've kept you up." Joe Hardwicke was apologetic.

"Not at all." Archie took the empty glasses and went to place them on the tray that stood on the grand piano. ". . . I'm not much of a sleeper. The shorter the night, the better."

"I . . . " Joe hesitated. "I hope you don't think I'm being impertinent, but I see that you're lame. Did you have an accident?"

"No. My leg was shot off in Northern Ireland."

"You have an artificial leg?"

"Yes. Aluminium. Marvellous piece of engineering. Now, what time do you want breakfast? Would eight-fifteen do you? That would give you time before the car comes to collect you and take you to Gleneagles. And shall I call you in the morning?"

"If you would. About eight o'clock. I sleep like the dead in this mountain air."

Archie moved to open the door. But Joe Hardwicke was offering to dispose of the tray of drinks. Could he perhaps carry it to the kitchen for Archie? Archie was grateful but firm. "Not at all. House rule. You're guests. Not allowed to lift a finger."

They went out into the hall. "Thank you," said Joe Hardwicke, standing at the foot of the staircase.

"Thank *you*. Goodnight. And sleep well."

He stayed at the foot of the stairs until the American had disappeared and Archie had heard the opening and the shutting of his bedroom door. Then he returned to the drawing room, settled the fire, put on the fireguard, drew back the heavy curtains, checked the window catches. Outside, the garden lay washed in moonlight. He heard an owl. He went out of the room, leaving the drinks tray where it was, switched off lights. He crossed the hall to the dining room. The table had been cleared of all traces of dinner, and was now set for breakfast. He felt guilty, for this was, by tradition, his job, and Isobel had accomplished it all alone, while he had sat talking.

He went on to the kitchen. Here again, all was neat and orderly. His two black Labrador bitches slumbered by the Aga in their round baskets. Disturbed, they woke and raised their heads. Thump, thump, went their tails.

"Have you been out?" he asked them. "Did Isobel take you out before she went to bed?"

Thump, thump. They were content and comfortable. There was nothing left for him to do.

Bed. He found himself, all at once, very tired. He climbed the staircase, switching off lights as he went. In his dressing-room, he took off his clothes. His dinner jacket, his bow-tie, his studded white shirt. Shoes and socks. Trousers were the most complicated, but he had perfected a routine for their removal. The tall mirror in his wardrobe reflected his image, but he made a point of not looking at it, because he so hated to see himself unclothed; the livid stump of his thigh, the shining metal of the leg, the screws and hinges, the belts and strappings that kept it in place – all revealed, shameless and somehow obscene.

Quickly he reached for and pulled on his night-shirt, easier to deal with than pyjamas. He went to the adjoining bathroom, peed, and cleaned his teeth. In their vast bedroom, no lights burned but moonlight flowed through the uncurtained window. On her side of the wide double bed, Isobel slept. But as he moved across the room, she stirred and woke.

"Archie?"

He sat down on his side of the bed.

"Yes."

"What time is it?"

"About twenty past one."

She thought about this. "Were you talking?"

"Yes. I'm sorry. I should have been helping you."

"It doesn't matter. They were nice."

He was unstrapping the harness, gently easing the

129

padded leather cup away from his stump. When it was free, he bent to lay the hateful contraption on the floor beside the bed, the webbing arranged neatly, so that in the morning he could put it on again with the least possible inconvenience. Without it, he felt lopsided and strangely weightless, and his stump burned and ached. It had been a long day.

He lay beside Isobel and pulled the cool sheets up to his shoulders.

"Are you all right?" Her voice was drowsy.

"Yes."

"Did you know that Verena Steynton's going to throw a dance for Katy? In September."

"Yes. Violet told me."

"I shall have to get a new dress."

"Yes."

"I haven't got anything to wear."

She drifted back to sleep.

As soon as it started, he knew what was going to happen. It was always the same. Forsaken, bleak streets, plastered with graffiti. Dark skies and rain. He wore a flak jacket and drove one of the armoured Land-Rovers, but there was something amiss because he should have a companion and he was on his own.

All he had to do was to get to the safety of the barracks. The barracks was a requisitioned Ulster Constabulary police station, fortified to the hilt, and bristling with armoury. If he could get there, without them coming, he would be safe. But they were there. They always came. Four figures, spread out across the road ahead, shrouded by the rain. They had no faces, only black hoods, and their weapons were trained upon him. He reached for his rifle, but it had gone. The Land-Rover had stopped. He could not remember stopping it. The door was open and they were upon him, dragging him out. Perhaps this time they were going to beat him to death. But it was the same. It was the bomb. It looked like a brown paper parcel but it was a bomb, and they loaded it into the back of the Land-Rover, and he stood and watched them. And then he was back behind the wheel and the nightmare had truly begun. Because he was going to drive it in through the open gates of the barracks, and it would explode and kill every man in the place.

He was driving like a lunatic and it was still raining, and he could see nothing, but would soon be there. All he had to do was to get through the gates, drive the explosive vehicle into the bomb pit and somehow get out and run like Jesus before the bomb went off.

Panic was destroying him, and his ears roared with the sound of his own breathing. The gates swung up, he was through them, down the ramp, into the bomb pit. Its concrete walls rose on either side of him, shutting out the light. Escape. He tugged at the door handle but it was stuck. The door wouldn't open, he was trapped, the bomb was ticking like a clock, lethal and murderous, and he was trapped. He screamed. Nobody knew he was there. He went on screaming . . .

He awoke, screaming like a woman, his mouth open, sweat streaming down his face . . . arms caught him . . .

"Archie."

She was there, holding him. After a little, she drew him gently down on to the pillows. She comforted him like a child, with small sounds. She kissed his eyes. "It's all right. It was a dream. You're here. I'm here. It's all over. You're awake."

His heart banged like a hammer and he streamed with sweat. He lay still in her embrace and gradually his breathing calmed. He reached for a glass of water, but she was there before him, holding it for him to drink, setting the glass back on the table when he had had enough.

131

When he was quiet, she said, with a ghost of a smile in her voice, "I hope you haven't woken anybody up. They'll think I'm murdering you."

"I know. I'm sorry."

"Was it . . . the same?"

"Yes. Always the same. The rain, and the hoods and the bomb and that fucking pit. Why do I have nightmares about something that never happened to me?"

"I don't know, Archie."

"I want them to stop."

"I know."

He turned his head, burying his face in her soft shoulder. "If only they would stop, perhaps then I could make love to you again."

❧ AUGUST ❧

12

Monday the Fifteenth

The arrival of the morning post at Croy was a movable feast. Tom Drystone, the postman, driving his scarlet van, covered, during the day, an enormous area. Long, winding single-track roads led up into the glens, to remote sheep farms and distant crofts. Young wives, isolated with small children, would watch for his coming while hanging out lines of washing in the cold, fresh wind. Old people, living on their own, depended on him to deliver their prescriptions, pause for a chat, even sit down and drink a cup of tea with them. In wintertime, he swapped his van for a Land-Rover, and only the worst of blizzards prevented him from somehow getting through and delivering the long-awaited letter from Australia, or a new blouse ordered from the Littlewoods catalogue, and when the howling north-west gales damaged telephone lines and power cables, he was very often the only source of communication with the outside world.

Because of this, even if he had been a dour-faced man with no small talk and a sharp tongue on him, Tom's daily appearance would always be welcome. But he was a cheerful fellow, born and bred in Tullochard, and so unfazed by anything that the wild country or the elements could throw at him. As well, when he was not being a postman, he was greatly admired for his ability to play the accordion, and was a kenspeckle figure at local ceilidhs, up on the platform with a glass of beer on the floor beside him, and leading the band in an endless round of jigs and reels. This catchy music went with him everywhere, because, as he delivered the mail, he whistled.

It was now the middle of August. A Monday. A blowy day with a good deal of cloud. Not hot but, at least, not raining. Isobel Balmerino, tied up in an apron, sat at one end of the kitchen table at Croy and plucked three brace of grouse. They had been shot on Friday and hung in the game larder for three days. They should, perhaps, hang a little longer, but she wanted to be shed of the messy job and have the grouse safely in the deep-freeze before the next lot of Americans arrived.

The kitchen was vast and Victorian, filled with every evidence of her busy life. A dresser was stacked with a set of chipped ironstone dinner-ware, a noticeboard was pinned with postcards, addresses, scribbled reminders to ring the plumber. The dogs' baskets lay near the great four-oven Aga, and large bunches of drying flowers hung from hooks in the ceiling, once employed for curing hams. Over the Aga was a drying rack, on a pulley, where sodden tweeds were hoisted after a day on the hill, or ironed linen, still not quite dry, put to air. This was not a wholly satisfactory arrangement because if there were kippers for breakfast, then pillowcases smelled faintly of fish, but as Isobel had no airing cupboard, there was nothing to be done about it.

Once, a long time ago in old Lady Balmerino's day, this pulley had been the source of a long-standing family joke. Mrs Harris was then resident cook; a splendid cook but not one troubled by any silly prejudices concerning hygiene. Her habit had been to keep, on the Aga, an enormous black iron stockpot simmering with bones and the remains of any vegetable she thought fit to scrape off a plate. With this, she made her famous soups. One year a house party stayed for the shooting. The weather was appalling, so the rack above the Aga constantly drooped with soaked jackets, knickerbockers, sweaters, and hairy stockings. The soup that fortnight got better and better, more and more tasty. Guests begged for recipes. "How do you do it, Mrs Harris? The flavour! Quite delicious." But Mrs Harris simply bridled and smugly said that it was just a wee knack she'd picked up from her mother. The week ended and the house party left, tucking large tips into Mrs Harris's boiled red hand as they left. When they had gone, the stockpot was finally emptied for scouring. At the bottom was found a felted and none-too-clean shooting stocking.

Four birds plucked and two to go. Feathers floated everywhere. Isobel gathered them cautiously, bundling them into newspaper, stowing the bundles into a black plastic dustbin bag. Spreading fresh newspaper and starting in on number five, she heard whistling.

The back door flew open, and Tom Drystone burst cheerfully in on her. The draught caused a cloud of feathers. Isobel let out a wail, and he hastily shut the door behind him.

"I see the Laird's keeping you busy." The feathers settled. Isobel sneezed. Tom slapped a pile of mail down on the dresser. "Can you not get young Hamish to give you a hand?"

"He's away. Gone to Argyll for a week with a school-friend."

"What kind of day did they have at Croy on Friday?"

"Disappointing, I'm afraid."

"They got forty-three brace over at Glenshandra."

"They were probably all ours, flown over the march fence to call on their friends. Do you want a cup of coffee?"

"No, not today, thanks. I've a full load on board. Council circulars. Well, I'll be off . . ."

And he was away, whistling before he had even banged the door shut behind him.

Isobel went on tearing feathers out of the grouse. She longed to go and inspect the letters, see if there was anything exciting, but was firm with herself. She would finish the plucking first. Then she would clear away all the feathers. Then she would wash her hands and look at the mail. And then she would embark upon the bloody job of cleaning the birds.

The post-van sped away. She heard footsteps approaching down the passage from the hall. Painful and uneven. Down the few stone steps, one at a time. The door opened and her husband appeared.

"Was that Tom?"

"Didn't you hear the whistle?"

"I'm waiting for that letter from the Forestry Commission."

"I haven't looked yet."

"Why didn't you tell me you were doing those grouse?" Archie sounded more accusing than guilty. "I'd have come to help."

"Perhaps you'd like to clean them for me?"

He made a distasteful face. He could shoot birds, and wring the neck of an injured runner. He could, if pressed, pluck them. But he was squeamish about cutting them open and pulling out their innards. This had always been a small cause of friction between himself and Isobel, and so he swiftly changed the subject. As she had known he would.

"Where is the mail?"

"He put it on the dresser."

He limped over to collect it, brought it back to the other end of the table, well out of reach of the general mess. He sat down and leafed through the envelopes.

"Hell. It's not here. I wish they'd put their skates on. But there's one from Lucilla . . ."

"Oh, good, I hoped there would be . . ."

". . . and something very large and stiff and thick, which might be a summons from the Queen."

"Verena's writing?"

"Could be."

"That's our invitation."

"And two more, similar, to be forwarded on. One for Lucilla, and another for" – he hesitated – "Pandora."

Isobel's hands were still. Down the long, feather-strewn table, their eyes met. "Pandora? They've asked Pandora?"

"Apparently."

"How extraordinary. Verena never told me she was going to ask Pandora."

"No reason why she should."

"We'll have to send it on to her. Open ours and let's see what it looks like."

Archie did so. "Very impressive." He raised his eyebrows. "Embossed, copperplate, and gold edges. The sixteenth of September. Verena's left it pretty late, hasn't she? I mean, that's scarcely a month away."

"There was a disaster. The printers made a mistake. They printed the first batch of invitations on the wrong side of the paper, and so she sent them all back and they had to be done again."

"How did she know they were printed on the wrong side?"

"Verena knows about things like that. She's a perfectionist. What does it say?"

"It says, 'Lord and Lady Balmerino. Mrs Angus Steynton. At Home. For Katy. Blah Blah. Dancing at ten. RSVP.' " He held it up. "Impressed?"

Without her glasses, Isobel screwed up her eyes and peered.

139

"Very impressed. It'll look splendid on the mantel-piece. The Americans will think we've been invited to something Royal. Now, read me Lucilla's letter. That's much more important."

Archie slit the flimsy envelope with the French stamp and postmark and unfolded two sheets of cheap, lined, and very thin paper.

"Looks as though she's written it on lavatory paper."

"Read it."

"Paris. August sixth. Darling Mum and Dad. Sorry I've been such ages in writing. No time for news. This is just a short note to let you know my movements. Am leaving here in a couple of days and going down to the south. I am travelling by bus, so no need to anguish about hitch-hiking. Going with an Australian boy I've met called Jeff Howland. Not an art student but a sheep-farmer from Queensland, with a year off to bum round Europe. He has friends in Ibiza, so we might possibly go there. I don't know what we'll do when we get to

140

Ibiza, but if there is the chance of getting over to Majorca, would you like me to go and see Pandora? And if you would, will you send me her address because I've lost it. And I'm a bit short of cash, so could you possibly float me a loan till my next allowance comes through. Send all c/o Hans Bergdorf, PO Box 73, Ibiza. Paris has been heaven but only tourists here just now. Everybody else has disappeared to beaches or mountains. Saw a blissful Matisse exhibition the other day. Lots of love, darlings, and DON'T WORRY. Lucilla. PS. Don't forget the money."

He folded the letter and put it back into the envelope.

Isobel said, "An Australian."

"A sheep-farmer."

"Bumming round Europe."

"At least they're travelling by bus."

"Oh well, I suppose it could be worse. But thinking that she might go and see Pandora . . . isn't that extra-ordinary? We don't mention Pandora's name for months and all at once it keeps popping up everywhere we turn. Is Ibiza very far from Majorca?"

"Not very."

"I wish Lucilla would come home."

"Isobel, she's having the time of her life."

"I hate her being short of money."

"I'll send her a cheque."

"I miss her so."

"I know."

She was done with plucking, the feathers all painfully collected and stowed in the black rubbish bag. The six small corpses lay in a pathetic row, their heads askew, their clawed feet pointed like dancers. Isobel reached for her lethally sharpened knife and without ado sliced into the first little flaccid body. Then she laid down the knife and plunged her hand into the bird. She withdrew it, red with blood, drawing out a long string of pearly, greyish entrails. These piled in surprising profusion on to the newspaper. The smell was overwhelming.

Archie sprang to his feet. "I'll go and write that cheque." He gathered the mail. "Before I forget." And he headed for his study, firmly closing the kitchen door behind him, shutting away the small scene of domestic carnage.

At his desk, he held Pandora's envelope for a moment or two. He thought about writing to her. Tucking a letter from himself in with Verena's invitation. It's a party, he would say. It'll be fun. Why not come home for it, and stay with us at Croy? We would so love to see you. Please, Pandora. Please.

But he had written thus before and she had scarcely bothered to reply. It was no good. He sighed and carefully readdressed the envelope. He added a few stamps for good measure and an airmail sticker, then laid it aside.

He wrote a cheque payable to Lucilla Blair, for a hundred and fifty pounds. He then began a letter to his daughter.

Croy, August 15th,

My darling Lucilla.

Thank you very much for your note which we received this morning. I hope you will have a good journey to the South of France, and are able to raise enough cash to get you to Ibiza, as I am sending this cheque there as you asked me to. As for Pandora, I am sure she would be delighted to see you but suggest that you telephone before you make any plans, and let her know that you propose to visit her.

Her address is Casa Rosa, Puerto del Fuego, Majorca. I haven't got her telephone number but I am sure you will be able to find it in the phone book in Palma.

As well, I am forwarding on an invitation to a party that the Steyntons are throwing for Katy. It's only a month off and you may have other and better things to do, but I know that your mother would be so happy if you could be there.

A good day on the twelfth. They were driving, and so I joined the guns for the morning only. Everybody was kind and I was allowed the bottom butt. Hamish came with me to carry my gun and my game bag, and help his old father up the hill. Edmund Aird shot exceptionally well, but at the end of the day the bag was only twenty-one and a half brace, and two hares. Hamish went off yesterday for a week in Argyll with a schoolfriend. He took his trout rod, but hopes for some deep-sea fishing. My love, my darling child. Dad.

He read this missive through, then folded it neatly. He found a large brown envelope and into this put the letter, the cheque, and Verena's invitation. He sealed and stamped it and addressed it to Lucilla at the Ibiza address that she had given them. He took both letters out into the hall and laid them on the chest that stood by the door. The next time that anyone went to the village they would be posted.

13

Wednesday the Seventeenth

The Steyntons' invitation was delivered to Ovington Street on the Wednesday of that week. It was early morning. Alexa, barefoot and wrapped in her bathrobe, stood in the kitchen, waiting for the kettle to boil. The door to the garden was open, and Larry was out there, having his routine sniff-around. Sometimes he found traces of cat and became very excited. It was a grey morning. Perhaps later the sun would come out and burn the mist away. She heard the rattle of the letterbox and, looking up through the window, saw the postman's legs as he strode on down the pavement.

She laid a tray, put tea-bags into the teapot. The kettle boiled and she made the tea, and then, leaving her little dog to his own devices, carried the tray up the basement stairs. The letters lay on the doormat. Juggling with the tray, she stooped to gather them up and push them into the capacious pocket of her robe. Up again, the thick carpet soft beneath her bare feet. Her bedroom door stood open, the curtains already drawn back. It was not a very large room, and almost completely filled by the bed that Alexa had inherited from her grandmother, an impressive bed, wide and downy, with tall brass bedheads at either end. She put the tray down and climbed back between the sheets.

She said, "Are you awake, because I've brought you a cup of tea?"

The hump on the other side of the bed did not instantly respond to this summons. Then it groaned and heaved. A bare brown arm appeared from the covers, and Noel turned to face her.

"What's the time?" His hair, so dark on the white linen pillow, was tousled, his chin rough with stubble.

"A quarter to eight."

He groaned again, ran his fingers through his hair. She said, "Good morning," and bent to kiss his unshaven cheek. He put his hand on the back of her head and held her close. He said, mumbling, "You smell delicious."

"Lemon shampoo."

"No. Not lemon shampoo. Just you."

He took his hand away. Released, she kissed him again, and then turned to the domestic business of pouring his tea. He pummelled pillows, heaved himself up to lean against them. He was naked, brown-chested as though he had just returned from some tropical holiday. She handed him the steaming Wedgwood mug.

He drank slowly, in silence. He took a long time to come to in the mornings, and scarcely said a word before breakfast. It was something she had found out about him, one of his small routines of existence. Like the way he made coffee, or cleaned his shoes, or mixed a dry martini. At night he emptied his pockets, laying their contents in a neat row on the dressing-table, always in the same order. Wallet, credit cards, penknife, small change, the coins tidily stacked. The best of all was lying in bed and watching him do this; then watching him undress, waiting for him to be ready, to come to her.

Each day brought new knowledge; each night fresh, sweet discovery. All the good things piled up so that every moment, every hour, was better than the moment and the hour before. Living with Noel, sharing this blissful blend of domesticity and passion, made her understand for the first time why people ever wanted to get married. It was so that it would go on for ever.

145

And once . . . only three months ago . . . she had thought herself perfectly satisfied. Alone in the house, with only Larry for company, occupied with her work, her little routine, occasional evenings out, or visits to friends. No more than half a life. How had she endured it?

You never miss what you've never had. Edie's voice, loud and clear. Thinking of Edie, Alexa smiled. She poured her own mug of tea, stood it beside her, and then reached into her pocket for the letters. She spread them on the eiderdown. A bill from Peter Jones, a circular for double glazing, a postcard from a woman who lived in Barnes and wanted some goodies concocted for her deep-freeze, and finally the huge stiff white envelope.

She looked at it. A Scottish postmark. An invitation? To a wedding, perhaps . . .

She ripped open the envelope with her thumb and took out the card.

She said, "Goodness me."

"What is it?"

"An invitation to the ball. 'You *shall* go to the ball' said the Fairy Godmother to Cinderella."

Noel reached out and took it from her.

"Who's Mrs Angus Steynton?"

"They live near us in Scotland. About ten miles away."

"And who's Katy?"

"Their daughter, of course. She works in London. You've maybe met her . . ." Alexa thought about this and then changed her mind. "No. I don't think you would have. She's inclined to go round with young men in the Guards . . . lots of race meetings."

"Sixteenth of September. Are you going to go?"

"I shouldn't think so."

"Why not?"

"Because I wouldn't want to go without you."

"I haven't been invited."

"I know."

146

"Will you say, 'I shall come if I can bring my lover with me'?"

"Nobody knows I've got a lover."

"You still haven't told your family that I've moved in with you?"

"Not yet."

"Any particular reason?"

"Oh, Noel . . . I don't know." But she did know. She wanted to keep it all to herself. With Noel, she inhabited a secret magic world of love and discovery, and she was afraid that if she let anybody in from the outside, then it would all dissolve and somehow be spoiled.

As well . . . and this was a pathetic admission . . . she lacked any form of moral courage. She was twenty-one but that didn't help, because she still felt, inside, about fifteen, and as anxious to please as she had ever been. The thought of possible family reactions filled her with agonised distress. She imagined her father's disapproval, Vi's horrified astonishment, and Virginia's concern. Then, the questions.

But who is he? Where did you meet him? You've been living together? At Ovington Street? But why is this the first we've heard of it? What does he do? What is his name?

And Edie. *Lady Cheriton must be turning in her grave.*

It wasn't that they wouldn't understand. It wasn't that they were strait-laced or hypocritical in any way. Nor was it that they didn't all love Alexa – she just couldn't bear any of them to be upset.

She drank some tea.

Noel said, "You're not a little girl any longer."

"I know I'm not. I'm an adult. I just wish I wasn't such a wet adult."

"Are you ashamed of our sinful cohabitation?"

"I'm not ashamed of anything. It's just . . . the family. I don't like hurting them."

"My sweet, they'll be much more hurt if they hear about us before you've got around to telling them."

Alexa knew that this was true. "But how could they find out?" she asked him.

"This is London. Everybody talks. I'm astonished your father hasn't got the buzz already. Take my advice and be a brave girl." He gave her his empty mug and a swift kiss on the cheek. Reaching for his bathrobe, he swung his legs over the side of the bed. "And then you can write to Mrs Stiffden, or whatever her name is, and say yes, please, you'd love to come to the ball, and you're bringing Prince Charming with you."

Despite herself, Alexa smiled. "Would you come?"

"Probably not. Tribal dances are scarcely my scene." And with that he took himself off to the bathroom. Almost at once Alexa heard the gushing of the shower.

So what was all the fuss about? Alexa picked up the invitation again, and frowned at it. I wish you'd never come, she told it. You've just stirred up a lot of trouble.

14

Monday the Twenty-second

That August, the entire island simmered in an unpre-
cedented heat wave. The mornings started hot, and
by midday the temperatures had risen to unbearable
heights, driving any person with sense indoors for
the afternoon, to loll breathless upon a bed, or
sleep on some shady terrace. The old town, up in the
hills, quiet and shuttered, slumbered through the
hours of siesta. The streets were empty and the shops
closed.

But, down in the port, it was a different story. There
were too many people about, and too much money
being spent, to respect this time-honoured custom. The
tourists did not want to know about siestas. They did
not want to waste a moment of their costly holiday in
sleeping. And the day visitors had nowhere to go. So,
instead, they sat about in droves, red and perspiring, in
the pavement cafés; or wandered aimlessly in air-
conditioned gift arcades. The beach was littered with
palm-thatch umbrellas and half-naked, kippering
bodies, and the marina packed with seagoing craft of
every description. Only the boat people seemed to know
what was good for them. Usually bustling with activity,
the yachts and launches dipped lazily in the swell of the
oily water, and in the shade of canvas awnings supine
bodies, brown as mahogany, lay about on the decks, as
though already dead.

Pandora awoke late. She had tossed and turned her way through the night and finally, at four in the morning, taken a sleeping pill and fallen at last into a heavy, dream-troubled sleep. She would have slept on but the sound of Seraphina clattering away in the kitchen disturbed her. The clatter shattered the dream, and after a little, reluctantly, she opened her eyes.

The dream had been of rain, and brown rivers, and cold wet scents, and the sound of wind. Of deep lochs and dark hills with boggy paths leading to their snow-capped summits. But most important was the rain. Not falling straight, not thunderous and tropical as it was when it fell here, but gentle and misty. Rolling in on clouds, insidious as smoke . . .

She stirred. The images dissolved, were gone. Why should she dream of Scotland? Why, after all these years, did those old chilly memories come back to tug at her sleeve? Perhaps it was the heat of this cruel August, the endless days of relentless sunshine, the dust and the dryness, the hard-edged black shadows of noon. One yearned for that gentle, scented mist.

She turned her head on the pillow and saw, beyond the sliding glass doors that had stood open all night, the balustrade of the terrace, the glaring brilliance of geraniums, the sky. Blue, cloudless, already brazen with heat.

She propped herself up on an elbow and reached across the wide, empty bed to the bedside table and her watch. Nine o'clock. More racket from the kitchen. The sound of the dishwasher churning. Seraphina was making her presence heard. And if she was here, that meant that Mario – her husband and Pandora's gardener – was already scratching away with his archaic hoe in the garden. Which precluded all possibilities of an early

150

skinny-dip. Mario and Seraphina lived in the old town and came to work each morning on Mario's moped, roaring full-throttle up the hill. Mario drove this noisy brute of a contraption with Seraphina perched behind him, riding, modestly, side-saddle, and with her strong brown arms wrapped around his waist. It was a wonder that the daily assault of din that proclaimed their arrival had not woken Pandora before this, but then the sleeping pills were very strong.

It was too hot to go on lying in this rumpled, messy bed. She had been here long enough. Pandora threw aside the thin sheet and, barefoot and naked, crossed the wide expanse of marbled floor and went into her bedroom. She collected her bikini – no more than two scraps of knotted handkerchief – climbed into it, and then walked back through her bedroom, out on to the terrace, and down the steps that led to the swimming pool.

She dived. It was cool, but not cool enough for true refreshment. She swam. She thought of diving into the loch at Croy and coming up screaming with agony because the cold bit into every painful pore of one's body; it was a numbing cold that took all breath away. How could she have swum in what was virtually snow-water? How could she and Archie and all the rest of them have indulged in such masochistic pleasures? But what fun it had been. And then coming out, and struggling damply into warm sweaters, and lighting a fire on the pebbly shore of the loch, and cooking the best trout in the world over the smoky embers. Trout, ever since, had never tasted so good as at those impromptu camp-fire meals.

She swam on. To and fro, up and down the long pool. Scotland again. Not dreams now but conscious memories. So what? She let them have their way. Let them lead her away from the loch, down the rough turfy track that followed the course of the burn, tumbling and spilling its way down the hill, finally to join the Croy.

151

Peaty water brown and frothy as beer, spilling over rocks and splashing into deep pools where the trout lurked in the shadows. Over the centuries this stream had cut for itself a little valley, and the banks of this were green and verdant, sheltered from the north winds and bright with wildflowers. Foxgloves grew, and starwort, sweet green bracken and tall purple thistles. One particular spot was special. They called it the Corrie and it was the venue for many spring and winter picnics when the winds from the north were too cold to light camp-fires by the loch.

The Corrie. She did not let her memories linger there but hurried them on. The track steepened, winding between great rock formations, cliffs of granite older than time. A final turn and the glen lay spread far below, sunlit, rolling with cloud shadows, revealed in all its pastoral beauty. The Croy a glittering thread, its two arched bridges just visible through the trees; the village reduced by distance to a child's plaything, set out on some nursery carpet.

A pause for contemplation and then on again. The track levelled off. The deer-fence lay ahead and the tall gate. Now visible, the first of the trees. Scots pines, and beyond them the green of the beeches. Then Gordon Gillock's house, with Mrs Gillock's washing-line flying a bunting of laundry, and the gun dogs, disturbed, exploding into a cacophony of frenzied barking from their kennels.

Nearly home. The track a proper road now, tar-macked, leading between farm buildings, stone stead-ings, and barns and byres. The smell was of cattle and dung. Another gate and past the farmhouse with its bright cottage garden and drystone wall smothered in honeysuckle. The cattle-grid. The drive lined with rhododendrons . . .

Croy.

Enough. Pandora jerked her wayward memories back into line as though they were over-eager children. She had no wish to go further. Enough of self-indulgence.

152

Enough of Scotland. She swam a final length and then climbed the shallow steps up and out of the pool. The stones beneath her bare feet were already hot. Dripping, she made her way back into the house. In her bathroom, she showered, washed her hair, put on a fresh dress, loose and sleeveless, the coolest garment she owned. She left her bedroom, crossed the hall, went into the kitchen.

"Seraphina."

Seraphina swung round from the sink where she was busily engaged in scrubbing a bucket of mussels. She was a small, squat, brown woman with sturdy bare legs thrust into espadrilles, and dark hair drawn back into a knot at the nape of her neck. She always wore black because she was perpetually in mourning. No sooner was she out of mourning for one old grandparent or distant relation than another of her clan passed on and she was back in mourning again. The black dresses all looked exactly the same, but as if to make up for their gloom, her pinafores and aprons were invariably brightly coloured and hectically patterned.

Seraphina went with the Casa Rosa. Previously, she had worked for fifteen years for the English couple who had originally built the villa. When, two years ago, due to family pressures and uncertain health, they had reluctantly returned to England, Pandora, searching for some place to live, had bought the property from them. Doing this, she discovered that she had inherited Seraphina and Mario. At first Seraphina was not certain whether she wished to work for Pandora, and Pandora was in two minds about Seraphina. She was not exactly attractive and very often looked quite grumpy. But tentatively they tried out a month together, and then the month stretched to three months, and then to a year, and the arrangement, quite comfortably, settled itself, without anything actually being said.

"*Señora. Buenos días.* You are awake."

After fifteen years with her previous employers, Ser-

153

aphina spoke reasonable English. Pandora was grateful for this small mercy. Her French was fluent but Spanish a closed book. People said it was easy because of having done Latin at school, but Pandora's education did not include Latin and she was not about to start now.

"Any breakfast?"

"Is on the table. I bring the coffee."

The table was set on the terrace, which faced out over the driveway. Here it was shady and cooled by any breeze that blew from the sea. Crossing the sitting room, Pandora's eye was caught by a book that lay on the coffee-table. It was a large and lush volume, sent as a present from Archie for her birthday. *Wainwright in Scotland*. She knew why he had sent it. He never stopped, in his simple and transparent way, trying to lure her home. Because of this, she had not even opened it. But now she paused, her attention caught. *Wainwright in Scotland*. Scotland again. Was this a day to be drenched in nostalgia? She smiled at herself, at this weakness that had suddenly come upon her. Why not? She stooped and picked up the book and carried it out on to the terrace. Peeling her orange, she opened it on the table.

It was indeed a coffee-table book, built for browsing. Pen-and-ink drawings, beautifully executed maps, and a simple text. Coloured photographs sprang from every page. The silver sands of Morar. Ben Vorlich. The Falls of Dochart. The old names resounded satisfactorily, like a roll of drums.

She began to eat the orange. Juice dripped on the pages of the book, and she brushed it carelessly away, leaving stains. Seraphina brought her coffee but she never looked up, so engrossed was she.

Here the river, after a long and sedate journey, suddenly erupts into a furious rage, descending in a turbulent cataract of white

foam along a wide and rocky channel in a remarkable display of thrashing waters. The flow of the rapids is interrupted by wooded islands, one of which was the burial place of the clan MacNab, and a bower of lovely trees enhances a scene of outstanding beauty . . .

She poured coffee, turned a page and read on.

Wainwright in Scotland consumed her day. She carried it from the breakfast table to a long chair by the pool and then, after lunch, took it to bed with her. By five o'clock, she had read it from cover to cover. Closed at last, she let it drop to the floor.

It was cooler now, but for once she had scarcely been troubled by the heat. She got off her bed and went out of doors and swam once more, then dressed in white cotton trousers and a blue-and-white shirt. She did her hair, her eyes, found earrings, a gold bracelet. White sandals. She sprayed on scent. Her bottle was nearly finished. She would have to buy more. The prospect of this small luxurious purchase filled her with pleasure.

She said goodbye to Seraphina and went out of the front door and down the steps to where her car was parked in the garage. She got in and drove down the winding hill and so out on to the wide road that led to the port. She parked her car in the courtyard of the post office and went in to collect her mail. She put this in her leather-strapped basket and then left her car and walked slowly through the still-crowded streets, pausing to glance into shop windows, to assess a dress, to price a delectable lacy shawl. At the scent shop, she went in and bought a flagon of Poison, then went on, always walking in the direction of the sea. She came at last to the wide, palm-fringed boulevard that ran parallel to the beach. At the end of the day it seemed as busy as ever, the sands crowded and people still swimming. Far out, windsurfers' sails caught the evening breeze, dipping like birds' wings out across the surface of the water.

She came to a little café where a few tables stood empty on the pavement. The waiter came and she

155

ordered coffee and cognac. Then, leaning back in the uncomfortable iron chair, pushing her sunglasses up on to the top of her head, she reached into the basket and took out her letters. One from Paris. One from her lawyer in New York. A postcard from Venice. She turned it over. Emily Richter, still staying at the Cipriani. A large, stiff white envelope, addressed to Croy and readdressed in Archie's handwriting. She opened it and read, in disbelief and then with some amusement, Verena Steynton's invitation.

At Home
For Katy

Extraordinary. As though she were receiving a summons from another age, another world. And yet a world which, by some strange coincidence, like it or not, she had inhabited for the whole of the day. She knew uncertainty. Was it an omen of some sort? Should she pay heed? And if it was an omen, did she believe in omens in the first place?

At Home for Katy. She remembered other invitations, "stiffies" she and Archie had called them, propped on the mantelpiece of the library at Croy. Invitations to garden parties, cricket matches, dances. Dances galore. There had been a week in September when one scarcely slept, somehow surviving with stolen naps in the backs of cars, or a doze in the sun while others played tennis. She remembered a wardrobe filled with ball-dresses, and she herself perpetually complaining to her mother that she had nothing to wear. Everybody had seen the ice-blue satin because she'd worn it at the Northern Meetings, and anyway, some man had spilled champagne all down the front and the stain wouldn't come out. And the rose-pink? The hem was torn and one of the straps had come loose. Whereupon her mother, the most indulgent and patient of women, instead of suggesting that Pandora find a needle and thread and

156

mend the rose-pink, would put her daughter into the car and drive to Relkirk or Edinburgh and there suffer the traumas of Pandora's capricious whims, trudging from shop to shop until the most beautiful – and inevitably most costly – dress was finally run to earth.

How spoiled Pandora had been, how adored, how cherished. And in return . . .

She laid down the card and looked up at the sea. The waiter came with her coffee and brandy on a little tray. She thanked him and paid. As she drank the bitter, black, scalding coffee, Pandora watched the windsurfers and the slow ambling flow of passers-by. The evening sun slipped down out of the sky and the sea became like molten gold.

She had never gone back. Her own decision. Nobody else's. They had not come chasing after her but they had never lost touch. Always letters, still filled with love. After her parents died, she thought the letters would stop but they didn't, because then Archie took over. Detailed descriptions of shoots, news of his children, scraps of village gossip. Always they ended in the same way. "We miss you. Why don't you come and stay for a few days? It is too long since we have seen you."

A yacht was moving out of the marina, motoring gently until it was clear of the beach and able to fill its sails with wind. Idly, she watched its passage. She saw it, but her inner eye was filled with images of Croy. Her thoughts, once more, ran ahead and this time she did not pull them back, but let them go. To the house. Up the steps to the front door. The door stood open. Nothing to stop her. She could go . . .

She set down her coffee-cup with some force. What was the point? The past was always golden because one recalled only the good times. But what about the darker side of memory? Happenings better left where they were, shut away, like sad mementoes stuffed in a trunk, the lid closed down, the key turned in the lock. Besides, the past was people, not places. Places without people

157

were like railway stations where no trains ran. I am thirty-nine. Nostalgia drains all energy from the present, and I am too old for nostalgia.

She reached for her brandy. As she did this, a shadow came between herself and the sun, to lie across her table. Startled, she looked up and into the face of the man who stood beside her. He gave a little bow.

"Pandora."

"Oh, Carlos! What are you doing creeping up on me?"

"I have been to the Casa Rosa but found nobody there. You see, if you don't come to me, then I have to come to you."

"I *am* sorry."

"So I tried the port. I thought that I should find you somewhere here."

"I was shopping."

"May I join you?"

"Of course."

He drew out a chair and sat facing her. He was a tall man in his mid-forties, formally attired in collar and tie and a light jacket. His hair was dark, as were his eyes, and even on this sultry evening his appearance was cool and crisp. He spoke impeccable English and looked, Pandora always thought, like a Frenchman. But he was, in fact, a Spaniard.

He was also extremely attractive. She smiled. She said, "Let me order you a brandy."

15

Wednesday the Twenty-fourth

Virginia Aird shouldered her way through the swing-
doors of Harrods and stepped out into the street. In the
store, the heat and the hassle had become oppressive.
Outside, it was scarcely better. The day was humid, the
air heavy with petrol fumes and the claustrophobia of
surging humanity. Brompton Road stood solid with
traffic, and the pavements were choked with a slow-
moving river of people. She had forgotten that city
streets could contain so many people. Some had to
be Londoners, one supposed, going about their daily
business, but the general impression was of some global
immigration from all points of the compass. Tourists and
visitors. More visitors than one could have believed
possible. Great blond students with back packs passed
by. Entire families of Italians or possibly Spaniards; two
Indian ladies in brilliant saris. And, of course, Americans. My fellow countrymen, thought Virginia wryly.
They were instantly recognisable by their clothes and
the plethora of camera equipment slung about their
necks. One huge man was even wearing his ten-gallon
hat.

It was four-thirty in the afternoon. She had been
shopping all day and was now laden with loot, carrier
bags, and parcels. Her feet hurt. But still she stood there,
because she had not yet made up her mind what she
was going to do next.

There were two alternatives.

Either she would return forthwith, by any means of transport that made itself available, to Cadgwith Mews, where she was staying in great comfort with her friend Felicity Crowe. She had been given a doorkey, so even if the house was empty – Felicity out shopping, or taking her dachshund for a turn around the gardens – Virginia could let herself in, kick off her shoes, make a cup of tea, and fall, in a stupor of exhaustion, on to her bed. The prospect of such a course of action was immensely tempting.

Or she could go to Ovington Street and risk finding Alexa out. This was what she *ought* to do. Alexa was not exactly on her conscience, but there could be no question of returning to Scotland without having made contact with her stepdaughter. She had already tried to do this, telephoning last night from Felicity's, but there had been no answer to the call and she had finally replaced the receiver deciding that, for once, Alexa was out on some spree. Then she had tried again this morning, and at lunch-time, and again from the hairdresser's, boiled with heat from the blow-drier. Still no reply. Was Alexa perhaps out of London?

At that moment a small Japanese, gazing in the opposite direction, barged into her and knocked one of her parcels to the ground. He apologised profusely in his polite Japanese way, picked up the parcel, dusted it off, returned it to her, bowed, smiled, raised his hat, and went on his way. Enough. A taxi drew up to unload its cargo and, before anyone else could claim it, Virginia did so.

"Where to, love?"

She had made up her mind. "Ovington Street." If Alexa was not at home, she would keep the taxi and go on to Felicity's. With the small decision taken, she felt better. She opened the window, sat back, thought about taking off her shoes.

It was a short journey. As the taxi turned into Ovington Street, Virginia sat forward to search for Alexa's car. If her car was there, then, in all probability, Alexa would be at home. It was – a white Mini van with a red stripe was parked at the pavement outside the blue front door. Relief. She directed the cab driver and he drew up in the middle of the street.

"Can you wait a moment? I just want to make sure somebody's in."

"Okay, love."

She gathered up her shopping and bundled out, climbed the steps and pressed the bell. She heard Larry barking, Alexa's voice telling him to be quiet. She dumped her parcels on the doorstep and, opening her bag, went back to pay off the taxi.

Alexa was in her kitchen, dealing bravely with the detritus of her day's work, all of which she had brought back from Chiswick in the back of her van. Saucepans, plastic containers, wooden salad bowls, knives, eggwhisk, and a cardboard wine crate filled with dirty glasses. When all was clean, dried, and put away, she planned to go upstairs, strip off her crumpled cotton skirt and shirt, take a shower, and then put on an entirely fresh set of clothes. After that, she would make a cup of tea . . . Lapsang Souchong with a slice of lemon . . . and then she would take Larry for a little stroll, and later start thinking about dinner. On the way back from Chiswick, she had stopped off at the fishmonger and bought rainbow trout, Noel's favourite. Grilled, with almonds. And perhaps . . .

She heard the taxi approaching slowly down the street. Standing at the sink, visibility was limited. The taxi stopped. A woman's voice. High-heeled footsteps tapped across the pavement. Alexa, rinsing a wineglass under the tap, waited, listening. Then her doorbell rang.

161

Larry hated the doorbell and burst into an aria of barking. And Alexa, so occupied and busy, resented the interruption and was equally unenthusiastic. Who on earth could this be? "Oh, be quiet, you stupid creature." She set down the glass, untied her apron and went upstairs to find out. Hopefully, it would be no one of importance. She opened the door to a pile of expensive-looking parcels. The taxi made a U-turn and trundled away. And . . .

She gaped. Her stepmother. Dressed for London but still instantly recognisable. She wore a black dress and a scarlet jacket and patent pumps, and her hair, fresh from the hands of some exclusive expert, had been dressed in a new style, drawn back from her face and clasped in a huge black velvet bow.

Her stepmother. Looking fantastic but unannounced and entirely unexpected. The implications of this caused every thought but one to fly from Alexa's head.

Noel.

"*Virginia.*"

"Don't die of shock. I kept the taxi waiting because I thought you might be out." She kissed Alexa. "I've been shopping," she explained unnecessarily, and stooped to gather up the parcels. Alexa, with an effort, pulled herself together and helped.

"But I didn't even know you were in London."

"Just for a day or two." They dumped it all on the hall table. "And don't say why didn't you ring me up, because I've been calling nonstop. I thought you must be away."

"No." Alexa shut the door. "We . . . I went out for dinner last night, though; and I've been out on a job all day. I was just washing up. That's why I'm looking such a mess . . ."

"You look great." Virginia eyed her. "Have you lost weight?"

"I don't know. I never weigh myself."

"What was the job?"

162

"Oh, a lunch for an old man's ninetieth birthday. In Chiswick. A lovely house, right on the river. Twenty guests, and all relations. Two great-grandchildren."

"What did you give them?"

"Cold salmon and champagne. That's what he wanted. And a birthday cake. But why didn't you tell me you were coming . . .?"

"Oh, I don't know. It was all done on the spur of the moment. I just felt I wanted to get away for a day or two. I've been shopping all day."

"It looks like it. And I love your hair. You must be exhausted. Go on in and take the weight off your feet . . ."

"That's all I want . . ." Pulling off her jacket, Virginia went through the open door, tossed her jacket aside, headed for the largest armchair, collapsed into it, kicked off her shoes and placed her feet on a stool. "Heaven."

Alexa stood and looked at her. How long did she plan to stay? Why . . .? "Why aren't you staying here with me?" Thank heavens she wasn't, but it was the obvious question to ask.

"I would have invited myself, of course, but I promised Felicity Crowe next time I came to London I'd stay with her. You know, she's my childhood friend. She'd have been my bridesmaid if I'd had bridesmaids. And we never see much of each other, and when we do we talk and giggle nonstop."

So that was all right. "Where does she live?"

"A dear little house in Cadgwith Mews. But I must say, it's not as pretty as this."

"Would you . . . would you like a cup of tea?"

"No, don't bother. A cold drink would do."

"I've got a can of Coke in the fridge."

"Perfect."

"I . . . I'll just get it."

She left Virginia and went down to the kitchen. She opened the fridge and took out the can of Coke. Virginia was here and it was necessary to be cool and objective.

163

Being cool and objective was not Alexa's strong point. Downstairs, evidences of Noel were scarce. His Barbour jacket and a tweed cap hung in the downstairs loo. A *Financial Times* lay in the drawing room. That was all. But upstairs was different. His personal belongings were everywhere, and the bed, very obviously, made up for the occupancy of two people. There could be no question of trying to hide it all away. If Virginia went upstairs . . .

She found herself overwhelmed with indecision. On the one hand, perhaps this was the best way to do it. She hadn't planned anything but it had happened; and Virginia was here. As well, Virginia was young and not even, strictly speaking, family. She would hopefully understand, and perhaps even approve. She, after all, had had strings of men in her life before she married Fa. Virginia could be Alexa's advocate, the best person of all to break the news gently that the shy and puddingy Alexa had not only found a man of her own at last but had taken him into her heart and her home, and was openly living with him.

On the other hand, if she did this, then the secret was out and Alexa would be expected to share Noel. Speak about him and allow them all to meet him. She imagined her father coming to London, ringing up. "I'll take you both to Claridge's for dinner." The prospect caused her knees to shake, but in the end, she knew that she would be able to cope with such a situation. The unanswered question was how Noel would react. Would he, perhaps, feel that he was being pressurised in some way? Which would be disastrous because, after three months of living with him and learning all the capricious twists of another person's character, Alexa knew that this was the one thing in life that Noel could not stand.

At a loss, totally out of her depth, she made a huge effort to be rational. There is nothing you can do about it, she told herself in Edie's voice. You'll just need to take things the way they come. Thinking of Edie made

164

her feel a bit stronger. She closed the door of the fridge, found a glass, and went back upstairs.

"Sorry I've been so long." Virginia was smoking. "I thought you'd given up cigarettes."

"I did but I've started again. Don't tell your father."

Alexa opened the Coke and poured it, and handed Virginia the glass.

"Oh, marvellous. Delicious. I thought I was going to die of thirst. Why are all the shops so hot? Why are there so many people everywhere?"

Alexa curled up in the corner of the sofa.

"Visitors. It took me hours to get back from Chiswick. And you've got on the wrong sort of shoes for shopping. You should be wearing trainers."

"I know. It's crazy, isn't it? Dressing up to come to London. Habit, I suppose."

"What have you been buying?"

"Clothes. Basically something for the Steyntons' party. I see you've got your invitation."

"I haven't answered it yet."

"You're coming, of course."

"I . . . I don't know . . . I'm pretty busy round then."

"But of course you must come. We're counting on you . . ."

Alexa diverted her. "What sort of a dress did you get?"

"It's dreamy. Sort of voile, white, in layers, with black spots everywhere. Tiny shoestring straps. I'll have to try to step up my suntan."

"Where did you find it?"

"Caroline Charles. I'll show it to you before I go. But, Alexa, do try to come. It's September, so everybody will be there and it'll be a great do."

"I'll see. How's Fa?"

"He's fine." Virginia turned away to stub out her cigarette in the ashtray. Alexa waited for her to enlarge on this flat statement, but she didn't say any more.

"And Henry?"

"Henry's great too."

"Are they both at home?"

"No. Edmund's spending this week in the flat in Edinburgh, and Henry's taken his sleeping-bag and gone to stay at Pennyburn with Vi. I took him to Devon for his summer holidays. We had three weeks, and it was a success. I took him riding for the first time in his life, and he liked all the farm animals and going fishing with my father." Another pause, not entirely comfortable, or was that Alexa's imagination? Then Virginia went on, "I really wanted to take him out to the States. I suddenly got this yen for Leesport and Long Island. But Gramps and Grandma had taken themselves off for a long cruise, so there wasn't much point our going."

"No, I suppose not." A car started up and sped away down the street. "So what's happening at home?"

"Oh, not a lot. The usual. We had the church sale in July, to try to raise money for the electrics. It was more work than you can possibly imagine, and we ended up with around four hundred pounds. I thought it was scarcely worth the effort, but Archie and the rector seemed quite satisfied. Henry won a bottle of rhubarb wine in the raffle. He's going to give it to Vi for her birthday."

"Lucky Vi. How is she? And how's Edie?"

"Oh, *Edie*. That's a real problem. Haven't you heard?"

It sounded disastrous. "Heard what?"

"She's got this dreadful cousin come to stay with her. She arrived last week and Edie's already looking demented."

The idea of Edie looking demented was enough to fill Alexa's heart with chill. "*What* dreadful cousin?"

Virginia told her, in some detail, the saga of Lottie Carstairs. Alexa was horrified. "I remember the Carstairs. They were very old, and they lived in a croft up the hill from Tullochard. And sometimes on Sundays they used to come to Strathcroy to have their dinner with Edie."

"That's right."

"They used to drive a tiny, rattly car. The two little old people sitting in the front and the great gawky daughter in the back."

"Well, the two little old people are now dead and the gawky daughter has gone witless. Which is putting it mildly."

Alexa was indignant. "But why should Edie have to look after her? Edie's got enough to do without such a responsibility."

"That's what we all told her, but she wouldn't listen. She says there's nowhere else for the poor soul to go. Anyway, last week she arrived in an ambulance and she's been with Edie ever since."

"But not for ever? She'll surely go back to her own house?"

"Let's hope so."

"Have you seen her?"

"Have I? She wanders round the village and talks to everybody. And not just the village. I took the dogs up to the dam the other day, and I was just sitting there on the bank when, all of a sudden, I had this queer feeling and I turned round, and there was Lottie sneaking up behind me."

"How spooky."

"Spooky's the word. Edie can't keep track of her. And that's not the worst of it. She goes out at night too, and drifts around the place. I suppose she's quite harmless, but the thought of her peering through windows is enough to put the fear of God into anybody."

"What does she look like?"

"She doesn't *look* mad. Just a bit strange. With very pale skin and eyes like boot buttons. And she's always smiling, which makes her spookier than ever. Ingratiating. I think that's the word. Edmund and Archie Balmerino say she was always like that. She worked at Croy one year as a housemaid. I don't think Lady Balmerino could find anybody else. Vi said it was the year Archie

167

and Isobel were married. Archie swears every time you opened the door, Lottie was always lurking behind it. And then she smashed so much china that Lady Balmerino sacked her. So all in all, as you can gather, it's something of a problem."

The telephone rang.

"Oh, bother." Alexa, engrossed in the drama of Strathcroy, resented the interruption. Reluctantly she got to her feet and went to her desk to answer the call.

"Hello?"

"Alexa Aird?"

"Speaking."

"You won't remember me – Moira Bradford – but I was a guest at the Thomsons' dinner party last week . . . and I wondered . . ."

Business. Alexa sat down, reached for her notepad, her biro, her engagement diary.

". . . not until October, but thought it better to fix things right away . . ."

Four courses, for twelve people. Perhaps, Mrs Bradford suggested delicately, Alexa could give her some idea of cost?

Alexa listened, answered questions, made notes. Behind her, she was aware that Virginia had got out of her chair and was making for the door. She looked up. Virginia made gestures, mouthed "Just going to the john . . ." and before Alexa had the opportunity to tell her to use the cloakroom and not go upstairs, was gone.

". . . of course, my husband will see to the wine . . ."

"I beg your pardon?"

"I said my *husband* will see to the *wine*."

". . . oh, yes, of course . . . look, shall I get back to you?"

"But can't we decide everything now? I'd rather do it that way. And another thing is serving. Do you have a colleague, or do you do the serving yourself?"

Virginia had gone upstairs. She would see everything, draw the obvious conclusions, guess the truth. In a strange way, Alexa felt a sort of resigned relief. There wasn't much point in feeling anything else because it was too late to do anything about it.

She took a deep breath. She said, in her most capable voice, "No. I don't have a colleague. But you don't have to worry, because I can manage it all very easily on my own."

Virginia, in stockinged feet, climbed the staircase, reflecting, as she always did, that this was one of the prettiest of small London houses. So fresh, with its wallpaper and shining white paint. And so comfortable, with thick carpets and extravagantly generous curtains. On the landing, the doors to the bedroom and the bathroom both stood open. She went into the bathroom and saw that Alexa had new curtains here, a quilted chintz patterned with leaves and birds. Admiring them, she looked around for other signs of refurbishment.

There were none, but other unexpected objects caught her eye and the implication of these drove all other thoughts from her head. Two toothbrushes in the toothmug. Shaving-tackle on the glass shelf, a wooden bowl of soap and a shaving-brush. A bottle of aftershave – Antaeus by Chanel – the same that Edmund used. By the side of the bath was a huge Turkish sponge, and hanging from the tap a ball of soap on a cord. From hooks behind the door hung two towelling robes, one large, blue-and-white-striped, the other smaller and white.

By now she had totally forgotten her reason for coming upstairs. She went out of the bathroom, back on to the landing. Downstairs was silent. The telephone call apparently was finished, and Alexa's voice stilled. She looked at the bedroom door, and then put out her hand, pushed it open and went in. Saw the bed, piled with double pillows; Alexa's nightgown neatly folded on one set, a man's sky-blue pyjamas on the other. On the bedside table a pigskin travelling clock softly ticked. That clock did not belong to Alexa. Her eyes moved around the room. Silver brushes on the dressing-table, silk ties slung on the mirror. A row of masculine shoes. A wardrobe door, perhaps faulty, hung open. She saw rows of suits on hangers, and on the chest of drawers a pile of immaculately ironed shirts.

A step on the stair behind her. She turned. Alexa stood there, in her crumpled cotton clothes, looking much as she had always looked. Yet different. "Have you lost weight?" Virginia had asked, but she knew now no diet was responsible for that indefinable radiance about Alexa that she had noticed the moment she saw her.

Their eyes met, and Alexa's were steady. She did not look away. There was no guilt there, no shame, and Virginia was glad for her. Alexa was twenty-one. It had taken long enough, but now it seemed that, at last, she had grown up.

Standing there, she remembered Alexa as a child, as she had first known her, so shy, so unsure, so eager to please. Then, the newly married Virginia had trod with the greatest of care, chosen her words, always painfully aware of the pitfalls of impetuously saying or doing the wrong thing.

It was the same now.

In the end it was Alexa who spoke first. She said, "I was going to tell you to use the downstairs loo."

"I'm sorry. I didn't mean to pry."

"You didn't have to. It's pretty obvious."

"Do you mind me knowing?"

"No. You would have found out some time."

"Want to talk about it?"

"If you like."

Virginia came out of the bedroom and closed the door

behind her. Alexa said, "Let's go back downstairs and I'll tell you there."

"I haven't been to the john yet." And all at once they were both laughing.

"He's called Noel Keeling. I met him in the street. He'd come to dinner with some people called Pennington – they live a couple of doors down – but he'd got the wrong night, so he was at a loose end."

"Was that the first time you'd ever seen him?"

"Oh, no, we'd met before that, but not very memorably. At some cocktail party, and then I did a directors' lunch for his firm."

"What does he do?"

"He's in advertising. Wenborn & Weinburg."

"How old is he?"

"Thirty-four." Alexa's face became dreamy, the very picture of a girl able to talk at last about the man she loves. "He's . . . oh, I can't describe him. I was never any good at describing people."

A pause fell. Virginia waited. And then, in an effort to get Alexa back to the point of the story, said, "So, he'd come to dine in Ovington Street on the wrong night."

"Yes. And he was tired out. You could see how tired he was. He'd just flown in from New York and he hadn't had any sleep, and he looked so down in the mouth, I asked him in. And we had a drink, and then something to eat. Chops. And then he went to sleep on the sofa."

"You can't have been very entertaining."

"Oh, Virginia, I *told* you. He was tired."

"Sorry. Go on."

"And then the next evening was the night he was meant to have dinner with the Penningtons, so he dropped in for a moment first, and brought me a great bunch of roses. A sort of thank-you. And then a couple of nights later, we went out for dinner. And . . . well, it sort of snowballed from there."

Virginia wondered if "snowballed" was, under the circumstances, an appropriate word. But she said, "I see."

"And then a weekend came along and we drove out into the country for a day. And it was very warm and blue-skyed, and we took Larry and walked for miles over the Downs, and we had dinner on the way back to London, and then we went to his flat for coffee. And then . . . well . . . it was dreadfully late . . . and . . ."

"You spent the night with him."

"Yes."

Virginia reached for another cigarette and lit it. Snapping out her lighter, she said, "And the following morning, you had no regrets?"

"No. No regrets."

"Was it . . . the first time? For you?"

"Yes. But you didn't have to ask that, did you?"

"Oh, honey, I know you very well."

"It made everything a bit embarrassing to begin with. Because I couldn't just let him find out. I couldn't pretend. It would have been like pretending you can swim frightfully well, and then jumping into the deep end and drowning. I didn't want to drown. So I told him. I was sure he would think I was dreadfully schoolgirlish or prissy. But do you know what he said? He said it was like being given a really splendid and unexpected present. And the next morning he woke me up by opening a bottle of champagne with a tremendous pop and a flying cork. And we sat in bed and drank it together. And after that . . ."

She paused, having apparently run out of both breath and words.

"More snowballing . . .?"

"Well, you know. We were always together, I mean when we weren't working. And after a bit, it seemed

172

ludicrous, at the end of the evening, driving off in different directions or having to borrow the other person's toothbrush. So we talked about it. He's got a very nice flat in Pembroke Gardens and I would happily have gone there, but I couldn't leave this house empty when it's so full of Granny Cheriton's precious things. And for the same reason I didn't feel very keen to let it. It was a bit of a dilemma but then Noel met up with these friends who'd just got married and wanted a place to rent until they'd found somewhere of their own. So he let them have his flat and moved in with me."

"How long has he been here?"

"About two months."

"And you never let on."

"It wasn't that I was ashamed or secretive. It was just that it was all so incredibly marvellous, I wanted to keep it to ourselves. Somehow that was part of the magic."

"Does he have family?"

"His parents are both dead but he's got two sisters. One's married and lives somewhere in Gloucestershire. The other's in London."

"Have you met her?"

"No, and I don't really want to. She's much older than Noel and she sounds rather frightening. She's Editor-in-Chief of *Venus*, and terribly high-powered."

"So when I get home, do you want me to say anything?"

"It's up to you."

Virginia thought about it. "It would surely be better to tell Edmund before he hears about it from some other person. He's in London a lot and you know how people talk. Especially men."

"That's what Noel says. Would you mind telling Fa? And Vi? Would it be very difficult to tell them?"

"Not difficult at all. Vi's amazing. She takes everything in her stride. And as for your father, at the moment I don't really care what I have to say to him."

Alexa frowned. "What *do* you mean?"

173

Virginia shrugged. She was frowning. When she frowned, all the fine lines on her face sprang into relief and she no longer looked so young. "I suppose you might as well know. We're not on the best of terms at the moment. We have a running row going on, no harsh words, but a certain frigid politeness."

"But . . ." Noel was forgotten and Alexa filled with apprehension. She had never heard Virginia speak about Fa in that cold tone of voice, could not remember them ever having quarrelled. Virginia adored him, fell in with all his plans, agreed with everything he suggested. There had never been anything but loving accord, every evidence of physical affection, and always – even from behind closed doors – much laughter and chat when they were together. They never seemed to run out of things to talk about, and the stability of their marriage was one of the reasons Alexa returned home to Balnaid whenever she could grab a holiday. She liked to be with them. The very thought of their falling out, not speaking, not loving, was unendurable. Perhaps they would never love again. Perhaps they would divorce . . . ". . . I can't *bear* it. What's happened?"

Virginia, seeing all the joy flow from Alexa's face, felt guilty and knew she had said too much. It was just that, talking about Noel, she had forgotten that Alexa was her stepdaughter and had allowed herself to speak bluntly and coldly about her problems, as though confiding in some old and intimate friend. A contemporary. But Alexa was not a contemporary.

She said quickly, "Don't look so horrified. It's not as bad as that. It's just that Edmund is insisting on sending Henry to boarding school and I don't want him to go. He's only eight, and I think he's too young. Edmund has always known how I feel, but he settled it all without consulting me and I was very hurt. It's got to a pitch where we can't even talk about it. The subject is never mentioned. We've both dug our toes in and that seems to be it. Which is one of the reasons I took Henry away

174

to Devon. He knows he's got to go away to school, and he knows that we're angry with each other. For his sake, I try to have fun with him, and do things with him the way I always have. And I would never dream of saying a word to him against Edmund. You know how he adores his father. But it's not easy."

"Oh, poor little Henry."

"I know. I thought maybe a day or two with Vi would make things better for him. You know what buddies they are. So I made the excuse of a new dress and seeing you, and came to London for a few days. I don't really need a new dress, but I've seen you, and the way things have turned out, that's made it worthwhile."

"But you've still got to go home to Balnaid."

"Yes. But perhaps things will be better."

"I am sorry. But I do understand. I know how Fa can be once he's made up his mind about something. Like a brick wall. It's the way he works. I suppose it's one of the reasons that he's been so successful. But it's not easy if you're on the other side of the fence and you've got a point of view of your own."

"That's right. I sometimes think he would be a little more human if, just once in his life, he made a real cock-up of something. Then he could admit to the possibility of being mistaken. But he never has and he never does."

In total agreement, they gazed at each other glumly. Then Alexa said, without much conviction, "Perhaps Henry will love school, once he gets there."

"Oh, I hope so much that he will. For all our sakes. For Henry's sake in particular, I'd be grateful to be proved wrong. But I'm terribly afraid that he'll hate it."

"And you . . .? Oh, Virginia. I can't imagine you without Henry."

"That's the trouble. Neither can I."

She reached for another cigarette and Alexa decided that the time had come to take some positive action.

She said, "Let's have a drink. After all this, I think we

could both do with one. What for you? A Scotch?"

Virginia looked at her watch. "I should go. Felicity's expecting me for dinner."

"There's heaps of time. And you must stay and meet Noel. He won't be long now. Now that you know about him, please don't go. And it'll make it much easier for you, telling Fa, if you've met Noel and can say how much you like him."

Virginia smiled. Alexa was twenty-one and now a woman of some experience but still wondrously naïve.

"All right. But don't make it too strong."

Noel had bought the flowers from a street vendor near the office. Carnations and sweet peas and a misting of gypsophila. He had not intended to buy flowers but had seen them as he passed, thought about Alexa, and then gone back to take a second look. The flowerlady was anxious to be home and let him have two bunches for the price of one. Two bunches made a good show.

Nowadays, living in Ovington Street, he walked home from the office each evening. It gave him the chance to stretch his legs and yet was not too great a distance to be tiring at the end of a day's work. It was pleasant to turn in at the end of the street and know that this was where he now belonged.

Domesticity with Alexa, he had discovered, had many advantages, for she had proved to be not only a charming, compliant lover but the most undemanding of companions. At first Noel had harboured fears that she might become possessive, and jealous of any time that he spent away from her. He had suffered such resentments before, and had ended up feeling as though he had a millstone hanging round his neck. But Alexa was different, generous and understanding about evenings when he was committed to giving dinner to some overseas

176

client, or the regular twice-weekly games of squash at his club.

Now, he knew that when he opened the blue front door she would be there, waiting for the sound of his key in the door, running up the stairs from the basement to greet him. He would relax with a drink, take a shower, eat an excellent dinner; later, watch the news, perhaps, or listen to some music. And, finally, bear Alexa off to bed.

His pace quickened. He took the steps in a single stride, juggling with the flowers in order to reach into his trouser pocket for his doorkey. The door, well-oiled, swung silently inwards, and he heard at once the voices from beyond the open drawing-room door. Alexa apparently had a caller. Which was unusual because ever since Noel had moved into Ovington Street, she had firmly kept all visitors at bay.

". . . I wish you'd stay for dinner," she was saying. He closed the door, being careful to make no sound. "Can't you ring Felicity and make some excuse?"

The hall table was piled with some person's expensive-looking shopping. He put his briefcase down on the floor.

"No, it would be too rude." A female visitor. He paused for a second to check on his appearance, sagging at the knees in front of the oval mirror, smoothing back his hair with his hand.

"It's grilled trout and almonds . . ."

He went through the open door. Alexa was on the sofa with her back to him, but her visitor saw him at once, and their eyes met across the room. She had the most astonishingly blue eyes that he had ever seen, and their bright glitter was cool as a challenge.

She said, "Hi!"

Alexa, alerted, sprang up. "Noel. I never heard you come in." She looked rosy and faintly grubby but very sweet. He gave her the flowers and stooped to kiss the top of her head.

177

"You were talking too hard," he told her, and turned to the guest, who was now on her feet, a tall and stunning blonde, wearing a slender black dress and a huge black velvet bow at the back of her head. "How do you do. I'm Noel Keeling."

"Virginia Aird." Her handshake was firm and friendly and, it occurred to him, at variance with the light in those brilliant eyes. He knew then that Alexa had been confiding, and that this glamorous creature was totally *au fait* with their situation. It was up to him to carry it off.

"And you're . . .?"

"My stepmother, Noel." Alexa spoke quickly, which meant that she was a little agitated and somewhat out of her social depth. "She's just down from Scotland to do some shopping. She dropped in out of the blue. It was the most lovely surprise. Oh, what gorgeous flowers. You are dear." She buried her nose in them and sniffed luxuriously. "Why do carnations always make me think of bread sauce?"

Noel smiled at Virginia. "She's got a one-track mind. Food."

"I'll go quickly and put them in water. We're having a drink, Noel."

"So I see."

"Do you want one?"

"Yes, of course, but don't worry, I'll help myself."

She left them, bearing her bouquet, headed for the kitchen. Alone with Virginia, Noel turned to her. "Do sit down again. I didn't mean to disturb you." She did so, arranging her long limbs with some grace. "Tell me, when did you come to London? And how long are you staying?"

Virginia explained. A spur-of-the-moment decision, an invitation from an old friend. Her voice was deep, with the attractive trace of an American accent. She had tried to get in touch with Alexa by telephone but had not been successful. Finally, she had just come round and taken Alexa by surprise.

As she told him all this, Noel fixed his drink. Now he brought it back to where she sat, and settled himself in the chair facing her. She had, he noticed, exceptional legs.

"And when are you going back to Scotland?"

"Oh, tomorrow, maybe. Or the day after."

"I heard Alexa inviting you to dinner. I wish you'd stay."

"That's kind of you, but I'm already committed. I shall have to go very soon, but Alexa wanted me to be here when you got home." Her eyes were bright as sapphires, unblinking. "She wanted me to meet you." She was splendidly direct, with no beating about the bush. He decided to meet her challenge head-on.

"I imagine that she's explained the situation to you."

"Yes, she has. I am entirely in the picture."

"I'm glad. It will make things much easier for all of us."

"Have they been difficult?"

"Not at all. But I think her conscience was troubling her."

"Her conscience has always troubled her."

"She's been a little worried about her family."

"Her family mean a lot to her. She's had a strange upbringing. It's left her in some ways quite mature, and in others still childlike."

Noel wondered at her saying this. She must realise, surely, that he had already found that out for himself. He said, "She didn't want anybody hurt."

"She's asked me to tell her father."

"I think that's a splendid idea. I have been urging her to do so." He smiled. "Do you imagine that he will appear at our door with a horsewhip?"

"I shouldn't think so." Virginia reached for her handbag, took a cigarette and lit it with a gold lighter. "He's

179

not a man who gives way to his emotions. But I think that, as soon as possible, you should make his acquaintance."

"It was never I who balked at the idea."

She eyed him through the drifting smoke of her cigarette. "I think it would be best if you were to come to Balnaid. Then we would all be around you, and Alexa would have a little moral support."

He realised that he was being invited to stay. In that solid old Edwardian house with the dogs and the conservatory and the country all around. Alexa had spoken to him, with great enthusiasm and at some length, of the joys of Balnaid. The garden, the picnics, the small brother, the grandmother, the old nanny. He had shown polite interest but not much more. It did not sound like a place where amusing things might happen, and Noel's greatest horror was to be trapped, a guest in another person's house, and bored.

But now, faced by Virginia Aird, he found his preconceptions of Balnaid doing a swift about-turn. For this elegant and sophisticated woman, with her mesmerising eyes and her charming suggestion of a transatlantic drawl, could never be dull. Perceptive enough to leave you alone with *The Times*, if that was what you wanted, but still the sort of hostess who could, on the spur of the moment, think up some new and amusing ploy or ask a party of entertaining friends round for an impromptu drink. His imagination moved on to other delights. There would probably be some fishing. And shooting, too. Although that wouldn't be much use to Noel because he had never shot. Nevertheless . . .

He said, "How very kind of you to invite me."

"It would be best if we kept it very casual . . . as though, for some reason, you were coming anyway." She thought about this, and then her face lit up with bright inspiration. "Of course. The Steyntons' dance. What could be more natural than that? I know Alexa is in two minds about coming, but . . ."

180

"She said she wouldn't go without me and of course I haven't had an invitation."

"That's no problem. I'll have a word with Verena Steynton. There are never enough men at these affairs. She'll be delighted."

"You may have to persuade Alexa."

As he said this, Alexa came back into the room, bearing a pink-and-white jug in which she had loosely arranged Noel's offering. "Are you talking about me behind my back?" She put the jug on the table behind the sofa. "Don't those look lovely? You are kind, Noel. It makes me feel special, being brought flowers." She fiddled with a stray carnation, and then abandoned the arrangement and returned to her seat in the corner of the sofa. "Persuade Alexa to do what?"

"Come to the Steyntons' dance," said Virginia, "and bring Noel with you. I'll fix an invitation for him. And stay with us at Balnaid."

"But perhaps Noel doesn't want to go."

"I never said I didn't want to go."

"You did so!" Alexa was indignant. "The morning the invitation came you said tribal dances were scarcely your scene. I thought that was the end of the matter."

"We never really discussed it."

"You mean you *would* come?"

"If you want me to, of course."

Alexa shook her head in disbelief. "But Noel, it *will* be tribal dances. Reels and things. Could you bear that? It's no fun if you can't do them."

"I'm not totally unexperienced. That year I fished in Sutherland, there was a hooley in the hotel one evening and we all leapt around like savages, and as far as I remember, I leapt with the best of them. A couple of whiskies are all I need to lose my inhibitions."

Virginia laughed. "Well, if it all becomes too much for the poor man, I'm sure there'll be a nightclub or a disco, so he can go and smooch in there." She stubbed out her cigarette. "What do you say, Alexa?"

181

"There doesn't seem to be much for me to say. Between the two of you, you've fixed the whole thing up."

"In that case, that's our little dilemma solved."

"What little dilemma?"

"Noel, casually, meeting Edmund."

"Oh, I see."

"Don't look so miserable. It's the perfect plan." She glanced at the clock, laid down her glass. "I must go."

Noel got to his feet. "Can I drive you somewhere?"

"No. You're sweet, but if you could find me a taxi, that would be great . . ."

While he was gone on this errand, Virginia put her shoes back on, checked on her beautiful hairdo, reached for her scarlet jacket. Fastening the buttons, she caught Alexa's anxious gaze and smiled encouragingly.

"Don't worry about a thing. I'll make it okay for you before you've even set foot in the house."

"But you and Fa. You won't still be having a row, will you? I couldn't bear it if there was a hateful atmosphere and the two of you being angry with each other."

"No, of course not. Forget that. I shouldn't have told you in the first place. We'll have a great time. And your being there will cheer me up after poor Henry's gone to school."

"Poor little boy. I can't bear to think about it."

"Like I said, neither can I. However, there doesn't seem to be much either of us can do about it." They kissed. "Thank you for the drink."

"Thank you for coming. And for being so marvellous. You . . . you do like him, don't you, Virginia?"

"I think he's dishy. You'll answer the invitation now?"

"Of course."

"And, Alexa, buy yourself a peachy new dress."

16

Thursday the Twenty-fifth

Edmund Aird drove his BMW into the car-park of Edinburgh airport just as the seven o'clock shuttle from London drifted down out of the clouds and lined up for landing. Unhurriedly, he found a slot for himself, got out of the car and locked the door, watching, as he did so, the approach of the plane. He had timed things exactly, and this gave him much satisfaction. Standing around and waiting, for anything or anybody, filled him with impatience. Every moment of time was precious, and to fill in so much as five minutes kicking his heels and doing nothing caused him considerable frustration and anguish.

He walked through the car-park, crossed the road, entered the terminal. The aircraft, with Virginia on board, had landed. A number of people stood around, come to meet friends or relations. They were a mixed bunch and appeared to be either in a state of wild excitement or total unconcern. A young mother with three small children milling noisily around her knees lost her patience and slapped one of them. The child roared in indignation. The carousel began to move. Edmund stood jingling the loose change in his trouser pocket.

"Edmund."

He turned to see a man he met most days lunching at the New Club. "Hello, there."

"Who are you meeting?"

"Virginia."

"I've come to pick up my daughter and her two children. They're coming to stay for a week. There's some wedding on and the wee girl's going to be bridesmaid. At least the plane's on time. I caught the three o'clock shuttle from Heathrow last week and we didn't take off until half past five."

"I know. It's hell, isn't it?"

The doors at the top of the stairway had opened, the first trickle of passengers started to descend. Some searched for the one who had come to meet them; some looked lost and anxious, laden by too much hand-luggage. There was the usual proportion of businessmen returning from London conferences and meetings, complete with briefcases, umbrellas, folded newspapers. One, quite unselfconsciously, bore a sheaf of red roses.

Edmund watched them, waiting for Virginia. His appearance, tall and elegantly suited, his demeanour, the heavily lidded eyes and expressionless features gave nothing away, and a stranger observing him would glean no clue as to his inner uncertainties. For the truth was that Edmund could not be sure either of his welcome from Virginia, nor what her reactions would be when she saw him standing there.

Relations between them, ever since the evening he had broken the news of his plans for sending Henry away to school, had been painfully strained. They had never had a row before, never quarrelled, and although he was a man who could exist very well without other people's approval, he was bored by the whole business, longed for a truce, and for this chill politeness that lay between them to come to an end and be finally finished.

He was not hopeful. As soon as the Strathcroy Primary had broken up for the summer, Virginia had packed Henry up and taken him to Devon to stay there with her parents for three long weeks. Edmund had hoped that this extended separation would somehow heal the

184

wounds and bring Virginia's sulks to an end, but the holiday, spent in the company of her beloved child, appeared only to have hardened her attitude, and she returned home to Balnaid as cool and uncommunicative as ever.

For a limited time, Edmund could deal with this, but he knew that the chill atmosphere that existed between himself and Virginia did not go unnoticed by Henry. He had become uncommunicative, prone to easy tears, and more dependent than ever on his precious Moo. Edmund hated Moo. He found it offensive that his son was still unable to sleep without that disgusting old scrap of baby blanket. He had been suggesting for some months that Virginia should wean Henry from Moo, but Virginia, as far as he could see, had ignored his advice. Now, with only three weeks to go before Henry left for Temple-hall, she was going to have her work cut out.

After the debacle of the Devon holiday, and becoming frustrated with Virginia's resolute non-communication, Edmund had considered precipitating another row with his young wife, so bringing matters to a head. But then he decided that this could do nothing but worsen the situation. In her present state of mind, she was quite capable of packing her bags and hightailing it off to Leesport, Long Island, to stay with her devoted grand-parents, now returned from their cruise. There she would be petted and spoiled as she had always been, and vociferously reassured that she was in the right and Edmund a hard-hearted monster even to contemplate sending small Henry away from her.

And so Edmund had kept his counsel and decided to ride out the emotional storm. He was, after all, not about to change his mind nor make any compromises. It was, at the end of the day, up to Virginia.

When she announced that she was going to London by herself for a few days, Edmund greeted the news with nothing but relief. If a few days of fun and shopping did not put her in a more sensible frame of mind, then

185

nothing would. Henry, she told him, was going to stay with Vi. He could do what he pleased. And so he put the dogs into kennels with Gordon Gillock, closed Balnaid, and spent the week in his flat in Moray Place.

The time alone had come as no hardship to him. He simply cleared his mind of all domestic problems, allowed himself to become absorbed in his work, and enjoyed being able to put in long and productive days at his office. As well, the word went swiftly around that Edmund Aird was in town and on his own. Extra attractive men were always at a premium, and the invitations to dinner had poured in. During Virginia's absence he had not once spent an evening in the flat.

But the hard truth was that he loved his wife and deeply resented this constraint that had lain for so long, like a fetid bog, between them. Standing waiting for her to appear, he hoped devoutly that the time spent enjoying herself in London had brought her to her senses.

For Virginia's sake. Because he had no intention of living under the cloud of her disapproval and umbrage for so much as one more day, and had already made the decision to stay in Edinburgh, and not return to Balnaid, if she had not relented.

Virginia was one of the last to appear. Through the door and down the stairs. He saw her at once. Her hair was different and she was dressed in unfamiliar and obviously brand-new clothes. Black trousers and a sapphire-blue shirt, and an immensely long raincoat that reached almost to her ankles. She was carrying, along with her flight bag, a number of shiny and extravagant-looking boxes and carriers, the very picture of an elegant woman fresh from a mammoth shopping spree. As well, she looked sensationally glamorous and about ten years younger.

And she was *his* wife. Despite everything, he realised all at once how dreadfully he had missed her. He did not move from where he stood, but he could feel the drumbeat of his own heart.

She saw him and paused. Their eyes met. Those blue and brilliant eyes of hers. For a long moment they simply looked at each other. Then she smiled, and came on down towards him.

Edmund took a long, deep breath in which relief, joy, and a surge of youthful well-being were all inextricably mingled. London, it appeared, had done the trick. Everything was going to be all right. He felt his face break into an answering, unstoppable smile, and went forward to greet her.

Ten minutes later, they were back in the car, Virginia's luggage stowed in the boot, doors closed, seat belts fastened. Alone and together.

Edmund reached for the car keys, tossed them in his hand. "What do you want to do?" he asked.

"What suggestions do you have?"

"We can head straight back to Balnaid. Or we can go to the flat. Or we can go and have dinner in Edinburgh and then drive back to Balnaid. Henry is spending another night with Vi, so we are completely free."

"I should like to go out for dinner and then go home."

"Then that is what we shall do." He inserted the car key, switched on the ignition. "I have a table booked at Rafaelli's." He manoeuvred the crowded car-park, drove to the tollgate, paid his dues. They moved out on to the road.

"How was London?"

"Hot and crowded. But *fun*. I saw masses of people, and went to about four parties, and Felicity had got tickets for *Phantom of the Opera*. I spent so much money, you're going to pass out when the bills come in."

"Did you get a dress for the Steyntons' dance?"

"Yes. At Caroline Charles. A really dreamy creation. And I got my hair done."

"I noticed."

"Do you like it?"

"Very elegant. And that coat is new."

"I felt such a country frump when I got to London, I went slightly mad. It's Italian. Not much use in Strathcroy, I admit, but I couldn't resist it."

She laughed. His own, sweet-tempered Virginia. He was filled with grateful satisfaction, and swore to himself that he would remember this when the inevitable American Express account came in. She said, "I can see I shall have to go to London more often."

"Did you see Alexa?"

"Yes, and I've lots to tell you, but I'll save that up till we're having dinner. How's Henry?"

"I rang up a couple of evenings ago. He's having, as usual, the time of his life. Vi asked Kedejah Ishak to tea at Pennyburn, and she and Henry made a dam in the burn and sailed paper boats. He was quite happy to spend an extra night with Vi."

"And you? What have you been doing?"

"Working. Going out to dinner. I've had a social week."

She glanced at him wryly. "I'll bet," she said without rancour.

He drove into Edinburgh by the old Glasgow road, and as they approached, the city looked its most impressive, etched like a romantic engraving beneath the immense and steely sky. The wide streets were verdant with leafy trees, the skyline pierced by spires and towers, and the castle on its rock brooded over all, with flag snapping at the masthead. Coming to the New Town, they entered the gracefully proportioned purlieus of Georgian terraces and spacious crescents. All had been newly sandstoned, and the buildings, with their classic windows and porticoes and airy fanlights, stood honey-coloured in the evening light.

Circling the one-way system, Edmund made his way through a labyrinth of hidden lanes and turned at last into a narrow cobbled street to draw up at the pavement's edge outside the little Italian restaurant. On the opposite side of this street stood one of Edinburgh's many beautiful churches. High up on the tower, above the massive arched doorway, the hands of a golden clock moved to nine o'clock, and as they got out of the car, its chimes pealed out across the rooftops, striking the hours. Flocks of pigeons, disturbed from their airy roosts, exploded upwards in a flurry of flight. When the last chime had struck, they settled again, on sill and parapet, cooing to themselves, folding their wings, pretending nothing had happened, as though ashamed of their silly agitation.

"You'd think," said Virginia, "that they'd get used to the din. Become blasé."

"I never met a blasé pigeon. Did you?"

"Come to think of it, no."

He took her arm and led her across the pavement and through the door. Inside the restaurant was small, dimly lighted, smelling of fresh coffee and garlic and delicious Mediterranean food. The place was pleasantly busy and most of the tables were occupied, but the head waiter spied them at once and made his way across the floor to welcome them.

"Good evening, Mr Aird. And Madame."

"Good evening, Luigi."

"I have your table ready."

The table Edmund had particularly asked for; in the corner, tucked under the window. A starched pink damask cloth, pink damask napkins, a single rose in a slender vase. Charming, intimate, seductive. The ultimate ambience for the ending of a feud.

"Perfect, Luigi. Thank you. And the Moët Chandon?"

"No problem, Mr Aird. I have it on ice."

They drank the chilled champagne. Virginia filled in the details of her social activities, the art exhibitions she had been to, the concert at the Wigmore Hall.

189

They ordered in a leisurely fashion. Eschewed the ravioli and tagliatelli, and went instead for duck pâté, and cold Tay salmon.

"Why do I bring you to Italian restaurants, when you can eat Tay salmon at home?"

"Because there is nothing in the world so delicious, and after my whirl in London I seem to have had my fill of ethnic food."

"I shall not ask with whom you have been dining."

She smiled. "Nor I you."

Without haste, they ate their way through the perfect meal, ending with fresh raspberries coated in thick cream, and a Brie of exactly the right consistency. She told him of the exhibition at Burlington House, Felicity Crowe's plans to buy a country cottage in Dorset, and tried to explain, with a certain amount of confusing detail, the plot of *Phantom of the Opera*. Edmund, who knew the plot anyway, listened with absorbed interest, simply because it was so marvellous to have her back, to listen to her voice, to have her sharing her pleasures with him.

Finally, their plates were cleared, and coffee brought, black and fragrant, steaming in the tiny cups, as well as a dish of chocolate peppermints thin as wafers.

By now most of the other tables had emptied, the diners gone home. Only one other couple sat, as they sat, but drinking brandy. The man smoked a cigar.

The Moët Chandon was finished, up-ended in the ice-bucket. "Would you like a brandy?" Edmund asked.

"No. Not a thing more."

"I'd have one, but I have to drive."

"I could drive."

He shook his head. "I don't need a brandy." He leaned back in his chair. "You've told me everything, but you still haven't told me about Alexa."

"I was keeping it to the end."

"Does that mean it's good?"

"I think it's good. I'm not sure what you'll think."

"Try me."

"You won't become Victorian, will you?"

"I don't think I ever am."

"Because Alexa's got a man. He's moved in with her. He's living with her in the house in Ovington Street."

Edmund did not at once reply to this. Then he said, quite calmly, "When did this happen?"

"In June, I think. She didn't tell us because she was afraid we would all be upset or disapproving."

"Does she think we wouldn't like him?"

"No. I think she thinks you'd like him very much. It's just that she wasn't sure how you'd take it. So she gave me the job of telling you."

"Have you met him?"

"Yes. Just for a little while. We had a drink together. There wasn't time for more."

"Did you like him?"

"Yes. I did. He's very good-looking, very charming. He's called Noel Keeling."

Edmund's coffee-cup was empty. He caught Luigi's eyes and asked for it to be refilled. When this was done, he stirred it thoughtfully, his eyes downcast, his handsome features giving nothing away.

"What do you think?" Virginia asked.

He looked up at her and smiled. "I think I'm thinking that I thought it would never happen."

"But you're pleased that it has?"

"I'm pleased that Alexa has found someone who is sufficiently fond of her to want to spend much time with her. It would be easier for everybody if it could have taken a less dramatic course, but I suppose nowadays it's inevitable that they should shack up together and give it a try before making any momentous decision." He took a mouthful of the scalding coffee, set down the cup. "It's just that she's such an extraordinarily unsophisticated child."

"She isn't a child any more, Edmund."

"It's hard to think of Alexa as anything else."

191

"We have to."

"I realise that."

"She was in rather a state about my telling you all. She *asked* me to tell you, but I know, in a funny way, she was dreading the secret coming out."

"What do you think I should do?"

"You don't have to do anything. She's going to bring him up to Balnaid in September for the weekend of the Steyntons' dance. And we'll all behave as casually as all-get-out . . . just as though he were an old childhood chum or a schoolfriend. I don't think we can do more. After that, it's up to them."

"Was that your idea or Alexa's?"

"Mine," Virginia told him, not without pride.

"What a clever girl you are."

"I told her other things as well, Edmund. I told her that, over the last few weeks, we haven't exactly been the best of friends."

"That must be the understatement of the year."

She fixed him with her brilliant gaze. She said, "I haven't changed my mind. I haven't changed my attitude. I don't want Henry to go and I think he's too young, and I think you're making a dreadful mistake; but I know that Henry's been upset by all this ill feeling, and I've decided we've got to stop thinking about ourselves and think about the children instead. Think about Henry and Alexa. Because Alexa said that if we were still glowering at each other, then she wasn't going to come up with Noel because she couldn't stand the idea of any sort of bad atmosphere between us." She paused, waiting for Edmund to make some sort of comment. But he said nothing and so she continued. "I've been thinking about that. I tried to imagine going back to Leesport and finding my grandparents snapping each other's heads off, but it was unimaginable, and that's the way we've got to make it for Henry and Alexa. I'm not giving in, Edmund. I'll never come round to your way of thinking. But what can't be cured must be endured. Besides, I've missed you. I don't really like being on my own. In London I kept wishing you were there." She put her elbows on the table, her chin in her hands. "You see, I love you."

After a little, Edmund said, "I'm sorry."

"Sorry I love you?"

He shook his head. "No. Sorry I went to Templehall and settled the whole affair with Colin Henderson without consulting you. I should have had more consideration. It was overbearing."

"I've never heard you admit to being in the wrong before."

"I hope you never have to again. It's painful." He reached out and took her hand in his. "It's a truce then?"

"With one proviso?"

"What would that be?"

"That when the terrible day comes and poor Henry has to go to Templehall, I am not asked nor expected to take him. Because I don't think that I could physically bear to do that. Later on maybe, when I've got used to being without him. But not the first time."

"I'll be there," said Edmund. "I shall take him."

It was growing late. The other couple had departed, and the waiters were standing around trying not to look as though they were longing for Edmund and Virginia, too, to go home and let them close up for the night. Edmund called for the bill and, while this was coming, leaned back in his chair, put his hand in the pocket of his jacket and brought out a small package wrapped in thick white paper and sealed with red wax.

"It's for you." He put it on the table between them. "It's a welcome-home present."

17

If Henry could not be at home, at Balnaid, then the next best thing was staying with Vi. At Pennyburn, he had his own bedroom, a tiny room over what had once been the front door, with a narrow window looking out over the garden and the glen and the hills beyond. From this window, if he screwed his neck around a bit, he could even see Balnaid, half-hidden in trees beyond the river and the village. And in the mornings when he awoke and sat up, he could watch the rising sun stretching long fingers of early light across the fields, and listen to the song of the blackbird that had its nest in the top branches of the old elder tree by the burn. Vi did not like elder trees, but she had let this one stand, because it was a good tree for Henry to climb. That was how he had found out about the blackbird's nest.

The room was so small, it was a little like sleeping in a Wendy house, or even a cupboard, but that was part of its charm. There was space for his bed and a chest of drawers with a mirror hanging over it, but no more. A couple of hooks on the back of the door did duty as a wardrobe, and there was a neat little light over his bedhead, so that he could read in bed if he wanted to. The carpet was blue and the walls were white. There was a nice picture of a bluebell wood, and the curtains were white with bunches of field flowers spattered all over them.

This was his last night with Vi. Tomorrow, his mother was going to come and fetch him, and take him home. It had been a funny sort of few days, because the Strathcroy Primary had already opened for the winter term, and all his friends were back at their lessons. And so Henry, destined for Templehall, had nobody to play with. But somehow it hadn't mattered. Edie was there most mornings, and Vi was always full of bright ideas for a small boy's amusement and entertainment. They had gardened together, and she had taught him how to make fairy cakes, and for the evenings she had produced a mammoth jigsaw puzzle with which they had struggled together. One afternoon Kedejah Ishak had come for tea after school, and she and Henry had built a dam in the stream and become extremely wet. Another day he and Vi had taken a picnic lunch up to the loch and made a collection of twenty-four different wildflowers. She had shown him how to press them dry between leaves of blotting paper and thick books, and when they were ready he was going to stick them into an old exercise book with bits of Sellotape.

He had had his supper and his bath, and was now in bed reading his library book, which was by Enid Blyton and called *The Famous Five*. He heard the clock in the hall strike eight o'clock, followed by the sound of Vi's footsteps treading heavily up the staircase, which meant that she was coming to say goodnight to him.

His door was open. He laid down his book and waited for her to come through it. She appeared, tall and large and solid, and settled herself comfortably on the foot of his bed. The springs creaked. He was cosy in his own sleeping-bag, but she had tucked a blanket over the top of it, and he thought that it was one of the best feelings, having someone sit on your bed, with the blanket pulled tight over your legs. It made him feel very safe.

Vi wore a silk blouse with a cameo brooch at the collar, and a soft, heathery-blue cardigan, and she had brought her spectacles with her, which meant that she was quite prepared, if he wished, to read aloud a chapter or two from *The Famous Five*.

She said, "This time tomorrow, you'll be back in your own bed. We've had a good time, though, haven't we?"

"Yes." He thought of all the fun they had had. Perhaps it was wrong to want to go home and leave her, but at least he knew that she was safe and happy alone in her little house. He wished that he could feel the same about Edie.

Lately, Henry had stopped dropping in on Edie, because he was frightened of Lottie. There was something witchy about her, with her strange dark eyes that never blinked, and her ungainly, unaccountable movements, and her endless flood of chat that was too disjointed to be called conversation. Most of the time Henry hadn't the least idea what she was talking about, and he knew that it exhausted Edie. Edie had told him to be nice to Lottie, and he had done his best, but the truth was that he hated her, and could not bear to think of Edie closeted with her scary cousin, and having to deal with her, day in and day out.

From time to time he had seen headlines in the newspapers about poor people being murdered with axes or carving knives, and felt certain that Lottie, if roused or thwarted, was perfectly capable of attacking darling Edie – perhaps late at night, in the dark – and leaving her, dead and bloodstained, on the kitchen floor.

He shivered at the thought. Vi noticed the shiver. "Is something worrying you? A ghost just went over your grave."

This observation was too close for comfort. "I was thinking about Edie's cousin. I don't like her."

"Oh, Henry."

"I don't think Edie is safe with her."

Vi made a little face. "To be honest, Henry, I'm not very happy either. But I think that it's just a great trial for Edie. We talk about her cousin in the mornings, over coffee. Lottie's certainly a very tiresome lady, but apart from driving Edie to distraction with her ways, I don't think Edie's in any real danger. Not the kind you're imagining."

He hadn't told her what he imagined, but she knew. Vi always knew things like that.

"You will take care of her, won't you, Vi? You won't let anything happen?"

"No, of course I won't. And I shall make a point of seeing Edie every day, and keeping an eye on the situation. And I'll ask Lottie for tea one day, and that'll give Edie a bit of a breather."

"When do you think Lottie will go away?"

"I don't know. When she's better. These things take time."

"Edie was so happy, on her own. And now she's not happy a bit. And she has to sleep on the Put-U-Up. It must be horrid not being in her own room."

"Edie is a very kind person. More kind than most of us. She is making a sacrifice for her cousin."

Henry thought of Abraham and Isaac. "I hope Lottie doesn't make a sacrifice of her."

Vi laughed. "You're letting your imagination run away with you. Don't go to sleep worrying about Edie. Think about seeing your mother again tomorrow."

"Yes." That was much better. "What time do you think she'll come?"

"Well, you've got a busy day tomorrow, out with Willy Snoddy and his ferrets. I should think about tea-time. When you get back, she'll be here."

"Do you think she'll bring me a present from London?"

"Sure to."

"Perhaps she'll bring you a present, too."

"Oh, I don't expect a present. Besides, it's my birthday soon, so I'll get one then. She always gives me something quite special, something that I never realised how much I wanted."

"What day is your birthday?" He had forgotten.

197

"The fifteenth of September. The day before the Steyntons' party."

"Are you going to have the picnic?"

Vi always arranged a picnic for her birthday. Everybody came, and they all met up at the loch and lit a fire and cooked sausages, and Vi brought her birthday cake in a big box, and when she cut it, the assembled party stood around and sang "Happy Birthday to You". Sometimes it was a chocolate cake, and sometimes it was an orange cake. Last year it had been an orange cake.

He remembered last year. Remembered the inclement day, the racing wind and the scattered showers that had dampened nobody's enthusiasm. Last year he had given Vi a picture that he had drawn with his felt pens, and which his mother had had framed and mounted, just like a proper picture. Vi had it hanging in her bedroom. This year he was giving her the bottle of rhubarb wine that he had won in the raffle at the church sale.

This year . . . He said, "This year, I shan't be there."

"No. This year, you'll be at boarding school."

"Couldn't you have your birthday earlier, so that I could be there?"

"Oh, Henry, birthdays don't work that way. But it won't be the same without you."

"Will you write me a letter, and tell me all about it?"

"Of course I will. And you shall write to me. There'll be such a lot that I will want to hear."

He said, "I don't want to go."

"No. I don't suppose you do. But your father thinks that you should go, and he nearly always knows best."

"Mummy doesn't want me to go, either."

"That's because she loves you so. She knows that she'll miss you."

He realised then that this was the first time he and Vi had talked about his going away. This was because Henry did not even want to think about it, let alone discuss it, and Vi had never brought the subject up. But now they had started speaking about it, he discovered that he felt easier. He knew that he could say anything to Vi, and knew, too, that she would never repeat it.

He said, "They've been quarrelling. They've been cross with each other."

"Yes," said Vi. "I know."

"How do you know, Vi?"

"I may be old, but I'm not stupid. And your father is my son. Mothers know lots about their sons. The good bits and the not-so-good bits. It doesn't stop them loving them, but it makes them a little bit more understanding."

"It's been so horrid, with them so unkind to each other."

"It must have been."

"I don't want to go away to school, but I *hate* them being cross with each other. I simply *hate* it. It makes the house feel all headachy and ill."

Vi sighed. "If you want to know what I think, Henry, I think they've both been very short-sighted and selfish. But I haven't been able to say anything, because it's none of my business. That's another thing a mother mustn't do. She must never interfere."

"I really want to go home tomorrow, but . . ." He gazed at her, his sentence left unfinished, because he didn't really know what he was trying to say.

Vi smiled. When she smiled her face creased into a thousand wrinkles. She laid her hand on his. It felt warm and dry, and rough from all the gardening she did.

She said, "There's an old saying, that parting makes the heart grow fonder. Your mother and father have had a few days apart, on their own, with time to think things over. I'm sure they'll both have realised how wrong they have been. You see, they love each other very much, and if you love someone, you need to be with them, close to them. You need to be able to confide, to laugh together. It's just about as important as breathing. By now, I'm certain that they will have found this out. And I'm just as certain that everything will be just as it was before."

"Really certain, Vi?"

"Really certain."

She sounded so certain that Henry felt that way too. Such a relief. It was as though a huge weight had dropped from his shoulders. And this made everything much better. Even the prospect of leaving home and parents and being sent to board at Templehall had lost some of its fearfulness. Nothing could be as bad as thinking that his home would never be the same again. Reassured, and filled with grateful love for his grandmother, he held out his arms, and she leaned forward, and he embraced her, hugging her tight around her neck and pressing kisses on her cheek. When he drew back, he saw that her eyes were very shiny and bright.

She said, "It's time to sleep."

He was ready for it, now suddenly drowsy. He lay back on the pillow and felt beneath it for Moo.

Vi laughed at him, but gently, teasing him. "You don't need that old bit of baby blanket. You're a grown-up boy now. You can make fairy cakes, and do jigsaw puzzles, and remember the names of all those wildflowers. I think you can do without Moo."

Henry screwed up his nose. "But not tonight, Vi."

"All right. Not tonight. But tomorrow, maybe."

"Yes." He yawned. "Maybe."

She stooped to kiss him, and then got up off the bed. The springs creaked once more. "Goodnight, my lamb."

"Goodnight, Vi."

She turned out his light and went out of the room, but she left the door open. The darkness was soft and blowy and smelled of the hills. Henry turned on his side, curled up in a ball, and closed his eyes.

18

Friday the Twenty-sixth

When, ten years ago, Violet Aird bought Pennyburn from Archie Balmerino, she had become owner of a sad and drab little house with little to commend it save its view and the small stream that tumbled down the hill on the western march of its land. It was from this stream that the house took its name.

It stood in the heart of Archie's estate, on the face of the hill that sloped up from the village, and access was by the Croy back drive and then a rutted track overgrown with thistles and fenced by sagging posts and broken barbed wire.

The garden, such as it was, lay on the slope to the south of the house. This too was surrounded by rotting posts and straggling wire, and consisted of a small drying-green, a weedy vegetable patch, and dismal evidences of hen-keeping – leaning wooden sheds, much wire-netting, and nettles grown waist-high.

The house was built of dull-coloured stone, with a grey-tiled roof and maroon paintwork in a sad state of repair. Concrete stairs led up from the garden to the front door, and inside were small and lightless rooms, hideous peeling wallpaper, the smell of damp, and the persistent drip of some faulty tap.

In fact, so unattractive was the entire property that Edmund Aird, viewing it for the first time, strongly recommended that his mother should abandon the idea of ever living there and start to look for somewhere else.

But Violet, for reasons of her own, liked the house. It had stood empty for some years, which accounted for its dereliction, but despite the mould and the gloom, it had a pleasant feel to it. And it had that little burn within its lands, tumbling away down the hill. And, as well, the view. Inspecting the house, Violet would pause from time to time to glance out, rubbing a clear space on the dusty glass of the windows, seeing the village below, the river, the glen, the distant hills. She would never find another house with such a view. The view and the burn seduced her, and she disregarded her son's advice.

Doing it all up had been tremendous fun. It had taken six months to complete the work, and during that time Violet – politely spurning Edmund's invitation to remain at Balnaid until such time as she could move into her new abode – camped in a caravan that she had rented from a tourist park a few miles up the glen. She had never lived in a caravan before, but the idea had always appealed to her gypsy instincts and she leapt at the chance. The caravan was parked at the back of the house, along with the concrete mixers and barrows and shovels and daunting piles of rubble, and from the open door she could keep an eye on the workmen, and dash out to have a word with the long-suffering architect the moment she spied his car come bumping up the road. For the first month or two of this cheerfully vagabond existence, it was summer, and the only hazards were the midges and a leaky roof whenever it rained. But when the winter gales blew, the caravan trembled beneath their blast and rocked unsteadily at its temporary mooring, not unlike a small boat in a storm. Violet found this quite exciting and relished the dark and gusty nights. She could lie in her bunk, which was far too short and too narrow for such a sizy lady, listening to the keening wind and watching the clouds racing across the cold, moonlit skies.

But she did not spend all her time alternately bullying

and cajoling the builders. To Violet, a garden was even more important than a house. Before the workmen had started in on their labours, she had already engaged a man with a tractor, who tore up all the old fence posts and broken wire. In their place she planted a beech hedge on either side of her driveway and all around her small plot of land. After ten years, this was still not high, but thick and firm, always leafy, and so providing good shelter for birds.

Within this hedge, she planted trees. To the east, conifers. Not her favourites, but quick-growing and good for keeping the worst of the coldest wind at bay. On the west, overhanging the stream, grew gnarled elder, willows, and double white cherries. At the foot of the garden she had kept her planting low, in order to conserve the view. Azaleas grew there, and potentillas, with drifts of spring bulbs in the rough grass.

There were two curving flower-beds, one herbaceous and one filled with roses, and between them a good-sized lawn. This was on the slope and tricky to cut. Violet had bought an electric lawnmower, but Edmund – interfering again – decided that she was likely to sever the flex and so electrocute herself, and had engaged the services of Willy Snoddy to come once a week and do the job for her. Violet knew perfectly well that Willy was a great deal less competent than she herself at handling complicated equipment, but she went along with the arrangement as being the line of least resistance. Every now and then Willy, being laid low with a killing hangover, did not turn up, and then Violet, quite happily and efficiently, cut the grass herself.

But she did not tell Edmund that she had done so.

As for the house, that she had transformed, turning it back-to-front and opening out all the poky and ill-proportioned rooms. Now the main entrance stood to the north and the old front door had become a glassed garden door, opening straight out of her sitting room.

203

The concrete stairs she had demolished, and in their place stood a semi-circular flight of steps built of old stone salvaged from a fallen dyke. Aubretia and scented thyme grew from crannies between these rocks and smelled delicious when one trod upon them.

After some consideration, Violet decided that she could not bear the dull colour of the stone walls of Pennyburn, and so had them all harled and painted white. Windows and doorways were outlined in black, which gave the face of the house a crisp and down-to-earth appearance. To embellish it, she had planted a wisteria, but, after ten years, it had scarcely grown as high as her shoulder. By the time it reached the roof, she would probably be dead.

At seventy-seven one was perhaps better off sticking to hardy annuals.

All that was missing was a conservatory. The one at Balnaid had been built at the same time as the house. Its erection was due to the insistence of Violet's mother, Lady Primrose Akenside, a woman not addicted to the great outdoors. It was Lady Primrose's opinion that, if forced to live in the wilds of Scotland, a conservatory was absolutely essential. Quite apart from the fact that it was useful for keeping the house supplied with pot plants and grapes, it was somewhere to sit when the sun shone and yet the wind blew with an edge like ice to it. Such days, everybody knew, occurred with amazing frequency during the winter and spring and autumn months. But Lady Primrose spent a good deal of the summers in her conservatory as well, entertaining her friends and playing bridge.

Violet had loved the Balnaid conservatory for less social reasons, relishing the warmth, the peace, the smell of damp earth and ferns and freesias. When the weather was too inclement to garden, you could always potter about in the conservatory, and what better place to sit down after lunch and try to do the *Times* crossword?

Yes, she missed it, but after deliberation had decided

that Pennyburn was too small and modest for such an extravagant addition. It would make the house look pretentious and foolish, and she was not about to inflict such an indignity upon her new home. And it was scarcely a hardship to sit in her sheltered and sunny garden and try to do the crossword there.

She was in her garden now, and had been out working all afternoon, staking clumps of Michaelmas daisies before the autumn winds arrived to fell them flat. It was a day to start thinking about autumn. Not cold but fresh, with a certain smell about the air, a briskness. The farmers were harvesting, and the distant rumble of combine harvesters working in tall fields of barley was seasonal and strangely reassuring. The sky was blue but sailing with clouds blown in from the west. A blinking day, the old country people called it, as the sun went in and out.

Unlike many people, Violet did not mourn the passing of the summer and the prospect of a long dark winter ahead. "How can you bear to live in Scotland?" she was sometimes asked. "The weather so unpredictable, so much rain, so cold." But Violet knew that she could not bear to live anywhere else, and never yearned to move away. When Geordie was alive they had travelled together extensively. They had explored Venice and Istanbul, paced the art galleries of Florence and Madrid. One year they had taken an archaeological cruise to Greece; another time had sailed the fjords of Norway, as far north as the Arctic Circle and the midnight sun. But without him, she knew no urge to journey abroad. She preferred to stay right here, where her roots were deep, surrounded by a countryside that she had known since she was a child. As for the weather, she disregarded it, caring not if it froze or snowed or blew or rained or scorched, provided she could be out of doors and part of it all.

Which was proved by her complexion, weather-beaten and lined as an old farmworker's. But again, at seventy-seven, what did a few wrinkles matter? A small price to pay for an energetic and active old age.

She drove in the last stake, twisted the last length of wire. Finished. She stepped back on to the grass to survey her work. The canes showed, but once the Michaelmas daisies had thickened out a bit, they would be concealed. She looked at her watch. Nearly half past three. She sighed, always reluctant to stop gardening and go indoors. But she stripped off her gloves and dropped them into her wheelbarrow, then collected her tools, the last of the canes, the drum of wire, and barrowed the lot around the house to her garage, where all was stowed neatly away until the next day's labour.

Then she went into the house by the kitchen door, toeing off her rubber boots and hanging her jacket on a hook. In the kitchen, she filled the kettle and switched it on to boil. She laid a tray with two cups and saucers, a milk jug, a sugar bowl, and a plate of chocolate digestive biscuits. (Virginia would not eat anything at teatime but Violet was never averse to a small snack.)

She went upstairs to her bedroom, washed her hands, found a pair of shoes, tidied her hair, slapped a bit of face-powder on to her shining nose. As she did this, she heard the car come up the hill and turn into the lane. A moment later came the slam of its door, her own front door opening, and Virginia's voice.

"Vi!"

"Just coming."

She settled her pearls, fixed a stray wisp of hair, and went downstairs. Her daughter-in-law stood in the hall waiting for her; her long legs were in corduroys and a leather jacket was slung around her shoulders. She had a new hairdo, Violet noticed, drawn back from her brow and fastened at the nape of her neck with a ribbon bow.

She looked, as always, casually elegant, and happier than Violet had seen her for a long time.

"Virginia. How lovely to have you home again. And how chic you look. I love the hair." They kissed. "Did you have it done in London?"

"Yes. I thought perhaps it was time I changed my image." She looked about her. "Where's Henry?"

"He's out ferreting with Willy Snoddy."

"Oh, *Vi*."

"It's all right. He'll be home in half an hour."

"I didn't mean that. I meant what's he doing spending his time with that old reprobate?"

"Well, there are no children to play with because they're all in school. And he got talking to Willy when he came to cut the grass this week, and Willy invited him to go ferreting. He seemed very keen to go, so I said he could. You don't disapprove, do you?"

Virginia laughed and shook her head. "No, of course not. It's just rather unexpected. Do you think Henry realises what ferreting entails? It's quite a bloodthirsty business."

"I've no idea. We'll doubtless hear all about it when he gets back. Willy will see that he's on time, I know."

"I always thought you thought the old drunk was quite undependable."

"He wouldn't dare break his promise to me, and he never gets drunk in the afternoons. Now, how are you? Did you have a good time?"

"A great time. Here . . ." She thrust a flat package, impressively wrapped, into Violet's hands. "I brought you a present from the big city."

"My dear, you didn't need to."

"It's a thank-you for having Henry."

"I've loved having him. But he's longing to see you and go home to Balnaid. He was all packed up and ready long before breakfast this morning. Now, I want to hear all about everything. Come and watch me open my present."

She led the way into her sitting room and settled herself in comfort in her own fireside chair. It was a relief to get the weight off her feet. Virginia perched herself on the arm of the sofa and watched. Violet undid the ribbon bow and unwrapped the paper. A flat box, orange and brown, was revealed. She removed the lid. Inside, folded and silken beneath the layers of tissue paper, was a Hermès scarf.

"Oh, Virginia. This is far too much."

"No more than you deserve."

"But having Henry was a *treat*."

"I've brought him a present, too. It's in the car. I thought he could open it here, before I take him home."

The scarf was all pinks and blues and greens. Just the thing for brightening up that grey woollen dress. "I can't thank you enough – I'm really delighted with it. And now . . ." She folded the scarf, returned it to its box, and set it aside. "Let's have a cup of tea, and you can tell me everything that's happened in London. I want to hear all the details . . ."

"When did you get back?"

"Yesterday evening, on the shuttle. Edmund met me at Turnhouse and we went into Edinburgh and had dinner at Rafaelli's, and after that we drove home to Balnaid."

"I hope" – Violet fixed Virginia with a firm stare – "that you used the time together to sort out your differences."

Virginia had the grace to look abashed. "Oh, Vi. Did it show so much?"

"It was obvious to anyone but a blind man. I didn't say anything, but you must realise that it's very worrying for Henry if you and his father are not on good terms."

"Did Henry talk to you about it?"

"Yes, he did. He's much upset. I think he feels that going to Templehall is bad enough, but having you and Edmund at each other's throats is more than he can bear."

"We weren't exactly at each other's throats."

"Icy politeness is almost worse."

"I know. And I'm sorry. And Edmund and I have made it up. By that I don't mean anything's changed. Edmund won't budge from his decision, and I still think it's a dreadful mistake. But at least we've called a truce." She smiled and held out a slender wrist circled by a wide bracelet of gold. "Over dinner, he gave me this. It's a welcome-home present. So I'd be churlish to carry on sulking."

"That is a great relief to me. I managed to persuade Henry that you would both have come to your senses and would be friends again. And I'm grateful to you both, because now I don't feel that I am letting him down. He needs a lot of reassurance, Virginia. A lot of security."

"Oh, Vi, don't I know it?"

"And there's another thing. He's very bothered about Edie. He's frightened of Lottie. He thinks that Lottie might harm Edie in some way."

Virginia frowned. "Did he say so?"

"We talked about it."

"Do you think he's right?"

"Children are perceptive. Like dogs. They recognise evil where, perhaps, we adults don't see it."

"Evil is a strong word, Vi. I know she gives me the shivers, but I've always told myself she's just harmlessly dotty."

"I really don't know," said Violet. "But I've promised Henry that we will all keep a weather eye on the situation. And if he talks to you about it, you must listen to him, and try to set his mind at rest."

"Of course."

"Now." With that necessary exchange safely disposed

of, Violet steered the conversation in a more cheerful direction. "Tell me about London. Did you get a dress? And what else did you do? And did you see Alexa?"

"Yes." Virginia leaned forward to refill her cup from the teapot. "Yes, I did get a dress, and yes, I did see Alexa. That's what I want to talk to you about. I've already told Edmund."

Violet's heart sank. What on earth was happening now?

"She's all right?"

"Never better." Virginia leaned back in her chair. "There is a man in her life."

"Alexa has a young man? But that's splendid news! I was beginning to think that nothing exciting was ever going to happen to the dear child."

"They're living together, Vi."

For an instant, Violet was silenced. Then: "*Living* together?"

"Yes. And I'm not telling tales out of school. She particularly asked me to let you know."

"And *where* are they living together?"

"At Ovington Street."

"But . . ." Violet, flustered, sought for words. "But . . . how long has this been going on?"

"About two months."

"Who is he?"

"He's called Noel Keeling."

"What does he do?"

"He's in advertising."

"How old is he?"

"About my age. Good-looking. Very charming."

About Virginia's age. A dreadful thought occurred to Violet. "I hope he's not already married."

"No. A very eligible bachelor."

"And Alexa . . .?"

"Alexa is radiantly happy."

"Do you think they will marry?"

"I have no idea."

210

"Is he kind to her?"

"I think so. I only saw him for a little while. He came home from the office and we all had a drink together. He brought Alexa flowers. And he didn't know I was going to be there, so he didn't buy them to impress me."

Violet fell silent, trying to come to terms with this astonishing revelation. They were living together. Alexa was living with a man. Sharing a bed, sharing a life. Unmarried. She did not approve but her own opinions were best kept to herself. All that mattered was that Alexa should know that they all would support her, whatever might happen.

"What did Edmund say when you told him?"

Virginia shrugged. "Not a lot. He's certainly not about to fly to London with a loaded shotgun. But I think he is concerned, if only for the fact that Alexa is a girl of some wealth . . . she has that house and she has the money she inherited from Lady Cheriton. Which, as Edmund pointed out, is considerable."

"He's afraid this young man is after her money?"

"It's a possibility, Vi."

"You've met him. What do you think of him?"

"I liked him . . ."

"But you have reservations?"

"He's so personable. Cool. Like I said, charming. I'm not *certain* if I trust him . . ."

"Oh dear."

"But that's just me talking. I may be making a total misjudgment."

"What can we do?"

"We can't do anything. Alexa is twenty-one, she must make her own decisions."

Violet knew that this was true. But Alexa . . . so far away. In London.

"If only we could *meet* him. That would put everything on a much more normal footing."

"I entirely agree with you, and you will meet him." Violet glanced at her daughter-in-law and saw that she was smiling, looking as pleased with herself as the cat that got the cream. "I'm afraid I stuck my oar in and made noises like a mother. I talked to the two of them and they've agreed to come north together for the weekend of the Steyntons' dance. They're going to stay at Balnaid."

"Oh, what a clever idea!" Violet could have kissed Virginia, so delighted was she. "What a brilliant girl you are. Quite the best way of doing things, without making too much of an occasion of it."

"That's what I thought. And even Edmund approves. But we'll have to be very casual and tactful and matter-of-fact. No suggestive glances or meaningful remarks."

"You mean I'm not to say anything about their getting married?" Virginia nodded. Violet thought about this. "I wouldn't, you know. I'm sufficiently modern to know when to hold my tongue. But, by living together, young people create for themselves such difficult situations. They make it so difficult for *us*. If we make too much of the young man, then he will think he is being pressurised and he'll back off and break Alexa's heart. And if we don't make enough of him, Alexa will think we disapprove and *that* will break her heart."

"I wouldn't be too sure about that. She's grown up a lot. She has much more confidence. She's changed."

"I couldn't bear her to be hurt. Not Alexa."

"I'm afraid we can't protect her any longer. The affair has already gone too far."

"Yes," said Violet, feeling in some way admonished. This was no time for apprehensive sentiment. If she was to be of any use to anybody, then she must remain sensible. "You are absolutely right. We must all – "

But there was no time for more. They heard the front door open and slam shut. "*Mummy!*"

Henry was back. Virginia laid down her teacup and sprang to her feet, Alexa forgotten. She made for the door but Henry was there first, bursting in on them, red-cheeked with excitement and the effort of running up the hill.

"Mummy!"

She held out her arms, and he flung himself, bodily, into them.

19

Saturday the Twenty-seventh

Edmund was frequently asked, by well-meaning fellow-guests at dinner parties, if he did not find the long commute between Edinburgh and Strathcroy an almost unbearable strain, every morning and evening each day of the week that he was working in Edinburgh. But the truth was that Edmund thought nothing of the miles that he covered. Getting home to Balnaid and his family was more important than the considerable effort that it involved, and only a late business dinner in Edinburgh, an early plane to catch, or impassable winter roads persuaded him to stay in town and spend the night in the flat in Moray Place.

Besides, he enjoyed driving. His car was both powerful and safe, and the motorway, slicing over the Forth and through Fife to Relkirk, had become as familiar as the back of his hand. Once through Relkirk, he was on to country roads that necessitated slowing down to a more prudent speed, but even so the journey rarely took him more than an hour.

He used this time to switch off at the end of a day of stress and decision-making, and to let his mind concentrate instead upon the many other, but equally absorbing, facets of his busy life. In winter-time, he listened to the radio. Not the news nor political discussions . . . he had had enough of both by the time he finally cleared his desk and locked away all confidential documents . . .

but Radio Three, classical concerts and erudite plays. For the rest of the year, as the hours of daylight lengthened and he no longer made the journey in the dark, he found much pleasure and solace in simply watching the unfolding seasons of the countryside. The ploughing, the sowing, the greening of the trees, the first young lambs in the fields, the crops turning gold, the raspberry pickers out in the long drills of canes, the harvest, the autumn leaves, the first of the snows.

They were harvesting now, on this fine blowy evening. The scenery was both peaceful and spectacular. Fields and farmlands were washed in fitful sunlight, but the air was so clear that every crag and corrie on the distant hills presented itself with startling visibility. The light flowed over these hills, touching their summits with reflected radiance; the river running alongside the road glittered and sparkled; and the sky, skimming with clouds, was infinite.

He felt more content than he had for a long time. Virginia was back, restored to him. His gift to her was the nearest he could get to an apology for the things that he had said on the day of the original explosion: accusing her of smothering Henry; wanting to keep him by her side for selfish reasons; never thinking of any person but herself. She had accepted the bracelet with gratitude and love, and her unqualified pleasure was as good as forgiveness.

Last night, after their dinner at Rafaelli's, he had driven her home to Balnaid through a twilit countryside and beneath the banner of a spectacular skyscape, rose-pink to the west, and streaked as though by some gargantuan paintbrush with dark charcoal clouds.

They had returned to an empty house. He could not remember when this had last happened, and it made their homecoming even more special. No dogs, no children; just the two of them. He had dealt with the luggage, then taken two malt whiskies up to their bedroom and sat on the bed and watched her unpack. There was

215

no sense of urgency, because the whole of the house, the night, the sweet darkness belonged to them. Later, he showered; Virginia took a bath. She came to him, scented and cool, and they made the most satisfying and blissful love.

He knew that the bone of contention still lay between them. Virginia did not want to lose Henry, and Edmund was determined that he should go. But for the time being they had ceased snarling over this particular bone and, with a bit of luck, it would stay buried and forgotten.

As well, there were other good things to look forward to. This evening, he would see his small son again after a week of separation. There would be much to tell and much to hear. And then, in a few days' time, it would be September, when Alexa was bringing her young man to stay.

Virginia's bombshell about Alexa had caught Edmund unawares, rendering him confounded but not shocked nor disapproving. He was extremely fond of his daughter, and recognised her many sterling qualities; but during the last year or two he had privately wished, more than once, that she would take her finger out and start to grow up. At twenty-one, her lack of sophistication, her shyness, her dumpy shape had become an embarrassment to him. He was used to being surrounded by elegant and worldly women (even his secretary was a stunner) and disliked himself for his own impatience and irritation with Alexa. But now, all by herself, she had found a man, and a personable one, if Virginia was to be believed.

Possibly he should be taking a tougher line. But he had never relished the image of himself as a paterfamilias, and was more concerned with the human side of the situation than the moral.

As always, when faced with a dilemma, he planned to go by his own set of rules. Act positively, plan negatively, expect nothing. The worst that could happen would be Alexa's getting hurt. For her, it would be a

216

frightening new experience, but at least she would come out of it more adult and, hopefully, stronger.

He drove into Strathcroy as the church clock was striking seven. He thought, in pleasant anticipation, of getting home. The dogs would be there, rescued from the kennels by Virginia; and Henry, in his bath or eating his tea in the kitchen. He would sit with Henry while he consumed his fishfingers or beefburgers or whatever horror he had chosen to eat, listening to all that Henry had been up to during the week, and drinking, meanwhile, a very long and strong gin and tonic.

Which reminded him that they were out of tonic. The drinks cupboard had been allowed to run dry of this precious commodity, and Edmund had meant to stop off and buy a crate before he left Edinburgh, but had forgotten to do this. And so he passed the bridge that led to Balnaid and drove on into the village, drawing up outside the Pakistani supermarket.

All the other shops had long since shut their doors and closed their shutters, but the Pakistanis never seemed to close. Long after nine o'clock in the evening they were still selling cartons of milk and bread and pizzas and frozen curries to anybody who wanted to buy them.

He got out of the car and went into the shop. There were other customers but they were filling their own wire baskets from the shelves or being assisted by Mr Ishak, and it was Mrs Ishak who dimpled at Edmund from behind the counter. She was a comely lady, with huge dark eyes ringed in kohl, and this evening dressed in butter-yellow silk, with a paler yellow silk scarf draped around her head and shoulders.

"Good evening, Mr Aird."

"Good evening, Mrs Ishak. How are you?"

"I am very well, thank you for asking."

217

"How's Kedejah?"

"She is watching television."

"I hear she had an afternoon at Pennyburn with Henry."

"That is true, and my God, she came home soaking wet."

Edmund laughed. "They were building dams. I hope you weren't annoyed."

"Not at all. She has had a most lovely time."

"I want some tonic water, Mrs Ishak. Have you got some?"

"But of course. How many bottles do you need?"

"Two dozen?"

"If you wait, I will fetch them for you from the store."

"Thank you."

She went. Edmund, unimpatient, stood waiting for her to return. A voice spoke from behind him.

"Mr Aird."

It was so close, just behind his shoulder, that he was much startled. He swung round and found himself faced by Edie's cousin, Lottie Carstairs. Since she had come to stay with Edie, he had glimpsed her once or twice, pottering about the village, but had taken some pains and avoiding action, not wishing to be confronted by her. Now it seemed she had him cornered and there was no escape.

"Good evening."

"Remember me?" She spoke almost coyly. Edmund did not relish finding himself so close to her with her pallid, bloodless skin and the strong suggestion of a moustache upon her upper lip. Her hair was the colour – and roughly the texture – of steel wool, and under wildly arched eyebrows her eyes were brown as currants, and round and quite unwinking. Apart from all this, her appearance was reasonably normal. She wore a blouse and skirt, a long green cardigan perkily embellished with a sparkling brooch, and shoes with high heels upon which she tottered slightly as she engaged

Edmund in conversation. "I used to be with Lady Balmerino, staying with Edie Findhorn right now I am. Seen you around the village, never had the chance of an old chinwag . . ."

Lottie Carstairs. She must be nearly sixty now, and yet she had not changed so much since those days when she had worked at Croy and caused every person in the house untold annoyance and aggravation, with her stealthy tread and her habit of always appearing just when least wanted or expected. Archie always swore that she listened at keyholes, and he had been perpetually throwing doors open in the expectation of catching Lottie there, crouched and eavesdropping. In the afternoons, Edmund remembered, she had always worn a brown woollen dress with a muslin apron tied over it. The muslin apron was not Lady Balmerino's idea but Lottie's. Archie said it was because she wanted to appear servile. The brown dress had stains under the armpits, and one of the worst things about Lottie was her smell.

The family complained vociferously and Archie demanded that his mother take some step to rectify the situation. Either sack the bloody woman or do something to ensure a little personal daintiness. But poor Lady Balmerino, with Archie's wedding on her mind, every bed filled with guests and a party planned at Croy on the evening of the great day, did not feel strong enough to sack her housemaid. And she was far too kind-hearted actually to send for Lottie, face her fair and square, and tell her that she smelled.

Under attack, she fell back on feeble excuses.

"I must have someone to clean the rooms and make the beds."

"We'll make our own beds."

"Poor thing, she's only got one dress."

"Well, buy her another."

"Perhaps she's nervous."

"Not too nervous to wash. Give her a bar of Lifebuoy."

"I'm not certain that that would make much differ-

219

ence. Perhaps . . . for Christmas . . . I could give her some talcum powder . . .?"

But even this timid notion came to nothing, for, soon after the wedding, Lottie dropped the tray and broke the Rockingham china, and Lady Balmerino was finally driven to firing her. By Christmas Lottie was gone from Croy. Now, trapped in Mr Ishak's shop, Edmund wondered if she still smelled. He was not about to risk finding out. Trying not to make it too obvious, he moved a pace or two away from her.

"Yes," he said, sounding as pleasant and friendly as he could. "Of course, I remember you . . ."

"Those days at Croy! The year Archie was wed to Isobel. Oh my, what times those were. I remember you coming up from London for the wedding and around the place all that week, helping Lady Balmerino with one thing and another."

"It seems a long time ago."

"Yes."

"And all of you so young. And old Lord and Lady Balmerino so good and kind. Croy's changed now, I hear, and not for the better. But then, hard times come to everybody. It was a sad day when Lady Balmerino died. She was always so good to me. She was good to my parents too. My mother and my father died. You knew that, didn't you? I've been wanting to talk to you, but somehow I missed you in the village. And all of you so young. And Archie with his two good legs . . . fancy getting his leg shot off! Never heard of anything so ridiculous . . ."

Oh, Mrs Ishak, come back quickly. Please, Mrs Ishak, come back to me.

". . . hear all your news from Edie, of course; very worried about Edie, she's grown so fat, can't be good for her heart. And all of you so young. And that Pandora! Flying around the place like a spinning top. Dreadful way she went, wasn't it? Funny she never came home. Always thought she might come back for Christmas, but no. And not to be there for Lady Balmerino's funeral, well, I'm sorry and I don't like to say such things, but in my view, it was downright unchristian. But then, she always was a wee fly-by-night . . . in more ways than one . . . you and I know that, don't we?"

At this point she burst into a peal of manic laughter and actually struck Edmund a playful, but quite painful, blow on his arm. His immediate and instinctive reaction was to hit her right back, a good punch, bang, square on the end of her long, inquisitive nose. He imagined it crumpling, concertinaed, into her face. He imagined the headlines in the local newspapers. 'Relkirkshire Landowner Assaults Strathcroy Lady In Village Supermarket.' He thrust his hands, the fists balled, into his trouser pockets.

". . . and your wife's been in London? Nice. And the wee boy with his gran. Seen him sometimes around the place. He is peaky, isn't he?" Edmund could feel the blood rising to his cheeks. He wondered how long he could continue to control himself. He could not remember when any person had cast him into such a confusion of impotent rage. ". . . small for his age, I'd say . . . not strong . . ."

"I am sorry, Mr Aird, to keep you so long." It was Mrs Ishak's soft voice that finally stilled the flood of Lottie's mindless malice. Mrs Ishak, bless her darling heart, come to his rescue with the cardboard crate of tonic water borne before her like a votive offering.

"Oh, thank you, Mrs Ishak." And not a moment too soon. "Here, let me take that." He went to relieve her of the heavy load. "I wonder, can you put that down on my account?" He could easily pay in cash but did not wish to linger a moment longer than he had to.

"Of course, Mr Aird."

"Thank you." The crate was transferred. With its weight safely in his arms, he turned to take his leave of Lottie and make his escape.

But Lottie had jumped the gun and was gone. Abruptly and disconcertingly, she had simply disappeared.

221

20

Tuesday the Thirtieth

"Has she always lived in Majorca, this aunt of yours?"

"No. She's only been here for about two years. She lived in Paris before that, and New York before that, and then California before that," Lucilla said.

"A rolling stone."

"Yes. I suppose you could call her that, except that she's gathered lots of lovely moss."

Jeff laughed. "What's she like?"

"I don't know because I've never seen her. By the time I was born, she was gone, married to an immensely wealthy American and living in Palm Springs. It seemed to me that she must be the most glamorous woman in the world. So wicked and sophisticated like someone out of those old 1930 plays, with men falling for her like ninepins, and always unashamedly outrageous. She eloped when she was eighteen. Such a frightfully brave thing to do. I'd never have had the nerve. *And* she was beautiful."

"Will she still be beautiful?"

"I don't see why not. After all, she's only about forty, not over the hill yet. There's a portrait of her at Croy in the dining room. It was painted when she was about fourteen and even then she was a stunner. And photographs too, all over the place, in frames or the old albums that my grandfather used to fill with snapshots. I used to welcome wet afternoons because then I could spend

222

them poring over those old albums. And when people talked about her, even if they started by being disapproving because she'd been so thoughtless and uncaring to her parents, they always ended up by remembering some funny anecdote about Pandora, and then of course there could be nothing but laughter."

"Was she surprised when you spoke to her on the telephone?"

"Of course she was. But pleased surprised, not horrified surprised. You can always tell. At first she could hardly believe it was me. But then she just said 'Of course you can come. As soon as possible. And stay for as long as you like.' And she gave me directions and hung up." Lucilla smiled. "So you see, we're good for at least a week."

They had hired a car, a little Seat, the cheapest they could get, and were now well on their way across the island, driving over flat, intensely cultivated countryside, dotted here and there with slow-moving windmills. It was afternoon, and the road ahead of them shimmered in the heat. On their left, far-distant and hazy, marched a range of impassable-looking mountains. On the other side, somewhere out of sight, lay the sea. For air, they had opened all the windows of the car, but the wind was scorching and dusty and very dry. Jeff was driving and Lucilla sat beside him, holding the scrap of paper on which she had scribbled the directions that Pandora had given her over the telephone.

She had rung Pandora from Palma, having arrived with Jeff that morning in a boat from Ibiza. They had spent a week in Ibiza, staying with Jeff's friend, Hans Bergdorf. Hans was a painter and *his* house had taken some finding, being at the very top of the old town, within the ancient walls of the fortified city. Finally discovered, it had proved very picturesque. It was thick-walled and whitewashed, but primitive beyond belief. The views from its jutting stone balcony took in the whole panorama of the old town, the new town, the

223

harbour, and the sea, but even this delight scarcely made up for the fact that any cooking had to be done on a miniature Calor gas stove and the only running water came from a single cold tap. Consequently, both Jeff and Lucilla were extremely dirty, if not to say smelly, and the bulging back packs piled on to the back seat of the car were stuffed with unsavoury, soiled and sweaty clothes. Lucilla, never a girl to spend time worrying about her appearance, had started to have fantasies about washing her hair, and Jeff in desperation had allowed his beard to grow. It was blond like his hair, but uneven and straggly and made him look more like a down-and-out than a Viking. In fact, the pair of them presented such a disreputable picture that it was a wonder that the hire-car man had agreed to rent them the Seat. Lucilla had noticed a certain suspicion on his face, but Jeff had produced a wad of pesetas and, with cash safely in hand, he could scarcely refuse.

She said, "I hope Pandora's got a washing machine."

"I'd settle for a pool."

"You can't wash your clothes in a pool."

"Want a bet?"

Lucilla gazed through the open car window. She saw that the mountains had drawn closer and the countryside become more lush. There were pine trees, and the smell of warm resin blew in through the open windows along with the dust. They came to a junction joining another main road. They paused for traffic to pass. The road sign was marked 'Puerto del Fuego'.

"Well, we're on the right track. What happens now?"

"We take the Puerto del Fuego road, but we have to turn off to the left in another mile or so. It's a little road and it's signposted to 'Cala San Torre'." The traffic thinned. Taking his chance Jeff cautiously negotiated the junction. "If we find ourselves in the port, then we've gone too far."

"That follows."

Now she could smell the sea. Houses appeared, a new

apartment block, a garage. They passed a riding stable with scrubby paddocks where sad, bony horses tried to graze.

"Oh, poor creatures," said the tender-hearted Lucilla, but Jeff had eyes only for the road ahead.

"There's a sign. 'Cala San Torre'."

"That's it!"

They turned off the sunbaked dual carriageway and found themselves, abruptly, in a green and verdant countryside totally unlike the flat and exposed land through which they had been travelling. Umbrella pines threw shade across the road, speckled by sun splashes, and from ramshackle farms came the contented cackle of hens and the bleat of goats.

"It's suddenly gone pretty," Lucilla observed. "Oh, look at that sweet little donkey."

"Keep your eyes on the map, girl. What happens next?"

Lucilla obediently consulted her notes. "Well, *next* is a very sharp turn to the right, and then we go right up a hill to the last house at the very top."

They came upon the turning around the next corner. Jeff changed down and made the turn. The Seat, sounding as though at any moment it might boil like a kettle, ground painfully up the steep and winding lane. There were other houses, large villas scarcely glimpsed beyond closed gates and burgeoning gardens.

"This," said Lucilla, "is what estate agents call a much-sought-after neighbourhood."

"You mean snob."

"I think I mean expensive."

"I think you do too. Your aunt must be loaded."

"She's got a Californian divorce," Lucilla told him and her voice implied that there was no need to say more.

Another hundred yards or so, another hairpin bend or two, and they had reached their destination. Casa Rosa. The name, embellished on decorated tiles, was set into a high stone wall and clearly visible despite a cloak

225

of pink-blossomed mesembryanthemum. Open gates lay ahead. A driveway, deeply bordered, sloped up to a garage. The garage had a car parked in it, and another car – an enviable dark-red Mercedes – was parked in the shade of a gnarled olive tree. Jeff switched off the engine. It was very quiet. Then Lucilla heard water splashing, as though from a fountain, and the distant, gentle clangour of sheep bells. The mountains now were close by, their summits bleached and barren, their lower slopes silvery with groves of olive.

They got slowly and gratefully out of the car, stretching their sweaty limbs. Up here, so high, there was a breeze blowing off the sea, cool and refreshing. Lucilla, looking about her, saw that the Casa Rosa stood on a rocky bluff above them, the main entrance reached by a flight of steps. The risers of these steps were set with blue-and-white tiles, and pots of geraniums stood sentry all the way to the top. As well, all was entwined by a torrent of purple bougainvillaea; and hibiscus grew, and plumbago, and a tangle of azure-blue morning glory. The air was sweet with flowery scents mingled with the damp smell of newly watered earth.

So amazing was it all, so unlike anything they had previously experienced, that for a moment neither of them could think of anything to say. Then Lucilla whispered, "I'd no *idea* it would be as grand as this!"

"Well, one thing's for sure, we can't stand here all day."

"No." He was right. Lucilla turned towards the steps, leading the way. But before she had mounted the first step, the silence was broken by the sound of sharp heel-taps, hurrying along the terrace above them.

"Darlings!" A figure appeared at the head of the stairs, arms outstretched in welcome. "I heard the car. You've come. And you've not lost the way. How clever you are and how perfect to see you."

226

Lucilla's first impression of Pandora was one of insubstantial thinness. She looked ethereal, as though at any moment she might blow away. Embracing her was like holding a little bird. You didn't want to hug too hard in case she snapped in two. Her hair was chestnut brown, swept back from her forehead and falling, in frondy curls, to her shoulders. Lucilla guessed that Pandora had worn her hair that way when she was eighteen and had never seen any reason to change the style. Her eyes were dark grey, shadowed by sooty black lashes, and her curving mouth full and sweet. On her right cheek, just above the corner of her upper lip, was a round dark beauty spot, too sexy to be called a mole. She was dressed in loose pyjamas of the brilliant pink of the hibiscus flowers, and there were gold chains around her neck and knots of gold in her ears. She smelled . . . Lucilla knew that scent. Poison. She had tried wearing it herself but could never decide whether she loved it or hated it. Smelling it on Pandora, she was still not certain.

"I'd have known you were Lucilla, even if nobody had told me. You look so like Archie . . ." It seemed that she did not even notice their unsavoury appearance, their soiled cut-off shorts and grubby T-shirts. And if she did, she gave no indication of objecting. "And you must be Jeff . . ." She held out a pink-tipped hand. "How wonderful that you could come with Lucilla."

He took it in his own enormous paw and, looking a bit overwhelmed by her welcome and her dazzling smile, said, "Pleased to meet you."

She picked up his accent at once. "You're an Australian! How heavenly. I don't think I've ever had an Australian here before. Did you have a hideous drive?"

"No. Not at all. Just hot."

"You must be longing for a drink . . ."

227

"Shall we get our stuff out of the car . . .?"

"You can do that later. A drink first. Come along, I've a friend here for you to meet."

Lucilla's heart sank. It didn't matter about Pandora, but they were certainly in no shape to be introduced to company. "Pandora, we're dreadfully dirty . . ."

"Oh, heavens, that doesn't matter. He won't mind . . ." She turned from them and led the way, and there was no alternative but to follow, down a long, shaded and airy terrace furnished with white cane chairs with butter-yellow cushions and great blue-and-white porcelain jars planted with palms. "He can't stay for very long and I want you to meet him . . ."

They turned the corner of the house and, hard on Pandora's tapping heels, stepped out into blinding sunshine. Lucilla longed for her sunglasses, left in the car. In a dazzle, she saw the wide, open terrace, shaded by striped awnings and paved in marble. Shallow steps led down from this to a spacious garden, massed with flowering trees and shrubs. Grass paths were set with flagged stepping-stones, and these encircled a swimming pool, aquamarine and still as glass. Just seeing it made Lucilla feel cooler. An inflatable sunbed floated upon the surface of the water, drifting with the undercurrent of the filter.

At the far end of the garden, half hidden by hibiscus, she saw another house, small and single-storeyed, but with its own little terrace facing out over the pool. This was shaded by a tall umbrella pine, and beyond the ridge of its roof there was nothing to be seen but the brazen blue sky.

"Here they are, Carlos, safely arrived. My directions can't have been as confusing as we'd feared." At the top of the steps, in the shade of the awning, stood a low table. On this was a tray with glasses and a tall jug. An ashtray, a pair of sunglasses, a paperback. More cane chairs, yellow-cushioned, stood about, and as they approached, a man rose from one of these and stood,

228

smiling, waiting to be introduced. He was tall and dark-eyed and very handsome. "Lucilla, darling, this is my friend Carlos Macaya. Carlos, this is Lucilla Blair, my niece. And Jeff . . .?"

"Howland," Jeff supplied for her.

"And he's Australian. Isn't that exciting? Now, let's all sit down and have a lovely drink. This is iced tea, but I can get Seraphina to bring something stronger if you'd like. Coke maybe? Or wine?" She began to laugh. "Or champagne? What a good idea. But perhaps a little early in the day. Let's save the champagne till later."

They told her that iced tea would be perfect. Carlos drew forward a chair for Lucilla and then settled himself beside her. But Jeff, who could soak up sun like a lizard, went to lean on the balustrade of the terrace, and Pandora perched herself beside him, legs swinging and one high-heeled sandal dangling from a toe.

Carlos Macaya poured iced tea and handed Lucilla her glass.

"You have come from Ibiza?"

"Yes, this morning, on the boat."

"How long were you there?" His English was perfect.

"A week. Staying with a friend of Jeff's. It was a lovely house but dreadfully primitive. Which is why we look so filthy. Because we are. I'm sorry."

He made no comment on this; simply smiled in an understanding way. "And before Ibiza?"

"I've been in Paris. That's where I met Jeff. I'm meant to be a painter, but there was so much to see and so much to do, I didn't achieve very much."

"Paris is a wonderful city. Was this your first visit?"

"No, I'd been once before. I spent some time as an au pair, to learn the language."

"And how did you get from Paris to Ibiza?"

"We thought of hitch-hiking but in the end we travelled by bus. We did the journey in stops and starts, staying in *gîtes*, and taking time to do some sightseeing. Cathedrals and wine châteaux – that sort of thing."

"You have not been wasting your time." He glanced at Pandora, chattering away to Jeff, who watched her intently as though she were some strange species of wildlife that he had never before observed. "Pandora tells me that this is the first time you have met each other."

"Yes." Lucilla hesitated. This man was probably Pandora's current lover, which meant that now was neither the time nor the place to enlarge on Pandora's youthful elopement and subsequent life-style. "She was always abroad, you see. I mean, living abroad."

"And your home is in Scotland?"

"Yes. In Relkirkshire. That's where my parents live." A small pause fell. She took a mouthful of iced tea. "Have you ever been to Scotland?"

"No. I studied in Oxford for a couple of years" (that explained his English), "but I never found time to go to Scotland."

"We're always wanting Pandora to come back and see us, but she never will."

"Perhaps she doesn't like the cold and the rain."

"It isn't cold and rainy *all* the time. Only some of the time."

He laughed. "Whatever. It is a splendid thing that you have come to keep her company. And now . . ." He pushed back his silk cuff and glanced at his watch. It was a handsome and unusual watch, the numbers marked by tiny replicas of yachting pennants, and was strapped to his wrist by a heavy gold bracelet. Lucilla wondered if Pandora had given it to him. Perhaps the pennants spelled out "I Love You" in naval code. " . . . it is time for me to take my leave. I hope you will excuse me but I have work to do . . ."

"Of course . . ."

He rose once more to his feet. "Pandora, I must go."

"Oh dear, what a shame." She fixed her sandal and hopped down off the balustrade. "Never mind, you've

230

had time to meet my guests. We'll come and see you off."

"Don't disturb everybody."

"They've got to get their luggage anyway. They're dying to unpack and have a swim. Come . . ." She took his arm.

And so they all made their way back to where his car was waiting in the shade beneath the olive tree. Goodbyes were said, he sketched a kiss over the back of Pandora's hand, and then got in behind the wheel of the Mercedes.

He started up the engine, and Pandora stood back. But before he drove away, he said, "Pandora."

"Yes, Carlos?"

"You will let me know if you change your mind."

She did not answer immediately, and then shook her head. "I shan't change my mind," she told him.

He smiled, shrugged resignedly, as though good-naturedly accepting her decision. He put the car into gear and, with a final wave, left them, driving away, through the gates, down the hill, out of sight. They stood waiting until the sound of the Mercedes could be heard no longer. Only the splash of water from that unseen fountain, the tinkle of sheep bells.

You will let me know if you change your mind.

What had Carlos been asking of Pandora? For an instant Lucilla toyed with the idea that he had been proposing marriage, but almost at once put this notion out of her head. It was too prosaic for such a sophisticated and glamorous pair. More likely, he had been trying to persuade her to join him on some romantic trip, to the Seychelles or the palm-fringed beaches of Tahiti. Or perhaps he had simply asked her out for dinner and she didn't feel like going.

Whatever, Pandora was not about to enlighten them. Carlos was gone and now she sprang into practical activity, giving a little clap with her hands. "So. Down to business. Where's your luggage? Is that all? No suitcases or cabin trunks or hatboxes? I take more than that if I go away for a single night. Now, come along . . .''

She started up the steps once more, going at a great pace, and yet again they followed her, Lucilla carrying her leather satchel, and Jeff lugging the two bulging back packs.

"I've put you in the guest house. You can make yourselves at home, and then be quite independent. And I'm not frightfully good in the mornings, so you'll have to get your own breakfast. The fridge is full of goodies, and there's coffee and stuff in the cupboard.'' They were now back on the terrace. "You'll be all right?''

"Of course.''

"And then I thought we'd have dinner about nine o'clock. Just something cold, because I can't cook to save my life, and Seraphina, my maid, goes home each evening. But she'll leave everything ready for us. Come over at half past eight and we'll have a drink. Now I'm going to have a little nap, so I'll leave you to find your own way and settle yourselves in. Later, I might swim before I change for dinner.''

The prospect of Pandora, dressed in an even grander outfit than the pink silk pyjamas, reminded her of the vexing question of clothes.

"Pandora, we haven't got anything to change into. Nearly everything's dirty. Jeff's got one clean shirt, but it hasn't been ironed.''

"Oh, darling, do you want to borrow something?''

"A clean T-shirt?''

"Of course, how stupid of me. I should have offered. Wait a moment.''

They waited. She disappeared through wide sliding glass doors into what was presumably her bedroom, and returned almost at once bearing a midnight-blue silk shirt splashed with a rocket-fall of sequins. "Have this, it's frightfully vulgar but rather fun. You can keep it if you want, I never wear it.'' She tossed it over and Lucilla caught it. "And now, off you go and dig yourselves into

232

your little nest. If you want anything, ring through on the house phone and Seraphina will bring it to you." She blew a kiss. "Half past eight. See you then."

And she was gone, leaving Lucilla and Jeff to their own devices. But still Lucilla hesitated, savouring the anticipation of what was about to happen next.

"Jeff, I can't believe it. We've got a whole house to ourselves."

"So what are we waiting for? If I don't get into that pool in two minutes flat, I'm going to explode."

Lucilla went first, leading the way down the steps and along the length of the garden. The little house awaited them. They crossed the terrace and opened the door into a living room. Curtains had been drawn, and Lucilla went to pull them back. Light streamed in and she saw the little patio on the far side, the sheltered scrap of garden.

"We've even got our own place to sunbathe!"

There was an open fireplace, filled with logs. There were a few comfortable chairs, a tray of drinks and glasses, a coffee-table stacked neatly with magazines, and a wall shelved with books. Opening other doors, they found two double bedrooms, a bathroom of marvellously spacious proportions.

"I think *this* is the nicest bedroom. It's certainly the biggest." Jeff dumped the back packs on to the tiled floor and Lucilla drew back more curtains. "We can see the sea from here. Just a little scrap, a triangle, but still a view of the sea." She opened cupboard doors, saw rows of padded hangers, smelled lavender. She put the borrowed shirt on to one of the hangers, where it hung in lonely style.

Jeff had toed off his trainers and was stripping off his T-shirt.

"You can play house as much as you like. I'm going to swim. You joining me?"

"I will in a moment."

He departed. An instant later she heard the splash as

233

he took his running dive, and imagined the silken bliss of the cool water. But later. Just now she wanted to explore.

On detailed inspection Pandora's guest house proved to be quite perfectly complete, and Lucilla was filled with admiration for such meticulous thought and planning. Someone . . . and who else but Pandora? . . . had somehow thought of everything that a visitor might want or need, from fresh flowers and lovely new books right down to spare blankets for chilly nights and hot-water bottles for possibly unsettled tummies. The bathroom was supplied with every sort of soap, scent, shampoo, aftershave, body lotion, and bath oil. There were thick white bathtowels and bathmats, and, hanging from the back of the door, a pair of voluminous and snowy-white towelling bathrobes.

Leaving all this luxury, she crossed the sitting room and went in search of the kitchen, and found it sparkling neat, and lined with dark wooden cupboards filled with Spanish pottery, shining saucepans, casseroles, and a complete *batterie de cuisine*. If one wanted – which Lucilla didn't – it would be quite possible to concoct a dinner party for ten. There were an electric cooker and a gas cooker and a dishwasher and a fridge. She opened the fridge and discovered there, along with all the fixings for a robust breakfast, two bottles of Perrier water and a bottle of champagne. A second door led out of the kitchen. She opened this and found . . . joy of joys . . . a compact laundry with clothes washer, drying-lines, an ironing board, and an iron. The sight of these homely items gave her more satisfaction than all the other luxuries put together. Because now, at last, they could be clean.

She set to work, losing no time. Went back to the bathroom, stripped off her clothes, put on one of the towelling robes and then started in on the unpacking. Which consisted of emptying the contents of the back packs on to the bedroom floor. At the bottom of her own back pack were her wash-bag, her brush and comb, her sketchpad, a book or two, and the envelope from her father, which had contained his cheque, his letter, and the invitation to a dance from Verena Steynton. She took this out of the envelope and propped it on the empty dressing-table. By now it was a bit dog-eared but bestowed, she decided, a personal note to the room, as though Lucilla had put her name to it and claimed it as her own.

Lucilla Blair
Mrs Angus Steynton
At Home
For Katy

Why did it seem so ludicrous? She laughed. Another life, another world away. She gathered up armfuls of dirty socks, shorts, jeans, pants, and T-shirts, and headed back to the laundry. Without bothering to sort any of these garments (her mother would have a fit if she could see red socks going in with white shirts, but her mother was not here to remonstrate so what did it matter?), Lucilla stuffed the open face of the washing machine, poured in detergent, slammed the door, and switched it on. Water gushed and the drum revolved, and she stood back and observed this with as much delight as if it had been a longed-for programme on television.

Then she kicked aside the remainder of the dirty clothes, went to find her bikini, and joined Jeff in the pool.

She swam for a long time. After a bit Jeff got out and lay in the sun to dry off. Another two lengths and she saw he was gone, had taken himself indoors. She came out of the pool and wrung the water out of her long dark hair. She went indoors. She found him in the bedroom, flat out on one of the beds. He looked as though he might be going to sleep. She did not want him to go to

235

sleep. She said his name and took a running jump, and landed flat on top of him.

"Jeff."

"Yeah?"

"I told you she was beautiful."

"Who?"

"Pandora, of course." Jeff did not immediately reply to this. He was drowsy and on the edge of sleep, and not inclined to conversation. His arm, out-flung, pillowed Lucilla's head. His skin smelled of chlorine and swimming pool. "Don't you think she's beautiful?"

"She's certainly one sexy sheila."

"You think she's sexy?"

"Bit too old for me."

"She doesn't *look* old."

"And a bit too skinny as well."

"Don't you like skinny ladies?"

"No. I like my women with big tits and fat bums."

Lucilla, who had inherited her shape from her father and was tall and thin and almost breastless, gave Jeff a thump with her fist. "You do *not*."

He laughed. "Well, what do you want me to say?"

"You know what I want you to say."

He pulled her face towards his own and kissed her soundly. "Will that do?"

"I think you'll have to shave that beard off."

"Now why should I do that?"

"Because my face is going to start looking as though it's been cleaned off with sandpaper."

"I'll have to stop kissing you then. Or start kissing you some place where it doesn't show."

They fell silent. The sun was dropping in the sky, and soon, quite suddenly, it would be dark. Lucilla thought of Scottish summer twilights that went on until mid-

236

night. She said, "Do you think they're lovers? Do you think they're having a raging affair?"

"Who?"

"Pandora and Carlos Macaya."

"I wouldn't know."

"He's terribly handsome."

"Yeah. A real smoothie."

"I thought he was nice. Rather cosy. Easy to talk to."

"I liked his car."

"You have a one-track mind. What do you think it was he asked her?"

"Come again?"

"He said, 'Let me know if you change your mind.' And she said, 'I won't change my mind.' He must have asked her something. He must have wanted her to do something with him."

"Well, whatever it was, she didn't look too bothered."

But Lucilla was not satisfied. "I'm certain it was something terribly significant. A turning-point in both their lives."

"You have a runaway imagination. More likely he was trying to fix a tennis game."

"Yes." But somehow, Lucilla did not feel that this was so. She sighed, and the sigh turned into a yawn. "Perhaps."

At half past eight they were ready to join Pandora, and Lucilla decided that, after all her anxiety, they didn't look too bad. Both of them had showered and scrubbed and now smelled sweetly of the gratuitous shampoo. Jeff had neatened up his beard with a pair of nail scissors, and Lucilla had ironed his one clean shirt and salvaged from the pile of clothes on the laundry floor his tidiest pair of jeans.

As for herself, she had washed her long dark hair and

brushed it dry, pulled on a pair of black leggings, and now buttoned up the borrowed shirt. The heavy silk felt deliciously cool against her bare skin, and the sequined embroidery, viewed in the mirror through half-closed eyes, was not nearly as outrageous as she had first imagined. Perhaps it had something to do with these unaccustomed surroundings. Perhaps the ambience of enormous luxury helped absorb such small vulgarities. It was an interesting notion and one that she would have liked to discuss at length, but right now there was no time.

"Come on," Jeff told her. "Time to be off. I need a drink."

He made for the door and she followed him, first making sure that all the lights in the guest house were switched off. She was fairly certain that Pandora would not give a damn if every light was left burning, but, brought up by a thrifty Scottish mother, such small housewifely economies were engrained in Lucilla, as though her subconscious were a programmed computer. She found this strange, because later strictures had left as little impression as water on a duck's back. Another interesting thought worth chewing over at a later date.

Out of doors, they stepped into a blue night, star-bright and soft and warm as velvet. The garden was headily fragrant, the swimming pool floodlit, and lamps lit the way along the stepping-stones of the path. Lucilla heard the incessant chirp of the cicadas, and there was music coming from Pandora's house.

Rachmaninoff. The Second Piano Concerto. Banal, maybe, but perfect for just such a Mediterranean night. Pandora had set the scene and now she was waiting for them on the terrace, lying in a long chair with a wineglass on the table beside her.

"There you are!" she called as they approached. "I've already opened the champagne. I couldn't wait any longer."

They went up the steps and into the pool of light that illuminated their hostess. She had changed into something black and cobwebby and wore gold sandals on her bare feet. The smell of Poison was even stronger than the scents of the garden.

"Don't you both look sleek! I can't think why you were so worried about yourselves. And Lucilla, the shirt is divine on you, you must keep it. Now, find chairs and settle down. Oh, blast, I've forgotten the glasses. Lucilla, darling, go and get some, will you? The little bar's just behind the door, you'll find everything there. There's a second bottle of bubbly in the fridge, but we'll leave it there till we've finished this one. Now, Jeff, you come and sit *here*, beside me. I want to hear all about what you and Lucilla have been up to . . ."

Lucilla left them and obediently went in search of the wine-glasses, stepping indoors through wide, curtained doors. The bar was immediately to hand, no more than a large closet fitted with everything that any human being could need to fix a drink. She took two wineglasses from the shelf but did not at once return to the terrace. This was the first time she had actually been inside Pandora's house, and she found herself in a room so spacious and spectacular that she was momentarily diverted from her errand. All was cool and creamy, sparked here and there with touches of brilliant colour. Sky-blue and turquoise cushions, and coral-pink lilies massed in a square glass vase. Alcoves, cunningly lit, displayed a collection of Dresden figures and Battersea enamel. A plate-glass coffee-table was stacked with books and magazines, more flowers, a silver cigarette box. There was an open fireplace faced with blue-and-white tiles, and above this hung a mirror-framed flower painting. At the other end of the room the dining table – glass again – was set for dinner with candles and crystal and yet more flowers, and to Lucilla's bemused eyes it all seemed more like a stage set than a room designed for living in. And yet, she realised, there were homely touches too. An open paperback tossed on to a sofa; a half-finished tapestry lying close at hand for an empty moment. And there were photographs. Archie and Isobel on their wedding day. Lucilla's grandparents, sweet old things in their tweeds, standing in front of Croy with their dogs beside them.

Lucilla found these evidences of nostalgia immensely touching. For some reason, she had not expected them, perhaps not imagining Pandora capable of such sentiment. Now she pictured Pandora taking them everywhere with her, all through her wayward love affairs and her turbulent nomad's life. Saw her unpacking them from her suitcase in houses in California, hotel bedrooms, apartments in New York and Paris. And now, Majorca. Setting the seal of her past and her identity upon yet another temporary home.

(There did not seem to be any pictures of the men who had owned these apartments and occupied so much of Pandora's life, but perhaps she kept those in her bedroom.)

Warm dark breezes blew through the opened windows, and Rachmaninoff emanated from some unseen stereo, concealed by a gold-latticed trellis. The piano solo dripped its notes, pure as raindrops. From the terrace came the low murmur of comfortable conversation, Pandora and Jeff sounding peaceful and unimpatient.

There were other photographs on the mantelpiece, and Lucilla crossed the floor to inspect these more closely. Old Lady Balmerino, resplendent in a feathered tam-o'-shanter, apparently opening a village fête. A snapshot of Archie and Edmund Aird, two very young men sitting in the boat at the edge of the loch with their rods and their creels stowed on the thwarts. Finally, a studio portrait of herself and Hamish, Lucilla in smocked Liberty lawn and Hamish a fat baby on her knee. Archie must have sent that one to Pandora with one of his letters and she had framed it in silver and set it in the

240

place of honour. Tucked into this silver frame was an invitation whose format was instantly familiar.

> Pandora Blair
> *Mrs Angus Steynton*
> *At Home*
> *For Katy*

Lucilla's first thought was, how nice. And then, how ridiculous. A waste of a card, a waste of a stamp, because there was not the slightest possibility that Pandora would accept. She had gone from Croy when she was eighteen and never returned. Resisted all pleading, first from her parents, and then from her brother, and stayed resolutely away. It was scarcely likely that Verena Steynton, of all people, would achieve what Pandora's own family had so abjectly failed to do.

"Lucilla!"

"Coming . . ."

"What are you doing?"

Lucilla, bearing the wineglasses, joined them on the terrace. "Sorry. I've been snooping round that beautiful room. And listening to the music . . ."

"Oh, darling, don't you love Rachmaninoff? It's one of my most favourites. I know it's a bit hackneyed, but I seem to go for hackneyed things."

"I'm just the same," Lucilla admitted. "Songs like 'Oh, Lovely Moon' and 'The Barcarolle' leave me quite weak-kneed. And some of the old Beatles records. I've got them all at home at Croy. And if I'm feeling *really* blue, I've got a tape of a Fiddlers' Rally in Oban and I play it and I can feel my spirits rise visibly, like mercury in a thermometer when you've got a temperature. All those dear old men and little boys in their kilts and their shirtsleeves, and an endless round of jigs and reels, as though they didn't know how to stop and didn't want to anyway. I usually end up dancing all by myself and leaping around the room like an idiot."

Jeff said, "I've never seen you do that."

"Well, if you hang around long enough, you probably will. But seriously, Pandora, this is the most beautiful place you've got. And our guest house is perfection."

"It is rather sweet, isn't it? I was so lucky to snap it all up. The people who lived here before had to go back to England; I was looking for somewhere to live and it seemed that it was just waiting for me. Jeff, you're meant to be pouring champagne . . ."

"And the furniture? Is that all yours too?"

Pandora laughed. "Oh, darling, I haven't got any furniture, just little bits and pieces that I've gathered on my travels and cart about with me. Most of the furniture here I took over with the house, but of course I've changed almost everything. The sofas were the most hideous blue, and there was a carpet with swirls on. Got rid of that pretty sharpish. I took Seraphina over with the house as well, and she's got a husband who does the garden. All I'm missing out on is a little doggie, but doggies in Majorca are inclined to get shot by youths with airguns, or else they get ticks, or they get stolen, or run over. So there's not really much point." All the glasses were now brimming full. Pandora raised hers.

"Here's to you both, and what heaven it is to have you here. Lucilla, Jeff's been telling me all about your journey down through France. How fascinating it must have been. And you got to see Chartres, such an experience. I'm longing to hear more, get all the details; but first, and most important, I want to be told all about home, and my precious Archie and Isobel and Hamish. Hamish must be enormous now. And Isobel, with those tedious Americans to stay. I hear all about them in Archie's letters, when he isn't telling me about the latest grouse-bag, or the size of the salmon he caught last week. It's a miracle he's able to do so much with that terrible leg. Tell me how the poor leg is."

"He can't actually do that much," Lucilla told her bluntly. "He just writes you positive letters because he doesn't want you to be upset. And his leg isn't anything. It's tin, full stop. It can't get any better, and we all pray it'll never get any worse."

"Poor darling. Beastly, beastly IRA. How they dare to do such things, and to Archie, of all people."

"They weren't necessarily gunning for *him*, Pandora. They were waiting, over the border, to blast off at a lot of British jocks, and he happened to be one of them."

"Did he know they were there? Or was it an ambush?"

"I don't know. And if I asked, he wouldn't tell me. He won't talk about it. He won't talk about it to anybody."

"Is that a good thing?"

"I don't suppose it is, but there's not much we can do about it."

"He was never a great talker. The most darling man, but even as a little boy he always kept everything to himself. We never even knew he was courting Isobel, and when he told our mother that he wanted to marry her, Mama nearly dropped dead with astonishment because she'd got him lined up for some entirely different female. Never mind, she made the best of it. Just as she always made the best of everything . . ." Her voice faded. She fell silent, then swiftly emptied her glass. "Jeff, is there any more left in that bottle, or shall we open another?"

But the bottle was not yet empty and Jeff refilled Pandora's glass, and then topped up Lucilla's and his own. Lucilla was now beginning to feel not only light-hearted but light-headed as well. She wondered how much Pandora had already consumed before they joined her. Perhaps the champagne was why she seemed to be talking so much.

"Now tell me . . ." She was off again. "What are the two of you going to do next?"

Jeff and Lucilla looked at each other. Making plans was not one of their strong points. Doing things on the spur of the moment was half the fun.

It was Jeff who replied. "We don't really know. Only

243

thing is, I have to go back to Australia at the beginning of October. I've a flight booked with Qantas on the third."

"Where do you fly from?"

"London."

"So, some time, you'll have to go back to England."

"Right."

"Is Lucilla going with you?"

Again they looked at each other. "We haven't discussed it," Lucilla said.

"So you're free. Free as air. Free to come and go as you wish. The world is your oyster." She made an expansive gesture with her hand and spilled some of her champagne.

"Yes," Jeff agreed cautiously, "I suppose it is."

"Then let us make plans. Lucilla, would you like to make plans with me?"

"What sort of plans?"

"When you were snooping, as you put it, around my drawing room, did you notice that large and pretentious copperplate invitation on my mantelpiece?"

"From Verena Steynton? Yes, I did."

"Have you been asked?"

"Yes. Dad sent my invitation on to me and I got it in Ibiza."

"Are you going?"

"I . . . I hadn't actually thought about it."

"*Might* you go?"

"I don't know. Why?"

"Because . . ." She laid down her glass. "I think that I shall go."

The shock of this announcement stunned Lucilla out of her delightful tipsiness and into a state of cold sobriety. She stared at Pandora in total disbelief, and Pandora stared back, her grey eyes with their huge black pupils bright with a strange elation, as though delighting in the expression of blank incredulity she had brought to Lucilla's face.

"You'd go?"

"Why not?"

"Back to Scotland?"

"Where else?"

"For Verena Steynton's *dance*?" It did not make sense.

"It's as good a reason as any."

"But you've never come before. Dad asked you and begged you, and you've never come. He told me."

"There has to be a first time. Perhaps now is the right time." All at once she stood up and walked away from them to stand looking out over the garden. She stayed there for an instant, quite still, silhouetted against the light that shone upwards from the pool. Her dress, her hair moved in the breeze. Then she turned to face them, leaning against the balustrade. She said, and she spoke now in quite a different voice, "I've been thinking so much about Croy. Just lately, I've been thinking so much about it. I dream about it, and wake up, and start remembering things I hadn't thought of in years. And then the invitation came. Like yours, Lucilla, forwarded on from Croy. And it brought back a million memories of the fun we used to have at those ridiculous dances and hunt balls. And house parties, and the hills ringing with the crack of guns, and every evening an enormous dinner party. How my poor mother coped with us all, I cannot imagine." She smiled at Lucilla, and then at Jeff. "And you two arriving. Phoning from Palma and turning up out of the blue, and Lucilla so like Archie. Omens. Do you believe in omens, Lucilla?"

"I don't know."

"Neither do I. But I'm certain, with the Highland blood that courses through our veins, that we should." She came back to her chair and sat on the footrest, her face close to Lucilla's. Beneath the beauty, Lucilla could discern the years stamped on Pandora's lovely features: the lines around her eyes and mouth, the papery skin, the sharp angle of her jawbone. "So, let us make plans.

245

Will you both make plans with me? Would you mind if I asked you to do that thing?"

Lucilla looked across at Jeff. He shook his head. She said, "We wouldn't mind."

"Then that is what we'll do. We'll stay here for a week, just the three of us, and you shall have the time of your lives. And then we'll take my car, and we'll catch the ferry to Spain. And we'll drive through Spain and France, taking our time and making a pleasure of the journey. When we get to Calais, we'll cross over to England. And we'll head north, and we'll go to Scotland, and we'll go home. Back to Croy. Oh, Lucilla, say you think it's a wonderful idea."

"It's certainly totally unexpected," was all Lucilla could come up with, but if Pandora noticed a certain lack of enthusiasm in her voice, she gave no indication of doing so. Swept along on her own excitement, she turned to Jeff. "And you? How does it sound to you? Or do you think I'm out of my mind?"

"No."

"You wouldn't mind coming to Scotland with us?"

"If that's what you and Lucilla want, I'd be delighted."

"Then it's all settled!" She was triumphant. "We'll all stay at Croy with Isobel and Archie, and we'll all go to the Steyntons' lovely party."

"But Jeff hasn't been asked," Lucilla pointed out.

"Oh, that's no problem."

"And he won't have anything to wear."

Pandora dissolved into laughter. "Darling, you do disappoint me. I thought you were an unworldly artist, and all you seem to do is worry about clothes! Don't you see, clothes don't matter. Nothing matters. The only thing that matters is that we're going back home, together. Just think what fun we're going to have. And now we must celebrate!" She sprang to her feet. "The perfect moment to open that second bottle of champagne!"

SEPTEMBER

21

Thursday the Eighth

Isobel Balmerino, at her sewing machine, stitched the last name-tape, HAMISH BLAIR, on to the last new handkerchief, cut the thread, folded the handkerchief, and laid it on top of the pile of clothes that stood on the table beside her. All done. All that remained were those garments which required that the name-tapes be hand-sewn . . . rugger stockings, an overcoat, and a grey polo-necked pullover, but these could be done at leisure, in the evening, and by the fireside.

She had not had such a session of name-tapes since Hamish first went to Templehall, four years ago, but he had grown during the summer holidays to such an alarming extent that she had been forced to drag him into Relkirk, school-clothes list in hand, and start all over again. The expedition, as she had known it would be, had been both painful and expensive. Painful because Hamish did not want to think about going back to school, hated shopping, hated new clothes, and miserably resented being done out of a single day of his holiday freedom. And expensive because the regulation uniform could only be purchased at the most up-market and costly shop in the town. The overcoat, the polo-necked sweater, and the rugger stockings were bad enough, but five new pairs of enormous leather shoes were almost more than Isobel, and her bank balance, could take.

With some idea of cheering Hamish up, she had

bought him an ice-cream, but he had devoured this morosely and without joy, and they had returned to Croy in an uncommunicative and mutually unfriendly silence. Once home, Hamish had immediately taken himself off, armed with his trout rod, and wearing an expression which implied that he had been grossly mistreated. Isobel was left to hump the parcels and boxes upstairs, where she had slung them into the foot of his wardrobe and firmly shut the door, then made her way to the kitchen to boil a kettle for a cup of tea and start preparing dinner.

The horrible experience of spending vast quantities of money that she could not afford left her feeling quite sick, and Hamish's patent ingratitude did not help. Peeling potatoes, she said a silent goodbye to any dreams of buying herself a new dress for the Steyntons' dance. The old navy taffeta would have to do. Letting herself feel martyred and ill done by, she toyed with the notion of freshening it up with a touch of white at the neck.

But that had all happened two weeks ago, and now September was here. That made everything better, and for a number of reasons. The most important was that, until next May, she was finished with the business of paying guests. Scottish Country Tours had shut up shop for the winter, and the last lot of Americans, complete with baggage, souvenirs, and tartan bonnets, had been waved away. The tiredness and depression that had dogged Isobel all summer was dissolved almost instantly by her sense of freedom and the knowledge that, once more, she and Archie had Croy to themselves.

But this was not all. Born and bred in Scotland, she experienced each year this lifting of the spirits as August slipped away, off the calendar, and one could stop pretending that it was summer. Some years, it was true, there came seasons like the old days, when the lawns grew dry from lack of rain and golden evenings were spent watering the roses and sweet peas and the rows of young lettuces in the vegetable garden. But too frequently the months of June, July, and August were nothing but a long and soggy endurance test of frustration and disappointment. Grey skies, chill winds, and dripping rain were enough to dampen the enthusiasm of a saint. The worst were those dark and muggy days when, in desperation, one eventually retreated indoors and lit a fire, whereupon the sky instantly cleared and the late afternoon sun dazzled out over the sodden garden, tantalisingly too late to be of use to anybody.

This summer, in particular, had been specially disappointing, and with hindsight Isobel realised that the weeks of dark clouds and sunlessness had done much to contribute to her low spirits and physical exhaustion. The first snap of frost was actually welcome, and she was able to put away her cotton skirts and shirts with some satisfaction and revert once more to friendly old tweeds and Shetland pullovers.

But even after splendid summers, September in Relkirkshire was special. Those first light frosts cleared the air, so that the colours of the countryside took on a stronger and richer hue. The deep blue of the skies was reflected in loch and river, and with the harvest safely in, the fields stood golden with stubble. Harebells grew in wayside ditches, and the scented heather, coming into full bloom, stained the hills with purple.

And then, most important of all, September meant fun. A packed season of socialising before the darkness of a long winter closed in on them all, when the bitter weather and snow-packed roads isolated scattered communities and precluded any form of contact. September meant people. Friends. For this was when Relkirkshire came truly into its own.

By the end of July, the last of the annual invasion of family holidaymakers had, by and large, left; tents were

251

packed up and caravans towed away, as the tourists headed for home. In their stead, August brought the vanguard of a secondary immigration from the south, regular visitors who returned each year to Scotland for the sport and the parties. Shooting lodges that had stood forlornly empty for most of the year were once more opened up, and their owners, driving north up the motorway in Range-Rovers loaded to the gunwales with rods, guns, small children, teenagers, friends, relations, and dogs, took happy and grateful repossession.

As well, local households swelled, not with Americans nor paying guests but with young families who belonged to these establishments and had, by necessity, moved south to London to live and work, saving their yearly vacations to return home at just this time. All bedrooms were occupied, attics turned into temporary accommodation for gangs of grandchildren, and sparse bathrooms worked overtime. Huge quantities of food were produced, cooked, and eaten every day at dining-room tables elongated by extra leaves.

And then, September. In September, all at once, everything came to life, as though some celestial stage manager had made his countdown and pulled the switch. The Station Hotel in Relkirk was transformed from its customary Victorian gloom to a cheerful, crowded meeting-place for old friends, and the Strathcroy Arms, taken over by the syndicate of businessmen who paid Archie reassuring sums of money for the privilege of shooting grouse over his moor, fairly buzzed with activity and sporting talk.

At Croy, the invitations stood stacked on the mantelpiece in the library, covering every type of convivial occasion. Isobel's contribution to the general jollity was an annual buffet lunch party before the Strathcroy Games. Archie was Chieftain of these Games and led the opening parade of village worthies, their stride tactfully slowed to match his halting gait. For this important ceremony, he wore his regimental balmoral and carried a drawn sword. He took his responsibilities with great solemnity and, at the end of the day, presented prizes, not only for piping and Highland dancing but also for the sweater most expertly knitted from hand-spun wool, the lightest of sponge cakes,and the winning pot of home-made strawberry jam.

Isobel kept her sewing machine in the old linen room at Croy, mostly for reasons of convenience but also because it was her favourite and most private retreat. Not large, but quite spacious enough, it had windows facing west, out over the croquet lawn and the road that led up to the loch, and on bright days was always filled with sunshine. The curtains were white cotton, the floor brown linoleum, and the walls were lined with large white-painted cupboards in which were stowed all the household sheets and towels and spare blankets and fresh bedcovers. The solid table on which stood the sewing machine was also useful for cutting out and dressmaking, and the ironing board and the iron stood ready for instant use. In here there was always a comforting nursery smell of laundered linen and the lavender bags that Isobel tucked in with her crisp piles of pillowcases, and this contributed in no small way to the room's extraordinary aura of timelessness and tranquillity.

Which was why, with the name-tapes finished, she made no immediate effort to move but stayed, sitting on the hard chair, with her elbows on the table and her chin in her hands. The view beyond the open window led, up beyond the trees, to the first gentle summits of the hills. All was washed in golden sunlight. The curtains stirred in the breeze, and that same breath of air shivered through the branches of the silver birches that stood on the far side of the lawn.

A leaf dropped, drifting like a tiny kite.

It was half past three and she was alone in the house. Indoors all was still, but from the farmyard she heard distant hammering and the barking of one of the dogs. For once in her life she had time to herself, there being no commitment nor person urgently requiring her attention. She could scarcely remember when she had last found herself in such a situation, and her thoughts drifted back to childhood and youth and the lazy, aimless joys of empty days.

A floorboard creaked. Somewhere a door slammed shut. Croy. An old house with a heartbeat all its own. Her home. But she remembered the day, over twenty years ago, when Archie had first brought her here. She was nineteen and a tennis party had been arranged, with afternoon tea served in the dining room. Isobel, the daughter of an Angus solicitor, and neither beautiful nor assured, had found herself overwhelmed by the size and grandeur of the place, and also by the glamour and sophistication of Archie's other friends, all of whom seemed to know each other frighteningly well. Already hopelessly in love with Archie, she could not imagine why he had bothered to include her in the general invitation. Lady Balmerino appeared to be equally perplexed, but had been kind, making certain Isobel sat next to her at the tea-table, and taking pains to see that she was not left out of any conversation.

But there was another girl, long-legged and blonde, who seemed already to have claimed Archie for her own, and made this very clear to the assembled company, teasing him, and catching his eye across the table as though they shared a million private secrets. Archie, she was telling them all, belonged to her, and no other person would be permitted to take possession.

But, at the end of the day, Archie had made up his own mind to marry Isobel. His parents, once they had got over their astonishment, were patently delighted and welcomed Isobel into the family not as Archie's wife but as another daughter. She was fortunate. Gentle,

254

funny, hospitable, unworldly, and totally charming, the Balmerinos were adored by everybody and Isobel was no exception.

From the farm, she heard one of the tractors starting up. Another leaf fluttered to the ground. It occurred to Isobel that now could be an afternoon that had happened long ago, as though time had slipped backwards. The sort of afternoon when dogs sought for shade, and cats basked on windowsills, their furry bellies turned to the sun. She thought of Mrs Harris, with one of the younger maids in tow, emerging from the kitchen and headed for the walled garden, there to fill a bowl with the last of the raspberries, or reach for the bloomy Victoria plums, capturing their sweetness before the wasps got at them.

All of Croy the way it once had been. Nobody had gone away. Nobody had died. They were still alive, those two dear old people; Archie's mother out with her roses, snipping away at the dead heads and finding time to chat with one of the gardeners while he raked the dusty gravel; and Archie's father in the library, stealing a little snooze with his silk handkerchief spread across his face. Isobel only had to go and find them. She imagined doing this, making her way down the stairs, crossing the hall to stand at the open front door. She saw Lady Balmerino in her straw gardening hat coming in from the garden, carrying the basket filled with snippings and faded rose petals. But when she looked up and saw Isobel, she would frown and show some confusion because the middle-aged Isobel would be unfamiliar to her as a ghost . . .

"Isobel!"

The voice, raised, impinged upon her daydreams. Isobel was aware that it had already called, more than once, but she had scarcely heard. Who was wanting her now? Reluctantly she collected herself, pushed back the chair and got to her feet. Perhaps to be left alone for more than five minutes was too much to expect. She went out of the room and down the nursery passage to the head of the stairs. Leaning over the banister, she saw below her the foreshortened view of Verena Steynton standing in the middle of the hall, having walked into the house through the open front door.

"Isobel!"

"I'm here."

Verena tilted her head and looked up. "I was beginning to think there was nobody in."

"Only me." Isobel started down the stairs. "Archie's taken Hamish and the dogs to the Buchanan-Wrights' cricket match."

"Are you busy?" Verena did not look as though she had been busy. As usual, she was immaculately and suitably turned out, and surely had just been to the hairdresser.

"I've been sewing Hamish's name-tapes for school." Instinctively, Isobel put a hand to her hair, as though the casual gesture might improve her own tousled head. "But I've finished now."

"Can you spare me a moment?"

"Of course."

"I've got lots to tell you and two favours to ask. I meant to phone but I've been in Relkirk all day and then, driving home, I thought much simpler and nicer just to call in."

"Do you want a cup of tea?"

"In a moment. No hurry."

"Let's go and be comfortable." Isobel led her visitor into the drawing room, not with any intentions of grandeur but simply because it was full of sunlight, and the library and the kitchen, at this time of day, were inclined to be gloomy. The windows stood open, the room felt cool, and a mass of sweet peas, which Isobel had picked that morning and arranged in an old soup tureen, filled the air with their fragrance.

"Heaven." Verena sank into a corner of the sofa and stretched out her long and elegantly shod legs. "What a day for the cricket match. Last year it bucketed with rain and they had to pull stumps in the middle of the afternoon because the pitch was flooded. Are those your own sweet peas? What colours! Mine were a bit of a failure this year. Do you know, I really hate Relkirk on a warm afternoon? The pavements were banked three deep with fat girls in jeans pushing babies in buggies. And all the babies seemed to be howling."

"I know the feeling. How's everything going?"

She had already made up her mind that Verena wanted to talk about the dance and she was not mistaken.

"Oh . . ." Verena, for a moment, became quite dramatic, groaning as though in pain and closing her eyes. "I'm beginning to wonder why I ever *thought* about throwing a party. Do you know, half the invitations haven't even been answered yet? People are so thoughtless. I think they leave them curling on mantelpieces, waiting to die of old age. It makes trying to arrange dinner parties and find beds for everybody quite impossible."

"I wouldn't worry." Isobel tried to sound soothing. "I'd let them make their own arrangements."

"But that would mean utter chaos."

Isobel knew that it wouldn't, but Verena was a perfectionist. "Yes, I suppose so. It must be awful." She added, almost afraid to ask, "Has Lucilla replied yet?"

"No," Verena told her bluntly.

"We did send your invitation on, but she's travelling so she may not even have got it. She sent us a rather vague address in Ibiza, but we haven't heard from her since she was in Paris. She thought she might go and see Pandora."

"I haven't heard from Pandora either."

"I'll be surprised if you do. She never answers anything."

"But Alexa Aird's coming, and bringing a boyfriend. Did you know that Alexa has found herself a man?"

257

"Vi told me."

"Extraordinary. I wonder what he's like."

"Virginia says he's dishy."

"Can't wait to see him."

"When is Katy arriving?"

"Next week some time. She phoned last night. Which is one of the favours that I have to ask you. Have you got a houseful of people staying over the dance?"

"So far, nobody. Hamish will be back at school and I don't know whether Lucilla will be here or not . . ."

"Well, could you be an angel and have a stray man to stay? Katy told me about him last night. She met him at some dinner party, and liked him. He's an American – a lawyer, I think – but his wife's just died, and he's come over here for a bit of a holiday. He's coming to Scotland anyway to stay with some people who live in the Borders, and she thought it would be friendly to send him an invitation. We can't put him up at Corriehill because I'm full, with all Katy's friends, and Toddy Buchanan hasn't a room free at the Strathcroy Arms, so I thought you could give him a bed? Would you mind? I don't know anything about him except the bit about his wife dying, but if Katy liked him I don't suppose he'd be *dreadfully* heavy weather."

"Poor man. Of course he can come."

"And you'll bring him to the party? You are sweet. I'll ring Katy tonight, and tell her to tell him to get in touch with you."

"What's his name?"

"Something funny. Plucker. Or . . . Tucker. That's it. Conrad Tucker. Why do you suppose Americans always have such peculiar names?"

Isobel laughed. "They probably think Balmerino's pretty odd. What else is happening?"

"Nothing really. We've persuaded Toddy Buchanan to do the catering and run the bar, and produce some sort of a breakfast. For some reason, Katy's generation are always ravenously hungry around four in the morn-

258

ing. And darling Tom Drystone is organising the band."

"Well, it wouldn't be a party without our whistling postman up on the platform. Are you having a disco?"

"Yes. A young man from Relkirk is doing that. He provides everything. A sort of job lot. Flashing lights and amplifiers. What the noise is going to be like, I dread to think. And we're going to have fairy lights all the way up the drive. I thought it would look festive, and if it's a miserably dark evening, it'll help people find the way."

"It'll look wonderful. You've thought of everything."

"Except flowers. That's the other favour I've got to ask you. Would you help with the flowers? Katy will be there, and I've press-ganged one or two others, but nobody does flowers the way you do, and I'd be endlessly grateful if you'd help."

Isobel felt flattered. It was nice to think that there was something that she could do better than Verena, and gratifying to be asked.

"The thing is," Verena went on before Isobel had a chance to speak, "I can't think how to decorate the marquee. The house isn't so difficult, but the marquee presents something of a problem because it's so enormous and ordinary flower arrangements would simply be dwarfed. What do you think? You're always full of bright ideas."

Isobel searched for a bright idea but drew a blank. "Hydrangeas?"

"They'll be over by then."

"Hire some potted palms."

"Too depressing. Like the ballroom of some provincial hotel."

"Well, why not make it really countrified and seasonal? Sheaves of ripe barley and branches of rowan. Lovely red berries and those pretty leaves. And the beeches will be turning as well. We can soak the stems in glycerine and simply cover the tent-poles, make them look like autumn trees . . ."

"Oh, a brainwave. You're brilliant. We'll do it all the

259

day before the party. The Thursday. Will you write it down in your diary?"

"It's Vi's birthday picnic that day, but I can give that a miss."

"You're a saint. What a weight off my mind. The relief of it." Verena stretched luxuriously, swallowed a yawn, fell silent.

The clock on the mantelpiece ticked gently, and the quiet of the room closed in on the two women. Yawns were catching. And it was a mistake ever to sit down in the middle of the afternoon because you didn't feel like ever getting up again. Summer afternoons and nothing in particular to do. Once more Isobel drifted back into that illusion of timelessness in which she had been lost before Verena's interruption. She thought again of old Lady Balmerino, who used to sit here, as she and Verena sat, reading a novel or peacefully sewing her tapestry. Everything now as once it had been. Perhaps in a moment there would come a discreet tap on the door and Harris the butler would enter, pushing before him the mahogany trolley laid with the silver teapot and the eggshell china cups; the covered dishes of scones, fresh from the oven, the bowl of cream, the strawberry jam, the lemon sponge-cake, and the dark, sticky gingerbread.

The clock, with silver notes, struck four, and the illusion dissolved. Harris was long gone and would never return. Isobel yawned again and then, with some effort, pulled herself to her feet. "I'll go and put the kettle on," she told Verena, "and we'll have that cup of tea."

22

Friday the Ninth

". . . That was the year my cousin Flora had her bairn.
Did you know her parents? Uncle Hector was my father's
brother, much younger, of course, and married to a girl
from Rhum. Met her when he was a policeman; she was
always a shiftless creature, lost all her teeth when she
was scarcely out of her twenties. When my granny
heard, she was up to high doh, didn't want any candle-
bearing Catholics in the family; she'd been brought up
Wee Free. I knitted a matinee coat for the bairn. Pink
silk with a fern pattern, but she put it in the boiler with
the sheets, it just about broke my heart . . ."

Violet stopped listening. It didn't seem necessary to
listen. One just nodded, or said "Oh, yes," every time
Lottie paused for breath, and then she was away again
on some other confusing tack.

". . . went into service when I was fourteen, over in
a big house in Fife; I cried buckets, but my mother said
I had to go. I was the kitchen maid and the cook was a
bisom; I've never been so tired in my life, up at five
o'clock in the morning and slept in the attic with a
moose."

This at least caught Violet's attention. "A *moose*, Lottie?"

"I think it was a moose. One of those stuffed heads.
On the wall. Too big for a stag. Mr Gilfillan had been
in Africa, a missionary. You wouldn't have thought a

missionary would have gone round killing mooses, would you? Christmas they had roast goose, but all I got was a bit of cold mutton. Mean. Wouldn't give you the drippings off their noses. The attic was that damp, my clothes were wringing wet, caught pneumonia. The doctor came, Mrs Gilfillan sent me home, never been so glad to get back. Had a cat at home. Tammy Puss. He was that quick. Open the larder door and in with the cream; once we found a dead mouse in the cream. And Ginger had a litter of kittens, half-wild, scratched the skin off my mother's hands . . . she was never good with animals. Hated my father's dog . . .''

They sat, the two elderly ladies, on a bench in the big park in Relkirk. Before them, the river flowed, heavy with floodwater and stained brown with peat. A fisherman, up to his hips in water, flogged his salmon rod. So far he did not seem to have had so much as a nibble. Across the river stood large Victorian houses, deep in spacious gardens with lawns that ran down to the water. One or two had little boats moored. There were ducks on the water. A man, passing with his dog, threw crusts and the ducks came gobbling, squabbling, to snatch the crusts up.

'. . . the doctor said it was a stroke, said she'd got nerves. I wanted to go and be a volunteer, with the war on and everything, but if I'd gone there'd be no one to stay with my mother. My father was a worker out of doors, he grew lovely turnips, but indoors, sit down and take off his boots and that was it . . . never seen a man who could eat so much. He was never a talker, some days never said a word. Trapped rabbits. Ate a lot of rabbits, we did. 'Course that was before mixamytoasties. Filthy things now . . .''

Violet, having made her promise to Henry that she would take Lottie off Edie's hands for an afternoon, had suffered an uneasy conscience until she had finally decided to take the plunge and get it over, and had invited Lottie to come shopping with her in Relkirk and to have high tea. She had duly collected Lottie from Edie's cottage, packed her into the car, and driven her into the town. For the occasion Lottie had dressed in her best, a beige Crimplene coat and a hat the shape of a cottage loaf. She carried a huge handbag and wore her tottery high-heeled shoes. From the moment she got into the car, she had not stopped talking. She had talked as they made their way around Marks & Spencer, talked as they waited in the queue to buy fresh vegetables, talked as they searched the crowded streets for what Lottie insisted on calling a haberdasher's.

"I don't think there are any haberdasher's any longer, Lottie . . ."

"Oh, yes, a little one down that street . . . or was it the next? Mother always came for her knitting wool."

Never believing they would find it, Violet allowed herself to be led around in circles, getting more hot and footsore by the moment, and was torn between annoyance and relief when Lottie finally ran the shop to earth. It was very old and dusty, and crammed with a collection of cardboard boxes containing crochet hooks, faded embroidery silks, and out-of-date knitting patterns. The old woman behind the counter looked as though she had just managed to make it out of a geriatric home, and it took her fifteen minutes to find what Lottie wanted, which was a yard of boiling knicker elastic. Finally, however, it was produced from a drawer filled with odd buttons, put shakily into a paper bag, and paid for. They stepped out on to the pavement, and Lottie was triumphant. "Told you so," she crowed to Violet. "Didn't believe me, did you?"

With their shopping over and it not yet being time for tea, Violet had suggested a walk in the park. They had made their way back to her car, dumped their purchases in the boot, and then crossed the wide sward of grass that led to the river. At the first bench, Violet had firmly sat down.

"We'll have a little rest," she told Lottie, and so here

they were, side by side in the golden sunshine, and Lottie still with plenty to say.

"That's the Relkirk Royal, that's where I was, you can just see it through the trees. Nice enough place, but I couldn't stand the nurses. The doctor was good enough, but no more than a young student, don't imagine he knew anything, although he pretended he did. Lovely gardens, though, just as nice as the Cremmy. I wanted Mother cremated, but the minister said she wanted to lie by my father in the churchyard at Tullochard. Though I don't know how he should know more than me."

"I expect your mother told him . . ."

"More likely made it up himself, always liked to interfere."

Violet looked across the river to where the Relkirk Royal stood high on the hill, its red stone turrets and gables scarcely visible through the leafy trees that surrounded it. She said, "The hospital certainly has a lovely position."

"That's doctors for you. They can pay for anything."

Casually, "What was he called, the young doctor who took care of you?"

"Dr Martin. There was another, Dr Faulkner, but he never came near me. It was Dr Martin who said I could go and live with Edie. I wanted a taxi but it was an ambulance."

"Edie is very kind."

"*She*'s had a good-enough life, some people have all the luck. Different living in a village to being stuck away up the hill."

"Perhaps you could sell your parents' house and move into a village?"

But Lottie ignored this sensible suggestion and went on, full flood, as though Violet had never made it. It occurred to Violet then that Lottie was more astute than any of them suspected. "Worry about her being so fat, it's a heart attack she'll have one morning, carrying all that flab around with her. And always flying out of the

264

house, off to your house or Virginia's, never sits down for a bit of peace or a chat or to watch the telly. Ought to think of herself sometimes. She told me that Alexa's coming up for Mrs Steynton's party. Bringing a friend. That's nice, isn't it? But you'll need to watch, men are all the same, after what they can get their hands on . . ."

"What do you mean, Lottie?" Violet was sharp.

Lottie turned dark round eyes upon her. "Well, she's no pauper, is Alexa. Old Lady Cheriton was never short of sixpence. I read the newspapers, know all about *that* family. Nothing like a bit of cash to start a man leering at a young girl."

Violet found herself assailed by a helpless rage that seemed to surge up from the soles of her feet and, reaching her cheeks, burn them red. Rage at Lottie's impertinence, and helplessness because Lottie was, after all, only voicing what all Alexa's family, obscurely, feared.

She said, "Alexa is very pretty and very dear. The fact that she is also independent has nothing to do with the friends she chooses."

But Lottie either ignored or missed the snub. She gave a little laugh, tossing her head. "I wouldn't be too sure about that. And coming from London, too. Lot of money-grubbers. Yuppies," she added with some force, saying the word as though it were dirty.

"Lottie, I don't think you know what you're talking about."

"All these girls are the same. Always were, see a handsome man and they're away like a bitch on heat." She shivered suddenly, as though the excitement of the thought had reached every nerve-end of her gangling frame. Then she put out a hand and closed it over Violet's wrist. "That's another thing. Henry. See him about the place. He's small, isn't he? Comes to Edie's and never says a word. Looks funny to me sometimes. I'd worry if I were you. Not like other little boys . . ."

Her bony fingers were strangely strong, the grip vice-

265

like. Violet, repelled, knew an instant of panic. Her immediate instinct was to prise the fingers loose, get to her feet and escape, but just then a girl walked by pushing a child in a buggy, and common sense came to Violet's rescue. The panic, the annoyance, faded. It was, after all, just poor Lottie Carstairs, to whom life had not been kind, letting her sad, sexual frustrations and her rambling imagination run away with her. And if Edie could stand having her cousin to live with her, surely Violet could cope calmly for a single afternoon.

She smiled. She said, "It's good of you to be concerned, Lottie, but Henry is a very ordinary little boy and sound as a bell. Now . . ." She shifted slightly, glancing at her watch, and felt Lottie's fingers loosen their manic grip and slip away. Violet, unhurried, reached for her handbag. ". . . I think it's time we went and found somewhere pleasant to have our tea. I'm feeling quite peckish. I fancy fish and chips. How about you?"

23

Friday the Ninth

As Isobel, worn out with the daily demands of her busy life, retreated from time to time to the linen room, so her husband found solace in his workshop. This was in the basement of Croy, an area of stone-flagged passages and dimly lighted cellars. The old boiler lived down here, a brooding, smelly monster that looked large enough to drive a liner, and demanded constant and regular attention and enormous quantities of coke. As well, one or two other rooms were still employed – to store unused china, unwanted items of furniture, the coal and the logs, and a much-diminished wine cellar. But mostly, the basement stood deserted, hung with cobwebs and invaded each year by families of fieldmice.

The workshop was next door to the boiler room, which meant that it was always pleasantly warm, and it had large windows, barred like a jail's, which faced south and west and let in sufficient light for cheerfulness. Archie's father, neat with his hands, had set it all up, with heavy benches, racks for tools, vices, and clamps. And it was here that the old man had liked to potter, repairing his children's damaged toys, dealing with various inevitable breakages that occurred about the house, and concocting his own salmon flies.

After he died, the workshop had stood empty for some years, unused, neglected, and gathering dust. But when Archie came back to Croy after his eight months

267

in hospital, he painfully made his way down the stone stairs, limped the length of the echoing passage, and took repossession. The first thing he saw as he entered the room was a broken balloon-back chair, its back legs shattered by the weight of some corpulent occupant. It had been brought down to the workshop before old Lord Balmerino died. He had made a start on its repair but never finished the job, and the chair had been left, forgotten and untended, ever since.

Archie stood and looked at the forlorn piece of furniture for some time. Then he shouted for Isobel. She came. She helped him sweep away the dirt and the cobwebs and the mouse-droppings and the drifts of old sawdust. Scuttling spiders were sent packing, as were solidified pots of glue, piles of yellowed newspapers, ancient tins of paint. Isobel cleaned the windows and somehow forced them open, letting in the sweet fresh air.

Meanwhile Archie, having wiped and oiled all the fine old tools, the chisels and hammers, saws and planes, replaced them in orderly fashion in their racks. With that done, he sat down and wrote out a list of all that he needed, and Isobel went into Relkirk and bought it for him.

Only then was he able to get down to work and finish the job that his father had started.

Now he sat at that same bench, the afternoon sun slanting through the top half of the window, and finished priming the carving he had been working on, from time to time, over the last month or two. It was about ten inches high and depicted the figure of a girl sitting on a boulder with a small Jack Russell terrier leaning against her knee. The girl wore a sweater and a kilted skirt, and her hair was windblown. It was, in fact, Katy Steynton and her dog. Verena had given Archie a photograph of her daughter, taken up on the moor last year, and from this he had made the drawings for the carving. With the primer dry, he would paint it, reproducing as closely as possible the muted colours of the photograph. And then it would be given to Katy as a twenty-first birthday present.

It was done. He laid down the brush and leaned back in his chair to stretch the aches out of his limbs, and assess his creation over the top of his half-moon spectacles. He had never before attempted the complications of a sitting figure, and a female one at that, and was inordinately pleased with the way it had turned out. Girl and dog made a charming composition. Tomorrow he would paint it. He looked forward with some satisfaction to applying the final touches.

From upstairs, he heard the faint sound of the telephone ringing. It was only just audible, and for months he and Isobel had been talking about the sense of installing another bell in the basement so that he could hear the sound more easily, should he be alone in the house. But they had done nothing about this and he was alone in the house now and wondered how long the telephone had been ringing, and if there was time for him to make his way upstairs and pick up the receiver before the caller, losing heart, hung up. He thought about ignoring it but the ringing continued. Perhaps it was important. He pushed back his chair and made his slow way down the passage and up the stairs to answer the wretched instrument. The nearest receiver was in the kitchen and it was still ringing shrilly as Archie crossed over to the dresser and picked it up.

"Croy."

"Dad!"

"Lucilla!" His heart leapt with joy. He reached for a chair.

"Where were you? The phone's been ringing for hours."

269

"Down in my workshop." He settled himself, taking the weight off his leg.

"Oh, I'm sorry. Is Mum not there?"

"No. She and Hamish have gone blackberrying. Lucilla, where are you?"

"I'm in *London*. And you'll never guess where I'm ringing from. You'll never guess in a thousand years."

"In that case you'd better tell me."

"The Ritz."

"What the hell are you doing there?"

"Staying the night. And then we're driving up tomorrow. We'll be home tomorrow night."

Archie took off his spectacles; he could feel the grin of delight spreading over his face. "Who's 'we'?"

"Jeff Howland and me. And . . . wait for it . . . *Pandora*."

"*Pandora?*"

"I thought that would surprise you . . ."

"But what's Pandora doing with you?"

"She's coming home. She says it's for Verena Steynton's dance, but I suspect it's really to see Croy and all of you again."

"Is she there now?"

"No. She's having a toes-up. I'm phoning from my room. I'm all alone except for Jeff. I've got so much to tell you and Mum, but I won't do it now because it's all so complicated . . ."

But Archie would not let her off with this excuse. "When did you get to London?"

"This morning. Just before lunch. We've all been driving through Spain and France in Pandora's car. We've had the most amazing time. Then we caught the ferry early this morning and came to London. I was all ready to head north right away, but Pandora wanted to draw breath, so she brought us here. Insisted. And don't worry about the bill because she's footing it. She footed the whole trip, ever since we left Palma. Paid for all the petrol, the hotels, everything."

270

"How . . ." His voice broke. It was ridiculous, unmanly, to be so emotional. He tried again. "How is she?"

"She's fine. Terribly pretty. Lots of fun. Oh, Dad, you are pleased I'm bringing her home, aren't you? It's not going to be too much for Mum? Pandora's not what you call madly domesticated and I don't suppose she'll ever raise a finger to do anything to help, but she's so excited about seeing you both again. It will be all right, won't it?"

"More than all right, my darling. It's like a miracle."

"And don't forget, I'm bringing Jeff as well."

"We look forward to meeting him."

"See you tomorrow then."

"What time?"

"About five? But don't worry if we're a little late."

"We won't."

"I can't wait."

"Nor me. Drive carefully, my darling."

"Of course." She sent him a kissing noise down the hundreds of miles of wire, and rang off.

Archie was left sitting on the hard kitchen chair and holding the buzzing receiver in his hand. Lucilla and Pandora. Coming home.

He replaced the receiver. The buzzing ceased. The old kitchen clock ticked slowly. For a few moments he sat where he was, and then got to his feet and went out of the kitchen and down the passage to his study. Sitting at his desk, he opened a drawer and took out a key. Using this key, he opened another, smaller drawer. From this he withdrew an envelope, yellowed with the years and addressed in Pandora's large and immature scrawl to himself, at the headquarters of the Queen's Loyal Highlanders, in Berlin. The date of the postmark was 1967. It contained a letter, but he did not take this letter out to read because he knew it by heart. Which meant that there was no reason not to have torn it to shreds, nor flung it on the fire years ago, except that he could not bring himself to destroy it.

271

Pandora. Coming back to Croy.

From the distance came the sound of a car, growing louder, approaching the house, up the hill from the main road. The noise of its engine was unmistakable. Isobel and Hamish returning in the minibus from their black-berrying expedition. Archie put the envelope back into its drawer, locked it away, disposed once more of the key, and went to meet them.

Isobel had driven the minibus around the back of the house and parked it in the yard and, by the time Archie returned to the kitchen, they were there, his wife and his son, flinging open the door and staggering triumphantly through it, each weighed down by two huge baskets brimming with dark fruit. After a session in the bramble thickets they were both disreputable, dirty, and mud-stained, and looked, Archie decided fondly, no better than a pair of tinkers.

Every time he set eyes on Hamish, he knew a small shock of surprise, because the boy, these summer holidays, had grown like a young tree, getting taller and larger by the day. At twelve, he now topped his mother, and his out-at-elbow sweater was strained across a pair of muscular shoulders. His shirt hung out of his jeans, purple juice stained his hands and mouth, and his abundant corn-coloured hair was sorely in need of a cut. Archie, eyeing him, was filled with pride.

"Hi, Dad." Dumping the baskets on to the kitchen table, Hamish groaned. "I'm starving."

"You're always starving."

Isobel, too, set down her load. "Hamish, you've been eating blackberries all afternoon." She wore her baggy corduroys and a shirt that Archie had long since discarded. "You can't be hungry."

"I am. Blackberries don't fill you up." Hamish was headed for the dresser where the cake-tins were stacked. He removed a lid with a clatter and reached for a knife.

Archie admired their harvest. "You've done frightfully well."

"We must have picked about thirty pounds. I've never seen so many. We went over to the other side of the river where Mr Gladstone grows his turnips. The hedgerows around those fields are groaning with fruit." Isobel pulled out a chair and sat down. "I'd die for a cup of tea."

Archie said, "I have news for you."

She looked up quickly, always fearing the worst. "Good news?"

"The best," he told her.

"But when did she call? What did she say? Why didn't she let us know before?" Isobel, alight with excitement, gave Archie no time to answer any question. "Why didn't they call us from Palma, or France, and give us more notice? Not that I need a moment's notice, it doesn't matter; all that matters is that they're coming. And staying at the *Ritz*. I don't think that Lucilla's ever stayed in a hotel in the whole of her life. Pandora is ridiculous. They could easily have gone somewhere a little less grand . . ."

"Pandora probably doesn't know anywhere else."

"And they're staying over the dance? And she's bringing the sheep-farmer? Do you suppose she actually persuaded Pandora to come? It's so extraordinary, after all these years, that it's taken *Lucilla* to persuade her. I'll have to get all the bedrooms ready. We'll be quite a house party because we've got that American friend of Katy's coming as well. And food. I think there are still some pheasants in the deep-freeze . . ."

They were, by now, sitting around the table and drinking tea. Hamish, in famished desperation, had put the kettle on and made this. While his parents talked, he had set the table with three mugs, the tins that contained the cakes and biscuits, and a loaf of bread on its wooden board. He had also found butter and a jar of Branston Pickle. Hamish had, just now, a passion for Branston Pickle and spread it on everything. He was, at this moment, engaged in concocting a sandwich, the dark pickle oozing out between two enormous doorsteps of bread.

". . . did she tell you about Pandora? Did she say anything at all about her?"

"Not very much. Just sounded pleased with life."

"Oh, I wish I'd been here to talk to her."

"You can talk to her tomorrow."

"Have you told anyone else they're coming?"

"No. Just you."

"I'll have to call Verena and tell her she's got three more people coming to her party. And I must tell Virginia. And Vi."

Archie reached for the teapot and refilled his mug.

"I was thinking. Perhaps it would be a good idea to ask all the Airds for lunch on Sunday? What do you say? After all, we don't know how long Pandora's going to be staying, and next week's going to be like a three-ring-circus with one thing and another. Sunday might be a good day."

"That's a brilliant idea. I'll ring Virginia. And I'll order a sirloin from the butcher."

Hamish said "Yum yum" and reached for another slice of gingerbread.

". . . and if it's a fine day we can play croquet. We haven't played croquet all summer. You'll have to cut the grass, Archie." She set down her mug, businesslike. "Now. I've got to make bramble jelly, and I'll have to get all the bedrooms ready. But I mustn't forget to ring Virginia . . ."

"I'll do that," said Archie. "You can leave that to me."

But Isobel, with the great jelly-pan set on the Aga and the blackberries simmering, knew that if she did not share her exciting news with somebody, she would burst, and so found time to call Violet. At first there was no reply from Pennyburn, so she hung up and called again half an hour later.

"Hello."

"Vi, it's Isobel."

"Oh, my dear."

"Are you busy?"

"No, I'm sitting down with a drink in my hand."

"But, Vi, it's only half past five. Have you taken to the bottle?"

"Temporarily. I've had the most exhausting day of my life, wheeling Lottie Carstairs around Relkirk and giving her tea. Never mind, it's all over now and I've done my good deed for the week. But I did feel I deserved a large whisky and soda."

"You certainly do. Or even *two* large whiskies and soda. Vi, something really exciting has happened. Lucilla rang from London and she's coming home tomorrow and she's bringing Pandora with her."

"She's bringing *who*?"

"Pandora. Archie's over the moon with delight. Just think. He's been trying to get her back to Croy for the past twenty years and now she's actually coming."

"I can't believe it."

"Incredible, isn't it? Come for lunch on Sunday and see them all. We're asking all the other Airds as well, you can come with them."

"I'd love to do that. But . . . Isobel, why did she suddenly decide to come? Pandora, I mean."

"No idea. Lucilla said something about the Steyntons' party, but it seems a fairly feeble excuse."

"How extraordinary. I . . . I . . . wonder what she will look like?"

"No idea. Probably smashing. Except that she's thirty-nine now, so there are bound to be a few wrinkles.

275

Anyway, we'll soon see for ourselves. I must go, Vi. I'm making bramble jelly and it's just about to boil over. See you Sunday."

"So kind. And I'm thrilled about Lucilla . . ."

But the bramble jelly claimed Isobel. "'Bye, Vi," And she rang off.

Pandora.

Vi put down the receiver, took off her spectacles, and rubbed her aching eyes. She had been tired before, but Isobel's news, delivered with such joy, left her with the sensation that she was being beleaguered. As though impossible demands were about to be made of her, and vital decisions would need to be taken.

She lay back in her chair and closed her eyes, wished that Edie were here, her old and dearest friend, so that she could confide, and discuss, and be comforted. But Edie was in her cottage, lumbered with Lottie, and even a telephone call was out of the question, with Lottie listening to every word and drawing her own dangerous conclusions.

Pandora. Now thirty-nine, but because Violet had not seen her since she was eighteen, she had stayed, in Violet's mind, perpetually that enchanting teenager. Like a person already dead. People who had died never aged, just stayed in the memory the way they had once been. Archie and Edmund had matured to middle age, but not Pandora.

Which was ridiculous. Everybody grew older at the same speed, like people at airports being carried along by those moving walkways. Pandora was thirty-nine and had lived a life, if all accounts were to be believed, that was anything but quiet and peaceful. Experience would have left its mark, drawing lines, wrinkling skin, dulling the bright lustre of that amazing hair.

But it was almost impossible to imagine. Violet sighed, opened her eyes, reached for her drink. This would not do. She must pull herself together. The implications of the situation had nothing to do with her. She would

276

make no decision because there was none to be made. She would simply continue to do what she had always done, which was to observe, disregard, and keep her counsel.

Edmund Aird, returning home to Balnaid from Edinburgh at seven o'clock in the evening, walked through his front door just as the telephone started to ring. Standing in the hall, he paused, but when no one immediately answered the call, he laid his briefcase down on the table and went to the library, to sit at his desk and pick up the receiver.

"Edmund Aird."

"Edmund. Archie here."

"Yes, Archie."

"Isobel asked me to call you. She wants you and Virginia and Henry to come for lunch on Sunday. We've asked Vi as well. Can you make it?"

"How very kind of Isobel. I think so . . . just a moment . . ." He reached in his pocket for his diary, laid it on the blotter, turned the pages. "As far as I'm concerned, that would be fine, but I'm only just back and I haven't spoken to Virginia yet. Do you want me to go and find her?"

"No, don't bother. You can ring me if you can't come, and if we don't hear, we'll expect you all at about a quarter to one."

"We look forward to it." Edmund hesitated. "Is this for some occasion we should know about, or just a routine invitation?"

Archie said, "No." And then said, "Yes. I mean, it is an occasion. Lucilla's coming home tomorrow . . ."

"That's great news."

"She's bringing some Australian with her."

"The sheep-farmer?"

comment on either their luck or the stunning scenery. She had known Jeff for long enough to discover that he did not appreciate, and was even embarrassed by, over-effusion.

They had set off at ten o'clock this morning, checking out of the Ritz, and watching the majestic porters load Pandora's dark-red Mercedes with her impressive array of matched luggage, along with their own humble back packs. Pandora had forgotten to tip the porters, so Lucilla had had to do it for her. She knew that she would never get it back, but after a night of total luxury with dinner and breakfast thrown in, she felt that it was the least she could do.

To begin with, Pandora had sat in the front of her magnificent car, cosy in her mink, because after the nailing heat of a Majorcan August, she felt in need of its opulent comfort. The cold and the rain were not what she had expected. While Jeff drove them out of the city, jousted with traffic, achieved the motorway, she kept up an endless stream of inconsequential chat. Later, she fell silent, gazing out of the window at the grey and dull countryside through which they swept, in the fast lane, at eighty miles an hour. The windscreen wipers worked flat out, immense juggernauts sent up blinding, muddy showers of spray, and even Lucilla had to admit that it was all thoroughly disagreeable.

"Goodness, it's ugly." Pandora snuggled deeper into her fur.

"I know. But it's just this bit."

For lunch, they stopped at a motorway service station. Pandora wanted to leave the motorway and go in search of some wayside pub, preferably thatched, where they could sit by an open fire and drink cheering concoctions like whisky and ginger ale. But Lucilla knew that if they allowed themselves to be so diverted, they would never get back to Croy.

"There isn't time. This isn't Spain, Pandora. It isn't France. We've no time to waste on frivolities."

"Darling, hardly a *frivolity*."

"Yes, it is. And you'd get talking to the barman and we'd be there for ever."

So the motorway service station it was, which proved just as unenjoyable as Lucilla had feared it would be. Queuing with trays for sandwiches and coffee; and then sitting on orange plastic chairs at a Formica table, hemmed in by irritable families with fractious children, punky youths in pornographic T-shirts, and muscular truck drivers, all seemingly content to wrap themselves around mind-boggling platefuls of fish and chips, evilly coloured trifles, and cups of tea.

After lunch, Pandora and Lucilla had changed places; Pandora had made herself comfortable on the back seat and fallen instantly asleep. She had been asleep ever since, which meant that she had missed the dramatic crossing of the border, the clearing of the sky, and the miraculous excitement of actually coming home.

They drove through a small country town. "Where's this?" Jeff asked.

"Kirkthornton."

The pavements were crammed with Saturday-afternoon shoppers, the municipal gardens bright with dahlias. Old men sat on benches enjoying the kindly warmth. Children licked ice-cream. A bridge curved high over a tumbling river. A man fished. The road led on up the hill. Pandora, bundled in mink, was curled up like a child, her head supported by Jeff's jacket rolled into a pillow. A lock of bright hair fell across her face, her lashes lay black on her jutting cheekbones.

"Do you think I should wake her up?"

"Up to you."

This had been her pattern, her routine, all through the long journey from Palma, through Spain and France. Spurts of immense energy, activity, conversation, much laughter, and sudden impetuous suggestions.

We really should see that cathedral. It's only ten kilometres out of our way.

281

Look at that delicious river. Why don't we stop for a moment and have a skinny-dip? There's no one to see.

You know, we've just passed the most enchanting café. Let's turn round and go back and have a drink.

But the drink would spin out into a long and leisurely lunch, with Pandora falling into conversation with any person who happened to be within earshot. Another bottle of wine. Coffee and cognac. And then . . . out. Sleep. She could catnap anywhere, and though this was sometimes embarrassing, it meant, at least, that she stopped talking, and Lucilla and Jeff had learned to be grateful for these respites. Without them Lucilla was not certain whether they would have survived the passage. Travelling with Pandora was a little like travelling with an ebullient child, or a dog – entertaining and companionable but quite dauntingly draining as well.

The Mercedes crested the slope. At the summit, the countryside opened and the views were magnificent. Beeches, fields, scattered farms, grazing sheep, the river far below them, the faraway hills bloomy and purple as ripe plums.

"If I don't wake her now she'll still be asleep when we get home. It's only about ten minutes away."

"Then wake her."

Lucilla stretched out her arm, laid her hand on the soft fur of Pandora's shoulder and gave her a little shake.

"Pandora."

"Um."

"Pandora." Another shake. "Wake up. We're almost there. We're almost home."

"What?" Pandora's eyes fluttered open. They stared blankly, disorientated, confused. She closed them again, yawned, stirred, stretched. "What a lovely sleep. Where are we?"

"Heading for Caple Bridge. Almost home."

"Almost home? Almost at Croy?"

"Sit up and you'll see. You've missed the best bit of the drive, snoring away on the back seat."

"I wasn't snoring. I never snore." But after a bit she made an effort and did sit up, pushing her hair out of her eyes, gathering her furs around her as though chilled. She yawned again, stared from the window. Blinked. Her eyes brightened. "But . . . we're nearly *there*!"

"I told you."

"You should have woken me hours ago. And the rain's gone. It's all sunshiny. And the green. I'd forgotten such greenness. What a welcome. 'Caledonia, stern and wild, fit nurse for a poetic child.' Who wrote that? Some stupid old fool. It's not stern and wild, it's just utterly beautiful. How perfectly sweet of it to be looking so lovely." She groped for her bag, her comb; tidied her hair. A mirror, some lipstick. A generous splash of Poison. "I must smell good for Archie."

"Don't forget about his leg. Don't expect him to come running to sweep you up in his arms. If he sweeps you up in his arms, he'll probably fall flat on his back."

"As if I'd suggest such a thing." She looked at her tiny diamond watch. "We're early. We said we'd be there at five and it's not four o'clock yet."

"We've made fantastic time."

"Dear Jeff." Pandora gave his shoulder an appreciative thump, as though she were patting a dog. "What a clever driver."

Now they were running downhill. At the bottom of the incline, they took the steep hump of Caple Bridge, turned left, and were at the start of the glen. Pandora leaned forward in her seat. "But it's amazing. Absolutely nothing seems to have changed. Some people called Miller used to live in that cottage. They were terribly old. He'd been a shepherd. They must be dead by now. They used to keep bees and sell jars of heather honey. Oh dear, I'm getting so fraught, I think I might have to stop for a pee. No, of course I don't want to. Just imagination." She gave Jeff another thump on his shoulder. "Jeff, you're doing your silent act again. Can't you think up one small word of appreciation?"

"Sure," he grinned. "It's great."

"It's more than that. It's *our* country now. The Balmerinos of Croy. Really heart-stirring, like a roll of drums. And we're coming home. We should be wearing feathers in our bonnets, and there should be a piper playing somewhere. Why didn't you think of that, Lucilla? Why didn't you arrange it? After twenty years, surely it's the least you could have done for me."

Lucilla laughed. "I'm sorry."

Now the river once more ran alongside the road, its banks verdant with green rushes, the pastures on the other side grazed by peaceful herds of Friesian cows. Harvested fields were carpets of gold in the sunlight. The Mercedes swept around the curve of the road and the village of Strathcroy came into view. Lucilla saw the cluster of grey stone houses, smoke rising straight from chimneypots, the tower of the church, the pleasing groups of ancient and shady beeches and oaks. Jeff slowed down to a prudent speed and they passed the war memorial, the small Episcopal church, and were into the long straight main street.

"The supermarket's new." Pandora sounded quite accusing.

"I know. It's run by people called Ishak. They're Pakistanis. Now, Jeff, it's here . . . turn right . . . up through the gates . . ."

"But the park's gone! It's not parkland any more. It's all ploughed up."

"Pandora, you knew that happened. Dad wrote and told you."

"I suppose I forgot. But it does look strange."

Up the back drive. The hill reared ahead of them, the tumbling waters of the Pennyburn splashed and tumbled down under the little stone bridge. Then the avenue . . .

"We're here," said Lucilla, and leaned across Jeff to put the heel of her hand on the horn.

284

At Croy, Lucilla's family filled in the long waiting hours of the afternoon. Isobel was upstairs seeing to the final details of the visitors' bedrooms, checking clean towels and arranging flowers for dressing-tables and mantelpieces. Hamish had decided to take the dogs for a walk, disappeared after lunch and had not been seen since. And Archie, Lord Balmerino, was in the dining room laying the table for dinner.

He had been finally forced into doing this. Waiting for anything or anybody was not his strong point, and as the day wore on, he had become increasingly restless, impatient, and anxious. He hated the thought of his loved ones belting up the murderous miles of the motorway, and his imagination had no difficulty at all in presenting hideously detailed pictures of pile-ups, mangled metal, and dead bodies. He had spent much time looking at his watch, going to the window at the faintest sound of a car engine, and was patently unable to settle for a moment. Isobel had suggested that he mow the croquet lawn but he had turned this down because he wanted to be certain of being on the spot when the car actually drew up in front of the house. Retreating to his study, he had sat down with *The Scotsman* but could not concentrate either on the news or the crossword. He tossed the paper aside and started prowling again.

At last Isobel, who had enough to do without her husband getting under her feet, lost her patience.

"Archie, if you can't sit still, then make yourself useful. You can lay the table for dinner. The clean mats and the napkins are on the sideboard." And she had gone upstairs quite crossly, and left him to it.

Not that he minded laying tables. In the old days, Harris used to perform the task, so there could be nothing unmanly about it. And when the American paying guests stayed, laying the table for dinner was always Archie's job, and he got a certain pleasure from doing it with military thoroughness, knives and forks precisely aligned, and napkins folded into mitres.

The wineglasses looked slightly dusty, so he had found a tea-towel and was engaged in giving them a bit of a polish when he heard the car coming up the hill. His heart lurched. He looked at the clock, which told him four o'clock. Too early surely. He set down the glass and the cloth. It could not be . . .

The blast of the car horn, a long continuous blare, tore the quiet afternoon and his own uncertainty into shreds.

Lucilla's traditional signal.

He could not move fast, but he moved as fast as he could. Down the length of the dining room, through the door.

"Isobel."

The front door stood open. He was crossing the hall as the car appeared, a thundering great Mercedes scattering gravel beneath its wheels.

"Isobel! They're here."

He got to the door but no further. Pandora was quicker than he, out of the car almost before it had drawn to a halt, running across the gravel towards him. Pandora with that same bright hair flying all over the place and those same long spindly legs.

"Archie!"

She wore a fur coat that reached almost to her ankles but that did not stop her bounding two at a time up the steps, and if he could no longer lift her off her feet and whirl her around the way he used to when she was a child, there was nothing the matter with his arms, and his arms were ready and waiting for her.

286

Isobel . . . dear, uncomplicated, hospitable, unchanging Isobel . . . had allocated Pandora the best spare bedroom. This was in the front of the house, with tall sash windows, facing south down the hill and over the glen and the river. It was furnished much as Pandora remembered it in her mother's day. Twin brass bedsteads, high off the ground, each wide as a small double bed. A faded carpet patterned with roses and an ornate dressing-table with many small drawers and a swing-mirror.

The old curtains, however, were gone, and heavy cream linen draperies hung in their place. The refurbishment had probably been planned with American paying guests in mind. They would scarcely appreciate threadbare chintz with sun-rotted linings. For them as well, the adjoining dressing-room had been converted into a bathroom. Not that it looked very different, because Isobel had simply installed a bath and a basin and a lavatory, and left the rugs, the laden bookshelves, and the comfortable armchair where they were.

Pandora was meant to be unpacking. "Unpack and make yourself comfortable," Isobel had told her. She and Jeff, between them, had humped all Pandora's luggage upstairs. (Archie, of course, could not hump luggage on account of his leg. Pandora decided not to think about Archie. His grey hairs had shocked her, and she had never seen a man so thin.) "Have a bath if you want. There's gallons of hot water. Then come down and have a drink. We'll eat about eight o'clock."

But that was fifteen minutes ago and Pandora had got no further than carrying her dressing-case into the bathroom and putting a few bottles out on the marble washstand. Her pills and potions, her Poison, bath oil, creams and cleansers. Later she would have a bath. Not now.

Now, she still had to convince herself that she was really home. Back at Croy. But it was difficult because in this room she did not feel as though she belonged. She was a guest come to stay, a bird of passage.

Abandoning her bottles, she went back to the bedroom, to the window, to lean out with her elbows on the sill, to gaze at the oft-remembered view and be quite, quite certain that it was not all a dream. This took some time. But what had happened to her own room, the room that had been Pandora's since babyhood? She decided to go and have a nose-around.

She went out of the room, went to the top of the stairs, paused. From the direction of the kitchen came cheerful domestic sounds and muted voices. Lucilla and Isobel busy with preparations for dinner and probably talking about Pandora. They were bound to talk. It did not matter; she did not mind. She crossed the landing and opened the door of what had been her parents' room, and was now Archie and Isobel's. She saw the huge double bed, the chaise longue at the foot of it with a sweater of Isobel's flung down, a pair of shoes, carelessly discarded. She saw the family photographs, the silver and crystal on the dressing-table, bedside books. There was the smell of face-powder and eau-de-cologne. Sweet and innocent scents. She closed the door and went on down the passage. She found the room that had been Archie's, swept and garnished with Jeff's back pack and his jacket set down in the middle of the carpet. The next room . . . Lucilla. Still filled with all the cherished flotsam of a schoolgirl . . . posters thumbtacked to the walls, china ornaments, a tape player, a guitar with a broken string.

And finally her own room. Her old room. Perhaps Hamish slept here? She had not yet met Hamish. Cautiously she turned the knob and pushed the door open. Not Hamish. Not anybody. Empty of any personal possession. New furniture, new curtains. No trace of Pandora.

What had they done with her books, her records, clothes, diaries, photographs . . . her *life*? All probably swept upstairs to some attic when the room was stripped and emptied, repainted, re-wallpapered, and given that beautiful new, blue, fitted carpet.

It was as though Pandora had ceased to exist, was already a ghost.

There was no point in asking why, because it was patently obvious. Croy belonged to Archie and Isobel, and to keep the place going as a viable proposition, every room must be put to good use. And Pandora had given up any claim to it by the simple act of going away and never coming back.

Standing there, she thought of those last miserable weeks when she had been beyond herself with an unhappiness that she was not allowed to talk about. Misery had made her cruel, and she was cruel to the two people she loved most in the world; snapping at her father, ignoring her mother, sulking for days on end and generally making their lives a misery, too.

In this room, she had spent hours lying face downwards on her bed with her record player churning out, over and over again, the saddest songs she knew. Matt Monro telling some female to "Walk Away". And Judy Garland tearing her guts out with "The Man That Got Away".

> The road gets tougher,
> It's lonelier and rougher,
> With hope you burn up,
> Tomorrow he will turn up . . .

Voices.
Darling, do come and eat some lunch.
I don't want any lunch.
I wish you'd tell me what's troubling you.
I just want to be left alone. It wouldn't be any good telling you. You'd never understand . . .

She saw again her mother's face, confused and dreadfully hurt. And was ashamed. At eighteen, I should have known better. I thought that I was adult and sophisticated, but the truth was that I knew less about life than a child. And it took me too long to find out.

289

Too long, and too late. All over. She closed the door and went back to her unpacking.

Dinner was over. They had sat, the six of them, around the candlelit table, and eaten their way through Isobel's lovingly prepared celebratory meal. If she had not exactly killed a fatted calf, she had gone to great pains to produce a suitable feast. Cold soup, roast pheasant, *crème brûleé*, and a splendid Stilton, all washed down by the best wine that Archie could bring up from his father's depleted cellar.

Now it was nearly ten o'clock, and Isobel, with Pandora in attendance, was in the kitchen dealing with the last of the washing-up – the pots and pans, the ivory-handled knives and vegetable dishes too large to fit into the dishwasher. Pandora was meant to be helping, but after drying up a knife or two and putting three saucepans into the wrong cupboard, she had laid aside the tea-towel, made herself a mug of Nescafé, and sat down to drink it.

Conversation during dinner had been nonstop, for there was much to hear and much to tell. The adventure of Lucilla and Jeff's bus journey down through France from Paris; their bohemian sojourn in Ibiza; and at last the bliss of Majorca and the Casa Rosa. Isobel's mouth had watered, hearing Lucilla's description of the garden there.

"Oh, I would love to see it."

"You should come. Lie in the sun and do nothing."

Archie laughed at this. "Isobel lie in the sun and do nothing? You must be mad. Before you could blink, she'd be bottoms-up in the flower-beds, tearing at weeds."

"I haven't got any weeds," said Pandora.

And then, home news. Pandora was avid for every scrap of gossip. The latest on Vi, the Airds, the Gillocks,

Willy Snoddy. Did Archie still hear from Harris and Mrs Harris? She listened with some dismay to the saga of Edie Findhorn and her cousin Lottie.

"Heavens! That ghoul. Don't say she's come back into our lives. I'm glad you warned me. I shall take pains to cross the road if I see her coming."

She was told about the Ishak family, exiled from Malawi and arriving in Strathcroy with scarcely a penny between them.

". . . but they had some relations in Glasgow who'd already managed to do quite well for themselves, and with a bit of financial help from them, they managed to take over Mrs McTaggart's newsagent's shop. You wouldn't recognise the place. It's a proper supermarket. We didn't think they'd last, but we were all mistaken. They're as industrious as ants, never seem to close their shop, and business booms. As well, we like them. They're all so helpful and kind."

And so on to the Balmerinos' slightly grander neighbours, which meant anybody living within a radius of twenty miles: the Buchanan-Wrights, the Ferguson-Crombies, the new people who had come to live at Ardnamoy; whose daughter had married; whose unlikely son had become a money-broker in the City and was coining millions.

No detail was unimportant. The only topic that was never brought up, as though by tacit agreement, was Pandora and what she had been doing with herself for the past twenty-one years.

She did not mind. She was back at Croy and for the moment that was all that mattered. The wayward years faded into unreality, like a life that had happened to another person, and surrounded by family she was happy to consign them to oblivion.

Sitting at the kitchen table, she sipped coffee and watched Isobel at the sink, scouring the roasting pan. Isobel wore red rubber gloves and a blue-and-white apron tied over her tidy dress, and it occurred to Pandora that she was an exceptional woman, peacefully labouring away and quite unresentful of the fact that the rest of her family had taken themselves off, and she was left to clear up the detritus of the meal by herself.

For, after dinner, the others had all dispersed. Archie, excusing himself, had gone down to his workshop. Hamish, with the promise of financial reward, had agreed to take advantage of the long evening light and mow the croquet lawn. He had gone to do this with good grace, and Pandora was much impressed. What she did not realise was how impressed Hamish had been by her. An aunt to stay was not an exciting prospect. Hamish had had visions of a Vi-type person with grey hair and laced-up shoes, and had received the shock of his life when he was introduced to Pandora. A stunner. Like a film star. Over his pheasant, he entertained fantasies of showing her off to the other seniors in his class at Templehall. Perhaps Dad would bring her over to watch some match or other. Hamish's stock with schoolmates would go sky-high. He wondered if she liked rugger.

"Isobel, I do love Hamish."

"I'm quite keen on him myself. I just hope he doesn't grow too enormous."

"He's going to be divinely handsome." She took another mouthful of coffee. "Do you like Jeff?'

Jeff, predictably sated by two weeks of female company and unaccustomed gracious living, had wheeled Lucilla down to the Strathcroy Arms for a restoring jar of Foster's lager downed in comfortably masculine surroundings.

"He seems really nice."

"Terribly kind. And all through that long drive, he never once lost his patience. A bit laconic, though. I

292

suppose all Australians are strong and silent. I wouldn't really know. Never met any others."

"Do you think Lucilla's in love with him?"

"No, I don't think so. They're just . . . that awful phrase . . . very good friends. Besides, she's terribly young. You don't want to start thinking about permanent relationships when you're only nineteen."

"You mean marriage."

"No, darling. I don't mean marriage."

Isobel fell silent. Pandora decided that she had, perhaps, said the wrong thing and cast about for a more amusing and less touchy topic. "Isobel, I know who you haven't told me about. Dermot Honeycombe and Terence. Are they still running the antique shop?"

"Oh dear." Isobel turned from the sink. "Didn't Archie tell you in one of his letters? So sad. Terence died. About five years ago."

"I don't believe it. What did poor Dermot do? Find himself another nice young man?"

"No, never. He was heartbroken, but faithful. We all thought he might leave Strathcroy, but he stayed; all by himself. Still running the antique shop, still living in their little cottage. Every now and then he asks Archie and me over for a meal, and gives us tiny helpings of frightfully dainty food with amusing sauces. Archie always comes home starving and has to be given soup or cornflakes before he goes to bed."

"Poor Dermot. I must go and see him."

"He'd love that. He's always asking after you."

"I can buy some trinket from him to give Katy Steynton for her birthday. We haven't talked about that either. The dance, I mean." Isobel, finished at last, pulled off her rubber gloves, laid them on the draining board, and came to sit down with her sister-in-law. "Are we going to be a huge house party?"

"No. Just us. No Hamish because he'll be back at school. And some sad American Katy met in London and took pity on. Verena hasn't got space for him, so he's coming here."

"Goodness! How nice. A man for me. Why is he sad?"

"His wife's just died."

"Oh dear, I hope he's not too gloomy. Where's he going to sleep?"

"In your old bedroom."

Which settled that question. "And what about the night of the party? Where are we having dinner?"

"Here, I think. We could ask the Airds to join us, and Vi. They're coming for lunch tomorrow; I thought I'd speak to Virginia then."

"You never said."

"What, that they're coming for lunch? Well, I've told you now. That's why Hamish is cutting the croquet lawn."

"Lovely afternoon entertainment, all laid on. What are you going to wear for the dance? Have you got a new dress?"

"No. I've run out of money. I had to buy Hamish five new pairs of shoes for school . . ."

"But, Isobel, you must have a new dress. We'll go and find one for you. Where shall we go? To Relkirk. We'll have a day out . . ."

"Pandora, I told you . . . I really can't afford it."

"Oh, darling, the least I can do is stand you a little gift." The back door opened and Hamish appeared, having finished his mowing just before darkness fell, and once again in his usual state of ravenous hunger. "We'll talk about it later."

Hamish collected his snack. A bowl of Weetabix, a glass of milk, a handful of chocolate biscuits. Pandora finished her coffee, set down the mug. She yawned. "I think I must go to bed. I'm bushed." She got to her feet. "Goodnight, Hamish."

She did not attempt to kiss him and Hamish was torn between relief and disappointment.

"Will I find Archie in his workshop? I'll just pop down

and have a word." She stooped and kissed Isobel. "And goodnight to you, darling. Heaven to be here. Delicious dinner. See you all in the morning."

In the basement, Archie, absorbed and concentrated, worked by a strong bulb with a wide shade that threw a bright circle on to his workbench. Painting the carving of Katy and her dog was both tricky and fiddly. The muted check of the skirt, the texture of the sweater, the subtle, varying streaks of colour in the hair, each presented a challenge and took all his dexterity to accomplish.

He laid down one sable brush and took up another, then heard Pandora approach. Her step was unmistakable, descending the stone stair that led down from the kitchens, as was the sharp tap of her high heels down the ill-lighted stone-flagged passage. He paused in his work to look up and saw the door open and Pandora's head come around the edge of it.

"Am I interrupting?"

"No."

"Goodness, it's gloomy. I couldn't find the light switch. Like a dungeon. But I must say, you're quite cosy in here." She found a chair and sat beside him. "What are you doing?"

"Painting."

"I can see that. What a charming little statue. Where did you get it?"

He told her, not without pride. "I made it."

"You made it? Archie, you are brilliant. I never knew you were so handy."

"It's for Katy's birthday. It's her. With her dog."

"What a lovely idea. You didn't used to be able to make things. It was always Pa who glued our toys together and mended broken china. Did you go to classes or something?"

"I suppose I did. After I was wounded . . ." He corrected himself. "After my leg was shot off and when I was finally discharged from hospital, I got sent to Headley Court. That's the Forces rehabilitation centre for chaps who've been disabled. Dismembered in some way. That's where they fit the artificial limbs. Legs, arms, hands, feet. Anything that you are missing is supplied for you. Within, of course, reason. And then they give you months of bloody hell until you've learned to use it properly."

"It doesn't sound very nice."

"It was all right. And there was always some poor bugger worse off than yourself."

"But you were alive. You weren't dead."

"True."

"Is it very horrible, having a tin leg?"

"Better than none at all, which seems to be the alternative."

"I never heard how it happened."

"Better not."

"Was it a nightmare?"

"All violence is a nightmare."

Forbidden ground. She backed off. "I'm sorry . . . go on telling me."

"Well . . . once I . . ." He had lost the thread of what he had been saying. He took off his spectacles, rubbed his eyes with his fingers. "Once . . . I was more or less ambulant, they taught me how to use a treadle jigsaw. Occupational therapy and good exercise for the leg. And from that, it sort of snowballed . . ."

It was all right. The dangerous moment was safely over. If Archie did not want to talk about Northern Ireland, then Pandora did not want to hear.

"Do you mend things, like Pa used to?"

"Yes."

"And that dear little figure. How do you start to make something like that? Where do you begin?"

"You start with a block of wood."

"What kind of wood?"

"For this one, I used beech. Beech from Croy, a wind-blown branch from years back. I squared it off into a block with the chainsaw. Then I made two drawings from the photograph, a front view and a side view. Then I transferred the front elevation on to the face of the block, and the side elevation on to the side of the block. Are you with me?"

"All the way."

"Then I cut it out on the band saw."

"What's a band saw?"

He pointed, "That's the band saw. It's electrically operated and lethally sharp, so don't start fiddling."

"I wasn't going to. What do you do then?"

"Start carving. Whittling."

"What with?"

"Woodcarver's chisels. A penknife."

"I'm amazed. Is this the first you've done?"

"By no means, but this was more difficult because of the composition. The girl sitting and the dog. That was quite difficult. Before, they've been standing figures. Soldiers mostly, in various regimental uniforms. I get the details of the uniforms from a book of plates I found up in Pa's library. It was that book that gave me the idea. They make quite good wedding presents if the bridegroom happens to be in the Army."

"Have you got any to show me?"

"Yes. There's one here." He pulled himself out of his chair, went to a cupboard, took out a box. "I didn't actually give this one away because I wasn't quite satisfied with it, so I made another. But it'll give you an idea . . ."

Pandora took the figure of the soldier from him and turned it in her hands. It was a replica of an officer in the Black Watch, every detail perfect – from brogues, to kilt, to the red hackle in his khaki bonnet. She thought it perfect and was filled with wordless admiration for

297

Archie's unsuspected talent, his precision, his undeniable artistry.

Also incredulous. "Do you mean to say you *give* these away? Archie, you're dotty. They're beautiful. Unique. Visitors from overseas would snap up just such a souvenir. Have you ever tried selling them?"

"No." He seemed quite surprised at the idea.

"Have you ever thought of it?"

"No."

She knew a burst of sisterly irritation. "You are hopeless. You always were a laid-back old stick, but this is ridiculous. There's Isobel slaving away, trying to keep everything going by having strings of Americans to stay, and you could be churning these things out and making a fortune."

"I doubt that. Anyway, it's not a case of churning. They take a lot of time."

"Well, get someone to help you. Get two people to help you. Start a little home industry."

"I haven't the space down here."

"What about the stables? They're empty. Or one of the barns?"

"It would mean reconstruction, equipping, electricity laid on, safety regulations, fire precautions."

"So?"

"So it would cost money. Which is a commodity pretty thin on the ground."

"Could you get a grant?"

"Grants, as well, are thin on the ground just now."

"You could *try* for one. Oh, don't be so hopeless, Archie. Be a bit more enterprising. I think it's the most wonderful idea."

"Pandora, you were always full of wonderful ideas." He took the soldier from her and laid him back in his box. "But you're right about Isobel. I do what I can to help, but I know she's got far too much on her plate. Before Northern Ireland, I thought about trying to get some sort of a job . . . as a factor, or something. I don't know who'd have employed me but I didn't want to leave Croy, and it seemed the only sort of work I could do . . . " His voice, ruminating, trailed to silence.

"But now you've learned a new trade. All this. Hidden talents have sprung to life. All you need is a little enterprise and a lot of determination."

"And a lot of money."

"Archie" – she spoke quite crossly – "whether you have one leg or two, you can't just shed responsibility."

"Are you speaking from experience?"

"*Touché.*" Pandora laughed and shook her head. "No. I'm the last to preach. Just talking off the top of my head." Abruptly, she abandoned the argument, yawned and stretched, reached upwards, spreading her fingers. "I'm tired. I came to say goodnight. I'm going to bed."

"I hope you have sweet dreams."

"What about you?"

"I want to get this finished and done with. Then, every spare moment I have I shall be able to spend with you."

"Dear man." On her feet, she stooped to kiss him. "I'm glad I came home."

"Me too."

She went to the door, opened it, hesitated, and turned back.

"Archie?"

"What is it?"

"I've often wondered. Did you get that letter I sent you in Berlin?"

"Yes."

"You never replied."

"By the time I'd decided what I was going to say, you'd gone to America and it was too late."

"Did you tell Isobel?"

"No."

"Did you . . . speak to anybody?"

"No."

"I see." She smiled. "The Airds are coming for lunch tomorrow."

"I know. I asked them."

"Goodnight, Archie."

"Goodnight."

The evening slipped into night. The house settled as the momentum of another busy day wound itself down. Hamish watched television for a bit and then made his way upstairs. Isobel, in the kitchen, laid the table for breakfast – the last chore of the day – and then let the dogs out for their last sniff around the dark garden, alert for scents of marauding rabbit. Lights were turned off, and she too headed for bed. Later still Jeff and Lucilla returned from the village. They let themselves in through the back door. Archie heard their voices above him in the hall. And then silence.

Past midnight, and he was finally finished. Another day and the enamel would be dry. He tidied up, put lids on small paint-pots, cleaned his brushes, turned off the light and closed the door. Slowly he made his way down the shadowy passage and up the stairs to do his nightly rounds, which he called putting the house to bed. He checked locks on doors and snibs on windows, fire-guards and electrical plugs. In the kitchen, he found the dogs asleep. He filled a tumbler with water and drank it. Finally he trod up the stairs.

But he did not go immediately to his own bedroom. Instead he walked down the passage and saw the shaft of light, still burning, beneath the door of Lucilla's room. He tapped and opened the door and found her in bed, reading by lamplight.

"Lucilla."

She looked up, marked her page and laid her book aside. "I thought you'd gone to bed hours ago."

"No. I've been working." He came to sit on the edge of her bed. "Did you have a good evening?"

"Yes, it was fun. Toddy Buchanan in his usual good form."

"I wanted to say goodnight, and I wanted to say thank you."

"What for?"

"Coming home. Bringing Pandora."

His hand lay on her eiderdown. She laid her own on top of it. Isobel's nightgowns were white lawn trimmed with lace, but Lucilla slept in a green T-shirt with "Save the Rain Forests" printed across the chest. Her long dark hair was spread like silk on her pillow, and he was filled with love for her.

"You're not disappointed?" she asked him.

"Why should I be disappointed?"

"Often when you've looked forward to something for years, you feel a bit let down when it actually happens."

"I don't feel let down."

"She is beautiful."

"But dreadfully thin, don't you think?"

"I know. There's nothing of her. But she's so hyper that she burns everything up."

"What do you mean?"

"Just that. She sleeps a lot, but when she's awake she's charging on every cylinder. Supercharging, I would say. Being with her all the time is really quite exhausting. And then she passes out as though sleep is the only thing that's going to top up her batteries."

"She was always like that. Mrs Harris used to say, 'That Pandora. Either up in the clouds or doon in the midden.'"

"Manic-depressive."

"Surely not as bad as that."

"Tending that way."

He frowned. And then asked the question that had been niggling around at the back of his mind all evening. "You don't think she's on drugs?"

"Oh, Dad."

He immediately wished that he had not mentioned his fears. "I only ask you because I imagine you know more about these things than I do."

"She's certainly not a junkie. But perhaps she does take something to bubble her along. A lot of people do."

"But she's not addicted?"

"Oh, Dad, I don't know. But worrying about Pandora isn't going to do any good. You've just got to accept her for what she is. The person she's turned into. Have fun with her. Lots of laughs."

"In Majorca . . . do you think she's happy?"

"She seems to be. And why not? A heavenly house, a garden, a pool, lots of money . . ."

"Does she have friends?"

"She has Seraphina and Mario, who take care of her . . ."

"That wasn't what I meant."

"I know. No, we didn't meet her friends, so I don't know if she has any or not. We didn't really meet anybody. Except one man. He was there the day we arrived, but after that we never saw him again."

"I thought she would have a resident lover."

"I think probably he was her lover and the reason he didn't come back was because we were there." Archie said nothing to this, and Lucilla smiled. "It's a different world out there, Dad."

"I know that. I know."

She put her arms around his neck and pulled him down and kissed him. She said, "You mustn't worry."

"I won't."

"Goodnight, Dad."

"Goodnight, my darling. God bless you."

25

Sunday the Eleventh

Sunday morning. Overcast, very still, very quiet, hushed with the weekly inertia of a Scottish Sabbath. It had rained during the night, leaving puddles by the roadside and gardens dripping with moisture. In Strathcroy, cottages slumbered, curtains stayed drawn. Slowly the occupants stirred, rose, opened doors, lit fires, made cups of tea. Plumes of peat-smoke rose, straight, from chimneypots. Dogs were walked, hedges clipped, cars washed. Mr Ishak opened up his shop for the sale of morning rolls, milk, cigarettes, Sunday newspapers, and any other commodity that a family might need to get through the empty day. From the tower of the Presbyterian church, the bell tolled.

At Croy, Hamish and Jeff were downstairs before anyone else and, between them, cooked their own breakfast. Bacon and eggs, sausages and tomatoes, racks of fresh toast, marmalade and honey, all washed down with large cups of very strong tea. Isobel, descending later, found their dirty breakfast dishes stacked by the sink, and a note from Hamish.

Dear Mum. Jeff and me have taken the dogs up to the loch. He wants to see it. Back about twelve thirty. In time for beef.

Isobel made coffee, sat and drank it, thought about peeling potatoes, making a pudding. She wondered if there was enough cream for a fool. Lucilla appeared, and finally Archie, wearing his good tweed suit because it was his day to read the lesson in church. Neither his wife nor his daughter offered to accompany him. With ten people for lunch, they had more than enough to do.

Pandora slept the morning through and did not put in an appearance until a quarter past twelve, by which time all the hard work in the kitchen had been accomplished. It was instantly clear, however, that she had not been idle, but busy titivating: painting her nails, washing her hair, doing her face, splashing herself in Poison. She wore a jersey dress patterned in diamonds of brilliant colour; it was so fine and supple and elegant that it had to be Italian. Discovering Lucilla in the library, she swore that she had slept the night through, but seemed perfectly happy to sink into the depths of an armchair and gratefully accept the offer of a glass of sherry.

At Pennyburn, Vi sat up in her bed, drank her early morning tea, and planned her day. She should perhaps go to church. There was plenty to pray for. She thought about this and then decided against it. Instead, self-indulgence. She would stay where she was, conserving her energy. She'd finish her current book and then, after a late breakfast, sit at her desk to deal with overdue bills, pension funds, and that incomprehensible demand from the Inland Revenue. For lunch, she had been invited to Croy. Edmund, with Virginia and Henry, would pick her up and drive her on up the hill.

She thought about this with more disquiet than delight and gazed from the window and assessed the mood of the weather: rain all night but now damp and still and muggy. Perhaps later it would cheer up. It was the sort of day, in more ways than one, that needed to be cheered up. For comfort, she decided, she would wear her grey wool. For courage, the new Hermès scarf.

At Balnaid, Virginia went in search of Henry.

"Henry, come and change."

He was on the floor of his playroom, constructing Space Lego, and resented the interruption. "Why do I have to change?"

"Because we're going out for lunch and you can't go looking like that."

"Why can't I?"

"Because your jeans are dirty, and your T-shirt's dirty, and your shoes are dirty, and you are dirty."

"Do I have to *dress up*?"

"No, but you have to put on a clean T-shirt and a clean pair of jeans and a clean pair of sneakers."

"What about socks?"

"Clean socks."

He sighed, hard done by. "Do I have to put my Space Lego away?"

"No, of course you don't have to. Leave it where it is. Just come, or Daddy'll start getting impatient."

She led him, lagging, to his bedroom, then sat on his bed and stripped off his T-shirt.

"Will there be any other children there?"

"Hamish."

"He won't want to play with me."

"Henry, you're such a ninny about Hamish. If you don't behave like a ninny, he'll like playing with you. Take off your jeans and your trainers."

"Who's going to be there?"

"Us. And Vi. And the Balmerinos. And Lucilla because she's come home from France. And her friend. He's called Jeff. And Pandora."

"Who's Pandora?"

"Archie's sister."

"Do I know her?"

"No."

"Do you know her?"

"No."

"Does Daddy know her?"

"Yes. He knew her when she was a little girl. Vi knows her too."

"Why don't you know her?"

"Because she's been living abroad for a long, long time. She lived in America. This is the first time she's come back to Croy."

"Does Alexa know her?"

"No. Alexa was only a tiny baby when she went to America."

"Does Pandora know your gramps and grandma at Leesport?"

"No. They live in Long Island, and Pandora lived in California. That's right over the other side of the United States."

"Does Edie know her?"

"Yes. Edie knew her when she was a little girl as well."

"What does she look like?"

"Heavens above, Henry, I've never met her, so I can't tell you. But you know that picture in the dining room at Croy? Of the pretty girl? Well, that's Pandora when she was young."

"I hope she's still pretty."

"You like pretty ladies."

"Well, I certainly don't like ugly ones." He screwed up his face, making a monster grimace. "Like that Lottie Carstairs."

Despite herself, Virginia had to laugh. "You know something, Henry Aird, you'll be the death of me. Now, hand me your hairbrush, and then go and wash your hands."

From the foot of the stairs, Edmund called, "Virginia."

"We're on our way!"

He waited for them, dressed for the occasion in grey flannels, a country shirt, a club tie, a blue cashmere pullover, his chestnut-polished Gucci loafers.

"We should go."

Reaching his side, Virginia kissed him. "You're looking handsome, Mr Aird. Did you know that?"

"You're not looking so gruesome yourself. Come along, Henry."

They got into the BMW and drove. They stopped for a moment in the village, where Edmund went into Mr Ishak's and emerged with the bulky wodge of the Sunday newspapers. Then on to Pennyburn.

Vi heard them coming and was ready for them, on the point of locking her front door. Edmund leaned over to open the car door for her and she got in beside him. Henry thought she was looking very smart and told her so.

"Thank you, Henry. This is the pretty scarf your mother brought me from London."

"I know. She brought me a cricket bat and a ball."

"You showed me."

"And she brought Edie a cardigan. Edie loves it. She says she's keeping it for best. It's sort of pinky blue."

"Lilac," Virginia told him.

"Lilac." He said the word over to himself because it had a pleasant sound. Lilac.

The powerful car left Pennyburn behind and sped on up the hill.

Arriving, they found Archie's old Land-Rover parked in front of the house. As Edmund drew up alongside and the Aird family disgorged from his car, Archie appeared at the open front door, come to greet them. They made their way up the steps.

"Well, here you are."

"You're looking very formal, Archie," Edmund told him. "I hope I'm not underdressed."

"Been to church. Read the lesson. I thought about

changing into something a little less stuffy, but now you've arrived so there isn't time. So you'll have to take me as I am. Vi. Virginia. Lovely to see you. Hello, Henry, good morning. How are you? Hamish is in his bedroom getting cleaned up. He's set his Scalectrix Road Race up on the floor of the playroom. If you want to go and have a look at it . . ."

The suggestion, casually made, was adroit and caught Henry's attention, as Archie knew it would. He had no qualms about his son, who had been warned that Henry was coming, and had it made clear to Hamish that he was to behave towards this small guest in an hospitable fashion.

As for Henry, it took only an instant to remember that Hamish, provided there was nobody else around to claim his attention, could be quite good company, even though Henry was four years younger. And Henry hadn't got a Scalectrix Road Race. It was one of the things he was thinking of putting on his Christmas list.

His face brightened. He said "All right" and set off at a fast clip, up the stairs, leaving the grown-ups to their own devices.

"Brilliant," murmured Vi, as though to herself. And then: "What sort of a congregation did you have this morning?"

"Sixteen, including the rector."

"I should have been there to swell the throng. Now I'm going to have a conscience for the rest of the day . . ."

"But it's not all bad news. The Bishop's come up trumps and ferreted out some obscure trust, set up years ago. He thinks he can wangle a sizy sum from that, which would pay off the balance of the bill for the electrics . . ."

"Wouldn't that be splendid?"

"But," said Virginia, "I thought that was why we had the church sale . . ."

"We can always divert funds . . ."

Edmund made no comment. It had been a long morning, deliberately filled with small and insignificant tasks that nevertheless had been demanding his attention for some weeks. Letters written, accounts paid, a query from his chartered accountant clarified and answered. Now, he found himself dealing with a growing impatience. At the far end of the wide hallway, the double doors of the library stood invitingly open. He looked forward to a gin and tonic, but Archie, Virginia, and Vi, loosely grouped at the foot of the stairs, had become absorbed by churchly problems. In these Edmund had little interest, having always taken great pains never to become involved.

". . . of course, we do need new kneelers."

"Vi, paying for the coke for the boiler is more urgent than new kneelers . . ."

The real reason for their coming to Croy appeared to have been forgotten by his wife and his mother. Stifling his irritation, Edmund listened. And then did not listen. Another sound caught his attention. From the library came the tap of high heels. He looked up, over the top of Virginia's head. Saw Pandora emerge.

Watching, assessing the situation, she paused, framed by the open doorway. Across the long space that divided them, her eyes met Edmund's. He forgot his impatience and found words flowing through his brain as though he had been abruptly asked to produce some sort of a report and was frantically searching for, and then abandoning, suitable adjectives with which to state his case: older, thinner, attenuated, elegant, *mondaine*, amoral, experienced. Beautiful.

Pandora. He would have seen her, recognised her, known her anywhere in the world. Still those wide and watchful eyes, the curving mouth with its provocative mole at the corner of her upper lip. The features, the bone structure, were untouched by the years that had passed, the profusion of chestnut hair still youthful.

He felt his face freeze. He could not smile. As though he were a gun dog pointing at a bird, the quality of his

309

stillness, his silence, obscurely reached the others. Their attention wandered, their voices died away. Vi turned her head.

"Pandora."

The church and its affairs were abandoned. She moved away from Virginia's side, across the polished parquet, her backview erect, her arms outflung, her bulging leather handbag dangling by its strap from her elbow. "Pandora, my dearest child. What a joy. What a delight to see you again."

". . . but Isobel, you can't possibly have us all for dinner. That's far too many."

"No. If my counting's right, we'll be eleven. That's only one more than we are now."

"Has Verena not lumbered you with people to stay?"

"Just one man . . ."

Pandora chipped in. "He's known as 'The Sad American' because Isobel can't remember what his name is."

"Poor chap," said Archie from the head of the table. "Sounds as though he's doomed before he's even arrived."

"Why is he sad?" asked Edmund, reaching for his glass of lager. At Croy, wine was never served at luncheon. This was not for any reason of parsimony but because of a family tradition, going back to Archie's parents, and his grandparents before that. Archie upheld it because he thought it a sound idea. Wine was apt to render guests both garrulous and comatose, and Sunday afternoons, in his opinion, were made to be spent in useful outdoor activities, not snoozing over the newspapers in some armchair.

"He probably isn't sad at all," Isobel told him. "He's probably a very sensible, cheerful fellow, but he's been

310

recently widowed and he's taken a couple of months off, and has come over here for a bit of a break."

"Does Verena know him?"

"No. But Katy does. She felt sorry for him and asked Verena to send him an invitation."

Pandora said, "I do hope he's not dreadfully solemn and sincere. You know how they can be. Show them round a sewage works and they'll go into polite ecstasies. Swearing it was all very very interesting, and wanting to know when it was built."

Archie laughed. "Pandora, how many times have you shown an American around a sewage works?"

"Oh, darling, never. Just giving a tiny example."

They sat around the dining-room table. The tender roast beef, perfectly cooked and pink in the middle, had been appreciatively consumed, along with fresh beans, fresh peas, roast potatoes, horseradish sauce, and dark gravy delicately laced with red wine. Now they were on to Isobel's blackberry fool and hot syrup tart, drooling with fresh cream.

Out of doors, the day, like a fickle woman, had ceased to sulk and decided, for no obvious reason, to brighten up. A wind had risen, freshening the air. From time to time, lozenges of sunlight fell upon the polished table, sparkling from silver and cut-glass tumblers.

"Well, if we all come to dinner," Virginia firmly led the conversation back to essentials, "you must let me help. I'll make a starter, or a pudding, or something."

"That would help," Isobel admitted. "Because the whole of the day before I'm going to be up at Corriehill helping Verena with the flowers."

"But that's my birthday." Vi was quite indignant. "That's the day of my picnic."

"I know, Vi, and I'm sorry, but for the first time in years I'm not going to be able to be there."

"Well, I hope nobody else is going to back out. You haven't got to go and do flowers, have you, Virginia?"

311

"No. I've just been asked to lend my biggest flower-pots and vases. But I can take them all up to Corriehill on Wednesday."

"When does Alexa arrive?" Lucilla asked.

"On Thursday morning. She and Noel are going to drive overnight. Noel can't get off before that. And of course they're bringing Alexa's dog. So *they*'ll all be at the picnic, Vi."

"I shall have to start writing all this down," said Vi, "otherwise I shall lose count and produce far too much food or too little." She leaned forward and looked down the length of the table to catch Henry's eye. Henry's expression was gloomy. He did not like people talking about Vi's birthday when they all knew he would not be there. She said, "I shall post two huge slices of birthday cake over to Templehall. One for Henry and one for Hamish."

"Well, make sure it's a cake that doesn't go squishy." Hamish scraped the last spoonful of syrup tart out of his plate. "Mum sent me a cake once and all the cream oozed out through the parcel, and Matron was livid. She threw the whole lot into the Sickbay dustbin."

"Mean old Matron," said Pandora sympathetically.

"She's a cow. Mum, can I have some more?"

"Yes, but hand it round first."

Hamish got to his feet and went to do this, a dish in either hand.

Lucilla said, "*We* have a small problem." Everybody looked at her, interested to know what it was but not particularly concerned. "Jeff hasn't got anything to wear. To the dance, I mean."

Eyes were now turned on Jeff, who had sat through the meal without taking much part in any conversation. He looked faintly abashed and seemed pleased for the diversion of Hamish arriving at his side with the offer of second helpings of pudding. He turned to dip the spoon into what remained of the blackberry fool.

312

He said, "When I left Australia I never thought I'd be asked to a formal do. Besides, there wasn't space in my back pack for a dinner jacket."

They all considered the problem.

Archie said, "I'd lend you mine, only I'm wearing it myself."

"Dad, yours wouldn't even go round Jeff."

"He could always hire one. There are places in Relkirk . . ."

"Oh, Dad, they're dreadfully expensive."

Archie was humbled. "Sorry. I wouldn't know."

Across the table, Edmund eyed the young Australian. "You're about the same size as I am. I'll lend you something if you like."

Violet, hearing this, was taken aback. Sitting next to her son, she turned her head to look at him. He seemed unaware of her piercing regard, and his profile, composed and unsmiling, gave nothing away. Trying to analyse her unmotherly astonishment, she realised that the truth of it was that she had never expected Edmund to come up with such a kindly and impetuous suggestion.

But why? He was her son, the child of Geordie. She knew that where important issues were concerned he would never be anything but generous – with both time and money – concerned and considerate. Violet could turn to him – and had done so many times – knowing that he would go to endless trouble to sort out a problem or help her make a decision.

But little things . . . little things were different, the small gesture, the tender word, the trivial gift that had cost nothing but a few pence and a moment of time, but was significant because of the thought behind it. Her eyes strayed across the table to Virginia and the heavy gold bracelet that she wore around her wrist. Edmund had given her that bracelet – and Violet did not like to think what it had cost – like a tube of glue, to patch up their disagreement. But how much better had they not

313

quarrelled in the first place, and so spared themselves weeks of unhappiness.

And now he was offering Lucilla's Jeff a favour. It would be no hardship to him, but the offer had been made so spontaneously that Violet was reminded of Geordie. Which should have filled her with pleasure, but instead left her sad because she could not remember when she had last looked at Edmund and recognised any characteristic inherited from his gentle father.

As for Jeff, he seemed as disconcerted as she was herself.

"No. I couldn't impose. I'll just hire something."

"No skin off my nose. I've some spare things at Balnaid. You can try them on, see how they fit."

"But won't you need them yourself?"

"I shall be decked out, like the man on a shortbread tin, in my kilt."

Lucilla, however, was deeply grateful. "You are a saint, Edmund. What a relief. Now all I have to do is find some garment to wear."

"Isobel and I are going shopping for finery in Relkirk," Pandora told her. "Why don't you come too?"

Lucilla, surprising everybody, said, "I'd love to." But their surprise was short-lived. "There's a wonderful market in Relkirk, and a stall stuffed with glorious 1930s tat. I'm sure I'll find something there."

"Yes," said her mother. "I am quite sure that you will."

"Dad, you are a brute! You've bashed me right into the rhododendrons."

"I wanted to get you out of the way."

"You didn't need to hit me *quite* so far."

"Yes, I did. You're far too cunning a player to be left

jostling around the hoop. Now, Virginia, you need to come just *here*."

"Which blade of grass did you have in mind?"

Isobel's lunch party, with coffee drunk, had amicably dispersed. The boys, abandoning Scalectrix, had gone to play in Hamish's tree-house, and swing on his trapeze. Isobel had taken Vi to look at her border . . . not as grand or imposing as it had been in the old days but still something that she was always quite proud to show off and have admired. Archie, Virginia, Lucilla, and Jeff had decided to take advantage of Hamish's labour and were engaged in a needle contest of croquet. Edmund and Pandora sat in the old swing-seat at the top of the grassy bank and watched them.

It had turned into a pleasant and blowy afternoon. Clouds, in layers, drifted across the sky, but there were wide patches of blue in between, and when the sun shone, it became very warm. Despite this, Pandora, on her way out into the garden, had collected from the cloakroom an old shooting jacket of Archie's, oiled khaki and lined with hairy tweed. Bundled in this garment, she sat with her legs tucked up beneath her. From time to time Edmund gave a push with his foot to set the old seat swinging. It needed to be oiled and made a hideous squeaking sound.

A wail from the middle of the rhododendrons. "I can't find the beastly ball and I've been scratched by a bramble."

"In a moment," Edmund observed, "family fur is going to fly."

"It always did. It's a lethal game."

They fell silent, rocking gently to and fro. Virginia took a swipe at her ball, which rolled placidly at least four yards beyond the spot that Archie had been indicating.

"Oh, sorry, Archie."

"You hit it too hard."

"Nothing," said Edmund, "is so obvious as the obvious remark."

315

Pandora made no comment. Squeak, squeak went the swing.

They watched in silence while Jeff played his shot. She said, "Do you hate me, Edmund?"

"No."

"But you despise me? Think little of me?"

"Why should I do that?"

"Because I made such a mess of everything. Running off with another woman's husband, and he old enough to be my father. Leaving no word of explanation, breaking my parents' hearts, never coming back. Sending waves of shock and horror to reverberate around the country."

"Is that what happened?"

"You know it is."

"I wasn't here at the time."

"Of course. You were in London."

"I never found out why you went flying off."

"I was miserable. I didn't know what to do with my life. Archie had gone and was married to Isobel, and I missed him. There didn't seem to be any way to turn. And then along came a little diversion, and it all seemed frightfully glamorous and grown-up. Exciting. My ego needed a boost and that's what he provided."

"How did you meet him?"

"Oh, at some party. He had a horse-faced wife called Gloria, but she scarpered pretty sharpish as soon as she saw the way the wind was blowing. Went off to Marbella and never returned. Which was another reason for eloping to California."

Lucilla, with bits of leaf in her hair, emerged from the rhododendrons and rejoined the game. "Who's been through the hoop, and who hasn't?"

The seat, gradually, stopped swinging. Edmund gave another push and started it up again. Squeak, squeak.

Pandora said, "Are you happy?"

"Yes."

"I don't think I was ever happy."

316

"I'm sorry."

"I liked being rich but I wasn't happy. I was homesick and I missed the dogs. Do you know what he was called, the man I ran away with?"

"I don't think I was ever told."

"Harald Hogg. Can you imagine anybody eloping with a man called Harald Hogg? After our divorce, the first thing I did was to change my name back to Blair. So I didn't keep his name, but I did keep most of his money. So lucky, to be divorced in California."

Edmund said nothing.

"And then, when it was all over, and after I'd changed my name back to Blair, do you know what I did?"

"I have no idea."

"I went to New York. I'd never been there before, didn't know anybody. But I checked in at the classiest hotel I could find and then I walked down Fifth Avenue and knew that anything I wanted I could buy. For myself. And then I didn't buy anything. That's a sort of happiness, isn't it, Edmund? Knowing that you can buy anything you want and then discovering that you don't want it."

"Are you happy now?"

"I'm home."

"Why did you come back?"

"Oh, I don't know. Reasons. Lucilla and Jeff were there to drive me. I wanted to see Archie again. And then, of course, the irresistible lure of Verena Steynton's party."

"I have a feeling that Verena Steynton has little to do with it."

"Perhaps. But it's a nice excuse."

"You never came home when your parents died."

"That was unforgivable, wasn't it?"

"You said it, Pandora. I didn't."

"I wasn't brave enough. I didn't have the nerve. I couldn't face funerals, graves, condolences. I couldn't face anybody. And death is so final, just as youth is so sweet. I couldn't bear to accept that it was all over."

"Are you happy in Majorca?"

"I'm home there too. All these years, and the Casa Rosa is the first home I've actually owned."

"Are you going back?"

All the time they had been talking, they had not looked at each other. Instead, they had watched, with patent intent, the croquet players. But now he turned to face her, and her head came around and her remarkable eyes, fringed with thick black lashes, stared into his own. Perhaps it was because she had become so painfully thin, but they seemed to Edmund more enormous and lustrous than they had ever been.

She said, "Why do you ask?"

"I don't know."

"Perhaps I don't know either."

She laid her head back on the faded striped cushions and returned her attention to the croquet. Their conversation, such as it was, appeared to be over. Edmund watched his wife. She stood in the middle of the verdant lawn, leaning on her mallet, while Jeff lined up to play a tricky shot. She wore a checked shirt and a short blue denim skirt, and her legs were long and bare and brown, and her canvas sneakers very white. Fit, slender, bursting into laughter at Jeff's abortive attempt to get his ball through the hoop, she radiated the sort of vitality that Edmund associated with glossy magazine advertisements for sports clothes, Rolex watches, or suntan oil.

Virginia. My love, he told himself. My life. But for some reason the words were empty as incantations that were never going to work, and he found himself racked by despair. Pandora had fallen silent. He could not imagine what she was thinking about. He turned to look at her and it took him no time at all to realise that she was fast asleep.

So much for his entertaining company. He was torn between chagrin and amusement, and this healthy reaction to her perfidy served to fend off for the time being the deadly sensation that he had come to the end of his rope.

26

Monday the Twelfth

Monday was one of Edie's mornings for helping Virginia at Balnaid, and Virginia was grateful for this arrangement. She had never relished Mondays, with the weekend over and Edmund gone from her once more, dressed in his city suit, and leaving the house at eight o'clock in order to get into Edinburgh and his office before the worst of the rush-hour traffic. His departure left an emptiness, a flatness, a sense of anticlimax, and it was always something of an effort to get down to day-to-day living again and cope with all the tedious demands of simply keeping the house going. But hearing the bang of the back door as Edie let herself in always made everything, instantly, a bit more bearable. To know that Edie was *there*. There was someone to talk to, someone to laugh with, someone to dust the library and vacuum the dog hairs off the hall carpet. The clatter from the kitchen was comforting. Edie, dealing with the breakfast dishes, loading the washing machine with a weekend's worth of dirty clothes, and talking to the dogs.

"Now don't you get under my feet, or you'll get your tail trodden on."

Virginia, in her bedroom, changed the sheets on their big double bed, her regular Monday-morning chore. Henry had gone shopping. His mother had given him five pounds, and he had set off for the village, to visit Mrs Ishak and buy the allotted amount of sweets, chocolates, and biscuits that he was permitted to take to Templehall in his tuck-box, and which were meant to last him for a full term. He had never before been given so much money to spend on sweets, and the novelty of this, for the moment, had diverted his attention from the fact that tomorrow he was leaving home for the first time. Eight years old and going away. Not for ever, it was true. But Virginia knew that when she saw him again, he would already be a different Henry because he would have seen things and done things and learned things totally dissociated from his mother's life. Tomorrow, he was going. The first day of ten years of regular separation from his parents and his home. The beginning of his growing up. Up and away from her.

She folded pillowcases. They had only another twenty-four hours. All through the weekend she had resolutely put his inevitable departure out of her mind; pretended to herself that Tuesday was never going to happen. Henry, she guessed, had done the same, and her heart bled for his innocence. Last night, saying goodnight to him, she had steeled herself for a dam-burst of tears and lamentations. *The weekend's over. Our last weekend. I don't want to go to school. I don't want to leave you.* But Henry had simply told her that he'd quite liked playing with Hamish, he'd hung by one leg from Hamish's trapeze; and then, worn out by the day's activity, had fallen almost instantly asleep.

She spread crisp, ironed sheets. I'll get through today and make it fun for him, she told herself. And then, somehow, I'll get through tomorrow. After Edmund has taken Henry, after they've driven away and I can't hear the car any longer, I'll think of something diverting or industrious to do. I'll go and see Dermot Honeycombe and spend hours looking for a present for Katy Steynton. A bit of china, or an antique lamp, or perhaps a little piece of Georgian silver. I'll write a long letter to Gramps and Grandma. I'll turn out the linen cupboard, sew

321

buttons on Edmund's shirts . . . And then Edmund will come home, and after that the worst will be over, and I can start counting the days until Henry's first weekend home.

She bundled up the soiled sheets and flung them out on to the landing, then put away a few random clothes and shoes, straightened a cushion. The telephone rang. She went to answer it, sitting on the edge of the freshly made bed.

"Balnaid."

"Virginia." It was Edmund. At a quarter past nine in the morning?

"Are you in the office?"

"Yes. Got here ten minutes ago. Virginia. Look. I have to go to New York."

She was not particularly perturbed. His flying off to New York was a regular occurrence.

"When?"

"Now. Today. I'm catching the first shuttle down to London. Flying out of Heathrow this afternoon."

"But –"

"I'll be back at Balnaid on Friday in time for the party. Probably about six in the evening. Earlier if I can make it."

"You mean . . ." It was difficult actually to take in what he was telling her. "You mean you'll be away all week?"

"That's right."

"But . . . packing . . . clothes . . ." Which was ridiculous because she knew that he kept a duplicate wardrobe in the flat at Moray Place, with suits, shirts, and underclothes suitable for any capital and any climate.

"I'll do that here."

"But . . ." The implication, the truth of what he was saying, broke at last. *He can't do this to me.* The bedroom window was open and the air that flowed through it was not cold, but Virginia, hunched over the telephone, shivered. She saw the knuckles of her hand, clenched

322

around the receiver, grow white. "Tomorrow," she said. "Tuesday. You're taking Henry to Templehall."

"I can't do that."

"You promised."

"I have to go to New York."

"Somebody else can go. Not you."

"There's nobody else who can. There's a panic on and it has to be me."

"But you *promised*. You said that you would take Henry. I told you that it was the one thing that I wouldn't do. It was my condition and you accepted it."

"I know, and I'm sorry. But what's happened is beyond my control."

"Send somebody else to New York. You're the boss. Send some underling."

"It's because I am who I am that I have to go."

"You are who you are!" She heard her own voice, shrill with scathing. "Edmund Aird. You think of nobody but yourself and nothing but your hateful job. Sanford Cubben. I hate Sanford Cubben. I realise I come fairly low on your priority list, but I thought Henry rated a little higher. You didn't only promise me, you promised Henry. Does that mean nothing to you?"

"I didn't promise anything. I just said that I'd take him, and now I can't."

"I call that a commitment. If you made such a commitment in business, you'd kill yourself to see it through."

"Virginia, be reasonable."

"I will *not* be reasonable! I will not sit here and listen to you and be told to be reasonable. And I will not deliver my child to a boarding school that I never wanted him to go to in the first place. It's like asking me to take one of the dogs to the vet to be put down. I won't do it!"

By now she was sounding like a fishwife, and did not care. But Edmund's voice remained, as always, infuriatingly cool and dispassionate.

"In that case, I suggest that you call Isobel Balmerino

and ask her to take Henry. She's driving Hamish. She'll have plenty of space for Henry.''

"If you think I'm going to palm Henry off on to Isobel –"

"Then you'll have to take him yourself."

"You're a bastard, Edmund. You know that, don't you? You're behaving like a selfish bastard."

"Where is Henry? I'd like to speak to him before I go."

"He's not here," Virginia told him with a certain malicious satisfaction. "He's buying his sweets from Mrs Ishak."

"Well, when he comes home, tell him to ring me at the office."

"You can ring him yourself." And on this biting exit line, she slammed down the receiver and put an end to the miserable exchange.

Her raised voice had penetrated to the kitchen.

"What was that all about?" Edie asked, turning from the sink as Virginia stormed in with a face like thunder, and arms filled with rumpled linen, to stride across the kitchen towards the open door of the utility room and hurl her burden in the general direction of the washing machine.

"Is something wrong?"

"Everything." Virginia pulled out a chair and sat, her arms folded and her expression mutinous. "That was Edmund, and he's going to New York *today*. *Now*. And he's going to be away all week, and he promised me . . . he *promised*, Edie . . . that he'd drive Henry to school tomorrow. I told him that it was the one thing I *wouldn't* do. I've hated the *whole* idea of Templehall from the very beginning, and the only reason I finally relented was because Edmund *promised* that he would take Henry tomorrow."

Edie knew a nasty temper when she saw one. She said reasonably, "Well, I suppose if you're an important businessman these things are bound to happen."

"Only to Edmund. Other men manage their lives without being so bloody selfish."

"You don't want to take Henry yourself?"

"No, I do not. It's the last thing in the world I want to do. It's inhuman of Edmund to expect it of me."

Edie, wringing out her dishcloth, considered the problem.

"Could you not ask Lady Balmerino to take him with Hamish?"

Virginia did not let on that Edmund had already made this sensible suggestion and got an earful for his pains.

"I don't know." She thought about it. "I suppose I could," she admitted sulkily.

"Isobel's very understanding. And she's been through it herself."

"No, she hasn't." It was obvious to Edie that she could say nothing right. "Hamish was *never* like Henry. You could send Hamish to the moon, and all he'd worry about would be when he was going to get his next meal."

"That's true enough. But if I were you, I'd have a word with Isobel. It's no good working yourself up into a state if there's nothing to be done. What –"

"I know, Edie. What can't be cured must be endured."

"That's true enough," said Edie placidly, and went to get the kettle and fill it with water. A cup of tea seemed to be in order. There was nothing, in times of stress, like a good hot cup of tea.

They were drinking the tea when Henry returned, his carrier bag bulging with goodies.

"Mummy, look what I got!" He emptied the contents out on to the kitchen table. "Look, Edie. Mars Bars, and Smarties, and Cadbury's Dairy Milk, and some jellybabies, and Jaffa Cakes, and chocolate digestives, and treacle toffees, and Rolos; and Mrs Ishak gave me a lollipop for going away. I didn't have to pay for the lollipop, so can I eat it now?"

Edie surveyed his loot. "I hope you're not going to eat

325

that lot all at once, otherwise you won't have a tooth left in your head."

"No." He was already unwrapping the lollipop. "It's got to last a long time."

By now Virginia's fury had simmered down. She put her arm around Henry and said, in consciously cheerful tones, "Daddy phoned."

He licked. "What about?"

"He has to go to America. Today. He's flying from London this afternoon. So he won't be able to take you to school tomorrow. But I thought I'd . . ."

Henry stopped licking. His pleasure flowed from his face, and he turned enormous, apprehensive eyes upon his mother.

She hesitated, and then started up again. ". . . I thought I'd ring Isobel and ask if she'd take you with Hamish . . ."

She got no further. His reaction to the news was even worse than she had dreaded. A wail of dismay and floods of instant tears . . .

"I don't want Isobel to take me . . ."

"Henry . . ."

He jerked himself out of her embrace and flung his lollipop on to the floor. "I'm not going to go with Isobel and Hamish. I want my mother or my father to take me. How would you like it, if you were me and . . ."

"Henry . . ."

". . . you had to go away with people who weren't your own mother and father? I think you are being very unkind to me . . ."

"I'll take you."

"And Hamish will be horrid and not talk because he's a senior. It's not *fair*!"

Furiously weeping, he turned and fled for the door.

"Henry, I'll *take* you . . ."

But he was gone, his footsteps stamping up the stairs to the sanctuary of his bedroom. Virginia, gritting her teeth, closed her eyes and wished that she could close her ears as well. It came. The deadly slam of his bedroom door. Then silence.

She opened her eyes and met Edie's across the table. Edie gave a long sigh. She said, "Oh, dearie dear."

"So much for *that* bright idea."

"Poor wee soul. He's upset."

Virginia leaned her elbow on the table and ran a hand through her hair. All at once the situation had become more than she felt able to cope with.

She said, "This is the very last thing I wanted to happen." She knew, and Edie knew, that Henry's tantrums, though rare, left him vulnerable and touchy for hours. "I wanted this to be a *good* day and not miserable. Our last day together. And now Henry's going to spend it bursting into tears and blaming me for everything. As if things weren't bad enough. Damn Edmund. What am I going to do, Edie?"

"How would it be," said Edie, "if I just came back this afternoon and took Henry off your hands? He's never so bad with me. Have you finished packing yet? Well, I could finish his packing and do any wee bits that need to be done, and he can just be around the place and have time to collect himself. A quiet day, that's what he needs."

"Oh, Edie." Virginia was filled with grateful love. "*Would* you do that?"

"No trouble. Mind, I'll have to go home and see to Lottie, give her her dinner, but I'll be here again by two."

"Can't Lottie see to her own dinner?"

"Well, she can, but she makes such a hash of it, burns the pans, and leaves my kitchen in a midden, I'm better to do it myself."

Virginia was repentant. "Oh, Edie. You do so much. I'm sorry I shouted at you."

"Good thing I was here for you to shout at." She heaved herself on to her swollen legs. "Now, I must get on, or we won't get the baby bathed at this rate. Up you go and have a word with Henry. Tell him he can spend

327

the afternoon with me, and what I'd really like would be one of his bonny pictures.''

Virginia found Henry, as she knew she would, under his duvet with Moo.

She said, ''I'm sorry, Henry.''

Racked with huge sobs, he did not reply. She sat on his bed. ''It was a silly thing to suggest. Daddy suggested it to me, and I thought it was silly then. I had no right even to mention it to you. Of course you won't go with Isobel. You'll come with me. I'll take you in the car.''

She waited. After a bit, Henry rolled on to his back. His face was swollen and tear-stained, but he seemed to have stopped crying.

He said, ''I don't mind so much about Hamish, but I want *you*.''

''I'll be there. Perhaps we'll take Hamish with *us*. It would be kind. Save Isobel a journey.''

He sniffed. ''All right.''

''Edie's coming back after lunch. She said she'd like to spend the afternoon with you. She wants you to draw her a picture.''

''Have you packed my felt pens?''

''Not yet.''

He put out his arms, and she gathered him up and held him close, rocking him gently, pressing kisses on to the top of his head. After a bit, he emerged from beneath his duvet, and they found a handkerchief and he blew his nose.

It was not until then that she remembered Edmund's message. ''Daddy wanted you to ring him up. He's at the office. You know the number.''

Henry went to her bedroom to do this, but Virginia had left it too late and Edmund had already gone.

The playroom was peaceful and warm. Sun poured through the wide windows, and the breeze sent the wisteria branches tapping at the panes. Henry sat at the big table in the middle of the room, and drew. Edie was on the window-seat, stitching the last of the name-tapes on to his new socks. In the mornings, for work, Edie wore her oldest clothes and a pinafore, but this afternoon she had turned up looking quite smart, and had put on her new lilac cardigan. Henry felt flattered, because he knew that she was keeping it for best. As soon as she arrived, she had set up the ironing board, and ironed the morning's load of washing, fresh from the line. This was now stacked, crisp and folded, on the other end of the table, and gave off a pleasant smell.

Henry laid down his felt pen and searched in his pen-box, making scrabbling sounds. He said, "Bother."

"What is it, pet?"

"I want a biro. I've drawn people with balloons coming out of their mouths, and I want to write what they're saying."

"Look in Edie's bag. There's a pen in there."

Her bag was on the chair by the fireside. It was large, made of leather, and bulged with important things: her comb, her fat housekeeping purse, her old age pension book, her post office savings book, her railcard, her bus pass. She didn't have a car, so she had to go everywhere by bus. Because of this she had a timetable, a little booklet, "Relkirkshire Bus Company". Henry, rootling for the pen, came upon this. It occurred to him, out of the blue, that it might be a sensible and useful thing to own. Edie probably had another at home.

He looked up at Edie. She was intent on her sewing, her white head bowed. He removed the booklet from her bag and slipped it into the pocket of his jeans. He found the biro, closed her bag, and went back to his work.

Presently, Edie asked, "What would you like for your tea?"

He said, "Macaroni cheese."

Dermot Honeycombe's antique shop stood at the far end of the village street, beyond the main gates of Croy, and at the foot of a gentle slope that leaned between the road and the river. Once it had been the village smithy, and the cottage where Dermot lived, the blacksmith's house. Dermot's cottage was painfully picturesque. It had tubs of begonias at the door, latticed windows, and a thickly thatched roof. But the shop was much as it had always been, with walls of dark stone and blackened beams. Outside was a yard of cobbles where once the patient farm horses had stood, waiting to be shod, and here Dermot had set up his shop sign, an aged wooden cart, painted blue, with DERMOT HONEYCOMBE ANTIQUES emblazoned tastefully on its side. It was an eye-catching gimmick, and brought in much casual trade. It was also useful for tying dogs to. Virginia clipped the leads on to the spaniels' collars, and knotted the ends around one of the cartwheels. The dogs sat, looking reproachful.

"I shan't be long," she told them. They thumped their stumpy tails, and their eyes made her feel like a murderer, but she left them and went across the cobbles and in through the door of the old smithy. Here Dermot sat, in his paper-piled birdcage of an office. He was on the telephone but spied her through the glass, raised a hand, and then reached out to turn on a switch.

Within the shop, four dangling bulbs sprang to light, doing a little to alleviate the gloom, but not very much. The place bulged with every sort of junk. Chairs were piled on tables, on the tops of chests of drawers. Huge wardrobes towered. There were milk churns, jelly-pans, stacks of unmatched china, brass fenders, corner cupboards, curtain rails, cushions, bundles of velvet, threadbare rugs. The smell was damp and musty and Virginia knew a small frisson of anticipation. Visits to

Dermot's were always something of a lottery because you never knew – and neither did Dermot – what you might, by chance, turn up.

She moved forward, edging her way between the tottering stacks of furniture, with the wary caution of a pot-holer. Already, she felt marginally more cheerful. Browsing was a comforting therapy, and Virginia allowed herself the self-indulgence of putting Edmund, the morning's traumas, and tomorrow, all out of her mind.

A present for Katy. Her eye wandered. She priced a chest of drawers, a wide-lapped chair. Searched for the silver mark on a battered spoon, poked through a box of old keys and brass doorknobs, turned the pages of a dignified old wreck of a book. Found a lustre cream jug, and wiped the dust from it, searching for chips or cracks. There were none.

She was joined by Dermot, finished with his telephone call.

"Hello, my dear."

"Dermot. Hello."

"Looking for something in particular?"

"A present for Katy Steynton." She held up the lustre jug. "This is sweet."

"It's a pet, isn't it? The Garden of Eden. I love that dark gentian blue." He was a rotund, smooth-faced man of mature years, but strangely ageless. His cheeks were pink, and his fluffy pale hair airy as dandelion down. He wore a faded green corduroy jacket, much adorned with drooping poachers' pockets, and had a red-spotted kerchief tied in a jaunty knot around his neck. "You're the second person I've had in today looking for something for Katy."

"Who else has been here?"

"Pandora Blair. Popped in this morning. Lovely to see her again. Couldn't believe it when she walked through the door. Just like old times. And after all these years!"

"We had lunch at Croy yesterday." Virginia thought

331

about yesterday, and knew that it had been a good day, the sort they would all remember when they were old and there was nothing much left to do but reminisce. *It was the time when Pandora came home from Majorca, and Lucilla was there and some young Australian. Can't remember his name. And we played croquet. And Edmund and Pandora sat in the swing-seat, and Pandora went to sleep, and we all teased Edmund for being such a boring companion.* "That's the first time I'd met Pandora."

"Of *course.* Amazing. How the years fly by."

"What did she buy for Katy? I mustn't get the same."

"A lamp. Chinese porcelain, and I'd made the shade for it myself. White silk, lined in palest pink. Then we had a cup of coffee and caught up on all the news. She was ever so sad when I told her about Terence."

"I'm sure." Virginia was afraid that Dermot's eyes were about to swim with tears, and went on hurriedly, "Dermot, I think I'll have this jug. Katy can use it either for cream or flowers, yet it's pretty enough on its own."

"Don't think you could find anything nicer. But stay for a bit. Have a snoop around . . ."

"I'd love to, but I'm taking the dogs for a walk. I'll pick the jug up on my way home, and write you a cheque for it then."

"Righty-ho." He took the jug from her and led the devious way back towards the door. "Are you going to Vi's picnic on Thursday?"

"Yes. Alexa will be there too. She's bringing a friend up for the dance."

"Oh, lovely. Haven't seen Alexa for months. I'm going to see if I can get someone to mind the shop for me that day. If I can't, I'll shut it up. Wouldn't miss Vi's picnic for anything."

"I hope it's a good day."

They emerged and stepped out into the sunshine. The dogs, spying them, wheeked blissfully and leapt to their feet, tangling the leads. "How's Edmund?" asked Dermot.

"On his way to New York."

"I don't *believe* it! What a thing! I wouldn't have his job for all the tea in China."

"Don't waste your sympathy. He loves it."

She rescued the dogs, waved goodbye to Dermot, walked on, leaving the last straggling cottages of Strathcroy behind her. Another half-mile and she had come to the bridge that spanned the river at the west end of the village. The bridge was ancient, steeply hump-backed, and once used by cattle-drovers. On the far side, a winding, tree-shaded lane followed the convolutions of the river, and led the way back to Balnaid.

On the crest of the bridge she paused to loosen the dogs and let them run free. They shot off at once, noses enticed by the smell of rabbits, to plunge into a thicket of bracken and brambles. Every now and then, as though to prove they were not wasting their time, they made hunting calls, or bounced high out of the tall bracken, with ears flying like furry wings.

Virginia let them go. They were Edmund's gun dogs, patiently trained, intelligent and obedient. A single whistle and they would return to her. The old bridge was a pleasant spot to loiter. The stone wall felt warm in the sunshine, and she leaned her arms on this and gazed downwards at the flowing peat-brown water. Sometimes she and Henry played Pooh-sticks from this bridge, flinging sticks upstream and then racing back to watch for the first, the winning stick, to appear. Sometimes the sticks never did appear, having been caught up in some unseen obstruction.

Like Edmund.

Alone, with only the river for company, she felt strong enough to think about Edmund, by now probably winging his way over the Atlantic towards New York, drawn, as though by a magnet, away from his wife and his son, just at a time when he was most needed at home. The magnet was his work, and right now Virginia felt as jealous and resentful and lonely as if he were gone to keep an assignation with a mistress.

Which was strange because she had never been jealous of other women, never tortured herself with imaginings of infidelity during the long periods when Edmund was away from her, in far-flung cities on the other side of the world. Once, teasing, she had told him that she didn't care what he did, provided she wasn't expected to watch. All that mattered was that he always came home. But today, she had slammed down the telephone receiver and never said goodbye, and then forgotten, until too late, to give Henry his father's message. Experiencing a twinge of guilt, she gathered her hurt feelings about her. *It's his own fault. Let him brood. Perhaps another time he'll –*

"Out for a walk, are you?"

The voice came from nowhere. Virginia thought, oh, God, let a few seconds pass, and then slowly turned. Lottie stood only a few feet away. She had come up the slope of the bridge from the village, the way that Virginia had, soft-footed, unheard. Had she seen Virginia in the street, watching from Edie's window, reached for her horrible beret, her green cardigan, and followed? Had she been waiting while Virginia was with Dermot, ducking out of sight and then dogging Virginia's footsteps, always just out of earshot? The very idea was spooky. What did she want? Why could she not leave people alone? And why, beyond Virginia's irritation, did there lurk, like a ghost, a sense of presentiment, a foreboding of fear?

Ridiculous. She pulled herself together. Imagination. It was only Edie's cousin, avid for company. With some effort, Virginia put a friendly expression on her face. "What are you doing here, Lottie?"

"Fresh air belongs to everybody, I always say. Looking at the water?" She moved to Virginia's side, to lean over the wall as she had been doing. But she was not as tall as Virginia and had to stand tiptoe, and crane her neck. "Seen any fish?"

"I wasn't looking for fish."

"Been to Mr Honeycombe's, haven't you? Lot of rubbish he's got in there. Most of it only fit for a bonfire. But then, there's no accounting for tastes. And as for what I'm doing, I'm out for a walk, same as you. On your own, Edie tells me over dinner. Edmund gone to America."

"Just for a few days."

"That's not so nice. On business, is he?"

"He wouldn't go for any other reason."

"Oh, ho, ho, that's what you think. Saw Pandora Blair this morning. Thin, isn't she? Like a scarecrow. And that hair! Looks like dyed to me. Called out to her but she didn't see *me*. Had dark glasses on. Could have had a good old chinwag about the old days. I was up at Croy, you know, resident housemaid. Old Lady Balmerino then. She was a lovely lady. Felt sorry for her, with a daughter no better than she should be. That was the time of the wedding. Lord and Lady Balmerino, but they were Archie and Isobel then. There was a dance at Croy the evening of the wedding. What a work. So many people staying you couldn't turn round. 'Course, Mrs Harris was cook, old Lady Balmerino didn't have to cook. There were some fine goings-on, but no doubt you've been told."

"Yes," said Virginia, and tried to think of some way in which she could escape this unwelcome flood of words.

"Scarcely out of school she was, Pandora, but she knew a thing or two, I can tell you. Men. She'd eat them for breakfast, and leave them chewed. A right wee whore."

She was smiling, her tone inconsequent and chatty, almost approving, so that the archaic word caught Virginia unawares and surprised her into saying, quite

335

sharply, "Lottie, I don't think you should say that about Pandora."

"Oh, you *don't*?" Lottie was still smiling. "Not pleasant, is it, hearing the truth? Nice Pandora's back, everybody is saying. But if I were you, I wouldn't be too happy. Not with your husband. Not with her. Lovers they were, Edmund and Pandora. That's why she's back, mark my words. Come back for him. Eighteen years old, and Edmund a married man and the father of a wee bairn, but that didn't stop them. That didn't stop him, rutting in her own bed. Night of the wedding it was, and everybody dancing. But *they* weren't dancing. Oh, no. They were up the stairs and thinking nobody noticed. But I noticed. Not much missed me." Pink spots burned on Lottie's sallow cheeks, her boot-button eyes were like a pair of nails, hammered into the sockets of her head. "I went after them. Stood at the door. It was dark. I heard. Never heard anything like it. You didn't guess, did you? He's a cool fish, that Edmund. Never let on. Never said a word. Just like the rest of them. They all knew. Well, it was obvious, wasn't it? Edmund back in London and Pandora sulking in her bedroom, face swollen with tears, wouldn't eat. And the way she spoke to her mother! But, of course, they're all thick as thieves. That's why Lady Balmerino gave me my notice. Didn't want *me* around. I knew too much."

Still smiling. Hot with excitement. Mad. I must, Virginia told herself, keep very calm. She said, "Lottie, I think you are making all this up."

Lottie's demeanour, with quite startling suddenness, changed. "Oh, am I?" The smile was wiped from her face. She backed away from Virginia and stood, four-square, facing up to her as though they were about to engage in a contest of physical strength. "And why do you think your husband's suddenly taken himself off to America? You ask him when he comes home to you, and I'll doubt you enjoy his answer. I'm sorry for you, do you know that? Because he'll make a fool of you, same as he did his first wife, poor lady. There's no streak of decency in him."

And then, abruptly, it was over. Her venom spent, Lottie seemed to slump within herself. The colour seeped from her cheeks. She pursed her lips, brushed a scrap of lichen from the front of her cardigan, tucked a wisp of hair under her beret, patted it into place. Her expression became complacent, as though all was now well, and she was content to prink.

Virginia said, "You are lying."

Lottie tossed her head and gave a little laugh. "Ask any of them."

"You are lying."

"Say what you please. Sticks and stones may break my bones . . ."

"I shall say nothing."

Lottie shrugged. "In that case, what's all the fuss about?"

"I shall say nothing and you are lying."

Her heart was banging in her chest, her knees trembling. But she turned her back on Lottie and began to walk away; walking steadily and without haste, knowing that Lottie watched, determined to give her no satisfaction. The worst was never looking back. Her scalp crawled with terrified apprehension, the fear that, at any moment, she would feel Lottie's weight leap upon her shoulders, dragging her to the ground with all the inhuman strength of a clawed monster from childhood nightmares.

This did not happen. She reached the far bank of the river, and felt a little safer. She remembered the dogs and pursed her lips to whistle for them, but her mouth and her lips were too dry for whistling, and she had to try again. A tiny piping sound, a pathetic effort, but Edmund's spaniels had had enough of abortive rabbiting, and almost immediately appeared, bounding through the bracken towards her, trailed with goose-grass and with twigs of thorny bramble entwined in their feathery fur.

She had never been so glad to see them, so grateful for their instant obedience. "Good dogs." She stopped to fondle them. "Good to come. Time to go home."

They ran ahead, down the lane. Leaving the bridge behind her, Virginia went after them, her pace still resolutely unhurried. She did not allow herself to look back until she reached the bend of the river, where the lane curved away beneath the trees. There, she stopped and turned. The bridge was still visible but there was no sign of Lottie.

She was gone. It was over. Virginia took a deep breath and let it all out in a whimpering sigh that was not far from panic. Then the panic took over, and all thought of the cream jug flew out of her mind. Without shame, she bolted for home. Ran to Edie, to Henry, to the sanctuary of Balnaid.

Back to the beginning.

You are lying.

Two o'clock in the morning and Virginia was still awake, her eyes, scratchy with fatigue, wide open, staring out into the soft darkness. She had tossed and turned, been either too hot or too cold, fought with pillows lumpy with pummelling. From time to time, she got out of the bed, wandered about in her nightgown, fetched a glass of water, drank it, tried again to sleep.

It was no good.

On the far side of the bed, Edmund's side, Henry slumbered peacefully. Virginia, defiantly breaking one of Edmund's strictest rules, had taken her son to bed with her. Every now and then, as though for reassurance, she put out a hand to touch him, to feel his gentle

338

breathing, his warmth through the flannel of his striped pyjamas. In the huge bed, he seemed small as a baby, scarcely alive.

She'd eat them for breakfast, and leave them chewed. A right wee whore.

She could not get the appalling scene out of her mind. Lottie's words went on and on, round and round like some scratchy old gramophone record, worn with playing. Circles of torment, never ceasing, never coming to any sort of conclusion.

Lovers they were. Edmund a married man, and the father of a wee bairn.

Edmund and Pandora. If it was true, Virginia knew that she had never imagined nor suspected it for a single instant. In her innocence, she had not watched for evidence, had read no inner meaning into Edmund's casual words, his easy demeanour. "Pandora's home," he had told her, pouring himself a drink and going to the refrigerator to search for ice. "We've been asked for lunch at Croy." And Virginia had said, "How nice," and gone on frying beefburgers for Henry's supper. Pandora was simply Archie's errant young sister, back from Majorca. And when the great reunion happened, she had paid little regard to the brotherly kiss Edmund had planted on Pandora's cheek, their laughter, and the understandable affection of his greeting. And as for the rest of the day, Virginia had been more interested in the croquet game than curious to know what it was that Edmund and Pandora, watching from the swing-seat, were talking about.

And what did it matter what they talked about? Be sensible. So what if they had had a wild and impetuous affair and ended up in Pandora's bed? Pandora at eighteen must have been sensational, and Edmund at the height of his virility. This is today, and adultery is no longer called adultery but extramarital sex. Besides, it was all a long time ago. Over twenty years. And Edmund had not been unfaithful to Virginia, but to his first wife,

Caroline. And now Caroline was dead. So it didn't matter. There was nothing to agonise over. Nothing . . .

They all knew. All thick as thieves. Didn't want me around. I knew too much.

Who knew? Did Archie know? Did Isobel? Did Vi know? And Edie? Because if they knew, they would have been watching, fearing perhaps that it was all going to happen all over again. Watching Edmund and Pandora. Watching Virginia, their eyes filled with a pity that she had never seen. Did they worry for Virginia as they must have worried for Caroline? Did they talk amongst themselves, like conspirators, agreeing to keep the truth from Edmund's second wife? Because if they had, then Virginia had been betrayed, and by the very people she was closest to and most relied upon.

And why do you think your husband's suddenly taken himself off to America? He'll make a fool of you, same as he did his first wife, poor lady.

This was the worst. These were the most dreaded doubts. Edmund had gone. Had he really had to fly off like that, or was New York simply a trumped-up excuse to get away from Balnaid and Virginia and to give himself time to work out his problems? His problems being that he loved Pandora, had always loved her, and now she was back and as beautiful as ever, and Edmund was once more trapped in marriage with yet another woman.

Edmund was fifty, a vulnerable age for restlessness and mid-life crises. He was not a man for showing emotion, and most of the time Virginia had no idea what he was thinking about. Her own self-doubt grew to terrifying proportions. Perhaps this time he would cut his losses and run, leaving Virginia with her marriage and her life tumbling in ruins. Leaving her and Henry lost in the rubble of what she had once thought totally impregnable.

It did not bear thinking about. She rolled over, burying her face in the pillow, shutting out the ghastly prospect.

340

She would not acknowledge it. Would not let it be true.

You are lying, Lottie.

This is where we came in. Back to the beginning.

27

Tuesday the Thirteenth

The rain was cruel, relentless, and unwelcome. It had started before daybreak, and Virginia awoke to the sound of it, and had known an awful sinking of the heart. As if things weren't bad enough on this dreaded day, without the elements turning against her. Perhaps it would stop. But the gods were not on anybody's side and the downpour continued, monotonously streaming down from a charcoal-grey sky, right through the long morning and the early afternoon.

Now, it was half past four, and they were on their way to Templehall. Because she had the two boys with her, and all their clobber – trunks, tuck-boxes, duvets, rugger balls, and book-bags – Virginia had left her own little car in the garage, and instead drove Edmund's Subaru, a four-wheel-drive workhorse that he used when he went into rough country, or up the hill. She was not used to driving this vehicle, and its unfamiliarity and her own uncertainty only served to heighten the sense of doom and hopelessness that had dogged her for nearly twenty-four hours.

Conditions were miserable. What light there had been was already seeping from the sky, and she drove with headlights on and the windscreen wipers working full-tilt. Tyres hissed on flooded patches of road, and on-coming cars and lorries sent up great waves of blinding mud. Visibility was almost nil, which was frustrating, because under normal conditions, the road that led from Relkirk to Templehall was an exceptionally scenic drive – through prosperous farmlands, alongside the banks of a wide and majestic river famous for its salmon, and past large estates, with distant glimpses of stately homes.

It would have eased the atmosphere had they been able to observe any of this. Remarking on beauty spots, pointing out some distant peak would have given Virginia something to talk about. As it was, she had tried engaging Hamish in lively conversation, hoping that this would divert Henry from his speechless misery, and that he might even join in. But Hamish was in a bad mood. Knowing that the freedom of summer holidays was over was bad enough, but worse was having to go back to school in the company of a new boy. A babe. That's what they called the little ones. The babes. Travelling with a babe was beneath Hamish's dignity, and he just prayed that none of his contemporaries would be around to witness his humiliating arrival. He was not going to be made responsible for Henry Aird, and had made this fact vociferously clear to his mother while she helped him lug his trunk down the stairs of Croy, and flattened, with a brush, his gruesome short haircut.

Accordingly, he had decided upon a course of non-communication, and had soon put a stop to Virginia's advances by answering her in a series of noncommittal grunts. She got the message, and after that the three of them had lapsed into a stony and wordless silence.

Which made Virginia wish that she hadn't brought the wretched boy; had let Isobel drive her own sulky son. But without him there, Henry might well have succumbed to tears, sobbed throughout the journey and arrived at Templehall sodden with weeping and in no fit state to deal with the rigours of his new and daunting future.

The prospect she found almost unendurable. I am hating this, she told herself. It is even worse than I imagined it would be. It is inhuman, hellish, unnatural.

343

And worse is to come, because the moment awaits when I have to say goodbye to Henry and drive away, and leave him standing there, alien and alone. I hate Templehall, and I hate the headmaster, and I could strangle Hamish Blair. I have never had to do anything in my life that I have hated so much. I am hating the rain, hating the entire educational system, hating Scotland, hating Edmund.

Hamish said, "There's a car behind us. It wants to get past."

"Well, it can bloody well wait," Virginia told him, and Hamish was silenced.

An hour later, she was back on the same road, driving the empty vehicle in the opposite direction.

It was over. Henry was gone. She felt numb. Nonexistent, as though the trauma of parting from him had robbed her of all identity. Just now, she would not think about Henry, because if she did she would weep, and the combination of tears, half-darkness, and relentless rain would most likely cause her to drive the Subaru off the road, or into the back of a ten-ton lorry. She imagined the crunch of metal, her own body flung like a broken doll to the side of the road, flashing lights, the howl of ambulance and police cars.

She would not think about Henry. That part of her life was over. But what was happening to her life? What was she doing here? Who was she? What was the reason for driving home to a house that stood dark and empty? She did not want to go home. She did not want to go back to Strathcroy. But where? Somewhere perfectly gorgeous, a million miles from Archie and Isobel and Edmund and Lottie and Pandora Blair. A place of sunlight and calmness and no responsibilities, where people would tell her she was marvellous, and she could be young again instead of about a hundred years old.

Leesport. That's it. She was driving to an airport to catch a jet to Kennedy, a limousine to Leesport. It wouldn't be raining there. It would be Long Island autumn weather, with blue skies and golden leaves and a crisp breeze blowing in over the Sound from the Atlantic. Leesport, unchanged. The wide streets, the crossroads, the hardware store and the drugstore, with the kids outside, wheeling about on their bicycles. Then, Harbor Road. Picket fences and shade trees and sprinklers out on lawns. The road sloping to the water, the yacht anchorage a coppice of masts. The gates of the country club, and then Grandma's house. And Grandma in the garden, pretending to rake leaves but in reality watching for the car, so that she could be out on the sidewalk the moment it drew up.

"Oh, honey, you're back." The soft, wrinkled cheek, the scent of White Linen. "It's been too long. Did you have a good journey? What a treat to see you!"

Indoors, and the other smells. Wood-smoke, sun oil, cedar, roses. Braided rugs and faded slip-covers. Cotton curtains blowing at open windows. And Gramps coming in from the sundeck, with his glasses on top of his head and *The New York Times* under his arm . . .

"Where's my sweetheart?"

Through the murky gloom, clusters of lights now shone ahead. Relkirk. Back to reality, and Virginia now realised that here she was going to have to stop for a little. She needed to go to the loo, freshen up. Find a bar, have a drink, be made to feel human again. She needed warmth and the syrupy comfort of musak and low lights. No reason to hurry home because there was nobody there to hurry to. A sort of freedom, perhaps. Nobody to care how late she was, nobody to worry about what she was doing.

She drove into the old city. Cobbled streets were awash, rain shimmered in the streetlights, pavements were crowded with shoppers and workers, booted, mackintoshed, carrying umbrellas and bags, all hurrying home to the comfort of their firesides and tea.

She made for the King's Hotel because it was familiar and she knew where to find the Ladies'. It was an old-fashioned edifice and in the middle of the town, so had no car-park of its own. Instead, Virginia found a space on the opposite side of the road and parked the Subaru there, beneath a dripping tree. As she locked the door, a taxi drew up outside the hotel. A man got out, wearing a raincoat and a tweed hat. He paid the driver off, and, carrying a grip, went up the steps that led from the pavement to the revolving door. He disappeared. Virginia paused for traffic to pass, and then ran across the road and followed him inside.

The Ladies' was on the far side of the foyer, but the man had paused at the reception desk. He had taken off his hat and was shaking the rain from it.

"Yes?" The receptionist was a sulky-looking girl, with fat pink lips and frizzy straw-coloured hair.

"Good evening. I have a room booked. I called about a week ago, from London."

An American. His voice husky but lightly pitched. Something about it caught Virginia's attention, as though a hand had tugged at her sleeve. Halfway across the floor, she paused to glance at him. Saw a tall, broad-shouldered backview, dark hair streaked with grey.

"What name did you say?"

"I didn't, but it's Conrad Tucker."

"Oh, yes. If you'd like to sign here . . ."

Virginia said, "Conrad."

Startled, he swung round to face her. Across the space that divided them, they stared at each other. Conrad Tucker. Older, going grey. But Conrad. The same heavy horn-rimmed spectacles, the same indelible tan. For a second his expression remained blank, then slowly, incredulously, he smiled.

"Virginia."

"I don't believe this . . ."

"Well, I'll be goddamned."

"I thought I recognised your voice."

"What are you doing here . . . ?"

The boot-faced girl was not amused. "Excuse me, sir, but would you mind signing?"

"I live near here."

"I never knew . . ."

"And you . . . ?"

"I'm staying . . ."

"And how will you be paying, sir?" Boot-face again. "By credit card or cheque?"

"Look," said Conrad to Virginia, "this is hopeless. Give me five minutes and I'll meet you in the bar and we'll have a drink. Can you do that? Have you time?"

"Yes, I have time."

"I'll get settled, wash up, and then join you. How's that?"

"Five minutes."

"No more."

The ladies' room, frilled and chintzy, was mercifully empty. Virginia had shed her grotty old Barbour, been to the loo, and now stood at the mirror gazing at her own reflection, and feeling more disorientated than ever by the astonishing unexpectedness of her encounter with Conrad. Conrad Tucker, not seen nor thought of for twelve years or more. Here, in Relkirk. Come from London, and for what reason she could not imagine. She only knew that she had never been so glad to see a known face, because now, at least, she had someone to talk to.

She was not dressed for socialising, defiant in blue jeans and an old grey cashmere sweater with a muffler of a collar. Her appearance was scarcely better. Hair lank with rain, her face clean of make-up. She saw the lines on her forehead and at the corners of her mouth, and the dark bruises beneath her eyes, evidence of her sleepless night. She reached for her bag, found a comb, fixed her hair, fastened it back from her face with an elastic band.

Conrad Tucker.

Twelve years. She had been twenty-one. So long ago, and so much, since, had taken place, that it took some effort to recall the details of that particular summer. They had met at the country club in Leesport. Conrad was a lawyer, in business in New York with his uncle. He had an apartment in the East Fifties, but his father owned an old house in Southampton, and Conrad had come from there to Leesport to play in some tennis championships.

So far, so good. How had he played? That was lost in the mists of time. Virginia simply remembered that she had watched the match and cheered for him, and afterwards he had sought her out and bought her a drink, which was exactly what she had intended should happen.

She searched in her bag, in vain, for a lipstick, but found scent and splashed it on.

It had been a good summer. Conrad turned up in Leesport most weekends, and there were midnight barbecues and clambakes on the Fire Island beach. They played a lot of tennis, sailed Gramps' old sloop out on to the blue waters of the Bay. She remembered Saturday nights at the club, and dancing with Conrad on the wide terrace with the sky full of stars and the band playing 'The Look of Love'.

Once, mid-week, she had driven up to the city with her grandmother, to stay at the Colony Club, do a bit of shopping, and take in a show. And Conrad had phoned, and taken her out to dinner at Les Pléiades, and after that they had gone on to the Café Carlyle and stayed until the small hours listening to Bobby Short.

Twelve years. Light years ago. She picked up her bag and her Barbour and went out of the room and up the stairs and into the bar. Conrad had not yet reappeared.

348

She bought herself a whisky and soda, a packet of cigarettes, and carried her drink to an empty table in the corner of the room.

She drank half the whisky at a single go, felt at once warmed, comforted, and marginally stronger. The day was not yet over, but at least she was being offered a little respite, and she wasn't alone any longer.

She said, "You start, Conrad."

"Why me?"

"Because before I say a single word, I have to know what you're doing here. What has brought you to Scotland, to Relkirk? There has to be some logical explanation, but I can't think what it is."

He smiled. "I'm not in fact doing anything. I'm on a long vacation. Not exactly a sabbatical, just an extended break."

"Are you still a lawyer in New York?"

"I am."

"Working with your uncle?"

"No. I'm the top of the heap now."

"How impressive. Go on."

"Well . . . I've been away about six weeks. Travelling England, staying with various acquaintances. Somerset, Berkshire, London. Then I came north and I've been in Kelso for a few days with some distant cousins of my mother's. It's a great place. Great fishing. Left them after lunch today. Caught the train up here."

"How long are you staying in Relkirk?"

"Just tonight. Tomorrow morning I'm hiring a car, and driving on north. I have to go to a party."

"And where is the party?"

"Some place called Corriehill. But I'm staying at another house called Croy. With –"

"I know," Virginia interrupted. "Archie and Isobel Balmerino."

"How do you know?"

"Because they're our closest friends. We all live in the same village, Strathcroy. And . . . you know Katy Steynton?"

"I met her in London."

"You're the Sad American." Virginia said this without thinking and could at once have bitten out her tongue.

"Sorry?"

"No, Conrad. *I'm* sorry. I shouldn't have said that. It's just that nobody could remember your name. That's why I didn't know it was you who was coming."

"You've lost me."

"We had lunch with the Balmerinos on Sunday. Isobel told me about you then."

Conrad shook his head. "I knew you'd married and I knew you'd married a Scotsman, but no more than that. I never imagined we'd meet up like this."

"Well, here I am, Mrs Edmund Aird." *At least I think I am.* She hesitated. "Conrad, I didn't mean to say that. The Sad American bit, I mean. It's just that Isobel didn't seem to know anything about you. Except that Katy had met you in London. And that your wife had died."

Conrad was holding his whisky tumbler. He turned it in his hand, watching the amber liquid swirl. After a bit he said, "Yes. That's right."

"I am so very sorry."

He looked up at her. He said, "Yes."

"Can I ask? What happened?"

"She had leukaemia. She was ill for a long time. That's why I came over. After the funeral."

"What was she called?"

"Mary."

"How long were you married?"

"Seven years."

350

"Do you have children?"

"A daughter. Emily. She's six. Right now she's with my mother in Southampton."

"Getting away . . . has that made things better for you?"

"I'll know when I get back."

"When are you going?"

"Next week some time." He tossed back the last of his drink, got to his feet. "I'll get us the other half."

She watched him as he stood at the bar, ordering and paying for their second round of drinks, and tried to work out why he was so unmistakably American, when he didn't actually chew gum or sport a crew cut. Perhaps it was his shape, the broad shoulders, narrow hips, long legs. Or his clothes. Polished loafers, chinos, a Brooks Brothers shirt, a blue Shetland sweater discreetly tagged with the Ralph Lauren logo.

She heard him ask the barman for some nuts. He did this quietly and politely, and the barman found a packet and emptied them into a little dish, and Virginia remembered that Conrad seldom raised his voice and was always mannerly to any person who happened to be doing a job for him. Gas-station attendants, barmen, waiters, cab drivers, doormen. The old black odd-job man who carried the trash and did all the dirty jobs down at the Leesport anchorage was much taken with Conrad, because Conrad had gone to the trouble to find out his Christian name, which was Clement, and always addressed him thus.

A kindly man. She thought about his dead wife, and was certain that the marriage must have been a happy one, and was angry for him. Why did tragedy always aim its venom at the couples who least deserved it, while others were spared to make each other miserable and everybody else as well? Seven years. It wasn't very long. But at least he had his little daughter. She thought of Henry, and was glad that he had a child.

351

He was coming back to their table. She put a smile on her face. The whiskies looked very dark. She said, "I only meant to have one drink. I'm driving."

"How far?"

"About twenty miles."

"Do you want to call your husband?"

"He's not at home. He's in New York. He works for Sandford Cubben. I don't know if that got through to you on the grapevine or not."

"I think I did know. How about your family?"

"If by family you mean kids, there's no family at home either. I have one child, a little boy, and I have just, this very afternoon, abandoned him to start his first term at boarding school. That is how I have spent this ghastly day. The most awful day of my life. That's why I came in here. To go to the john and gather up my courage before travelling on." Even to herself, she sounded truculent.

"How old is your boy?"

"Eight."

"Oh, God!" His voice was despairing, which Virginia found comforting. Here at last was a twin soul, someone who thought the way she thought.

"He's just a baby. I never wanted him to go, and I fought every inch of the way. But his father was adamant. It's tradition. Good old British stiff-upper-lip tradition. He thinks it's the right thing to do, and he was all set to take Henry himself. But then he had to go to New York. So it had to be me. I don't know which of us was most miserable, Henry or myself. I don't know which of us I feel most sorry for."

"Was Henry okay? Being left, I mean. Saying goodbye."

"Conrad, I don't know. I honestly don't know. It was the fastest turn-round you could imagine. Split-second timing. Not a moment to stand, no time for a tear. I'd hardly stopped the car before two burly chaps were there, opening the back door and manhandling all the

352

luggage on to trolleys. And then the Matron . . . quite young and quite pretty . . . took Henry by the arm and led him indoors. I don't think he even looked back. I was standing there with my mouth open, all set to have a scene, and suddenly the headmaster appeared from nowhere, shook me by the hand and said, 'Goodbye, Mrs Aird.' So I got back into the car and drove away. Do you know something? I felt like a dead chicken on a conveyor belt. Do you think I should have asserted myself?"

"No, I don't. I think you did the right thing."

"Nothing could have made it any better." She sighed, drank whisky, set down the glass. "At least neither of us had the chance to disgrace ourselves."

"I guess that's what it's all about." He smiled. "But you could still do with a bit of cheering. So why don't we have dinner together?"

". . . I never thought I'd live in Scotland. To me it was a place one came to at the end of the summer for a bit of jollity and the odd hunt ball or two; but never somewhere one would spend the rest of one's life . . ."

The King's Hotel was not famous for its food, but it was warm and friendly, and the darkness and the streaming rain out of doors offered no inducement to tramp the windy streets in search of some place a little more sophisticated. They had already eaten their Scotch broth, and were now ploughing their way through steaks, onions, chips, and mixed veg. For pudding, there was a choice of trifle or various ices. The waitress had already told them that the trifle was 'offly guid'.

Conrad had ordered wine, which was perhaps a mistake, and Virginia was drinking it, which was a bigger one, because she didn't usually talk as much as this, and, for the life of her, she couldn't think how to stop.

Even if she'd wanted to. Because Conrad was a sympathetic listener, and so far had not started to look bored. On the contrary, he seemed to be fascinated.

She had already explained about Edmund, and his first wife, and Vi and Alexa. She had told him about Henry, about Balnaid, about the almost indescribable remoteness, and yet closeness, of their existence in Strathcroy.

"What goes on there?"

"Nothing, really. It's just a little place on the way to somewhere else. And yet everything. You know how small communities are. And we have a pub and a school, and shops, and two churches, and a dear queer who sells antiques. There always seems to be something going on. A jumble sale, or a garden opening, or a school play." It sounded dreadfully dull. She said, "It sounds dreadfully dull."

"Not a bit. Who lives there?"

"The village people, and the Balmerinos, and the minister and his wife, and the rector and his wife, and the Airds. Archie Balmerino is the Laird, which means that he owns the village and thousands of acres of land. Croy is enormous, but he's not in the least grand, and neither is Isobel. Isobel works harder than any woman I know, which is saying something in Scotland because all the women beaver away endlessly. If they're not running huge houses, or bringing up children, or gardening, then they're organising enormous charity events or engaged in some home industry or other. Like running farm shops and selling all their own produce, or drying flowers, or keeping bees, or restoring antiques, or making the most beautiful curtains for people."

"Don't they ever have fun?"

"Yes, they have fun, but it's not Long Island fun, and it's not even Devon fun. In August and September, everything comes to a rising boil and there's a party most nights, and hunt balls and shooting and things.

You've come at the right time, Conrad, though you'd never believe it on a dismal evening like this. But then the winter closes in and everybody hibernates.''

"How do you see your girlfriends?''

"I don't know." She tried to work this one out. "It's not like anywhere else. We all live such miles apart, and there's no club life. I mean, there aren't country clubs like there are in the States. And pubs aren't the same as they are in the south. Women don't really go into pubs. There are golf clubs, of course, but those are mostly male-orientated, and women are strictly personae non gratae. You might go to Relkirk and meet a girl-friend there, but most of the socialising is done in people's private houses. Lunch parties for the girls, and dinner parties for the couples. We all get dressed up, and like I said, drive for forty miles or more. Which is one of the reasons that life more or less stops during the winter. That's when people escape. They go to Jamaica, if they can afford it, or Val-d'Isère for the skiing.''

"And what do you do?''

"I don't mind the winters. I hate the wet summers, but the winters are beautiful. And I go skiing up the glen. There's a ski-area only about ten miles on from Strathcroy, with a couple of tows and some good runs. The only thing is that if there's a lot of snow you can't get up the road. Which rather defeats the purpose.''

"You used to ride.''

"I used to hunt. For me, that was the whole purpose of riding. When I first came to Balnaid, Edmund said I could keep a couple of horses, but there didn't seem any point if there was to be no hunting.''

"So how do you fill your days?''

"So far,'' she told him, "I've filled them with Henry.'' She gazed at Conrad, in glum hopelessness, across the table, because he had nailed with a single question the sum total of all her apprehension. Henry was gone, torn from her against her will. *You smother him*, Edmund had

355

told her, and she had been furiously hurt and angry, but the smothering and the mothering had been her daily occupation and her greatest joy.

Bereft of Henry, there was only Edmund.

But Edmund was in New York, and if he wasn't in New York, then he was in Frankfurt or Tokyo or Hong Kong. Before, she had coped with these long separations, partly because there had always been Henry for comfort and companionship, but also because she had been totally confident, wherever he might be, in Edmund's strength and constancy and love.

But now . . . the doubts and dreadful possibilities of last night's waking nightmares crowded in on her again. Lottie Carstairs, that madwoman . . . but perhaps not so mad . . . telling Virginia things that she had never thought to hear. Edmund and Pandora Blair. *Why do you think he's taken himself off to America? He'll make a fool of you, same as he did his first wife, poor lady.*

Suddenly, it was all too much.

To her horror, she felt her mouth tremble, her eyes prick with tears. Across the table, Conrad watched her, and for a mad instant she thought about confiding in him, spilling out all the anguish of her miserable uncertainties. But then the tears swam into her eyes and his face dissolved into a watery mist, and Virginia thought, oh, bugger, I'm pissed. Just in time. The moment mercifully was over, and the dangerous temptation behind her. She must never speak about it to anybody, because if she did, then the words, said aloud, might make it all true. Might make it happen.

She said, "I'm sorry. So silly." She sniffed lustily, searched for a handkerchief, couldn't find one. Across the table, Conrad offered his own, white and clean and freshly ironed, and she took it gratefully and blew her nose. She said, "I'm tired and I'm miserable." She tried to make light of it. "I'm also slightly pissed."

He said, "You can't drive yourself home."

356

"I have to."

"Stay here the night and go back in the morning. We'll get a room for you."

"I can't."

"Why not?"

Tears poured again. "I have to get back for the dogs."

He did not laugh at her. He said, "Stay here for a moment. Order coffee. I just have to make a telephone call."

He laid down his napkin, pushed back his chair, and went. Virginia mopped her face, blew her nose again, glanced around the dining room, anxious that no other person had noticed her sudden attack of weepy emotion. But the other diners were all absorbed in their dinners, munching stolidly at fried fish, or spooning their way through the 'offly guid' trifle. The tears, thankfully, receded. The waitress approached to remove their plates.

"Did you enjoy your steak?"

"Yes, it was delicious."

"Are you taking sweet?"

"No. I don't think so, thank you. But if we could have some coffee?"

She had brought the coffee, and Virginia was already drinking the black and noxious stuff, which tasted as though it had been made out of a bottle, when Conrad returned to her. He drew back his chair and sat down. She looked at him inquiringly, and he said, "That's all settled."

"What have you settled?"

"I've cancelled my room, and cancelled the hire car for tomorrow. I'll drive you back to Strathcroy. I'll drive you home."

"Will you go to Croy?"

"No. They're not expecting me until tomorrow morning. I can go to the pub you mentioned."

"No, you can't, because they won't have a room. They're filled with grouse-shooting visitors who've taken Archie's moor." She sniffed away the last of her weeping, poured his coffee. "You can come to Balnaid. Stay the night there. The guest-room beds are all made up." She looked up, and caught the expression on his face. She said, "There's no problem," but even as she said this, knew that there was.

In the darkness, Conrad drove. It had stopped raining, as though the skies had run out of water, but the wind was from the south-west, and still damp, and the night stayed overcast. The road climbed and wound and dipped, and in the hollows lay pools of floodwater from the overflowing ditches. Virginia, bundled in her Barbour, thought of the last time that she had made this journey; the evening Edmund had met her off the shuttle and they had had dinner together in Edinburgh. Then the sky had been an artist's wonder of rose-pink and grey. Now the darkness was sombre and menacing, and the lights that shone from the windows of farmhouses scattered over the surrounding braes of Strathcroy gave little relief, seeming distant and unreachable as stars.

Virginia yawned.

"You're sleepy," Conrad told her.

"Not really. Just too much wine." She reached out and rolled down the window, and felt the cold, wet, mossy air pour over her face. The tyres of the Subaru hissed on the wet tarmac; out of the darkness came the long call of a curlew.

She said, "That's the sound of coming home."

"You certainly live a long way from anywhere."

"We're just about there."

The street of the village stood empty. Even Mr Ishak had closed up his shop, and the only lights were those that burned from behind drawn curtains. On such a night people stayed at home, watched television, made tea.

"We turn left, over this bridge."

They crossed the river, turned into the lane beneath the trees, came to the open gates, the drive that led to the house. All was, predictably, in darkness.

"Don't go around to the front, Conrad. Park just here, at the back. I don't use the front door when I'm on my own. I've got the back-door key."

He drew up, turned off the engine. While the headlights still burned, she climbed down and went to unlock the back door, reach inside and switch on a light. The dogs had heard the car and were waiting, and showed gratifying excitement at her return, hurling themselves at her feet and uttering small welcoming noises in the back of their throats.

"Oh, what good doggies." She crouched to fondle them. "I'm sorry I've been such a long time. You must have thought I was never coming home. Go on, out you both go and spend pennies, and I'll give you lovely biscuits before you go to bed."

They bundled happily out into the darkness, barked at the alien figure alighting from the Subaru, went to smell him, were patted and spoken to, and then, reassured, bounded off into the trees.

Virginia went on, switching on more lights. The big kitchen slumbered, the Aga was warm, the refrigerator gently hummed to itself. Conrad joined her, carrying his grip.

"Do you want me to put the car away?"

"No matter. We'll leave it in the yard for the night. Just take the keys out . . ."

"I have . . ." He laid them on the table.

In the uncompromising brightness, they regarded each other, and Virginia found herself overcome, quite suddenly, by a ridiculous shyness. To deal with this, she became businesslike and hostessy.

359

"Now. You'd like a drink? A nightcap. Edmund has some malt whisky he keeps for these occasions."

"I'm okay."

"But you'd like one?"

"Yes, I would."

"I'll get it. I won't be a moment."

When she came back bearing the bottle, he had taken off his coat and hat, and the dogs had returned from their nightly expedition and were already curled up on the beanbags by the Aga. Conrad, hunkered down, was making friends with them, talking softly, smoothing their high-domed well-bred heads with a gentle hand. As Virginia appeared, he stood up.

"I've closed the door, and locked it."

"How kind. Thank you. Actually, we often forget to lock doors. Thieves and robbers don't seem to be a problem in Strathcroy." She set the bottle down on the table, found a glass. "You'd better pour it yourself."

"You're not joining me?"

She shook her head, rueful. "No, Conrad, I've had enough for this evening."

He poured the malt and filled the tumbler from the cold tap. Virginia fed the dogs with biscuits. They took them politely, not snapping nor grabbing, and munched them up appreciatively.

"They're beautiful spaniels."

"Edmund's gun dogs, and very well-behaved. With Edmund in charge, they don't dare be anything else." The biscuits were finished. She said, "If you'd like to bring your drink upstairs with you, I'll show you where you're sleeping." She gathered up his hat and coat, and Conrad collected his grip, and she led the way out of the kitchen, turning lights off and on as she went. Down the passage, across the big hall, and up the stairs.

"What a lovely house."

"It's big, but I like it that way."

He followed behind her. Below them, the old grand-father clock ticked the minutes away, but their feet made

360

no sound on the thick carpets. The spare room faced over the front of the house. She opened the door and turned on the switch, and all was illuminated by the cold brilliance of the overhead chandelier. It was a large room, furnished with high brass bedsteads and a mahogany suite of Victorian furniture that Virginia had inherited from Vi. Taken unawares, it presented an impersonal face, without flowers or books. As well, the air was stuffy and unused.

"I'm afraid it doesn't look very welcoming." She dropped his hat and coat on a chair and went to fling open the tall sash window. The night wind flowed in, stirring the curtains. Conrad joined her and they leaned out, gazing into the velvety darkness. Light from the window drew a chequered pattern on the gravel beyond the front door, but all else was obscured.

He took a deep lungful of air. He said, "It all smells so clean and sweet. Like fresh spring water."

"You have to take my word for it, but we're looking at a wonderful view. You'll see it in the morning. Out over the garden to the fields and the hills."

From the trees by the church, an owl hooted. Virginia shivered and withdrew from the window. She said, "It's cold. Shall I close it again?"

"No. Leave it. It's too good to shut away."

She drew the heavy curtains, settling them so that there should be no chinks. "The bathroom's through that door." He went to investigate. "There should be towels, and the water's always hot if you want to take a bath." She turned on the small lights on the dressing table, and then the bedside light, and then went to switch off the cold brilliance of the chandelier. At once the high-ceilinged room was rendered cosier, even intimate. "I'm afraid there's no shower. This isn't a very modern establishment."

He emerged from the bathroom as Virginia turned back a heavy bedcover, revealing puffy square pillows encased in embroidered linen, a flowered eiderdown.

361

"There's an electric blanket if you want to turn it on." She folded the cover, laid it aside. "Now."

There was nothing more to occupy her hands, her attention. She faced Conrad. For a moment neither of them spoke. His eyes, behind the heavy horn-rims, were sombre. She saw his rugged features, the deep lines on either side of his mouth. He was still holding his drink in his hand, but now moved to set it down on the table beside the bed. She watched him do this, and thought of that hand gently fondling the head of one of Edmund's dogs. A kindly man.

"Will you be all right, Conrad?" An innocently intended question but as soon as the words were spoken she heard them as loaded.

He said, "I don't know."

There's no problem, she had told him, but knew that the problem had lurked between them all evening and now could no longer be pushed out of sight. It was no good prevaricating. They were two grown-up people, and life was hell.

She said, "I'm grateful to you. I needed comfort."

"I need you . . ."

"I had fantasies about Leesport. Going back to Grandma and Gramps. I didn't tell you that."

"That summer, I fell in love with you . . ."

"I imagined getting there. In a limousine from Kennedy. And it was all the same. The trees and the lawns, and the smell of the Atlantic blowing in over the Bay."

"You went back to England . . ."

"I wanted someone to tell me I was great. That I was doing all right. I wanted not to be alone."

"I feel like a shit . . ."

"It's two worlds, isn't it, Conrad? Bumping, and then moving apart. Light years away from each other."

". . . because I want you."

"Why does everything have to happen when it's too late? Why does everything have to be so impossible?"

"It's not impossible."

"It is, because it's over. Being young is over. The moment you have a child of your own being young is over."

"I want you."

"I'm not young any more. A different person."

"I haven't slept with a woman . . ."

"Don't say it, Conrad."

"That's what loneliness is all about."

She said, "I know."

Outside in the garden, nothing moved. Nothing stirred the dripping leaves of the rhododendrons. Eventually, a figure slipped away down the narrow paths of the shrubbery, leaving a trail of footmarks on the sodden grass, the indentations of high-heeled shoes.

28

Wednesday the Fourteenth

Isobel sat at her kitchen table, drank coffee and made lists. She was an inveterate list-maker, and these small inventories of things to be done, food to be bought, meals to be cooked, telephone calls to be made, as well as reminders to herself to split the polyanthus or dig up the gladioli, were constantly pinned to her kitchen noticeboard, along with postcards from friends and children, and the address of a man prepared to clean the outside of the windows. At the moment she was working on three lists. Today, tomorrow, and then Friday. With one thing and another, life had suddenly become very complicated.

She wrote: "Dinner Tonight." There were some chicken joints in the deep-freeze. She could grill these or make some sort of a casserole.

She wrote: "Get chicken legs out. Peel potatoes. String beans."

Tomorrow was more complicated, with her house party committed in three different directions. Isobel herself would be at Corriehill for most of the day, helping Verena and her band of ladies to arrange flowers and somehow decorate that enormous marquee.

She wrote: "Secateurs. String. Wire. Wire-cutters. Beech branches. Rowan branches. Pick all the dahlias."

But, as well, there was Vi's birthday picnic by the loch to think about, and a day's shooting for Archie, because tomorrow they were driving grouse over Creagan Dubh, which meant that he would be joining the other guns.

She wrote: "Baps and cold ham for Archie's piece. Gingerbread. Apples. Hot soup?"

As for Vi's picnic, Lucilla, Jeff, Pandora, and the Sad American would probably want to go to that, which meant a hefty contribution of goodies from Croy.

She wrote: "Sausages for Vi's barbecue. Make some beefburgers. Slice tomato salad. French bread. Two bottles wine. Six cans lager."

She poured more coffee, went on to Friday. "Eleven people for dinner," she wrote, and then underlined the words and sat debating over grouse or pheasant. Pheasant Theodora was spectacular, cooked with celery and bacon and served with a sauce of egg yolks and cream. As well as being spectacular, Pheasant Theodora could be concocted in advance, which precluded a lot of last-minute labour while the dinner guests were drinking cocktails.

She wrote: "Pheasant Theodora." The door opened and Archie appeared.

Isobel scarcely raised her head. "You like Pheasant Theodora, don't you?"

"Not for breakfast."

"I didn't mean for breakfast, I meant for dinner the night of the party."

"Why can't we have roast grouse?"

"Because it's a fiddle to serve. Little last-minute bits and pieces, like scraps of toast to arrange and gravy to stir."

"Roast pheasant then?"

"Same objections."

"Is Pheasant Theodora the one that looks like sick?"

"It does, a bit, but I can cook it ahead."

"Why don't you just cook *a head*?"

"Ha ha."

"What's for breakfast?"

"It's in the bottom oven."

Archie went over to the Aga and opened the oven door. "A red-letter day! Bacon, sausages, and tomatoes. What's happened to the porridge and boiled eggs?"

"We have visitors staying. Bacon, sausages, and tomatoes are what we always give visitors." He brought his plate over to the table and settled himself beside her, pouring coffee, reaching for the toast and the butter.

"I thought," he said, "that Agnes Cooper was coming to help on Friday evening."

"So she is."

"Why can't she roast the pheasant?"

"Because she's not a cook. She's a washer-up."

"You could always ask her to cook."

"All right. I will. And we'll have mince and tatties for dinner because that's all the poor woman's capable of."

She wrote: "Clean silver candlesticks. Buy eight pink candles."

"I just wish Pheasant Theodora didn't look like sick."

"If you say it looks like sick in front of all our guests, I shall cut your throat, there and then, with a fruit knife."

"What are we going to have for starters?"

"Smoked trout?"

Archie put half a sausage into his mouth and chewed it thoughtfully. "And pudding?"

"Orange sorbet."

"White or red wine?"

"A couple of bottles of both, I think. Or champagne. We'll be drinking champagne for the rest of the evening. Perhaps we'd better stick to that."

"I haven't got any champagne."

"I shall order a crate today, in Relkirk."

"Are you going to Relkirk?"

"Oh, Archie!" Isobel laid down her biro and gazed at her husband in hopeless exasperation. "Do you never listen to anything I tell you? And why do you think I'm all dressed up in my posh clothes? Yes, I am going to Relkirk today. With Pandora and Lucilla and Jeff. We're going shopping."

366

"What are you going to buy?"

"Lots of things for Friday night." She did not say, a new dress, because she still hadn't made up her mind about this extravagance. "And then we're going to lunch in the Wine Bar, and then we're coming home again."

"Will you get me some cartridges?"

"I'll get you anything you need if you'll write me a list."

"So I'm not expected to come." He sounded pleased. He hated shopping.

"You *can't* come because you've got to be here when the Sad American arrives. He's driving a hired car from Relkirk, and he's due sometime this morning. And you're not to go wandering off, otherwise he'll be faced by a deserted house and think he's not expected and go away again."

"Might be as well. What shall I give him for lunch?"

"There's soup and pâté in the larder."

"Which room's he sleeping in?"

"Pandora's old room."

"What's his name?"

"I can't remember."

"So how am I supposed to greet him? Hail, Sad American." Archie seemed to find this funny. He made his voice enormously deep. "Big Chief Running Nose Speaks with Forked Tongue."

"You've been watching too much television." But luckily she found it funny too. "He'll think he's come to a madhouse."

"Wouldn't be all that far off the mark. What time are you setting off for Relkirk?"

"About half past ten."

"Lucilla and Jeff seem to be on the move, but you'd better prise Pandora out of bed or you'll still be waiting for her at four o'clock in the afternoon."

"I already did," Isobel told him. "Half an hour ago."

"She's probably climbed back into bed and gone to sleep again."

But Pandora had done no such thing. The words were scarcely out of Archie's mouth when they heard the tap of her high heels coming down the passage from the hall. The door opened and she burst into the kitchen, her profusion of hair bright as a flame, and face filled with laughter.

"Good morning, good morning, here I am, and I bet you thought I'd gone back to bed." She kissed the top of Archie's head and settled herself beside him. She was wearing dark-grey flannel trousers and a pale-grey sweater patterned with pink knitted sheep, and was carrying a magazine. This, it appeared, was the root cause of her amusement. "I'd forgotten this marvellous mag. Papa used to take it every month. *The Country Landowners' Journal.*"

"We still take it. I never got around to cancelling the subscription."

"I found this copy in my bedroom. It's simply fascinating, full of mind-boggling articles about something called Flea-Beetle Dust, and how we've all got to be terribly kind to badgers." She began to riffle through the pages. Isobel poured her a cup of coffee. "Oh, thank you darling, heaven. But the best are the ads at the back. Do listen to this one: 'For Sale. Titled Lady Wishes to Dispose of Underclothes. Peach-Pink Directoire Knickers and Silk Opera-Top Vests. Hardly Worn. Offers.'"

Archie finished munching his bit of toast. "Who do we write to?"

"Box number. Do you suppose that because she's titled, she's simply *stopped* wearing underclothes?"

"Perhaps somebody's died," Isobel suggested. "An old aunt. And she's cashing in on the loot."

"Some loot. *I* think she's having a mid-life crisis and has changed her image. Gone on a diet and lost stones of weight and become all flighty. She's into satin camiknickers now with lace round the legs, and His Lordship doesn't know what's hit him. And here's another marvellous one. Do listen, Archie. 'Work Wanted. Person-

368

able Farmer's Son. (Does that mean the farmer's personable or the son is?) Thirty Years Old. Some Experience in Draining. Driver. Fond of Shooting and Fishing.' Just *think*!" Pandora's eyes became enormous. "He's only *thirty* and he's able to drive a car. I'm sure he'd be frightfully useful to you, Archie. 'Some Experience in Draining.' He'd be able to take care of all the plumbing. Ballcocks and such. Why don't you drop him a line and offer to take him on?"

"No. I don't think so."

"Why ever not?"

Archie thought about it. "He's over-qualified."

Simultaneously, their shared sense of the ridiculous bubbled to the surface and brother and sister dissolved into giggles. Isobel, observing them, shaking her head at their idiotic paroxysms of mirth, was nevertheless filled with grateful wonder. Since Pandora's arrival, Archie had been in better spirits than Isobel had seen him for years, and now, sitting at her own breakfast table, she recognised once more that attractive and blissfully funny man she had fallen in love with over twenty years ago.

Pandora was not the perfect guest. Domestically speaking, she was a dead loss, and Isobel spent much time clearing up after her – making her bed, cleaning her bath, tidying away her clothes, and doing her laundry. But Isobel would forgive her anything, because she knew that it was his sister who had brought about the miraculous change in Archie, and for this could be nothing but grateful, for somehow Pandora had rekindled Archie's youth and brought, like a gust of fresh wind, laughter back to Croy.

The shopping party, one by one, mustered. Jeff, having eaten his way through Isobel's enormous breakfast, went to collect Pandora's Mercedes from the garage, and drive it around to the front of the house. Isobel, armed with shopping baskets and the inevitable lists, joined him. Pandora was the next to appear, wearing her mink coat and her dark glasses and reeking of Poison.

It was another windy day with flashes of sunshine, and they all stood around in the breeze and waited for Lucilla. She came at last, shouted for by her father, and then shooed out through the door by him, just as he shooed his dogs. But she turned back to say goodbye, embracing and kissing him as though she were never going to see him again, before running down the steps with her dark hair flying.

"Sorry, I didn't know you were waiting."

Lucilla was dressed in old and faded jeans with slits at the knees that had been ineptly patched with some red-spotted material. With these, she wore a crumpled cotton shirt with much embroidery and drooping sleeves. The tails of this hung down below a very small leather waistcoat, dangling with fringe. She looked, thought her mother, as though she had just been raped by a Sioux.

"Darling, aren't you going to change?" She spoke rashly.

"Mum, I *am* changed. These are my best jeans. I bought them in Majorca when I was staying with Pandora."

"Oh yes, of course." They all got into the car. "I am sorry, Lucilla. How silly of me."

Having reached Relkirk and found a place to park, the shoppers split up, because Lucilla and Jeff wanted to case the antique shops and browse around the famous street market.

"We'll meet you for lunch in the Wine Bar," Isobel told them. "At one o'clock."

"Have you booked a table?"

"No, but we should get one."

"Right. We'll be off then." They walked away across the cobbled square. As Isobel watched them go, she saw Jeff put his arm around Lucilla's thin shoulders. Which surprised her, because he had struck her as a most undemonstrative young man.

"That's got rid of them," said Pandora, sounding like

a wicked child who, having disposed of the grown-ups, was ripe and ready for mischief. "Now, where are all the dress shops?"

"Pandora, I haven't quite made up my mind . . ."

"We're going to get you a dress for the dance, and that's it. And stop looking agonised because it's going to be my present to you. I owe it. I'm paying a debt."

"But . . . shouldn't we do all the important shopping first? The food for Friday, and . . ."

"What could be more important than a new dress? We can leave all the boring stuff until the afternoon. Now, stop standing around and dithering, or we'll waste the day away. Head us in the right direction . . ."

"Well . . . there's McKay's . . ." said Isobel doubtfully.

"Not a dreary department store. Isn't there somewhere exclusive and expensive?"

"Yes, there is, but I've never been into it."

"Well, now is the time to start. Come on."

And Isobel, feeling all at once carefree and pleasantly sinful, abandoned her Calvinistic tendencies and followed.

The shop was narrow and deep, thickly carpeted, lined with mirrors, and sweetly scented like a glamorous woman. They were the only customers, and as they came through the plate-glass door, a woman rose from behind an enviable little marquetry desk and came to meet them. Dressed for work, she wore the sort of outfit that Isobel would have happily gone out to dinner in.

"Good morning."

She was told what they searched for.

"What size are you, madam?"

"Oh." Isobel, already, was flustered. "I think a twelve. Or maybe a fourteen."

"Oh, no." A professional eye was cast over Isobel, gauging. Isobel hoped that her tights hadn't laddered. "I'm sure a twelve. The ball-gowns are through here, if you'd like to come."

They followed her into the back of the shop. She swept aside a curtain and revealed open wardrobes bulging with racks of evening dresses. Some short, some long; silk and velvet, glimmering satin, chiffon, and voile; and every beautiful colour under the sun. She rattled the hangers along the rail.

"These are twelves, here. But of course, if you find something you like in another size, I could always get it altered for you."

"We haven't time," Isobel told her. Her eyes moved to the darker gowns. Dark colours didn't date, and you could always add bits to them to make them look different. There was a brown satin. Or a navy-blue ribbed silk. Or maybe black. She took down a black crêpe with jet buttons, and moved to the mirror to hold it in front of her . . . a bit governessy perhaps, but she saw it standing her in good stead for years . . . She tried squinting at the price ticket but was not wearing her glasses.

"This is nice."

Pandora scarcely gave it a glance. "Not black, Isobel. And not red." She pushed more hangers aside, and then pounced. "Now, *this*."

Isobel, still listlessly holding the black crêpe, looked – at the most beautiful dress she had ever imagined. Sapphire-blue Thai silk shot with black, so that as the light moved over the material, it shimmered like the wings of some exotic insect. The skirt was huge, puffed out with petticoats, and it had a low neck. The sleeves were finished at the elbow with narrow ruffles of the same silk, and an identical ruffle bordered the hem.

Scarcely daring to imagine herself owning such a garment, Isobel eyed the tiny waist. "I'll never get into that."

"Try."

It was as though she had lost all will of her own. Bundled into a curtained changing-room, stripped, like some votive sacrifice, of all her outer clothes. "Now."

372

She stood in her bra and tights, and the profusion of whispering silk was lowered cautiously over her head; sleeves pulled up over her arms; the zip . . .

She sucked in her breath, but there was no problem. The waistline hugged her snugly, but she could breathe. The saleslady settled the shoulders, bouffed out the skirt, stepped back to admire.

Isobel saw herself full-length in the mirror, and it was like seeing another person. A woman from another age, stepped down from the frame of an eighteenth-century portrait. The hem of the dress swept the floor, the stiff silk arranging itself in gleaming folds. The sleeves were infinitely flattering, and the deep neckline revealed Isobel's best points, which were her pretty plump shoulders and the swelling curve of her breasts.

Overwhelmed with desire, she tried to remain practical. "It's too long."

"It won't be with high heels," Pandora pointed out. "And the colour makes your eyes as blue as ink."

Isobel looked and saw that this was true. But she put her hands to her tanned and weathered cheeks. "My face is all wrong."

"Darling, you're wearing no make-up."

"And my hair."

"I'll do your hair for you." Pandora narrowed her eyes. "You need jewellery."

"I could wear the Balmerino earrings. The diamond drops with the pearls and sapphires."

"Of course. Perfection. And Mama's pearl choker? Have you got that as well?"

"It's in the bank."

"We'll get it out this afternoon. You're beautiful in it, Isobel. Every man in the room will be in love with you. We couldn't have found anything more becoming." She turned to smile at the silent but satisfied saleslady. "We'll have it."

The dress was unzipped, gently removed, and taken away to be parcelled up.

"Pandora!" Isobel whispered urgently, reaching for her Marks & Spencer petticoat. "You never even asked the price."

"If you have to ask the price, you can't afford it," Pandora whispered back and disappeared. Isobel, torn between excitement and guilt, was left to put on her blouse and skirt, button up her jacket and lace up her shoes. By the time she had done this, the cheque had been written, the price-tag removed, and the ravishing dress packed into a huge box.

The saleslady went to open the door for them.

"Thank you so much," said Isobel.

"I'm glad you found something you liked."

The whole transaction had taken no more than ten minutes. Pandora and Isobel stood on the pavement in the sunshine.

"I can't thank you . . ."

"Don't thank me . . ."

"I've never in my life owned such a dress . . ."

"Then it's about time you did. You deserve it . . ."

"Pandora . . ."

But Pandora did not want to hear any more. She looked at her watch. "It's only a quarter to twelve. What shall we go and buy now?"

"But haven't you spent enough money?"

"Heavens no, I've only just started. What's Archie going to wear to the party? His kilt?"

They began slowly to walk down the pavement.

"No. He hasn't worn his kilt since his leg was shot off. He says a horrible tin knee sticking out is an obscenity. He'll just wear his dinner jacket."

Pandora stopped dead. "But Lord Balmerino can't go to a Highland dance in his dinner jacket."

"Well, he's been doing it for years."

A fat lady with a basket, annoyed by the obstruction they were causing, said "Excuse *me*," and pushed her way between them. Pandora ignored her.

"Why doesn't he wear tartan trews?"

374

"He hasn't got any."

"Why ever not?"

Isobel tried to think why this obvious solution had not solved the problem years ago, and realised that, along with his leg, Archie had lost all pride and pleasure in his appearance. It was as though it didn't matter any longer. As well, luxury clothes cost money, and there always seemed to be something else more essential to spend it on.

"I don't know."

"But he always used to look so yummy at dances. And what's more, knew he did. In a boring old dinner jacket, he'll look like an undertaker, or a part-time waiter. Or worse, a Sassenach. Come on, let's go and buy him something brilliant. Do you know what size he is?"

"Not offhand. But his tailor will."

"Where's his tailor?"

"In the next street."

"Would he have tartan trews? Off-the-peg?"

"I should think so."

"Then what are we waiting for?" And Pandora was off again, striding away with her mink coat open and flying. Isobel, lugging her parcel, had to run to keep up with her.

"But even if we find some trews, what's he going to wear with them? He can't wear a dinner jacket."

"Papa had a very handsome velvet smoking jacket. Faded bottle green. What's happened to that?"

"It's up in the attic."

"Well, we'll go and find it. Oh, how exciting. Just imagine how majestic the dear man is going to look."

They found the old tailor working away at his table in the back regions of the shop, a Gentleman's Outfitters Specialising in Highland Dress for All Occasions. Disturbed, he raised his head from an unrolled bolt of tweed, saw Isobel, laid down his scissors and favoured her with a beaming smile.

"Lady Balmerino."

375

"Good morning, Mr Pittendriech. Mr Pittendriech, do you remember my sister-in-law, Pandora Blair?"

The old man looked at Pandora over the top of his spectacles. "Yes, I remember. But it's a long time ago. You couldn't have been more than a wee girl." Across the table, he and Pandora shook hands. "Very pleased to see you again. And how is His Lordship, Lady Balmerino?"

"He's very well."

"Is he able to get up the hill?"

"Not very far, but . . ."

Pandora, impatient, interrupted. "We've come to buy him a present, Mr Pittendriech. A pair of tartan trews. You know his measurements. Would you come and help us choose a pair?"

"Most certainly. It would be a pleasure." He abandoned his cutting and emerged from behind his table to lead them back to the main shop, where a plethora of tartans, leather sporrans, skean dhus, diced hose, lace jabots, silver-buckled shoes, and Cairngorm brooches fairly dazzled the eye.

Mr Pittendriech obviously felt that all this was a little beneath his dignity.

"Would it not be better if I were to tailor His Lordship a pair of trews? He's never been a gentleman to buy his clothes off-the-peg."

"We haven't time," Isobel said for the second time that morning.

"In that case, would it be regimental tartan, or family tartan?"

"Oh, family tartan," said Pandora firmly. "Anyway, it's such a pretty one."

It took a little time to find the right tartan, and then more time fiddling with a tape measure to ensure that the inside leg was the correct length. Finally, Mr Pittendriech made his choice.

"This pair should do His Lordship very nicely."

Isobel considered them. "They aren't going to be too

narrow, are they? Otherwise he won't be able to get them over his tin leg."

"No, I think they should be amply comfortable."

"In that case," said Pandora, "we'll have them."

"And how about a cummerbund, Miss Blair?"

"He can wear his father's, Mr Pittendriech." She turned her dazzling smile upon him. "But perhaps a really lovely new white cotton shirt?"

More parcels, more cheques. Out on the pavement again. "Time for lunch," said Pandora, and they headed, mutually delighted with themselves, in the direction of the Wine Bar. Propelled into this popular rendezvous by the revolving door, they came up against the first obstacle of the day. There was no sign of Lucilla and Jeff, most of the tables were occupied, and those that weren't had "Reserved" notices placed upon them.

"We want a table for four," Pandora told the superior-looking woman behind the high desk.

"Have you resairved?"

"No, but we still want a table for four."

"I'm afraid if you haven't resairved, then you will have to await your turn."

Pandora opened her mouth to argue, but before she could say anything the telephone on the desk began fortuitously to ring and the woman turned aside to pick up the receiver. "This is the Waine Bar."

Behind her back, Pandora dug Isobel in the ribs, and then, looking unconcerned, stalked over to where an empty and reserved table stood by the window. Reaching it, she unobtrusively whisked the "Reserved" sign up and pushed this deep into the pocket of her coat. A brilliant and professional piece of sleight of hand. She then settled herself gracefully, disposed of her bag and parcels, spread the mink over the back of the chair, and reached for the menu.

Isobel, horrified, hovered. "Pandora, you *can't* . . ."

"I have. Bloody woman. Sit down."

377

"But someone's *reserved* it."

"But we've got it. Possession is nine-tenths of the law." Isobel, who dreaded any sort of a scene, continued to hesitate, but Pandora took no notice of her waffling, and after a bit, with no alternative, she sat down as well, facing her blatantly criminal sister-in-law. "Oh, look, we can have a cocktail. And we can eat quiche and salad, or an omelette *aux fines herbes*."

"That woman's going to be *livid*."

"I hate cocktails, don't you? Do you suppose they have any champagne? Let's ask when she comes gunning for us."

Which she did, almost immediately.

"Excuse me, madam, but this table is resairved."

"Oh, *is* it?" Pandora's eyes were bland and innocent orbs. "But there's no sign."

"This table is resairved, and there was a sign upon it."

"Where can it be?" Pandora craned her neck to look under the table. "It's not on the floor."

"I'm sorry, but I'm afraid you will have to move and await your turn."

"I'm sorry, but I'm afraid we're not going to. Will you take our order, or would you rather send one of the waitresses?"

The woman's neck was growing red, like turkey wattles. Her mouth worked. Isobel felt rather sorry for her.

"You know perfectly well that there was a resairved notice upon this table. The manager put it there himself this morning."

Pandora raised her eyebrows. "Oh, there's a manager, is there? Then perhaps you would like to go and find him, and tell him that Lady Balmerino is here and wishes to order lunch."

Isobel, hot with embarrassment, felt her cheeks burn. Pandora's adversary by now looked as though she was about to burst into tears. Humiliation stared her in the

378

face. "The manager is not in this afternoon," she admitted.

"In that case, you are obviously in charge, and you have done all you can. Now, perhaps you will send a waitress over and we can order."

The poor woman, reduced to pulp by such nerveless authority, dithered for a moment, but finally collapsed, her ire deflating like a pricked balloon. In silence, gathering her tattered dignity about her, and with lips pressed together, she turned to go. But Pandora was remorseless. "Just one more thing. Would you be very kind and tell the barman that we'd like a bottle of his best champagne." Her smile dazzled. "Iced."

No more objections, no more argument. It was over. Isobel stopped blushing. She said, "Pandora, you are shameless."

"I know, darling."

"Poor female. She's practically in blubs."

"Silly old cow."

"And the Lady Balmerino bit . . ."

"That's what did the trick. These sort of people are the most appalling snobs."

It wasn't any good trying to scold her. She was Pandora, generous, loving, laughing . . . and ruthless if she didn't get her own way. Isobel shook her head. "I despair of you."

"Oh, darling, don't be cross. We've had such a heavenly morning, and I'll be good for the rest of the day and hump all your grocery boxes. Oh, look, there are Lucilla and Jeff. Laden with rather tatty carrier bags. What could they have been buying?" She waved, flapping a red-nailed hand. "Here we are!" They saw her, and came over. "We've ordered champagne, Jeff, so you're not to be boring and say you'd rather have a can of Foster's."

Over the champagne, Lucilla and Jeff were told, in lowered tones and with a certain amount of muffled mirth, the saga of the resairved table.

Lucilla was amused, but at the same time almost as shocked as her mother, and Isobel was glad to see this. "Pandora, that's dreadful. What's going to happen to the poor people who *did* reserve the table?"

"That's the old bag's problem. Oh, don't worry, she'll tuck them in somewhere."

"But it's frightfully dishonest."

"I think you're being very ungrateful. If it wasn't for my quickthinking enterprise, we'd all be standing in a queue with aching shoppers' feet. Anyway, she was offhand and rude to me. And I don't like being told I can't have anything I really want."

Archie, left on his own and forbidden by his wife to leave the purlieus of the house, decided to fill in the time before their guest arrived by clearing up the first of the fallen leaves that littered the lawn beyond the gravel sweep. He would then perhaps find time to cut it, and all would look orderly for the party on Friday night. With only his dogs for company, he duly drove his garden tractor out of the garage and set to work. The Labradors, who had imagined that he was about to take them for a small walk, sat about and looked bored, but diversion was on its way, for Archie had only completed a couple of runs before a Land-Rover came spinning up the front drive, turned in over the cattle-grid, and came to a halt a few yards from where he laboured.

It was Gordon Gillock, the Croy keeper, with his two spaniels penned into the back of the vehicle. A cacophony of barking instantly erupted, from both inside and outside the Land-Rover, but all four dogs were swiftly silenced by a stream of routine abuse from Gordon, and quiet was once more achieved.

Archie stopped his machine and switched off the engine, but stayed where he was, seated, because that was as good a place as any to engage in conversation.

"Hello, Gordon."

"Good morning, milord."

Gordon was a lithe and stringy Highlander in his early fifties but looking, with his black hair and dark eyes, a good deal younger. He had come to Croy as an under-keeper in the days of Archie's father, and had been in the family's employ ever since. Today he wore his working clothes, which meant an open-necked shirt and a tweed hat, stuck with fishing flies, that had seen many years of windy weather. But on shooting days, he wore a collar and tie and a knickerbocker suit with a deerstalker of the same tweed, and was a good deal better-dressed than most of the other gentlemen out on the moor.

"Where have you come from?"

"Kirkthornton, sir. I took thirty brace of birds down to the game dealer."

"Did you get a good price?"

"Not so bad."

"What's happening tomorrow?"

"That's why I'm here, sir. Wanted a word. Mr Aird's not going to be with us. He's away in America."

"I know. He rang me before he left. We're shooting Creagan Dubh?"

"That's right, the main glen. I thought, first thing we'd drive the Clash, and then come in the other way over Rabbie's Naup."

"What about the afternoon? Should we try the Mid Hill?"

"It's up to you, sir. But mind, the birds are getting pretty wild. They'll be coming in fast over the butts and the guns will need to keep their wits about them."

"They know they're responsible for seeing that all the shot birds are picked up and brought down the hill? No runners abandoned. I don't want any wounded birds left to die."

381

"Oh aye, they know that. Mind, there are some good dogs this year."

"You were walking on Monday. How did you get on?"

"There was a fair wind and a lot of water about. Then an eagle and a buzzard started working overhead, and that scared the daylights out of the grouse. They either wouldn't get up or they flew in all directions. But there was some good shooting. We finished with thirty-two brace."

"Any deer?"

"Oh aye, a big herd. Saw them on the skyline sticking their heads up over the Sneck of Balquhidder."

"And how about that damaged bridge over the Taitnie burn?"

"I've seen to that, sir. It was just about down, with the rain we've been having and the water in spate."

"Good. We don't want any of the London gentlemen suffering a ducking. How about beaters for tomorrow?"

"I've got sixteen."

"And flankers? The last time we drove, a lot of the birds slipped away because of poor flanking."

"Aye, they were a useless pair of buggers. But tomorrow I've got the schoolmaster's son and Willy Snoddy." The keeper caught Archie's eye and the two of them grinned. "He's an unreliable old villain but a rare flanker." Gordon shifted his weight, took off his hat, scratched the back of his neck, and then put his hat on again. "I was up at the loch early yesterday morning. Caught him there with that old lurcher of his, lifting your trout out of the water. He's there evenings forbye, making full use of the late rise."

"Do you see him?"

"He sneaks up the back lane from the village, but, aye, I've spied him more than once."

"I know he poaches, Gordon, and so does the local bobby. But he's done it all his life, and he's not going to stop now. I don't say anything. Besides" – Archie smiled – "if he's flung into jail, we're short of a flanker."

"True enough, sir."

"What about the beaters' money?"

"Went to the bank this morning, sir, collected it then."

"You seem to have got it all well organised, Gordon. Thank you very much for dropping in. And I'll see you tomorrow . . ."

Gordon and his dogs departed, and Archie continued with his leaf-sweeping. He had just about completed the task when he heard a second car coming up the back drive from the village, and decided that this time, in all likelihood, it would be the Sad American in his hired car. He wished to hell he knew what the bloody man was called. In preparation, he once more stopped the tractor and switched off the engine, and as he eased himself cautiously on to his two feet, the car came down the avenue towards him and he realised that it was Edmund's Subaru, and so not the Sad American after all. Virginia was at the wheel, but a man sat beside her. The Subaru drew to a halt, and as Archie, awkwardly stiff, limped forward, they got out of the car and came to meet him.

"Virginia."

"Hello, Archie. I've brought your guest to stay with you." Archie, at a loss, turned to the stranger. Tall, well-built, quite handsome in a weathered sort of way. Not young, and wearing heavy horn-rimmed spectacles. "Conrad Tucker; Archie Balmerino."

The two men shook hands. Archie said, "I'm sorry . . . I thought you were coming under your own steam, in a hired car . . ."

"I intended doing that, but . . ."

Virginia interrupted. "I'll explain. It's the most extraordinary coincidence, Archie. I met Conrad yesterday evening in the King's Hotel, in Relkirk. Out of the blue. And of course we're very old friends. We knew each other in Long Island when we were young. So instead

383

of spending the night at the hotel as he'd planned, he came back to Balnaid with me and stayed there."

So all was clear. "But what a fortuitous meeting, and what a good idea." And then Archie added, for Conrad's benefit, "The ridiculous thing is that my wife was either never told, or forgot, your name, and so Virginia would never have known that our house guest was yourself. I'm afraid sometimes we're dreadfully vague."

"It's very good of you to have me."

"Anyway . . ." Archie hesitated, wishing that Isobel was here. ". . . this is all splendid. Come along. Let's go indoors. There's nobody here but me because the others have all gone shopping. Have you got a bag, Conrad? What's the time? A quarter to twelve. The sun's not over the yardarm yet, but I think we could have a gin and tonic . . ."

Virginia said, "No, Archie," and she sounded jumpy and unlike herself. Archie looked at her with closer attention and saw the pallor beneath her tan and the dark rings under her eyes. She seemed upset and he was concerned for her, and then remembered that only yesterday she had had to take Henry to Templehall and leave him there. Which explained everything.

He felt very sympathetic and said kindly, "Why not? It'll do you good."

"It's not that I don't want to stay, but I have to take some stuff up to Corriehill for Verena. Flower vases. Things like that. If you don't mind, I think I'd better get home."

"Whatever you want."

"We'll all see each other tomorrow at Vi's picnic."

"Not me. I'm shooting. But Lucilla and Jeff and Pandora will take Conrad along with them."

Conrad had retrieved his bag from Virginia's car and was standing waiting for what was going to happen next. Virginia went to him and gave him a kiss. "See you tomorrow, Conrad."

"Thanks for everything."

384

"It's been great."

She got back into the Subaru and drove away, back under the trees and down the hill. When she had gone, Archie turned to his guest. "How very nice that you already know Virginia. Now, come along and I'll show you where you're sleeping . . ."

He led the way up to the door and into the house, and Conrad, slowing his pace down to his host's halting step, followed him.

Back at Balnaid, in her flower pantry, searching for jugs, urns, bowls, old soup tureens, Virginia was grateful for domestic occupation. At the moment she needed neither idle hands nor an empty mind. Especially an empty mind. She assembled her loot and then collected pin-holders and screwed-up pieces of chicken wire, essential for keeping top-heavy flower arrangements in place. Making two or three trips, she carried everything out to the Subaru and stowed it all neatly into the back of the car.

Meanwhile, she made plans. Tomorrow morning early, Alexa and Noel and Alexa's dog would be arriving, having driven up from London overnight. They would be at Balnaid for breakfast. When I come back from Corriehill, she told herself, I shall get the bedrooms ready for Alexa and Noel. Bedrooms. Not a bedroom. In London they slept together, in a double bed, but Virginia knew that if she were to put them in a double bed at Balnaid, Alexa would be embarrassed, and even more put out than her father.

Tomorrow. She would think about tomorrow. She would not think about yesterday, nor the day before. Nor last night. They were over. Finished with. Done. Nothing could be changed and nothing could be altered.

When the bedrooms were finished, she would emulate

385

Isobel and make lists, visit Mrs Ishak and do an enormous shop. The dogs would have to be walked. After that she might do some cooking, make a cake or a pot of soup. Or brownies for tomorrow's picnic. By then it would be evening, and then night, and the long, lonely, soul-searching days would be over. She would sleep in her empty bed, in her empty house. Without Edmund, without Henry. But the morning would bring Alexa and Noel, and with them for company surely things must get better; life would seem less impossible and easier to bear.

She drove to Corriehill and found the place in a turmoil. Alien vans and lorries were parked on the gravel outside, and inside, the house appeared to have been taken over by armies of workmen, as though the family were on the point of moving out, or moving in. In the hall, most of the furniture and the rugs had already been shunted aside, electric cables snaked in all directions, and the open doors of the dining room revealed that this, by means of festoons of darkly striped material, had been transformed into a lightless cave. The nightclub. She paused to admire but was almost instantly asked to move aside by a young man with long hair who staggered, with bent knees, beneath the weight of some piece of audio equipment.

"Do you know where I can find Mrs Steynton?"

"Try the marquee."

Picking her way through the confusion, Virginia made for the library and saw, for the first time, the gargantuan tent that had been erected on the lawn the day before. It was very tall and very wide, and took most of the daylight from the rooms inside. The french doors of the library had been removed, and house and marquee were joined by the umbilical cord of a wide, tented passageway. She went down this and stepped into the aqueous, filtered gloom that was the interior of the marquee, saw the soaring tent-poles, tall as masts, the yellow-and-

386

white striped lining. On the top of tall ladders, more electricians were perched fixing the overhead lights, and at the far end a couple of burly men were constructing, with trestles and planks, a platform for the band. There was the smell of trodden grass and canvas, rather like an agricultural show, and in the middle of it all she found Verena with Mr Abberley, who was in charge of the entire operation, and apparently being given a piece of Verena's mind.

". . . but it's ridiculous to say we've got the measurements wrong. You *took* the measurements."

"The thing is, Mrs Steynton, that the floor comes in prefabricated units. Six-by-three. I explained when you ordered my largest tent."

"I never imagined there would be a problem."

"And there's another thing. Your lawn's not level."

"Of course it's level. It used to be a tennis court."

"I'm sorry, but it's not. Sinks down in that corner a foot or more. That means wedges."

"Well, use wedges. Just be certain the floor doesn't collapse."

Mr Abberley looked hurt. "My floors never collapse," he told her, and took himself off to mull over the situation.

Virginia said, "Verena." Verena turned. "I don't seem to have come at a very good time."

"Oh, Virginia." Verena ran fingers through her hair in a most uncharacteristic fashion. "I'm going demented. Have you ever seen such a mess?"

"I think it looks fantastic. Terribly impressive."

"But it's so *huge*."

"Well, you're having a huge party. When it's full of flowers and people and the band and everything, it'll be quite different."

"You don't think it's all going to be the most dreadful flop?"

"Of course not. It'll be the dance of the century. Look, I've brought the flower vases. If you tell me where to put them, I'll bring them into the house and then get out of your way."

"You are a dear. If you go into the kitchen, you'll find Katy and some friends of hers. They're making silver stars, or streamers, or something, to decorate the night-club. She'll show you where to put them."

"If there's anything else you're needing . . ."

But Verena's attention was already wandering. "If I think of anything, I'll call you . . ." She had too much on her mind. "Mr Abberley! I've just remembered. There's something else I want to ask you . . ."

Virginia drove home. By the time she reached Balnaid again, it was nearly two o'clock. She was beginning to feel ravenously hungry, and decided that before she did anything else, she must have something to eat. A cold beef sandwich, perhaps, some biscuits and cheese, and a cup of coffee. She parked the Subaru at the back door and walked indoors and into the kitchen.

All thoughts of food instantly flew out of her head. She stopped dead, her empty stomach contracting in a spasm of shock and outrage.

For Lottie was there. Waiting. Sitting at the kitchen table. She did not look abashed in the very least, but smiled as though Virginia had asked her to drop by, and Lottie, graciously, had taken up the invitation.

"What are you doing here?" This time Virginia made no effort to keep the irritation out of her voice. She was startled but she was also enraged. "What do you want?"

"Just waiting for you. And I wanted a wee word."

"You have no right to walk into my house."

"You should learn to lock your doors."

Across the kitchen table, they faced each other.

"How long have you been here?"

"Ooh, about half an hour." Where else had she been? What had she been doing? Had she been snooping around Virginia's house, gone upstairs, opened cupboards, opened drawers, touched Virginia's clothes? "I thought you'd not be long, leaving the doors open like that. 'Course, the dogs barked, but I soon quieted them down. They can always tell a friend."

A friend.

"I think that you should go at once, Lottie. And please don't ever come back unless you are asked."

"Oh, Miss Hoity-Toity, is it? Am I not good enough for the likes of you?"

"Please go."

"I'll go in my own time when I've said what I have to say."

"You have nothing to say to me."

"But that's where you're wrong, Mrs Edmund Aird. I have plenty to say to you. Up to high doh you were, when I met you out for a walk on the bridge. Didn't like what I had to say, did you? I could tell. I'm not stupid."

"You were telling lies."

"And why should I tell lies? I have no reason to tell lies because the truth is black enough. 'Whore' was what I called Pandora Blair, and you buttoned up your lips as though I'd said a dirty word, pretending to be so pure yourself, and high and mighty."

"What do you want?"

"I want to see no evil and fornicating," Lottie droned, and she sounded like a Wee Free minister promising his congregation Eternal Damnation. "The vileness of men and women. Lustful practices . . ."

Infuriated, Virginia cut her short. "You're talking drivel."

"Oh, drivel, is it?" Lottie became herself again. "And is it drivel that when your man's away, and you're rid of your wee boy, you bring your fancy men home with you and take them to your bed?" It was impossible. She was making it up. Letting her crazy twisted imagination feast on her own carnal fantasies. "Aha, I thought that would silence you. Mrs Edmund Aird indeed. You're no better than a street-walker."

Virginia took hold of the edge of the table. She said,

and kept her voice quite cold and quite calm, "I don't know what you're talking about."

"And who's lying now, may I ask?" Lottie, with her hands clasped in her lap, leaned forward, her strange eyes fixed on Virginia's face. Her skin was waxy as a candle and the faint shadow of her moustache darkened her upper lip. "I was there, Mrs Edmund Aird." Her voice dropped, and now she spoke in the hushed tones of a person telling a ghost story, and making it as scary as possible. "I was outside your house when you came home last night. I saw you coming back. I saw you, switching on all the lights and making your way up the stairs with your fancy man. I saw you at the bedroom window, leaning out like a pair of lovers and whispering between the two of you. I saw you draw the curtains, and shut yourselves away, with your lust and your adultery."

"You had no right to be in my garden. Just as you have no right to be in my house. It's called trespass, and if I wanted I could call the police."

"The police." Lottie gave a cackle of laughter. "Fat lot of good they are. And wouldn't they be interested to know what goes on when Mr Aird is in America. Missing him, were you? Thinking of him and Pandora? Told you about them, didn't I? Makes you wonder, doesn't it? Makes you wonder who you can trust."

"I want you to go now, Lottie."

"And *he's* not going to be pleased when he knows what's been going on."

"Go. Now."

"One thing's for certain. You're no better than the rest of them, and don't try to convince me you're not guilty, because your face gives you away . . ."

Virginia finally lost her cool. Through clenched teeth she screamed at Lottie, "GET OUT!" She flung out an arm, pointing at the open door. "Get out and stay out and never come back, you creeping old bag."

Lottie was silenced. She did not budge. Across the

table, she stared at Virginia, her eyes hot with hatred. Virginia, dreading what might happen next, stood, tense as strung wire. If Lottie made one move to touch her, she would turn the heavy table on top of the old lunatic and squash her flat as a beetle. But, far from becoming physically violent, Lottie's face assumed an expression of deep complacency. The glitter went out of her eyes. She had said her piece, achieved what she'd set out to do. Without hurry, in her own time, she got to her feet and neatly buttoned up her cardigan. "Well," she announced, "I'll be off then. Bye-bye, doggies, nice to have met you."

Virginia watched her go. Lottie, on her high heels, tapping jauntily across the kitchen. At the open door she paused to look back. "That's been very nice. No doubt I'll see you around."

And then she was gone, quietly closing the door behind her.

Violet, in her own little kitchen at Pennyburn, stood, aproned, at the table, and iced her birthday cake. Edie had made the cake, which was large and had three tiers, but Violet had been left to do the decorating. She had made chocolate-butter icing and with this had stuck the three tiers together. Now she was engaged in spreading what remained of the sticky goo over the outside of the cake. She was not an expert at cake-decorating and, when it was completed, it had a fairly rough-and-ready appearance, more like a newly ploughed field than anything else, but by the time she had stuck a few brightly coloured Smarties into the icing and added the single candle that was all she allowed herself, it would be quite festive enough.

She stood back to eye the finished cake, licking a few gobs of icing off her fingers. At that moment she heard a car coming up the hill and then turning into her own driveway. She looked up and out of the window and saw that her visitor was Virginia, and was pleased. Virginia was on her own, and Violet was always gratified when her daughter-in-law unexpectedly dropped in, uninvited, because it meant that she wanted to come. And today was specially important, because they would have time to sit down and talk, and Violet would be able to hear all about Henry.

She went to wash her hands. Heard the front door open and close.

"Vi!"

"I'm in the kitchen." She dried her hands, reached to untie her apron.

"Vi!"

Violet tossed her apron aside and went out into the hall. Her daughter-in-law stood there at the foot of the stairs, and it was immediately obvious to Violet that something was very wrong. Virginia was as pale as paper, and her brilliant eyes were hard and bright, as though they burned with unshed tears.

She was filled with apprehension. "My dear. What is it?"

"I have to see you, Vi." Her voice was controlled, but there was unsteadiness there. She was not far from weeping. "I have to talk."

"But of course. Come along. Come and sit down . . ." She put her arm around Virginia and led her into the sitting room. "There. Sit down. Be quiet for a moment. There's nothing to disturb us." Virginia sank into Vi's deep armchair, laid her head back on the cushion, closed her lovely eyes, and then, almost immediately, opened them again.

She said, "Henry was right. Lottie Carstairs is evil. She can't stay. She can't stay with Edie. She must go away again."

Vi lowered herself into her own wide-lapped fireside chair. "Virginia, what has happened?"

392

Virginia said, "I'm frightened."

"That she will do Edie some harm?"

"Not Edie. Me."

"Tell me."

"I . . . I don't quite know how to start."

"Everything, from the beginning."

Her quiet tones had effect. Virginia gathered herself, visibly making some effort to keep control and stay sensible and objective. She sat up, smoothing back her hair, pressing her fingers to her cheeks as though she had already wept and was wiping tears away.

She said, "I've never liked her. Just as none of us has ever liked her, or been happy with the fact that she's living with Edie. But, like the rest of us, I told myself that she was harmless."

Violet remembered her own reservations about Lottie. And the frisson of panic she had experienced, sitting with Lottie by the river in Relkirk, with Lottie's hand closed around her wrist, the fingers strong and steely as a vice.

"But now you believe that we were all wrong?"

"The day before I took Henry to school . . . Monday . . . I took a walk with the dogs. I went to Dermot's to buy something for Katy, and then on and over the west bridge. Lottie appeared out of nowhere. She'd been following me. She told me that you all knew – all of you – you and Archie and Isobel and Edie. She said that you knew."

Violet thought, oh, dear God. She said, "Knew what, Virginia?"

"Knew that Edmund and Pandora Blair had been in love with each other. Had been lovers."

"And how did Lottie know this?"

"Because she was working at Croy at the time of Archie and Isobel's wedding. There was a dance that night, wasn't there? She said that she followed them upstairs in the middle of the party, and listened at Pandora's bedroom door. She said that Edmund was

393

married and had a child, but that made no difference, because he was in love with Pandora. She said that everybody knew because it was so blatantly obvious. She said that they are still in love with each other, and that is why Pandora has come back."

It was even worse than Violet had dreaded, and for once in her life she found herself at a total loss for words. What could one say? What could one do to comfort? How to salvage a single grain of comfort from those muddy depths of scandal, stirred up by a madwoman who had nothing to do with her pathetic life but make trouble?

Across the small space that divided them, her eyes met Virginia's. And Virginia's were filled with pleading, because all she wanted was for Violet to assure her that the whole fabrication was a pack of lies.

Violet sighed. She said, with total inadequacy, "Oh dear."

"It's true then. And you did know."

"No, Virginia, we didn't know. We all had a pretty shrewd idea, but we didn't know, and we never spoke about it to each other, and we all went on behaving as though it had never happened."

"But *why*?" It was a cry of despair. "Why did you all shut *me* out? I'm married to Edmund. I'm his wife. How did you imagine that I wouldn't find out? And from that dreadful woman, of all people. It's a sort of betrayal, as though you didn't trust me. As though you thought I was some sort of innocent child, not old enough nor mature enough to deal with the truth."

"Virginia, how could we tell you? We didn't even know for certain. We simply suspected, and being the people that we are, we brushed it all away under the carpet and hoped that it would stay there. She was eighteen, and Edmund had known her since she was a child. But he'd been in London, and he'd married and had Alexa, and he hadn't seen Pandora for years. And then he came north for Archie's wedding, and there she was again. Not a child any longer but the most ravishing, wicked, delicious creature you've ever seen in your life. And I have an idea that she had always been in love with Edmund. When they met again, it was like an explosion of fireworks. We all saw the fireworks but we turned away and did not watch. There was nothing we could do except hope that the fireworks would burn themselves out. And it wasn't as though there was any chance of it going on for ever. Edmund had commitments in London. His wife, his child, his job. When the wedding was over, he went away, back to his own responsibilities.''

"Did he go willingly?"

Violet shrugged. "With Edmund it's impossible to know. But I remember seeing him off, in his car, from Balnaid, and saying goodbye, and very nearly saying something more. Something ridiculous. Like 'I'm sorry' or 'Time is a great healer' or 'You'll forget Pandora', but at the end of the day I lost my nerve and I never said anything.''

"And Pandora?"

"She went into a sort of teenage decline. Tears, sulks, misery. Her mother confided in me, and was in the greatest distress about it all, but truly, Virginia, what could we say? What could any of us do? I suggested sending Pandora away for a little . . . to do some sort of a course, or perhaps go to Paris or to Switzerland. At eighteen she was still very young in many ways, and some worthwhile project . . . learning a language or working with children . . . might have diverted her misery. Given her the chance to meet other young people and the chance to get over Edmund. But I'm afraid she'd always been most dreadfully spoiled, and in a strange way her mother was frightened of Pandora's tantrums. Whether anything was ever said, I don't know. All I do know is that Pandora simply hung around Croy for a month or two, making everybody's lives utterly miserable, and the next thing was she'd run off with that dreadful Harald Hogg, rich as Croesus and old enough to be her father. And that, tragically enough, was the end of Pandora."

"Until now."

"Yes. Until now."

"Were you concerned when you knew she was coming back?"

"Yes. A little."

"Do you think they are still in love with each other?"

"Virginia, Edmund *loves* you." Virginia said nothing to this. Violet frowned. "You *surely* know that."

"There are so many different sorts of love. And sometimes, when I really need it, Edmund doesn't seem to have it to give."

"I don't understand."

"He took Henry away from me. He said I smothered him. He said I only wanted to keep Henry because he was some sort of a possession, a toy I wanted to go on playing with. I begged and pleaded and finally had that dreadful row with Edmund, but nothing made any difference. It was like arguing with a brick wall. Brick walls don't love, Vi. That isn't love."

"I shouldn't say this, but I am on your side as far as Henry is concerned. But he *is* Edmund's child, and I truly believe that Edmund is doing what he thinks best for Henry."

"And then this week he swanned off to New York, just when I really needed him here. Taking Henry to Templehall and leaving the poor little scrap was the worst thing I've ever had to do in the whole of my life."

"Yes," said Vi inadequately. "Yes, I know." They fell silent. Violet considered the miserable situation, went back in her mind over all they had been saying. And then realised that there was a small discrepancy. She said, "Virginia, all this happened on *Monday*. But you came to see me today. Has something else occurred?"

"Oh." Virginia bit her lip. "Yes. Yes, it has."

"Lottie again?" Violet scarcely dared to ask.

"Yes. Lottie. You see . . . Vi, you remember last Sunday, having lunch at Croy and all of us teasing Isobel about her house guest, the Sad American? Well, on my way back from Templehall, I stopped off at the King's Hotel to go to the loo, and I met him there. And I know him. I know him quite well. He's called Conrad Tucker and we used to play tennis together in Leesport, about twelve years ago."

This was about the most cheerful thing Violet had been told since Virginia appeared. She said, "But how very nice."

"Anyway, we had dinner together, and then it seemed silly, his staying in Relkirk when he was coming to Croy the next day, so he came back to Balnaid with me, and stayed there. I took him up to Croy this morning and left him with Archie. And then I went to Corriehill with some flower vases for Verena. And then I came home and I found Lottie in the kitchen."

"In the kitchen at Balnaid?"

"Yes. She was waiting for me. She told me . . . that last night she'd been at Balnaid, standing in the garden, in the dark and the rain, when Conrad and I came back. She watched us. Through the windows. None of the curtains were drawn. She watched us going upstairs . . ." Virginia met Violet's horrified gaze, opened her mouth and shut it again. Finally, she said, "She called me a whore. Called Conrad a fancy man. Raved on about lust and fornication . . ."

"She is obsessed."

"She must go, or she will tell Edmund." Before Violet's eyes, Virginia all at once went to pieces, her face crumpling like a child's, tears brimming into her blue eyes and overflowing, streaming down her cheeks. "I can't bear any more, Vi. I can't bear everything being so horrible. She's like a witch, and she hates me so much . . . I don't know why she hates me . . ."

She groped for a handkerchief but could not find one,

397

so Violet handed over her own, lawn and lace-trimmed and little use for damming such a flood of misery.

"She is jealous of you. Jealous of all normal happiness . . . As for telling Edmund, he will know, as we all know, that it is nothing but a pack of lies."

"But that's just it," Virginia wailed. "It's true. That's what's so ghastly. It's true."

"*True?*"

"I did sleep with Conrad. I went to bed with him because I wanted to, and I wanted him to make love to me."

"But *why?*"

"Oh, *Vi*. I suppose we needed each other."

It was a desperate admission, and watching her weeping daughter-in-law, Violet found herself flooded with compassion. That Virginia, of all people, should have been driven to such lengths was a clear indication of the state that her marriage had been allowed to reach. But, thinking it over, it was perfectly understandable. The man, Conrad Tucker or whatever he was called, had just lost his wife. Virginia, in a turmoil over Edmund's motivations, had just lost her beloved son. They were old friends. For comfort, people turned to old friends. She was a desirable woman, sexual and attractive, and the unknown American was in all probability a personable man. But still, Violet wished, beyond all else, that it had never happened. More than that, she wished that she had never been told.

Only one essential stood out, crystal-clear.

She said, "You must never tell Edmund."

Virginia blew her nose on the sodden handkerchief. "Is that all you have to say?"

"It's the only important thing to say."

"No reproaches? No recriminations?"

"What took place is none of my affair."

"It was wrong."

"But, under the circumstances, understandable."

"Oh, Vi." Virginia slipped out of the chair, on to her

398

knees, put her arms around Violet and buried her face in Violet's considerable bosom. "I'm sorry."

Violet laid a hand on her hair. She said sadly, "We are all of us human."

For a little they stayed as they were, comforted by closeness. Virginia's sobs gradually stilled. Presently, she drew away from Violet and sat back on her heels. She blew her nose in a final sort of fashion.

She said, "There's just one more thing, Vi. When Edmund's back, and the dance is all over, I'm thinking of going back to Long Island for a little. To stay with Gramps and Grandma. I need to get away. I've been wanting to go for some months but it never worked out, and now that I have no Henry, it seems a good time."

"And Edmund?"

"I thought . . . Edmund could stay with you."

"When did you think of leaving?"

"Next week?"

"Is that wise?"

"You tell me."

"Just remember that you can't run away from reality any more than you can run away from guilt."

"Reality being Edmund and Pandora?"

"I didn't say that."

"But that's what you're thinking, isn't it? You just told me she'd always been in love with him. And I'm certain that she's no less beautiful now than she was at eighteen. And they share something that I can't share with Edmund, which is a thousand memories of youth. And in a funny way, those are always the most enduring and the most important."

"You are important, and I don't think you should leave Edmund just now."

"I've never minded before. All the times he has to go away and leave me, I've never known jealousy or worried about what he was up to. I tell him I don't care what he does provided I don't have to watch him doing

399

it. A joke. But it's not a joke now. If anything's going to happen, I don't want to be a witness."

"You underestimate your friends, Virginia. Do you imagine that Archie would stand by and watch, and do nothing?"

"If Edmund wants his own way, then Archie would be no match for him."

"Pandora will not stay at Croy for ever."

"But she's there *now*. And *now* is going to be my problem."

"Do you dislike her?"

"I think she's charming."

"But you don't trust her?"

"At the moment I don't trust anybody, least of all myself. I need to stand back, make a reappraisal, get things in perspective. That's why I'm going back to the States."

"I still think that you shouldn't go."

"I think I have to."

There did not seem to be anything more to be said. Violet sighed. "In that case, we'll talk no more about it. Instead, we must be practical and take steps. One thing, very clear, is that Lottie must go. Back to hospital. She is a deadly mischief-maker and I fear for Edie. I shall see to that immediately. And while I'm making my telephone call, I suggest that you go and wash your face and tidy your hair, and then find my brandy bottle, which is in the dining-room sideboard, and a couple of glasses. We shall both have a cheering medicinal tot and then we shall feel much stronger and much better."

Virginia did as she was told. While she was out of the room, Violet heaved herself out of her chair and went to her desk. She looked up the number of the Relkirk Royal, dialled, and asked to be put through to Dr Martin. A little wait while the telephonist bleeped him, and then he came on the line.

"Dr Martin?"

Violet, at some length, explained who she was, and her connection with Lottie Carstairs.

"You know who I'm talking about, Dr Martin?"

"Yes, of course."

"I'm afraid that she is really not fit to be out of hospital. She behaves in a most irrational fashion, and is distressing and upsetting a lot of people. As for Miss Findhorn, with whom she is staying, I think it is really all too much for her. She's not a young woman, and Lottie is too much of a responsibility for her."

"Yes." The doctor sounded thoughtful. "I see."

"You don't seem surprised."

"No, I'm not surprised. I discharged her into the care of Miss Findhorn because I thought that maybe going back into ordinary life and living in a regular household would help to restore her to some sort of normality. But it was always a risk."

"It seems that the risk has not paid off."

"No, I realise that."

"Will you take her back into your care?"

"Yes, of course. I'll speak to my ward sister. Will you be able to drive Miss Carstairs into the hospital? It might be better than sending an ambulance. And bring Miss Findhorn with you. It's important that she is there, as she is the patient's next of kin."

"Of course. We'll be with you some time this afternoon."

"If there's any trouble, let me know."

"I certainly will," Violet promised him, and put down her receiver.

Knowing that the dilemma of Edie's cousin had been dealt with and that Lottie was probably being returned to the Relkirk Royal that very afternoon did more than the slug of Violet's best brandy to restore Virginia's equilibrium.

"When are you taking her?"

"Now," Violet told her. She had already changed her shoes and was buttoning herself into her jacket.

401

"Supposing Lottie refuses to go?"

"She won't."

"Supposing she has a tantrum in the car and tries to strangle you?"

"I shall have Edie with me, and she will stop her. I know this will be a great relief to dear Edie. She can't object."

"I'd come with you, only . . ."

"No, I think *you* must keep well out of the way."

"You'll give me a ring when it's all safely over?"

"Of course."

"Just take care." Virginia put her arms around Violet and kissed her. "And thank you. I love you, and I never get around to telling you."

Violet was touched, but had other things now on her mind. "Dear girl." Absently, she patted Virginia's shoulder, as she laid her plans for dealing with Lottie and Edie. "I'll see you tomorrow at the picnic."

"Of course. And Alexa and Noel will be there too."

Alexa and Noel. More family, more friends arriving. So many people, so many demands, so many decisions, so much to be resolved. I am seventy-eight tomorrow, Violet reminded herself, and wondered why she was not sitting peacefully in a wheelchair with a lace cap on her head. She reached for her handbag, found her car keys, opened the front door. Alexa and Noel.

"I know," she told Virginia. "I hadn't forgotten."

She had feared a terrible scene with Lottie, but at the end of the day it was all quite painless. She found Lottie sitting in Edie's armchair watching television and looking as though butter wouldn't melt in her mouth. Violet paused to exchange a few pleasantries with her, but Lottie was far more interested in the fat lady on the screen who was demonstrating how to make a pleated lampshade out of an old piece of wallpaper. Through the kitchen window, Violet spied Edie in her garden, pegging out her daily line of washing. She went to join her and tell her, quietly and out of earshot of her cousin, all that had been decided and all that had been arranged.

Edie, who had been, of late, looking tireder by the day, now looked as though she was about to cry.

She said, "I'm no' wanting to send her away."

"Edie, it's getting too much for all of us. It's always been too much for you, and now she's started persecuting Virginia and spreading the most distressing rumours. You know what I'm talking about."

Of course Edie knew, but between them nothing needed to be spoken.

"I was afraid," Edie admitted.

"She's sick, Edie."

"Have you told her?"

"Not yet."

"What will you say?"

"Just that Dr Martin wants to see her again. To keep her in the Relkirk Royal for a day or two."

"She'll be furious."

"I don't think so."

Edie pegged out the last of her washing, stooped to pick up the empty laundry basket. She did this as though it weighed a ton, as though she were hefting all the worries of the world.

She said, "I should have kept an eye on her."

"How could you?"

"I blame myself."

"Nobody could have done more." Violet smiled. "Come. We'll all have a cup of tea, and then I'll tell her what's happening while you put her belongings into a suitcase."

Together they made their way up the long garden and back to the cottage.

"I feel," said Edie, "like a murderer. She's my cousin and I've failed her."

"It's she who's failed you, Edie. You haven't failed her. Just as you've never failed any of us."

By six o'clock in the evening, the whole distasteful

episode was over, and Lottie was once more incarcerated in the Relkirk Royal under the care of a kindly ward sister, and the incredibly youthful Dr Martin. Mercifully, she had made no objections when Violet told her what was about to happen, simply announced that she hoped that Dr Faulkner would take a bit more notice of her, and then raised her voice to remind Edie not to forget to pack her best green cardigan.

She had even come to the door of the hospital, with the ward sister in attendance, and waved them a cheerful goodbye as Violet drove Edie away down the road between the dismally formal gardens that Lottie had thought so beautiful.

"You mustn't worry about her, Edie."

"I can't help it."

"You have done all you can. Been a saint. You can always visit Lottie. It's not the end."

"She's such a poor soul."

"She needs professional care. And you have more than enough to do. Now you must put it all behind you and enjoy yourself again. It's my picnic tomorrow. No long faces for my birthday."

Edie, for a little, sat silent. And then, "Have you iced your cake?" she asked, and they made plans for the picnic, and by the time Violet dropped her back at her cottage, she knew that they were over the worst.

She drove back to Pennyburn, let herself indoors through the back door and heaved a sigh of relief because she was safely home again. The birthday cake still sat on the table where she had left it. Seventy-eight years old. No wonder she was feeling utterly drained. The icing had become too hard for Smarties, so it would have to do just the way it was. She put it in a tin, then went into her sitting room, poured herself a large, strong whisky and soda, sat at her desk, and made the last, but vitally important, telephone call of the day.

"Templehall School."

"Good evening. This is Mrs Geordie Aird speaking. I

am Henry Aird's grandmother, and I would like to speak to the headmaster."

"This is the headmaster's secretary speaking. Can I take a message?"

"No, I'm afraid you can't."

"Well, the headmaster's busy at the moment. Perhaps I could ask him to ring you?"

"No. I should like to speak to him now. If you would go and find him, and tell him that I am waiting."

The secretary hesitated, and then said reluctantly, "Oh. Very well. But it may take some minutes."

"I shall wait," Violet told her majestically.

She waited. After a long time, she heard, from some distant uncarpeted passageway, the approaching tread of footsteps.

"Headmaster speaking."

"Mr Henderson?"

"Yes."

"It's Mrs Geordie Aird, Henry Aird's grandmother. I'm sorry to bother you, but it's important that you give Henry a message from me. Will you do that?"

"What is the message?" He sounded rather impatient, or cross.

"Just tell him that Lottie Carstairs is back in hospital, and no longer living with Edie Findhorn."

"Is that all?" He sounded disbelieving.

"Yes, that's all."

"And it's important?"

"Vitally important. Henry was very worried about Miss Findhorn. He will be most relieved to know that Lottie Carstairs is no longer living with her. It will be a weight off his mind."

"In that case, I'd better write it down."

"Yes, I think you had better. I shall repeat it." Which she did, raising her voice and enunciating clearly, as though the headmaster might be stone-deaf. "LOTTIE CARSTAIRS. IS BACK IN HOSPITAL. AND NO LONGER LIVING. WITH EDIE FINDHORN. Have you got that?"

405

"Loud and clear," said the headmaster, revealing a thin vein of humour.

"And you'll tell Henry, won't you?"

"I'll go at once and find him."

"You're very kind. I'm sorry I bothered you." She thought about asking for Henry, inquiring as to his well-being, and then decided against it. She didn't want to be labelled as an old fusspot. "Goodbye, Mr Henderson."

"Goodbye, Mrs Aird."

At the top of the long climb where the roughly bulldozed road crested the summit of Creagan Dubh, Archie halted the Land-Rover and the two men climbed down and stood to survey the wondrous view.

They had come, that afternoon, from Croy by way of the track that led through the farmstead and the deer-fence, alongside the loch, and so up into the wilderness of the hills. Now, the Wester Glen lay far behind and below them, the waters of the loch blue as a jewel. Ahead, the main glen of Creagan plunged down in a succession of corries and spurs to where the purling waters of a narrow burn glittered like a bright thread in the spasmodic sunshine. To the north, ramparts of empty countryside folded away into infinity. The light was fitful, constantly changing, so that distant peaks were shadowed with a blue bloom, and cloud lay upon them like a blanket of smoke.

In the gardens of Croy, it had felt pleasantly warm, with sunlight streaming down through golden trees and only a faint breeze to cool the air. But here, so high had they come, that same air blew pure and clear as iced water, and the north-west wind had a cutting edge to it, buffeting across the open moorland with no tree nor any sort of obstruction to stand in its way.

Archie opened the back of the Land-Rover and his two dogs, who had been waiting for some time for just this moment, leapt down. He reached in and pulled out two disreputable old weatherproof coats, much dirtied and torn, but with thick woollen linings.

"Here." He tossed one over to Conrad, and then, propping his stick against the rear of the Land-Rover, pulled on the other. Its pockets were ripped and there were bloodstains down the front of it, witness to some long-since slaughtered hare or rabbit.

"We'll sit down for a bit. There's a spot a few yards in . . . we can get out of the wind . . ."

He led the way, stepping off the stony surface of the road and into the high heather, using his stick as a third leg to get him through the thick of it. Conrad followed, observing his host's painful progress but making no offer to assist. After a little, they came to an outcrop of granite, weathered by a million years of exposure, crusted with lichen and jutting like some ancient monolith from its deep bed of heather. Its natural shape provided a place to sit and a not-very-comfortable backrest against which to lean but, settled, they achieved some shelter from the worst of the wind.

The dogs had been ordered to heel, but the younger one was not as disciplined as her mother, and as Archie made himself as comfortable as he could, and reached for his field-glasses, she scented game, bolted off in high excitement and put up a covey of grouse. Eight birds exploded out of the heather only yards from where they sat. *Go-Back Go-Back* they called, sailing down into the depths of the glen, jinking beneath the skyline, settling far below, disappearing.

Conrad, in amazed delight, watched their flight. But Archie snarled at the dog, and, drooping with shame, she returned to his side, leaning her head against his shoulder and apologising profusely. He put his arm around her and drew her close, forgiving her small misdemeanour.

407

"Did you mark them?" he asked Conrad.

"I think so."

Archie handed over his glasses. "See if you can find them."

With the field-glasses to his eyes, Conrad searched. Distance sprang into detail. In the deep clumps of heather at the foot of the glen, he scanned painfully for the vanished birds, but could see no trace, mark no movement. They had gone. He gave the glasses back to Archie.

"I never imagined I'd see grouse so close."

"After a lifetime, they never fail to amaze me. So wily and brave. They can fly at eighty miles an hour, and use every trick to outwit a man with a gun. They're the most demanding adversaries, which is why they provide such incomparable sport."

"But you shoot them . . ."

"I've shot grouse all my life. And yet, as I grow older, I shoot less frequently and, I must admit, with some reservation. My son Hamish, so far, has shown no qualms, but Lucilla hates the whole business and refuses to come out with me." He sat hunched in his ragged old coat, with his good leg drawn up and his elbow resting on his knee. His worn tweed cap was pulled low over his forehead, shading his eyes against the fitful blasts of sunlight. "She feels very strongly that they are wild birds, and so part of God's creation. By wild, I mean that they are self-perpetuating. It is impossible to rear them as one might rear pheasants, because to put chicks from a hatchery out on to these moors would mean instant and certain death from predators."

"What do they feed on?"

"Heather. Blaeberries. But mostly heather. Because of that, a well-keepered moor is regularly burned in strips. By law, burning is controlled. It's only allowed during a few weeks in April, and if you haven't burned by then, it has to be left for another year."

"Why do you burn?"

"To encourage new growth." He pointed with his stick. "You can see the black strips on the Mid Hill where we burned this year. The longer heather is left to give the birds good protective cover."

Conrad gazed in some bewilderment at the rolling miles all about him. "It's a hell of a lot of land for what seems to me an awfully few birds."

Archie smiled. "It does appear to be a bit of an anachronism, in this day and age. But if it wasn't for the great sporting estates in Scotland, enormous tracts of land would become neglected, or decimated either by intensive farming of some sort or other, or else commercial forestry."

"Is planting trees such a bad thing?"

"It's a touchy subject. The Scots pine is our indigenous tree, not Sitka spruce from Norway, nor lodgepole pine from North America. And it depends on how well the woodland is husbanded. But a tightly packed stand of Sitka spruce destroys the breeding ground of upland birds because they won't nest within nine hundred yards of it. It harbours too many predators – foxes and crows. And I'm not simply talking about grouse but redshank and golden plover and curlews as well. And other forms of wildlife. Bugs, insects, frogs, adders. And plantlife. Harebells, cotton-grass, rare mosses and fungi, bog asphodel. Properly cared for, the moor is a powerhouse of rational ecology."

"But isn't the image of the rich guy on the grouse moor blasting away at the birds the subject of some ridicule?"

"Of course it is. The chinless aristocrat loading his gun with ten-pound notes. But I believe that image is fading, as even the greenest of politicians becomes aware that the link between country sports and conservation is of immense importance if the basic ecosystem of the Highlands is going to survive."

They fell silent. Stealthily, that silence was filled with small sounds, as seeping water will fill a void. The faint piping and drumming of the wind. The whisper of the distant burn, running in spate. Across the glen, scattered over the side of the hill, sheep grazed, moved, bleated. And as these sounds filled the quiet, so Conrad, at ease with his companion, found himself pervaded by tranquillity, a peace of mind that he had forgotten even existed.

Maybe this was wrong. Maybe after what had taken place last night, he should be suffering agonies of remorse and guilt. But his conscience was dormant, even self-satisfied.

"I feel like a shit," he had told Virginia, "because I want you."

And he *had* felt guilty, aching with the physical need to make love to another man's wife, behind that other man's back, and in that other man's house. But he could do little to quench his desire, and even less when it became perfectly clear that Virginia's need for comfort and love were just as great as his own. It had been, for him, a night of joyous release after months of enforced celibacy. And for her, perhaps an assuagement of loneliness and a last impetuous taste of lost youth.

Last night, coming to Balnaid, she had become shy, keeping Conrad at arm's length with her hostessy busyness, aware as a young animal of potential danger. But this morning, she was composed. He had woken late, having slept more deeply than he had for months, and found her gone. Dressed, he made his way downstairs and discovered Virginia in the kitchen cooking breakfast, perking coffee, talking to the two spaniels. She still looked pale, but far less strained, and greeted him with a smile. Over bacon and eggs, they talked of trivial matters, and he respected her reticence. Perhaps it was better that way, with neither of them indulging in heart-searching analysis, or trying to rationalise the events of the previous evening.

A one-night stand. For Virginia, perhaps, that was it. Conrad could not be sure. For himself, he simply felt

410

immensely grateful to the fates that had flung them together at a time when both were vulnerable, bereft, and deeply in need of each other. Matters had taken their own course in a natural progression as basic as breathing.

No regrets. For Virginia he had no real worry. For himself, he only knew that twelve years ago he had been in love with her, and now he could not be too certain that anything had changed.

A movement caught his eye. A buzzard appeared, floating in the sky, then began its descent, spiralling in flight. A second later, another covey of grouse burst from the heather halfway down the hill and flew southward, at amazing speed, with the wind on their tails. The two men watched them go.

Archie said, "I hoped we'd see more birds. We're shooting this glen tomorrow. Driving over the butts."

"Will you be there?"

"Yes. It's about all I can manage, provided I can get myself to the bottom butt. It's one of the things I really regret, not being able to walk the hill any longer. Those were the best days; walking up with a few friends and half a dozen dogs. Now just a thing of the past."

Conrad hesitated. The two men had spent most of the day in each other's company, but Conrad, not wishing to appear curious or impertinent, had deliberately not brought up the subject of Archie's obvious disability. Now, however, it seemed a sensible opportunity. "How did you lose your leg?" he asked casually.

Archie watched the buzzard. "It was shot off."

"An accident?"

"No. Not an accident." The buzzard hovered, dived, swept back up into the sky, its prey, a small rabbit, dangling from its beak. "An incident in Northern Ireland."

"What were you doing there?"

"I was a regular soldier. I was there with my regiment."

411

"When was this?"

"Seven, eight years ago." The buzzard had gone. Archie turned his head to look at Conrad. "The Army has been in Northern Ireland now for twenty years. Sometimes I think the rest of the world forgets how long that bloody conflict has been going on."

"Twenty years is a long time."

"We went to stop the violence, to keep the peace. But we haven't stopped the violence, and peace still seems a long way off." He shifted his position, laid down his glasses, leaned on his elbow. He said, "During the summers, we have Americans to stay, as paying guests. We give them beds, arrange diversions for them, wine them and dine them, and make conversation. During these conversations, the subject of Northern Ireland is frequently raised, and inevitably, some joker comes out with the opinion that Northern Ireland is Great Britain's Vietnam. I have learned swiftly to change the subject and talk about something else."

"I wasn't going to say that. About Vietnam, I mean. I wouldn't be so presumptuous."

"And I didn't mean to sound aggressive." He eyed Conrad. "Were you in Vietnam?"

"No. I've worn glasses since I was eight years old, so I was labelled medically unfit."

"Would you have fought, without that legitimate let-out?"

Conrad shook his head. "I don't know. But my brother went. He joined the Marines. He flew a gunship. He was killed."

"What a flaming, bloody, useless war. But then, all war is flaming and bloody and useless. And Northern Ireland most useless of all because the troubles have their roots in the past, and nobody is willing to pull those roots up and throw them away, and start planting something decent and new."

"By the past, you mean Cromwell?"

"I mean Cromwell, and William of Orange, and the

412

Battle of the Boyne, and the Black-and-Tans and the young men who went on hunger strike and died of starvation. And I mean long and bitter memories, and unemployment, and segregation and no-go areas and religious intolerance. And worst of all, the impossibility of being able to apply logic to the situation."

"How long were you there?"

"Three months. It should have been four, but I was in hospital when the battalion came home."

"What happened?"

"To me, or to the battalion?"

"To you."

Archie's response to this was a deep and reluctant telling silence. Looking at him, Conrad saw that once again his attention had been caught by some distant movement, far away out on the opposite hill. His profile was gaunt, seemingly frozen in concentration. Conrad sensed the other man's reluctance to talk, and swiftly retracted from his question.

"I'm sorry."

"Why sorry?"

"I sound curious. I don't mean to be."

"That's all right. It was an incident. That's the euphemistic term for bombings, murders, ambushes, general mayhem. You hear the word every other day over the evening news. An incident in Northern Ireland. And I was involved."

"You were operational?"

"Everybody was operational, but my actual job was Officer Commanding HQ company."

"One reads of such incidents, but, still, it's hard to imagine how it must be out there."

"I hear it's a very pretty country." Conrad was on the point of saying, "I didn't mean that," and then thought better of it, and let Archie continue.

"Parts of Northern Ireland are very beautiful. Sometimes my job took me out of HQ for the best part of the day, visiting units in their posts all over the countryside.

413

Some of those on the border were in beleaguered forts made from old police stations which one could only get to by helicopter for fear of ambush on the roads. It was great, flying over that country. I was there in spring and early summer. Fermanagh with all its lakes, and the Mountains of Mourne." He stopped, and grinned wryly, shaking his head. "Although one had to realise that they not only swept down to the sea, but to the badlands as well. The border."

"Is that where you were?"

"Yes. Right in the thick of it. And different country again. Very green, small fields, winding country roads, lachans and streams. Sparsely populated. Tiny farms dotted about the place, grotty little homesteads surrounded by dead and broken machinery; old cars and tractors left to rot. But all quite pastoral. Peaceful. I found it impossible, sometimes, to relate such surroundings with what was going on."

"It must have been rough."

"It was all right. We were all in it together. Being with your own regiment is a little like being with your own family. You can cope with most things if you have your family around you."

Archie fell silent again. The granite boulder made a painful resting place, and he had become uncomfortable. He shifted his position slightly, easing the strain on his leg. The younger dog, alert, moved in beside him, and Archie fondled her head with a gentle hand.

"Did you have your own barracks?" Conrad asked.

"Yes. If you can call a requisitioned clothing factory a barracks. It was all fairly rough and ready. We lived behind barbed wire, corrugated iron and sandbags, seldom saw daylight, and had little chance of exercise. We worked on one floor, went downstairs to eat, and upstairs to sleep. Scarcely the Ritz. I had a batman-cum-bodyguard who went everywhere with me, and even in plain clothes, we were never unarmed.

"One existed in a state of siege. We were never actually

414

attacked, but there was always the threat of some sort of ambush or assault, so one was prepared for any of the various ploys for blowing a police or military establishment off the face of the earth. One of these was to hijack an armed Land-Rover, load it with high explosives and then get the poor bugger at the wheel to drive it through the open gates of the barracks, park it and set it off from a distance. This actually happened once or twice, whereupon a device was conceived to deal with such a contingency. A solid concrete pit with a steep ramp. The idea was to drive the vehicle into the pit, and then run, shit-for-ginger and screaming warning like a maniac, before the whole caboodle blew up. The resultant devastation was still pretty formidable, but by and large, lives were saved."

"Did that happen to you?"

"No, that didn't happen to me. I have nightmares about those bloody bomb pits, and yet it was never an experience that I had to endure. Strange, isn't it? But then there can be no explanation for the workings of one's own subconscious."

By now Conrad had abandoned his inhibitions about curiosity. "So what *did* happen?"

Archie put his arm around his young dog, and she settled, to lie with her head on her master's tweeded knee.

"It was early in June. Sunshine and blossom everywhere. Then an incident on the border at the crossroads near Keady. A bomb buried beneath the road, in a culvert. Two armoured vehicles – we call them Pigs – were out on border patrol, four men in each Pig. The bomb was detonated by remote control from over the border. One Pig was blown to smithereens and all four men with it. The other was badly damaged. Two men dead and two wounded. One of the wounded was the sergeant in charge, and it was he who radioed back to HQ to report. I was in the Operations Room when the message and the details came through. On such occasions, for security reasons, no names are ever mentioned over the radio, but every man in the battalion has his own Zap code, a number for identification purposes. So, as the sergeant gave us the numbers, I knew exactly who had been killed and who was still alive. And they were all my men.''

''*Your* men?''

''I told you, I was Officer Commanding the Administrative company rather than a rifle company. That meant I was in charge of the Signals, the Quartermaster, the Pay Office and the Pipes and Drums.''

''Pipes and Drums?'' Conrad could scarcely keep the disbelief out of his voice. ''You mean you had a band out there?''

''But of course. The Pipes and Drums are an important part of any Highland regiment. They play Reveille and the Last Post, beat retreat on ceremonial occasions, provide the music for dancing and smoking concerts, and guest nights in the Officers' and Sergeants' Messes. And pipe the lament at funerals. 'The Flowers of the Forest.' The saddest sound on earth. But apart from being an integral part of the battalion, every Piper and Drummer is, as well, an active service soldier and trained as a machine-gunner. It was some of these men who were trapped in that ambush. I knew them all. One of them was a boy called Neil MacDonald, who was twenty-two years old and the son of the head keeper at Ardnamore – that's up at the head of our glen, beyond Tullochard. I first heard him piping at the Strathcroy Games, when he was about fifteen. That year he walked away with all the prizes, and I suggested that when he was old enough, he should join the regiment. And that day, I listened to those Zap codes coming in, and I knew that he was dead.''

Conrad could think of no suitable comment to make, and so sensibly said nothing. A pause fell, not uncompanionable, and after a little, Archie, unprompted, went on.

416

"To deal with such emergencies there is always an Air Reaction Force at full alert. Two bricks of men . . ."

"Bricks?"

"You'd call them squads, and a Lynx helicopter ready and waiting for takeoff. That day, I told the sergeant to stand down, and I took his place and went with them. There were eight of us in the helicopter, the pilot and a crewman, five Jocks, and myself. It took less than ten minutes to get to the scene. When we reached the area, we circled to suss out exactly what had happened. The explosive, which had totally destroyed the first Pig, had left a hole in the road the size of a crater, and the second Pig was arse-over-tit in this. All around was littered with scraps of metal, mess-tins, bits of camouflage netting, bodies, clothing, burning tyres. A lot of smoke, flames, the stench of burning rubber and fuel and paint. But no sign of movement. No sign of anything or anybody."

Once more Conrad found himself astonished by what he thought of as an obvious discrepancy.

"You mean no local people, farmers, or ploughmen, hearing the explosion and running to investigate?"

"No. Nothing. In that part of the world no person goes within arm's length of that sort of trouble, unless of course he wishes to be dead or kneecapped within the week. There was nobody, just the smoke and the carnage.

"There was a patch of grass, like a layby, alongside the road. The helicopter landed and we all piled out. Our immediate task was to stake out the area, and get out the wounded while the helicopter flew back to base to bring in the MO – the Medical Officer – and his boys. But the helicopter had scarcely taken off, and before we had time to shake out, we were caught in a hail of machine-gun fire from across the border. They were waiting for us, you see. Watching and waiting. Three of my Jocks were killed instantly, another was wounded in the chest, and I caught it in the leg. Shot to pieces.

"When the helicopter returned with the MO on board,

myself and the worst of the wounded were flown straight to hospital in Belfast. The sergeant didn't make it, he died on the way. In the hospital my leg was amputated above the knee. I stayed there a few weeks, and then was flown back to England to begin the long business of rehabilitation. Finally I returned to Croy, pensioned off with the rank of Lieutenant Colonel.''

Conrad endeavoured to make a mental tally of the casualties, but lost count and gave up. ''So what did that particular incident achieve?'' he asked.

''Nothing. A hole in the road. A few more British soldiers dead. The next morning, the IRA officially claimed responsibility.''

''Do you feel bitter about it? Angry?''

''Why? Because I've lost my leg? Because I have to hump myself around on this aluminium contraption? No. I was a regular soldier, Conrad. Being shot to ribbons by an implacable enemy is one of the occupational hazards of being a soldier. But I could just as easily have been an ordinary civilian, a run-of-the-mill guy, trying to get peacefully on with his own life. An old father, perhaps, gone to Enniskillen to mourn his dead son on Armistice Day, and ending up dying beneath a pile of rubble. A young boy, taking his girlfriend to a Belfast pub for a drink, and seeing her blown to kingdom come by a booby-trap bomb. I could have been an off-duty service-man, in the wrong car, at the wrong place, at the wrong time; dragged by a mob into a patch of wasteground, stripped, clubbed nigh to death, and finally shot.''

Conrad shuddered. He chewed his lip, shamed by his own queasiness. He said, ''I read about that. It made me want to vomit.''

''Mindless, pointless, bloody violence. And there are other outrages that never reach the papers, are never made public. Do you know, one time a man went into a pub for a few beers. Just an ordinary young man, except that he happened to be a member of the IRA. One of the lads he was drinking with suggested it might

418

be a laugh if he shot off somebody's kneecaps. Which was something he had never actually done, but after three beers he was ready to have a go. He was given a gun, and left the pub, and walked up to the local housing estate. He saw a young girl who was walking home from a friend's house. He hid in a passageway, and as the young girl came past, he grabbed hold of her and pushed her to the ground. He then shot off both her knees. That girl will never walk again.

"Just another incident. But it haunts me because it could have been any man's daughter, and more personally, it could have been my Lucilla. So you see I don't feel bitter and I don't feel angry. Just desperately sad for the people of Northern Ireland, the ordinary decent people who are trying to make a life for themselves, and bring up their children under this terrible, perpetual shadow, of blood and revenge and fear. And I feel sad for the whole human race, because if such senseless cruelty is accepted as the norm, then I can see no future for us all. It is frightening. And I am frightened for myself because, like a child, I still get nightmares that terrify me, and leave me screaming. And there is still worse. Guilt and remorse for that young man I told you about. Neil MacDonald. Twenty-two years old and dead as a doornail. Nothing left of his body, nothing to bury. His parents left without even the consolation of a funeral, or a grave to visit. I knew Neil as a soldier, and a good one, too, but I remember him as a boy, standing on the platform at the Strathcroy Games, piping his Pibroch. I remember the day, the sun shining down on the grass, and the river, and hills, and he and his Pibroch part of it all. Just a boy. With all his life before him, and standing there making that marvellous music."

"You can't blame yourself for his death."

"It was because of me that he became a soldier. If I hadn't shoved my oar in, he would still be alive now."

"No way, Archie. If he was meant to join your regiment, he'd have done it, with no prompting from you."

419

"You think that? I find it hard to be a fatalist. I wish I could be, because then I might be able to lay his ghost and leave him in peace, and stop asking myself, why? Why should I be here, on the top of Creagan Dubh, seeing, breathing, touching, feeling, when Neil Mac-Donald is dead?"

"It is always worst for the one who is left to carry on."

Archie turned his head and looked at Conrad. Across the small space which divided them, the eyes of the two men met. Then Archie said, "Your wife died."

"Yes. Of leukaemia. I watched her die and it took a long time. And all that time I was resentful and bitter, because it wasn't me who was dying. And when she died, I hated myself because I was alive."

"You too."

"I think, probably, it's an inevitable reaction. One simply has to come to terms with it. It takes time. But at the end of the day, all those self-accusing and soul-searching questions are unanswerable. And so, as you Brits would say, it's bloody silly even to ask them."

There was a long pause. Then Archie grinned. "Yes. You are right. Bloody silly." He turned his face up and surveyed the sky. "You are right, Conrad." The sky was darkening. They had sat for too long, and it was becoming cold. "Perhaps we should make tracks for home. And I must apologise. For a moment, I admit, I forgot that you had tragedies of your own to deal with. I hope you will believe me when I tell you that I didn't bring you up here in order to unload my troubles on to your shoulders."

Conrad smiled. "I asked for them," he reminded Archie. He realised then that he was chilled and stiff with sitting, tucked into that hard and inhospitable perch. He rose painfully to his feet, stretching the cramps out of his legs. Out of the shelter of the rock, the wind pounced upon him, stinging his cheeks, sneaking down the back of his collar. He shivered slightly. The dogs, stirring at

420

this promise of activity, and already thinking of their dinners, sat up and gazed with hopeful eyes into Archie's face.

"So you did. But now let us both forget it all and not speak of it again. All right, you greedy bitches, I'll take you home and feed you." He held out an arm. "Give me a hand, would you, Conrad, old boy, and heave me to my feet?"

They left the hills at last, and trundled slowly homewards, down the main glen and so back to Croy. As they came through the front door, the grandfather clock by the staircase chimed the half-hour. Half past six. The dogs were ravenous. It was long past their dinner-time and they headed straight for the kitchen. Archie glanced into the library but there did not seem to be anybody about.

"What would you like to do?" he asked his guest. "We usually eat about half past eight."

"If it's okay with you, I think I'll go up and unpack my bag. Maybe take a shower."

"Fine. Use any bathroom that doesn't happen to be occupied. And come downstairs when you're ready. If there's still nobody around, you'll find a tray of drinks in the library. Help yourself. Make yourself at home."

"That's very kind." Conrad started up the stairs and then turned back. "And thanks for today. It was special."

"Perhaps it is I who should thank you."

Conrad continued on his way. Archie followed the dogs, and in the kitchen found Lucilla and Jeff, at sink and stove, both aproned and looking industrious and companionable. Lucilla turned from some pot she was stirring.

"Dad. You're back. Where've you been?"

"Up on the moor. What are you two up to?"

"We're cooking dinner."

"Where's Mum?"

"She went to have a bath."

"Would you feed the dogs for me?"

"Of course. No problem . . ." She returned to her stirring. "But they've got to wait a moment, otherwise this sauce is going to end up in lumps."

He left them to their cooking, shut the door, went back to the library, poured himself a whisky and soda and, carrying the glass, climbed the stairs in search of his wife.

He found her in the bath, soaking in scented steam and looking as comic as she always did in her blue-and-white-spotted shower-cap.

"Archie." He made himself comfortable on the lavatory seat. "Where have you been?"

"To the top of Creagan Dubh."

"It must have been heavenly. Did the Sad American turn up all right?"

"Yes, and he's not sad. He's very good company. And he's called Conrad Tucker, and he happens to be an old chum of Virginia's."

"I don't believe it! You mean they know each other? What an extraordinary coincidence. But what a lucky one. It'll make him feel not so strange, dumped in this alien household." She sat up and reached for the soap. "You obviously like him?"

"Delightful man. Exceptionally nice."

"What a relief. What's he doing now?"

"Same as you, I think."

"Has he ever been to Scotland before?"

"I don't think so."

"Because I've been thinking. Neither he nor Jeff are going to be able to do any of the dances on Friday night. Do you think it would be a good idea to have a bit of instruction after dinner this evening? Provided they can get themselves through an eightsome reel and one or two others, they can at least join in some of the fun."

"Why not? Good idea. I'll look for some tapes. Where's Pandora?"

"Crashed out, I think. We didn't get home till five. Archie, would you mind if she came up the hill with you

422

tomorrow? I told her about Vi's picnic but she said she'd rather spend the day with you. She wants to sit in your butt and chat."

"No, that's all right, provided she doesn't make too much noise. You'd better see she's got some warm clothes."

"I'll lend her my green wellies and my Barbour."

He drank whisky. Yawned. He was tired.

"How was the shopping? Did you get my cartridges?"

"Yes. And the champagne, and the candles, and enough food to feed a starving army. And I got a new dress for the dance."

"You bought a new dress?"

"No, I didn't buy it. Pandora bought it for me. And it's perfectly beautiful, and I wasn't allowed to know how much it cost, but I think probably an arm and a leg. She seems to be dreadfully rich. Do you think I should have allowed her to be so extravagant and generous?"

"If she wanted to give you a dress, there's no way you could have stopped her. She always loved giving presents. But it was kind. Am I allowed to see it?"

"No, not until Friday, when I shall astonish you with my beauty."

"What else did you do?"

"We had lunch in the Wine Bar . . ." Isobel, squeezing water from her sponge, considered telling Archie about Pandora and the reserved table, and then decided against it because she knew that he would disapprove. "And Lucilla bought a dress off a stall in the market."

"Oh God, it's probably full of fleas."

"I made her leave it at the cleaner's. Somebody will have to go to Relkirk on Friday morning to pick it up. But the most exciting bit of news I've kept to the end. Because Pandora bought *you* a present as well, and if you hand me my towel I shall get out of the bath and show it to you."

He did this. "A present for me?" He tried to imagine what on earth his sister had brought back for him. He

423

hoped not a gold watch, a cigar cutter, or a tiepin, none of which he would use. What he really needed was a new cartridge belt . . .

Isobel finished drying herself, pulled off the bathcap, shook out her hair, reached for her silk dressing-gown, knotted the sash around her waist. "Come and look." He pulled himself off the lavatory seat and followed her through to their bedroom. "There."

It was all laid out on the bed. Tartan trews, a new white shirt still in its cellophane wrapper, black satin cummerbund, and his father's remembered green velvet smoking jacket, which Archie hadn't set eyes on since the old man died.

"Where did that come from?"

"It's been in the attic, in mothballs. I hung it over the bath to get the wrinkles out. And the trews and the shirt are from Pandora. And I've polished your evening shoes."

He gaped. "But what's all this for?"

"Friday night, you goop. When I told Pandora you wouldn't wear your kilt, and you'd go to Verena's party in a dinner jacket, she was horrified. She said you'd look like a part-time waiter. So we visited Mr Pittendriech and he helped us choose these." She held up the trews. "Aren't they heaven? Oh, do try it all on, Archie, I can't wait to see how you look."

The last thing Archie wanted to do, at this particular moment, was to try on a lot of new clothes, but Isobel seemed so excited that he hadn't the heart to refuse her. And so he put his glass down on her dressing-table and obediently began to shed his old tweeds.

"Leave your shirt on. We don't want to open the new one in case you get it dirty. Take off your brogues and those smelly old stockings. Now . . ."

With her help, he pulled on the new trousers. Isobel dealt with zips and buttons, tucking in the tails of his blue country shirt and generally fussing around as if she were dressing a child for a tea-party. She fixed the

424

cummerbund, laced his evening shoes for him, held out the velvet smoking jacket. He put his arms into the silk-lined sleeves, and she turned him around and did up the frogged fastenings.

"Now." She smoothed his hair with her hands. "Go and look in the mirror."

For some reason, he felt like an idiot. His stump ached and he yearned for a hot bath, but he limped obediently over to Isobel's wardrobe, where a full-length mirror was set in the centre panel. Observing himself in mirrors was not his favourite occupation, because his reflection nowadays seemed·such a travesty of his former hand-some self, so thin and grey had he become, so graceless in his shabby clothes, so awkward with his lumbering, hated aluminium leg.

Even now, with Isobel's proud eyes upon him, it took some effort actually to face himself. But he did so, and it wasn't as bad as he thought it would be. It wasn't bad at all. He looked all right. Great, in fact. The trews, long and slim-legged, immaculately cut and sharply creased, had a crisp and almost military dash about them. And the marvellously rich and lustrous velvet of the jacket provided exactly the right touch of worn and gentle-manly elegance, the faded green picking up the thread of green in the tartan.

Isobel had tidied his hair, but now he smoothed it again, for himself; turned to see other aspects of his reflected finery. Undid the jacket to admire the satiny sheen of the cummerbund, sleek around his skinny middle. Did the jacket up again. Caught his own eye and smiled wryly, seeing himself preen like a bloody peacock.

He turned to his wife. "What do you think?"

"You look amazing."

He held out his arms. "Lady Balmerino, will you waltz with me?"

She came to him, and he held her close, his cheek resting on the top of her head, the way they used to

425

dance long ago, smooching in nightclubs. Through the thin silk of her gown his hands felt her skin, still warm from the bathwater, the curve of her hips, her neat waist. Her breasts, soft, unrestricted, pressed against him, and she smelled sweetly of soap.

They shifted gently from foot to foot, rocking in each other's arms, dancing, as best they could, to music which only the two of them could hear.

He said, "Have you, at this moment, got anything pressing that you have to go and do?"

"Not that I can think of."

"No dinner to cook, no dog to feed, no bird to pluck, no border to weed?"

"No."

He pressed a kiss on her hair. "Then come to bed with me."

She was still, but Archie's hand moved on, stroking her back. After a little, she drew away from him, looked up into his face, and he saw that her deep-blue eyes were bright with unshed tears.

"Archie . . ."

"Please."

"The others?"

"All occupied. We'll lock the door. Hang up a 'Do Not Disturb' sign."

"But . . . the nightmare?"

"Nightmares are for children. We are too old to allow dreams to stop us loving each other."

"You are different." She frowned, her sweet face filled with puzzlement. "What has happened to you?"

"Pandora bought me a present?"

"Not that. Something else."

"I found a guy who would listen. At the top of Creagan Dubh, with only the wind and the heather and the birds for company, and no person to obtrude. And so I talked."

"About Northern Ireland?"

"Yes."

426

"All of it?"

"All of it."

"The bomb blast, and the bits of body and the dead Jocks?"

"Yes."

"And Neil MacDonald? And the nightmare?"

"Yes."

"But you told *me*. You talked to *me*. And that didn't do us any good."

"That's because you are part of me. A stranger is different. Objective. There was never anybody like that before. Only relations and old friends who had known me all my life. Too close."

"The nightmare's still there, Archie. That won't go away."

"Maybe not. But maybe its fangs have been drawn."

"What makes you so sure?"

"My mother had a saying. Fear knocked at the door, Faith went to answer it, and no one was there. We'll have to see. I love you more than life itself, and that's all that's important."

"Oh, Archie." Her tears overflowed and he kissed them away, unloosened the sash of her gown and slid his hand beneath the soft silk, caressing her nakedness. His lips moved to her mouth, the lips opening for him . . .

"Shall we give it a try?"

"Now?"

"Yes. Now. Right away. Just as soon as you can get me out of these damned trousers."

427

29

Thursday the Fifteenth

Virginia, awake at five o'clock, waited for the dawn. It was Thursday, Vi's seventy-eighth birthday.

Vi, as she had promised, had rung in the evening just before the nine o'clock news. Lottie was back in the Relkirk Royal, she had told Virginia. Not at all upset, she seemed to take it in her stride. Edie had been distressed, but after some persuasion, had accepted the inevitable. And Vi had telephoned Templehall and instructed the headmaster to reassure Henry that he no longer needed to agonise over his beloved Edie. The horrendous episode was over at last. Virginia must put it out of her mind.

The conversation left Virginia in a state of confused emotions. The most important was one of thankfulness and overwhelming relief. Now she could face the darkness of the night, go to bed by herself in the large and empty house; sleep, in the certain knowledge that no ghoul haunted the shadows of the garden, hovering, watching, waiting to pounce. Lottie would not return; she was shut away with her dangerous secrets. Virginia was free of her.

However, she felt a certain uneasiness. It was hateful to imagine Edie's distress at having to admit failure, her reluctance to commit her cousin once more to the professional, but impersonal, care of the hospital. But surely, deep down, Edie must know some relief, if only for the fact that she was shed of that almost untenable responsibility and no longer had to endure listening to the seemingly endless spate of Lottie's conversation.

Finally, there was Henry, and here Virginia was filled with guilt. She knew how Henry felt about Lottie, and how he feared for Edie, and yet the sensible idea of making a telephone call to his school had never even occurred to her, and she realised that the shameful reason for this was that Henry had slipped out of her mind, so absorbed had she become in herself and the events of the last two days.

First, Edmund and Pandora. Now, Conrad.

Conrad Tucker. Here, in Scotland, in Strathcroy, already part of the Balmerino household and an important character in the dramatis personae of the next few days, Conrad's presence changed the shape of everything. Mostly herself, as though some unsuspected and hidden facet of her own personality had been, by him, revealed. She had slept with Conrad. They had made love with a mutual desire that had more to do with comfort than passion, and she had stayed with him, and spent the night in his arms. An act of infidelity; adultery. Call it the worst name in the world, and still Virginia regretted nothing.

You must never tell Edmund.

Vi was a wise old lady, and confession was not a penance but a self-indulgence. It was unloading your so-called sin on to another person, and thus shedding guilt. But her own total lack of remorse had taken Virginia by surprise, and she felt that in the last twenty-four hours she had somehow grown, not physically, but within herself. It was as though she had been struggling up some precipitous hillside, and now had time to pause for breath, to rest, to appreciate the widened prospects that her efforts had achieved.

For so long she had been content to be simply Henry's mother, Edmund's wife, one of the Airds, her existence shaped by clan, and all her time and energy and love

429

channelled into making a home for the family. But now Alexa was grown, Henry was gone, and Edmund . . .? For the moment, she seemed to have lost sight of Edmund. Which left only herself. Virginia. An individual, an entity with a past and a future, bridged by the fleeting years of marriage. Henry's going had not only ended an era, but freed her as well. There was nothing to stop her stretching her wings, flying. All the world was hers.

The visit to Long Island, which for months had been simply a dream, edging around at the back of her mind, was now possible, positive, even imperative. Whatever Vi said, it was time to go, and if excuses were needed she would plead her grandparents' advancing age and her own burning need to see them again before they grew too old to enjoy her company; before they became ill or infirm; before they died. That was the excuse. But the true reason had much to do with Conrad.

He would be there. He would be around. In the city, or Southampton, but never more than a telephone call away. They could be together. A man whom her grandparents had always known and liked. A kindly man. He was not one to leave abruptly, nor break promises, nor let you down just when you needed him most; nor love another woman. It occurred to her then that perhaps trust was more important than love if a relationship was to be truly enduring. In order to deal with these uncertainties, she needed time and space, some sort of an interlude in which to stand back and review the situation. She needed solace, and knew that she would find it in the company of one who had always been her friend and was now her lover. Her lover. An ambivalent word, loaded with meanings. Once more, she searched her conscience for that mandatory twinge of guilt, but found nothing but a sort of assurance, a comforting strength, as though Conrad had brought to her some sort of a second chance, another taste of youth, a whole new freedom. Whatever. She only knew that she was going to grab at it, before it eluded her for ever. Leesport

430

was there, just a jet flight away. Unchanged, because it was a place that never changed. She smelled the crisp autumn air, saw the wide streets scattered with fallen scarlet leaves, the smoke from the first fires rising from the chimneys of the stately white clapboard houses drifting sweetly upwards into the deep-blue sky of a Long Island Indian summer.

Recalling other years, she took stock. Labor Day was past, the kids back at school, the ferry no longer running to Fire Island, the shore bars closed. But Gramps would not yet have pulled his small motorboat out of the water, and the great Atlantic beaches were there, only a short trip distant. The dunes, combed by the wind; the endless sands littered with clam shells, and laced by the surf of the thundering rollers. She felt that blown spume on her cheeks. Saw herself, as though from a great distance, walking through the shallows, silhouetted against the evening sky, with Conrad at her side . . .

And then, despite everything, Virginia found herself smiling, not with romantic delight, but with healthy self-ridicule. For this was a teenager's image, culled from some television ad. She heard the soupy music, the deeply sincere masculine voice urging her to use some shampoo, or deodorant, or biodegradable washing powder. Too easy, it would be, to drift through this day on a cloud of fantasy. It was not that daydreams were the sole right of the young, it was just that their elders did not have the time to lose themselves in fantasy. They had too much to do, too much to see to, too much to organise. Like herself. Right now. Life, immediate and demanding, claimed her attention. Resolutely, she put Leesport and Conrad out of her mind and thought about Alexa. The first priority was Alexa. Alexa was due to arrive at Balnaid in an hour or two, and a month ago, in London, Virginia had made Alexa a promise.

". . . you and Fa," Alexa had pleaded. "You won't still be having a row, will you? I couldn't bear it if there was a hateful atmosphere . . ."

And, "No, of course not," Virginia had assured her. "Forget that . . . We'll have a great time . . ."

Promises were not made to be broken, and she had enough pride to know that this one was no exception. By Friday, Edmund would be home again. She wondered if he would bring her another gold bracelet and hoped that he would not, for now it was not only Henry who lay between them, like a bone to be snarled over, but Virginia's new knowledge, both of herself and her husband. She felt that nothing would be either simple or straightforward again, but somehow, for Alexa's sake, she would make it seem that way. It was basically a question of getting through the next few days. She imagined a series of hurdles; Alexa's arrival, Vi's picnic, Edmund's homecoming, Isobel's dinner party, Verena's dance, all to be taken, one by one, without betraying a single base emotion. No doubt, no lust, no suspicion, no jealousy. Eventually, it would all be over. And when the September visitors were gone, and life was back to normal, Virginia, freed of commitments, would make plans for departure.

She waited for the dawn, from time to time turning on her bedside light to check the hour, but by seven o'clock she had had enough of this pointless occupation and was grateful to abandon her bed with its twisted sheets.

She drew back the curtains and was met by a pale-blue sky, a garden streaked with long, early shadows, and a thin ground mist hanging over the fields. All these were potential signs of a fine day. As the sun rose, the mist would be burned away, and with a bit of luck, it might become really warm.

She knew a certain relief. To have been met by cold, grey, and rain, today of all days, would have been almost more than she could bear. Not simply because her spirits were low enough without extra depressions, but, as well, because whatever the elements threw at them, Vi's birthday picnic, willy-nilly, would take place. For Vi was a stickler for traditions, and cared not if all her guests had to crouch beneath golf umbrellas, paddle about in rubber boots, and cook their damp sausages over a smoking, rain-sizzled barbecue. This year, it seemed, they were to be spared such masochistic pleasures.

Virginia went downstairs, dealt with the dogs, and made a cup of tea. She thought about starting to cook breakfast, abandoned this idea, and went back upstairs to dress and make her bed. She heard a car, dashed to the window, saw nothing. Just some person passing the gates as they headed down the lane.

She returned to the kitchen and made a pot of coffee. At nine o'clock the telephone rang, and she sprang for it, expecting some explanation from Alexa, stuck in a motorway telephone kiosk. But it was Verena Steynton.

"Virginia. Sorry to ring so early. Are you out of bed?"

"Of course."

"Heavenly day. You haven't got any damask table-cloths, have you? White ones, and huge. It's the one thing we never thought of, and of course Toddy Buchanan can't produce them."

"I think I've got about half a dozen, but I'll have to look them out. They were Vi's; she left them behind when she moved out."

"Are they really long?"

"Banquet-sized. She had them for parties."

"You couldn't be an absolute saint and bring them up to Corriehill this morning, could you? I'd come and fetch them, only we're all going to be doing flowers, and I simply haven't got a moment to spare."

Virginia was glad that Verena could not see her face. "Yes. Yes, I could do that," she said, sounding as obliging as possible. "But I can't come until Alexa and Noel have arrived, and they aren't here yet. And then I've got to go to Vi's picnic . . ."

"That's all right . . . if you could just drop them in.

Endlessly grateful. You are a love. Find Toddy and give them to him . . . and see you tomorrow if not before. Bye-eee . . .''

She rang off. Virginia sighed in some exasperation, because this morning the last thing she wanted to do was to drive the ten miles to Corriehill and then back again. However, after years of living in Scotland, she had become programmed to the local customs, and one of these was that in times of stress it was a case of all hands to the wheel – even if it was somebody else's – and putting a cheerful face on inconvenience. She supposed throwing a dance counted as a time of stress, but even so wished that Verena had thought of table-cloths before the last moment.

She wrote ''Tablecloths'' on the telephone pad. She thought about the picnic and put a large chicken into the oven to roast. By the time it had cooked and cooled, hopefully Alexa would be here, and she would get her to carve it into handy chunks.

The telephone rang again. This time it was Edie.

''Would you be able to give me a lift to the picnic?''

''Yes, of course. I'll come and pick you up. Edie, I'm so sorry about Lottie.''

''Yes.'' Edie sounded curt, which was the way she always sounded when she had been much upset but didn't want to talk about it. ''I felt badly.'' Which left Virginia uncertain as to whether Edie felt badly because Lottie had had to go, or because of Virginia's involvement in the whole sorry affair. ''What time should I be ready?''

''I have to go to Corriehill with some tablecloths, but I'll try to be with you around twelve.''

''Has Alexa come yet?''

''No, not yet.''

Edie, imagining death and destruction, was instantly anxious. ''Oh my, I hope they're safe.''

''I'm sure. Perhaps heavy traffic.''

''Those roads scare the life out of me.''

434

"Don't worry. I'll see you at midday, and they'll be here by then."

Virginia poured another mug of coffee. The telephone rang.

"Balnaid."

"Virginia."

It was Vi. "Happy birthday."

"Aren't I lucky with the weather? Has Alexa come?"

"Not yet."

"I thought they'd have arrived by now."

"So did I, but they haven't shown up yet."

"I can't wait to see the darling child. Why don't you all come to Pennyburn early, and we'll have a cup of coffee and a chat before we head off up the hill?"

"I can't." Virginia explained about the tablecloths. "I'm not even certain where to find them."

"They're on the top shelf of your linen cupboard, wrapped in blue tissue paper. Verena is a nuisance. Why didn't she think of asking you earlier?"

"I suppose she's got a lot on her mind."

"So when will you all be here?"

Virginia made calculations and laid plans. "I'll send Noel and Alexa up to Pennyburn in the Subaru. And then I'll go to Corriehill in the small car, and on the way back I'll pick up Edie and bring her to Pennyburn. And then we'll pack all of us and all the picnic gear into the Subaru and go on from there."

"What a splendid organiser you are. It must have something to do with having an American mother. And you'll bring rugs, won't you? And wineglasses for yourselves." Under "Tablecloths", Virginia wrote "Rugs, Wineglasses". "And I'll expect Noel and Alexa at about eleven o'clock."

"I hope they're not too exhausted."

"Oh, they won't be exhausted," Vi assured her breezily. "They're young."

435

Noel Keeling was an urban creature, born and raised in London, his habitat the city streets and weekend forays into the diminishing countryside of the Home Counties. From time to time his pleasures took him further afield, and he'd fly to the Costa Smeralda or the Algarve, invited to join some house party, where he would play golf or tennis or indulge in a bit of yachting. Sightseeing, gazing at churches or châteaux, admiring great tracts of vineyards did not enter his plans for enjoyment, and if such an outing was suggested, he usually found good reason to opt out, and instead spent the time either lying by the swimming pool, or drifting down to the nearest town to sit beneath the awning of a pavement bar and watch the world go by.

Once, some years ago, when he had come to Scotland to join a few friends for a week of salmon fishing, he had flown to Inverness from London, where he had been met by another member of the fishing party, and driven to Oykel Bridge. It had been raining. It rained the whole way to the hotel, and continued to rain for the remainder of their stay, the downpour interrupted at infrequent intervals by a slight clearing of the mist, which revealed a great deal of brown and treeless moorland and very little else.

His memories of that week were mixed. Each day was spent thigh-deep in the flood of the river, flogging the swollen waters for the elusive fish. And each evening was passed in a cheerful blur of conviviality, eating quantities of delicious Scottish food and drinking even larger quantities of malt whisky. The surrounding scenery had left no impression whatsoever.

But now, at the wheel of his Volkswagen Golf, and driving the last few miles of their long journey, he

436

realised that he was not only on familiar ground, but also in unexpected territory.

The familiar ground was metaphorical. He was an experienced guest, with long years of country weekend house parties behind him, and this was by no means the first time he had approached an unknown house to stay with strangers. In years gone by, he had devised a rating for weekends, awarding stars for comfort and pleasure. But that was when he had been much younger and poorer, and in no position to turn down any invitation. Now, older and more prosperous, with friends and acquaintances to match, he could afford to be more selective, and was seldom disappointed.

But the game, if it was to be properly played, had its own appointed rituals. And so, in his suitcase, stowed in the boot, were not only his dinner jacket and a selection of suitably countrified clothes, but a bottle of The Famous Grouse for his host, and a generously large box of Bendicks handmade chocolates for his hostess. As well, this weekend involved birthday presents. For Alexa's grandmother, celebrating her seventy-eighth year this very day, there were shiny boxes of soap and bath oil from Floris – Noel's standard offering to elderly ladies, both known and unknown; and for Katy Steynton, whom he had never met, a framed sporting print depicting a sad-eyed spaniel with a dead pheasant in its mouth.

Thus, bearing gifts, he abided by the rules.

The unexpected territory was a physical thing, the astonishingly beautiful county of Relkirkshire. He had never imagined such rich and prosperous estates, such verdant farmlands, immaculately fenced and grazed by herds of handsome cattle. He had not expected avenues of beech, roadside gardens filled with flowers in such profusion and such colour. Driving overnight, he had watched the light creep into an overcast and misty dawn, but now the sun had done its work, and the greyness was dissolved into a morning of brilliant clarity. With

Relkirk behind them, the road was clear, fields gold with stubble, rivers sparkling, bracken turning to saffron-yellow, the skies enormous, the air crystal-clear, unpolluted by smoke or smog or any horror that the hand of man could produce. It was like going back in time to a world that one had thought gone for ever. Had he ever known such a world? Or had he known it once and simply forgotten that it had existed?

Caple Bridge. They crossed a river, deep in a ravine far below them, and then took the turning signposted "Strathcroy". The hills, still bloomy with heather, folded away on either side of the narrow winding road. He saw scattered farmsteads, a man driving a flock of sheep up through green pasture fields to the rough grazing beyond. Alexa, with Larry on her knee, sat beside him. Larry slept, but Alexa was palpably tense with the scarcely suppressed excitement of coming home. In truth, she had been in a state of happy anticipation for weeks, counting the days off on her calendar, getting her hair cut, buying presents and searching the shops for a new dress. This had proved an abortive business and she had finally abandoned the shops for an establishment which hired out marvellous creations – she had agonised over a delectable mini-dress spangled in glitter, but with the help of a sympathetic assistant had decided that she did not have the legs for a mini-skirt – and had happily allowed herself to be persuaded into a traditional gown, raw silk and splashed with flowers, in which Noel thought she looked both delectable and romantic. For the last two days, she had been spinning like a top with last-minute arrangements; packing for the pair of them, ironing all Noel's shirts, emptying the refrigerator, and leaving with a neighbour the spare keys of her house in case it should be invaded by vandalising bandits. All this was accomplished with the transparent enthusiasm and energy of a child, and Noel had witnessed her furious activity with fond tolerance, while refusing to pretend that he felt the same way.

Now, however, with the long journey behind them, with the sunlight streaming down from that vast and pristine sky, the clean air blowing through the opened window, the fresh prospects revealed at each bend of the road, her excitement suddenly became contagious, and he was filled with ridiculous elation – not happiness, exactly, but a surge of physical well-being that was perhaps the next-best thing. Impulsively, Noel took his hand off the wheel and laid it on Alexa's knee, and at once she covered it with her own.

She said, "I'm not saying 'Isn't it beautiful' all the time, because if I do, it'll just sound too banal for words."

"I know."

"And coming back is always special, but it's more special this time because you're with me. That's what I've been thinking." Her fingers twined with his. "It's never been quite like this before."

He smiled. "I'll be on my best behaviour and try to keep it that way."

Alexa leaned over and kissed his cheek. She said, "I love you."

Five minutes later, they had arrived. Reaching the little village, they crossed another bridge, passed through open gates and up a drive. He saw the lawns, the banks of rhododendrons and azaleas, glimpsed the open view through to the hills that lay to the south. He drew up in front of the house, the house familiar from Alexa's photograph, but now reality, standing before him, solid and substantial, with the towering conservatory jutting out at one side. Virginia creeper, now turning crimson, framed the open front door, and before Noel had even switched off the ignition the two spaniels were there, not posed obediently at the top of the steps, but racing down them, in full cry and with ears flying, come to investigate the new arrivals. Larry, rudely awoken, gave as good as he got, yapping from Alexa's arms as she got out of the car.

Almost at once, right behind the dogs, Virginia

appeared, wearing jeans and an open-necked white shirt and looking just as toothsome as she had in her sophisticated London clothes, that first and only time that Noel had met her.

"Alexa. Darling. I thought you were never coming." Hugs and kisses. Stretching the aches out of his arms and legs, Noel watched the loving reunion. "And Noel" – Virginia turned to him – "how lovely to see you." He was kissed as well, which was pleasurable. "Did you have a frightful drive? Alexa, I can't stand the din. Put Larry down and let them make friends right here in the garden, otherwise he'll pee all over my carpets. Why are you so late? I've been expecting you for hours."

Alexa explained. "We stopped in Edinburgh for breakfast. Noel's got some friends there called Delia and Calum Robertson. They live in the dearest little mews house just at the back of Moray Place. We woke them up by throwing stones at their window and they came down, let us in and cooked us bacon and eggs and weren't a bit cross at being woken up. I should have phoned you, but I never thought. I am sorry."

"It doesn't matter. All that matters is that you're here. But there's not a moment to spare because you've got to be with Vi at eleven, and have coffee with her before we all head up the hill for the picnic." She looked at Noel with some sympathy. "Poor man, you're really being thrown in at the deep end, but Vi's longing to see you both. Can you bear it? You're not too exhausted after the long drive?"

"Not a bit," he assured her. "We shared the driving and the one who wasn't at the wheel was able to have a kip . . ." He opened the boot of his car, and Virginia raised her eyebrows.

"Heavens, what a lot of luggage. Come on, let's hump it all in . . ."

440

He was in his bedroom, left with his bags to settle himself in. The door stood open, and from down the passage, he could hear the voices of Alexa and Virginia, still with plenty to talk about. From time to time there was a burst of laughter. He went to close the door, finding himself in need of a moment of privacy before the next lot of demands were made upon him. He was to drive the Subaru, he had been told. There was some complication about tablecloths, but he and Alexa would have coffee with her grandmother, and later Virginia and Edie would join them, whereupon the entire party would drive up the hill for the celebratory picnic.

He was not dismayed by the prospect; on the contrary, he found himself quite looking forward to anything that the day might bring. He opened his suitcase and began in a desultory fashion to unpack. He hung up his dinner jacket in the towering Victorian wardrobe, dug around for Vi's birthday present, his hairbrushes, his wash-bag. He put the brushes on the dressing-table and went to inspect the bathroom. There he was confronted by a seven-foot bath with gargantuan brass taps, a marbled floor, tall mirrors, fluffy white bathsheets neatly folded over a heated rail. He felt worn and grubby after his overnight drive, and, on an impulse, turned on the taps, tore off his clothes, and took the quickest, hottest bath of his life. Much refreshed, he dressed again, and, buttoning his clean shirt, walked to the window to observe the pleasing view beyond the boundary of the garden. Fields, sheep, hills. Out of the quiet came the liquid call of a curlew. It rose and died away, and he tried to remember when he had last heard that haunting, evocative sound, but could not.

Virginia Aird was half-American; young, vital, and chic. Once, on a business trip to the United States, Noel

441

had stayed in the home of a colleague who lived in New York State. The house was ranch-type, set in lawns that ran into the lawns of the next-door property, and had been designed with convenience and ease of maintenance as first priorities. Centrally heated, marvellously thought out, and equipped with every sort of modern appliance, it should have been the most comfortable place in the world in which to spend a winter weekend. But somehow, none of it added up, because his hostess, although delightful, hadn't the first idea about having guests to stay. Despite the fact that she was possessed of an all-singing, all-dancing kitchen, she never cooked a single meal. Each evening, they dressed up and went out to the local country club for dinner, and the only food that emerged from that kitchen was fried eggs or microwaved beefburgers. But that was not all. In the living room was an open fireplace, but the grate was filled with pot plants, and instead of a comfortingly blazing log fire, the sinfully comfortable couches and armchairs were arranged around the focal point of the television, and Sunday afternoon was spent gazing at a football match, the rules and shibboleths of which Noel found incomprehensible. There was another television set in his bedroom, and the bathroom off this was meticulously equipped with shower, shaving sockets, and even a bidet, but the largest of the navy-blue matching towels was so minute that it barely covered his private parts, and this small inconvenience caused Noel to yearn wistfully for the comfort of his own, immense, white, thirsty bathsheets. But worst of all was the discomfort and pain of blocked sinuses, caused by sleeping in a heated room, the window of which refused to open.

It was churlish and ungrateful to find fault, because they had been immensely kind, but he had never, in his life, been so glad to get away from anywhere.

The curlew called again. Peace. And . . . he turned back to the bedroom, stuffing his shirttails into his jeans . . . a marvellous, Edwardian opulence. As opulent as Ovington Street, but all on a massive and masculine scale. The great bath, built for the largest of men. The monster towels, the heavy curtains, swagged back with ropes of silk. He thought again about Virginia, and knew that although he had harboured no fears of a repeat of that sojourn in suburban America, he had scarcely expected her to be the mistress of a house that seemed to have been decorated and furnished fifty years ago and never altered since.

But he approved. He felt very much at home. He liked the feeling of the place, the solid comfort, the pleasant country-house smell, the gleam of polish on well-tended furniture, the crispness of fresh linen, the sense of family. Pulling on clean socks, a thick sweater, brushing his hair, he found himself whistling. He caught his own eye in the mirror and grinned at his reflection. Already, he had started to enjoy himself.

Finally ready, and bearing Vi's birthday present, he left his bedroom and went downstairs and, following the sound of feminine voices, found himself in Virginia's kitchen. Not all-singing, all-dancing, but large and homely, and filled, not only with sunshine, but with the fragrant smell of fresh coffee. Alexa, professionally, had carved a cold chicken and was packing the pieces into a plastic box, and Virginia, now wearing an apron over her jeans, was filling a vacuum flask with coffee. As Noel appeared, she set down the jug and screwed on the stopper.

"Everything all right?" she asked him.

"More than all right. I had a bath, and now I'm ready for anything."

"Is that a present for Vi? Put it in this big box, with all of ours . . ." It was a grocery carton already crammed with oddly shaped and brightly wrapped packages.

He added his own. "Somebody's given her a bottle."

"Henry. It's rhubarb wine. He won it at the church sale. Noel, the Subaru's out at the back. Perhaps you could put the box in with all the other stuff, and then you

443

can give it to Vi when you and Alexa get to Pennyburn."

Noel picked up the birthday box and carried it across the kitchen and out through the open back door. In the yard beyond, the Subaru, a sturdy four-wheel-drive vehicle, was parked, waiting, its rear compartment already half filled with assorted clobber. To Noel a picnic meant a sandwich eaten in a field, or perhaps a well-chosen hamper from Fortnum's, complete with champagne, to be ceremoniously opened on the lawns of Glyndebourne. Preparations for today, however, seemed to be more on the scale of an army manoeuvre. Rugs, umbrellas; fishing rods, creels, and bags; a paper sack of charcoal, another of kindling; grids and tongs; dogs' bowls; a bottle of water, cans of beer; a basket filled with brightly coloured plastic plates and a number of plastic wineglasses. There were a roll of paper towel, a bundle of rainproof gear, Alexa's camera, a pair of field-glasses.

He loaded the box of presents, and as he did this was joined by Alexa with yet another basket containing the coffee flask and the box of cold chicken, some mugs, dog-leads, and a whistle.

"It looks," he told her, "as though we are going camping for at least two weeks."

"We have to be prepared for all eventualities." He took the basket from her and found a corner for it. "And we should go. We're late already."

"What about the dogs?"

"They all come with us. We'll have to squash them in with all this stuff."

"Can't they sit on the back seat?"

"No, because there are five of us going up the hill, and neither Vi nor Edie is noticeably slender."

"We could take my car as well."

"We could, but we wouldn't get very far. Wait till you see the track. It's precipitous and very rough. This is the only car that will make it."

Noel was protective of his Volkswagen, and so this

ended the argument. The three dogs were rounded up, bundled aboard, and the doors shut in their faces. Their expressions were resigned. Alexa and Noel climbed up into the front seats, Noel at the wheel. Virginia, still in her apron, came to wave them away. "I'll be with you about twelve-fifteen," she told them. "Have a good time with Vi."

They set off, around the back of the house, through the gates, over the bridge. As he drove, Alexa gave him all the up-to-date local news. "Fa's in New York. I heard all about it while I was carving the chicken. But he's meant to be getting back some time tomorrow, so he'll be there for the party. And Lucilla Blair's at Croy . . . she's come back from France . . . and Pandora Blair. She's Archie Balmerino's sister, so you'll meet both of them."

"Will they all be at the picnic?"

"I expect so. Not sure about Pandora, though. I'm longing to see her because I never have. Just heard about her. She's the black ewe of the Balmerino family, with a wonderfully risqué reputation."

"Sounds interesting."

"Well, don't get too excited. She's at least ten years older than you."

"I always did go for the more mature lady."

"I don't think 'mature' is quite the right word for Pandora. And there's another man staying at Croy called Conrad Tucker. He's an American, and an old friend of Virginia's. Isn't that extraordinary? And poor Virginia had to take Henry to school herself, on account of Fa not being here. She said it was really horrible and she doesn't want to talk about it. And she hasn't yet heard from darling Henry, so we don't know how he's getting on. She says she doesn't want to ring the headmaster and ask in case he thinks she's a fussing parent." By now they were trundling down the village street. "I don't know why she shouldn't telephone. I don't see why she shouldn't talk to Henry if she wants to. Turn

445

left here, Noel, through these gates and up the hill. This is Croy now. Archie Balmerino's land. I think he's shooting today, but we're all going to dinner with them tomorrow, before the dance, so you'll meet him then . . ."

The road climbed steeply, through farmland that had once been parkland. The leaves of stately beeches were turning gold, and ahead the hills thrust their summits into the sparkling autumn sky. Despite the warmth of the sun, there was a nippy breeze, and Noel was glad of his thick sweater.

"Now we turn down this lane. It used to be really grotty, a broken-down track leading to an old gardener's cottage, but Vi did it all up when she bought the place from Archie. She's a manic gardener. I've told you that already. But just look at her view. Of course, she's in the teeth of the wind, but it's better now that the beech hedge has grown . . ."

The little house stood blinding white in the sunshine, set in a garden of green lawns and bright flower-beds. As Noel drew up at the front door, this opened and a large and well-built lady emerged to greet them, her arms outstretched, and the brisk breeze playing havoc with her grey hair. She wore a very old tweed skirt, a cardigan, ankle socks, and sturdy brogues, and Alexa, jumping down from the car, was almost instantly swept up into her grandmother's mammoth embrace.

"Alexa. My darling child, what a joy to see you."

"Happy birthday."

"Seventy-eight, my darling. Isn't it terrible? Old as Methuselah." She kissed Alexa, and then, looking over her granddaughter's head, watched as Noel came around the front of the Subaru. Their eyes met, and held. Violet's gaze was steady and bright; sharp, but not unkindly. I am, Noel told himself, being summed up. He put on his most open smile. "How do you do? I'm Noel Keeling."

Violet released Alexa and held out her hand. He took

it in his own, a healthy handshake, the palm warm and dry, the fingers strong. She was not a beautiful old lady, and probably had never been so, but he saw much liveliness and wisdom in her weather-beaten features, and all the lines on her face looked as though they had been put there by laughter. His liking for her, his immediate and wordless rapport with her, was instinctive, and he knew that she was the sort of person who, although quite capable of implacable enmity, could as well become the truest and most staunch of friends. All at once he wanted her on his side.

And then she said an odd thing. "We've never met?"

"I don't think so."

"Your name. Keeling. It rings a bell." She shrugged, let loose his hand. "No matter." She smiled, and he realised that if she had never been beautiful, then she had once been possessed of a great physical attraction. "How very nice of you to come and see us all."

"I must wish you a happy birthday. We've a box of presents for you."

"Bring them inside. I'll open them later."

He returned to the car, opened the doors, calmed the dogs, retrieved the birthday box, closed the doors again. By the time he had achieved all this, Alexa and her grandmother had disappeared into the house, and Noel followed them into a small hallway, and so through to an airy sitting room filled with light, and with a glassed door giving out on to the old lady's delectable garden.

"Put the box down there! I won't open them yet, because I want to hear all your news. Alexa, the coffee and the cups are in the kitchen, would you fetch the tray in for me?" Alexa disappeared to do this. "Now, Noel . . . I can't call you Mr Keeling because nobody does these days, and you must call me Violet . . . where would you like to sit?"

But he did not want to sit. As always in new surroundings, he wanted to prowl, nose, get the feel of things. It was a charming room, with pale-yellow walls, bright rose-chintzed curtains, and cream carpets, fitted snug to the wainscot. Violet Aird had not lived here for many years, he knew, and there was a freshness and a lightness about everything, evidence of recent refurbishment; but her furniture, her pictures, her bibelots, her books and her china had obviously all moved with her from some previous abode, presumably Balnaid. The chairs and sofa were loose-covered in coral linen, and an ebony cabinet, its doors standing open, was lined in that same coral, and contained a collection of Famille Rose porcelain. Everywhere he looked, Noel's eye fell upon a clutter of either enviable or practical objects, the squirrel hoard of an elderly lady, gathering about her, like a store of nuts, the comforting possessions of a lifetime. Here were hand-worked cushions, a wicker basket filled with logs, a brass fender, a pair of bellows, her sewing box, her little television set, stacks of magazines, bowls of pot-pourri. As well, every horizontal surface was cluttered with small and decorative objects. Enamel boxes, jugs of fresh flowers, a copper bowl filled with purple heather, silver-framed photographs, small arrangements of Dresden china.

She was watching him. He looked at her and smiled. He said, "You follow the rules of William Morris."

"And what do you mean by that?"

"You have nothing in your house that you don't know to be useful nor think to be beautiful."

She was amused. "Who taught you that?"

"My mother."

"It's an outmoded concept."

"But still viable."

In her grate, she had lighted a little fire. On the mantelshelf were a pair of Staffordshire dogs, and over the mantelpiece . . .

He frowned, moving to inspect the picture more closely. It was an oil painting of a child in a field of buttercups. The field was in shadow, but, beyond the field, the sun shone on rocks and sea and the distant

448

figures of two older girls. The illusionary effect of light and colour had caught his attention, not simply because it hummed with warmth but because the technique, the factual rendering of the three-dimensional form, sprang at him with all the familiarity of a face remembered from childhood.

It had to be. Noel scarcely needed to read the signature to know who it was.

He said, in wonder, "This is a Lawrence Stern."

"How clever of you to know. I love it more than anything."

He turned to face her. "How did you come to possess it?"

"You seem astonished."

"I am. There are so few about."

"My husband gave it to me many years ago. He was in London. He saw it in the window of a gallery, and went in and bought it for me, not minding that he had to pay a great deal more than he could afford."

Noel said, "Lawrence Stern was my grandfather."

She frowned. "Your grandfather?"

"Yes. My mother's father."

"Your mother's . . .?" She paused, still frowning, and then all at once smiled, the puzzlement gone, and her face filled with pleasure. "So *that* is how I knew your name! Noel Keeling. But I knew her . . . I met her . . . Oh, what has happened to Penelope?"

"She died about four years ago."

"I can't bear it. Such a lovely person. We only met once, but . . ."

They were interrupted by Alexa's reappearance from Violet's kitchen, bearing the tray with the coffee jug and cups and saucers upon it.

"Alexa, this is the most extraordinary thing! Just imagine, Noel isn't a stranger at all to me, because I once met his mother . . . and we made such friends. And I always hoped so much that we would meet again, but somehow we never did . . ."

This discovery, this revelation, the extraordinary small-world coincidence, claimed all attention. The picnic and the birthday were, for the moment, forgotten, and Alexa and Noel sat and drank scalding coffee and listened with fascination to Vi's story.

"It was all through Roger Wimbush, the portrait painter. When Geordie came back from the war, from prison camp, and went back to Relkirk to work, it was decided that, as chairman of the firm, he should have his portrait painted for posterity. And Roger Wimbush was given the commission. He came to Balnaid and stayed with us, and the portrait was accomplished in the conservatory, and duly hung, with some ceremony, in the boardroom at the office. As far as I know, it's still there. We made great friends, and when Geordie died, Roger wrote me such a dear letter, and sent me an invitation to the Portrait Painters' Exhibition at Burlington House. I didn't very often travel to London, but I felt the occasion deserved the long journey, so I went, and Roger met me there and showed me around. And all at once, he spied these two ladies. One was your mother, Noel, and the other, I think, an old aunt of hers whom she had brought to the exhibition as a little treat. A very old lady; tiny and wrinkled, but humming with vitality . . ."

"Great-Aunt Ethel," said Noel, because it could have been no one else.

"That's it. Of course. Ethel Stern, Lawrence Stern's sister."

"She died some years ago, but while she was alive she afforded us all an enormous amount of amusement."

"I can imagine it. Anyway, Roger and your mother were obviously old friends of long standing. I think she had taken him in as a lodger years before when he was a penniless young student, struggling to make his way. There was a great reunion between them, and then introductions, and I was told about the relationship with Lawrence Stern, and I was able to tell your mother about that picture. By now we were all on the best of terms, and we'd all seen all the portraits anyway, so we decided that we would have lunch together. I had a restaurant in mind, but your mother insisted that we all go back to her house and have lunch with her."

"Oakley Street."

"Absolutely. Oakley Street. We made noises about it being too much trouble, but she overrode all our objections, and the next thing we knew, all four of us were in a taxi and on our way to Chelsea. It was a beautiful day. I remember it so clearly. Very warm and sunny, and you know how pretty London can be on an early-summer day. And we had lunch in the garden, and the garden was big, and so leafy, and so sweet with the scent of lilac that it felt like being in another country, the South of France perhaps, or Paris, with the city sound of traffic muffled by trees, and everything spattered with sunlight and shadow. There was a terrace, nicely shaded, with a table and garden chairs, and we all sat and drank chilled wine, while your mother busied herself in that big basement kitchen, from time to time appearing to chat or pour more wine, or lay a cloth on the table, and set out the knives and forks."

"What did you eat?" asked Alexa, fascinated by the picture that Vi drew for them.

"Let me see. I have to think. It was delicious, I remember that. It was exactly right, and delicious. Cold soup – gazpacho, I think – and crusty home-made bread. And a salad. And pâté. And French cheese. And there was a bowl of peaches, which she had picked that morning from the tree that grew against the wall at the far end of the garden. We stayed all afternoon. We had no other engagement, or if we did, we forgot it. The hours just slid away, like an afternoon in a hazy delicious dream.

451

And then, I remember, Penelope and I left Ethel and Roger at the table, drinking coffee and cognac and smoking Gauloise cigarettes, and she took me around the garden and showed me all its delights. And as we walked, we talked, and never drew breath, and yet it is difficult to tell you what we talked about. I think she told me about Cornwall, and her childhood there, and the house that they used to own, and the life that they led before the war. And it all sounded so different to my own. And when the time came to leave at last, I didn't want it to end. I didn't want to say goodbye. But when I finally came home again, back to Balnaid and Strathcroy, that picture, which I always loved, took on an even deeper meaning, because once I had met Lawrence Stern's daughter."

"Didn't you ever see her again?" Alexa asked.

"No. So sad. I so seldom went to London, and then, I believe, she moved to the country. We lost touch. So silly and careless of me to lose touch with someone I liked so much, felt so close to."

"What did she look like?" Alexa, naturally fascinated by this unexpected insight into Noel's family life, was avid for detail. Vi looked at Noel. "You tell her," she said.

But he couldn't. Features, eyes, lips, smile, hair eluded him. He could not have drawn them had some man put a gun to his head. What stayed, and remained with him, after four years of living without his mother, was her presence, her warmth, her laughter, her generosity, her contrariness, and her maddening ways, her endless cornucopia of hospitality and giving. Vi's recalling of that long-ago luncheon party, spontaneous and informal but infused with such style that she had not forgotten a single detail of the occasion, brought back the old days at Oakley Street so vividly that he found himself pierced with nostalgia for everything that he had taken so for granted and never found time to appreciate.

He shook his head. "I can't."

Vi met his eyes. And then, as though accepting and acknowledging his dilemma, did not press him further. She turned to Alexa. "She was tall and very good-looking – I thought beautiful. She had dark-grey hair, drawn back from her face into a chignon pierced with tortoiseshell pins. Her eyes were dark, very large and lustrous, and her skin smooth and brown, as though she had always lived out of doors, like a gypsy. She wasn't in the least fashionable or chic, but she held herself so proudly, and that endowed her with a great elegance. She gave off an enormous charge of . . . enjoyment. An unforgettable woman." She turned back to Noel. "And you are her son. Imagine it. How strange life can be. At seventy-eight, you'd think that you'd stop being surprised, and something like this happens, and it's as though the world had only just begun."

The loch at Croy lay hidden in the hills, three miles north of the house, and accessible only by a primitive track of great steepness that wound up on to the moor in a series of precipitous hairpin bends.

It was not a natural stretch of water. Long ago, this glen, encircled by the northern hills and the towering hulk of Creagan Dubh, had been a place of remote solitude, the habitat of eagles and deer, wildcat, grouse and curlew. At Croy, there were still to be seen old sepia photographs of the glen the way it had once looked, with a burn running through it, flanked by steep banks where the rushes grew, and by the burnside the ruins of a small dwelling-house, with byres and sheepfolds reduced to roofless desolation and tumbled granite walls. But then the first Lord Balmerino, Archie's grandfather, with a fortune to spend and trout-fishing in mind, decided to create for himself a loch. Accordingly a dam was built, sturdy as a bastion, twelve feet high or more, and wide enough to allow passage for a carriage to drive along the top of it. Sluice-gates were integrated to deal with any overflow, and when the dam was completed, these sluice-gates were closed, and the burn was trapped. Slowly, the waters rose, and the abandoned croft was drowned for ever. Because of the bulk of the dam wall, any person approaching it for the first time did not see the water until the last rise was crested, when the huge expanse of the loch – two miles long and a mile wide – all at once was there. Depending on the hour and the season, it glittered blue in sunshine, was tossed with leaden-grey waves, or lay still as glass in the evening light, with a pale moon reflected in its mirror surface, broken from time to time by the disturbance of rising fish.

A boathouse was built, strongly constructed, and large enough to shelter two boats, with an extra apartment to one side where picnics could be enjoyed in inclement weather. But it was not only fishermen who made their way to the loch. Generations of children had claimed it as their special place. Sheep grazed on the surrounding hills, and the closely cropped grass that sloped to the water's edge made splendid places for setting up tents, playing ball games, organising cricket matches. Blairs and Airds, with attendant young friends, had learned to cast for trout from the shores of the loch, and mastered their first swimming strokes in its icy waters; and long happy days had been spent in building rafts, or make-shift canoes, which, paddled intrepidly out into the deep water, inevitably sank.

The overloaded Subaru, in four-wheel-drive, and with Virginia at the wheel, thumped and bumped up the last stretch of the track, its bonnet pointing skywards. Noel, after half an hour of total discomfort, decided that, going back, he would make the journey on foot. Virginia had opted to drive because she said, quite rightly, that she knew the way, which he did not, and Violet – also quite rightly – had been given the seat next to Virginia, with her birthday cake, in its large box, to hold on her knee. In the back, things were not so easy. Edie Findhorn, about whom Noel had heard so much, proved to be a lady of ample girth, and took up so much space that Noel was forced to take Alexa upon his knee. There she crouched, her weight growing heavier by the moment and threatening his thighs with incipient cramp, but as every bump in the road caused her to clout her head on the roof of the car, he felt that it would be churlish to add his complaints to hers.

They had made two stops. One at the great house of Croy, where Virginia had alighted to see whether the Balmerino party had already left. But the door was shut and the house deserted, so they obviously had. The second stop was to open and shut the deer-gate, and here Alexa had let out the two spaniels, who had run the rest of the way behind the slowly moving car. Noel wished that he had been let out to run with them, but by now it was a little too late to make such a suggestion.

For, it seemed, they were nearly there. Violet peered through the windscreen. "They've lit the fire!" she announced.

Alexa screwed herself around to look, causing Noel even more discomfort. "How do you know?"

"I can see smoke."

"They must have brought their own kindling," said Edie.

"Probably used burned heather," said Alexa. "Or rubbed two Boy Scouts together. I hope Lucilla's remembered the boathouse key. You can go fishing, Noel."

"At the moment, all I want to do is get a little feeling back into my legs."

"I'm sorry. Am I frightfully heavy?"

455

"No, not heavy at all. It's just that my feet have gone numb."

"Perhaps you're getting gangrene."

"Probably."

"It can happen in the wink of an eye, and then it spreads like wildfire, all through your body."

Edie was indignant. "For heaven's sake, Alexa, what a thing to say."

"Oh, he'll survive," Alexa told her airily. "Besides, we're very nearly there."

Which they were. The fiendish track levelled off, there were no more jolts, and the Subaru rolled on to smooth sloping grass, coming to a halt. Virginia switched off the ignition. At once Noel opened the door, bundled Alexa gently out, and gratefully followed her. Standing, stretching his aching legs, he found himself assaulted by a blast of light, air, brightness, blueness, water, space, scents, wind. It was cold . . . colder than it had been down in the shelter of the valley, but so dazzled was he by all that he saw that he scarcely noticed the chill. As well he was impressed, as he had been impressed by the grandeur and apparent magnificence of Croy. He had not thought that the loch would be so large, so beautiful, and found it hard to come to terms with the fact that this immense tract of countryside, the hills and the moors, all belonged to one man. Everything was on such a huge scale, so lavish, so rich. Looking about him, he saw the boathouse, intricately gabled and windowed, the Land-Rover already parked only a few yards away, the roughly constructed barbecue fireplace where smoke already rose into the clean air.

He saw two men down on the pebbly shore, searching for driftwood. He heard a grouse call high on the hill above him, and then, far distant, from some further glen, the crack of guns.

The others were now all out of the car. Alexa had opened the back door and let out her little dog. Virginia's two spaniels had not yet turned up, but probably would in a moment or two. Violet was already making her way down towards the boathouse, and as she did a girl emerged from its open doors.

"Hello," she called. "You've got here. Happy birthday, Vi!"

Introductions were made all round, and as soon as this small chore was accomplished, everybody set to work, and it became clear to Noel that there was a well-ordered pattern for these traditional occasions. The Subaru was unloaded, the fire built up with sticks and charcoal. Two large folding tables were manhandled from the boathouse and set up nearby, spread with large checkered cloths. Food, plates, salads, glasses were arranged on these. Rugs were spread on beds of heather. The two spaniels, out of breath and with tongues hanging, lolloped over the crest of the hill and headed straight for the water, where they cooled their feet, drank lustily, and then collapsed, exhausted. Edie Findhorn, tied up in a large white apron, unpacked sausages and beef burgers and, when the charcoal began to turn to ash, commenced her cooking. The smoke thickened. Her rosy cheeks grew rosier in the heat, and the wind blew her white hair into disarray.

One by one, other cars appeared, disgorging yet more guests. The wine was opened, and they stood about with glasses in their hands, or made themselves comfortable on the spread tartan rugs. The sun continued to shine. Then Julian Gloxby, the rector of Strathcroy, appeared over the brow of the hill with his wife and Dermot Honeycombe. Because none of them owned a vehicle tough enough to deal with the road from Croy, they had made the journey on foot, and turned up looking distinctly puffed, despite the fact that they all wore walking boots and carried sticks. Dermot had a rucksack on his back, and from this he produced his contribution to the feast, which proved to be six quail eggs and a bottle of elderberry wine.

Lucilla and Alexa stood at the table and buttered baps,

457

those sweet white bread rolls mandatory for any Scottish picnic. Violet chased wasps away from her cake, and Alexa's dog stole a red-hot sausage and burned his mouth.

The party was on its way.

Virginia said, "I shall make you a present." She pulled rushes, one by one, from a clump of reeds that grew on the bank.

"What will you make me?" asked Conrad.

"Wait, and watch, and see."

With the picnic consumed, and the coffee drunk, they had walked away from the others, along the length of the dam wall, and then made their way up the eastern shore of the loch where, over the years, the winds and high waters had eroded away the peaty bank and formed a narrow beach of shingly pebbles. No one else had followed them, and save for the two Balnaid spaniels, they were quite alone.

He stood, without impatience, and watched her. From the pocket of her corduroy trousers she took a scrap of sheep wool gleaned from a barbed-wire fence. She twisted this into a thread, and with it tied the rushes together into a bunch. Then she spread them, and started plaiting and folding, the rushes revolving like the spokes of a wheel. In her fingers, a little basket formed, which, finished, was about the size of a teacup.

He was fascinated. "Who taught you to do that?"

"Vi. And she was taught as a child by an old tinker woman. There." She tucked in the last of the rush-ends, and held it up for him to admire

"That's neat."

"Now I shall fill it with moss and flowers, and you will have an arrangement to put on your dressing-table."

She looked about her, spied moss growing on a rock,

tore it loose with her fingernails and crammed it into the little basket. They strolled on, Virginia pausing every now and then to pick a harebell, or a sprig of heather, or a stem of cotton-grass, which were added to her miniature creation. Finally satisfied, she held it out to him. "Here you are. A memento, Conrad. A souvenir of Scotland."

He took it. "That's really neat. Thank you. But I don't need a souvenir, because I'm not ever going to forget. Any of it."

"In that case," she said lightly, "you can throw it away."

"I wouldn't do that."

"So, put it in a tooth-mug of water, then it will neither wither nor die. You can take it back to America with you. But you'll have to hide it in your spongebag, or the customs man will get you for importing germs."

"Perhaps I could dry it, and then it would last for ever."

"Yes, perhaps you could."

They walked on, into the wind. Small brown waves ran up upon the shore, and out on the water, the two fishing boats drifted gently, the fishers silent, absorbed, casting their lines. Virginia paused, stooped for a flat stone and chucked it expertly, causing it to bounce half a dozen times before it finally sank.

She said, "When are you going?"

"Sorry?"

"When are you going back to the States?"

"I've a flight booked next Thursday."

She searched for another stone. She said, "I'll maybe come with you." She found one, threw it. A failure. It disappeared at once. She straightened, turned to face him. The wind blew her hair across her cheeks. He looked down into her amazing eyes.

He said, "Why should you do that?"

"I just feel a need to get away."

"When did you decide?"

459

"I've been thinking about it for some months."

"That doesn't answer my question."

"All right. Yesterday. I decided yesterday."

"How much have I got to do with this decision?"

"I don't know. But it's not just you. It's Edmund and Henry as well. Everything. Everything's on top of me. I need time on my own. I need to stand back, and take the long view and get things into perspective."

"Where will you go?"

"To Leesport. To the old house. To Gramps and Grandma."

"Will I be around?"

"If you want to be. I hope you will be."

"I'm not sure if you appreciate the implications."

"Don't I, Conrad?"

"We'll be skating on pretty thin ice."

"We don't need to go out on to the middle of the ice. We can stay around the edge."

"I don't think I'll want to do that."

"I'm not sure about me, either."

"With your husband and your family an ocean away, I won't just feel like a shit, but probably start behaving like one."

"That's a risk I'm prepared to take."

"In that case, I'll say no more."

"That's what I want you to say."

"Except that I'm flying Pan Am, eleven o'clock in the morning, out of Heathrow."

"I'll see if I can get on the same plane."

The worst of growing old, Violet decided, was that happiness, at the most inappropriate of times, eluded one. She should feel happy now, but did not.

Now was the afternoon of her birthday, and to all intents and purposes everything was perfect. No woman could ask for more. She sat, cushioned in heather, high above the loch, and, despite a sinister-looking bruise of cloud that gathered in the west, the sun continued to shine, streaming down from a pristine autumn sky. Far below, but clearly visible, as though viewed through the wrong end of a telescope, the picnic party went about its business; small groups had dispersed to engage in their own activities. The two boats were out on the water. Julian Gloxby and Charles Ferguson-Crombie fished from one of them, Lucilla and her young Australian friend from the other. Dermot had drifted off on his own to search for wildflowers. Virginia and Conrad Tucker had made their way out along the top of the dam wall, and now could be seen walking, side by side, along the narrow shore on the far side of the loch. Edmund's two spaniels accompanied them. From time to time they paused, as though deep in conversation, or stooped to pick up some small flat pebble and send it skimming and jumping out over the glittering water. The others had chosen to stay where they were, gathered about the remains of the fire, lazing in the sunshine. Edie and Alexa sat together. Mrs Gloxby, seldom seen off her feet, had brought her knitting and a book and was enjoying a spot of peace.

Small sounds reached Violet's ears. The buffet of the wind, a raised voice, the splash of oars, a birdcall. Every now and then the crack of guns from the far glen was carried towards them, borne on the wind across the summit of Creagan Dubh.

Everything just as it should be, and yet her heart lay heavy. It is because, she told herself, I know too much. I am the recipient of too many confidences. I should like to be ignorant, and so, blissful. I should like to be unaware of the fact that Virginia and Conrad Tucker . . . that personable and attractive American . . . are lovers. That Virginia has come to a certain crisis in her life; that, with Henry gone, she is capable of making some

461

disastrous decision. I should like to know that Edie is not still agonising over poor Lottie.

And at the same time, there were uncertainties that she would prefer resolved. I should like to feel confident that Alexa is not about to have her heart broken, that Henry is not eating *his* heart out for his mother. I should like to know exactly what is going on in Edmund's unfathomable mind.

Her family. Edmund, Virginia, Alexa, Henry, and Edie. Love and involvement brought joy, but could equally become a hideously heavy millstone slung about one's neck. And the worst was that she felt useless because there was not a mortal thing she could do to help resolve their problems.

She sighed. The sigh was clearly audible, and realising this, Violet, with some effort, pulled herself together, assumed a cheerful expression and turned to the man who lay propped on one elbow beside her.

She said the first thing that came into her mind. "I love the colours of the moor because they remind me of the most beautiful tweed. All russet and purple, and larch-green and peat-brown. And I love the beautiful tweeds because they remind me of the moor. How clever people are to be able to emulate nature so perfectly."

"Is that what you've been thinking?"

He was no fool. She shook her head. "No," she admitted. "I was thinking . . . that it's not the same."

"What isn't the same?" asked Noel.

Violet was not certain why he had come with her. She had not invited him to join her on her walk, and he had not suggested that he might accompany her. She had simply started out, up the hill, and he had fallen into step beside her, as though without words they had made some prearranged assignment. And they had climbed together, Violet leading the way up the narrow sheep-track, pausing every now and then to admire the expanding view, to watch the flight of a grouse, to pick a sprig of white heather. Reaching the summit, she had settled

462

herself down for a small breather, and he had made himself comfortable beside her. She was touched that he had chosen to be with her, and a little more of her reserve towards him melted away.

For, meeting him for the first time, she had been wary. Though prepared to like the young man whom Alexa had chosen to love, she had kept her defences well up, determined not to be taken in by any brittle veneer of too-obvious charm. His dark good looks, his tall frame, his bright and intelligent blue eyes had caught her slightly off-balance, and the fact that he was the son of Penelope Keeling had further taken the wind from her sails. That was another thing that had occurred to cloud her day, for Noel had told her that Penelope was dead, and for some reason she found it painful to come to terms with this. Filled with the regrets of hindsight, she knew that she had no person but herself to blame for the fact that she had never again got in touch with that vital and fascinating woman. And now it was too late.

"What isn't the same?" he prompted gently.

She gathered her flying thoughts. "My picnic."

"It's a splendid picnic."

"But different. Missing out. Henry is not here, nor Edmund, nor Isobel Balmerino. This is the first time she's missed my birthday celebration, but she had to go to Corriehill to help Verena Steynton arrange the flowers for the dance tomorrow evening. And as for my darling little Henry, he is now committed to boarding schools for at least ten years, and by the time he is free to come again, I shall probably be six feet under the turf. I hope I shall be. Eighty-eight scarcely bears thinking about. Too old. Perhaps dependent on one's children. My only fear."

"I can't imagine you being dependent on anybody."

"Senility comes to us all eventually."

They fell silent. Out of this silence another spatter of distant and sporadic gunfire echoed towards them over the hills.

Violet smiled. "They, at least, seem to be having a successful day."

"Who's shooting?"

"I suppose the members of the syndicate who happen to be here just now. And Archie Balmerino is with them." She turned to smile at Noel. "Do you shoot?"

"No. I never even owned a gun. I didn't have that sort of an upbringing. I grew up in London."

"In that wonderful house in Oakley Street?"

"That's right."

"What a fortunate young man you were."

He shook his head. "The shaming thing is that I didn't consider myself fortunate. I was sent to a day school and thought myself very hard done by, because my mother couldn't afford to send me to Eton or Harrow. As well, my father had taken off by the time I was ready for school, and married some other female. I didn't exactly miss him, because I'd hardly known him, but in some strange way it rankled."

She did not waste her sympathy on him. Instead, thinking of Penelope Keeling, she said, "It is not easy for a woman to bring up a family on her own."

"Growing up, I don't think that ever occurred to me."

Violet laughed, appreciating his honesty. "Youth is wasted on the young. But you enjoyed your mother's company?"

"Yes, I did. But from time to time we had the most stupendous rows. Usually about money."

"That's what most family rows are about. And I don't imagine that she suffered from materialism."

"The very opposite. She had her own philosophy for living, and a selection of homespun truisms which she would come out with in times of stress, or in the middle of some really acrimonious argument. One of them was that happiness is making the most of what you have and riches is making the most of what you've got. It sounded plausible, but I never quite worked out the logic."

"Perhaps you needed more than wise words."

"Yes. I needed more. I needed not to feel an outsider. I wanted to be part of a different sort of life, to have a different background. The Establishment. Old houses, old families, old names, old money. We were brought up to believe that money didn't matter, but I knew that it only didn't matter provided you had plenty of it."

Violet said, "I disapprove, but understand. The grass is always greener on the other side of the hill, and it is human nature to yearn for what you cannot have." She thought of Alexa's little jewel of a house in Ovington Street, and the financial security she had inherited from her maternal grandmother, and knew a small stirring of disquiet. "The worst is," she went on, "that when you achieve that green grass, you often discover that you never really wanted it at all." He stayed silent, and she frowned. "Tell me," she said abruptly, coming straight to the point, "what do you think of us all?"

Noel was taken aback by her bluntness. "I . . . I've scarcely had time to form an opinion."

"Rubbish. Of course you have. Do you think, for instance, that we are Establishment, as you term it? Do you think that we are all very *grand*?"

He laughed. Perhaps his amusement disguised a certain embarrassment. She could not be sure. "I don't know about grand. But you must admit that you live on a fairly lavish scale. To achieve such a life-style in the south, one would need to be a millionaire ten times over."

"But this is Scotland."

"Precisely so."

"So you *do* think we're grand?"

"No. Just different."

"Not different, Noel. Ordinary. The most ordinary of folk, who have been blessed with the good fortune to be raised and to live in this incomparable country. There are, I admit, titles, lands, huge houses, and a certain feudalism, but scratch the surface of any one of us, go back a generation or two, and you'll find humble crofters, millworkers, shepherds, small farmers. The Scottish clan system was an extraordinary thing. No man was any man's servant, but part of a family. Which is why your average Highlander does not walk through life with a chip on his shoulder. He is proud. He knows he is as good as you are, and probably a good deal better. As well, the Industrial Revolution and Victorian money created an enormous and wealthy middle class out of a lot of hard-working artisans. Archie is the third Lord Balmerino, but his grandfather made his pile in heavy textiles, and he was raised in the city streets. As for my own father, he started life as the barefoot son of a crofter from the Isle of Lewis. But he was blessed with brains and a talent for book-learning, and his ambitions led him to scholarships, and eventually to study medicine. He became a surgeon and prospered and attained great heights – the Chair of Anatomy at Edinburgh University and a knighthood. Sir Hector Akenside. A resounding name, don't you think? But he always remained a man without pride or pretension, and for this reason was not only respected but loved."

"And your mother?"

"My mother came from an entirely different background. I have to admit that she *was* rather grand. Lady Primrose Marr, the daughter of an ancient and well-connected family from the Borders, who had, through nobody's fault but their own, become totally impoverished. She was very beautiful. Famously so. Small and elegant and with silvery-blonde hair, piled up on her head, so that it looked as though her slender neck might break with the weight of it. My father set eyes on her at some ball or reception in the Assembly Rooms, and fell instantly in love. I don't think she was ever in love with him, but by then he was something of a personage, and well-to-do to boot, and she was intelligent enough to realise on which side her bread had been buttered. Her family, although they could scarcely approve of the match, raised no objections . . . they were

466

probably only too glad to get the girl off their hands."

"Were they happy?"

"I think so. I think they suited each other very well. They lived in a tall and draughty house in Heriot Row, and that is where I was born. My mother relished Edinburgh, with all its social life, the coming and going of friends, the theatre and the concerts, the balls and receptions. But my father remained a countryman with his heart in the hills. He had always loved Strathcroy, and had come every summer for his annual fishing holiday. When I was about five, he bought the land south of the river and built Balnaid. He was still working, and I was at school in Edinburgh, so to begin with, Balnaid was simply a holiday home, a sort of shooting lodge. To me it was paradise, and I lived for the summer months. When he finally retired, he retired to Balnaid. My mother thought it a rotten idea, but he had a stubborn streak to him, and in the end, she simply made the best of it. She filled the house with guests, thus ensuring a fourth for bridge, and a dinner party every night. But we kept the house in Heriot Row, and when the rain fell with unceasing venom, or the bitter winds of winter blew, she invariably found some excuse to return to Edinburgh, or take herself off to Italy, or the South of France."

"And you?"

"I told you. For me it was paradise. I was an only child, and a great disappointment to my mother because I was not only dreadfully large and fat, but plain as well. I towered over all my contemporaries, and was a total failure at dancing class because no boy ever wanted to be my partner. In Edinburgh society, I stuck out like a sore thumb, but at Balnaid it didn't seem to matter how I looked, and at Balnaid I could be just myself."

"And your husband?"

"My husband?" Violet's warm smile transformed her weathered features. "My husband was Geordie Aird. You see, I married my dearest friend, and at the end of

467

over thirty years of marriage, he was still my dearest friend. Not many women can say that."

"How did you meet him?"

"At a shooting party, up on the moors of Creagan Dubh. My father had been asked to shoot with Lord Balmerino, and because my mother was away on some Mediterranean cruise, he asked me to accompany him. Going shooting with my father was always the greatest of treats, and I went to great pains to be useful, carrying his cartridge bag, and sitting, quiet and still as a mouse, in his butt."

"Was Geordie one of the guns?" asked Noel.

"No, Noel. Geordie was one of the beaters. His father, Jamie Aird, was Lord Balmerino's head keeper."

"You married the gamekeeper's son?" Noel could scarcely keep the astonishment out of his voice, but there was admiration there as well.

"I did. It smacks a little of Lady Chatterley, doesn't it, but I can assure you it was not like that at all."

"But when did this happen?"

"The early 1920s. I was ten and Geordie was fifteen. I decided he was the most beautiful boy I had ever seen, and when it was time for the luncheon picnic, I took my sandwiches over to where the keepers and the beaters sat, and ate them with him. You could say that I set my cap at him. After that, he was my friend; I was his shadow, he took me under his wing. I wasn't alone any more. I was with Geordie. We spent whole days together, always out of doors. He taught me to cast for salmon and guddle for trout. Some days we walked for miles, and he showed me the hidden corries where the deer grazed, and the high peaks where the eagles nested. And after a day on the moor, he would take me home to the little house where his parents lived . . . where Gordon Gillock, Archie's keeper, lives now . . . and Mrs Aird would feed me bannocks and scones and pour me strong black tea from her best lustre teapot."

"Did your mother not object to this friendship?"

468

"I think she was quite glad to have me out of the way. She knew that I would come to no harm."

"And did Geordie follow in his father's footsteps?"

"No. Like my own father, he was a clever and academic boy and he did well at school. My father encouraged him in his ambitions. I think he recognised something of himself in Geordie. Because of this, Geordie won a place at the Grammar School in Relkirk, and after that was apprenticed to a firm of chartered accountants."

"And you?"

"Sadly, I had to grow up. All at once, I was eighteen, and my mother realised that her Ugly Duckling had become an Ugly Duck. Despite my size and my lack of social graces, she decided that I must 'come out' – do a season in Edinburgh and be presented to Royalty at Holyrood House. It was the last thing I wanted to do, but Geordie had gone from me and was living in lodgings in Relkirk, and I worked it out in my own mind that if I was complaisant about this dreadful scheme of hers, then perhaps she would in time accept the fact that Geordie Aird was the only man in the world I would think of marrying. The season and the coming-out were, as you can imagine, a total failure. A charade. Dressed in enormous evening gowns, all satin and glitter, I looked like a youthful pantomime dame. At the end of the season I remained unsought, unwanted, and unengaged. My mother, deeply ashamed, brought me home to Balnaid, and I did the flowers and walked the dogs . . . and waited for Geordie."

"How long did you have to wait?"

"Four years. Until he had qualified and was in a position to support a wife. I had money of my own, of course. A trust, which came to me when I was twenty-one, and we could quite easily have managed on that, but Geordie would not hear of it. So I went on waiting. Until the great day came and he passed all his final examinations. I remember I was in the wash-house at

Balnaid, giving the dog a bath. I'd taken him out for a walk, and he'd rolled in something disgusting, and there I was wrapped in an apron and soaking wet and smelling of carbolic. And the wash-house door was flung open, and there stood Geordie, come to ask me to marry him. It was the most romantic moment. And since then, I've always had a soft spot for the smell of carbolic."

"What was the reaction of your parents?"

"Oh, they'd seen it coming for years. My father was delighted and my mother resigned. Once she'd got over agonising about what her smart friends would say, I think she decided that it was better for me to marry Geordie Aird than stay a spinster daughter, getting under her feet and interfering with her butterfly life. So, on an early summer day in 1933, Geordie and I finally wed. And for my mother's sake, I submitted to being laced into stays, and buttoned into white satin so stiff and gleaming that it was like being encased in cardboard. And after the reception, Geordie and I got into his little Baby Austin and we trundled all the way to Edinburgh, where we spent our wedding night in the Caledonian Hotel. And I remember undressing in the bathroom and taking off my going-away dress, and unlacing my stays, and dropping them, with great ceremony, into the wastepaper basket. And I made a vow. No person was ever going to make me wear a corset again. And no person ever has." She burst into lusty laughter and struck Noel a thump on his knee. "So you see, on my wedding night, I said goodbye, not only to my virginity, but to my stays as well. It's hard to say which gave me most satisfaction."

He was laughing. "And you lived happily ever after?"

"Oh, so happily. Such happy years in a little terraced house in Relkirk. Then Edmund was born, and Edie came into our lives. Eighteen years old and the daughter of the Strathcroy joiner, she came to me as a nursery maid, and we've been together ever since. It was a good time. So good that I pretended not to notice the gathering

470

clouds of war looming up over our horizon. But the war came. Geordie joined up with the Highland Division and went to France. In May 1940, he was taken prisoner at Saint-Valéry, and I didn't see him again for five and a half years. Edie and Edmund and I moved back to Balnaid and sat out the war with my parents, but they were growing old, and by the time peace was declared, they had both died. So when Geordie finally came back to us, it was to Balnaid that he came, and it was there that we spent the rest of our life together."

"When did he die?"

"About three years after Edmund was married – for the first time, you understand, to Alexa's mother. It all happened with astonishing suddenness. We had such a good life. I made plans – for the garden, for the house, for holidays and trips that we would take together – as though both of us were going to live for ever. And so I was quite taken by surprise when I realised that, quite suddenly, Geordie was failing. He lost his appetite, lost weight, complained of vague discomforts and pains. At first, refusing to be frightened, I told myself that it was simply some digestive disorder, legacy of his long years in prisoner-of-war camps. But a doctor was finally consulted and then a specialist. Geordie was wheeled into Relkirk General for what were, at that stage, euphemistically known as 'tests'. The result of these tests was conveyed to me by the specialist. He sat across a desk from me in a sun-filled office, and he was very kind, and when he had finished telling me, I thanked him very much, and I got up, and went out of the room, and down the long rubber-floored corridors to where Geordie lay in a side-ward, propped up by pillows in the high hospital bed. I had brought him daffodils from Balnaid, and I arranged them for him in a jug, with plenty of water so that they should not wilt and die. But Geordie died two weeks later. Edmund was there with me, but not Caroline, his wife. She had started a baby, and was suffering from sickness. Knowing that Alexa was coming was one of the things I hung on to during those dreadful, dark days. Geordie was gone, but another new little life was on its way, to set the seal on the bonds of continuity. Which is one of the reasons that Alexa has always been so special to me."

After a while, Noel said, "You're special to her as well. She's talked to me so much about you."

Violet fell silent. A wind sprang up, shuddering through the grass. It carried with it the smell of rain. She looked, and saw the clouds rolling in from the west, blurring the hills and darkening their lower slopes with shadow.

She said, "We've had the best of the day. I hope you don't feel it has been wasted. I hope I haven't bored you."

"Not for a moment."

"I began by trying to prove a point to you, and ended up by telling you my life-story."

"I feel privileged."

She said, "Alexa is coming."

He sat up, dusting scraps of grass from the sleeves of his sweater. "So she is."

They watched her approach, making her way up the steep path with youthful speed and energy. She wore jeans and a dark-blue sweater, and her pale red hair was tousled and her cheeks were rosy with the wind and the sun and the effort of the climb. She looked, thought Violet, quite absurdly young. And, all at once, knew that she had to speak.

"I was so fortunate. I married the man I loved. I only hope that the same thing will happen to Alexa." Noel, slowly, turned his head, and their eyes met. "Virginia told me that I must keep my counsel and not interfere. But I think you know already how much she loves you and I cannot bear to see her hurt. I am not pressurising you, but I want you to be careful. And if you have to hurt her, then you must do it now, before it is too late. You are surely fond enough of her to be able to do that?"

His face was expressionless, but his gaze steady. After a bit, he said, "Yes. Yes, I am."

There was, perhaps mercifully, no time for more. Alexa was there, within earshot, pounding up the last few yards towards them, collapsing into the heather at Noel's side.

"What have you two been talking about? You've been up here for *ages*."

"Oh, this and that," her grandmother told her airily.

"I've been sent to come and tell you that perhaps it's time we thought about packing up. The Ferguson-Crombies have got to go to some dinner party, and they've offered to give the Gloxbys and Dermot Honeycombe a lift back to Croy. Anyway, before very long, it's going to start to rain; the sky's beginning to look really black."

"Yes," said Violet. She looked, and saw that the boats were coming in off the water. Someone had damped down the fire, and her guests were already on their feet, folding rugs, reloading the cars. "Yes, it is time to go."

She began to heave herself up, but Noel was on his feet before her and ready with a helping hand.

"Thank you, Noel." She dusted scraps of heather from her heavy tweed skirt, took a last lingering look. All over. All over for another year. "Come."

She led the way, down the path, off the hill.

Noel awoke to darkness and a raging thirst. And something more urgent. Analysed, this proved to be a rising physical longing for love and Alexa. He lay for a bit, dry-mouthed and lonely and frustrated, in the strange bed, in the unfamiliar bedroom, with the windows wide open on to a dark and blowy night, where no lights shone, and no cars passed, and the only sound was the soughing of the wind in the topmost branches of the trees. He thought nostalgically of London, of Ovington Street, where he had existed for the last few months, lapped in comfort and care. If he awoke thirsty in London, he only had to reach out a hand to find the tumbler of spring water which Alexa set out for him each night, spiked with a slice of lemon. If, in the small dark hours of the morning, he found himself desiring her, he only had to turn to the downy bed, reach out and draw her towards him. Awoken, she was never resentful nor too sleepy for his ardour, but responded with the gentle passion that he had taught her, glorying in her own new-found knowledge, confident in her own desirability.

These reflections helped not at all. At last, unable to bear his thirst a moment longer, he turned on the bedside light and climbed out of bed. Went into the bathroom, ran the cold tap and filled a tooth-mug with water. The water was ice-cold and had a sweet and clean taste to it. He drained the tumbler and refilled it, and then went back to the bedroom and stood in the howling draught, gazing out into the bloomy darkness.

He drank some more. His thirst was assuaged, but his other need stayed with him. Fresh water and Alexa. It occurred to him that these two basic necessities, which, immediately, were more urgent than anything else in life, were in some strange way a reflection of each other. Adjectives flowed through his mind. Clean, sweet, pure, transparent, good, innocent, unsullied. They applied to both the element and the girl. And then, the final accolade. Life-giving.

Alexa.

He prided himself that it was he who was responsible for her flowering from gawky youngster to confident woman – finding out that she was a virgin had been one of the most astonishingly disarming experiences of his life – but he knew as well that it had been a two-way deal, and he had been on the receiving end of a great cornucopia of love and companionship and undemanding acceptance, for although she had been blessed with worldly riches, her gifts had not all been material. Being with Alexa had been a good interlude in his life, one of the best, and whatever happened in the future, he knew that he would always remember it with gratitude.

And what *was* going to happen? But he did not, at the moment, wish to consider this. More pressing to concentrate on now – Alexa. She slept in her own bed, in her childhood bedroom, only a few yards distant, across the landing and down a passage. He thought about going in search of her, silently opening and closing her door, slipping in between the sheets beside her. She would make space for him, turn to him, her arms ready for him, her body waking for him . . .

He considered this course of action for a bit and then decided against it, for, he assured himself, practical rather than high-minded reasons. He knew from experience that it was all too easy to lose one's way in the unlit corridors of other people's country houses, and did not relish being discovered in some broom cupboard, along with the hoover and a lot of old dusters. And here, at Balnaid, he had not even got the watertight excuse of going to the loo, because he had a perfectly good bathroom of his own.

And yet, even without these excuses, and putting more worthy reasons out of his mind, he still found himself wondering if he had the nerve to go in search of her. It had something to do with this house. There was an atmosphere he had sensed as soon as he walked through the door, a feeling of family, which rendered the notion of clandestine corridor-creeping simply out of the question. His long conversation with Vi, out on the hill during the afternoon, had further strengthened his conception of Balnaid. It was as though all the generations who had lived here were still around the place, in residence, living and breathing, going about their daily occupations, watching, and perhaps judging. Not just Alexa and Virginia, but Violet and her stalwart and

475

much-loved Geordie. And before them, the old people, Sir Hector and Lady Primrose Akenside, solidly entrenched, highly principled, and still in charge of a house brimming with individuals; children in the nurseries, guests in the spare rooms, and housemaids and parlourmaids snoring away in the attics upstairs. This was the sort of enduring household that, as a boy, trapped in London, Noel had longed to be part of. A well-ordered and lavish life-style with all the attendant delights of the outdoors. Tennis parties and picnics on an even more elaborate scale than the one that had taken place this afternoon. Ponies, and guns and fishing-rods, and devoted gillies and keepers only too eager and ready to give the young gentleman a guiding hand.

This morning, driving up to Strathcroy with Alexa beside him, dazzled by the countryside and the colours and the sparkling air, he had been overwhelmed by the sensation that in some way he was driving back to the past, to a world that he had once known and yet forgotten. Now, he accepted that he had never known that world but, having found it, was reluctant to let it go. For the first time in his life, he felt that he belonged.

And Alexa?

He heard Violet's voice. *If you have to hurt her, then you must do it now, before it is too late.*

The words had an ominous ring to them. It was possible that it was already too late, in which case he had reached the watershed of his relationship with Alexa, and with Vi's warning ringing in his ears, knew that the time had come to take stock. Before the weekend was over, some sort of a decision had to be made.

He saw himself, as though from some great distance, teetering on that watershed, endeavouring to make the vital choice as to which path he would follow. He could go back the way he had come, which meant leaving Alexa, saying goodbye, trying to explain, packing his bags, moving out of Ovington Street; returning to the basement flat in Pembroke Gardens, placating his tenants, informing them that they must find some other place to roost. It meant going back to the old life, somehow getting himself back into social circulation. Calling up friends, meeting in bars, eating in restaurants, trying to find the telephone numbers of all those emaciated and beautiful women, feeding them, listening to their conversation. It meant driving to the country on Friday evenings, and then struggling back to London, on roads choked with traffic, the following Sunday night.

He sighed. But he'd done it all before, and there was no reason why he should not do it again.

The other alternative, the other path, led the way to commitment. And for Alexa, and everything she represented, he knew that, this time, it had to be total. A lifetime of assumed responsibility – marriage and probably children.

Perhaps it was time. He was thirty-four, but still bedevilled by the uncertainties of immaturity. Basic and deep-rooted insecurities rattled their bones at him, like a lot of gruesome skeletons lurking in a forgotten cupboard. Perhaps it was time, but the prospect filled him with terror.

He shivered. Enough. The wind was rising. A gust rattled the open window-frame. He discovered that he was chilled to the bone, but, like an icy shower, the cold air had finally stilled his unrequited ardour. Which settled at least one problem. He got back into bed, bundled on blankets, and turned off the light. For a long time he lay awake, but when he finally turned and slept again, had still made no decision.

30

Friday the Sixteenth

The rain started soon after Edmund left Relkirk. As the country road climbed, heading north, mist drifted down from the hilltops, and his windscreen was beaded with damp. He switched on the wipers. It was the first rain he had seen for over a week, for New York had sparkled in the warmth of an Indian summer, sunshine reflected from towers of glass, flags snapping in the breeze outside the Rockefeller Center, vagrants enjoying the last of the seasonal warmth, stretched out on the benches of Central Park, with their bags and bundles of meagre possessions gathered all about them.

Edmund had spanned two worlds in a single day. New York, Kennedy, Concorde, Heathrow, Turnhouse, and now back to Strathcroy. Under normal circumstances, he would have taken time to drop in at the office in Edinburgh, but this evening was the night of the Steyntons' dance, and for this reason he had elected to drive directly home. Getting out his Highland finery was apt to take some time, and there was the possibility that neither Virginia nor Edie had remembered to clean the silver buttons on his jacket and his waistcoat, in which case he would have to buckle down to the task himself.

A dance. They would, very likely, not get to bed until four o'clock in the morning. By now he had lost track of his own time-clock, and knew a certain weariness. Nothing, however, that a slug of whisky would not dispel. His wristwatch still stood at New York time, but the clock on his dashboard told him that it was half past five. The day was not yet dead, but the low clouds rendered visibility murky. He switched on his sidelights.

Caple Bridge. The powerful car hummed along the winding curves of the narrow glen road. Tarmac glistened in the damp, whins and gorse were wreathed in mist. He opened the window and smelled the cool and incomparable air. He thought about seeing Alexa again. Thought about not seeing Henry. Thought about Virginia . . .

Their tenuous truce, he feared, had collapsed, and their final exchange, as he was on the point of leaving for New York, had been acrimonious. She had blasted her temper at him down the telephone, accusing him of selfishness, thoughtlessness, broken promises. Refusing to listen to his perfectly reasonable explanations, she had finally slammed down the receiver. He had wanted to speak to Henry, but she had either forgotten this, or deliberately refrained from giving Henry his father's message. Perhaps, after five days without him, she would have cooled down, but Edmund did not feel hopeful. Lately, she had taken to nursing grievances as though they were babies.

His saving grace would be Alexa. For Alexa, he knew Virginia would put on her best face, if necessary play-act her way through the weekend, performing a charade of enjoyment and affection. For this small mercy, at least, he would be grateful.

The road sign came up at him out of the mist. 'Strathcroy'. He slowed, changed down, crossed the bridge by the Presbyterian church, drove beneath the high branches of the elms, clattering with rooks, and through the open gates of Balnaid.

Home. He did not go around to the front of the house, but turned into the old stableyard and parked the BMW there. Only one car, Virginia's, stood in the garage, and the back door, which led into the kitchen, was open. But this, he knew, did not necessarily mean that anybody was at home.

He switched off the ignition and waited, expecting, if not a delighted family spilling out of that door to greet him, then at least some sort of a welcome from his dogs. But he was met by silence. There did not appear to be anybody about.

He climbed wearily from his car, went to open the boot and collect his baggage. His suitcase, his bulging leather briefcase, his raincoat, the yellow plastic bag of duty-free. It was heavy with bottles, Scotch and Gordon's gin, and generous packages containing French perfume for his wife, his daughter, his mother. He carried these indoors, out of the rain. He found a kitchen warm, swept, orderly but empty, the only sign of his dogs their unoccupied baskets. The Aga hummed to itself. Into the sink, a tap dripped gently. He put his suitcase and his raincoat on the floor, the bag of duty-free on the table, went to the sink to tighten off the faulty tap. The dripping ceased. He listened for other sounds, but none disturbed the ensuing quiet.

Carrying his briefcase, he went out of the kitchen, down the passage, through the hall. There he paused for a moment, waiting for an opened door, footsteps, a voice, another person. The old clock ticked. Nothing more. He went on, his footsteps muffled by the thick carpet, past the drawing room, to open the door of the library.

Nobody here either. He saw cushions, smooth and fat, on the sofa, an empty fireplace, a neat pile of *Country Lifes*, an arrangement of dried flowers, their colours faded, smoky, and rusty. The window was open and let in a great draught of damp and chilly air. He set down his briefcase and went to close it, and then returned to his desk, where a week's mail was tidily stacked, awaiting his attention. He turned over an envelope or two, but knew that there was nothing there that could not wait for another day.

The telephone rang. He picked up the receiver. "Balnaid."

It clicked, buzzed, and then went dead. Probably some person dialling the wrong number. He put the receiver back, and all at once could not bear the gloom of the empty room for a moment longer. The library at Balnaid, without a fire for companionship, was like a person without a heart, and only on the hottest days of summer was it ever allowed to go out. He found matches, lit the paper in the hearth, waited until the kindling crackled, added logs. The flames leapt up the chimney, warming and lighting, bringing life. Thus he contrived his own welcome and felt marginally cheered.

He watched the flames for a bit, then put on the fireguard and made his way back to the kitchen. He unloaded the whisky and the gin and put them in the cupboard, and then carried his suitcase and the duty-free bag upstairs. The ticking of the grandfather clock accompanied his tread. He crossed the landing and opened the door of their bedroom.

"Edmund."

She was there, had been in the house all the time. She sat at her dressing-table and was engaged in painting her nails. The room, so spacious and feminine – dominated by the enormous king-size double bed draped in antique-white linen and lace – was, uncharacteristically, in a state of some disarray. Shoes lay about, a pile of folded clothes stood stacked on a chair, wardrobe doors hung open. On one of these doors, from a padded hanger, was suspended Virginia's new evening dress, the one she had bought in London especially for the occasion tonight. The skirt, flaring out in layers of some filmy material spattered with a confetti of black spots, without her inside it, looked a bit sad and empty.

Across the room, they eyed each other. He said, "Hi."

She wore her white towelling robe and had washed her hair and set it on the huge rollers that Henry always

481

told her made her look like some monster from outer space.

"You're back. I never heard the car."

"I parked it by the garage. I thought there was nobody around."

He carried the suitcase through to his dressing-room and set it down on the floor. All his evening clothes were laid out on the single bed. His kilt, stockings, skean dhu, evening shirt, jacket, and waistcoat. The buttons of these shone like stars, as did the silver buckles on his shoes.

He went back into the bedroom. "You cleaned my buttons."

"Edie did."

"That was kind." He went over to her side and stooped to give her a kiss. "A present for you." He put the box on her dressing-table.

"Oh, lovely. Thank you." She had finished painting her nails, but the varnish had not yet dried. She sat with fingers outspread, from time to time blowing on them to speed the process up. "How was New York?"

"Okay."

"I didn't expect you back so soon."

"I caught the early shuttle."

"Are you tired?"

"I won't be when I've had a drink." He lowered himself on to the edge of the bed. "Is there anything wrong with the telephone?"

"I don't know. It rang about five minutes ago, but only once, and then it stopped."

"I answered it downstairs, but it went dead."

"It's done that once or twice today. But it's working for outgoing calls."

"Have you reported it?"

"No. Do you think we should?"

"I'll do it later." He leaned back on the piles of pillows, his head against the quilted bedhead. "How have things been with you?"

482

She inspected her nails. "All right."

"And Henry?"

"I don't know about Henry. I haven't heard and I haven't telephoned." She looked at him, and her brilliant blue gaze was cool. "I thought that perhaps telephoning was not *quite* the right thing to do. Untraditional, perhaps."

Which made it abundantly clear that he was not forgiven. But this was not the time to pick up the gauntlet and precipitate yet another row.

"Did you get him to Templehall?"

"Yes. I drove him. He didn't want to go with Isobel, so we took Hamish with us. Hamish was in one of his most disagreeable moods, Henry never said a single word the entire journey, and it peed with rain the whole way. Apart from that, it was a picnic."

"He didn't take Moo with him, did he?"

"No, he didn't take Moo."

"Thank God for that. And Alexa?"

"She arrived yesterday morning, with Noel."

"Where are they now?"

"I think they took the dogs out for a walk. After lunch they had to go to Relkirk to pick up Lucilla's dress from the cleaner's. We had an SOS from Croy. The dress had been forgotten, and they're all so busy getting the dinner party together that nobody had time to go."

"So what else has been happening?"

"What else has been happening? Vi had her picnic. Verena's had us all at her beck and call like slaves, and Edie's cousin has gone back to hospital."

Edmund raised his head a fraction, as an alert dog will prick its ears. Virginia, her nails now satisfactorily dry and hard, took up the package that he had brought her, and began to tear off the cellophane wrapping.

"She's gone back?"

"Yes." She opened the box and drew out the bottle, square-cut and opulent, the stopper ringed with a bow of velvet ribbon. She unscrewed the stopper and dabbed

483

a little on her neck. "Delicious. Fendi. How kind. I've been wanting this scent, but it's too expensive to buy for oneself."

"When did this happen?"

"Lottie, you mean? Oh, a couple of days ago. She became so impossible that Vi insisted. She should never have been discharged in the first place. She's insane."

"What did she do?"

"Oh, talked. Meddled. Made mischief. She wouldn't leave me alone. She's evil."

"What did she say?"

Virginia turned back to the mirror and began, slowly, to take the pins out of her rollers. One by one, she laid them on the plate glass of the dressing-table. He watched her profile, the line of her jaw, the curve of her lovely neck.

"Do you really want to know?"

"I shouldn't ask if I didn't."

"All right. She said that you and Pandora Blair were lovers. Years ago, the time of Archie and Isobel's wedding, when Lottie was a housemaid at Croy. You always said that she listened at doors. She doesn't seem to have missed a trick. Describing it all to me, she made it quite vivid. She became quite excited. Turned on, one might say. She said that it was because of *you* that Pandora ran off with her married man and never came home again. That it was all your fault. And now . . ." One of the rollers was being stubborn, and Virginia jerked at it, trying to free it, tugging at and tangling her corn-coloured hair. ". . . now she is saying that *you* are the reason that Pandora has come back to Croy. Nothing to do with the party tonight. Nothing to do with Archie. Just you. She wants to start it up all over again. To get you back."

Another jerk and the roller was loose, and Virginia's eyes were watering with agony. Edmund watched her, scarcely able to bear the pain that she was inflicting upon herself.

484

He remembered the evening when he had encountered Lottie in Mrs Ishak's supermarket, and how she had buttonholed him. He had recoiled from her distasteful presence. He remembered her eyes, her pallid skin, her moustache, and the useless fury that she had kindled within him, so that he had come very close to losing his temper and inflicting upon her grievous bodily harm. He recalled the stirring of a dreadful apprehension. An apprehension well-founded, for now it seemed it had come to this.

He said coldly, "She is lying."

"Is she, Edmund?"

"Do you believe her?"

"I don't know . . ."

"Virginia . . ."

"Oh . . ." In a burst of exasperation, she jerked another roller free, flung it at her own reflection in the mirror, and then rounded on him. "I don't know. I don't know. I can't think straight any longer. And I don't care. Why should I care? What does it matter to me that you and Pandora Blair once had a raging love affair? As far as I'm concerned, it's all lost in the mists of time and absolutely nothing to do with me. I only know that it happened when you were already a married man – married to Caroline – and that you were the father of a child. The simple fact is that that doesn't make me feel very secure."

"You don't trust me?"

"Sometimes I think I don't even know you."

"That is a ludicrous statement."

"All right, so it's ludicrous. But unfortunately we can't all be as cold and objective as you. And if it is ludicrous, you can put it down to human frailty, except that I don't suppose you even know what that means."

"I'm beginning to realise I know only too well."

"It's *us* I'm talking about, Edmund. You and me."

"In that case, perhaps it would be better to postpone this conversation until you are a little less overwrought."

485

"I am *not* overwrought. And I am not a child any longer, I am not your *little* wife. And I think perhaps that this is as good a time as any to tell you that I'm going away for a bit. I'm going back to Long Island, to Leesport, to spend some time with my grandparents. I've told Vi. She says you can stay with her. We'll close the house."

Edmund said nothing. She looked at him and saw his poker-face empty of expression, the handsome features still, the hooded eyes giving nothing away. No hurt showed, no anger. She let the silence lengthen, waiting for him to react to her announcement. For a mad moment, she imagined him flinging reserve to the wind, coming to her side, taking her in his arms, covering her with kisses, loving her, making love to her . . .

"When did you plan all this?"

Tears pricked behind her eyes, but she set her teeth and willed them away.

"I've been thinking about going for months. I finally made up my mind after Henry went. Without Henry, there is no reason not to go."

"When are you leaving?"

"I've got a seat on a Pan Am flight out of Heathrow next Thursday morning."

"Thursday? That's less than a week away."

"I know." She turned back to her mirror, pulled free the last of the rollers, reached for her comb, began to draw it through the tangled curls, smoothing out the snarls. "But there is a reason, and you may as well be told that reason now, because if I don't tell you, some other person will. A strange thing has happened. You remember last Sunday Isobel telling us that she had some unknown American coming to stay? It turned out that he's a man called Conrad Tucker, and we knew each other years ago, in Leesport."

"The Sad American."

"Yes. And he is sad. His wife has just died of leukaemia, and he's been left with a little daughter. He's been over here for a month or more, but he's returning to the States on Thursday." She laid down the comb, tossing the shining, clean hair away from her face, turned back to face him. "It seemed," she said, "a good idea to make the journey together."

"Was that his idea or your idea?"

"Does it matter?"

"No. I don't suppose it makes any difference at all. When are you planning to return?"

"I don't know. I have an open-ended ticket."

"I don't think you should go."

"That has an ominous ring to it, Edmund. It wouldn't be a warning?"

"You're running away."

"No. I am simply taking advantage of a freedom that has been forced upon me. Without Henry, I am in a sort of limbo, and I've got to come to terms with being bereft of him, and I can't do that here. I need time to sort myself out. To be on my own. To be my own person. You have to try, just for once in your life, to see a situation from another person's point of view. In this case, mine. And perhaps, as well, you could try to give me some credit for being honest with you."

"I would have been astonished had you done anything else."

After that, there did not seem to be anything more to say. Beyond the open windows, the misty autumn evening sank into an early dusk. Virginia switched on the lights of her dressing-table, and then stood up and moved to close the heavy chintz curtains. From downstairs, sounds reached their ears. A door opening and shutting, dogs barking, voices raised.

She said, "Noel and Alexa. They're back from their walk."

"I'll go down." He got to his feet, stretched his arms, swallowed a yawn. "I need a drink. Do you want one?"

"Later."

He made for the door. "What time are we expected at Croy?"

"Half past eight."

"You can have your drink in the library before we leave."

"There's no fire."

"I lit it."

He went out of the room. Listening, Virginia heard him traverse the landing, start down the stairs. And then Alexa's voice. "Fa!"

"*Hello*, my darling."

He had left the door open. She went to shut it and then returned to her dressing-table, with some idea of starting to do something about her face. But tears, so long controlled, rose in her eyes, overflowed, streamed down her cheeks.

She sat and watched her own weeping reflection.

The country bus, stopping and starting and taking its time, trundled through the twilit countryside. Leaving Relkirk, it had been full, with every seat occupied, and one or two passengers standing. Some of the people were returning home from work, others had been shopping. A lot of them seemed to know each other, smiling and chatting as they climbed on board. Probably they travelled together every day. There was a man with a sheepdog. The dog sat between his knees and gazed without ceasing into the man's eyes. The man didn't have to buy a ticket for the dog.

Henry sat at the front, just behind the driver. He was squashed in by the window, because a hugely fat lady had chosen to sit beside him.

"Hello, pet," she'd said, as she settled herself, her massive bottom shunting him sideways and her bulging thighs taking up most of the space. She had two laden bags with her, one of which she put at her feet, and the other on her lap. From the top of this bag stuck out a head of celery and a bright pink celluloid windmill. Henry decided that she was taking it home for her grandchild.

She had a round, kind face, not unlike Edie's, and beneath the brim of her sensible hat, her eyes screwed up in a friendly way. But when she spoke to him, Henry did not answer her; simply turned away and gazed from the window, although there was nothing to be seen except rain.

He wore his school stockings and shoes, his new tweed overcoat, which was much too big for him, and his Balaclava helmet. The Balaclava helmet had been a good idea, and he was proud of himself for thinking of it. It was navy-blue and very thick, and he had pulled it right down over his face, like a terrorist, so that only his eyes showed. It was his disguise, because he did not want anybody to recognise him.

The bus made slow progress, and they had already been travelling for nearly an hour. Every mile or so, they drew to a halt at some crossroad, or lonely cottage, to allow people to get off. Henry watched as the seats emptied; passengers gathered up their possessions and alighted one by one, to set off on foot, to walk the last bit of their journey home. The fat lady beside him got out at Kirkthornton, but she didn't have to walk, because her husband had come to meet her in his little farm truck. As she struggled to her feet, she said, "Goodbye, pet," to Henry. He thought this very nice of her but, again, made no reply. It wasn't easy to say something with a Balaclava over your mouth.

Once more, they set off. Now, there were only half a dozen people on board. The engine of the bus made a grinding sound as they climbed the hill out of the little market town, and at the top of the hill it became quite foggy. The driver turned on his headlights, and thorn hedges and wind-bent beeches raced towards them out of the gloom, wreathed in mist and looking ghostly. Henry thought about the five empty miles between Caple Bridge and Strathcroy, which he was going to have to walk because Caple Bridge was where he had to get off the bus. The prospect scared him a bit, but not all that much, because he knew the road, and the difficult bit was over, and he was nearly there.

At Pennyburn, Violet prepared herself for the rigours of the evening that lay ahead.

She had not been invited to a proper dance for longer than she could remember, and, at seventy-eight, it was unlikely that she would ever be invited to another. For this reason, she had decided to make the most of the occasion. Accordingly, this afternoon, she had driven to Relkirk, and there had her hair professionally washed and waved. As well, she had indulged in a manicure, and the nice girl, with her cushion, had spent some time digging earth out of Violet's nails and pushing back her neglected cuticles.

After this little beautifying session, she had called in at the bank, and withdrawn from its vaults the battered leather box that contained Lady Primrose's diamond tiara. It was not very large, and had to be held together at the back with a loop of elastic, but she had brought it home and cleaned it up with an old toothbrush dipped in neat gin. This was a household tip that she had gleaned, long ago, from Mrs Harris. It worked well, but still seemed to Violet a terrible waste of gin.

Then, from her wardrobe, she had taken down her ball-dress, black velvet and at least fifteen years old. The frill of black lace at the neck had come away a little, and needed the attention of a needle and thread, and her evening shoes, black satin with diamanté buckles, proved, on inspection, to have grown a few whiskers around the toes, so she took up her nail scissors and gave them a trim.

When all was ready, she allowed herself a little relaxation. She was not due at Croy until half past eight. So, there was time to pour a restoring whisky and soda and settle down by the fire to watch the news on television and then 'Wogan'. She enjoyed Wogan. She liked his cheerful Irish charm, his blarney. This evening, he was interviewing a young pop star, who, for some reason, had become deeply involved in the preservation of rural hedgerows. People were really quite extraordinary, Violet decided, watching the young man, with his punk hair and his earring, burbling on about nesting yellow-hammers.

Then Wogan finished, and a quiz-show came on. Four people were meant to guess the value of various bits of antique junk which were set before them. Violet, all on her own, joined in the guessing game, and became certain that her assessments were far more accurate than anybody else's. She was beginning to enjoy herself when the telephone rang.

How tiresome. Why did the wretched thing always ring at the least opportune moment? She set down her glass, heaved herself out of her comfortable chair, turned down the television and picked up the receiver.

"Hello?"

"Mrs Aird?"

"Yes."

"This is Dr Martin. From the Relkirk Royal."

"Oh, yes."

"Mrs Aird, I'm afraid we have a little trouble on our hands. Miss Carstairs has disappeared."

"She's *disappeared*?" It sounded like some sort of dreadful conjuring trick, bringing visions of an explosion, a puff of smoke, and Lottie fading into nothing. "How could she *possibly* have disappeared?"

"She's gone. She went out for a walk in the garden, with another patient. She never returned."

491

"But that's perfectly terrible."

"We think she must have simply walked out through the gates. We've alerted the police, of course, and I'm certain that she cannot be far away. She'll probably come back here of her own accord. She's been quite content, responding to treatment, and not troublesome in any sort of way. There is no reason why she shouldn't return. But I felt I should let you know . . ."

Violet thought that he was being very feeble.

"Surely you should have taken more care of her?"

"Mrs Aird, we are overcrowded here and under-staffed. Under the circumstances, we do the best we can, but ambulant patients, whom we consider able, up to a point, to take care of themselves, have always been allowed a certain amount of freedom."

"So what do we do now?"

"There is nothing to be done. But, as I said, I thought you should know what has happened."

"Have you spoken to Miss Findhorn, her next of kin?"

"Not yet. I thought it better to have a word with you first."

"In that case, I shall tell Miss Findhorn."

"I'd be very grateful if you would."

"Dr Martin . . ." Violet hesitated. "Do you think that Lottie Carstairs will try to make her way back to Strathcroy?"

"It's possible, of course."

"She would go to Miss Findhorn's house?"

"Possibly."

"I shall be honest with you. I don't like the prospect at all. I fear for Miss Findhorn."

"I appreciate your fears but consider them groundless."

"I wish," Violet told him dryly, "that I could be so certain, but thank you, Dr Martin, for calling."

"If I have any news, I'll ring you."

"I shan't be here. But you will be able to reach me at Croy, because I shall be dining with Lord Balmerino."

"I'll make a note. Thank you. Goodbye, Mrs Aird. And I'm sorry to have bothered you."

"Yes," said Violet. "You have bothered me. Goodbye."

And she was more than bothered. All peace of mind had been shot to ribbons. She was not only bothered but filled with fear. The same reasonless panic she had experienced sitting by the river with Lottie that day in Relkirk, with Lottie's fingers clenched, vicelike, around her wrist. Then, she had been tempted to leap to her feet and run. Now, she felt the same way, her heart pounding in her chest. It was the fear of the unknown, the unimaginable, some lurking danger.

Analysed, she realised that this fear was not for herself, but for Edie. Her imagination leapt ahead. A knock on Edie's cottage door, Edie going to answer it, and Lottie, with her hands outstretched like claws, leaping upon her . . .

It didn't bear thinking about. On the television screen, a woman, presented with a flowered chamber pot, dissolved into silent, embarrassed laughter, her mouth open, her hand over her eyes. Violet turned her off, picked up the receiver and dialled Balnaid. Edmund must be back from New York by now. Edmund would know exactly what to do.

She heard the ringing sound. It continued to ring. She waited, became impatient. Why did none of them answer her call? What were they all doing?

Finally, exasperated, and by now in a state of fluster, she slammed the receiver down, and then picked it up again and dialled Edie.

Edie, too, was watching television. A nice Scottish programme, country dancing, and a comic in a kilt, telling rare stories. She sat with her supper tray on her lap, grilled chicken legs and chips and mushy peas. For afters, there was some leftover Apple Betty in the fridge. This evening, she was eating late. One of the good things about being on her own again was that she could eat

493

when it suited her, without Lottie on at her all the time about when was the next meal coming. There were other good things. Quiet was one of them. And being able to get a good night's rest in her own bed, instead of tossing and turning on the inadequate Put-U-Up. Getting a good night's rest had done more than anything to restore her energy and good spirits. She still felt guilty about poor Lottie, back in the hospital, but there could be no doubt that life was a great deal easier without her.

The telephone rang. She set aside her tray and got up to answer it.

"Yes?"

"Edie."

She smiled. "Hello, Mrs Aird."

"Edie . . ." There was something wrong. Edie could tell at once, just by the way Mrs Aird said her name. "Edie, I've just been speaking to Dr Martin from the hospital. Lottie's walked out. They don't know where she is."

Edie felt her heart sink into her boots. After a bit she said, "Oh dear, goodness," which was all she could think of to say.

"They've notified the police, and they are pretty certain she's not gone far, but Dr Martin agrees with me that there is a strong possibility that she'll make her way back to Strathcroy."

"Has she got money with her?" asked Edie, ever practical.

"I don't know. I hadn't thought about that. But I'm certain that she wouldn't have gone far without her handbag."

"No. That's true enough." Lottie was devoted to her handbag, and kept it by her side even when she was just sitting by the fire. "Poor soul. Something must have upset her."

"Yes. Maybe. But, Edie, I'm concerned for *you*. If she does come back to Strathcroy, I don't want you to be alone in your house."

"But I must be here. If she comes, I must be here."

"No. No, Edie, listen. You must listen. You must be sensible. We don't know what is going on in Lottie's mind. She may have got it into her head that you have let her down in some way. Done her some hurt, rejected her. If she is in one of her states, you cannot possibly deal with her on your own."

"And what harm could she do to me?"

"I don't know. I only know that you must get out of your house . . . come to me for the night, or go to Balnaid until such time as she has been located and is safely back in hospital."

"But . . ."

Her protest was overridden. "No, Edie, I will not take no for an answer, otherwise I shall not have a moment's peace. You must pack a nightdress and go to Balnaid. Or come here. I don't mind which. And if you don't agree, then I shall be forced to get into my car and come and fetch you myself. And as I have to be at Croy at half past eight, and am not yet bathed nor dressed, this will be extremely inconvenient for me. It's up to you."

Edie hesitated. The last thing she wanted was to cause a lot of inconvenience. Besides, she knew of old that Violet, once she had set her mind on something, was immovable. And yet . . .

"I should stay here, Mrs Aird. I'm her next of kin. She's my responsibility."

"You are also responsible to yourself. If you were to be distressed or threatened or hurt in any way, I should never forgive myself."

"And what will happen if she does come and finds the house empty?"

"The police have been alerted. I am certain that a patrol car will be around the place. It won't be difficult for them to pick her up."

Edie could think of no more arguments. She was defeated, her fate sealed. She sighed, and said quite

495

crossly, "Oh, very well. But in my opinion, you're making a mountain out of a molehill."

"Maybe so. I hope I am."

"Do they know at Balnaid that I'm coming?"

"No. I can't get through to them on the telephone. I think something must be wrong with the wires."

"Have you reported it to Faults?"

"Not yet. I called you right away."

"Well, I'll give Faults a ring, and let them know the number's not answering. They must be there. All getting ready for the party."

"Yes, Edie. You ring Faults. And when you've done that, you must promise me that you'll go to Balnaid. Your room there is always ready, and Virginia will understand. Explain to her what has happened. If there is any inconvenience, you can put the blame on me. I'm sorry, Edie, to be so dictatorial. But I really wouldn't enjoy myself in the very least if I knew that you were on your own."

"It seems to me a lot of fuss about nothing, but I suppose a night at Balnaid won't kill me."

"Thank you, Edie dear. Goodbye."

"Have a good party."

Edie rang off. And then, before she should forget, she lifted the receiver again and called Faults to report the dead line. She was answered by a helpful man, who said that he would investigate the trouble and ring her back.

Lottie gone. What was going to happen next? It was terrible to think of Lottie wandering around somewhere all on her own, perhaps frightened, lost. What was the stupid creature thinking about? Why could she not have stayed where she was, cared for by kindly folk? What wild idea had got into her head this time?

Edie would go to Balnaid, but not immediately. Her tray waited, with the cooling remains of her supper. She would finish it, then do her dishes, tidy the kitchen, and bank up the Rayburn with coke. After that, she would put a nightie into her leatherette message bag, and set off down the road.

She sighed in exasperation. That Lottie was a real nuisance, and no mistake, turning everybody's lives upside down. She settled herself once more with her supper tray on her lap, but the chicken had cooled and lost its tastiness, and even the Scottish programme could not claim her attention.

Once more the telephone rang. Once more she set aside the tray and got up to answer the call. The man from Faults told her that the Balnaid number did not seem to be ringing out, but that an engineer would be around to see to it tomorrow morning.

Edie thanked him. Nothing more could be done. She picked up her supper tray and carried it through to the kitchen. Scraping the remains on her plate into the rubbish bin, she washed up the few bits and pieces and stacked them on the draining board, all the time trying to work out where on earth her sad, half-witted cousin could have got to.

Archie Balmerino, bathed, shaved, groomed, dressed in his evening clothes, and, given a kiss of approval by his wife, left Isobel at her dressing-table, doing something complicated to her eyelashes, and emerged on to the landing from their bedroom.

For a moment he paused, listening for other signs of activity, but nobody but himself appeared to be about, and so he set off down the stairs, one step at a time, with a hand on the banister rail. All through the day, each occupant of Croy had been hard at it, with jobs allotted and tasks to be accomplished. Which was just as well, for there had been a hell of a lot to do. Now the house was ready, dressed for the party, a stage set for action, awaiting the raising of the curtain, the entrance of the dramatis personae.

He was the first. At the turn of the stair he paused, to stand, admiring with some satisfaction, the scene below him. The great entrance hall, cleared and tidied of all its normal day-to-day clobber, presented a face both impressive and welcoming. In the huge fireplace, with its carved overmantel, logs flamed, and the table that stood in the centre of the worn Turkey rug reflected, in its highly polished surface, the considerable arrangement of white chrysanthemums and scarlet rosehip berries which Isobel had concocted some time during the course of the afternoon.

Croy, dressed for entertaining. An excitement in the air, a promise of pleasures to come. For once austerity and necessary economies had been tossed overboard, and the old house could be sensed revelling in the indulgence of rare extravagance.

He thought of other evenings. His own twenty-first; and the evening when he and Isobel had celebrated their engagement. Birthdays, Christmases, hunt balls, his parents' silver wedding . . .

And then, frowning at himself, he shut the memories away. Nostalgia was his greatest weakness. One could look back for ever, but looking back was an old person's ploy and he was not old. He was not yet fifty. Croy was his and yet not his. It had come to him, through his father and his grandfather, to hold in trust for Hamish. And the strength of a chain was the strength of its weakest link.

He himself. The horrors of Northern Ireland would remain with him until the day he died, but the haunting ghosts and dreams had finally been laid to rest, and with them disposed of, he knew that there were no longer excuses to be made to himself. The time had come to stop vacillating and start constructing some practical plans for his inheritance and his family and their future. He had marked time for too long, and there were no more years to be wasted. He wasn't quite sure what he would do, but he would do something. Borrow money and start that factory that Pandora thought such a brilliant idea. Or grow soft fruit, raspberries and strawberries, on a huge commercial scale. Or go in for fish-farming. There were opportunities and possibilities all about him. All he had to do was make up his mind and go for it.

Go for it. The words had a heartening ring to them. He knew again some of his old, youthful confidence. Knew that the worst was over, and nothing could ever be quite so bad again.

He went on, down the stairs, into the dining room. He and Pandora had laid the table together, just the way it had always been arranged for important occasions, when Harris was in charge, and pleased to instruct the youthful Blairs on correct and time-honoured procedure. It had taken them most of the afternoon, with Archie polishing up the bubble-thin wineglasses, and Pandora folding the starched white napkins into mitres, each tipped with the embroidered coronet and the letter *B*.

Now he observed, with a critical eye, their work. The effect was splendid. The four heavy silver candlesticks marched down the centre of the table, and firelight shone and sparkled from gleaming silver and glass, for here, as well, the logs flamed, and Jeff Howland had been given the job of filling all the wood-baskets. The scent of dry and crackling pine was warm and spicy. Archie walked the length of the room, checking on the placement, straightening a fork, altering, very slightly, the position of a salt-cellar. Satisfied, he went on into the kitchen.

Here he found Agnes Cooper, up from the village for the evening. Agnes normally came to work in her tracksuit and a pair of trainers, but this evening she wore beneath her pinafore her best turquoise Crimplene dress, and she had had her hair done.

She was at the sink, dealing with the odd saucepan or two, but turned at his footstep.

"Agnes. Everything all right?"

"All under control. I've just got to keep my eye on the casserole, and put the wee bits of smoked trout on to the plates when Lady Balmerino says."

"It's good of you to come and help us."

"That's what I'm here for." She eyed him in some admiration. "I hope you don't mind my saying, but you're looking *fantaastic*."

"Oh, thank you, Agnes." He found himself a little embarrassed, and to cover his confusion, offered her a drink. "A glass of sherry. How would that be?"

Agnes was also a little taken aback. "Oh. Well. That would be very nice."

She reached for a towel and dried her hands. Archie found a glass, and the bottle of Harvey's Bristol Cream. He poured her a generous tot. "Here you are . . ."

"Thanks a lot, Lord Balmerino . . ." She raised the glass in a convivial fashion, saying, "Here's to having a good time," and then took a ladylike sip, folding her lips appreciatively around the rich taste. "Sherry's lovely," she said. "Like I say, it always gives you a beautiful glow."

He left her and went back, through the dining room, across the hall, and into the drawing room. Another fire, more flowers, soft lights, but no guests. His house party, it seemed, were taking their time. The drinks tray had been set out, and placed on top of the grand piano. He considered the situation. They would be on champagne for the remainder of the evening, but he needed a Scotch. He poured himself a drink, and then poured a second one, and, carrying the two glasses with a certain amount of care, painfully made his way upstairs again.

On the landing he came upon his daughter, who, for some reason, was wandering around in her under-clothes.

"Lucilla!" he reproached her.

But she was more concerned over his appearance than her own.

500

"Goodness, Dad, you look *gorgeous*. Really romantic and distinguished. The Lord Balmerino in full fig. Are those new trousers? They're heaven. I wouldn't mind a pair of those. And Grandpa's old smoking jacket. Quite perfect." She put her naked arms around his neck and pressed a kiss on his newly shaved cheek. "And you smell delicious as well. All sleek and barbered and yummy. Who are the drinks for?"

"I thought I'd better make sure that Pandora's awake. Why haven't you got any clothes on?"

"Just on my way to borrow a petticoat from Mum. My new dress is a bit flimsy."

"You'd better get a move on. It's twenty-five past eight."

"I'm ready now." She went to throw open the door of her parents' bedroom. "Mum! I'm going to *have* to wear a petticoat . . ."

Archie crossed the landing to the door of the guest room. From within came faint strains of music, which meant that Pandora had turned on her radio, but did not necessarily mean that she was awake. He juggled the two glasses into one hand, gave a cursory thump on the panel, and opened the door.

"Pandora?"

She was not in bed, but she was on it, lying draped in a silk-and-lace wrapper. Clothes were scattered about all over the place, and the room was heavy with the smell of that strange scent which had become so much part of her presence.

"Pandora."

She opened her beautiful grey eyes. She had put on her make-up, and her thick lashes were heavy with mascara. She saw him and smiled. She said, "I'm not asleep."

"I've brought you a drink."

He set the glass down on her table, alongside the little lamp, and went to sit on the edge of the bed. Her radio crooned softly away to itself, a programme of dance

501

music that sounded as though it came from a long way back.

She said, "How kind."

"It's almost time to come downstairs." Her shining hair spilled over the pillow, almost as though it had a life of its own, but lying there she looked so thin, so insubstantial, so weightless that, all at once, he felt concern. "Are you tired?"

"No. Just lazy. Where is everybody?"

"Isobel's dealing with her face, and Lucilla's wandering about in her knickers wanting to borrow a petticoat from her mother. So far, there's no sign of either of the men."

"It's always a good moment, isn't it? Just before a party. Time to have a toes-up and listen to nostalgic tunes. Do you remember this one? It's so pretty. Rather sad. I can't remember the words."

Together they listened. The tenor saxophone carried the melody. Archie frowned, trying to capture the elusive lyric. The music carried him back twenty years, to Berlin and some regimental ball. Berlin was the clue.

"Something about a long long time from May to December."

"Yes, of course. Kurt Weill. 'But the days grow short when you reach September.' And then autumn leaves, and the days running out, and there not being time for the waiting game. So dreadfully poignant."

She sat up, bunching her pillows behind her. She reached for her drink, and he saw her narrow wrist, and her red-tipped hand, so fine and pale and blue-veined that it seemed to Archie almost transparent.

He said, "Are you nearly ready?"

"Nearly. I've only got to slip my dress on and zip up the zip." She took a mouthful of whisky. "Oh, delicious. This will get me going." Over the rim of the glass her eyes appeared enormous. "You look amazing, Archie. Just as dashing as you ever did."

"Agnes Cooper said I looked *fantaastic*."

502

"What a compliment. Darling, I wasn't asleep. I was just having a little quiet think about yesterday. It was all so perfect. Just like it used to be. The two of us. Sitting in the butt, and having time to chat. Or not chat, as the case might be. Perhaps I talked too much, but twenty years is a long time to tell. Was it dreadfully boring?"

"No. You made me laugh. You always made me laugh."

"And the sun and the blue sky and the heather linties cheeping away, and the guns going *crack*, and the poor little grouse tumbling out of the sky. And all those clever doggies. Weren't we lucky to have such a day? Like being given the most gorgeous present."

He said, "I know."

"It's nice to think those sort of days come back again. That they haven't gone for ever."

"We must reform. Kick this invidious family habit of dwelling in the past."

"It was such a good past, it's difficult not to. Besides, what else is there to think about?"

"Now. Yesterday is dead and tomorrow not yet born. We only have today."

"Yes."

She took another sip from her glass. They fell silent. From beyond the closed door came sounds of activity. A door opened and shut. And then Lucilla's voice. "Conrad. How smart you look. I don't know where Dad is, but go downstairs and we'll all be with you in a moment . . ."

"I hope," said Archie, "that she's wearing Isobel's petticoat."

"Conrad is such a gentleman that even if Lucilla is stark-naked, he'll pay no regard. Such a nice Sad American. It would have been too awful for all of us if he'd been a crashing bore."

"You must make a point of dancing with him."

"I'll twirl him through a Dashing White Sergeant and introduce him to all the nobs as we move around the room. That's the only thing about this evening that makes me a little unhappy. You won't be able to dance."

"Don't worry about that. Over the years, I've perfected the art of sparkling conversation . . ."

They were interrupted at last by Lucilla opening the door and putting her head around the edge of it.

"Sorry to barge in, but there's a crisis. Dad, Jeff can't tie Edmund's bow-tie. He's only worn a bow-tie once in his life, and that was a made-up one on an elastic. I tried to help, but it was a total failure. Can you come and assist?"

"Of course."

Duty called. He was needed. The quiet moments were over. He gave Pandora a kiss. "See you." And then got to his feet and followed Lucilla out of the room. Pandora, left alone, slowly finished her drink.

These precious days I'll spend with you.

The song was ended.

Violet, with Highland blood coursing through her veins, always stoutly averred that she was not superstitious. She walked under ladders, disregarded Friday the thirteenth, and never touched wood. If some sort of an omen presented itself, she usually told herself firmly that it was probably for the best, and looked for good news. She was grateful that she had not been blessed – or cursed – with second sight. It was better not to know what the future held.

Having dealt with Edie, and bullied that promise out of her, she expected her anxieties to be resolved, and her mind once more at rest. But this did not happen, and she returned to her fireside chair in a state of grave apprehension. What was amiss? Why did she feel all at once haunted by nameless, lurking fears? Bundled in her old dressing-gown, she sat forward, staring into the flames, searching for the root-cause of her sudden chill, the unease that, like a weight, lay deep in her being.

Hearing that Lottie was on the loose, wandering about, up to heaven knew what, was bad enough; but, ridiculously, the fact that she could not get through to Balnaid and speak to Edmund disturbed her a good deal more. It wasn't just the frustration of non-communication. Often, during the winter blizzards, Violet was cut off at Pennyburn for a day or more, and isolation did not worry her in the very least. It was just that the breakdown had occurred at such a startlingly inappropriate time. As though some uncontrollable and malevolent force were at work.

She was not superstitious. But misfortunes invariably happened in threes. First Lottie, then the faulty telephone. What next?

She let her imagination move forward to the evening ahead, and knew that there lay a veritable minefield of potential disaster. For the first time, the players in the drama that had been boiling up over the last week would all come together, gathered around the dining-room table at Croy. Edmund, Virginia, Pandora, Conrad, Alexa and Noel. All, in their various ways, confused and restless, searching for some elusive happiness, as though it could be found, like a pot of gold, at the end of a fairy-tale rainbow. But in their efforts all they seemed to have unearthed was a useless cache of destructive emotion. Resentment, distrust, selfishness, greed, and disloyalty. Adultery, too. Only Alexa, it seemed, stayed unsullied. For Alexa, there was only the pain of love.

A log, burning through, collapsed with a whisper into the bed of ashes. An interruption. Violet looked up at her clock, and was horrified to see that she had sat, brooding, for too long, for it was already a quarter-past eight. She would be late arriving at Croy. Under usual circumstances, this would have bothered her, for she

505

was a stickler for punctuality, but this evening, with so much else on her mind, it scarcely seemed to matter. For fifteen minutes or so, she would not be missed, and Isobel would not lead them into the dining room until at least nine o'clock.

She realised, too, that the last thing she wanted to do was go out. Smile, chat, conceal her apprehensions. She did not want to leave the safe haven of her house, her fireside. Something, somewhere, was lying in wait, and her frail human instinct was to bolt herself indoors, in safety, sit by the telephone, and keep watch.

But she was *not* superstitious.

She pulled herself together, got out of her chair, put the guard on the dying fire, and went upstairs. Swiftly, she bathed, and then dressed herself for the party. Silk underclothes and black silk stockings, the venerable black velvet gown, the satin court shoes. She dressed her hair, and then took up her diamond tiara and settled it on her head, fixing, with a bit of difficulty, the loop of elastic at the back. She powdered her nose, found a lacy handkerchief, sprayed a little eau-de-cologne about her person. Moving to her long mirror, she gauged, with critical eyes, the general effect. Saw a large and stout dowager for whom the word "dignified" seemed the kindest description.

Large and stout. And old. All at once, she felt very tired. Tiredness did funny things to one's imagination, for, staring into the mirror, she saw beyond her own reflection the cloudy image of another woman. Never beautiful, but unlined, and brown-haired, and filled with a raging energy for life. Herself, wearing the crimson satin ball-gown that had been her most favourite. And beside that other woman, stood Geordie. For an instant the mirage stayed, so real that she could have touched it. And then it faded and was gone, and she was left alone. For years, she had not felt so alone. But there was no time to stand and feel sorry for herself. Others were waiting for her, as always, demanding her company, her attention. She turned from the mirror, reached for her fur coat and pulled it on, picking up her evening bag and switching off the lights. Downstairs, she went out through the kitchen door, locking it behind her. The night was dark, and damp with a drizzling mist. She crossed over to the garage and got into her car. Lifts had been offered by all and sundry, but she had chosen to drive herself to Croy, and after dinner, she would drive herself to Corriehill. That way she would be totally independent of any person and able to return home whenever she chose.

You should always leave a party just when you are most enjoying yourself.

That had been one of Geordie's maxims. Thinking of Geordie, hearing his dear voice in her head, filled her with a certain comfort. On such occasions, she never felt that he was very far away. How amused he would be by her now, seventy-eight years old, dolled up in velvet and diamonds and fur, and driving herself in her mud-stained motor car to . . . of all things . . . a ball.

Headed up the hill, watching the road ahead contained by the beam of her headlights, she made Geordie a promise.

I know this is a ludicrous situation, my darling, but it is the last time. After this evening, if any person is kind enough to ask me to a dance, I shall tell them no. And my excuse will be that I am really far too old.

Henry walked. Darkness had fallen and a thin rain drifted into his face. The river, the Croy, kept him company, flowing alongside the winding road. He could not see it, but was aware all the time of the presence of moving water, the rippling sound as the shallows tumbled downhill in a series of little pools and waterfalls. It was comforting to know that the Croy was there. The

507

only other noises to reach his ears were familiar, but strangely magnified by his own solitude. The wind, stirring the branches of trees, and the curlew's lonely call. His footsteps sounded enormous. Sometimes he imagined other footsteps, following some way behind him, but it was probably just an echo of his own tread. Any alternative was too scary to contemplate.

He had been passed by only three cars, driving from Caple Bridge and heading, as he was headed, up the glen. On each occasion, aware of the approaching headlights, he had bundled himself down into the ditch, hiding until the car was gone, zipping past with a hiss of tyres on the wet road. He did not wish to be observed, and as well, he did not wish to be offered a lift. Accepting lifts from strangers was not only dreadfully dangerous, but totally forbidden, and at this stage of his long journey, Henry was not about to risk being driven somewhere he did not want to go, and murdered.

However, when he was less than a mile from Strathcroy, and could actually see the lights of the village pricking like welcome stars through the gloom, he did get a lift. A massive double-deckered sheep-float came grinding up the road behind him, and Henry somehow hadn't the energy to jump for the ditch before being caught in its headlights. Even as it passed Henry, the sheep-float was already slowing down. It drew to a throbbing halt, and the driver opened the door of his high cab and waited for Henry to catch up with him. He squinted down into the murky dusk and saw Henry's Balaclava-ed face staring up at him.

"Hello, sonny." He was a great burly man in a tweed bonnet. A familiar sort of person. Not a stranger. By now, Henry's legs were beginning to feel wobbly, like cooked spaghetti, and he was not certain whether he was going to be able to make that last bit of the road to Strathcroy.

"Hello."

"Where are you off to?"

"Strathcroy."

"Did you miss the bus?"

This seemed a good excuse. "Yes," fibbed Henry.

"Want a ride?"

"Yes, please."

"Up you come, then."

The man reached down a horny hand. Henry put his own hand into it and was heaved upwards, as though he weighed no more than a fly, on to the big man's knee, and then over and on to the other seat. The cab was warm and snug and very dirty. It smelled fuggy, of old cigarettes and sheep, and there were sweet-papers and match-ends littered around the floor, but Henry didn't mind this, because it was good to be there, with another person for company, and to know that he didn't have to walk any further.

The driver slammed his door shut, shoved his engine into gear, and they moved forward.

"Where have you walked from?"

"Caple Bridge."

"That's a long walk on a wet night."

"Yes."

"Do you live in Strathcroy?"

"I'm going to see someone there." Before he could be asked any more questions, Henry decided to ask one himself. "Where have you been?"

"To the market in Relkirk."

"Did you have a lot of sheep?"

"Aye."

"Were they your own?"

"No, I've no sheep. I'm just the driver."

"Where do you live?"

"Inverness."

"Are you going there tonight?"

"Oh, aye."

"It's a long way."

"Maybe so, but I like to sleep in my own bed."

The windscreen wipers swung to and fro. Through

the clear fan of glass, Henry watched as the lights of Strathcroy came closer. Then they passed the thirty-miles-an-hour sign, and then the war memorial. Around the last curve of the road, and the long main street of the village stretched ahead into the darkness.

"Where do you want me to drop you off?"

"Just here will do very nicely, thank you."

Once more, the sheep-float ground to a juddering halt.

"You'll be all right, now?" The man reached over to open Henry's door.

"Yes, of course. Thank you very much indeed. You've been very kind."

"You mind yourself, now."

"I will." He clambered down the great height to the road. "Goodbye."

"Goodbye, sonny."

The door slammed shut. The massive vehicle went on its way, and Henry stood and watched it go, its red taillight winking, like a friendly eye. The sound of the engine faded into the darkness, and after it was gone, everything seemed very quiet.

He started off again, walking down the middle of the deserted street. He felt extremely tired, but that didn't matter, because he was almost there. He knew exactly where he was going and what he was going to do, because he had laid his secret plans with the greatest possible thought and care. He'd mulled over every eventuality, and left nothing to chance. He was not going to Balnaid, nor Pennyburn, but to Edie's. He was not going to Balnaid because there would be nobody there. His mother his father, Alexa and her friend were all at Croy, having dinner with the Balmerinos before going to Mrs Steynton's party. And he was not going to Pennyburn because Vi was at Croy too. And even if they had all been at home, he would still have made for Edie's cottage because Edie would be there.

Without Lottie. Horrible Lottie was back in hospital. The news had been relayed to Henry by Mr Henderson, and the relief of knowing that Edie was safely on her own again had filled Henry with courage and finally precipitated his illegal flight. It made all the difference, knowing that he had somewhere safe to go. Edie would take him in her arms, ask no questions, make him hot cocoa. Edie would listen to him. She would understand. She would be on his side. And with Edie on his side, surely everybody else would take notice of what she had to say and would not be angry with him.

The lights still burned in Mrs Ishak's supermarket, but he kept to the far side of the road, so that Mrs Ishak, by chance, would not see him as he passed by. The rest of the street was dark, lit only by the curtained windows of the wayside houses. From behind these windows Henry could hear muffled voices of music from people's television sets. Edie would be sitting in her armchair, watching television, busy with her knitting.

He came to her little cottage with its thatch, crouched down between its neighbours. The window of her sitting room was dark, which meant she wasn't watching television. But from her bedroom window, light streamed brightly out, and it seemed that she had forgotten to draw her curtains.

She had other curtains, lace ones, for privacy, but it was perfectly possible to see through these. Henry went close to the window and peered inside, cupping his hands to the sides of his face as he had seen grown-ups do. The lace curtains veiled the interior a bit, but he saw Edie at once. She was standing at her dressing-table, with her back to him. She was wearing her new lilac cardigan and looked as though she was putting powder on her face. Perhaps she was going out. Dressed in her best lilac cardigan . . .

He balled his fist and rapped on the glass to catch her attention. She turned from the mirror with a start and came towards him. The overhead light shone down on her face, and his heart leapt in a spasm of horror, because something dreadful had happened to her. She had got

511

a different face, with staring black eyes and a mouth red with lipstick, all smeared as though it were blood. And her hair was wrong, and her cheeks pale as paper . . .

It was Lottie.

Those staring eyes. A revulsion, stronger than fear, jerked him away from the window. He backed off across the street, out of the patch of yellow light that lay across the wet pavement. Every exhausted limb in his body was shaking, and his heart thumped against his chest as though it were trying to fight its way out. Petrified with terror, he thought he would probably never be able to move again. The terror was for himself, but mostly it was for Edie.

Lottie had done something to her. His very worst nightmare was true, was happening. Somehow, Lottie had come creeping secretly back to Strathcroy and burst in on Edie when Edie wasn't looking. Somewhere in the cottage Edie lay. On the kitchen floor perhaps, with a meat chopper in the back of her neck and blood all over the place.

He opened his mouth to scream for help, but the only sound that emerged was a trembling, faint whisper.

And now Lottie was there, at the window, raising the lace curtain to peer out into the street, her horrible face pressed against the glass. In a moment, she would go to the door, she would be after him.

He forced his legs to move; backed away up the road, and then turned and ran. It was like running in a dreadful, treacly dream, but this time he knew that he would never wake up. His ears were filled with the thud of his own footsteps and the rasping of his breath. It was difficult to breathe. He tore off the Balaclava helmet and the cold air streamed down on his head and cheeks. His brain cleared, and ahead, he saw his refuge. The bright windows of Mrs Ishak's shop, stacked with the usual colourful display of soap powders and cereal packets and cut-price bargains.

He ran to Mrs Ishak.

Mrs Ishak's long day was winding itself down. Her husband, having emptied the till of a day's takings, had disappeared into the stockroom, where each evening he totted up all the cash, and then locked it away in his safe. Mrs Ishak had been around the shelves, replacing tins and goods, and filling up the gaps left by the day's customers. She was now busy with her broom, sweeping the floor.

When the door burst open so suddenly and with such force, she was a little startled. She looked up from her sweeping, her brows raised over her kohl-rimmed eyes, and was even more startled when she saw who it was.

"Henree."

He looked terrible, wearing a mud-stained tweed coat sizes too big for him, and with his socks falling down and his shoes covered with dirt. But Mrs Ishak was less concerned by his clothes than the state of Henry himself. Gasping for breath, ashen-white, he stood there for a second, before slamming the door shut and setting his back against it.

"Henree." Mrs Ishak laid down her broom. "What has happened?" But he had no breath for words. "Why are you not at school?"

His mouth worked. "Edie's dead." She could scarcely hear him. And then again, only this time he shouted it at her, "Edie's *dead*."

"But . . ."

Henry burst into tears. Mrs Ishak held out her arms and Henry fled into them. She knelt to his height, holding him close to her silken breast, her hand cupped around the back of his head. "No," she murmured. "No. It is not true." And when he went on crying, hysterically asserting that it *was*, she tried to soothe him, speaking to him in *katchi*, that intimate and unwritable dialect

513

that all the Ishak family used when they spoke among themselves. Henry had heard the soft sounds before, when Mrs Ishak comforted Kedejah, or sat her on her knee to pet her. He could not understand a word but he was comforted too, and Mrs Ishak smelled musky and delicious, and her lovely rose-pink tunic was cool against his face.

And yet he had to make her understand. He pulled away from her embrace and stared into her confused and troubled face.

"Edie is dead."

"No, Henry."

"Yes, she *is*." He gave her a little thump on her shoulder, maddened that she was being so stupid.

"Why do you say this?"

"Lottie's in her house. She's killed her. She's stealing her cardigan."

Mrs Ishak stopped looking confused. Her face sharpened. She frowned.

"Did you see Lottie?"

"Yes. She's in Edie's bedroom, and . . ."

Mrs Ishak got to her feet. "Shamsh!" she called to her husband, and her voice was strong and urgent.

"What is it?"

"Come quickly." He appeared. Mrs Ishak, in a long stream of *katchi*, gave him instructions. He asked questions; she answered them. He went back to his stockroom, and Henry heard the sound as he dialled a number on his telephone.

Mrs Ishak fetched a chair and made Henry sit on it. She knelt beside him and held his hands.

She said, "Henree, I do not know what you are doing here but you must listen to me. Mr Ishak is telephoning the police now. They will come in a patrol car and fetch Lottie and take her back to hospital. They have been warned that she left the hospital without permission, and have been told to watch out for her. Now, do you understand that?"

514

"Yes, but Edie . . ."

With her gentle fingers, Mrs Ishak wiped away the tears that dribbled down Henry's cheeks. With the end of her rose-pink chiffon scarf, which she wore draped around her shining black hair, she dabbed at his snivelling nose.

She told him, "Edie is at Balnaid. She is staying there for the night. She is safe."

Henry stared in silence at Mrs Ishak, terrified that she was not telling him the truth.

"How do you know?" he asked her at last.

"Because on her way there, she dropped in to see me, to buy an evening newspaper. She told me that your granny, Mrs Aird, had told her about Lottie, and also that Mrs Aird did not want her to stay alone in her own cottage."

"Vi was frightened of Lottie, too?"

"Not frightened. Mrs Aird would not be frightened, I think. But concerned for your dear Edie. So you see, it is all right. You are safe."

From the back of the shop, they could hear Mr Ishak speaking on the telephone. Henry turned his head to listen, but could not catch the words. Then Mr Ishak stopped speaking and rang off. Henry waited. Mr Ishak came through the door.

"All right?" asked Mrs Ishak.

"Yes. I have spoken to the police. They will send a patrol car. It should be in the village in about five minutes."

"Do they know where to go?"

"Yes. They know." He looked at Henry, and smiled reassuringly. "Poor boy. You have had a bad fright. But it is over now."

They were being very kind. Mrs Ishak still knelt, holding Henry's hands, and he had stopped shaking. After a bit, he asked, "Can I ring Edie up?"

"No. It is not possible to do that because your telephone at Balnaid is out of order. Edie reported it to

Faults before she left her home, but they said that they could not attend to the matter before tomorrow morning. But we will wait a little, and I will make you a hot drink, and then I will walk with you to Balnaid and you will be with your Edie."

It was only then that Henry was truly convinced that Edie was not dead. She was at Balnaid, waiting for him, and the knowledge that soon he would be with her was almost more than he could bear. He felt his mouth trembling like a baby's, and the tears filling his eyes, but he was too tired to do anything about them. Mrs Ishak said his name and once more gathered him into her silk and scented embrace and he wept for a long time.

Finally, it was all over, except for a few troublesome sobs. Mr Ishak brought him a mug of hot chocolate, very sweet and brown and bubbly, and Mrs Ishak made him a sandwich with jam in the middle.

"Tell me," said Mrs Ishak, when Henry was feeling much stronger and more composed, "because you still have not answered my first question. Why are you here and not at school?"

Henry, with his fingers locked around the hot mug, gazed into her dark and liquid eyes.

"I didn't like it," he told her. "I ran away. I've come home."

The clock on the mantelpiece stood at twenty to nine as Edmund walked into the drawing room at Croy. He had expected to find it filled with people, but instead discovered Archie and an unknown man, whom, by the simple process of elimination, he assumed to be the Sad American, Conrad Tucker, and the root-cause of Edmund's immediate disagreement with Virginia.

Both men were resplendent in their evening gear, Archie looking better than Edmund had seen him look

516

in years. They sat by the fire, companionably, glasses in their hands. Conrad Tucker occupied an armchair, and Archie perched, with his back to the fire, on the club fender. As the door opened, they stopped talking, looked up, saw Edmund, and got to their feet.

"Edmund."

"We're late, I'm sorry. We've had dramas."

"As you can see, not late at all. Nobody else, yet, has appeared. Where's Virginia?"

"Gone upstairs to shed her coat. And Alexa and Noel will be here in a moment. At the last minute Alexa decided to wash her hair, and she was still drying it when we left. God knows why she didn't think of doing it before."

"They never do," said Archie bleakly, speaking from years of experience. "Edmund, you've not met Conrad Tucker."

"No, I don't think I have. How do you do."

They shook hands. The American was as tall as Edmund, and heftily built. His eyes, behind the heavy horn-rims, met Edmund's in a steady gaze, and Edmund found himself torn by an uncharacteristic uncertainty.

For, deep within him, concealed by a civilised veneer of good manners, burned a smouldering rage and resentment against this man, this American, who appeared to have taken over while Edmund's back was turned, rekindled Virginia's remembered youth, and was now calmly planning to fly back to the States with her – Edmund's wife – in tow. Smiling politely into Conrad Tucker's open face, Edmund toyed with the lovely idea of balling his fist and smashing it into that craggy and suntanned nose. Imagining the consequent mayhem, the blood and the bruising, filled him with shameful relish.

And yet on the other hand he knew that, under different circumstances, this was the sort of person that it would be perfectly possible to like instantly.

Conrad Tucker's friendly expression mirrored Edmund's own. "How very nice to meet you." Damn his eyes.

Archie was headed for the tray of bottles.

"Edmund. A small whisky?"

"Thank you. I could do with one."

His host reached for the Famous Grouse. "When did you get back from New York?"

"About five-thirty."

Conrad asked, "Did you have a good trip?"

"More or less. A bit of troubleshooting, a few well-chosen words. I believe you're an old friend of my wife's?"

If he had hoped to throw the other man off-balance, he did not succeed. Conrad Tucker gave nothing away, showed no discomfiture.

"That's right. We were dancing partners in our long-ago and misspent youth."

"She tells me you're travelling back to the States together."

Still no reaction. If the American guessed that he was being needled, he betrayed no sign. "She got a seat on that plane?" was all that he said.

"Apparently so."

"I hadn't heard. But that'll be great. It's a long trip on your own. I'll be going to the city straight from Kennedy, but I can see her through immigration and baggage claim, and then be certain that she has transportation to Leesport."

"That's more than kind of you."

Archie handed Edmund his drink. "Conrad, I didn't know you'd planned all this. I didn't even know Virginia was thinking of going to the States . . ."

"She's going to visit her grandparents."

"And when are *you* off?"

"I'm staying here until Sunday, if that's all right by you, and then flying out of Heathrow on Thursday. I need a day or two in London to see to some business."

518

"How long have you been in this country?" Edmund asked him.

"A couple of months."

"I hope you've enjoyed your visit."

"Thank you. I've had a fine time."

"I'm glad." Edmund raised his glass. "Cheers."

At this point they were interrupted by the appearance of Jeff Howland who, having finally solved the problem of the bow-tie, had completed his dressing and come downstairs. He obviously felt ill at ease and self-conscious in his unaccustomed gear, and his face wore a faintly abashed expression as he walked into the room, but indeed he looked more than presentable in the outfit that he and Lucilla had gleaned from Edmund's wardrobe. Edmund was amused to see that Jeff had picked out a cream hopsack jacket, purchased in a moment of crisis in Hong Kong. It had proved to be a mistaken buy, for Edmund had worn it only once.

"Jeff."

The young man craned his neck and ran a finger around the restricting collar of the starched evening shirt. He said, "I'm not used to this sort of thing. I feel a real berk."

"You look splendid. Come and have a drink. We're on to the whisky before the women turn up and demand champagne."

Jeff relaxed a little. He was always happier in purely masculine company. "There wouldn't be a can of Foster's?"

"There most certainly would. On the tray. Help yourself."

Jeff relaxed a bit more, reached for the can, poured the long glass. He said to Edmund, "It was good of you to kit me out. I'm grateful."

"A pleasure. The jacket is perfect. Dressy, but with just the right touch of outback informality."

"That's what Lucilla said."

"She was quite right. And you look a great deal better

519

in it than I did. Wearing it, I resembled an elderly barman
. . . the useless variety that doesn't even know how to
fix a dry martini.''

Jeff smiled, took a heartening swallow, and then
looked about him. "Where are all the girls?''

"Good question," said Archie. "God knows." He had
settled himself once more on the fender, seeing no
reason to stand about for a moment longer than he had
to. "Buttoning themselves into their evening gowns, I
suppose. Lucilla was searching for underclothes, Pandora decided to go to bed, and Isobel's in a state of panic
about her evening shoes." He turned to Edmund. "But
you said that you had dramas. What's been happening
at Balnaid?''

Edmund told him.

"Our phone's on the blink, which is one thing. We
can make calls, but nobody can get through to us. However, it's been reported, and some guy's coming to see
to it in the morning. But that's the least of our worries.
Edie turned up out of the blue, with her nightie in a bag,
and the news that Lottie Carstairs is on the loose again.
She walked out of the Relkirk Royal and hasn't been
seen since.''

Archie shook his head in exasperation. "That bloody
woman is more trouble than a bitch on heat. When did
this happen?''

"I don't know. Some time this afternoon, I suppose.
The doctor rang Vi to let her know. Then Vi tried to ring
Balnaid but couldn't get through. So she called Edie,
and proceeded to order her out of her cottage for the
night, and come to us. Which is what Edie has done.''

"Vi surely doesn't think that lunatic is dangerous?''

"I don't know. Personally, I think she's capable of
almost anything, and if Vi hadn't told Edie to come to
Balnaid, then I should have done so myself. Anyway,
Alexa will leave her bolted in with the dogs for company.
But as you can imagine, it's all taken a bit of time.''

"No matter." Archie, with domestic problems dealt

with, changed the subject to more absorbing and important matters. "We missed you yesterday, Edmund. We
had a great day. Thirty-three and a half brace, and the
birds flying like the wind . . ."

Violet was the last to arrive. She knew that she was the
last, because as she drew up on the gravel sweep in front
of Croy, she saw five other vehicles already parked there.
Archie's Land-Rover, Isobel's minibus, Edmund's BMW,
Pandora's Mercedes, and Noel's Volkswagen. A bit, she
decided, like the car-park at a point-to-point, and an
awful lot of traffic for just two families.

She got out of her car, bundled her long skirts up out
of the damp, and made for the front door. As she went
up the steps, this was opened, and she saw that Edmund
waited for her, standing in the bright light of the hall.
With his silver hair, and wearing kilt, doublet, and diced
hose, he looked even more distinguished than usual,
and despite all her dratted anxieties, Violet found time
to experience a dart of motherly pride, and the relief
of having him actually around again filled her with
gratitude.

"Oh, Edmund."

"I heard your car." He gave her a kiss.

"What a time I've had." She went indoors, he closed
the door behind her, and came to help her off with her
fur coat. "Your telephone. It's not working . . ."

"It's all right, Vi. All under control. It's being fixed
tomorrow morning . . ."

He laid the coat on a chair while Vi shook out her
ample velvet skirts and readjusted the lace frill at her
shoulders. "Thank heavens for that. And my darling
Edie? She's at Balnaid?"

"Yes. Safe and sound. You look trachled. Stop worrying now, or you're not going to enjoy yourself."

"It's impossible not to. That wretched Lottie. Just one thing after another. But you're home and safe, and that's all that matters. I am dreadfully late, aren't I?"

"This evening, everybody's late. Isobel's only just appeared. Now, come and have a glass of champagne, and then you'll feel much better."

"Is my tiara straight?"

"Perfect." He took her arm and led her into the drawing room.

"*I* think," said Pandora, "that Verena's missed out. We should all have been issued with darling little dance programmes, and tiny pencils hanging off them . . ."

"That just shows," Archie told her, "how long you've been away. Dance programmes are a thing of the past . . ."

"That's a *shame*. They were always half the fun. And then you kept them, all tied up in ribbon, and brooded over your lost beaux."

"It was all right," Isobel pointed out, "if one was a social butterfly, with lots of admirers. Not so much fun if nobody wanted to dance with you."

"I'm certain," said Conrad, with a certain transatlantic gallantry, "that never happened to *you*."

"Oh, Conrad, how kind of you. But every now and then there did occur a disastrous evening when one had a spot on one's nose, or a horrid dress."

"So what did you do?"

"Hid in shame in the ladies' cloakroom. The Ladies' was always filled with sad wallflowers . . ."

"Like Daphne Brownfield," Pandora chipped in. "Archie, you have to remember Daphne Brownfield. She was the size of a house and her mother always dressed her in white net . . . she was madly in love with you and blushed like a lobster whenever you came within spitting distance . . .''

But Archie was more charitable. "She played a splendid game of tennis.''

"Oh, jolly hockey sticks," Pandora scoffed.

The room rang with voices, and now, laughter. Violet, sitting at Archie's right hand, and with a glass of champagne inside her, was already feeling a little less edgy. She listened to Pandora's teasing, but with only half an ear, because it was far more fascinating to watch than to listen. The dining room at Croy this evening presented a splendid spectacle. The long table was dressed overall, like a battleship, for ceremony, laden with gleaming silver, starched linen, green-and-gold china, sparkling crystal. Silver pheasants stood as a centrepiece, and all was illuminated by the flames of fire and candles.

"It wasn't just the girls who suffered," Noel pointed out. "For a young man, dance programmes could be dreadfully limiting. No chance to play the field, and by the time you'd spied some dishy chick, it was too late to do very much about her . . .''

"How did you become so experienced?" Edmund asked him.

"Doing my circuit as a Debs' Delight, but those days, thank God, are over . . .''

They ate smoked trout, with wedges of lemon and thin brown bread and butter. Lucilla moved around the table pouring white wine. Lucilla appeared, to Violet, to have raided the dressing-up box. Her flea-market dress was gunmetal-grey voile, sleeveless and hanging straight from her bony shoulders, with a skirt that drooped below her knees in a series of handkerchief points. It was so dreadful that she should have looked hideous, but for some reason she looked perfectly sweet.

And the others? Violet sat back in her chair and observed them covertly over her spectacles. Close family, old friends, new friends, come together for this long-anticipated celebration. She disregarded the undercurrents of tension that she could feel charging the atmosphere like electric wires, and kept her gaze objective. Saw the five men; two of them come from the other sides of the world. Different ages, different cultures, but all groomed and barbered and dressed up to the nines. She saw the five women, each, in her own way, beautiful.

Colour assaulted her eye. Ball-gowns of dark silk or flower-garden chintz. Virginia cool and sophisticated in black and white, Pandora ethereal as a dryad in sea-green chiffon. She saw jewels. Isobel's inherited pearls and diamonds, the silver-and-turquoise chain that encircled Pandora's slender neck, the gleam of gold that shone from Virginia's ears and at her wrist. She saw Alexa's face, laughing across the table at some remark of Noel's. Alexa wore no jewels but her pale-red hair shone like a flame, and her peachy face was alight with love . . .

All at once, it wasn't any good. Violet was too involved with all of them to remain objective, to continue to observe them with a stranger's dispassionate eye. Her heart agonised for Alexa, so vulnerable and transparent. And Virginia? Across the table she faced her daughter-in-law, and knew that although Edmund was home again, nothing had been resolved between the two of them. For Virginia, this evening, was at her most animated. There was a brilliant and brittle sheen about her, and a dangerous brightness in her blue eyes.

I mustn't imagine the worst, Violet told herself. I must simply hope for the best. She reached for her glass and drank a little wine.

The first course was over. Jeff rose to his feet to act as butler and clear the plates. As he did this, Archie turned to Virginia.

"Virginia, Edmund tells me that you're going back to the States to see your grandparents?"

"That's right!" Her smile was too swift, her eyes too wide. "Such fun. I can't wait to see the darling old things."

524

So, despite Violet's warnings, she had done it. It was definite, official. Knowing that the worst of her fears was confirmed, Violet felt her heart sink.

"So you are going?" She did not try to keep the disapproval from her voice.

"Yes, Vi. I am. I told you I was. And now it's all fixed. I leave on Thursday. Conrad and I are travelling together."

For an instant Vi said nothing. Across the table their eyes met. Virginia's gaze was defiant and did not waver.

"How long will you be away?" Violet asked her.

Virginia shrugged her bare brown shoulders. "Not certain yet. I've got an open-ended ticket." She turned back to Archie. "I always wanted to take Henry, but now that he is no longer with us, I decided that I might as well go on my own. Such a funny feeling, being able to do things on the spur of the moment. No responsibilities. No ties."

"And Edmund?" Archie asked.

"Oh, Vi will take care of Edmund for me," Virginia told him airily. "Won't you, Vi?"

"Of course." She repressed an impulse to take her daughter-in-law by the shoulders and shake her until her teeth rattled. "It will be no trouble at all."

And with that Violet turned away from them both, and talked instead to Noel.

". . . my grandfather had a young underkeeper by the name of Donald Buist. Twenty years old and a fine, lusty lad . . ."

They were now on to the second course, Isobel's Pheasant Theodora. Jeff had handed round the vegetable dishes, and Conrad Tucker refilled the wineglasses. Archie, primed and prompted by Pandora, was engaged in telling a classic family anecdote, which, like the saga of Mrs Harris and the shooting stocking, had become, over the years, an oft-repeated family joke. Blairs and Airds had heard it many times before, but for the sake of the newcomers Archie had been persuaded to recount it again.

"... he was an excellent underkeeper, but he had one failing, and the net result of this was that every girl within twenty miles became, unfortuitously, pregnant. The shepherd's daughter at Ardnamore, the butcher's daughter in Strathcroy; even my grandmother's parlour-maid fainted clean away one lunch-time while serving the chocolate soufflé."

He paused. From beyond the closed door that led to the pantry and into the kitchen could be clearly heard the ringing of the telephone. It rang twice, and then ceased. Agnes Cooper was dealing with the interruption. Archie continued with his story.

"Finally, my grandmother put her foot down and insisted that my grandfather take Donald Buist to task. So he was sent for and duly marched into my grandfather's office for the distasteful interview. My grandfather named half a dozen of the ladies who were bearing, or had borne, the young man's little bastards, and finally demanded to know what Donald had to say for himself, and what possible excuse he could give for his behaviour. There was a long silence while Donald thought about this, and finally he came up with his defence. 'Well, you see, sir, I've got a bicycle!' "

As the laughter died, there sounded a cursory thump on the pantry door. It was at once opened, and Agnes Cooper put her head around the edge of it.

"Sorry to disturb you, but that's Edie Findhorn on the telephone; wants to speak to Mrs Geordie Aird."

Misfortunes always came in threes.

Violet instantly felt very cold, as though the opened door had admitted not only Agnes, but a freezing, icy draught as well. She rose to her feet so abruptly that she would have knocked over her chair had not Noel put out a hand to steady it.

Nobody spoke. They were all looking at her, their faces mirroring her own concern. She said, "If you will excuse me . . ." and was ashamed of the shake in her voice ". . . I won't be a moment."

She turned and left the table. Agnes held the door open for her, and she went through it, through to Isobel's big kitchen. Agnes followed her, but that didn't matter . . . privacy was, at the moment, the last thing to worry about. The telephone stood on the dresser. She picked up the receiver.

"Edie."

"Oh, Mrs Aird . . ."

"Edie, what is it?"

"I'm sorry to get you out of your dinner party . . ."

"Is Lottie there?"

"It's all right about Lottie, Mrs Aird. You were right. She did make her way to Strathcroy. Caught a bus. She went to my cottage. She got in through the back door . . ."

"You weren't there?"

"No, I was no' there. I was here at Balnaid."

"Thank God for that. Where is she now?"

"Mr Ishak telephoned the police and in five minutes they were there in a wee Panda car and picked her up."

"So where is she now?"

"Safely back in the hospital . . ."

Relief made Violet feel quite weak. Her knees shook. She glanced about for a chair, but there was none within reach. However, Agnes Cooper, seeing her need, came forward with one, and Violet was able to take the weight off her legs.

"And you're all right, Edie?"

"I'm fine, Mrs Aird." She stopped. Violet waited. There was something else. She frowned. "How did Mr Ishak know about Lottie? Did he see her?"

"No. Not exactly." Another long pause. "You see,

527

that's not all. You'll need to tell Edmund. He and Virginia must come back. Henry's here. He's run away from school, Mrs Aird. He's come home."

Edmund drove, too fast, in the rain and the darkness, away from Croy and down the hill to the village. Virginia, her chin buried in the fur collar of her coat, sat beside him, staring ahead at the swinging windscreen wiper. She did not speak. Not because there was nothing to say, but because so distanced had they become from each other, so shocking was the situation in which they found themselves, that there was no way of saying it.

The short journey took only moments. They sped through the gates of Croy and out into the village street. Another hundred yards or so, and then over the bridge. The trees; the open gates; Balnaid.

Virginia spoke at last. She said, "You mustn't be angry with him."

"Angry?" He could scarcely believe that she could be so unperceptive.

She said no more. He turned the BMW into the backyard, slammed on the brakes, switched off the engine. He was out of the car before she was, leading the way to the house, flinging open the door.

They were in the kitchen, Edie and Henry, sitting at the table. Waiting. Henry faced the door. His face was very white, and his eyes round with apprehension. He wore his grey school sweater and looked pathetically small and defenceless.

How the hell had he managed that long and solitary journey? The thought flashed through Edmund's mind, and was gone.

He said, "Hello, Henry."

Henry hesitated for only an instant, and then slipped off the chair and bolted for his father. Edmund scooped him up into his arms, and the boy, it seemed, weighed nothing, no more than a baby. Henry's arms were locked about his neck, and he could feel Henry's tears wet on his own cheek.

"Henry." Virginia was there, beside him. After a bit, gently, Edmund set Henry down on his feet. Henry's stranglehold loosened. He turned to his mother, and Virginia, in one graceful fluid movement, dropped to her knees, with no regard for her evening gown, and gathered him into her soft and furry embrace. He buried his face in her collar.

"Darling. Darling. It's all right. Don't cry. Don't cry . . ."

Edmund turned to Edie. She had risen to her feet, and down the length of the scrubbed kitchen table she and Edmund faced each other in silence. She had known him all his life, and he was grateful to her because there was no reproach in her eyes.

Instead she said, "I'm sorry."

"What for, Edie?"

"Spoiling your party."

"Don't be ridiculous. As if it could possibly matter. When did he get here?"

"About fifteen minutes ago. Mrs Ishak brought him."

"Has anybody phoned from the school?"

"The phone's broken. Nobody can call."

He had forgotten. "Of course." So there were things to be seen to, practical matters of the utmost urgency. "In that case, I must go and do some telephoning."

He left them, Henry still weeping. Made his way through the quiet house to the library, switched on the lights, sat at his desk, dialled the number for Templehall.

The ringing sounded only once before the receiver was snatched up.

"Templehall."

"Headmaster?"

"Speaking."

"Colin, it's Edmund Aird."

"Oh . . ." The sound came down the line on a sigh of audible relief. Edmund found time to wonder how long the poor man had been trying to make some sort of contact. "I've been going insane trying to get in touch with you."

"Henry's here. He's safe."

"Thank God for that. When did he turn up?"

"About a quarter of an hour ago. I haven't heard the details. We're only just back ourselves. We were out for dinner. The message came through there."

"He disappeared just after bed-time. Seven o'clock. I've been trying to get hold of you ever since."

"Our phone's on the blink. No incoming calls."

"I finally found that out. When I did, I rang your mother, but there was no reply from her number either."

"She was at the same dinner party."

"Is Henry all right?"

"He seems to be."

"How the devil did he get home?"

"I've no idea. Like I told you, I've only just this minute got here myself. I've hardly spoken to him. I wanted to talk to you first."

"I'm grateful."

"I'm sorry you've been put to so much trouble."

"It's I who should apologise. Henry's your son, and I was responsible for him."

"You" – Edmund leaned back in his chair – "you don't know if anything in particular precipitated his flight?"

"No, I don't. Nor do any of my senior boys. Nor do any of my staff. He didn't seem either happy or un-happy. And it always takes a week or two for a new boy to settle down and get used to his new life; accept the change, and the unfamiliar environment. I kept an eye on him, of course, but he showed no signs of taking such dramatic action."

He sounded as upset and as puzzled as Edmund himself. Edmund said, "Yes. Yes, I see."

The headmaster hesitated, and then he asked, "Will you send him back to us?"

"Why do you say that?"

"I just wondered if you wanted him to return."

"Is there any reason why he shouldn't?"

"From my point of view, absolutely no reason at all. He's a very nice boy, and I know I could make something of him. I, personally, would like to welcome him back at any time, but . . ." He paused, and Edmund got the impression that he was choosing his words with the utmost tact. ". . . but, you know, Edmund, every now and then a boy comes to Templehall who really shouldn't be away from home in the first place. I haven't had Henry long enough to be perfectly certain, but I think he is one of those children. It isn't just that he's young for his age; it's that he is not ready for the demands of boarding school life."

"Yes. Yes, I see."

"Why don't you take a day or two to think it over? Keep Henry there till you've made up your mind. Remember, I really want him back. I'm not trying to shed my responsibility, nor renege on my commitments, but I would seriously suggest that you reconsider the situation."

"And do what?"

"Return him to his local primary. It's obviously a good school, and he's been well-grounded. By the time he's twelve you can think again."

"You're saying exactly what my wife has been telling me for the past year."

"I am sorry. But with hindsight, I think she is right. And I think that you and I are to blame and that we have both been mistaken . . ."

They talked a little more, agreed to be in touch in a couple of days, and finally rang off.

He is one of those children. He is not ready for the demands of boarding-school life. We have both been mistaken.

Mistaken. That was the word that hammered home,

531

like a nail driven into a block of wood. Your wife is right, and you are mistaken. It took a bit of time to accept the word, to accept the implications. He sat at his desk, slowly coming to terms with the fact that he had been almost disastrously wrong. It was not an exercise that he was accustomed to, and it took a little time.

But after a bit, he got to his feet. The fire had, he saw, died. He crossed the room and fed it with logs, as he had already done earlier in the evening. When the dry wood had caught and the comforting flames were once more leaping, he left the library and returned to the kitchen.

Here, he found things more or less back to normal. Once more, they were all sitting around the table, Henry on his mother's knee. Edie had made a pot of tea, and cocoa for Henry. Virginia still wore her fur coat. As he came in, they all looked towards him, and he saw that Henry's tears had dried and a little colour had come back into his cheeks.

Edmund put a cheerful expression on his face.

"That's done then . . ." He tousled his son's hair and pulled out a chair. "Is there a cup of tea for me?"

"What have you been doing?" Henry asked.

"Speaking to Mr Henderson."

"Was he very cross?"

"No, not cross. Just a bit worried."

Henry said, "I'm very sorry."

"Are you going to tell us about it?"

"Yes. I suppose so."

"How did you get home?"

Henry took another mouthful of the steaming, sweet cocoa, and then laid his mug on the table. He said, "I caught a bus."

"But how did you get out of school?"

Henry explained. He made it all sound ridiculously simple. At bed-time, he'd dressed under the bedclothes, and then put his dressing-gown on. And then when the lights went out, he'd pretended he wanted to go to the lavatory. In the bathroom there was a large airing cupboard, and at the back of this he had hidden his overcoat. He'd swapped his dressing-gown for his overcoat and then climbed out of the window on to the fire escape. After that, he'd made his way down the back drive, and so on to the main road where the buses ran.

"But how long did you have to wait for a bus?" Virginia asked him.

"Only a little bit. I knew there was one coming."

"How did you know?"

"I had a bus timetable." He looked at Edie. "I took it out of your bag one day. I kept it."

"I *wondered* what had happened to my wee timetable."

"I took it. I looked up the bus for Relkirk, and I knew it would come. And it did."

"But didn't anybody ask you what you were doing all on your own?"

"No. I had on my Balaclava helmet and it was my disguise and only my eyes showed. I didn't look like a schoolboy because I didn't wear my school cap."

"How did you pay the fare?" Edmund asked.

"Vi had given me two pounds when she said goodbye to me. I didn't hand it in. I kept it in the inside pocket of my overcoat. I put the timetable there too, so that nobody would find it."

"And then you got to Relkirk?"

"Yes. I got to the bus station. And it was getting dark, and I had to find the other bus, the one that goes past Caple Bridge. There was a Strathcroy bus too, but I didn't want to catch that one in case somebody saw me, somebody who knew me. And it was quite difficult to find that bus because there were lots of buses and I had to read the names on all the fronts of them. But I did find it, but we had to wait for quite a long time before it started."

"Where did you get off that bus?"

"I told you. Caple Bridge. And then I walked."

"You walked from Caple Bridge?" Virginia looked at

her son in wonder. "But, Henry, that's five miles . . ."

"I didn't walk the whole of the way," he admitted. "I know I'm not allowed to get lifts, but I did get one at the very end from a very nice man in a sheep-float. And he took me to Strathcroy. And then . . ." His voice, which had sounded so clear and confident, began to shake again. "And then . . ." His eyes turned to Edie.

Edie took over. "Don't cry, pet. We won't talk about it if you don't want to . . ."

"I want *you* to tell them."

So Edie did, in her most practical and down-to-earth fashion, but even this did not assuage the horror of Henry's terrible experience. At mention of Lottie, the colour seeped from Virginia's cheeks, and she drew Henry close and pressed her face to the top of his head and laid her hands across his eyes, as though she could shut out for ever the sight of Lottie Carstairs coming across Edie's bedroom floor to find out who stood beyond the window.

"Oh, Henry." She rocked him like baby. "I can't bear it . . . What a thing to happen. What a thing to happen to you."

Edmund, equally shaken, kept his voice calm.

"So what did you do, Henry?"

His father's level tones restored, a little, Henry's courage. He emerged, ruffled, from Virginia's embrace. He said, "I went to Mrs Ishak. Her shop was still open and she was sweeping the floor. And she was very kind. And Mr Ishak telephoned the police, and they came with the siren going and a blue light flashing. We saw it from the shop. And then, when the police car had gone again, back to Relkirk, Mrs Ishak put on her coat, and she and me walked here. And she rang the bell because the door was locked, and then the dogs barked, and Edie came." He reached for his cocoa and drained the mug, and then set the empty mug down on the table. He said, "I thought she was *murdered*! Lottie had put on

534

her lilac cardigan and her mouth was all red, and I thought that she had killed Edie . . ."

His face crumpled. It was all too much for him. He wept again, and they let him cry, and Edmund did not tell him to be a man but simply sat there, regarding his small and sobbing son with a growing admiration and pride. For Henry, at eight years old, had not only run away from school, but accomplished his flight in a certain style. He'd planned the whole operation with undreamed-of courage, good sense, and forethought. He appeared to have been prepared for any contingency, and it was only the disastrous and unfortuitous appearance of the wretched Lottie Carstairs that had finally defeated him.

Eventually, the tears ceased. Henry had cried himself dry. Edmund gave him his clean linen handkerchief, and Henry sat up and blew his nose. He said, "I think I should like to go to bed now."

"Of course." Virginia smiled down at him. "Do you want a bath first? You must be feeling very cold and dirty."

"Yes, all right."

He got off her knee. Blew his nose again, went to his father to return the handkerchief. Edmund took it, and drew Henry close, and bent to kiss the top of his head.

He said, "There's just one thing you haven't told us." Henry looked up. "Why did you run away?"

Henry thought. And then he said, "I didn't like it. It felt all wrong. Like being ill. Headachy."

"Yes," said Edmund after a bit. "Yes, I see." He hesitated, and then went on. "Look, old boy, why don't you go up with Edie and get into the bath. Mummy and I have got to go to this party, but I'll ring Vi first and tell her you're in great shape, and we'll come up and say goodnight before you go to sleep."

"All right." Henry put his hand into Edie's and they made for the door. But he turned back. "You will come, won't you?"

"Promise."

The door closed behind him. Edmund and Virginia were left alone.

With Henry gone, she sat slumped in the hard kitchen chair. There was no longer need to conceal the trauma of shock and strain, and beneath her make-up he saw her face pale and drawn, and her eyes shadowed, no longer bright with the evening's laughter.

She looked drained. He stood up and took her hand and pulled her to her feet. "Come," he said, and he led her out of the kitchen and along the passage to the empty library. The fire that he had rekindled still blazed, and the big, shadowy room was warm. She was grateful for the warmth. She went towards it, sank down on the fireside stool, and spread her hands to the flames. Her long, many-layered skirts flowed about her, and the collar of her fur coat supported her head, her clear-cut profile.

"You look like a particularly well-heeled Cinderella." She glanced up and sent him the ghost of a smile. "Would you like a drink?"

She shook her head. "No. I'm all right."

He went to his desk, switched on the lamp, and dialled the number for Croy. It was Archie who answered the call.

"Archie. Edmund here."

"Is Henry all right?"

"Yes, he's fine. Had a bit of an experience, but don't say anything to Vi. Just tell her that Edie's with him, and he's on his way to bed."

"Are you coming back here?"

Edmund watched his wife, sitting with her back to him, silhouetted against the firelight. He said, "No, I think not. We'll go straight to Corriehill and meet you all there."

"Right. I'll tell everyone. See you later, Edmund."

"Goodbye."

He put down the phone, went back to the fire, and

536

stood, with one foot on the fender and a hand on the mantelpiece, gazing, as his wife gazed, at the flames. But the silence that lay between them was no longer one of enmity, but the peaceful communion of two people who, having together survived a crisis, felt no need for words.

It was Virginia who broke that silence. She said, "I'm sorry."

"What are you sorry about?"

"I'm sorry I said that. In the car. Telling you not to be angry. It was stupid. I should have known that you would never be angry with Henry."

"On the contrary, I feel proud of him. He did very well."

"He must have been so miserable."

"I think he just felt lost. I was wrong. You were right. Colin Henderson said as much. He's not ready, yet, for boarding school."

"You mustn't blame yourself."

"That's a generous thing to say."

"No, it's not generous. I'm grateful. Because now we can stop arguing and quarrelling and destroying each other. And you had only the best intentions in mind. You thought it would be best for Henry. Everybody makes mistakes, sooner or later. A man who never made a mistake never made anything. It's over now. Let's leave it behind. Just be thankful that nothing dreadful happened to Henry, and that he's safe."

"Lottie happened to him. I should think that experience would be enough to give him nightmares for the rest of his life . . ."

"But he dealt with it. Very sensibly. He got himself to Mrs Ishak. Took care of himself, gave the alarm. It's no good brooding about it, Edmund."

He said nothing to this. After a bit, he moved away from the fire and sank down at one end of the great sofa, his long legs, in their red-and-white tartan stockings and silver-buckled shoes, stretched out in front of him. The

537

firelight winked on polished buttons and the jewelled hilt of his sporran.

She said, "You must be exhausted."

"Yes. It's been a long day." He rubbed his eyes. "But I think we have to talk."

"We can talk tomorrow."

"No. It has to be now. Before it's too late. I should have told you this evening, when I got back and you started telling me about Lottie. Lottie and her talk, her gossip. I said she was lying but that wasn't strictly true."

"You are going to tell me about Pandora." Virginia's voice was cool, resigned.

"It has to be done."

"You were in love with her."

"Yes."

"I'm frightened of her."

"Why?"

"Because she is so beautiful. Mysterious. Under that flood of chat, you never know what she's thinking. I can't begin to imagine what goes on inside her head. And because she knew you always, when I didn't know you, and that makes me feel left out and insecure. Why did she come back to Croy, Edmund? Do you know why she came?"

He shook his head. "No."

"I'm afraid of her still being in love with you. She still wants you."

"No."

"How can you be so sure?"

"Pandora's motives, whatever they are, have no importance. To me, all that matters is you. And Alexa. And Henry. You seem to have lost sight of that basic priority."

"You were married when you loved Pandora. You were married to Caroline. You had a baby. Was that so different?"

It was an accusation, and he accepted it.

"Yes. And I was unfaithful to both of them. But Caroline wasn't like you. If I tried to explain to you why I

538

married her in the first place, I don't suppose you'd understand. It was something to do with the way things were at that time, the swinging sixties, and all of us young, and a certain restless materialism in the air. I was making my way, making money, making my mark on London society. She was part of my ambitions, part of what I wanted. Her parents were immensely wealthy and she was an only child, and I craved the security of being established, and the reflected dazzle of success.''

"But you *loved* her?''

Edmund shook his head. "I don't know. I didn't think about it all that much. I only know that she was wonderful to look at, immensely elegant, the sort of woman that would always turn heads, who excites a certain envy. I liked being seen around with her. I was very proud of her. The sexual, loving part of our relationship wasn't quite so smooth. I don't quite know when it all started to go wrong. I'm sure it was as much my fault as Caroline's, but she was a strange girl. She used sex as a weapon and frigidity as a punishment. Before the first year was over, I was sleeping as often as not in my dressing-room, and when she realised that she was pregnant with Alexa, there was no joy, only tears and recriminations. She didn't want a baby, because she was frightened of childbirth, and as things turned out, she had every reason to be afraid. Because after Alexa was born, she went into a post-natal depression that lasted for months. She was in hospital for a long time, and when she was fit to travel, her mother took her off to Madeira to spend the winter there. In the early summer of that year, Archie and Isobel were married. He was my oldest, closest friend. I'd seen little of him after I went to London, but I knew that I had to be at his wedding. I took a week's leave and came home. I was twenty-nine. I came back to Strathcroy on my own. I stayed here, at Balnaid, with Vi, but Croy was filled with house guests and alive with activity, and on my first day home I went up to see Archie and become involved in all the fun.

"And Pandora was there. I hadn't seen her for five years. She was eighteen, finished with schools, finished with childhood. I'd known her for ever. She was part of my life, always there. A baby in a pram, a little girl tagging along with Archie and me, never missing a trick. Spoiled as hell, wayward, wicked, but utterly enchanting and endearing. I saw her again, and knew that she hadn't changed. All that had happened was that she had grown up. I saw her coming towards me across the hall at Croy, and I saw her eyes and her smile, and her long legs, and an aura of sexuality about her, so potent, almost visible. And she put her arms around my neck and kissed my mouth and said, 'Edmund, you horrible man. Why didn't you wait for me?' And that was all she said. And I felt as though I was drowning, and the deep waters had already closed over the top of my head."

"You were lovers."

"I didn't seduce her. She was only eighteen, but somewhere along the line, she had already lost her virginity. It wasn't difficult to be together. There was so much going on, so many people in the house, that nobody missed us if we went off on our own."

"She was in love with you."

"So she said. She said she always had been, ever since she was a small girl. The fact that I was married only made her more obdurate. She'd never been denied anything that she wanted, and when I tried to talk reason to her, she put her hands over her ears and closed her eyes and refused to listen. She couldn't believe that I would leave her. She couldn't believe that I wouldn't come back.

"The wedding was on a Saturday. I had to drive back to London on the Sunday afternoon. On the Sunday morning, Pandora and I walked up the hill, on the road to the loch. But we stopped at the Corrie and lay on the grass, with the sound of the burn trickling at our feet. And I finally convinced her that I had to go, and she wept and protested and clung to me, and at last, to quieten her, I promised that I would come back, that I would write, that I did love her. All the stupid bloody things you say when you haven't the courage to end something. When you haven't the courage to be strong. When you can't bring yourself to destroy another person's dream.''

"Oh, Edmund.''

"I made such a fucking cock-up of it all. I was such a bloody coward. I went back to London, and as the miles lengthened behind me, I started to hate myself for what I'd done to Caroline and Alexa, and for what I was doing to Pandora. By the time I got back to London, I determined I would write to Pandora and try to explain that the whole episode had been a sort of fantasy; stolen days that had no more substance, no more future, than a soap bubble. But I didn't write. Because the next morning I went into the office, and by that evening I was in an aeroplane with my chairman, flying to Hong Kong. A huge financial deal was on the stocks, and I'd been picked to handle it. I was away for three weeks. By the time I returned to London, that time at Croy had dissolved into a sort of distant unlikelihood, like days stolen from another person's life. I could scarcely believe that it had happened to *me*. I was my own hard-headed businessman, not that indecisive romantic, swept off his feet by a fleeting sexual infatuation. And there was too much at stake. My job, I suppose. A way of life that I'd worked my guts out to achieve. Alexa. Losing Alexa did not bear thinking about. And Caroline. My wife, for better, for worse. Back from Madeira, suntanned, well, recovered. We'd gone through a bad time together, but we'd come out on the other side. We were together again, and it wasn't the right time to blow it all apart. We picked up the threads of life, the warp and woof of a convenient marriage.''

541

"And Pandora?"

"Nothing. Finished. I never wrote that letter."

"Oh, Edmund. That was cruel."

"Yes. A sin of omission. Do you know that dreadful feeling, when there is something immensely important that you should do, and you haven't done? And with each day that passes, it becomes more and more difficult to accomplish, until finally it passes the bounds of possibility and becomes impossible. It was over. Archie and Isobel went to Berlin, and immediate ties with Croy were severed. I heard nothing more. Until that day that Vi called from Balnaid to say that Pandora had gone. Run away, eloped to the other side of the world with a rich American old enough to be her father."

"You blame yourself?"

"Of course."

"Did you ever tell Caroline?"

"Never."

"Were you happy with her?"

"No. She wasn't a woman who engendered happiness. It worked all right, because we made it work, we were those sort of people. But love, of every sort, was always thin on the ground. I wish we had been happy. It would have been easier to accept her death if we'd had a good life, and I could have been certain that it hadn't all been just a" – he searched for words – "waste of ten good years."

There did not seem to be anything more to say. Across the distance that divided them, husband and wife regarded each other, and Virginia saw Edmund's hooded eyes filled with despair and sadness. She got up then, off the low stool, and went to sit beside him. She touched his mouth with her fingers. She kissed him. He reached out his arm and pulled her close.

She said, "And us?"

"I never knew how it could be, until I met you."

"I wish you'd told me all this before."

"I was ashamed. I didn't want you to know. I'd give

my right arm to be able to change things. But I can't, because they happened. They become part of you, stay with you for ever."

"Have you spoken to Pandora about this?"

"No. I've scarcely seen her. There's been no opportunity."

"You must make it right with her."

"Yes."

"She is, I think, still very precious to you."

"Yes. But she's part of life the way it used to be. Not the way it is now."

"You know, I've always loved you. I suppose if I hadn't loved you so much, you wouldn't have been able to make me so miserable. But now that I realise you are human and frail and make the same idiotic blunders as the rest of us, it's even better. I never thought you needed me, you see. I thought you were quite self-sufficient. Being needed's more important than anything."

"I need you now. Don't go away. Don't leave me. Don't go to America with Conrad Tucker."

"I wasn't running *away* with him."

"I thought you were."

"No, you didn't. He's actually a very nice man."

"I wanted to kill him."

You must never tell Edmund. Still untouched by guilt, she felt protective of her husband, holding her secret like a proud and private trophy. She said lightly, "That would have been a dreadful waste."

"Will your grandparents be very disappointed?"

"We'll go some other time. You and me together. We'll leave Henry with Vi and Edie and we'll go and see them on our own."

He kissed her. Leaned his head back on the deep cushions of the sofa and sighed. "I wish we didn't have to go to this bloody dance."

"I know. But we must. Just for a little."

"I would very very much rather take you to bed."

543

"Oh, Edmund. We've lots of time for love. Years and years. The rest of our lives."

Presently Edie came to find them, knocking on the door before she opened it. The light from the hall shone from behind her and turned her white hair into an aureole.

"Just to say Henry's in bed and waiting for you . . ."

"Oh, thank you, Edie . . ."

They went upstairs. In his own room, Henry lay in his own bed. His night-lamp burnt dimly, and the room lay in shadows. Virginia sat on the edge of the bed and bent to kiss him. He was already half asleep.

"Good night, my darling."

"Good night, Mummy."

"You'll be all right."

"Yes. I'll be all right."

"No dreams."

"I don't think so."

"If dreams come, Edie's downstairs."

"Yes. I know."

"I'll leave you with Daddy."

She stood up and moved towards the door.

"Have a good party," Henry told her.

"Thank you, my darling. We will." She went through the door. Edmund took her place.

"Well, Henry, you're home again."

"I'm sorry about the school. It really wasn't right."

"No. I know. I realise that. Mr Henderson does as well."

"I don't have to go back to it, do I?"

"I don't think so. We'll have to see if the Strathcroy Primary will take you on again."

"Do you think they'll say no?"

"I shouldn't think so. You'll be back with Kedejah."

"That'll be good."

"Good night, old boy. You did well. I'm proud of you."

Henry's eyes were closing. Edmund stood up and

moved away. But at the open door, he turned back, and realised, with some surprise, that his own eyes were moist.

"Henry?"

"Yes?"

"Have you got Moo in there with you?"

"No," Henry told him, "I don't need Moo any more."

Out of doors, Virginia realised that the rain had stopped. From somewhere a wind had sprung up, chill and fresh as snow, stirring the darkness, causing the high elms of Balnaid to rustle and creak and toss their heads. Looking up, she saw stars, for this wind was blowing all clouds away to the east, and in their wake the sky was clear and infinite, pricked with the jewel glitter of a million constellations. Sweet and cold, the clean air struck her cheeks. She took deep breaths of it and was revitalised. No longer tired. No longer miserable, angry, resentful, lost. Henry was home and staying home, and Edmund, in more ways than one, returned to her. She was young and knew that she looked beautiful. Dressed to the nines and off to a party, she was ready to dance all night.

They drove into the beam of the headlights, the narrow country roads twisting away behind them. As they approached Corriehill, the night sky was bathed in reflected brilliance from the spotlights which had been directed on to the front of the house. Drawing closer, they saw Verena's strings of fairy lights looped from tree to tree all the way up the long drive, and as well, every twenty yards or so, the bright flares of Roman candles that grew from the grass verges.

The BMW swung around the last bend, and the house was revealed in its full glory, towering up against the dark backdrop of the sky. It looked enormously impress-ive and proud.

Virginia said, "It must be feeling really good tonight."

"What must?"

"Corriehill. Like a monument. In memory of all the dinner parties, and wedding feasts and dances and balls that it must have known in the course of its history. And christenings. And funerals too, I suppose. But mostly parties."

Three brilliant searchlights were beamed upwards, lighting Corriehill from basements to chimneys. Beyond stood the marquee, lit from inside, like a shadow theatre. Distorted silhouettes moved and turned against the white canvas. They heard the beat of music. The dancing, clearly, was already well under way.

Another spotlight hung from a tree to the left of the drive, illuminating the big paddock. Here, cars were parked, in long, well-ordered rows, as far as the eye could see. A figure approached through the gloom, flashing a torch. Edmund stopped the car and rolled down his window. The torchbearer stopped to peer in. Hughie McKinnon, the Steyntons' old handyman, press-ganged for the evening into the role of car-park attendant, and already reeking of whisky.

"Good evening, sir."

"Good evening, Hughie."

"Oh, it's yourself, Mr Aird! I'm sorry, I didna' recognise the car. How are you, sir?" He craned a little further in order to cock his eye at Virginia, and the whisky fumes flowed afresh. "And Mrs Aird. How are you keeping yourself?"

"Very well, thank you, Hughie."

"Very good, very good," said Hughie. "You're awfully late. The rest of your party were all here an hour ago."

"I'm afraid we were unavoidably detained."

"Oh, well, no matter. The night's long enough. Now, sir" – with pleasantries over, he steadied his legs – "if you would just like to take your good lady to the front of the house, and drop her off there, you can come back here, and I'll be here, and I'll help you park the car

546

over *there*." His torchbeam wavered haphazardly in the direction of the field, and he belched discreetly. "And see that you both enjoy yourselves, and have a rare time."

He stepped back. Edmund rolled up the window.

"I doubt that Hughie is going to last the evening."

"At least he's well centrally heated. He won't die of hypothermia."

The car moved forward to pull up at the front door behind a large Audi with a personalised number-plate, disgorging its load of very young men and girls, all flushed and laughing from some extended and lavish dinner party. Virginia followed them up the steps while Edmund drove to find Hughie again and park his car.

She entered the house and was assailed by light, warmth, music, the smell of flowers, greenery, wood-smoke; the sound of voices, raised in greeting, laughter, and high-pitched conversation. As she slowly made her way up the stairs, she looked down over the banisters at the carnival scene. People everywhere. Many she knew, and others strangers, come from all parts of the country especially for the occasion. A log fire blazed in the huge fireplace, and around this, young men in kilts and evening dress stood talking to each other, drinks in hand. Two of them were officers from the Relkirk barracks, flamboyant in their scarlet regimental mess-jackets.

From the dining room, its doors festooned in draperies of deep-blue silk, came the powerful beat of the disco music. A steady flow of two-way traffic passed through these doors. Eager boys, their partners in tow, disappeared into the darkness, while others emerged, the young men as hot and sweaty as if they had just completed a fast game of squash, while the girls, casual with assumed sophistication, raked their fingers through tousled hair, and reached for cigarettes. The lowered lights and the din were clearly engendering a certain sexual excitement.

547

On one of the sofas that guarded the entrance to the library sat old General Grant-Palmer, kilted, and with his knees indecently wide apart. He talked to a formidable lady with a huge bosom, whom Virginia did not recognise. Past them, others made their way through to the library, and so to the marquee at the front of the house. "Virginia!" Some man, spying her, called her name.

She waved, smiled, continued on up the stairs. She went into the bedroom that had the sign 'Ladies' on the door, shed her fur and laid it on top of the coats already piled on the bed. She went to the mirror to comb her hair. Behind her the bathroom door burst open and a girl appeared. She had hair pale and fine as dandelion fluff, and eyes blackened like a panda's. Virginia was about to tell her kindly that she'd inadvertently got her dress tucked up into her knickers, and then realised that she was wearing a puffball skirt. Wishing that Edmund were with her so that they could share the joke together, she did a quick turn to spin the creases out of her skirt, put her comb back in her bag, and went out of the room.

Edmund was waiting for her at the bottom of the stairs. He took her hand. "All right?"

"I've got something lovely and funny to tell you. Did you get the car parked?"

"Hughie found a place for me. Come on, let's go and see what's going on."

She had seen it all before, the morning that she had delivered her flower vases, when the marquee stood empty and unfinished, and there had been workmen everywhere. Now all was transformed, and Verena's months of planning, agonising, and sheer hard labour had paid off. Corriehill, Virginia decided, might have been especially designed for just this occasion. From the library, the lead-out to the tent took in the stone garden steps. The urns that stood at the top and the bottom of these contained great masses of greenery and white chrysanthemums, and the lamps illuminating them

548

swayed in the thin draught that blew beneath the enclosed awning.

At the top of the steps, a natural vantage spot, they paused to regard in some wonder and admiration the scene before them.

The tall tent-poles had been transformed into veritable trees of barley sheaves, beech branches, and rowan bright with scarlet berries. High overhead hung four sparkling chandeliers. At the far end, a platform had been erected and strung with silver helium balloons, and on this sat Tom Drystone and his band, thumping out an eightsome reel, 'The Soldiers' Dance'. Tom with the accordion sat, as leader, in the middle, and around him were grouped the others. A pianist, two fiddlers, and a young boy with a drum set. In white jackets and tartan trews, they presented a fine sight, and Tom caught Virginia's eye and sent her a wink and a crack of his head. His long tumbler of beer stood brimming on the floor beside him.

The sets of dancers, some in eightsome, some in sixteensome, circled and swung, linking arms, changing partners, clapping hands and stamping feet in time to the hypnotic pulse of the music. In the middle of one set was a huge young man making a fine exhibition of himself. He looked strong enough to be a shot-putter or caber-tosser, but this evening was putting all his energy into his dancing. Kilt flying, arms held high over his massive shoulders, shirt bursting from his scarlet waistcoat, he was giving it his all, and his muscled legs flailed as he leapt, uttering manic cries, high off the floor.

"If he doesn't watch out," remarked Edmund, "he's going to do himself an injury."

"More likely kill off one of the girls."

But the girls loved him, they screamed with glee, were lifted off their feet, or spun like tops. Virginia half-expected to see one of them tossed, like a doll, high up into the roof of the tent.

Edmund nudged her. "Look at Noel."

549

Virginia followed his pointing finger, saw Noel, and dissolved into laughter. He stood, with a bemused expression on his handsome face, in the centre of one of the sets, having clearly lost his bearings and any idea of what he was meant to do next. Alexa, quite undeterred, and in a state of giggles, was trying to point him in the direction of his next partner, while she, in her turn, was being deliberately non-co-operative and wore a look of mock boredom.

They searched for the others. Found Vi, Conrad and Pandora, and Jeff and Lucilla, all dancing in a big sixteen-some together. Vi's partner was a retired Law Lord from Edinburgh, about half her size and perhaps the only person in the room older than she was. Vi, so large and so stout, moved, when she danced, lightly as a feather, gracefully swinging from man to man and never a step out of beat. As they watched, she took her place in the ring again, and two other ladies moved to dance together in the centre. Vi looked up, over their heads, and caught sight of Edmund and Virginia, standing hand in hand at the head of the stone steps.

For an instant, her cheerful, flushed face clouded. She raised her brows in fearful question. In answer, Edmund held their clasped hands up, as if in triumph. She got the message. A smile lit her homely features. The tempo of the catchy music quickened, she and the old judge linked arms to swing again, and Violet gave him such an almighty spin that he was nearly sent flying off his spindly legs.

At last the Grand Chain, a final turn, a long chord from the band, and the eightsome reel was over. Applause for the musicians instantly broke out, clapping, cheering, and stamping. The dancers, hot, breathless, sweating, wanted more. There were noisy demands for an encore, another round.

But Violet had had enough. Excusing herself, she had abandoned her partner and was already on her way across the dance floor to where Edmund and Virginia

550

waited. They went down the stone steps to meet her, and Violet embraced her daughter-in-law.

"You're here at last. I've been so worried. Is everything all right?"

"Everything, Vi."

"Henry?"

"Safe and well."

Violet fixed her son with a beady stare.

"Edmund. You're not going to send him back?"

"With that look in your eye, I don't think I'd dare. No, we're going to keep him at home for a little while longer."

"Oh, thank heavens for that. You've come to your senses. And in more ways than one, if I'm not mistaken. I can tell, just by the look of the pair of you." She opened her bag, took out her handkerchief, mopped her beaded forehead. "I," she announced, "have now had enough. I shall take myself home."

"But, Vi," Edmund protested, "I haven't danced with you."

"Then you must be disappointed, because I'm on my way. I've had a splendid evening, a splendid dinner, and I've danced an eightsome reel. Done the hat trick. I'm enjoying myself thoroughly, and this is the moment to call it a day."

She was obdurate. "If you like," Edmund offered, "I'll fetch your car and bring it to the door."

"That would be kind. I'll go upstairs and rescue my coat." She kissed Virginia again. "We have so much to talk about, but this is neither the time nor the place. But I am so happy for you both. Goodnight, my dear. Enjoy yourselves."

"Goodnight, Vi."

Edmund, after some searching, finally ran Pandora to earth in the drawing room, where a long bar had been set up down one side of the room, and sofas and chairs disposed in convenient conversational groups. Here, it was comparatively quiet, although impossible to escape totally from the pervasive beat of music from both marquee and disco. Standing in the door, he saw that a number of Verena's guests had chosen to sit out a dance or two, take a breather and have a drink. Very young girls sat on the floor . . . a good position for gazing up into the eyes of attendant young men. One of them had already caught Edmund's attention, for she wore the smallest black sequin dress he had ever seen in his life, its minimal skirt barely concealing her crotch. Inquiring as to her identity, he had been told she was an old schoolfriend of Katy's, which was hard to believe. The provocative sequins and the endless black silk legs didn't seem to go with hockey sticks.

He spied Pandora at last, tucked into the corner of the sofa near the fire, and deep in conversation with some man. Edmund picked his way across the floor towards them, and she sensed his coming and turned her head at his approach.

"Edmund."

"Come and dance."

"Oh, darling, I'm exhausted. I've been leaping up and down like a yo-yo."

"The disco, then. They're playing 'Lady in Red'."

"Heavenly tune. Edmund, you know Robert Bramwell, don't you? Yes, of course you do, because he's one of the guns in your syndicate. Silly me."

"Sorry, Robert. You don't mind if I steal her away?"

"No, of course not . . ." He had some difficulty in heaving himself out of the sofa, being both well-built and portly. ". . . Anyway, it's time I went in search of my wife. Said I'd do something called Hamilton House with her. Don't know how the hell to do it, but suppose I'd better report for duty . . ."

"Such a lovely drink . . ." Pandora thanked him vaguely.

"A pleasure."

They watched him go. Across the crowded room, out through the door. Then Edmund, shamelessly, took his place.

"Oh, darling, you are naughty. I thought you wanted to dance."

"Poor chap. It probably took much sneaky manoeuvring to get you to himself, and now I've spoiled it all."

"You haven't spoiled it for *me*. You haven't got a drink."

"I'm laying off for the moment. I've already consumed far too much this evening."

"Poor darling, you've had such a horrid time. How is Henry?"

"Considering what he's been through, in great shape."

"Terribly brave to run away from school. Terribly brave, actually, to run anywhere."

"You did."

"Oh, darling, are we back to that? I thought we'd stopped talking about that."

"I'm sorry."

"Sorry for talking about it?"

"No. Sorry for everything that happened. For the way I behaved. I never explained to you, and I suppose it's too late to start explaining now."

"Yes," she told him, "I think it is a little late."

"You've never forgiven me?"

"Oh, Edmund, I don't forgive people. I'm not good enough to forgive people. 'Forgive' is a non-word in my vocabulary. How could I forgive, when during the course of my life *I* have made so many people desperately unhappy?"

"That's not the point."

"If you want to talk about it, let's be objective. You

553

said you would write, be in touch, love me for ever, and you didn't do any of those things. It wasn't like you to break your word, and I could never understand . . ."

"If I had written it would have been to tell you that my promises were empty and I was backing out. And I left it too long, and when I finally plucked up the nerve, it was too late . . . So I took the easy way out."

"That was the bad bit. I thought you never took the easy way out of anything. I thought I knew you so well, and that was why I loved you so much. And I couldn't believe that you didn't love me. I wanted you. So stupid. But all my life, everything I'd wanted I'd been allowed to have, I'd been given. To be denied anything I wanted was a new and cruel experience. And I wouldn't accept it. I couldn't believe that some miracle wouldn't happen, and everything that you'd done – going to London, and marrying Caroline, and having Alexa – couldn't be magically absolved, dissolved, swept under the carpet. So stupid. But then, I was only eighteen, and I never had much brain."

"I'm sorry."

She smiled at him, touched his cheek with her fingers. "Do you blame yourself for the mess I made of everything? Don't. I was born disaster material. We both know that. If it hadn't been you, it would have been somebody else. And if Harald Hogg hadn't been there, stinking-rich and panting with lust, then I'm certain I would have found some other equally impossible man to elope with. I would never have made you happy. I don't think Caroline made you happy. But now, I think, with Virginia, you are happy at last. So that makes me happy."

"What else makes you happy?"

"Even if I knew, I wouldn't tell you."

"Why did you come back to Croy?"

"Oh, a whim. An impulse. To see you all again."

"Will you stay?"

"I think not. Too restless, darling."

"That makes me feel guilty."

"Why?"

"I don't know. We all have so much."

"Me too. But mine are different things."

"I hate you being alone."

"Better that way."

"You are part of us all. You know that?"

"Thank you. That's the nicest thing you could say to me. That's just the way I want it to be. Just the way I want it to stay." She leaned forward and kissed his cheek, and his senses were assaulted by her closeness, the touch of her lips, the scent of her perfume.

"Pandora . . ."

"And now, darling, we've sat here long enough . . . Don't you think we should go and find the others?"

It was past one o'clock in the morning, with festivities at their peak, when Noel Keeling, unable and unwilling to deal with the complexities of a dance called the Duke of Perth, found himself abandoned and alone, decided that he was in need of liquid refreshment, and headed for the bar. He was offered champagne, but his mouth was dry and he settled instead for a glass of ice-cold lager. He had just set the glass to his lips and taken a long and refreshing swig when, all at once, Pandora Blair appeared at his elbow.

Since the dinner party, he had scarcely seen her all evening, which was a shame, because he thought her good news, and quite the most decorative and amusing female he had met for a long time.

"Noel."

It was gratifying to be sought out. He instantly laid down his glass and made space for her, and she settled herself beside him on an empty bar-stool and, having made herself comfortable, smiled conspiratorially into his face.

She said, "I have a favour to ask."

"But of course. Have a drink?"

She reached for a brimming glass of champagne and drank it like water.

He laughed. "Have you been on that the whole evening?"

"Of course."

"What's the favour?"

"I think it's time I went home. Would you take me?"

Noel was, in truth, a little taken aback. It was the last thing he had expected.

"But why do you want to go home?"

"I think I've stayed long enough. Danced with everybody, said all the right things, and now I'm longing for my beddy-byes. I'd ask Archie to take me, but he's having such a jolly time, closeted in Angus Steynton's office with old General Grant-Palmer and a bottle of Glen Morangie, it seems a shame to spoil his fun. And everybody else is leaping about in the tent, doing tribal dances. Even Conrad, our friendly Sad American."

"I'm surprised he knows how to do them."

"Archie and Isobel organised a little class at Croy on Wednesday evening and gave us lessons, but I never imagined he'd become totally hooked. Will you take me, Noel? Is it a perfectly horrid thing to ask?"

"No, of course not. Of course I'll take you."

"I've got my car, but I'm truly not fit to drive and I'm sure I'd fall asleep on the way back and end up in a ditch. And the others will need to get home. So perhaps I should leave it behind for them . . ."

"I'll drive you in my car."

"You're an angel." She finished her champagne. "I'll go and get my coat. Meet you at the front door."

He thought of telling somebody what he was about to do, and then decided against it, because the drive to Croy wouldn't take longer than half an hour, and most likely he would never be missed. At the foot of the staircase he waited for her and was amused to find

556

himself in a pleasant state of anticipation, as though he and Pandora were embarking on a small shared and secret assignation, one with possible romantic connotations. Which, on analysis, he realised had much to do with her, and he guessed that she had probably always had this effect on any man on whom she chose to beam her attention.

"Ready." She ran down the stairs, wrapped in her long, voluptuous mink. He took her arm and they went out, down the steps and across the gravel. The grass of the paddock was cold and wet, and the ground muddy, and he offered to sweep her up into his arms and carry her to his car, but she only laughed at him and pulled off her fragile sandals and walked beside him in her bare feet.

Old Hughie had disappeared, but they finally located Noel's Golf. He turned up the heater to warm her toes. "Do you want music?"

"Not particularly. It might interfere with the stars."

He backed, turned, drove away from Corriehill, down the fairy-lit driveway, and into the dark countryside. The warm interior of the car was pervaded with the scent of her perfume, and he had a strange feeling that in the future, whenever he smelled it again he would remember *now*, this journey, this woman.

She began to talk. "It was a lovely party. Exactly right from beginning to end. Just the way they used to be, only even better. We used to have dances like that at Croy, ages ago, when we were all young. Christmas and birthdays. Magic. You'll have to come back to Croy, because things will get better now. They won't be gloomy any longer. Archie's better. He's his own man again. He's had a horrible, nightmare time, but he's over that. Come to terms with it."

For a little, she was silent. She sat, with her head turned away from him, her hair spilling over the soft fur of her coat. She stared through the window, as the lightless, empty road streamed away behind them.

557

After a bit, she said, "*Will* you come back to Croy, Noel?"

"Why do you ask that?"

"Perhaps I'm asking something else. Perhaps I'm asking you about Alexa."

He was cautious. "What are you asking me?"

"I think you're wavering, dithering. You don't know what to do."

He was surprised by her perception. "Have you been talking to Vi?"

"Darling, I never talk to anyone. Not about things that matter."

"Alexa matters."

"That's what I thought. You see, I have a funny feeling that you and I are rather alike. I never really knew what I wanted, and then when I got it, I discovered I'd never really wanted it at all. And that's because I was looking for something that didn't exist."

"Are you talking about a particular man, or a way of life?"

"Both, I think. Don't they go together? And perfection. The ultimate. But it never happens, because it doesn't exist. Loving isn't finding perfection, but forgiving horrible faults. I suppose it's all a matter of compromise. And recognising the moment when it's time to decide whether you're going to fish or cut bait."

Noel said, "I love Alexa, but I am not in love with her." He thought about this statement and then smiled. "You know, I've never said those words aloud before. Not to myself. Not to anybody. Not about anybody."

"How does it feel, saying them aloud?"

"Frightening. I'm afraid of making promises, because I've never been much good at keeping them."

"Fear is the worst reason for doing anything, or for doing nothing. It's negative. Like not doing something because of what people will say. Pandora, you can't behave like that! *Whatever* will people *say*? As if it mat-

558

tered. No, that won't do. You'll have to think of a better excuse."

"All right, how about this one? Uncommitted, I stay in charge of my own life."

"That's all right when you're young. But the unattached men about town very often end up as lonely and pathetic old bachelors, if they're not very careful. The sort that hostesses invite to dinner parties to make up the numbers. And afterwards, they drive themselves home to an empty flat and only a faithful doggie to take to bed."

"That's a jolly prospect."

"You only have one life. You don't get second chances. Let something really good slip through your fingers and it's gone for ever. And then you spend the rest of your life trying to find it again . . . lurching from one unsatisfactory affair to another. And after a bit the day comes when you know it's all for nothing. Useless. Just a waste of time and effort."

"So what is the answer?"

"I don't know. I'm not you. I suppose a little courage and a lot of faith." She thought about this. "I sound just like a headmistress on Speech Day. Or a politician. 'Let us put our hands to the plough, and look forward, for there lies the way ahead.' " She began to laugh. " 'Vote for Blair, and get free corn plasters.' "

He said, "You are advocating compromise."

Her laughter died. "There are worse things. This evening is the first time I ever met Alexa, but I watched her at dinner . . . watching you, and her face filled with love. She is a giver. She is gold."

"I know all that."

"So, I rest my case."

Silence once more, and now just a little way left to go. Down the long glen, and the lights of Strathcroy were dimmed, only the sparse street-lamps shed their glow. The interior of the car had become very warm. Noel lowered the window a little and felt the fresh cold air

559

on his face and heard the sound of the river running alongside the road.

They reached the first of the cottages, the gates of Croy, the front drive. He changed down, sped up the hill. The house awaited them, its windows dark. Only Archie's Land-Rover stood parked in solitary state outside the front door. Noel drew up, switched off the ignition. The night was quiet; only the wind moved.

"There you are. Safely home."

She turned to him, her smile full of gratitude. "You've been really sweet. I hope I haven't ruined your fun. And I'm sorry if I've interfered."

"I can't quite work out why you said all those things."

"Probably because I've drunk too much champagne." She leaned over and kissed his cheek. "Goodnight, Noel."

"Will the door be open?"

"Of course. It's never locked."

"I'll see you in."

"No." She restrained him with a hand on his arm. "I'll be all right. Don't come. Go back to Alexa."

She got out of the car and slammed shut the door. In the beam of his headlamps she walked away from him across the gravel and up the steps. He watched her go. The big door opened, she turned to wave, slipped inside. The door closed. She was gone.

Even Tom Drystone could not play for ever. At the end of two rousing rounds of 'The Duke of Perth', finishing off with the distinctly non-Scottish strains of 'The Girl I Left Behind Me', he pulled a long and breathless chord from his accordion, laid it on the floor, rose to his feet, and announced, over the microphone, that he and his colleagues were away for their supper. Despite exaggerated groans of despair and a good deal of derogatory badinage, he stuck to his guns and led his perspiring team of musicians across the dance floor and in the general direction of well-earned refreshment.

In the resultant lull the abandoned dancers, for a moment, stood about in aimless fashion, but almost at once were assailed by mouth-watering smells of frying bacon and fresh coffee drifting through from the house. These reminded the assembled company that it was some hours since they had last eaten, and there started a general exodus, headed for sustenance. However, as the marquee slowly emptied, a young man – spontaneously, or perhaps previously instructed by Verena – stepped up on to the platform, took his place at the piano, and began to play.

"Virginia . . ." She was already halfway up the stone steps that led into the house. She turned and saw Conrad behind her. "Come and dance with me."

"Don't you want bacon and eggs?"

"Later. This is too good to miss."

It was good. The sort of soft, pervasive mood music that went back a long way, a long time, to expensive, sophisticated restaurants and darkened nightclubs and sentimental movies that left you with tear-filled eyes and a wad of damp Kleenex.

'Bewitched'. "I'm wild again, beguiled again . . ."

She gave in. "All right."

She turned back, stepped into his arms. Conrad drew her close, laid his cheek against her hair. They danced, scarcely moving, hardly aware of other couples, who, succumbing to the seduction of the plangent piano, had taken once more to the floor.

He said, "Do you think this guy knows how to play 'The Look of Love'?"

She smiled to herself. "I don't know. You could ask him."

"It's been a good party."

"I'm impressed by your reeling."

561

"If you can do a square dance, I guess you can do anything."

"Just needs guts."

"Do they still have Saturday-night dances at the Leesport Country Club?"

"I expect so. A whole new generation smooching around the terrace under the stars."

"We're not doing too badly right now."

She said, "I'm not coming back, Conrad. I'm not coming back with you."

She felt his hand, against her ribcage, moving, gentle as a caress. She looked up into his face. "You knew already, didn't you?"

"Yeah," he admitted. "I guessed."

"Everything's changed. Henry's home. We've talked. It's different now. We're together again, Edmund and I. It's all right again."

"I'm glad."

"Edmund's my life. I lost sight of him, but he's back and we're together."

"For you, I'm really glad."

"Right now isn't the time to go away and leave him."

"He's a lucky man."

"No, not lucky. Just special."

"He's also a nice guy."

"I am sorry, Conrad. Whatever you feel, I don't want you to think that I was just using you."

"I think we used each other. We levelled off with our mutual need. At exactly the right time, the right person was there. At least, for me it was the right person. It was you."

"You're a special man, too. You know that, don't you? And one day, sooner or later, you'll meet someone. Someone just as special as you are. She won't fill Mary's place, because she'll have a place of her own. And she'll fill it for all the right reasons. You've got to remember that. For your own sake, and for the sake of your little daughter."

562

"Okay. A positive approach."

"I don't want you to be sad any longer."

"No longer the Sad American."

"Oh, don't *remind* me! How crass I was to blurt that out."

"When will I see you again?"

"Oh, soon. We'll come out to the States, Edmund and I. Some time. We'll all get together then."

She laid her head on his shoulder. "Bewitched, bothered, and bewildered, am I." The last notes of the song trickled away off the piano.

He said, "I love you."

"Me too," Virginia told him. "It's been great."

Noel drove back to Corriehill. With the wind pouring in through the open window, the Golf headed back into the hills, and he took his time and did not speed. Being on his own was strangely peaceful, a small breathing space in which to collect some of his thoughts and let others wander. Leaving Croy, he had toyed with the idea of putting on a tape for company, and then decided against it because, for once, quiet was what he craved. Besides, it seemed almost blasphemous to intrude on the infinite, bloomy darkness of the night by letting loose a blast of rock.

The countryside, all about him, was obscured, desolate, and scarcely habited, and yet he felt that his passage, in some inexplicable way, was being observed. This was an ancient land. The hilltops thrusting up into the sky had held those shapes since the beginning of time, and his immediate surroundings had probably looked for hundreds of years much as they looked now.

Ahead, the narrow road twisted away from him. Long

ago, when its course was first laid, it would have followed the boundaries of a farmer's land, circumvented the drystone dykes of a crofter's smallholding. Now, others owned these lands, and tractors and milk-floats and buses came this way, yet the road wound and climbed and dipped, to no apparent purpose, just the way it had always done.

Unable to shrug off the sensation that he was being watched, he thought about those long-gone crofters pitting their energies against the cruel climate, the stubborn land, the barren soil. Ploughing the thin soil behind a horse, harvesting, with sickles, the meagre crops; braving blizzards in search of sheep, cutting peat to stack for fuel. He imagined just such a man making his way home, along the road Noel was now travelling, headed up the empty glen, on horseback maybe, but more likely on foot. Slogging up the hill, bent against the wind that blew from the west. The road, then, would have seemed very long, and the labours of survival endless.

He found it impossible to imagine such hardships, such a tenuous existence. Safe in the twentieth century, taking both necessities and luxuries for granted, the problem of surviving was not one that Noel had ever contemplated, let alone had to deal with, and in comparison his own uncertainties seemed so unimportant that he felt diminished by their triviality.

And yet, it was his life. *You only have one life*, Pandora had told him. *You don't get second chances. Let something really good slip through your fingers and it's gone for ever*.

Which brought him back to Alexa. *Alexa was gold*. Pandora was right, and he knew she was right. *If you have to hurt her, then you must do it now* . . . That was old Vi, sitting on the hill above the loch and opening her heart to him.

He thought about Vi, and Pandora, and the Balmerinos and the Airds. Together they constituted a way of life that he had never before truly experienced. Family, friends, neighbours; involved and interdependent. He thought about Balnaid and once more was assailed by the reasonless conviction that here was where he belonged.

Alexa was the key.

Now, taking him by surprise, his mother joined in the argument. *Happiness is making the most of what you have.* Penelope's robust and certain tones rang clear in his head, brooking no argument, laying down the law as she always had when she felt strongly about some issue.

So what had he got?

The answer was painfully straightforward. A girl. Unsophisticated and not particularly beautiful. In fact, the very antithesis of every woman who had gone before. A girl who loved him. Not to distraction; never nagging him with demands. But with a constancy that burned bright as a steady flame. He thought about the last few months, during which he had lived with Alexa in her little house in Ovington Street, and a series of random images floated, unsummoned, into his mind. And these took him by surprise, because for some reason his subconscious did not come up with any of those rich and material possessions which had first caught his attention that evening, so long ago, when Alexa had invited him in for a drink. The pictures, the furniture, the books and the porcelain; the handsome coasters on the sideboard, and the two silver pheasants which stood in the middle of her dining-room table. Instead, he saw delicious and domestic objects. A bowl of fresh apples, a loaf of newly-baked bread, a jug crammed with tulips, the gleam of evening sunshine on the copper pans that hung in the kitchen.

And then the other good things which they had shared together. Kiri te Kanawa at Covent Garden, the Tate Gallery at weekends. Sunday lunches at San Lorenzo. Making love. He thought of the peaceful feeling of walking home in the evenings, back from the office, turning into Ovington Street and knowing that she was there, waiting for him.

That was what he'd got. Alexa. There. Waiting for

him. That was all he wanted. That was all that mattered. So what the hell was he dithering about? What the hell was he looking for? All at once the questions were of so little importance that he didn't even bother to attempt to think up the answers.

Because the prospect of a future without her was unimaginable.

He knew then that he was over the watershed and on the path of commitment. For better, for worse. Till death us do part. But the daunting words no longer rendered him shit-scared. Instead, he found himself filled with an unaccustomed and unexpected sense of purpose and elation.

And urgency. No more reason to linger. Instead, a new impatience. He had wasted enough time. He took a deep breath, accelerated. The engine responded and the car sped up the hill. Along the road that led to Corriehill.

His mother was still around somewhere. "All right," he said, "I heard you. You've made your point. I'm on my way." And he said the words aloud, and the wind snatched the words from his mouth and tossed them away behind him. He shouted, "I'm coming!" And the reassurance was for the two of them, his dead mother and his living love.

The first of the guests were on their way home from the dance. The headlights of their cars could be seen from far off, moving away from Corriehill, down between the trees and out of the imposing gates. Driving up the hill towards the house, Noel passed a couple of these cars, but there was plenty of space on the wide driveway and time, as well, for a certain amount of badinage; derisive remarks about Noel's apparently tardy arrival at the party, and assurances that it was better to be late than never.

The home-goers had clearly been enjoying themselves.

As the exodus had already begun, Noel did not bother to park the car in the field, but instead, took it to the side of the gravel sweep of the front door. As he went up the steps, an old couple emerged, and he stood aside, to hold the door open for them and let them by. The husband thanked him courteously, and bade him goodnight, and then tucked his arm solicitously into his wife's, and helped her on her way. Noel watched them go, stepping cautiously, and deep in conversation. He heard their laughter. Elderly, perhaps, but they too had enjoyed themselves, had a fine time, and now together were going home. He thought again, till death us do part. But death, after all, was simply a part of life, and it was the living bit that was important.

He went through the doors and in search of Alexa. She was not in the disco, nor the drawing room. Emerging from the drawing room, he heard his name being spoken.

"Noel."

He stopped and turned, and saw a girl to whom he had not been formally introduced, but whom he knew to be Katy Steynton, because Alexa had pointed her out to him. She was blonde and very slender, with features the quintessence of Englishness; a beautiful complexion, a long face, pale blue eyes and a tiny mouth. She wore a dress of slipper satin in exactly the same shade as her eyes, and held the hand of a man who was obviously impatient to get her into the throbbing, strobe-lit den of the disco.

"Hello, there."

"You are Noel Keeling, aren't you? Alexa's friend?"

For some reason, Noel felt faintly foolish. "That's right."

"She's in the marquee. I'm Katy Steynton."

567

"Yes, I know."

"She's dancing with Torquil Hamilton-Scott."

"Oh, thanks." Which sounded a bit abrupt, so Noel added tactfully, "Wonderful party. You must be thrilled. So kind of you to ask me."

"Not a bit. It was super . . ." she was already being towed away from him " . . . that you could come."

A waiter bustled by with a trayful of brimming champagne glasses. As he passed, Noel adroitly lifted one off the tray, and then made his way through the library towards the marquee. The beat of the music there had reached a crescendo, for the band was on its second run through the dance, and the pace seemed to quicken with every moment that passed. At the top of the steps, he paused, to search for Alexa, but then, despite his anxiety to find her, and his impatience, found himself diverted, captivated by the sight before him. He had no great love of dancing, let alone Scottish country dancing, but the atmosphere had become electric, with a charge that could not be ignored. As well, his professional, creative instincts automatically responded to this visual assault on his senses, the whirling circles of colour and movement, and he wished, more than anything, that he were able to capture it on camera. For this dancing had about it an aggressive symmetry that reminded him of the precision of some oft-rehearsed military tattoo. The false floor of the marquee audibly groaned as one hundred pairs of feet banged down on it in perfect rhythm, and the centre of each ring was a vortex, sucking a dancer from the side of the set, and then throwing him out a second later with the full impact of centrifugal force. Bare-armed girls wryly displayed bruises inflicted by the silver cuff-buttons of a partner's kilt-jacket, but to all intents and purposes, they were mesmerised by the intricacies of the reel, concentrating and waiting for their next turn to be pulled into the spinning inferno.

He saw Alexa at last, in her flower-splashed dress, with her cheeks rosy and her hair flying. She was un-

568

aware of his presence, and dancing with one of the young soldiers, a handsome figure with his raven-black hair and his scarlet mess jacket. Noel saw her engrossed, excited, blissfully happy, her face tilted up to her partner's, and filled with laughter.

Alexa.

"It's a hell of a dance, isn't it?"

Startled, Noel looked round and saw the man who stood beside him, come, presumably, to enjoy the spectacle, as he was.

He said, "It certainly is. What is it they're doing?"

"The Reel of the Fifty-First Highland Division."

"Never heard of it."

"It was devised in a German prison camp during the war."

"It looks extremely complicated."

"Well, why not? They had five and a half years to make the bloody thing up."

Noel smiled politely, and went back to watching Alexa. But now his patience was wearing thin, and he longed for it all to be over. Which, in a moment or two, it was. A rousing last few bars, and then a final, shattering roll of drums. Applause, clapping, and cheers took the place of the music, but Noel wasted not a moment. He laid down his glass in a handy plant pot, and shouldered his way across the crowded floor to her side, where he found her being gratefully and robustly embraced by her overheated partner.

"Alexa."

She looked and saw him, and her flushed face lighted up, and she disentangled herself, reaching out her hand to him.

"Noel. Where have you been?"

"I'll explain. Come and have a drink . . ." And he took her hand, and pulled her firmly off the dance floor, Alexa meanwhile calling her thanks to the young soldier over her shoulder, but doing nothing to resist Noel's masterful progress. He led her out of the tent, through

569

the library; he searched for a peaceful spot, and decided that halfway up the staircase was as good a place as any.

"But, Noel, I thought we were going to have a drink."

"We will in a moment."

"You're taking me to the Ladies."

"No, I'm not."

On the half-landing it was quiet, and softly lit. He sat on the wide, Turkey-carpeted stair and drew her down beside him, and took her head between his hands and kissed her warm, flushed cheeks, and her brow, and her eyes, and then her sweet and open mouth, thus stilling her laughing protests.

It took a long time. They drew apart at last. After a bit, he said, "I watched you dancing, yet that was all I wanted to do."

"I don't understand, Noel."

He smiled. "Nor do I."

"What has happened?"

"I took Pandora home to Croy."

"I didn't know where you'd gone."

"I love you."

"I looked for you, but . . ."

"I want you for always."

"You have me."

"Till death us do part."

She looked, quite suddenly, almost frightened. "Oh, Noel . . ."

"Please."

"But that's for ever."

He thought of the old couple, arm in arm, setting off in the darkness for home. Together. "I know." He had never felt so confident, so unafraid, so certain in the whole of his life. "You see, my darling Alexa, I am asking you to marry me."

Pandora shut the door behind her. Inside the house, with curtains drawn and doors closed, it was very dark, the great hall illuminated only by the glow of red ashes from the dying fire. She was alone. It was the first time in her life that she had had Croy to herself. Always, there had been others around the place. Archie, Isobel, Lucilla, Conrad, Jeff. And long before them, her parents, their servants, the constant stream of visitors and friends; always somebody, coming or going. Distant voices, distant laughter.

She switched on the light. Went upstairs, down the upper passage to her room. She found it all just as she had left it, flung with clothes, the bed crumpled, the empty whisky glass still on the bedside table, along with her radio and a dog-eared paperback. The dressing-table was littered with bottles and jars, dusted with spilled face-powder; the wardrobe door hung open, and random shoes lay about the floor.

She tossed her bag on to the bed, and went over to the bombé desk. Here lay the letter that she had been writing before succumbing to exhaustion and taking to her bed to have one of her little toes-ups. She picked it up and read it through. It did not take very long. She folded it and put it into an envelope and licked the flap and pressed it down. She left the envelope on the blotter.

She went into the bathroom. This, too, was in its habitual state of disorder, with damp bathmat and towels on the floor, and the soap lying, forgotten and soggy, in the bottom of the bath. At the basin, she filled a glass with water and drank it down, watching her own reflection in the tall plate-glass mirror. Her jars of pills stood on the shelf below this, and she reached for one of them, but clumsily, or perhaps her hand was shaking, because, inadvertently, she knocked over the bottle of Poison that stood alongside. It tipped and fell, and she watched this happen, and it all seemed to happen quite gradually, like watching a slow-motion film. It wasn't until it hit the basin and had smashed into smithereens that she put out her hand as though to save it.

Too late. All gone. The basin filled with shards of glass, and she herself, almost anaesthetised by the concentrated scent of the precious golden perfume . . .

Bugger.

No matter. No good trying to clean it up, because she'd only cut her fingers to ribbons. Isobel would deal with it. In the morning. Tomorrow morning, Isobel would deal with it.

She stowed the jar of pills safely away, deep into the pocket of her mink coat, and then, carefully switching off all the lights, and closing her bedroom door, went back downstairs and into the drawing room. She turned on the main switch, and the huge chandelier, suspended from the centre of the ceiling, sprang into a thousand facets of glittering crystal light. Here again, the fire was nearly dead, but the room was still warm and comfortingly shabby and familiar with its crimson damask walls hung with the old portraits and oil paintings that Pandora had known all her life. It was all so dear. The battered armchairs and sofas, the mismatched cushions, the little green velvet footstool where she had sat, as a child, while her father read aloud to her before she went to bed. And the piano. Mama used to play the piano in the evenings, and Pandora and Archie would sing the old songs. Scottish songs. Songs of loyalty and love and death . . . nearly all of them quite dreadfully sad.

> *Ye banks and braes of bonnie Doon,*
> *How can ye bloom sae fresh and fair . . .*

How lovely to be able to play as Mama had. But then, being given lessons, the young Pandora had swiftly tired of them, and her gentle mother, as always, had allowed her to have her own way. And so she had never learned.

Another regret to add to all the others. Another missed opportunity of joy.

She went to the piano and lifted the lid and haltingly picked out the notes with a single finger.

It's a long long time
From May to December
But the days grow short . . .

Wrong note, try again.

. . . short
When you reach September.

Not much of a performance.

She shut the piano lid, went out of the room, across the hall and into the dining room. Here, more detritus. The table uncleared, empty coffee-cups, port glasses, crumpled napkins, chocolate wrappings, the scent of cigar smoke. The sideboard was laden with decanters, and she found an open bottle of champagne, still three-quarters full, which Archie had capped for future consumption with some patent stopper. Carrying this, she went back across the hall and out through the front door.

Archie's Land-Rover waited for her. She climbed up behind the wheel, into its smelly and battered interior. She had never driven it before, and it took a moment or two to work out the complexities of ignition, gears, and lights. But finally, she got the hang of them. With only sidelights burning, the old engine chuntered into life, and she was off.

Down the drive between the dark masses of the rhododendrons, across the cattle-grid, up to the right, headed for the hills. She drove very slowly, with immense care, feeling her way by the dim lights, as though she walked on tiptoe. Past the farmhouse, through the steadings. And then, Gordon Gillock's house. She had been afraid that the sound of the car engine would disturb Gordon's

573

dogs, and they would start raging and barking and wake their master. But this did not happen.

Now she switched on the full beam of the headlights and was able to pick up a little speed. The road wound and twisted, but she knew every inch of the way. After a bit she reached the deer-fence with its tall gates. The last obstacle. She drew to a halt, pulled on the hand-brake, and, leaving the engine throbbing, climbed down and went to open the gates. The bolt was rusted and awkward to pull free, but she finally achieved this, and the gates, weighted, swung open of their own accord. Back into the Land-Rover, through the gap in the fence, and then the whole procedure all over again – pulling the gates shut, and bolting them closed behind her.

Free. Now she was free. Nothing more to be afraid of. Nothing more to worry about. Lurching and bumping, the Land-Rover crawled its way up the unmade track, headlights pointing to the sky, and the sweet damp air pouring through the ill-fitting windows cool upon her cheeks.

Behind, the world dropped away, became smaller, infinitesimal, unimportant. The hills closed ranks, drew her close, like comforting arms. This was Pandora's country. She had carried it all through the wasted years in her heart, and now she was back for good. This was reality. The darkness, the feeling of belonging. Warm and safe and comforting as the womb.

You are my womb, she told the hills. I am returning to the womb. She began to sing.

> Ye banks and braes of bonnie Doon,
> How can ye bloom sae fresh and fair . . .

Her voice, thin and cracked and out of tune, sounded lonely as a curlew's cry. Too banal. Something cheerful.

> Oh, the black cat piddled in the white cat's eye
> And the white cat said "Gorblimey."

574

"I'm sorry, sir, if I piddled in you eye
But I didn't know you were behind me."

It was some time before she reached the loch, but time didn't matter, because there was no hurry now, no stress, no urgency, no panic. All had been attended to, nothing forgotten. Familiar landmarks came and went. The Corrie was one of them. She thought of Edmund, and then did not think of him.

She knew at last that she was drawing close to the loch when the bumping ceased and the land levelled out, and the wheels of the Land-Rover ran smoothly over close-cropped grass.

In the beam of the headlights the dark waters lay revealed, the further shores invisible, melding into the moors. She saw the black shape of the boathouse, the pale sickle of the pebbled beach.

She switched off the engine and the lights, reached for the bottle of champagne, and climbed out on to the grass. The heels of her sandals sank into the soft turf and the high air was very cold. She pulled her mink close about her and stood for a moment listening to the silence. Then she heard the piping of the wind, the ripple of water on shingle, the distant soughing of the tall pines that stood at the far end of the dam.

She smiled, because it felt just as it had always felt. She walked down to the water and sat on the turfy bank above the little beach. She set the champagne bottle beside her, then took the jar of sleeping pills from her coat pocket, unscrewed the cap and shook the lot out into her palm. There seemed to be an awful lot of them. She put her hand to her mouth and shovelled them in.

Their taste and texture caused her to shudder and gag. Impossible to chew or to swallow. She reached for the champagne bottle, tore off the stopper, tilted it to her lips and washed the noxious mouthful down. The wine still fizzed and bubbled. It was important not to start

575

vomiting. She drank more champagne, rinsing out her mouth as though she'd just endured a tiresome session at the dentist.

An amusing thought came to mind. How smart to do it with champagne. Like being poisoned by an oyster or run over by a Rolls-Royce. What else was smart? She'd once heard of somebody's mother who'd died of a heart attack in the Food Hall at Fortnum & Mason. Presumably she'd been laid out . . .

Her mind wandered. There really wasn't time to sit here, remembering that poor dead lady.

. . . laid out by some kindly swallow-tailed gentleman; stowed away behind the jars of Larks' Tongues in Aspic . . .

She stopped to jerk off her high-heeled sandals and, straightening, felt her head reel as though some person had struck her a blow on the back of the neck. There is, she told herself with some deliberation, no time to lose. She shed her coat, left it lying, got to her feet, and walked the little distance that separated her from the loch. The stones were agony beneath her bare feet, but somehow it was a detached sort of agony, as though it were happening to another person.

The loch was cold, but no colder than other times, other remembered summers, other midnight swims. Here, the shore shelved steeply. A step and she was ankle-deep, another, and she was up to her knees. The filmy skirts of her dress dragged heavy with the weight of the water. Another step. And another, and that was it.

She plunged forward, out of her depth, and the water closed over the top of her head. She surfaced, gasping and spluttering for air. Her long wet hair clung to her naked shoulders, and she began to swim, but her arms felt feeble, and her legs were shrouded and tangled in layers of sodden chiffon. She could perhaps kick them free, but she was too tired . . . always too tired . . . to make the effort.

More restful, surely, just to float with the tide.

The hills were blurred now, but they were there, and that was comforting.

Always tired. I'll just have a little toes-up.

She saw, with grateful wonder, the night sky filled with stars. She laid back her head to gaze at these, and the dark water flowed over her face.

31

Saturday the Seventeenth

It was five-thirty in the morning when Archie Balmerino looked at his watch, realised the time, and heaved himself reluctantly out of the armchair in which he had been sitting, placidly sipping the last of the malt whisky, and having a crack with young Jamie Ferguson-Crombie.

The party was over. There was no sign of Isobel or the rest of his house guests, the band had gone home, and the marquee was deserted. Only from the disco did the music still emanate and, glancing in, he observed two or three couples drooping around in the darkness, and looking as though they had fallen asleep on their feet. Nor was there any evidence of his hosts. From the kitchen could be heard voices, and he debated as to whether he should go and search for Verena, and then decided against it. It was time to head for home, and he would write his heartfelt thanks in a bread-and-butter letter the following morning.

He went out of the house, down the steps, set off in the direction of the car-park. The night had lightened, and the sky faded to grey. Dawn was not far off. It occurred to him then that perhaps he would find no form of transport waiting. The others, maybe returning to Croy in dribs and drabs, might well have forgotten all about Archie, and left nothing for him to drive. But then he saw Isobel's minibus standing in the middle of the field in lonely state, and knew that she had not forgotten him, and was filled with gratitude for her thoughtfulness.

He drove away from Corriehill. The Roman candles had burned themselves out, and the fairy lights had been extinguished. He knew that he was mildly tipsy, but, for some reason, felt totally clear-headed. He drove slowly, with concentrated care, only too aware that in the unlikely event of being stopped by the police, he hadn't a hope in hell of cheating the breathalyser. On the other hand, if he did meet a policeman, it would probably be young Bob McCrae from Strathcroy, and the last thing Bob would want to do would be to wheel the Laird in on a drunk-and-driving charge.

Dreadfully wrong; but one of the perks and privileges, he reflected wryly, of local gentry.

It had been a good party. He had enjoyed every moment of it. Seen a lot of old friends, made a lot of new ones. Drunk some excellent whisky, and eaten a splendid breakfast of bacon and eggs and sausages and black pudding and mushrooms and tomatoes and toast. Black coffee, too. Which was probably why he was feeling so wakeful and sparky.

All he had had to miss out on was the dancing. But he had taken great pleasure in watching some of the reels and listening to the toe-tapping music. The only time he had felt a little wistful was during the Duke of Perth. The Duke of Perth was the dance when, by tradition, your wife was your partner, and it had been a little galling to see Isobel being whirled off her feet by another man. No matter, she and Archie had shunted their way a couple of times around the floor of the disco, and very romantic and satisfactory it had been too, cheek to cheek, just like the old days.

The sun was edging its way over the eastern horizon as he turned into the front drive of Croy and mounted the hill. The sweep in front of the house was empty of cars. No Land-Rover. Jeff, good fellow that he was, must have put it away in the garage.

579

He climbed out of the minibus and went indoors. Physically, he was very tired, and his stump hurt like hell, as it always did when he had spent too much time standing about on it. Haltingly, holding the banister, he climbed the stairs. In their bedroom, he found Isobel, fast asleep. Evidence of her evening's finery lay across the floor in a little trail. Shoes, tights; the beautiful dark-blue dress abandoned on the sofa which stood at the foot of the bed. Her jewels on the dressing-table, her evening bag on a chair. He sat on the edge of the bed and watched her sleep. There was still mascara on her eyelashes, and her hair was tousled. After a bit, he stooped and kissed her, and she did not stir.

He left her sleeping, went into his dressing-room, and slowly took off his clothes. In the bathroom, he turned on the taps, and the boiling water filled the air with steam. He sat on the lavatory seat and unbuckled his harness and his tin leg, and laid the awkward contraption out on the bathmat. Then, with a cunning expertise perfected over the years, he lowered himself into the scalding bathwater.

He soaked for a long time, turning on the hot tap whenever the water threatened to turn chill. He soaped himself, shaved, washed his hair. He thought about going to bed, and then decided against it. The new day had begun, and he might just as well see it through.

Later, dressed in old corduroys and a polo-necked sweater of great age and thickness, he went back downstairs and into the kitchen. The dogs were waiting for him, ready for their morning outing. He put on the kettle. When he came indoors again he would make a cup of tea. He led the dogs across the hall and out through the front door. They raced ahead of him, over the gravel and off on to the grass, scenting the rabbits who had played there during the night hours. He stood at the top of the steps and watched them go. Seven o'clock and the sun was on its way up the sky. A pearly morning with only a little light cloud drifting about in the west. Birds were singing, and so still was it that he could hear the sound of a car, far below in the glen, starting up, and driving away through the village.

Another sound. Footsteps on the gravel, approaching from the direction of the cattle-grid. He looked and saw, in some surprise, the unmistakable figure of Willy Snoddy, his lurcher at his heels, walking towards him. Willy, as disreputable as ever in his tinker's cap and muffler and his old jacket with its bulging poacher's pockets.

"Willy," Archie went down the steps to meet him. "What are you up to?" A ridiculous question, because he knew perfectly well that Willy Snoddy, at this hour of the day, was up to only one thing, and that was no good.

"I . . ." The old man opened his mouth and then shut it again. His eyes met Archie's and veered away. "I . . . I was up at the loch . . . me and the dog . . . I . . ."

He stopped.

Archie waited. Willy put his hands in his pockets and took them out again. And then the dog, sensing something, began to whine. Willy swore at it and slapped its head, but a frisson ran down Archie's spine and he tensed, consumed by a dreadful apprehension.

"Well, what is it?" he demanded sharply.

"I was up at the loch . . ."

"You told me . . ."

"Just a wee troot or twa, ken . . ." But that wasn't what Willy had come to say. "Your Land-Rover. It's there. And the lady's furry coat . . ."

And then Willy did a strange thing. He took off his cap, an instinctive and touching gesture of respect. He held it, twisted in his hands. Archie had never seen him bareheaded before. Willy's cap was part of his image, and rumour had it that he even slept in it. But now he saw that Willy's head was balding, and his sparse white hair lay thin over the defenceless scalp. Without the rakish slant of his bonnet it was as though the graceless

581

poacher had been disarmed; no longer the well-kent villain, slouching about the place with his pockets full of ferrets, but simply an old countryman, uneducated and at a total loss, struggling to find the words to tell the untellable.

"Lucilla."

The voice came from a long way off. Lucilla decided to ignore it.

"Lucilla."

A hand on her shoulder, gently shaking.

"Lucilla, darling."

Her mother. Lucilla groaned, buried her head in the pillow. Slowly awoke. She lay for a moment and then rolled on to her back and opened her eyes. Isobel was sitting on the edge of her bed, her hand on Lucilla's T-shirted shoulder.

"Darling. Wake up."

"I am awake," Lucilla mumbled. She yawned and stretched. Blinked once or twice. "Why did you wake me up?" she asked resentfully.

"I'm sorry."

"What time is it?"

"Ten o'clock."

"Ten o'clock. Oh Mum, I wanted to sleep until lunch."

"I know. I'm sorry."

Lucilla slowly came to. The curtains had been drawn back, and morning sunlight slanted into the far corner of her room. She looked at her mother with sleepy eyes. Isobel was dressed, wearing a pullover and a Husky, but her hair was untidy, as if she had not found time to do more than run a comb through it, and her expression seemed strained. But then, she would be tired. Lacking sleep. They had none of them got to bed before four o'clock.

But she was not smiling. Was not her usual self.

Lucilla frowned. "Is something wrong?"

"Darling, I had to wake you. And yes, something is wrong. Something's happened. It's very sad. I have to tell you. You've got to try to be brave." Lucilla's eyes widened in apprehension. "It's Pandora . . ." Her voice faltered. "Oh, Lucilla, Pandora is dead . . ."

Dead. Pandora *dead*? "No." The instinctive reaction was one of denial. "She can't be."

"Sweetheart, she is."

Lucilla was now awake, all trace of drowsiness shattered by shock. "But when?" Noel Keeling had driven Pandora home from the dance. "How?" She imagined Pandora, like a wraith, not breathing, still, on her bed. A heart attack, perhaps.

But not dead. Not Pandora.

"She drowned herself, Lucilla. We think she drowned herself . . ."

"Drowned herself?" The implications were too horrifying to take in.

"In the loch. She took Dad's Land-Rover. She must have driven herself up the road. Right past Gordon Gillock's house, but the Gillocks never heard a thing. The gates of the deer-fence were bolted shut. She must have shut them behind her."

Pandora drowned. Lucilla thought of Pandora somewhere in France, skinny-dipping in a deep and fast-flowing river, swimming against the current, calling to Jeff and Lucilla that it was lovely, the water was lovely, why didn't they come in?

Pandora drowned. Bolting the heavy gates behind her. Surely that in itself was proof that she had not taken her own life? Surely no one, under such circumstances, would painstakingly trouble to close the deer-gates.

No.

"It must have been an accident. She would never, never have killed herself. Oh, Mum, not *Pandora* . . ."

"It wasn't an accident. We hoped it was. That she'd

583

come home from the dance, and taken it into her head to go for a swim. It was just the sort of dotty decision that she was quite capable of taking. An impulsive whim. But by the loch they found her mink coat and her sandals; and an empty sleeping-pill jar, and the last of a bottle of champagne.''

And the last of a bottle of champagne. The last of the wine. Like a final, terrible celebration.

'' . . . and when we went to her room, there was a letter for Dad.''

Lucilla knew then that it was true. She was dead. Pandora had drowned herself. She shivered. An old cardigan lay on a chair beside her bed. She sat up, reached for it, wrapped it around her shoulders. She said, ''Tell me what happened.''

Isobel took Lucilla's hands in her own. ''Willy Snoddy was up at the loch early, all set to lift a few trout out with the first rise. He'd walked up from the village with his dog. He saw the Land-Rover parked by the boathouse. And then her coat, lying on the bank. He thought, like us, that perhaps someone had just gone for a midnight swim. And then he saw her body, washed up against the sluice-gates.''

''I can't *bear* it for him. Poor old man.''

''Yes. Poor Willy. But for once in his life he did the right thing, and came straight to Croy to find Archie. By then it was seven o'clock, and Dad was out with the dogs. He never went to bed after the dance. Just took a bath and dressed again. And he was out with the dogs, and he saw Willy coming, and Willy told him what he'd found.''

Only too clearly, Lucilla could imagine the scene. She thought about her father, and then could not think about him, because Pandora was his sister, and he had loved her, and longed for her to come home to Croy. And she had come, and now she was gone for ever.

She said, ''What did Dad do?''

''I was still sleeping. He woke me. We went along to

584

Pandora's room, and she'd broken her bottle of scent in the bathroom basin. She must have knocked it over. The basin was filled with broken glass, and the smell filled the room, overpowering, like a sort of drug. So we drew back the curtains and threw open all the windows, and then we thought we must look for some sort of clue. We didn't have to look very far because she'd left an envelope on the desk, and there was a letter for Dad inside."

"What did it say?"

"Not very much. Just that she was sorry. And . . . something about money. Her house in Majorca. She said she was tired and she couldn't go on fighting any longer. But she didn't give any reason. She must have been so unhappy, and none of us knew. None of us had the slightest suspicion, the least idea of what was going on in her mind. If only I'd known. I should have been more perceptive, more sympathetic. I might have been able to talk to her . . . to help . . ."

"How could you? You mustn't for a moment blame yourself. Of course you didn't know what Pandora was thinking. Nobody could ever know what she was thinking."

"I thought we were close. I thought that I was close to her . . ."

"And you *were*. Just as close as any woman could be to Pandora. She loved you, I know. But I don't think she ever wanted to get too near to people. I think that was her defence."

"I don't know." Isobel, clearly, was distraught and bewildered. "I suppose so." Her grip on Lucilla's hands tightened. "I have to tell you the rest." She took a deep and steadying breath. "After we found the letter, Dad rang the police in Relkirk. He explained what had happened, and the difficulties of the location, the road to the loch. They sent, not an ambulance, but a police Land-Rover, with a four-wheel drive. And the police doctor came with it. Then they drove on up to the loch . . ."

"Who went?"

"Willy. And Dad. And Conrad Tucker. Conrad went with them. He was up and about by then, and he offered to go with Dad. So kind of him, such a kind man, because Archie didn't want me to go, and I couldn't bear the thought of his being on his own."

"So where are they now?"

"They're not yet back from Relkirk. They were going to take her – the body – there, to the Relkirk General. I suppose to the mortuary."

"Will there have to be an inquest?"

"Yes. A fatal-accident inquiry."

A fatal accident. The words had the chilling ring of officialdom about them. Lucilla imagined the courtroom, the cold and objective words of evidence and conclusion. Then newspapers, with accounts of the incident. Some old, blurred photograph of Pandora's lovely face. The headlines. "Death of Lord Balmerino's Sister."

The inevitable publicity, she knew, would be the final horror. "Oh, poor Dad."

Isobel said, "People always tell you, 'This will pass. Time will heal.' But at times like this one doesn't seem to be able to think more than a moment ahead. This is now. And it feels insupportable. There are no words of comfort."

"I can't take it in. It's all so *pointless*."

"I know, my darling. I know."

Isobel's voice was soothing, but Lucilla was not soothed. Instead, her distress blew up in an outburst of indignation. "It's all such a *waste*. Why did she have to? What on earth drove her to take such a step?"

"We don't know. We have no idea."

The little explosion of anger flickered and then died. Lucilla sighed. She said, "Does anybody else know? Has anybody been told?"

"There's really nobody to tell. Except Edmund. And Vi. I expect Dad will ring Edmund when he gets back from Relkirk. But Vi mustn't be told over the telephone.

586

Somebody will have to go and see her and break the news. Too great a shock for an old lady . . ."

"What about Jeff?"

"Jeff's downstairs in the kitchen. He appeared about five minutes ago. I'm afraid I'd forgotten all about him, and the poor man didn't get much of a welcome. Coming down to breakfast and being faced with such news. And there wasn't even any breakfast, because I hadn't got around to cooking anything. I think he's frying something up for himself right now."

"I must go and be with him."

"Yes. I think he could do with a little company."

"When will Dad and Conrad be back?"

"I suppose about half past ten or eleven. They'll be ravenous too, because there wasn't time to feed them before they left. I'll make them something when they come. And meantime . . ." She got to her feet. "I'm going to start clearing the dining room. The table's still laden with all the remains of dinner last night."

"It seems a lifetime ago, doesn't it? Why don't you leave it? Jeff and I will do it later, or we'll get Agnes back from the village . . ."

"No, I want something to do. Women are so much luckier than men. At ghastly times like this, they can always find something to occupy their hands, even if it's only scrubbing the kitchen floor. Washing glasses and polishing silver will fit the bill very nicely . . ."

Lucilla was alone. She got out of bed and dressed, pulling on jeans and a sweater. Brushed her hair, went to the bathroom to clean her teeth and wash her face. A flannel soaked in scalding water, pressed to her eyes and cheeks. The heat cleansed, refreshed, cleared her head. She ran downstairs.

Jeff sat at one end of the kitchen table, with a mug of

coffee and a plateful of bacon and sausages. He looked up as she came in, swallowed his mouthful, laid down his knife and fork, and got to his feet. She went to him, and he took her in his arms, and for a little while they just stood there. It felt warm and safe in his strong embrace, and the thick sheepy wool of his sweater smelled friendly and familiar. From the pantry came the sound of running water, the clink of glass. Isobel was already hard at work.

He didn't say anything. After a little they drew apart. She smiled her gratitude for his comfort, and reached for a chair and sat, leaning her elbows on the scrubbed table.

"Do you want something to eat?" he asked.

"No."

"You'd feel better with something inside you."

"I couldn't eat."

"A cup of coffee then." He went to the Aga and filled a mug, and brought it over and set it down before her. Then he sat down again and went on with his sausages.

She drank a little coffee. She said, "I'm glad we had that time with her."

"Yeah."

"I'm glad she came home with us."

"It was good." He reached over and took her hand. He said, "Lucilla, I think I should go."

"*Go*?" She stared at him in some dismay. "Go where?"

"Well, this isn't a very good time for your mother and father to have a stranger around the place . . ."

"But you're not a stranger . . ."

"You know what I mean. I think I should pack my bag and take myself off . . ."

"Oh, but you *can't* . . ." The very suggestion filled Lucilla with panic. "You can't leave us all . . ." Her voice rose, and he shushed her gently, aware of Isobel's presence beyond the open door, and not wishing his hostess to overhear the conversation. Lucilla dropped her voice to a furious whisper. "You can't leave me. Not

588

now. I need you, Jeff. I can't cope with everything being so utterly awful. Not on my own."

"I feel I'm intruding."

"You're not. You're *not*. Oh, please, don't go."

He looked into her beseeching face and relented.

"Okay. If I can be any help, I'll certainly stay around. But whatever happens, I can't stay for long, because the beginning of October I have to go back to Australia."

"Yes. I know. But don't talk about leaving us just yet."

He said, "If you like, you could come with me."

"Sorry?"

"I said, if you like you could come with me. To Australia, I mean."

Lucilla's fingers closed around her coffee-mug. "What would I do there?"

"We could be together. Go on being together. There's plenty of room in my parents' house. And I know they'd make you very welcome."

"Why are you asking me now?"

"Seems a good idea."

"And what would I do in Australia?"

"Whatever you wanted. Get a job. Paint. Be with me. We could find some place of our own."

"Jeff . . . I don't quite know what you're asking of me."

"I'm not asking anything. Just extending an invitation."

"But . . . it . . . it isn't like that, is it? You and me. Not for ever."

"I thought we could maybe find out."

"Oh, *Jeff*." A lump grew in her throat, and she felt her eyes swim with tears, which was ridiculous because she hadn't cried for Pandora, but now she was in floods just because Jeff was being so sweet, and asking her to go back to Australia with him, and because she wasn't going to go, because she wasn't in love with him, and knew that he was not in love with her.

"Come on, now, don't cry."

589

She reached for a tea-towel and unhygienically blew her nose on it.

"It's just that you're being so dear. And I would love to come. But not just now. Just now I have to stay here. Besides, I don't think you really want me hanging around when you go home. You're going to have enough to think about without me under your feet. Going back to work, getting on with your life, settling down . . ." She blew her nose again and managed a watery smile. ". . . and, somehow, I don't think I'm quite the right person for you. When you do settle down, and you will, it will be with some lovely Australian girl. A suntanned sheila with a fat bum and big tits . . ."

He cuffed her gently over the ear. He said, "That's not funny." But he was smiling.

She said, "It was the nicest invitation I've ever had in my life. And you are the dearest man I've ever met. And we've had just the best time ever since that day we met in Paris. And one day I *will* come to Australia, and I shall expect a huge welcome from you, red carpets, ticker tapes, the full treatment. But right now . . . and for ever . . . I can't come."

"Well, if you change your mind, the offer's open . . ."

He had finished his breakfast, laid the knife and fork together on the plate, and carried it over to the sink. From the dining room now could be heard the sounds of hoovering. Jeff crossed the kitchen and closed the pantry door. He returned to the table and sat facing Lucilla.

He said, "I don't like to ask this and it's none of my business, but did Pandora leave any sort of letter?"

"Yes, she did. For Dad. On the desk in her room."

"Did she say why she was going to kill herself?"

"No. Apparently not."

"What does your mother think?"

"At the moment she's too distressed even to try to think."

"So there's no obvious reason?"

"None."

"How about you?"

"I have no opinion, Jeff." His silence caught her attention. "Why? Have you?"

"I just thought. I was thinking. Remember that guy we met our first day at the villa? Carlos Macaya?"

"Carlos?" That suave and handsome man with his charming manners and his notable wristwatch. "But of course." She could not imagine why she had not thought of him before. "Jeff. Do you think he might know something?"

"Probably not. But he was obviously very close to Pandora. Perhaps she confided. Told him something that we don't know . . ."

Lucilla remembered. Recalled that puzzling remark that Carlos had made to Pandora as he drove away from the villa . . . *Let me know if you change your mind*, he had said. And she had replied, *I shan't change my mind*. And Lucilla and Jeff had discussed the exchange, and decided that Carlos and Pandora had probably been referring to something quite trivial – a cancelled tennis match, or a rejected invitation.

"Yes. You're right. I think they were very close. Lovers, probably. Maybe he does know something . . ."

"Even if he doesn't, if they were so close, perhaps he should be told what's happened."

"Yes." It was a perfectly viable suggestion. "But how can we tell him?"

"Ring him up."

"We don't know his number."

"Pandora must have had an address book . . . what's the betting we'll find Carlos Macaya's number in it?'

"Yes. You're right. Of course."

"If we're going to put a call through, we'd better do it now, before your father and Conrad get back, and while your mother's occupied. Is there a telephone where we won't be disturbed . . .?"

591

"Nowhere. Except, perhaps, Mum's bedroom. We'll use the phone by her bed . . ."

"Come on then." He got to his feet. "We'll do it now."

Isobel was still hoovering. They went out of the kitchen and soft-footed up the carpeted stairs. Lucilla led the way along the passage to Pandora's bedroom. They went inside and she closed the door behind them.

The room, with its unmade bed and litter of feminine possessions, was cold. Every window was open, and the curtains ballooned in the breeze. And yet that perfume still hung like a pall; the smell of Poison.

Lucilla said, "I never knew, I could never make up my mind if I loved that scent or if I hated it."

"Why is it so strong?"

"She broke the bottle in her basin." She looked around her, saw the filmy dressing-gown tossed on the bed, Pandora's evening bag, the wardrobe full of her clothes, the brimming wastepaper basket, the crowded dressing-table, the odd shoes that lay about on the carpet.

The shoes, expensive Spanish leather, high-heeled, impractical, were somehow the most personal and poignant of reminders, because they could never have belonged to anybody but Pandora.

Lucilla closed her mind to them.

She said, "Her address book. Where would we find her address book?"

They found it on the desk, alongside the blotter. It was large and leather-bound, with Pandora's initials in gold, and endpapers of Florentine paper. Lucilla sat, ran her finger down the index, and opened it at the letter M.

Mademoiselle, Dress Shop.
Maitland, Lady Letitia.
Mendoza, Philip and Lucia.
Macaya . . .

592

Carlos Macaya. She sat very still, staring at the page. She did not speak.

After a bit, Jeff said, "Have you found it?"

"Yes."

"What's wrong?"

"Jeff." She looked up at him. "Jeff, he's a doctor."

"A doctor?" He frowned. "Let's see."

She pointed. "Here, 'Macaya, Dr Carlos and Lisa.' Lisa must be his wife. Jeff, do you think he was Pandora's doctor?"

"Most probably. We'll find out." He looked at his watch. "It's ten-thirty. It'll be about eight-thirty in Majorca. We'll call him at home. It's a Saturday morning. Most likely we'll get him at home."

With the address book in her hand, Lucilla got to her feet. They went out of Pandora's room and along to her parents' bedroom where, on this unreal and disorientated morning, yet another bed had not been made. The telephone sat on the bedside table. Jeff found the phone book and looked up the international code for Spain, and carefully, digit by digit, Lucilla dialled the long and complicated number.

A wait. Various clickings and buzzings. And then the ringing sound. She thought about the Majorca morning, the Mediterranean sunlight already warm, the sky clear with the promise of yet another hot and cloudless day.

"*Hola?*" A woman's voice.

"Mrs . . ." Something had gone wrong with Lucilla's throat. She cleared it and started again. "Mrs Macaya? Señora Macaya?"

"*Sí?*"

"I'm so sorry, but do you speak English?"

"Yes, a little. Who is this?"

"My name is Lucilla Blair." She willed herself to calmness, deliberately spoke slowly and clearly. "I am calling from Scotland. I want to talk to your husband. Is he there?"

"Yes, he is here. *Uno momento . . .*"

The phone was put down. Footsteps receded, tapping across a polished tiled floor. From a distance, Lucilla heard her call, "Carlos!" And then a few unintelligible sentences in Spanish.

She waited. She reached out her hand, and Jeff took it in his own.

He came. "Dr Macaya."

"Oh, Carlos, this is Lucilla Blair. Pandora Blair's niece. I met you at her house in August. I came with a friend from Palma and you were there drinking tea. Do you remember?"

"But of course I remember you. How are you?"

"I'm all right. I'm calling from my home in Scotland. Carlos, please forgive me, but were you Pandora's doctor?"

"Yes, I was. Why?"

"Because . . . I'm terribly sorry, but I'm afraid it's very sad news. Because she is dead."

He did not speak immediately. And then he said, "How did she die?"

"She drowned. She drowned herself. She took all her sleeping pills and then drowned herself. Last night . . ."

Another pause. And then Carlos Macaya said, "I see." Was that all he had to say?

"You don't seem very surprised."

"Lucilla, I am devastated by your news. But I am not completely surprised. I was very afraid that something like this might happen."

"Why?"

He told her.

Over the roar of the hoover, Isobel heard Archie's Land-Rover returning from Relkirk, the familiar sound of its old engine grinding up the hill from the village and then turning down into the avenue. She turned off the

594

hoover, and its din slowly died. Glancing through the tall window, she saw the Land-Rover trundle past, with Conrad at the wheel.

She left the hoover standing in the middle of the floor and went to meet them. Out through the front door, and down the steps on to the gravel. The two men were already alighting from the Land-Rover, Archie limping badly, which was never a good sign. She went to him and put her arms around him and kissed him. His face was cadaverous, grey with fatigue, and felt very cold.

She said, "You're back. Come."

She took his arm and Conrad followed them and they mounted the steps and went indoors. Looking at the American, Isobel saw that he too showed signs of strain. She put questions aside, and concentrated on practicalities.

"You must be exhausted, and hungry as well. I didn't cook anything because I was waiting for you to come, but it won't take a moment. You'll both feel better when you've got something inside you."

Conrad said, "That sounds like a fine idea," but Archie shook his head.

"Isobel, in a moment. I must telephone first. I must ring Edmund Aird, their telephone should have been fixed by now."

"Darling, that can surely wait . . ."

"No." He raised his hand. "I'd rather get it over. You two go ahead. I'll be with you in a moment."

Isobel opened her mouth to argue, and then thought better of it and stayed silent. Archie turned and slowly, painfully, walked away from them, down the hall, headed for his study. In silence, Conrad and Isobel watched him go, and heard the door close behind him.

They looked at each other. Isobel said, "I think he probably wants to be alone for a moment."

"That's understandable." Conrad wore a borrowed pair of green rubber boots and an old jacket of Archie's.

595

His head was bare, his eyes, behind the heavy glasses, filled with sympathy.

"Was it *very* awful?" she asked.

"Yes," he told her, and his voice was gentle. "Yes. It was very sad."

"Where did you find her?"

"Just where Willy said she'd be. By the sluice-gate."

"Did she . . ." She tried again. "I mean, how long had she been there?"

"Only a few hours."

"Yes." Only a few hours. Not long enough to change, swell, putrefy. "I'm glad Willy found her so soon. It was good of you to go with Archie, and bring him back again. I can't tell you how grateful I am . . ."

"It was the least I could do."

"Yes. There isn't really very much anybody can do, is there?"

"Not very much."

"No. Well . . ." The subject, for the moment, had run its course. Breakfast. "I'm sure you must be ravenous."

"I am. But first, if I may, I'll shed these boots and wash my hands."

"Of course. I'll be in the kitchen."

Lucilla and Jeff had disappeared, taken themselves off somewhere. Isobel found frying pan, more sausages, bacon, tomatoes, and eggs. She put bread in the toaster, made a fresh pot of coffee, laid two places at the table. By the time Conrad joined her, his breakfast was just about ready. She poured a cup of coffee and set it by his place.

"Drink it while it's hot. I just have to fry you an egg. How do you like it? Sunny side up? Isn't that what they say in America?"

"That's what they say. Isobel . . ."

She turned from the Aga. "Yes?"

"I think I should leave you this afternoon. You have enough to think about without extraneous guests hanging around the place."

She was horrified. "But I thought you weren't leaving until tomorrow!"

"I can call a taxi, get myself to Turnhouse . . ."

"Oh, Conrad, please don't feel you have to go . . ."

"This is not a time for visitors . . ."

"I don't think of you as a mere visitor. I think of you as a friend. And I would be very distressed if you felt you had to leave us a day early. But if *you* would prefer to do that, I shall quite understand."

"It isn't that I would prefer it . . ."

"I know. You're thinking of us. But you know, at the moment, it's good for us to have friends around. This morning, for instance. What would we have done without you? And I am certain that Archie will want you to stay. At least for one more night."

"If you really mean that, I would like to stay."

"I do really mean it. And when I said I think of you as a friend, I really meant that as well. You came as a stranger to Croy, and we none of us knew you or knew anything about you. But now, after just a few days, I feel as though we'd known you all our lives. I hope you'll come back again and visit us some other time."

"I'd like that. Thank you."

Isobel smiled. "And you can bring your little daughter. This is a good place for children."

"Watch out. I may take you up on that."

Isobel professionally broke the egg into the pan.

"When are you flying back to your little daughter?"

"On Thursday."

"And Virginia's coming with you?"

"No. Not now that Henry's home again. She's cancelling her flight, and calling her grandparents to explain. She and Edmund will maybe come out next spring, and we're all going to get together then."

"That's disappointing for her. But perhaps better. More fun to go on holidays with your husband." She stooped to take his plate out of the low oven, added the egg to the pile of goodies already on it, and then set the

597

lot in front of him. "Now you wrap yourself around that, as my son Hamish always says." She glanced at the clock. "What *is* Archie doing? I think I'll take him a cup of coffee. You don't mind being left on your own, do you?"

"No, I'm perfectly all right. And this looks like the best breakfast I've ever eaten."

"You've earned it," Isobel told him.

Archie sat at his desk, in his study, in his father's chair, and surrounded by his father's possessions. The room faced west, and so, on this bright morning, was sunless. For the moment, he was grateful for quiet and solitude. Deadened by fatigue and his own despair, he waited until such time as he could muster enough moral courage to pick up the telephone, dial the Balnaid number, and speak to Edmund Aird.

From the moment that Willy Snoddy had finally managed to find the words with which to relay his dreadful tidings, Archie had experienced the grip of a mental numbness that precluded all intelligent incentive. Somehow, like a sleepwalker in the throes of a nightmare, he had gone through the motions of doing what he knew had to be done.

Waking Isobel, having her there beside him, had been the first priority. Only with Isobel could he share his grief. Then, together, they had gone to Pandora's bedroom, disordered in characteristic fashion, as though she had, just that moment, gone from the room. It was Isobel who had drawn back the heavy curtains and opened all the windows to set free the suffocating odour of the spilled and wasted perfume. It was Isobel who had spied the envelope on the desk, and handed it to Archie.

And, together, they had read Pandora's final letter.

After that the inevitable, painful procedures. Ringing

the police, and the seemingly endless wait until the official vehicle, with the police doctor on board, arrived. The long drive to the loch, crawling with agonising slowness up the steep and bumpy track. The gruesome and heartbreaking operation of retrieving from the loch his dead sister's body.

The irony of the situation was his own hopelessness. No sooner, it seemed, had he come to terms with his memories of Northern Ireland than he was fated to be burdened by this new horror. The sight of Pandora, like a sodden doll, washed up beneath the sluice-gates. Her face bloodless, her wet hair wound, like silken cords, around her neck. Her white arms, thin and bleached as drifting twigs, the skirts of her dress tangled in a flotsam of broken branches and broken reeds.

How great it would be if the impossible were rendered possible, and he could blank the image from his mind's eye for ever.

He sighed, and drew her letter towards him. The thick blue paper embossed with the Croy address, and Pandora's scrawly handwriting, unformed as a child's. A ghost of a smile touched his lips, because he remembered how she had never bothered to learn to do anything properly, and at the end of the day, she still could scarcely write.

Friday evening.
My darling Archie. I once went to a funeral and a man got up and read something so nice, about dead people having just slipped away into the next room, and not being miserable nor sorry, but going on laughing at the same old jokes. If, by chance, you give me a lovely Christian funeral (and who knows, you may be so cross, you'll just toss me on to Isobel's compost heap), then it would be nice if somebody could read that about me.

599

He laid the letter down, and gazed unseeing, over his spectacles, at the opposite wall. The strange thing was that he knew exactly the passage that Pandora referred to. He knew it because he had read it aloud in church during the course of his own father's funeral service. (But Pandora did not know that, because Pandora had not been there.) And moreover, wishing to be word-perfect and not make a hash of his emotional duty, he had privately rehearsed the reading a number of times, and ended up knowing it by heart.

Death is nothing at all. It does not count. I have only slipped away into the next room. Nothing has happened. Everything remains exactly as it was. I am I, and you are you, and the old life that we lived so fondly together is untouched, unchanged. Whatever we were to each other, that we are still. Call me by the old familiar name. Speak of me in the easy way which you always used. Put no difference into your tone. Wear no forced air of solemnity or sorrow. Laugh as we always laughed at the little jokes that we enjoyed together. Play, smile, think of me, pray for me. Let my name be ever the household word that it always was. Let it be spoken without an effort, without the ghost of a shadow upon it. Life means all that it ever meant. It is the same as it ever was. There is absolute and unbroken continuity. What is this death but a negligible accident? Why should I be out of mind because I am out of sight? I am but waiting for you, for an interval, somewhere very near, just round the corner. All is well.

All is well.
But then old Lord Balmerino had not taken his own life.

Archie, I have been very practical and sensible and made a will, and left all my worldly goods to you.

600

Perhaps you should get in touch with my New York lawyer. He is called Ryan Tyndall and you'll find his address and telephone number in my address book. (He's terribly nice.) I know I've seemed to spend money like water, but there ought to be lots left in the Bank, as well as various Stocks and Bonds and even a little California Real Estate. And of course, the house in Majorca. You can do what you want with this, sell it or keep it. (Lovely hols. for you and Isobel.) But whatever you do, just be sure that dear Seraphina and Mario are all right.

I like to think that you will use some of this money to turn the stables or the barn into a workshop, start manufacturing your clever little wooden people, and sell them all over the world at a socking profit. I know you can do it. It just needs a bit of get-up-and-go. And if the business side of it seems a bit daunting, I am sure that Edmund would help and advise.

Darling, I'm so dreadfully sorry about all this. It's just that everything's suddenly become so complicated and such an effort and I haven't the energy to fight any longer. I was never much use at being steadfast and brave.

It's been a funny old life.

I adore you both and I leave you my love.

Pandora

I am sure that Edmund would help and advise.
Back to Edmund.

He thought of the other letter, safe in the drawer of this desk. He found the key, and unlocked the drawer, and took out that letter. The airmail envelope, creased and dog-eared, addressed to himself in Berlin; the postmark 1967.

He withdrew the two flimsy sheets, scrawled with the same immature handwriting. Unfolded them.

My darling Archie. It was such a lovely wedding and I hope you and Isobel are happy, had a lovely honeymoon and are happy in Berlin, but oh, I miss you so much. Everything is horrible, because everybody I love has gone away. I have got nobody to talk to. I can't talk to Mama and Pa because it's about Edmund. This doesn't surprise you, does it, because you must have known. I don't know how I never knew it, but I must have loved him for ever, because when I saw him again, the few days before the wedding, I suddenly realised that there never had been, nor could be, anyone else, ever again. And the ghastly, tragic, unbearable thing is that he's married somebody else. But we love each other. I can write it in big letters. WE LOVE EACH OTHER. But I'm not allowed to tell anybody because of him being married to Caroline and having the baby and everything. He has gone back to her, but he doesn't love her, Archie. He loves me, and I am without him, stuck here, and I need you so badly and you're in Berlin. He said that he would write but he's been gone for a month and I haven't heard a word, and I can't bear it and I don't know what to do. I know it's wrong to break up a marriage, but I'm not doing that, because I had Edmund long before she did. I know you can't do anything to help but I just had to tell someone. I never knew Croy could be so lonely and I'm horrible to Mama and Pa, and I can't help it. I can't stay here for ever, I think I shall go mad. There's only you I can tell. With lots of love and tears, Pandora.

Before, he had always found the adolescent despair immeasurably poignant. Now, in the light of the morning's tragedy, it took on an even graver significance. He covered his eyes with his hand. Behind him, the door opened.

"Archie."

It was Isobel. "I've brought you some coffee." He did not turn. She reached over his shoulder and laid the steaming, fragrant cup on the desk in front of him, and then put her arms around his neck, and stooped to press her warm cheek against his own.

"Why are you taking so long? What are you doing?"

"Just reading." He laid the letter down.

She hesitated and then said, "That's the letter Pandora sent you just after we were married."

"Yes."

"I didn't know you'd kept it. Why did you, Archie?"

"I didn't have the heart to tear it up and throw it away."

"So sad. Poor little girl. Have you telephoned Edmund yet?"

"No. Not yet."

"You don't know what to say, do you?"

"I don't know what to think."

"Perhaps she *was* still in love with him. Perhaps that's why she came home. And then she saw him again, with Virginia and Alexa and Henry, and she realised it was hopeless."

She was voicing his own fears, his own unspoken dreads. He could not have spoken them, and hearing Isobel say the words aloud, bringing their shared suspicions out into the open, filled him with loving gratitude for her fearless good sense. Because now they could talk about it.

"Yes," he admitted. "That's what I'm afraid of."

"She was such a little sorceress. Always enchanting. Generous and funny. But you know, Archie, she could be ruthless. If she wanted something, she could be ruthless to get it. If she set her heart on something, other people didn't matter."

"I know. It was our fault. We all spoiled her, indulged her . . ."

"I think it would have been impossible not to . . ."

"She was only eighteen when they had that affair.

603

Edmund was twenty-nine. He was married and he had a child. I know Pandora flung herself at him, but instead of backing off, he reneged on his responsibilities, threw them to the wind. She was like a fire, and he added his own potent fuel to that fire; the result was an explosion."

"Have you ever talked to Edmund about it?"

"No. Once, I could have. But not after that. He was the reason she ran away. He was the reason she never came back."

"You've never forgiven him, have you, Archie?"

"No. Not really." It was a bleak admission.

"Is that why you're hesitating now? Is that why you haven't rung him?"

"If all our conjectures are true, I would be unwilling to unload such a burden of guilt on to my worst enemy."

"Archie, that's not your – "

She stopped abruptly, raised her head to listen. From beyond the closed door could be heard footsteps coming down the hall.

"Mum!" It was Lucilla.

"We're in the study."

The door opened a crack. "Can I come in? I'm not disturbing you, am I?"

"No, of course not, darling. Come in."

Lucilla closed the door behind her. She looked as though she had been crying, but had dried her tears. Archie held out his arm to her, and she took his hand and bent to kiss his cheek. She said, "I am so dreadfully sorry." She sat on the edge of the desk, facing her parents. She said, "I've got something to tell you. And it's very sad, and I hope you won't be too distressed . . ."

"Is it about Pandora?"

"Yes. I've found out why she did it." Waiting, they watched their daughter. "You see . . . she had terminal cancer."

Her voice was quiet, but quite calm and firm. Isobel looked into Lucilla's face and saw there, behind the youthful features, a great inner strength, and knew that,

604

at nineteen, she had quite suddenly grown up. The child was gone for ever. Lucilla would never be her child again.

"Cancer?"

"Yes."

"How do you know?"

"When Jeff and I went to stay with her in Majorca, the afternoon we arrived, there was a man with her called Carlos Macaya. I told you about him, Dad. He was very attractive, and Jeff and I were convinced he was her current lover. But he wasn't. He was her doctor. It was Jeff who remembered him, and suggested that we ring him up, just in case he knew something that we didn't know. We found his name and his telephone number in her address book, and it was then that we realised that he was a doctor, and not just a friend. So we put the call through, to Majorca, and spoke to him. And he told us everything."

"Had he been taking care of her?"

"Yes. But I think he found it a fairly difficult and thankless task. He realised that something was wrong when she started getting so thin, but he had a hard time of it getting her to agree to a consultation. And even then, she wouldn't face up to reality or keep appointments. By the time he finally managed to get her into his surgery, she had sat on her illness for a long time. As well, he discovered a carcinoma on one of her breasts. He did a needle biopsy, and sent it off to the hospital in Palma for a pathology report. It was malignant, and may well have spread. So he went to see Pandora and tell her that she would have to have surgery, a mastectomy, and then a course of chemotherapy. That was what he was telling her the day Jeff and I turned up. But she flatly refused. She said that nothing would induce her to have surgery, and nothing would induce her to endure the subsequent treatment, radiation chemotherapy. He could give her no real hope of a total cure . . . the disease was too far along, I suppose . . . but he did tell her that

605

if she went her own way, her expectation of life was not very long."

"Was she in pain?"

"Some. She was taking medication. Quite strong drugs. That's why she was always so tired. I don't think she suffered a great deal, but of course, in time, it would have got very bad."

"Cancer." Archie said the word, and it had about it the toll of finality. The end. The double line drawn at the foot of a column of figures. "I never thought. I never had the faintest suspicion. But we should have guessed. There was nothing of her. We should have known . . ."

"Oh, Dad . . ."

"Why didn't she *tell* us . . . We could have helped . . ."

"No, you couldn't have helped. And she would never have told you. Don't you see, the last thing she wanted was for you and Mum to know. She just wanted to be back at Croy, and everything just the way it used to be. September. And parties, and little shopping sprees to Relkirk, and people coming and going and the house full of guests. No sadness. No talk of dying. And that's what you gave her. Verena's dance was the perfect, timely excuse for Pandora to come home and to accomplish what I think she had planned all along."

"Did the doctor know this?"

"Not for certain. But he did say that he would never have allowed her to make that journey through Spain and France if Jeff and I had not been with her."

"But he guessed what she had in mind?"

"I don't know. I couldn't ask. But I expect that he did. He knew her very well. And I think that he was very fond of her."

Archie said, "How could he have let her simply go away?"

"You mustn't blame Carlos, Dad. He did everything he could to persuade her to go to hospital, to try to make

606

her grasp her only chance, however slight. But she was simply adamant."

"So she came home to die?"

"Not just that. She came home to be with you, to be at Croy. To give us all a good time, and lovely presents, and to make us laugh. She came back to her childhood and the places she remembered and loved. The house, the glen, the hills, the loch. If you think about it, it was a very brave thing to do. But that doesn't make it any easier for you. I'm sorry. I've hated telling you. I just hope it makes it all a bit easier to understand." Lucilla fell silent, thinking about this. Then she said, and her voice, which had been so strong, suddenly wavered, "Not that understanding helps very much." Isobel saw her face crumple like a child's and tears fill her eyes and overflow and stream down her cheeks. "She was so sweet to Jeff and me . . . we had such a good time together . . . and now it feels as though a light has gone out of all our lives . . ."

"Oh, darling," Isobel could not bear it. She went to Lucilla, put her arms around her daughter's thin and heaving shoulders. "I know. I'm so sorry. And you've been so brave . . . but you're not alone, because we're all going to miss her. And I think we must be grateful that she did come home. How awful if we had never seen her again. You brought her back to us, even if it was only for just a little time . . ."

After a bit, Lucilla calmed down and stopped crying. Isobel gave her a handkerchief, and she blew her nose. She said, "I've already had one blub, and I'd hoped that was the last of it. You see, Jeff asked me to go back to Australia with him, and I'm not going to go. For some idiotic reason that made me cry as well . . ."

"Oh, Lucilla . . ."

"I'm going to stay home for a bit. If you and Dad can stand having me under your feet."

"I can't think of anything we would love more."

"Nor me."

607

Lucilla gave her mother a watery smile, blew her nose in a final sort of way, and got to her feet. She said, "I'll leave you two together. But, Dad, please come soon and eat some breakfast. You'll feel better then."

"I'll come," he promised her.

She went to the door. "I'll make certain those two greedy men haven't helped themselves to all the bacon." She smiled. "Don't be too long."

"I won't, my darling. And thank you."

She was gone, leaving Isobel and Archie with only each other. After a bit, Isobel left Archie's side and went over to the long window. Beyond lay the garden, the croquet lawn, and the squeaky old swing-seat. The sun had not yet reached the grass, and it was still damp with the night's dew. She saw the silver birches, their leaves turned to gold. Soon the leaves would drop, and the branches be stripped bare for the winter.

She said, "Poor Pandora. But I think I understand."

She looked up at the hills, the sky, and saw the rain-clouds looming, blowing in from the west. Sun at seven, rain at eleven. They had had the best of the day.

"Archie."

"Yes."

"This exonerates Edmund, doesn't it?"

"Yes."

She turned from the window. He was watching her. She smiled. "I think you should ring him now. And I think now is the time to forgive. It's all over, Archie."

Edie, breathless after her climb up the hill, hurried on her way along the lane that led to Pennyburn.

It seemed a funny thing to be doing on a Saturday. Saturday was one of the few days of the week that Edie kept to herself, seeing to her own little house, doing a bit of gardening if it was fine, clearing out cupboards, baking. This morning, because the sun had shone, she had pegged out a long line of washing, and then walked down the street to Mrs Ishak's, to get a few groceries and the daily newspaper. As well, she had bought a *People's Friend* and a box of chocolates for Lottie, because she had planned to catch the afternoon bus into Relkirk and go to visit her poor cousin. She felt badly about Lottie, but also a little annoyed, because Lottie had nicked her new lilac cardigan. The police couldn't have known, of course, that it wasn't hers, but Edie was determined to get it back. She'd give it a good wash before she wore it again. Poor Lottie. Maybe, as well as the magazine and the box of chocolates, Edie would pick a few Michaelmas daisies out of her garden to liven up the impersonal ward. Not that she'd get any thanks for her pains, but still, her own conscience would be eased. Just because things had gone so wrong for Lottie, one couldn't simply abandon the poor soul.

Everything nicely organised.

But then, just as she was heating up a pot of broth for her dinner, Edmund had stopped by to see her. He had come straight to Edie's from Pennyburn, and before that, from Croy. He'd brought with him terrible tidings, and after hearing these, all thoughts of Lottie had flown from Edie's head, and she was left with her day fallen to pieces. She had picked up the bits and put them together again; only now everything was a different shape. A strange feeling. Upsetting.

From time to time she read in the papers of some family, setting out on an innocent and enjoyable outing in the car, perhaps to see friends, or simply to enjoy the countryside, only to have their lives blown apart for ever by an accident; a pile-up on the motorway, with dead drivers at the wheel, and shattered vehicles this way and that, all over the road. She felt, now, as though she had been, if not involved, then witness to such a disaster, and was standing there surrounded by wreckage,

609

knowing only that there had to be something that she could do to help.

"I've told my mother," Edmund had said, "but she's alone. I asked her to come back to Balnaid for lunch, and to spend the day with us all, but she declined. She said that she just wanted to be on her own."

"I'll go to her."

"I would be grateful. If there is one person in the world she will want to be with, it's you."

So Edie had taken the pot of soup off the hob, and put on her coat and her walking shoes. Into her capacious bag she had put her spectacles and her knitting, then locked her house and set off for Pennyburn.

Now, she was there. She went in through the kitchen door. All was neat and tidy. Mrs Aird had washed her own breakfast dishes this morning, and put them all away. Even swept the floor.

"Mrs Aird!" She laid her bag on the table and, still wearing her coat, went through the hall and opened the sitting-room door.

She was there. Sitting motionless in her chair, staring at the unlit fire. Not knitting, not doing her tapestry, not reading the paper – just sitting. And the room, as well, felt chill. The morning, which had started so brightly, had clouded over, and without the warmth of the sun pouring through the windows, felt strangely comfortless.

"Mrs Aird."

Disturbed, Violet turned her head, and Edie was shocked, because for the first time in her life, she saw Vi as old, lost, confused; even infirm. For a moment her expression remained blank, as if she scarcely recognised Edie. And then, at last, her eyes brightened, and an expression of immeasurable relief filled her face.

"Oh, *Edie*."

Edie shut the door behind her. "Yes, it's me."

"But why are you here?"

"Edmund dropped by to see me. To tell me about

Pandora. What a thing to do. He said you were on your own. Could maybe do with a bit of company . . ."

"Only you, Edie. Nobody else. He wanted me to go back to Balnaid with him. So kind. But somehow I didn't feel quite up to it. I didn't feel strong enough. With one's children one always has to put on a brave face, and be the person who does the comforting. And somehow, I think I've just run out of the energy to comfort anybody. Just for the moment. I shall be better tomorrow."

Edie glanced about her. "It's awful cold in here."

"I suppose it is. I really hadn't noticed." Violet looked at the fireplace. "I was up quite early this morning. I got everything done. Cleaned out the ashes myself, and relaid the fire and everything. I've just not got around to lighting it."

"Won't take a moment." Edie unbuttoned her coat and laid it over a chair, then knelt on the hearthrug, lowering her bulk on to her well-padded knees, and reached for the box of matches. The paper caught. The sticks, the little pile of coal. The flames flickered.

Violet said, "I am sitting here filled with shame, Edie. We should have been more perceptive. We should have realised that Pandora was ill, perhaps dying. She was so dreadfully thin. Just skin and bone. We should have seen for ourselves that something was wrong. But I, for one, have been so taken up with my own family that I never gave Pandora a passing thought. Perhaps if I had been a little less self-absorbed, I would have sensed that all was not well." She sighed, and shrugged. "And yet, she was just the way she had always been. Beautiful, flirtatious, funny. Bewitching."

"She was always a wee character."

Edie reached for a couple of logs and set them on the brightly burning coals. Then, with some effort, she pulled herself up off her knees and settled down in the chair facing Violet. She was wearing her best tweed skirt and her Shetland cardigan with the bright colours around the neck, and her dear face was rosy from the effort of the long walk up the hill. With the fire burning, and Edie there, sitting on the other side of the hearthrug, Violet was warmed, and felt no longer quite so desolate.

"I hear," said Edie, in her gossiping voice, "it was Willy Snoddy who found her?"

"Yes. Poor Willy. I don't doubt he'll be drunk for days after such an experience."

"Cancer's a terrible thing. But to take your own life . . ." Edie shook her head. "I cannot understand a body doing such a thing."

"I think we have to understand, Edie, otherwise we shall never forgive her . . ."

". . . but the Balmerinos. And wee Lucilla. Did she not think of them?"

"I am sure that she did. And yet, perhaps, she never thought very much about anybody except herself. And she was so pretty, so attractive to men. Little love affairs were always the excitement of her life. To understand, we have to try to imagine her future as she obviously saw it. Ill, maimed by surgery, fighting the disease, losing all her lovely hair, rendered unappealing." The fire now was crackling up the chimney. Violet spread her hands to its comfort. "No. She couldn't have coped with all of that, Edie. Not on her own, the way she was."

"And Edmund?" Edie asked.

They had no secrets from each other. It was a good feeling.

"You saw Edmund, Edie."

"But he didn't say very much."

"He said a great deal to me. He is naturally devastated about Pandora, as we all are, but, I think, no more than the rest of us. And I believe that now he will be all right, because he has Virginia and Alexa and Henry. Darling little Henry. And, who knows, perhaps even Noel Keeling as well. I have a feeling that, very soon, Noel is going to be a member of the family."

"Is that right?"

"Just a feeling, Edie. We'll have to wait and see. As

612

well, Edmund told me that he is going to take a bit of a holiday. He wants to spend some time with Virginia and Henry, and of course he must be around to support Archie Balmerino through the next few days. There will be so much to be seen to. A fatal-accident inquiry is inevitable, and then, after that hurdle has been taken, the funeral, and all the sad and heart-rending tying-up of the loose ends. Afterwards, when it is all over, he and Archie plan to go fishing together, to Sutherland perhaps for a little while. And you know, that fills me with satisfaction. I have always loved Edmund, Edie, but just lately I have found myself not liking him very much. But I think that everything has changed. Perhaps he's realised at last that the little things in life are sometimes infinitely more important than the big ones. And it's a comfort to know that out of this appalling and unnecessary tragedy has come at least one good thing. Which is that Archie and Edmund are good friends again, just the way they used to be."

"It's taken a long-enough time," Edie pointed out, down-to-earth as ever, and not afraid to speak her mind. "Over twenty years."

"Yes. But then Edmund behaved very badly. We both, I think, know that."

Edie was silent for a little, and then made her only comment. "Alexa's mother. She was a very cold lady."

It was not much of an excuse, but her loyalty to Edmund filled Violet with gratitude. "Well, you should know, Edie. You lived with them in London. You knew them both, perhaps better than any of us."

"A nice-enough girl, but cold."

On the mantelpiece, Violet's little gilt clock struck the hour. One o'clock. Edie glanced up at it in some surprise. The time had flown by.

"Just look at that," she said. "One o'clock already. You must be needing something to eat. I'll go into the kitchen and see what I can find. There was a pot of beef stew I left in the larder yesterday. I'll give it a heat-up.

613

There's plenty for the two of us. So what do you say? We'll have it here, on a tray, by the fire."

"I can't think of anything I'd like more. And perhaps a glass of sherry to cheer ourselves up?" Edie clicked her tongue in disapproval, but she was smiling. She rose to her feet and made for the door. "Oh, and Edie, you will stay with me, won't you? We'll spend the afternoon together, and talk about the old days."

"I'd like that," Edie told her. "I've no mind to be on my own today. And I've brought my knitting."

She went. A moment later Violet heard her clattering dishes in the kitchen, opening and shutting the larder door. Comforting and companionable sounds. She stood up, holding on to the mantelpiece until the stiffness left her knees. Behind the clock, she saw the invitation, which had stood there for so many weeks. Curling now, and a bit dusty from the smoke that rose from the fire.

Mrs Angus Steynton
At Home
For Katy

She took it out from behind the clock, and read it for the last time, then tore it into pieces and dropped the scraps on to the flames. They flared, burned, shrivelled to ashes, were gone.

She went to the door that led out into the garden, opened it, descended the steps and walked out on to the sloping lawn. With the sun gone, and the sky filled with sailing grey clouds, it felt very cold. Colder than it had been all autumn. September was passing, and soon the winter gales would begin.

She made her way to the foot of the garden, to stand by the gap in the hedge, looking out to the south, over the incomparable view. The glen, the river, the distant hills: sunless today, sombre, but beautiful. Always so beautiful. Never would she tire of them. Never would she tire of life.

She thought about Pandora. And Geordie. Geordie, wherever he was, would keep an eye on Pandora. She thought about Edie, and for the first time the dreadful possibility occurred to her that perhaps her dearest friend would die before she herself died, and she would be left with no contemporary, no person to turn to, to give her comfort; no person to talk to, remembering together the days that were gone.

She said a prayer. "I know I am a dreadfully selfish woman, but please let me go before Edie goes, because without her I don't think I could cope with living. I don't think I could cope with growing old."

A sound caught her ear. High up, far beyond the blowing clouds. A distant honking and gabbling, both haunting and familiar. The wild geese, returning. The first she had heard since they had flown away north at the end of the spring. She gazed up into the sky, screwing up her eyes, searching for them. And then the clouds momentarily parted, and she glimpsed the birds, a single skein, beating their way south, the vanguard of the many thousands already on their way.

They were early. They had left late, and were returning early. Perhaps it was going to be very cold. Perhaps it was going to be a hard winter.

But she had survived hard winters before, and this one would be no worse. In fact, it would be better, because she felt, in some strange way, that her family had been restored to her, and she knew that, together, the Airds were strong enough to withstand whatever the fates chose to hurl in their direction. That was the most important thing. Togetherness. There lay the greatest strength. Her family, putting the past behind them, and never losing sight of the fact that, beyond the winter, a new spring was already on its way.

"Mrs Aird."

She turned, saw Edie standing there at the open door.

615

She had tied one of Violet's aprons on over her good skirt, and her white hair blew in the breeze. "Come away in and get your dinner."

Violet smiled, raised her hand. "Coming, Edie." She walked . . . slowly at first and then briskly . . . back up the sloping lawn towards her house. "I'm coming."

ANOTHER VIEW

1

In Paris, in February, the sun was shining. At Le Bourget
Airport, it gleamed coldly from an ice blue sky, and this was
reflected, with much dazzle, from the runways, still wet after a
night's rain. From inside, the day looked inviting, and they had
been tempted out on to the terrace, only to discover that the
bright sun held no real warmth and the gay breeze that blew the
wind socks out at right angles had an edge to it like a knife.
Defeated, they withdrew to the restaurant to wait for Emma's
flight to be called, and sat now, at a small table, drinking black
coffee and smoking Christopher's Gauloises cigarettes.

Unselfconscious, absorbed in each other, they nevertheless
attracted a certain amount of attention. This was inevitable, for
they made an arresting pair. Emma was tall and very dark.
Her hair, worn back off her forehead and held in place by a
tortoiseshell band, fell in a straight black tassel to below her
shoulder-blades. Her face was not beautiful – it was too clearly
boned and strongly built for beauty, with a straight nose, and a
square and determined chin. But these features were redeemed
and given much charm by large and unexpectedly grey-blue
eyes, and a wide mouth, which, although it was quite capable of
drooping disconsolately if she did not get her own way, could
grin, from ear to ear, like a boy's, when she was happy. She

1

was happy now. She wore, on this cold bright day, a bitter green trouser suit and a white polo-necked sweater that made her face look very brown, but her sophisticated appearance was off-set by the mass of luggage with which she was surrounded, and which appeared, to the casual passer-by, to have been salvaged from some disastrous act of God.

It was, in fact, the accumulation of six years of living abroad, but no one was to know this. Three suitcases, at enormous expense, had already been checked in. But there was still a canvas grip, a Prisunic paper carrier sprouting long French loaves, a basket bulging with books and records, a raincoat, a pair of ski-boots and an enormous straw hat.

Christopher surveyed it all, speculating, in a detached and unbothered fashion, as to how it was all going to be conveyed into the aeroplane.

"You could wear the hat and the ski-boots and the raincoat. That would make three less things to carry."

"I've already got a pair of shoes on, and the hat would blow off. And the raincoat's disgusting. I look like a displaced person in it. I can't think why I bothered to bring it at all."

"I'll tell you why. Because it will be raining in London."

"It may not be."

"It always is." He lit another Gauloise from the stub of the first. "Another good reason for staying in Paris with me."

"We've had this out a hundred times. And I'm going back to England."

He grinned without rancour. He had been teasing her. When he smiled, his yellow-flecked eyes slanted upwards at the corners, and this, combined with his lanky, idle body, gave him a curiously feline appearance. His clothes were colourful, casual, faintly Bohemian. Narrow cord trousers, battered chukka boots, a blue cotton shirt worn over a yellow sweater, and a suède

2

jacket, very old and shiny about the elbows and the collar. He looked French, but in fact he was as English as Emma and even related to her in a tenuous way, for, years ago, when Emma was six and Christopher ten, her father, Ben Litton, had married Hester Ferris, Christopher's mother. The arrangement had lasted, with only the smallest degree of success, for eighteen months, before it finally fell apart, and now Emma remembered it as the only time in her life when she had ever known anything vaguely approaching an ordinary family life.

It was Hester who had insisted on buying the cottage at Porthkerris. Ben had owned a studio there for a number of years, since long before the war, but its conveniences were non-existent, and after one look at the squalor in which she was expected to live Hester went straight out and acquired two fisherman's cottages, which she proceeded, with taste and charm, to convert. Ben was disinterested in any such activity, so it became very much Hester's house, and it was she who insisted on a kitchen that would work, and a boiler that would heat water, and a big fireplace blazing with driftwood, a heart to their home, a focal point around which the children could gather.

Her intentions were splendid, her methods of carrying them out not so successful. She tried to make allowances for Ben. She had married a genius, and she knew his reputation and she was prepared to turn a blind eye to his love affairs, his disreputable companions and his attitude towards money. But in the end, as so often happens in quite ordinary marriages, she was defeated by the small things. By meals, forgotten and uneaten. By trivial bills left unpaid for months. By the fact that Ben preferred to drink in the local pub, rather than in a civilised fashion, at home, with her. She was defeated by his refusal to have a telephone, to own a car; by the stream of apparent derelicts whom he invited to sleep on her sofa; and finally by his total inability to show at any time any sort of affection.

She left him at last, taking Christopher with her, and sued almost immediately for a divorce. Ben was delighted to let her have it. He was delighted, too, to see the back of the small boy. The two of them had never got on. Ben was jealous of his male priority, he liked to be the only man of importance in his household, and Christopher, even at ten years old, was an individual who refused to be ignored. Despite all Hester's efforts, this antagonism endured. Even the boy's good looks, which Hester truly believed would charm Ben's painter's eye, had the very opposite effect, and when Hester tried to persuade Ben to do a portrait of him, he refused.

After their departure, life at Porthkerris slid easily back into its old seamy routine. Emma and Ben were cared for by a series of messy females, either models or student painters, who moved into and through and out of Ben Litton's life with the monotonous regularity of a well-ordered cinema queue. The only thing they had in common was an adulation of Ben, and a lofty disregard for housekeeping. They took as little notice of Emma as possible, but, in fact, she did not miss Hester as much as people thought she would. She had become weary – as Ben was – of being organised, and perpetually buttoned into clean clothes, but Christopher's going left a great void in her life which refused to be filled. For a little, she had mourned for him, tried to write him letters, but had not dared to ask Ben for his address. Once, in the desperation of loneliness, she ran away to find him. This entailed walking to the station and trying to buy a ticket to London, which seemed as good a place as any to look for him. But she had only one and ninepence in the world, and the stationmaster, who knew her, had taken her into his office which smelt of paraffin lamps and the black railway coal he burnt in his grate, and had given her a cup of tea out of an enamel pot, and walked her home. Ben was working, and had not noticed her absence. She never tried to look for Christopher again.

When Emma was thirteen, Ben was offered a teaching fellowship at the University of Texas for two years, which, without thought of Emma, he instantly accepted. There was a small hiatus while Emma's future was discussed. When taxed with the question of his daughter, he announced that he would simply take her to Texas with him, but someone – probably Marcus Bernstein – persuaded Ben that she would be better off away from him, and she was sent to a school in Switzerland. She stayed in Lausanne for three years – never returning to England, and then went to Florence to study Italian and Renaissance Art, for another year. At the end of this time, Ben was in Japan. When she suggested that she should join him, he replied by telegram. ONLY SPARE BED OCCUPIED BY CHARMING GEISHA GIRL WHY DONT YOU TRY LIVING IN PARIS.

Philosophically, for she was now seventeen and life was no longer surprising, Emma did as he suggested. She found herself a job with a family called Duprés who lived in a tall scholarly house in St Germain. The father was a professor of medicine, and the mother a teacher. Emma cared for their three well-behaved children, taught them English and Italian, and took them, in August, to the modest family villa at La Baule, and all the time waited patiently until Ben should return to live in England. He stayed in Japan for eighteen months, and when he did return it was by way of the United States, where he spent a month in New York. Marcus Bernstein flew out to meet him there, and it was typical that Emma learned the reason for this reunion, not from Ben himself, nor even from Leo, who was her usual source of information, but from a long and fully illustrated article in the French *Réalités*, which dealt with a newly built

5

Museum of Fine Arts in Queenstown, Virginia. This museum was a memorial created by his widow, to a rich Virginian called Kenneth Ryan, and the opening of the Art Section was to be a retrospective exhibition of the paintings of Ben Litton, ranging from his pre-war landscapes, right through to his latest abstractionisms.

Such an exhibition was an honour and a tribute, but inevitably suggested a painter to be revered, a Grand Old Man of the arts. Emma, studying one of the photographs of Ben, all angles and contrasts, dark-tanned skin and jutting chin and snowy hair, wondered how he felt about such veneration. He had been a rebel all his life against convention, and she could not imagine him tamely submitting to being a Grand Old anything.

"But what a man!" said Madame Duprés, when Emma showed her the photograph. "He is very attractive."

"Yes," said Emma, and sighed, because that had always been the trouble.

With Marcus, he returned to London in January, and went straight back to Porthkerris to paint. This was confirmed by a letter from Marcus. The day the letter arrived, Emma went to Madame Duprés and gave in her notice. They tried to coax, cajole, bribe her into changing her mind, but she was adamant. She had scarcely seen her father for six years. It was time they got to know each other again. She was going back to Porthkerris, to live with him.

In the end, because they had no option, they agreed to letting her go. Her flight was booked, and she started to pack, throwing out some of the accumulated possessions of six years, and cramming the rest into a variety of battered and much-travelled suitcases. But even these were sadly inadequate, and Emma was eventually driven to going out and buying herself a basket, a huge French marketing basket that would accommodate the number of awkwardly-shaped objects that refused to go into anything else.

It was a grey and cold afternoon, two days before she was due to fly home. Madame Duprés was at home, so Emma, explaining her errand, left the children with her, and went out alone. To her surprise, she found that it was raining, lightly, in a chill drizzle. The cobbled pavements of the narrow street shone with wet, and the tall bleached houses stood quiet and closed against the murk, like faces which give nothing away. From the river a tug hooted, and a solitary gull hung, high above, in the mist, screaming dismally. The illusion of Porthkerris was suddenly more real than the reality of Paris. The resolve to return, which had for so long been in the back of her mind, was crystallised now into the impression that she was already there.

This street would lead – not to the busy Rue St Germain, but out on to the harbour road, and it would be flood tide, the harbour full of grey sea and bobbing boats, and a heavy swell running out beyond the north pier, the Atlantic crested with white horses. And there would be familiar smells – fish from the market, and hot saffron buns from the baker's; and all the little summer shops would be shuttered and closed for the season. And back at the studio Ben would be working, hands mittened against the cold, the brilliance of his palette a scream of colour against the sweep of grey cloud that was framed by his towering north window.

She was going home. In two days, she would be there. The rain was wet on her face and all at once she felt that she could not wait, and this sense of happy urgency made her run, and she ran all the way to the little épicerie in the Rue St Germain, where she knew she would be able to buy the basket.

It was a tiny shop, fragrant with fresh bread and garlic-flavoured sausage meat, with onions strung like white beads from the ceiling, and jars of wine, which the local workmen bought by the litre. The baskets hung at the door, strung together and suspended by a single piece of rope. Emma did not dare untie it and choose herself a basket in case the whole lot fell to the pavement, so she went into the shop to find someone to do it for her. There was only the fat woman with the mole on her face, and she was busy with a customer, so Emma waited. The customer was a young man, fair haired, his raincoat streaked with damp. He was buying a long loaf and a pat of country butter. Emma eyed him and decided that, from the back at least, he looked attractive.

"*Combien?*" he said.

The fat woman did a sum with a stub of pencil. She told him. He felt in his pocket and paid, turned, smiled at Emma and made for the door.

And there he stopped. With his hand against the edge of the door, he swung slowly around, to take a second look. She saw the amber eyes, the slow, incredulous smile.

The face was the same, the familiar, boy's face on the unfamiliar man's body. With the illusion of Porthkerris so near and so strong, it seemed that he was simply an extension of that illusion, a figment of her own highly-stimulated imagination. This was not him. This could not be . . .

She heard herself say "Christo," and it was the most natural thing in the world to call him by the name that only she had ever used. He said, quietly, "I simply don't believe it," and then he dropped his parcels and held out his arms and Emma fell into them, pressed close against the shiny, wet front of his raincoat.

They had two days to spend together. Emma told Madame Duprés, "My brother is in Paris," and Madame, who was kind-hearted, and had, anyway, resigned herself to being without Emma, set Emma free to spend them with Christopher. They used up these two days in slowly walking the streets of the city;

8

hanging over the bridges to watch the barges slip away below them, bound for the south and the sun; sitting in the thin sunshine and drinking coffee at the small, round iron tables, and when it rained, taking refuge in Notre Dame or the Louvre, perched on the stairs beneath the Winged Victory and always talking. They had so much to ask and so much to tell. She learned that Christopher, after a number of false starts, had decided to become an actor. This was much against his mother's wishes – after eighteen months of Ben Litton she had had enough of artistic temperaments to last her for the rest of her life – but he had stuck to his guns and even managed to get a scholarship to RADA. He had worked for two years in a repertory theatre in Scotland, had moved, unsuccessfully, to London, done a little television work, and then had been diverted by an invitation from an acquaintance, whose mother owned a house in St Tropez.

"St Tropez in the winter?" Emma could not help asking.

"It was then or never. We'd never have been offered it in the summer."

"But wasn't it cold?"

"Freezing. Never stopping raining. And when the wind blew all the shutters rattled. It was like some ghastly film."

In January he had returned to London to see his agent, and had been offered a twelve-month contract with a small repertory company in the south of England. It was not the sort of work he wanted, but it was better than nothing, and he was running out of money, and it was not too far from London. The job, however, did not start until the beginning of March, and so he had returned to France, finished up in Paris, and finally met Emma. Now, it irked him that she was returning so soon to England, and did everything he could to make her change her mind, postpone her flight, stay in Paris with him. But Emma was adamant.

"You don't understand. This is something that I have to do."

"It's not even as though the old boy asked you to go. You're just going to get in his way, and interfere with all his amorous adventures."

"I never have before – interfered, I mean." She laughed at his stubborn expression. "Anyway, there's no point my staying, if you're coming back to England next month."

He made a face. "Wish I wasn't. That lousy little theatre at Brookford. I shall get lost in the jungle of fortnightly rep. Besides, I'm not due there for two weeks. Now if you would only stay in Paris . . ."

"No, Christo."

"We could rent a tiny attic. Think of all the fun we could have. Bread and cheese every night for supper and lots of rough red wine."

"No, Christo."

"Paris in the Spring . . . blue skies and blossom and all that rot?"

"It isn't spring yet. It's still winter."

"Were you always so unco-operative?"

But still she would not agree to staying, and in the end he admitted defeat. "Very well, if I can't persuade you to keep me company, I shall simply behave in a very well-bred and British way, and come and see you on to your plane."

"That would be perfect."

"It's very self-sacrificing of me. I hate saying goodbyes."

Emma agreed with this. Sometimes, it felt as if she had been saying goodbye to people all her life, and the sound of a train moving out of a station, gathering speed, was enough to reduce her to tears. "But this goodbye is different."

"How is it different?" he wanted to know.

"It isn't really goodbye. It's *au revoir*. A stepping stone between two hellos."

10

"My mother and your father are not going to approve."

"It doesn't matter if they approve or not," said Emma. "We've found each other again. For the moment, that's all that matters."

Above them, the loudspeakers gave a click, began to speak with a feminine voice.

"Ladies and gentlemen. Air France announce the departure of their flight Number 402 for London . . ."

"That's me," said Emma.

They stubbed out their cigarettes, stood up, began to gather in the baggage. Christopher took the canvas grip and the Prisunic paper carrier, and the great bulging basket. Emma slung the raincoat over her shoulder, carried her handbag, the ski-boots and the hat.

Christopher said, "I wish you'd wear the hat. It really would complete your ensemble."

"It would blow off. Not to say look funny."

They went downstairs, crossed the expanse of shining floor towards the barrier where a small queue of passengers was already forming.

"Emma, are you going down to Porthkerris today?"

"Yes, I'll get the first train I can."

"Have you got any money? Pounds, shillings and pence, I mean?"

She had not thought of this. "No. But it doesn't matter. I'll cash a cheque somewhere."

They joined the queue behind a British businessman who carried only his passport and a slim brief-case. Christopher leaned forward.

"Oh, sir, I wonder if you could help."

The man swung round, and found to his surprise Christopher's face only inches from his own. Christopher was wearing his sincere expression. "I am sorry, but we're in rather a predicament. My sister's returning to London, she's not been home for six years, and she has such a lot of hand luggage, and she's only just recovered from a serious operation . . ."

Emma remembered Ben saying that Christopher never told a small lie if he could get away with a bigger one. Looking at him as he came out with this outrageous fabrication, she decided that he had chosen his career wisely. He was a wonderful actor.

The businessman, thus approached, could make no excuse.

"Well, yes, I suppose . . ."

"It's more than kind of you . . ." The canvas grip and the carrier with the bread went under one arm, the basket in the other along with the slim brief-case. Emma felt sorry for him.

"It's just till we get on to the plane . . . it is so kind of you, and you see my brother isn't coming with me . . ."

The queue moved forward, they had reached the barrier.

"Goodbye, darling Emma," said Christopher.

"Goodbye, Christo." They kissed. A brown hand whipped away her passport, riffled the pages, stamped it.

"Goodbye."

They were divided by the barrier, by the formalities of the French government, by other travellers, surging forward.

"Goodbye."

She would have liked him to wait and see her safely on to the plane, but even as she waved, flapping the sun hat, he had turned, and was walking away from her, the light shining on his hair, and his hands buried deep in the pockets of his leather coat.

2

In London, in February, it was raining. It had started to rain at seven o'clock in the morning, and it had rained without ceasing ever since. By half past eleven only a handful of people had visited the exhibition, and those enthusiasts, one suspected, had simply come in order to get out of the rain. They shed wet raincoats and dripping umbrellas, and stood around, bemoaning the weather before they had even bought themselves a catalogue.

At eleven-thirty, the man came in to buy a picture. He was an American, staying at the Hilton, and he asked to see Mr Bernstein. Peggy, the receptionist, took the card which he proffered, asked him politely if he would mind waiting for a moment, and then came through to the office to speak to Robert.

"Mr Morrow, there's an American outside by the name of . . ." she glanced at the card. "Lowell Cheeke. He was here a week ago, and Mr Bernstein showed him the Ben Litton of the deer, and thought he was going to buy it, but he went off without making up his mind. Said he wanted to mull it over."

"Have you told him Mr Bernstein's in Edinburgh?"

"Yes, but he can't wait. He's going back to the States the day after tomorrow."

"I'd better see him," said Robert.

He stood up, and while Peggy went to open the door and

13

invite the American in, did a swift spring-clean of his desk, squaring some letters, emptying the ash-tray into the wastepaper basket and shoving the basket under the desk with the toe of his shoe.

"Mr Cheeke," said Peggy, announcing the visitor like a well-trained parlourmaid.

Robert came around the desk to shake hands.

"How do you do, Mr Cheeke? I'm Robert Morrow, Mr Bernstein's partner. I am sorry, I'm afraid he's in Edinburgh today, but perhaps I could help you . . . ?"

Lowell Cheeke was a short, powerful-looking individual in a dacron raincoat and a narrow-brimmed hat. Both of these were very wet, indicating that Mr Cheeke had not arrived in a taxi. He began divesting himself, with Robert's help, from these sodden garments, and revealed an uncrushable navy blue terylene suit and a pin-striped nylon shirt. He wore rimless spectacles and behind them his eyes were cool and grey, and it was impossible to assess any sort of potential either financial or artistic.

"Thank you very much . . ." said Mr Cheeke. "What a terrible morning . . ."

"It doesn't look as though it's going to let up either . . . A cigarette, Mr Cheeke?"

"No, thank you, I no longer smoke." He coughed self-consciously. "My wife made me give it up."

They grinned at this female idiosyncrasy. The grin did not reach Mr Cheeke's eyes. He reached for a chair and settled himself into it, hitching a polished black shoe across his knee. He already looked very much at home.

"I was in here a week ago, Mr Morrow, and Mr Bernstein showed me a painting by Ben Litton – your receptionist probably told you."

"Yes, she did, the deer painting."

"I'd like to see it again if I may. I'm returning to the States the day after tomorrow, and I have to make up my mind."

"But of course . . . !"

The picture waited for Mr Cheeke's decision, resting, where Marcus had left it, against the wall of the office. Robert drew the padded easel into the centre of the room, turned it towards the light, and gently lifted the Ben Litton into position. It was a large picture, an oil of three deer in a forest. Light filtered through the barely-suggested branches, and the artist had used a quantity of white which gave the work an ethereal quality. But its most interesting feature was the fact that it had been painted, not on stretched canvas, but on jute, and the coarser weave of this textile had blurred the artist's brush, like the outlines of an action photograph taken at high speed.

The American swung his chair into position, and turned the cold beam of his spectacles on to the painting. Discreetly, Robert removed himself to the back of the room so as not to obtrude in any way upon Mr Cheeke's own assessment, and his own view of the painting was obscured by the round crew-cut head of his potential customer. Personally, he liked the picture. He was not a fan of Ben Litton's. He thought his work affected and not always easy to understand – a reflection, perhaps, of the artist's own personality – but this swift sylvan impression was a thing to be looked at and lived with and never tired of.

Mr Cheeke got out of his chair, moved up to the painting, examined it minutely, backed away once more, and finished up leaning against the edge of Robert's desk.

"Why do you suppose, Mr Morrow," he said, without turning round, "that Litton was inspired to paint it on burlap?"

The word burlap made Robert want to laugh. He longed to say irreverently, *Probably had an old sack lying around* but Mr Cheeke did not look as though he would appreciate irreverence.

15

Mr Cheeke was here to spend money – always a serious business. Robert decided then that he was buying the Litton as an investment, and he hoped it would pay him off.

He said, "I'm afraid I have no idea, Mr Cheeke, but it does give a most unusual quality to the work."

Mr Cheeke turned his head to send Robert a cold smile over his shoulder.

"You are not as well informed on such aspects as Mr Bernstein."

"No," said Robert. "I'm afraid I'm not."

Mr Cheeke relapsed once more into contemplation. The silence settled and lasted. Robert's own concentration had begun to wander. Small sounds intruded. The ticking of his own wristwatch. A murmur of voices from the other side of the door. The thunderous rumble, like distant surf, that was Piccadilly traffic.

The American sighed gustily. He began to feel in his pockets, one by one, searching for something. A handkerchief, perhaps. Some change for his taxi ride back to the Hilton. His attention had strayed. Robert had not convinced him that the Litton was worth buying. He was going to make some excuse and go away.

But Mr Cheeke was simply searching for his pen. When he turned round, Robert saw that he already held his cheque book in the other hand.

Their business finally completed, Mr Cheeke relaxed. He became quite human and even took off his glasses and stowed them away in a tooled leather case. He accepted the offer of a drink, and he and Robert sat for a little, with two glasses of sherry, and talked about Marcus Bernstein and Ben Litton, and the two or three paintings which Mr Cheeke had purchased on his last visit to London, with which to form, with his latest acquisition, the nucleus of a small private collection. Robert told him about the retrospective Ben Litton exhibition which was being held in

16

Queenstown, Virginia, in April, and Mr Cheeke made a note of it in his diary, and then they both stood up, and Robert helped Mr Cheeke into his raincoat, and gave him his hat, and they shook hands.

"I've enjoyed meeting you, Mr Morrow, and doing business with you."

"I hope we'll see you next time you come to London."

"Most certainly I shall pay you a visit . . ."

Robert held the door open and they moved out into the Gallery. Bernstein's were showing, that fortnight, a collection of bird and animal paintings by an obscure South American with an unpronounceable name, a man of humble origins, who had somehow, sometime, incredibly, taught himself to paint. Marcus had met him last year in New York, had been instantly impressed by his work, and invited him then and there to stage a London exhibition. Now, his brilliant pictures lined the straw-green walls of the Bernstein Gallery and on this gloomy morning seemed to fill the room with the verdancy and sunshine of a more salubrious climate. The critics had loved him. Since the exhibition opened ten days ago, the Gallery had never once been empty, and within twenty-four hours there was not a picture that had not been sold.

At this moment, however, there were only three people in the Gallery. One of them was Peggy, neat and unobtrusive behind her kidney-shaped desk, busy with the proofs of a new catalogue. Another was a black-hatted man, stooped as a crow, doing a slow round of inspection. The last was a girl, who sat, facing the office door, on the circular buttoned sofa in the middle of the room. She wore a bright green trouser suit and was surrounded by luggage, and appeared to have wandered into Bernstein's under the mistaken impression that it was the waiting-room of a railway station.

Robert, with considerable self-possession, managed to behave as if she was not there. Together he and Mr Cheeke moved across the thick carpet towards the main door, Robert's head bent to catch the last of Mr Cheeke's small talk. The glass doors opened and swung shut behind them, and they were swallowed into the gloom of the dismal morning.

Emma Litton said, "Is that Mr Morrow?"

Peggy looked up. "That's right."

Emma was not used to being ignored. The single swift glance had made her feel uncomfortable. She wished that Marcus was not in Edinburgh. She crossed her legs and then uncrossed them again. From outside came the sound of the departing taxi. In a moment, the glass door opened, once more, and Robert Morrow came back into the Gallery. He did not make any comment, simply put his hands in his pockets, and calmly regarded Emma and her attendant chaos.

She decided that she had never, in her life, seen a man who looked less like an art dealer. His was the sort of face that, groggy and unshaven, is helped from a small sailboat at the end of a single-handed circumnavigation; or, darkly goggled, looks down from the peak of a previously unconquered mountain. But here, in the precious and rarefied atmosphere of the Bernstein galleries, he did not fit at all. He was very tall, wide-shouldered, long-legged; all this emphasised – and yet made incongruous – by his smoothly-tailored dark grey suit. In his youth his hair might have been red, but the years had tamed it to a tawny brown, and in contrast his grey eyes seemed pale as steel. He had high cheek-bones and a long, stubborn jaw, and she was diverted by the discovery that such a collection of features could be so attractive, and then remembered that Ben always averred that the character of a man lies, not in his eyes, where emotions are fleeting and can always be masked, but in the physical shape of his mouth, and this man's mouth was wide, with a jutting lower lip, and looked now as though it was trying, hard, not to laugh.

The silence became uncomfortable. Emma tried a smile. She said "Hello!"

For enlightenment, Robert Morrow turned to Peggy. Peggy was amused. "This young lady wants to see Mr Bernstein."

He said, "I am sorry, he's in Edinburgh."

"Yes, I know, so I've been told. The thing is, I only wanted him to cash me a cheque." He looked more puzzled than ever. Emma decided it was time to explain. "I'm Emma Litton. Ben Litton's my father."

His puzzlement cleared. "But why on earth didn't you say so? I am sorry, I had no idea." He came forward. "How do you do . . ."

Emma stood up. The straw hat, which had been on her knee, floated to the carpet and lay there, adding to the confusion which she had already wrought to the elegantly designed room.

They shook hands. "I . . . there wasn't any reason why you should know who I was. And I'm terribly sorry about all this stuff, but you see I haven't been home for six years, so there's bound to be quite a lot."

"Yes, I can see that."

Emma was embarrassed. "If you can just cash me a cheque, I'll take it all out of your way again. I only want enough to get back to Porthkerris. You see, I forgot to get any sterling when I was in Paris, and I've run out of traveller's cheques."

He frowned. "But how did you get this far? From the airport, I mean?"

"Oh." She had already forgotten. "Oh, there was a kind man on the plane, he helped me to carry my stuff on, and off

19

again at London, and he lent me a pound. I'll have to send it back. I've got his address here . . . somewhere.'' She felt vaguely in pockets, but could not find the man's card. ''Well, anyway, I've got it somewhere.'' She smiled again, hoping to disarm him.

''And when are you going down to Porthkerris?''

''There's a train at twelve-thirty, I think.''

He glanced at his wrist-watch. ''You've missed that. When's the next?''

Emma looked blank. Peggy broke into the conversation in her usual polite and practical fashion. ''I think there's one at two-thirty, Mr Morrow, but I can check.''

''Yes, do that, Peggy. Would the two-thirty be all right for you?''

''Yes, of course. It doesn't matter what time I arrive.''

''Is your father expecting you?''

''Well, I wrote him a letter and told him I was coming. But that doesn't mean he's *expecting* me . . .''

He smiled at this. ''Yes. Well . . .'' He glanced at his watch again. It was twelve-fifteen. Peggy was already on the telephone, inquiring about train times. His eyes returned to the turmoil of suitcases. In a feeble effort to improve the situation, Emma stooped and picked up her sun hat.

He said, ''I think the best thing would be to get all this out of the way . . . we'll pile it up in the office, and then . . . Have you had anything to eat?''

''I had some coffee at Le Bourget.''

''If you catch the two-thirty, there's time for me to give you lunch before you go.''

''Oh, you don't have to bother.''

''It's no bother. I have to eat anyway and you might as well eat with me. Come along now.''

20

He picked up two of the suitcases, and led the way into the office. Emma gathered up as much as she could carry, and followed him. The deer painting was still on the stand, and she saw it at once and was diverted.

"That's one of Ben's."

"Yes, I just sold it . . ."

"To the little man in the raincoat? It's good, isn't it?" She continued to admire it, while Robert toted the remainder of her luggage. "Why did he paint it on sacking?"

"You'd better ask him when you see him tonight."

She turned and grinned at him over her shoulder. "Influenced, do you think, by the Japanese school?"

"I wish," said Robert, "I'd thought of saying that to Mr Cheeke. Now, are you ready for lunch?"

He took an enormous black umbrella out of a stand, and stood aside for Emma to go out through the door ahead of him, and they left Peggy to hold the fort, sitting in a gallery restored once more to its usual ordered calm, and they went out into the rain and walked together, beneath the black umbrella, shouldering their way through the lunch-hour jostle of Kent Street, London, W1.

He took her to Marcello's where he normally lunched if he was not expected to entertain some important expense-account customer. Marcello was an Italian who ran a small upstairs restaurant, two streets from Bernstein's, and a table was perpetually reserved for either Marcus or Robert, or both of them, on the odd occasion when they were able to lunch together. It was a modest table, in a quiet corner, but today when Robert and Emma came up the stairs, Marcello took one look at her, with her long tassel of black hair, and her green trouser suit, and suggested that they might prefer to sit in the window.

Robert was amused. "Would you like to sit in the window?" he asked Emma.

"Where do you usually sit?" He indicated the small corner table. "Well, why don't we just sit there?"

Marcello was charmed by her. He led the way to the smaller table, held Emma's chair for her, gave them each an enormous menu written in dubious purple ink and went to fetch two glasses of Tio Pepe while they decided what they were going to eat.

Robert said, "My stock with Marcello will have gone up. I don't think I've ever brought a girl here for lunch."

"Who do you usually bring?"

"Just myself. Or Marcus."

"How is Marcus?" . . . her voice was warm.

"He's well. He'll be sorry to have missed you I know."

"It's my fault. I should have written and told him I was coming. But as you've probably realised, we Littons aren't very good at letting anybody know about anything."

"But you knew Ben had gone back to Porthkerris."

"Yes. Marcus wrote and told me that. And I know all about the retrospective exhibition, because I read an article on it in *Réalités.*" She smiled wryly. "Being the daughter of a famous father does have some compensations. Even if he never does anything except send telegrams, you can usually read up what is happening to him in some paper or other."

"When did you last see him?"

"Oh," she shrugged. "Two years ago. I was in Florence, and he stopped off on his way to Japan."

"I didn't know you went through Florence when you went to Japan."

"You do if you happen to have a daughter living there." She put her elbows on the table, and rested her chin in her hand. "I don't suppose you even knew Ben had a daughter."

"Yes, of course I did."

"Well, I didn't know about you. I mean, I didn't know Marcus

22

had a partner. He was still on his own when Ben went to Texas and I was bundled off to Switzerland.''

"It was about that time that I joined Bernstein's.''

"I . . . I never knew anyone who looked less like an art dealer. Than you, I mean.''

"Perhaps that's just because I'm not an art dealer.''

"But . . . you just sold that man Ben's painting.''

"No,'' he corrected her. "I simply accepted the cheque. Marcus had already sold it to him a week ago, but even Mr Cheeke didn't realise that.''

"But you must know something about painting.''

"Now, I do. One couldn't work with Marcus for all these years and not have some of his boundless knowledge rub off. But I'm basically a business man, and that's why Marcus asked me to join him.''

"But Marcus is the most successful business man I know.''

"Exactly, and so successful that the whole venture of the Gallery grew too big for him to handle on his own.''

Emma continued to regard him, a slight frown between her thickly-marked brows.

"Any more questions?''

She was not disconcerted. "Were you always a very close friend of Marcus?''

"What you really mean is, why did he take me into the firm? And the answer is that Marcus is not only my partner, but my brother-in-law as well. He married my older sister.''

"You mean Helen Bernstein is your sister?''

"You remember Helen?''

"But of course. And little David. How are they? You'll send them my love, won't you? You know I used to go and stay with them when Ben came up to London and there wasn't anyone to leave me with at Porthkerris. And when I went to Switzerland, it was Marcus and Helen who put me on to the plane, because Ben had already gone to Texas. Will you tell Helen I'm home, and that you gave me lunch?''

''Yes, of course I will.''

''Do they still have that little flat in the Brompton Road?''

''No, as a matter of fact, when my father died, they moved in with me. We all live in our old family house, in Kensington.''

''You mean you all live together?''

''Together and apart. Marcus and Helen and David live on the first two floors, and my father's old housekeeper lives in the basement, and I roost in the attics.''

''Aren't you married?''

Momentarily, he looked put out. ''Well, no, I'm not.''

''I was sure you'd be married. You have a very married look about you.''

''I don't quite know how to take that.''

''Oh, it wasn't meant in a derogatory fashion at all. It's really quite a compliment. I only wish Ben had that look about him. It would make life so much easier for all concerned. Especially me.''

''Don't you want to go back and live with him?''

''Yes, of course I do, more than anything. But I don't want it to be a failure. I was never very good at coping with Ben, and I don't suppose I'll be any better now.''

''Then why are you going?''

''Well . . .'' Under Robert Morrow's cool grey regard, it was difficult to be coherent. She picked up a fork and began to make patterns with it on the white damask cloth. ''I don't know. You only have one family. If people belong to each other, they should at least be able to live together. I want to have something to remember. When I'm old I want to be able to remember that once, even if it was only for a few weeks on end, my father

24

and I were making some sort of a life together. Does that sound crazy?"

"No, it doesn't sound crazy, but it sounds as if you might be disappointed."

"I learned all about being disappointed when I was a little girl. It's a luxury I can well do without. Besides, I only plan to stay until it becomes painfully obvious that we cannot stand each other's company for another hour."

"Or," said Robert gently, "until he prefers some other person's company."

Emma's head came up, her eyes a sudden furious blaze of blue. She was, in that instant, her father at his most unscrupulous, when there was no retort too cruel or too cutting to be made. But her anger provoked no reaction, and after a cold pause, she looked down again, and continued to draw patterns on the tablecloth, and only said, "All right. Until then."

The small tension was broken by the return of Marcello bringing their sherry and ready to take the order. Emma chose a dozen oysters and fried chicken; Robert, more conservatively, a consommé and a steak. Then, taking advantage of the interruption, he tactfully changed the subject.

"Tell me about Paris. How was it looking?"

"Wet. Wet and cold and sunny all at once. Does that convey anything to you?"

"Everything."

"You know Paris?"

"I go over on business. I was there last month."

"On business?"

"No, on my way back from Austria. I had three weeks' splendid ski-ing."

"Where did you go?"

"Obergurgl."

"So that's why you're so brown. That's one of the reasons you don't look like an art dealer."

"Perhaps, when my tan fades, I shall look more authentic and be able to command higher prices. How long did you spend in Paris?"

"Two years. I shall miss it. It's so beautiful, and doubly so now all the buildings have been cleaned. And somehow, at this time of the year, there's that special feeling in Paris. That the winter's nearly over and the sun's just a day or so away and it's going to be spring again . . ."

And buds unfolding, and the scream of gulls, swooping over the chopped brown waters of the Seine. And barges, strung like necklaces, slipping away beneath the bridges, and the smell of the Metro, and garlic, and Gauloises. And being with Christopher.

All at once it became important to talk about him, to speak his name, to reassure herself of his existence. She said, casually, "You never met Hester, did you? My stepmother? At least for eighteen months she was my stepmother."

"I know about her."

"And about Christopher? Her son? Do you know about Christopher? Because, quite by chance, Christopher and I met up again in Paris. Just two days ago. And he came, this very morning, and saw me off at Le Bourget."

"You mean . . . you just bumped into each other . . . ?"

"Yes, we really did . . . in a grocer's shop. It could only happen in Paris."

"What was he doing there?"

"Oh, filling in time. He'd been to St Tropez, but he comes back to England in March to join some repertory theatre or other."

"He's an actor?"

"Yes. Didn't I tell you that? There is just one thing . . . I'm not going to say anything to Ben. You see, Ben never liked Christopher, and I don't think Christopher lost any love over him. To be truthful, I expect they were a little jealous of each other. But there were other things as well, and Ben and Hester didn't exactly part company on the best of terms. I don't want to start off by having a row with Ben about Christopher, so I'm not going to say anything. At least not right away."

"I see."

Emma sighed. "You've got a very stuffy expression on your face. You obviously think I'm being underhand."

"I don't think anything of the sort. And when you've finished making patterns on the tablecloth, your oysters have arrived."

By the time they had finished lunch and drunk their coffee, and Robert had paid the bill, it was half past one. They got up from the table, and said goodbye to Marcello, and collected the big black umbrella and went downstairs. They walked back to Bernstein's, asked the doorman to get Emma a taxi.

"I'd come with you and put you on to the train, but Peggy has to go out and get herself some lunch."

"I'll be all right."

He took her into the office and unlocked the safe.

"Will twenty pounds be enough?"

She had already forgotten her reason for coming to the Gallery in the first place. "What? Oh, yes, of course . . ." She began to feel for her cheque book, but Robert stopped her.

"Don't bother. Your father has a sort of petty cash account with us. He's always running out of small change when he's in London. We'll put your twenty pounds down to that."

"Well, if you're sure . . ."

"Sure I'm sure. And, Emma, there is one other thing. The man who lent you the pound. Somewhere you have his address.

27

If you find it and give it to me now, I'll see he gets the pound back again.''

Emma was amused. Searching for the card, finding it at last, entangled with a French bus ticket and a book of matches, she began to laugh, and when Robert asked her what was so funny, she simply said, ''How well you know my father!''

3

It stopped raining at tea-time. There was a subtle lifting of the atmosphere, a freshness in the air. An errant shaft of sunlight even found its way into the Gallery, and by five-thirty, when Robert locked up his office, and went out to join the rush hour torrent of home-going humanity, he found that a small breeze had got up and blown the clouds away, leaving the city to sparkle beneath a pale, pellucid blue sky.

It was somehow more than he could bear to plunge into the subterranean stuffiness of the tube, so he walked as far as Knightsbridge, and then got on a bus and rode the rest of the way home.

His house, in Milton Gardens, was separated from the busy artery of the Kensington High Street by a maze of small streets and squares, a pleasant neighbourhood of miniature, early-Victorian houses, cream-painted, and with bright front doors and small gardens that in summer bloomed with lilac and magnolia. The streets had wide pavements where nannies pushed prams and small, well-dressed children walked to their expensive schools and the local dogs were rigorously exercised. After this, Milton Gardens came as something of a let down. It was a terrace of large and shabby houses, and Number Twenty-three, which was Robert's – the centre house, and crowned with the main pediment of the terrace – quite often looked the shabbiest. It had a black front door, and two dried-up bay trees in tubs, and a brass letter-box that Helen always meant to polish, but quite often forgot. The household cars were parked at the pavement's edge – a big dark-green Alvis coupé which was Robert's, and a dusty red Mini which was Helen's. Marcus did not own a car because he had never found time to learn how to drive.

Robert went up the steps, feeling in his pocket for his latch-key, and let himself in. The hall was large and spacious, a surprisingly wide and shallow staircase curved up to the first floor. Beyond the staircase, the hall continued in a narrow passage, which led to a glassed door, and the garden. This beguiling vista of distant grass and sun-touched chestnut trees gave the immediate impression of being in the country, and was one of the most endearing aspects of the house.

The front door slammed shut behind him. From the kitchen, his sister Helen called his name.

''Robert.''

''Hello!''

He chucked his hat on to the hall table, and went in through the door at the right of the hall. In the old days this room, facing out over the street, had been the family dining-room, but when Robert's father had died, and Marcus and Helen and David had moved in, Helen had converted it into a kitchen dining-room, with a scrubbed country table, and a pine dresser, crammed with patterned china and a counter, like a bar, behind which she could work. There were also a great many plants in pots, straggling geraniums, and herbs, and bowls of bulbs. Bunches of onions and marketing baskets hung from hooks, and there were recipe books, and racks of wooden spoons, and the cheerfulness of bright rugs and cushions.

Helen was behind her counter now, in a blue and white butcher's apron, peeling mushrooms. The air was filled with fragrant smells – of baking and lemons, and warm butter and the lightest suggestion of garlic. She was an exceptional cook.

She said, "Marcus called from Edinburgh. He's coming home tonight. Did you know?"

"What time?"

"There's a plane at a quarter past five. He was going to try and get a seat on that. It gets in to the terminal at half past seven."

Robert pulled a high stool up to the counter, and perched on it, like a man sitting at a bar.

"Does he want to be met at the airport?"

"No, he'll get the bus in. I thought one of us would go and pick him up. Are you in or out for dinner tonight?"

"It smells so good, I think I'm in."

She smiled. Facing each other across the counter, the family resemblance between them was very marked. Helen was a big woman, tall and heavy-boned, but when she smiled her face and her eyes lit up like a girl's. Her hair, like Robert's, was reddish, but softened by streaks of grey, and she wore it drawn tightly back into a knot, to reveal a small and unexpectedly neat pair of ears. She was proud of her pretty ears, and always wore earrings. She had a whole boxful of them in her dressing-table drawer, and if you didn't know what to give her for a present, you simply bought a pair of ear-rings. This evening they were green, some sort of semi-precious stone, set in a narrow rope of woven gold, and their colour brought out the green lights in her indeterminate, speckled eyes.

She was forty-two, six years older than Robert, and she had been married to Marcus Bernstein for ten years. Before that she had worked for him, as secretary, receptionist, book-keeper, and – on occasions when finances were shaky – as office cleaner as

31

well, and it was as much due to her efforts and faith in Marcus that the Gallery had not merely survived the initial lean patches, but had grown to achieve its present international reputation.

Robert said, ''Did Marcus tell you anything . . . about how he got on . . . ?''

''Not much, there wasn't time. But the old Lord of the Glens, whoever he is, has three Raeburns, a Constable and a Turner. So that should give you all something to think about.''

''Does he want to sell them?''

''Apparently. He says that at the current price of whisky, he can no longer afford to keep them hanging on the wall. Anyway, we'll hear all about it when Marcus gets back. How about you . . . what have you been doing today . . . ?''

''Nothing much. An American called Lowell Cheeke came in and wrote a cheque for a Ben Litton . . .''

''That's fine . . .''

''And . . .'' he watched his sister's face ''. . . Emma Litton's home.''

Helen had started to slice the mushrooms. Now, swiftly, she looked up and her hands were still.

''Emma. You mean Ben's Emma?''

''Flew back from Paris today. Came into the Gallery to collect enough money to get her back to Porthkerris.''

''Did Marcus know she was coming back?''

''No, I don't think so. I don't think she wrote to anyone except her father.''

''And of course Ben wouldn't say a word.'' Helen made an exasperated face. ''Sometimes I could just strangle that man.''

Robert was amused. ''What would you have done if you'd known she was coming?''

''Well, met her at the airport. Given her lunch. Anything.''

''If it's any comfort to you, I gave her lunch.''

32

"Well, good for you." She sliced another mushroom, considering this. "What does she look like now?"

"Attractive, in a rather unusual way."

"Unusual," Helen repeated dryly. "Tell me she's unusual and you tell me nothing I don't already know."

Robert picked up a slice of raw mushroom and ate it, experimentally. "Do you know about her mother?"

"Of course I do." Helen rescued her mushrooms, whisking them out of his reach, and taking them to her cooker, where a pan simmered with warm butter. With another deft movement, she spilled the mushrooms into the butter, and there were faint sizzling sounds and a delicious smell. She stood there, moving the mushrooms around with a wooden spatula, her strong features profiled.

"Who was she?"

"Oh, a little art student, half Ben's age. She was very pretty."

"Was he married to her?"

"Yes, he did marry her. I think, in his way, he was very fond of her. But she was simply a child."

"Did she leave him?"

"No, she died, having Emma."

"And then, later on, he married someone called Hester."

Helen turned to look at him, her eyes narrowed. "How do you know about that?"

"Emma told me today at lunch."

"Well, I never did! Yes, Hester Ferris. That was years ago."

"But there was a boy. A son. Called Christopher?"

"Don't say he's turned up again."

"Why do you sound so alarmed?"

"You'd sound alarmed, too, if you'd lived through those eighteen months when Ben Litton was married to Hester . . ."

"Tell me."

33

"Oh, they were murder. For Marcus, for Ben . . . I suppose for Hester, and certainly for me. If Marcus wasn't being roped in to referee some sordid domestic fracas, then he was being showered with ridiculous little bills which Hester said Ben refused to pay. And then, you know how Ben has this phobia about telephones, and Hester put one into her house and Ben tore it out by the roots. And then Ben ran into some sort of mental block and couldn't do any work, and spent all his time in the local pub, and Hester would get hold of Marcus and say that Marcus must come because he was the only person who could do anything with him, and so on, and so on. Marcus aged, visibly, before my eyes. Can you believe that?"

"Yes. But I don't see what it has to do with the boy."

"The boy was one of the bones of contention. Ben couldn't bear him."

"Emma said he was jealous."

"She said that? She was always a perceptive child. I suppose in a way Ben was jealous of Christopher, but Christopher was a devil. He looked like a saint, but his mother spoiled him rotten." She drew her pan of mushrooms away from the heat, and came back to lean her elbows on the counter. "What did Emma say about Christopher?"

"Just that they'd met in Paris."

"What was he doing there?"

"I don't know. I suppose having a holiday. He's an actor. Did you know that?"

"No, but I can well believe it. Was she looking very starry-eyed about him?"

"I should say so, yes. Unless it was the thought of going back to live with her father."

"That's the last thing in the world for her to be starry-eyed about."

34

"I know that. But when I started to say as much, I near as dammit got my head bitten off."

"Yes, you would. They're as loyal as thieves to each other." She patted his hand. "Don't get involved, Robert; I couldn't bear the strain."

"I'm not involved, simply intrigued."

"Well, for your own peace of mind, take my advice and keep it that way. And while we're on the subject of involvements, Jane Marshall called at lunch-time, and she wants you to ring her up."

"What about, do you know?"

"She didn't say. Just said she'd be in any time after six o'clock. You won't forget, will you?"

"No, I won't forget. But don't you forget, either, that Jane is not an involvement."

"What you're jibbing at, I cannot imagine," said Helen, who had never, with her brother at any rate, bothered to mince words. "She is charming, attractive and efficient."

Robert made no comment on this, and exasperated by his silence, she went on, justifying herself. "You have everything in common, interests, friends, a way of life. Besides, a man of your age should be married. There's nothing so pathetic as an elderly bachelor."

She stopped. There was a pause. Robert said politely, "Have you finished?"

Helen sighed deeply. It was hopeless. She knew, had always known, that no words would provoke Robert into any action that he did not choose to make. He had never been talked into anything in his life. Her outburst had been a waste of breath and she already regretted it.

"Yes, of course I've finished. And I apologise. It's none of my business and I have no right to interfere. It's just that I like

Jane, and I want you to be happy. I don't know, Robert. I can't work out what it is you're looking for.''

''I don't know either,'' said Robert. He smiled at his sister, and ran a hand over his head and down the back of his neck, a familiar gesture made when he was either confused or tired. ''But I think it has something to do with what exists between you and Marcus.''

''Well, I just hope you find it before you drop dead of old age.''

He left her to her cooking, collected his hat and the evening paper and a handful of letters, and went upstairs to his own flat. His sitting-room, which looked out over the big garden and the chestnut tree had once been the nursery. It was low-ceilinged, close-carpeted, lined with books, and furnished with as much of his father's stuff as he had been able to get up the staircase. He dropped his hat and the paper and the letters on a chair, and went to the antique bombé cupboard where he kept his drink, and poured himself a whisky and soda. Then he took a cigarette from the box on the coffee table, lit it, and, cradling his glass, went to sit at the desk, to lift the telephone receiver and dial Jane Marshall's number.

She took some time to answer. While he waited, he doodled on the blotting paper with a pencil, and glanced at his watch and decided that he would have a bath, and change before he went to pick Marcus up at the Cromwell Road terminal. And, as a peace offering to Helen, he would take a bottle of wine downstairs and they would have it with their dinner, the three of them, sitting round the scrubbed table in Helen's kitchen and, inevitably, talking shop. He discovered that he was very tired, and the prospect of such an evening was comforting.

The double burr stopped. A cold voice said, ''Jane Marshall here.''

She always answered the telephone in this manner, and Robert still found it chilling, although he knew the reason for it. At twenty-six, Jane, with a broken marriage and a divorce behind her, had been forced to start earning her own living, and had ended up with a modest interior decorating business which she ran from her own house. Thus, a single telephone number had to do double duty, and she had long since decided it was prudent to treat an incoming call as potential business until it proved to be otherwise. She had explained this to Robert when he complained about her frigid manner.

"You don't understand. It might be a client ringing up. What's he going to think if I sound all sexy and treacle-voiced?"

"You don't need to sound sexy. Just friendly and pleasant. Why don't you try it? You'd be ripping out walls and running up curtains and loose covers before you knew where you were."

"That's what you think. More likely to be fending him off with a curved upholstery needle."

Now he said, "Jane . . . ?"

"Oh, Robert." Her voice was at once its normal self, warm and obviously pleased to hear him. "I am sorry, did Helen give you my message?"

"She asked me to call you."

"It's just that I wondered . . . Look, I've been given two tickets for the ballet on Friday. It's La Fille Mal Gardée and I thought you might like to come. Unless you're going away or something."

He looked down at his own hand, drawing boxes, in perfect perspective, on the blotting pad. He heard Helen's voice. *You have everything in common. Interests, friends, a way of life.*

"Robert?"

"Yes. Sorry. No, I'm not going away. I'd love to come."

"Shall we eat here first?"

37

"No, we'll go out. I'll book a table."

"I'm glad you can make it." He could tell that she was smiling. "Is Marcus back yet?"

"No, I'm just going to meet him."

"Send him and Helen my love."

"I will."

"See you Friday, then. Goodbye."

"Goodbye, Jane."

After he had replaced the receiver, he did not get up from his desk, but sat there, his chin in his hand, putting the final touches to the last box. When it was finished, he laid down the pencil and reached for his drink, and sat, looking at what he had drawn, and wondered why it should make him think of a long line of suitcases.

Marcus Bernstein came through the glass doors of the terminal building looking, as he always looked, like a refugee or a street musician. His overcoat sagged, his old-fashioned black hat had somehow got turned up in the front, his long, lined face was sallow with tiredness. He carried his bulging brief-case, but his grip had travelled from the airport in the luggage compartment of the bus, and when Robert found him, he was standing, patiently, by the circular conveyor-belt, awaiting its arrival.

He managed to look both humble and dejected, and the casual passer-by would have found it hard to believe that this modest and unassuming man was, in fact, a powerful influence in the art world on both sides of the Atlantic. An Austrian, he had left his native Vienna in 1937, and after the horrors of an alien's war, had burst upon the post-war art world like a bright flame. His obvious knowledge and perception quickly drew attention, and his backing of young artists showed an example which other dealers were quick to follow. But his real impact upon the lay public was made in 1949, when he opened his own gallery in Kent Street with an exhibition of abstracts by Ben Litton. Ben, already famous for his pre-war landscapes and portraits, had been moving for some time towards this new medium, and the 1949 exhibition was the beginning of a working friendship which rode all personal storms and quarrels. It also marked the end of Marcus's initial struggles, and the start of a long, slow haul to success.

"Marcus!"

He gave a small start, and turned and saw Robert coming towards him, and looked surprised, as though he had not expected to be met.

"Hello, Robert. This is very kind of you."

After thirty years in England, his accent was still strongly marked, but Robert no longer noticed it.

"I would have come to the airport, but we weren't sure if you'd get on the plane. Did you have a good flight?"

"It was snowing in Edinburgh."

"It's been raining here all day. Look, there's your bag." He whipped it off the conveyor-belt. "Come on, now . . ."

In the car, waiting for the lights in the Cromwell Road to change, he told Marcus about Mr Lowell Cheeke returning to Bernstein's to buy the Litton of the deer. Marcus acknowledged this with a grunt, giving the impression that he had known all along that the sale was simply a matter of time. The lights went from red to yellow to green and the car moved forward and Robert said, "And Emma Litton is home from Paris. She flew in this morning. Didn't have any sterling, so she came to the gallery to get you to cash her a cheque. I gave her lunch and twenty pounds and sent her on her way."

"On her way to where?"

"Porthkerris, and Ben."

"I suppose he is there."

"She seemed to think he would be. For the time being, at any rate."

"Poor child," said Marcus.

Robert made no answer to this, and they drove home in silence, each busy with his own thoughts. Back at Milton Gardens, Marcus got out of the car, and went up the steps, feeling for his latchkey, but before he could run it to earth, the door was opened by Helen, and Marcus, in his sagging coat and comic's hat, was silhouetted against the hall light.

She said, "Well, how lovely!" and because he was so much smaller than she, stooped to embrace him, and Robert, extracting Marcus's grip from the boot of the Alvis, tried to work out why it was that they never looked ridiculous.

It seemed to have been dark for a long time. But when the London express came to the junction where she had to change for Porthkerris, and Emma got out of the train, she found that it was not really dark at all. The sky was bright with stars, and the night blown through with a buffeting wind that smelt of the sea. When she had unloaded all her luggage, she stood waiting on the platform for the express to pull out, and above her the tattered leaves of a palm tree rattled incongruously in this restless wind.

The train moved on, and she saw the single porter on the opposite platform, occupied, in a leisurely fashion, with a barrow-load of parcels. When at last he noticed her, he set down the handles of his barrow, and called, across the lines, "Want some help, do you?"

"Yes please."

He jumped down on to the tracks and walked across to her side, and somehow gathered all her belongings into his two arms, and then Emma followed him back across the tracks, and he gave her a hand up on to the other platform.

"Where are you going?"

"Porthkerris."

"Taking the train?"

"Yes."

The smaller train waited on the single line branch track that ran round the coast to Porthkerris. Emma appeared to be the only passenger. She thanked the porter and tipped him and collapsed into a seat. Exhaustion consumed her. Never had a day seemed so long. After a little she was joined by a country woman in a brown hat like a pot. Perhaps she had been shopping, for she carried a bulging, checked leather bag. Minutes passed, the only sound the wind thudding at the closed windows of the train. At last, the engine gave a single whistle and they were off.

It was impossible not to feel excited as familiar landmarks loomed up through the darkness, and were recognised, and then fled past. There were only two small halts before Porthkerris and then, at last, the steep cutting which in spring was quilted in primroses, and then the tunnel, and then the sea was below them, dark as ink, the tide out, the wet sands like satin. Porthkerris was a nest of lights, the curve of the harbour seemed strung with a necklace, and the riding lights of fishing boats were reflected in a maze of shimmering black and gold water.

They had begun to lose speed. The platform slid alongside. The name PORTHKERRIS passed and fell behind. They finally stopped alongside a shiny tin advertisement for boot polish which had been there ever since Emma could remember. Her companion, who had spoken not a word the entire journey, now stood up, opened the door, and stepped sedately out, disappearing into the night. Emma stood in the open door, looking for a porter, but the only visible official was up at the other end of the

41

train, unnecessarily shouting, "Porthkerris! Porthkerris!" She saw him stop to chat to the driver, pushing his cap back off his forehead, and standing with his hands on his hips.

There was an empty barrow by the boot polish advertisement, so she loaded her luggage on to this, and then abandoned it, carrying only a small overnight bag. She began to walk up the platform. In the stationmaster's office, the lights were on, they shone out in warm yellow patches, and a man sat on a bench, reading a newspaper. Emma walked by him, her footsteps ringing on the stone flags, but as she passed, he put down the newspaper and said her name.

Emma stopped, and slowly turned. He folded the newspaper and stood up, and the light seemed to turn his white hair into a halo.

"I thought you were never going to arrive."

"Hello, Ben," said Emma.

"Is the train late, or did I get the times all wrong?"

"I don't think we're late. Perhaps we were late starting from the junction. We seemed to wait there a long time. How did you know what train I'd be on?"

"I had a telegram from Bernstein's." *Robert Morrow*, thought Emma. *How kind.* Ben glanced at her bag. "You haven't much luggage."

"I have a barrow-load at the other end of the platform."

He turned to vaguely peer in the direction that Emma indicated. "Never mind. We'll fetch it some other time. Come on, let's get back."

"But someone might take it," Emma protested. "Or it might rain. We'd better tell the porter."

The porter had by now finished his social chat with the engine driver. Ben attracted his attention, told him about Emma's luggage. "Put it somewhere, would you, we'll collect it tomorrow.'' He gave him five shillings. The porter said, ''Yes, Mr Litton, don't worry, I'll do that,'' and went off down the platform whistling, tucking the money in the pocket of his waistcoat.

''Well,'' said Ben again, ''what are we waiting for? Come on, let's get moving.''

There was no suggestion of a car or a taxi, they were simply going to walk home. They did this by way of a series of narrow short-cuts, steep flights of stone steps, tiny sloping alleys, always leading downhill, until finally they emerged on to the brightly lighted harbour road.

Emma, trudging beside her father, still carrying the overnight bag which he had not thought to carry for her, took a long sideways look at Ben. It was the first time she had seen him for nearly two years, and she thought that no man changed as little as he. He was no fatter, no thinner. His hair, which had been snow-white as long as Emma could remember, was neither thinning nor receding. His face, weathered by years of working in the sun, in the outdoors, by the sea, was darkly tanned and netted with fine lines which could never be described as anything so prosaic as wrinkles. From him, Emma had inherited her strong cheekbones, and her square chin, but her pale eyes must have come from her mother, for Ben's were deep-set beneath craggy brows, and of so dark a brown that in certain lights they looked black.

Even his clothes did not seem to have changed. The sagging corduroy jacket, the narrowly cut trousers, the suède shoes of immense elegance and age – they could have belonged to no one else. Tonight his shirt was a faded orange wool, a paisley cotton handkerchief did duty as a necktie. He had never owned a waistcoat.

They came to his pub, the Sliding Tackle, and Emma half expected him to suggest that they should go in for a drink.

She did not want a drink, but she was ravenously hungry. She wondered if there was any food in the cottage. She wondered, in fact, if they were actually going to the cottage. It was quite within the bounds of possibility that Ben had been living in his studio, and would expect Emma to shake down there with him.

She said, tentatively, "I don't even know where we're heading for."

"The cottage, of course. Where did you imagine?"

"I didn't know." They were safely past the pub. "I thought perhaps you might have been living at the studio."

"No, I've been staying at the Sliding Tackle. This is the first time I've been to the cottage."

"Oh," said Emma, glumly.

He caught the inflexion in her voice and reassured her. "It's all right. When they knew at the Sliding Tackle that you were turning up there was a positive deputation of eager ladies all wanting to get the place ready for you. In the end Daniel's wife saw to it for me." Daniel was the barman. "She seemed to think that after all these years everything would be covered in blue mould, like Gorgonzola cheese."

"And was it?"

"No, of course it wasn't. A bit cobwebby, perhaps, but perfectly habitable."

"That was kind of her . . . I must thank her."

"Yes, she'd like that."

The cobbled road climbed steeply away from the harbour. Emma's tired legs ached. Suddenly, and with no word of explanation, Ben removed her bag from her grasp.

"What the hell have you got in this?"

"A toothbrush."

"It weighs like pig-iron. When did you leave Paris, Emma?"

"This morning." It seemed a lifetime ago.

44

"And how did Bernstein's know about you?"

"I had to go there to get some money. Some sterling. I was given twenty pounds out of your petty cash account. I hope you don't mind."

"I don't give a damn."

They passed his studio, shuttered and dark. "Have you started painting yet?" asked Emma.

"Of course I have. That's what I came back for."

"And the work you did in Japan?"

"I left it in America for the exhibition."

Now, the air was full of the sound of surf, of breakers rolling up on to the beach. The big beach. Their beach. And then the uneven roof of their cottage came into view, illuminated by the street lamp which stood by the blue gate. As they approached it, Ben felt in his jacket pocket for the key, and he went ahead of Emma, through the gate and down the steps, unlocking the door, and letting himself in, switching on the lights as he went, so that in a moment every window was blazing.

Emma followed more slowly. She saw at once the bright flicker of firelight and the almost inhuman cleanliness and order which Daniel's wife had somehow created out of neglect. Everything shone, was scrubbed and whitewashed and polished to within an inch of its life. Cushions had been plumped and placed with geometrical precision. There were no flowers, but the house was pervaded with a strong smell of carbolic.

Ben sniffed and made a face. "Like a bloody hospital," he said. He had put down Emma's bag, and now disappeared in the direction of the kitchen. Emma crossed the room and stood at the fireplace, warming her hands at the blaze. Cautiously, she was beginning to feel more hopeful. She had been afraid that there would be no welcome. But Ben had met her train and there was a fire in the fireplace. No human being could ask for much more.

Over the mantelshelf was the room's only picture, the painting that Ben had done of Emma when she was six years old. It was the first time in her life – and, it transpired, the last – that she had been the centre of his attention, and, for this reason alone she had borne uncomplaining the long hours of sitting, the boredom, the cramps, and his unleashed fury if she moved. For the picture, she had worn a wreath of marguerite daisies, and each day had brought the recurring pleasure of watching Ben's clever hands make a fresh wreath, and then the pride of having him place it on her head, solemnly, as though he were crowning a queen.

He came back into the room. ''She's a good woman, that wife of Daniel's. I shall tell him so. I told her to stock up with a few supplies.'' Emma turned, and saw that he had found himself a bottle of Haig and a tumbler. ''Get me a jug of water, would you, Emma?'' A thought occurred to him. ''And I suppose another glass, if you want a drink.''

''I don't want a drink. But I'm hungry.''

''I don't know if she laid in *those* sort of supplies.''

''I'll look.''

The kitchen, too, had been scoured and scrubbed and swept. She opened the fridge and found eggs and bacon and a bottle of milk, and there was bread in the bin. She took a jug off a hook on the dresser and filled it with cold water, and carried it back into the sitting-room. Ben was wandering about, fiddling with the lamps, trying to find something wrong. He had always hated this house.

She said, ''Do you want me to cook you some scrambled eggs?''

''What? Oh, no, I don't want anything. You know, it's odd being back here. I keep feeling Hester's going to appear and tell us to start doing something we don't want to.''

Emma thought of Christopher. She said, ''Oh, poor Hester.''

46

"Poor nothing. Interfering bitch."

She went back to the kitchen, found a saucepan, a bowl, some butter. From the living-room, she could hear the continued sounds of Ben's restlessness. He opened and shut doors, drew a curtain, kicked a log back on to the fire. Presently, he appeared in the kitchen doorway, a cigarette in one hand, his glass cradled in the other. He watched Emma, stirring eggs. He said, "You've grown up, haven't you?"

"I'm nineteen. Whether I've grown up or not, I really wouldn't know."

"It's odd, your not being a little girl any longer."

"You'll get used to it."

"Yes, I suppose so. How long are you going to stay?"

"Let's say I've made no plans for going away again."

"You mean, you want to live here?"

"For the time being."

"With me?"

Emma glanced at him, over her shoulder. "Would that be so painful?"

"I don't know," said Ben. "I've never tried it."

"That's why I came back. I thought perhaps it was time you did."

"You couldn't, by any chance, be reproaching me?"

"Why should I reproach you?"

"Because I abandoned you, and went off to teach in Texas. Because I never came to see you in Switzerland. Because I wouldn't let you come to Japan."

"If I really minded about those things, I shouldn't have wanted to come back."

"And supposing I decide to go away again?"

"Are you going to go?"

"No." He looked down at his drink. "Not for the moment.

47

At the moment I'm tired. I've come back for a bit of peace.'' He looked up again. ''But I shan't stay here for ever.''

''I shan't stay here for ever, either,'' said Emma. She put the toast on a plate, the egg on the toast, opened a drawer to find a knife and fork.

Ben watched all this with some agitation. ''You aren't going to be an efficient little housewife, are you? Another Hester? If so, I shall throw you out.''

''I couldn't be efficient if I tried. If it's any comfort to you, I miss trains, burn food, lose money, drop things. I had a sun hat, this morning, in Paris, but by the time I'd got to Porthkerris, it had gone. How could anyone lose a sun hat in this country, in February?''

But he was still not convinced. ''Won't you want to be driving around in a car all the time?''

''I don't know how to drive a car.''

''And television and telephones and all that rubbish?''

''They've never figured largely in my life.''

He laughed then, and Emma wondered if there was something wrong in thinking your own father so attractive.

He said, ''You know, I wasn't sure how well this was going to work. But under such favourable circumstances, I can only say I'm glad you came back. Welcome home.''

And he raised his glass to Emma and finished his drink, and then went back to the sitting-room to retrieve the bottle and pour himself the other half.

4

The bar of the Sliding Tackle was small and snug, blackly panelled, very old. It boasted only one tiny window, which looked out over the harbour, so that a visitor's first impression, as he came in from the glaring outside light, was one of utter darkness. Later, when his eyes became accustomed to the gloom, other peculiarities became evident, the most prominent being that there were not two parallel lines in the place, for over the centuries the little pub had settled into its foundations, like a deep sleeper in a comfortable bed, and various irregularities, like optical illusions, were apt to make potential customers feel intoxicated before they had even downed their first drink. The flagged floor sank in one direction, displaying a sinister gap between stone and wainscoting. The blackened beam, which formed the framework of the bar itself, sloped in another. And the whitewashed ceiling had such a lethal tilt to it that the landlord had been driven to put up notices saying "Watch That Beam" and "Mind Your Head".

Over the years the Sliding Tackle had remained, stubbornly, itself. Set in the old and unfashionable part of Porthkerris, slap on the harbour, with no space for chi-chi terraces or tea gardens, it had managed to resist the spate of summer tourism which engulfed the rest of the town. It had its regulars, who came to drink, and talk in comfortable, undemanding grunts, and play shove-ha'penny. It had a dart board and a small blackened grate where, winter and summer, a fire always burned. It had Daniel, the barman, and Fred, turnip-faced and squint-eyed, who was employed in the summer cleaning trash from the beaches and hiring out deckchairs, and spent the rest of the year blissfully drinking his takings.

And it had Ben Litton.

"It's a matter of priorities," said Marcus, as he and Robert set forth in the Alvis to run Ben Litton to earth. It was so fine that Robert had put the hood down, and so Marcus wore, with his habitual black overcoat, a tweed cap like a mushroom that looked as though it had been bought for some other person. "Priorities and timing. At mid-day on a Sunday, the first place to look is the Sliding Tackle. And if he isn't there, which I very much doubt, we'll go on to the studio, and then try the cottage."

"Or maybe, on such a wonderful morning, just out and about?"

"I don't think so. This is his drinking time, and as far as that is concerned, he has always been a creature of habit."

Still only March, it was indeed a freak day of unbelievable beauty. The sky was cloudless. The sea, driven obliquely into the curve of the bay by a buffeting north-west wind, lay streaked before them in every shade of blue, from deep indigo to palest turquoise. From the top of the hill, the view stretched to infinity, distant headlands merging into a haze that suggested the full heat of midsummer. And below, down the twisting road, the town dropped steeply, a jumble of narrow cobbled lanes, and whitewashed houses, and bleached, crooked roofs, clustered around the harbour.

Each year, during the three months of summer, Porthkerris

became a small hell on earth. Its inadequate streets were jammed with cars, its pavements overflowed with underdressed humanity, its shops spilled over with postcards, sun hats, sand-shoes, shrimping-nets, surfboards and inflatable plastic cushions. On the big beach the tents and the bathing huts went up, and the cafés opened, their terraces crammed with round iron tables, speared by umbrellas. Orange banners flapped in the wind, advertising Raspberry Sticks, and Frozen Chocolate-Coated Clusters and other horrors, and if these were not sustenance enough, there were Cornish splits for sale, and pasties, filled with soggy grey potato.

And around Whitsun, the amusement arcade opened up, with pin-ball machines and juke boxes blaring, and perhaps another cluster of ramshackle but picturesque houses would go down before the bulldozers, to clear the space for yet another car park, and the residents, and the people who loved the town, and the artists, would be horrified witnesses to this rape and say, *It's worse than ever. It is ruined. We can stay no longer.* But each autumn, once the last train had borne away the last peeling-nosed invader, Porthkerris settled back, miraculously, in its normal tempo. The shops put up their shutters. The tents came down, and the beaches were washed clean by the winter storms. The only flags which flew were lines of washing, flapping from house to house, like pastel-coloured bunting, or propped high over the greenswards where the fishermen spread their nets to dry.

And it was then that the old magic reasserted itself, and it became easy to understand why a man like Ben Litton should return time and time again, like a homing pigeon, for refreshment, and the security of familiar things, to be caught up once more in the painter's obsession with colour and light.

The Sliding Tackle was at the far end of the harbour road. Robert drew up outside its crooked porch and killed the engine.

51

It was very warm and quiet. The tide was out, the harbour full of clean sand and seaweed and screaming gulls. Some children, coaxed out by the sunshine, played with buckets and spades, watched over by a couple of knitting grannies in pinafores and hairnets, and a scrawny black cat sat on the cobbles and washed its ears.

Marcus got out of the car. "I'll go and see if he's inside. You wait here."

Robert took a cigarette from the packet on the dashboard and lit it, and watched the cat. Above his head the inn sign creaked in the wind, and a gull came and sat on it and eyed Robert with malevolence, screaming defiance. Two men came down the road, walking with the slow righteous gait of a restful Methodist Sunday. They wore navy blue guernseys and white cloth caps.

" 'Morning," they said as they passed.

"Lovely day," said Robert.

"Yes. Lovely."

After a little, Marcus appeared once more. "All right, I've found him."

"What about Emma?"

"He says she's back at the studio. Whitewashing."

"Want me to go and get her?"

"If you would. It's . . ." he glanced at his watch, "twelve-fifteen. Suppose you're back here at one. I said we'd lunch at one-thirty."

"Right. I'll walk. It's not worth taking the car."

"Can you remember the way?"

"Of course." He had been before, twice, to Porthkerris, chasing up Ben Litton for some reason or other when Marcus had not been available to do it for himself. Ben's phobia about telephones and cars and all forms of communication, presented, from time to time, the most hideous complications, and Marcus had long since accepted the fact that it was quicker to make the journey from London to Cornwall and beard the lion in his den than to wait for an answer to the most impassioned of reply-paid telegrams.

He got out of the car and slammed the door shut. "Do you want me to tell her what it's all about, or shall I leave that pleasant task to you?"

Marcus grinned. "You tell her."

Robert pulled off his narrow tweed cap and dropped it on to the driving seat. He said, amiably, "You bastard."

He had had a letter from Emma, a week or two after she passed through London.

Dear Robert,

If I call Marcus Marcus, I can't possibly call you Mr Morrow, can I? No, of course I can't, not possibly. I should have written at once to thank you so very much for the lunch and for letting me have the money, and for letting Ben know that I was on the train. He actually came to meet me at the station. Everything is going wonderfully well, so far we haven't had a row, and Ben is working like a fiend on four canvases at once.

I didn't lose any of my luggage except the sun hat, which I'm sure someone stole.

My love to Marcus. And you.
Emma.

Now, he made his way through the baffling maze of narrow streets and tightly-packed houses that led to the north shore of the town. Here, there was another beach, a bleak and unprotected bay only esteemed for the long surfing rollers which poured in,

53

straight from the Atlantic. Ben Litton's studio faced out over this beach. Once, long ago, it had been a net store and its only access was a cobbled ramp which sloped down from the street to a double, black-tarred door. There was a printed sign with his name, and an immense iron knocker, and Robert took hold of this and banged it, and called "Emma."

There was no reply. He opened the door, and it was immediately almost torn from his hand by a gust of wind which poured, like a torrent of water, through the open window on the far side of the studio. Once the door had slammed shut again behind him, the draught subsided. The studio was empty and bitterly cold. There was no sign of Emma, but a step ladder and whitewash brush and bucket bore witness to her recent occupation. She had finished the whole of one wall, but when he went to touch it with his hand, he found that it was still cold and damp.

From the middle of this wall protruded an ugly old-fashioned stove, empty now and unlit, and beside it a gas ring, a battered kettle, and an upturned orange box containing blue and white striped mugs and a jar of sugar lumps. On the opposite side of the room stood Ben's work table, littered with drawings and papers, tubes of paint, and hundreds of pencils and brushes all contained on sheets of corrugated cardboard. The wall above this table was dark and dirty with age, and smeared with the scrapings of countless palette knives, that had built up, over the years, into a crustaceous shell of colour. At the top of the desk was a narrow level shelf, and on this ranged a selection of *objets trouvés* which at some time or another had caught Ben's eye. A stone from the shore, a fossilised starfish. A blue jug of dried grasses. A postcard reproduction of a Picasso; a piece of bleached driftwood, carved by sea and wind to abstract sculpture. There were photographs, a fan of curling snapshots, arranged in an old silver menu-holder; an invitation to a private view that had taken place six years ago, and, finally, a heavy, old-fashioned pair of binoculars.

At floor level, the walls were stacked with leaning canvases, and in the middle of the room the current work stood, easeled and shrouded with a faded pink cloth. Turned towards the empty stove was a sagging sofa, draped in what looked like the remains of an Arabic rug. There was also an old kitchen table, with its legs cut short, and on this a tin of cigarettes, and an overflowing ash-tray, a pile of *Studios*, and a green glass bowl, full of painted china eggs.

The north wall was all glass, squared off by narrow wooden partitions and designed so that its lower portions would slide aside. Along the foot of this was a long seat, piled with cushions, and from beneath this protruded further ill-assorted flotsam. The spars of a boat, a stack of surfboards, and a crate of empty bottles, and, in the middle, beneath the open window, two iron hooks had been screwed into the floor, and on to those were looped the spliced ends of a rope ladder. This disappeared out of the window, and Robert, going to investigate, saw that it dropped straight down to the sand, twenty feet below.

The beach appeared to be empty. The ebb tide had left it a sweep of hard clean sand, divided from the sky by a narrow line of frothing white breakers. Further inshore, there was a stratum of rock, crusted with shellfish and seaweed, and over this the seagulls hovered, occasionally pouncing to fight and scream over some prize. Robert sat on the window-seat, and lit himself a cigarette. When he looked up again, a figure had appeared on the horizon, right on the edge of the sea. It wore a long white gown, like an Arab's, and as it walked back towards the studio, appeared to be wrestling with some large and unidentifiable red package.

He remembered the binoculars on Ben's table and went to

fetch them. Focused, the figure sprang into relief, and revealed itself as Emma Litton, long hair blowing, dressed in a huge white towelling robe and lugging, with some difficulty, for the wind kept catching it broadside and jerking it out of her grasp, a scarlet surfboard.

"You surely haven't been swimming?"

Emma, struggling with the surfboard, had not seen him at the window. Now, with a hand on the rope ladder, she nearly jumped out of her skin at the sound of his voice. She looked up, trailing the surfboard in the sand, her wet black hair ripped to ribbons by the wind.

"Yes, I have, and what a fright you gave me. How long have you been there?"

"About ten minutes. How are you going to get the surfboard up the ladder?"

"I was wondering that, but now you've turned up all my problems are solved. There's a rope under the seat. If you chuck one end down, I'll tie it on, and you can pull it up for me."

This was duly accomplished. Robert hauled the board through the open window, and hard on its heels came Emma herself, her face and hands and feet crusted with dry sand, and her black lashes spiked like starfish.

She knelt on the window-seat, and laughed at him. "Now, wasn't that the luckiest thing! What would I have done? I could hardly get it over the beach, let alone up the ladder."

Beneath the sand, her face looked blue with cold. He said, "Come along in, and get the window shut . . . that wind's freezing. How could you bear to go and swim? You'll die of pneumonia."

"No I won't." She stepped down on to the floor, and watched him furl the ladder in and slide the window shut. It did not fit

56

properly and there was still a draught like the edge of a knife. "Anyway, I'm used to it. We always used to swim in April when we were children."

"This isn't April. It's March. It's winter. What would your father say?"

"Oh, he wouldn't say anything. And it's such an utterly gorgeous day and I was sick of whitewashing . . . have you seen my lovely clean wall? The only thing is, it makes the rest of the studio look like a slum. Besides, I wasn't swimming, I was surfing, and the breakers kept me warm." And then, without any noticeable change of expression, "Have you come to see Ben? He's down at the Sliding Tackle."

"Yes, I know."

"How do you know?"

"Because I left Marcus there with him."

"Marcus." She raised her strongly-marked eyebrows, considering this. "Has Marcus come too? My goodness, it must be important business!"

She shivered slightly.

Robert said, "Do get some clothes on."

"Oh, I'm all right." She went to take a cigarette from the table, and lit it, and then collapsed on to the old sofa, flat on her back, with her feet propped on the arm.

"Did you get my letter?"

"Yes, I did." With Emma taking up all the sofa, there was nowhere to sit but on the table, so he eased the pile of magazines on to the floor, and sat there. "I was sorry about your sun hat."

Emma laughed. "But glad about Ben?"

"Of course."

"It's amazing how well it's working. Unbelievable. And he really likes having me around."

"I never imagined for a moment that he wouldn't."

"Oh, don't start being gallant. You know you did. At lunch that day, you were all quizzical eyebrows and scepticism. But you see, it really is the perfect arrangement. Ben doesn't have to pay me to keep house for him, or be bothered with tedious details like days off and insurance stamps, nor does he have to become emotionally involved. He never knew that life could be so simple."

"Have you heard from Christopher?"

Emma turned her head sideways to look at him. "How do you know about Christopher?"

"You told me yourself. At Marcello's. Remember?"

"So I did. No, I haven't heard. But he'll be at Brookford by now, in the thick of rehearsals. He won't have had time to write. Anyway, there's been such a lot to do here, getting the cottage organised and cooking and things. Don't believe people when they say that artists never eat. Ben's inner man is quite insatiable."

"Have you told him you met up with Christopher again?"

"Good heavens, no! And spoil the even tenor of our life? I haven't even mentioned his name. You know, you look much nicer in those tweedy sort of clothes than you do in the London kind. I thought when I first saw you that you weren't the type to spend his days buttoned up in a charcoal grey suit. When did you get down here?"

"We drove yesterday afternoon. We spent last night at The Castle."

Emma made a face. "In with all the potted palms and the cashmere cardigans. Ugh!"

"It's very comfortable."

"The central heating gives me hay fever. I can't even breathe."

She stubbed her half-smoked cigarette out in the overflowing ash-tray, and swung her feet off the sofa, and stood up and walked away from him, towards the window, untying the sash of the robe as she went. She took a pile of clothes from beneath a cushion, and with her back to him, started to dress. She said, "Why did you and Marcus come together?"

"Marcus doesn't drive."

"There are trains. And that wasn't what I meant."

"No, I know." He picked up one of the painted china eggs and began to play with it as an Arab handles a string of worry beads. "We've come to try and persuade Ben to go back to the United States."

There was a sudden great squall of wind. It broke over the glass window of the studio like a wave, poured, roaring over the roof above them, with the thunder of a passing train. A cluster of gulls rose screaming from the rocks, were flung across the sky. And then, as suddenly, it was over.

Emma said, "Why does he have to go back?"

"This retrospective exhibition."

She dropped the white towelling robe, and stood silhouetted, in jeans, pulling a navy blue sweater over her head.

"But I thought he and Marcus fixed all that when they were in New York in January."

"We thought so too. But you see, this exhibition is being sponsored by a private individual."

"I know," said Emma, turning, and flipping her dark hair free of the turtle-neck of the sweater. "I read all about it in *Réalités*. Mrs Kenneth Ryan. The widow of the wealthy man whose memorial is the Queenstown Museum of Fine Arts. You see how well informed I am. I hope you're impressed."

"And Mrs Kenneth Ryan wants a private view."

"Then why didn't she say so?"

"Because she wasn't in New York. She was sunning it in

59

Nassau or the Bahamas or Palm Beach or somewhere. They never met her. They only saw the curator of the museum.''

''And now Mrs Ryan wants Ben Litton to go back, so that she can throw a nice little champagne party and show him off, like a trophy, to all her influential friends. It makes me sick.''

''She's done more than decide, Emma. She's come to persuade him.''

''You mean come to England?''

''I mean come to England, come to Bernstein's, come to Porthkerris. She drove down with Marcus and me yesterday and at this very moment, is sitting in the bar of The Castle Hotel, drinking very cold Martinis and waiting for us all to go and have lunch with her.''

''Well, I for one am not going.''

''You have to. We're all expected.'' He glanced at his wrist-watch. ''And we're running late. Do hurry up.''

''Does Ben know about the private view?''

''He will by now. Marcus will have told him.''

She picked up a brown sailcloth smock off the floor and pulled it on over her sweater. As her head came through the neck, she said, ''Ben may not want to go.''

''You mean you don't want him to go?''

''I mean that he's settled down here again. He's not prowling, he's not restless, he's not even drinking very much. He's working like a young man, and what he's doing is fresh and new and better than ever. Ben is sixty, you know. Looking at him, it's hard to believe, but he's nearly sixty. Isn't it possible that all this hopping about all over the world may no longer stimulate him, but simply wear him out?'' She came back to the sofa to sit down, facing Robert, her earnest face on a level with his own. ''Please. If he doesn't want to go, don't try to persuade him.''

Robert still held the china egg. He looked at it intently as though its convolutions of blue and green would miraculously provide the answer to every problem. Then, with care, he laid it back in the glass dish, along with its fellows.

He said, ''You talk as though this were something important, as though he were returning to the States to teach again, as though he weren't going to come back for years. But it isn't. It's simply a party. He needn't be away for more than a few days.'' She opened her mouth with a fresh protest, but he talked her down. ''And you mustn't forget that this exhibition is a great tribute to Ben. A lot of money's been ploughed into it, and a great deal of organisation, and perhaps the least he can do . . .''

Furiously, Emma interrupted. ''The least he can do is go and parade up and down like a pet monkey for some fat old American. And what makes it so awful is that he likes that sort of thing. That's what I hate, that he likes it.''

''So he likes it. So, if he wants to, he'll go.''

She was silenced. She sat, eyes downcast, her mouth sulky as a child's. Robert finished his cigarette and stubbed it out, and stood up and said, more gently, ''Now, do come on or we're going to be late. Have you got a coat?''

''No.''

''Some shoes then, you must have some shoes.''

She felt under the sofa and produced a pair of thong sandals, and stood up, thrusting her bare feet into them. Her feet were still covered in sand, and the sailcloth smock spotted in whitewash.

She said, ''I can't go to The Castle, for lunch, looking like this.''

''Nonsense.'' He tried to sound bracing. ''You'll give the residents something to talk about. Brighten their dull lives no end.''

''Isn't there time to go back to the cottage? I haven't even got a comb.''

"There'll be a comb at the hotel."

"But . . ."

"There simply isn't time. We're late already. Now come along . . ."

They went together, out of the studio and up the ramp, and into the sunlit street, and began to walk back towards the harbour. After the chill of the studio the air felt warm, and the brightness of the sea was reflected from the whitewashed walls of houses, and assailed the eye like the glare of snow.

5

Emma did not want to go into the Sliding Tackle.

"I'll wait here. You go and prise them out."

"All right."

He went across the cobbles, and she noticed how he had to duck his tall head to get in under the porch. The door of the pub swung shut behind him. She wandered over to his car and inspected it with interest, because it belonged to him, and should therefore provide further clues to his character, as a shelf of book-titles will do, or the pictures that a man hangs on his walls. But, apart from the fact that it was dark-green, had fog lights and wire wheels and a couple of car-club badges, the Alvis gave little away. Inside on the driving-seat was a tweed cap; cigarettes in the dashboard cupboard, a book of maps. On the back seat, neatly folded, a thick, expensive-looking tartan rug. She decided that he was either trusting, or careless, but also lucky, for the rug had not been stolen.

A gust of wind blew in from the sea and Emma shivered. After the swim and the session in the draughty studio, she still was very cold. Her hands had gone numb, quite colourless, the fingernails tinged with blue. But the metal of the car was warm, and, for comfort, she leaned against it, spreadeagled across the bonnet, with her hands splayed like starfish.

63

The pub door opened and Robert Morrow emerged once more, ducking cautiously. He was alone.

"Aren't they there?"

"No. We're late, and they got fed up with waiting, so they got a lift back to the hotel." He opened the driving-seat door, picked up his cap and pulled it on, jerked down over his nose, to add yet another sharp angle to his formidable profile. "Come on . . ." And he leaned over and opened the other door, and Emma unpeeled herself from the bonnet, and slid in beside him.

They left the harbour behind and below them, roared up through the town, up the steep narrow streets, up between terraces of prim houses, and the signs which said Bed and Breakfast, and front gardens where sad palm trees tossed their heads in the alien wind. They came out on to the main road, still climbing, turned into the drive of The Castle Hotel; climbed on, between banks of hydrangeas, and landward-leaning elm trees, and at last came out at the very top of the hill, into an open space of tennis courts, and lawns, and a miniature golf course. The hotel had once been a country house, and prided itself on its authentic atmosphere. A white post and chain fence kept cars away from the gravel sweep in front of the hotel, and here, in deckchairs, sat a handful of hardy residents, scarved, gloved and swaddled in rugs, like the passengers of some trans-Atlantic liner. They read books or newspapers, but when the Alvis roared up the drive and drew up with a massive scrunch of gravel, these were lowered, and in some cases, spectacles were removed, and Robert and Emma's progress observed and noted as though they were visitors from another planet.

Robert said, "We're probably the first exciting thing to happen since the manager fell into the swimming-pool."

Once inside the revolving doors, the heat of the place struck like a newly-opened oven. Emma professed to despise such comfort, but today it was blissfully welcome.

She said, "I expect they'll be in the bar. You go, I'll be there in a moment. I must try and get rid of some of this sand."

In the Ladies', she washed her hands and her face, and rubbed the sand off her feet on to the back of her jeans, like a schoolboy trying to polish his shoes. There was a pretentious set of brushes and combs on a beruffled dressing-table, and she used the comb on the snarls of her hair, breaking half the teeth, but reducing the tangled mass into some sort of order. As she turned back for the door, she caught sight of herself in the long mirror. No make-up, faded jeans, whitewash stains. She pulled off the offending smock, and then was infuriated with herself for minding about anything so trivial as her own personal appearance, and pulled it on again. They would think she was a beatnik art student. A model. Ben Litton's mistress. Let them. As Robert Morrow had so rightly said, it would give them something to talk about.

But as she emerged from the Ladies' and went down the long, carpeted hall, she was grateful to see that Robert Morrow had not abandoned her and gone to join the others, as she had told him to, but was waiting for her by the porter's desk, reading a Sunday paper which had been left on a chair. When he saw her coming, he folded the paper and tossed it down again, and gave her a grin of encouragement.

"You've done splendidly," he said.

"I've ruined the hotel comb. Ever so nice it was, too, one of a matching set. You didn't need to wait. I've been before and I know the way . . ."

"Come along, then."

It was a quarter to two, and the busy Sunday lunch-time session was over. Only a few serious drinkers still sat at the bar, cradling their gin and tonics and beginning to look a bit red in the face. Ben Litton, Marcus Bernstein and Mrs Kenneth Ryan were over on the other side of the room, grouped in the bay formed by a huge picture window. Mrs Ryan was on the window-seat, against a backdrop like a travel agent's poster – a shout of blue sea, a sweep of sky, and the green undulations of the miniature golf course. The two men, Ben in his French workman's *bleus*, and Marcus in his dark suit, were talking, turned slightly towards her, so that it was Mrs Ryan who first saw Emma and Robert.

"Well, look who's here . . ." she said.

They turned. Ben remained sitting, but Marcus stood up and came to greet Emma, his arms outstretched, his pleasure at seeing her both genuine and demonstrative and very un-British. He could on occasion be almost embarrassingly Austrian.

"Emma, my darling child. Here you are at last." He put his hands to her shoulders and kissed her, formally, on both cheeks. "What a pleasure to see you again, after this very long time. How long is it? Five years? Six years? What a lot we have to talk about. Come along, and meet Mrs Ryan." He took her hand to lead her over. ". . . But your hand is like a block of ice. What have you been doing?"

"Nothing," said Emma, catching Robert's eyes, and daring him to say more.

"And your bare feet . . . how can you stand it? Mrs Ryan, this is Ben's daughter, Emma, but don't shake hands with her, or you will die of shock."

"I can think of worse ways to die," said Mrs Ryan, and held out her hand. "How do you do?"

They shook hands. "I must say, you are very cold."

On an insane impulse, Emma said, "I was swimming. That's why we're late. And why I'm so untidy. There wasn't time to go back to change."

"Oh, but you don't look untidy, you look charming. Sit down
. . . we have time for another drink, don't we? The dining-room
isn't going to shut down on us or anything like that. Robert,
would you be a darling, and order another round for us. What
would you like, Emma?"

"I . . . I don't really want anything." Ben gave a small cough.
"Well . . . a glass of sherry."

"And we're all drinking martinis, Robert. If you want one
too?" Emma lowered herself carefully on to the chair that
Marcus had vacated, aware of her father watching her from the
other side of the table.

"I simply don't believe," said Mrs Ryan, "that you really
have been swimming."

"Not really. I just went in and out again. There were huge
waves."

"But won't you get the most terrible chill? It can't be good
for you." She turned to Ben. "You don't approve, surely, of
swimming when it's as cold as this? Haven't you got any
influence on your daughter?"

Her voice was gay and teasing. Ben made some reply, and she
went on, telling him that he should be ashamed of himself . . .
that she could see he was an outrageous father . . .

Emma did not listen. She was far too busy looking. For Mrs
Ryan was not old and fat, but young and beautiful and very
attractive, and from the top of her smoothly-coiffed golden
blonde head to the tips of her shining crocodile pumps there
was no single detail that did not give active pleasure. Her eyes
were enormous and blue as violets, her mouth full and sweet-
tempered, and when she smiled, as she did now, revealed two
perfect rows of even, white, American teeth. She wore a most
becoming suit of rose-pink tweed, the collar and cuffs edged
with starched white pique. Diamonds sparkled from her ears,

her lapel, her neatly-manicured hands. There was nothing vulgar about her, nothing brash. Even her scent was flower-like.

"... The fact that she has been away from you for six years is all the more reason for you to take care of her now."

"I don't take care of her ... she takes care of me ..."

"Now there is a real man talking ..." Her soft, southern voice made the words sound like a caress.

Emma's eyes moved round to her father. His attitude was a characteristic one, legs crossed, right elbow resting on his knee, his chin supported by his thumb, a cigarette between his fingers, its smoke rising before his eyes. The eyes were dark as black coffee, deeply shadowed, and they watched Mrs Ryan as though she were a fascinating new specimen, caught between the glass plates of a laboratory slide.

"Emma, your drink."

It was Marcus. She dragged her eyes from Ben and Mrs Ryan and turned to him in relief.

"Oh, thank you ..."

He sat beside her. "Robert has told you about the private view?"

"Yes, he told me."

"Are you angry with us?"

"No." And this was true. You could not be angry with such an honest man who came so instantly to the point.

"But you don't want him to go?"

"Did Robert say that?"

"No, he didn't say. But I know you very well. And I know how long you've waited to be with Ben. But it's only for a little while."

"Yes." She looked down at her drink. "He really is going, then?"

"Yes, he really is going. But not until the end of the month."

"I see."

Marcus said, gently, ". . . if you wanted to go with him . . ."

"No. No, I don't want to go to America."

"Do you mind being alone?"

"No. It doesn't bother me. And, as you say, it won't be for long."

"You could come to London, and stay with Helen and myself. You could have David's room."

"Where would David sleep?"

"It is so sad, he is away at boarding school. It broke my heart, but I am now an Englishman and my son was torn from me at eight years old. Come and stay, Emma. In London, there is a lot to see. The Tate Gallery has been re-hung, and it is a masterpiece . . ."

Despite herself Emma began to smile.

"What are you laughing about, you horrible child?"

"I'm laughing at your shamelessness. You take my father away with one hand, and offer me the Tate Gallery with the other. And," she added, dropping her voice, "nobody bothered to tell me that Mrs Kenneth Ryan was the Beauty Queen of Southern Virginia."

"We didn't know," said Marcus. "We had never seen her. She flew to England on an impulse, she walked into the Bernstein Galleries the day before yesterday and said she wanted to see Ben Litton, and that was the first time I had ever set eyes on her."

"Well, she's certainly worth setting eyes on."

"Yes," said Marcus. He looked across at Mrs Ryan with his sad, hound's eyes. He looked at Ben. He looked back into his Martini, and touched the sliver of lemon peel with his forefinger. "Yes," he said again.

Their arrival, late, in the dining-room caused something of a stir. The best table had been reserved for them, the round one in the window, and it was necessary to cross the length of the floor to get there. Mrs Ryan led the way, aware of adulation from every eye in the room, and apparently unconcerned. She was quite used to it. Behind her came Marcus, shabby, but oddly distinguished and obviously interesting. Then Robert and Emma, and finally Ben. Ben fell behind to stub out his cigarette and made what amounted to a star entrance, stopping for a moment in the doorway to speak to the head waiter, so that by the time he did move forward into the room, he was the sole centre of attraction.

Ben Litton . . . There's Ben Litton, the whispers went up, as he walked between the tables, magnificent in his blue French overalls, the red and white scarf knotted at his throat, his white hair thick as a young man's, a quiff like a comma falling across his forehead.

Ben Litton . . . you know, the painter.

It was exciting. Everybody knew that Ben Litton had a studio in Porthkerris, but if you were determined to actually see him, you had to make your way down to the town, and find a fisherman's pub called the Sliding Tackle, and there sit, in the stuffy gloom, making a glass of warm beer last as long as possible, and wait for him to come. It was rather like a strange form of bird-watching.

But today, Ben Litton had abandoned his usual haunts, and was here, at The Castle Hotel, about to eat Sunday lunch, like any other ordinary human being. The mountain had come to Mahomet. An elderly lady stared openly at him through her lorgnette, and a visiting Texan was heard mourning the fact that he had left his flash camera in the bedroom.

Emma caught Robert Morrow's eye, and just managed to suppress a snort of laughter.

Ben reached the table at last, settled himself in the place of honour at Mrs Ryan's right, picked up a menu, and suggested, simply by raising a finger, that the wine waiter should be fetched. Gradually, the excitement in the dining-room died down, but it was obvious that for the rest of the meal they would be the object of all attention.

Emma said to Robert, "I know I shouldn't approve – I should be ashamed of such blatant exhibitionism, but somehow, he gets away with it every time."

"Well, at least it's made you laugh, and you've stopped looking all pinched and nervous."

"You might have told me Mrs Ryan was young and beautiful."

"She's certainly beautiful. But I don't think she's as young as she appears. Well-preserved more like it."

"That's the sort of bitchy remark a woman would make."

"I'm sorry. It was meant with the best will in the world."

"You still should have told me."

"You never asked."

"No, but I made some remark about fat old Americans, and even then you didn't put me right."

"Perhaps I didn't realise that it was so important to you."

"A beautiful woman and Ben Litton, and you didn't realise it was important? It's more than that; it's lethal. One thing, you and Marcus won't have to do any persuading. Ben is going to America. One sweep of those lashes, and he was already mid-Atlantic."

"I don't think you're being entirely fair. The longest lashes in the world wouldn't sweep him into anything he didn't want to do."

"No, but he could never resist a challenge."

Her voice was cold.

Robert said, "Emma."

She turned to look at him. "What?"

"Your resentment is showing." He measured between his forefinger and thumb. "Just the very smallest amount."

"Yes . . . well . . ." She decided to change the subject. "When do you go back to London?"

"This very afternoon." He glanced at his watch. "We're running late, as it is. We'll need to leave, as soon as I can coax Little Miss Millions away."

But Mrs Ryan was not to be hurried. The luncheon wore on through four courses, through wine and brandy and coffee, served in the now-empty dining-room, because she did not want to move from their table. At last, taking advantage of a pause in the conversation, Robert cleared his throat, and said, "Marcus, I am sorry to interrupt, but I really think we should make a start, we've got a three hundred mile drive."

Mrs Ryan seemed astonished. "But whatever time is it?"

"Nearly four o'clock."

She laughed. "Already! It's like being in Spain. I once went to a lunch party in Spain, and we didn't get up from the table until half past seven in the evening. Why does time have to go so fast when you're really enjoying yourself?"

"Cause and effect," said Ben.

Across the table, she smiled at Robert. "You don't want to leave right away, do you?"

"Well . . . as soon as possible."

"But I wanted to see the studio. I can't come all the way across the Atlantic, and all the way down to Porthkerris and not see Ben's studio. Couldn't we drop in just for a moment, on the way back to London?"

This light-hearted suggestion was received in silence. Robert and Marcus both looked momentarily confused; Robert, because he did not want to put off any more time, and Marcus, because he knew that of all things, Ben hated to have his studio inspected. Emma also experienced a sinking of the heart. The studio was in chaos – not Ben's chaos which was of no account, but her own chaos. She thought of the step ladder, and the whitewash bucket, the wet towelling coat, and the bathing-suit which she had left abandoned on the floor, the brimming ash-trays, and the sagging sofa, and the sand everywhere. She looked at Ben, praying for him to refuse. They all looked at Ben, waiting like puppets, to see which way he would jerk the strings.

But for once he did not let them down.

"My dear Mrs Ryan, despite the pleasure it would give me to show you my studio, I think I should point out that it is not on the way to London."

They all looked at her, to see how she would take this. But she merely pouted, and they laughed in relief, and Mrs Ryan laughed too, with good grace.

"All right, I know when I'm beaten." She began to collect her bag and gloves. "But there is just one thing. You've all been so sweet to me, and I don't want to feel like a stranger any longer. My name's Melissa. Do you-all think you could manage to call me that?"

And later, when the men were loading the car, she got Emma to herself.

"You've been specially sweet," she said. "Marcus told me that you'd come back from Paris to be with your father, and here I am, taking him away from you again."

Emma, who knew that she had not been specially sweet, felt guilty. "The exhibition has to come first . . ."

"I'll take good care of him," Melissa Ryan promised.

Yes, thought Emma, *I'm sure you will*. And yet, despite herself, she liked the American woman. And there was something

73

about the set of her chin and the clarity of her violet-blue eyes that made Emma wonder if perhaps, this time, Ben would not enjoy his usual walkover. And if things did not go his way from the very beginning he was apt to become discouraged. She smiled at Mrs Ryan. She said, "I don't suppose it'll be long before he's home again." And she picked up the honey-coloured mink which lay across the back of a chair and helped Mrs Ryan into it. They went out of the hotel together. It was colder now. The warmth of the sun had left the sky and a chill, like frost, swept up from the sea. Robert had put up the hood of the Alvis, and Melissa, wrapped in the mink, went to say goodbye to Ben.

"But it isn't goodbye," he told her, holding her hand, and gazing darkly down at her. "It's au revoir."

"Of course. And if you let me know when your flight arrives at Kennedy Airport, I'll arrange to have you met."

Marcus said, "I will do that. Ben has never in living memory let anybody know anything, least of all his time of arrival. Goodbye, Emma, my darling child, and don't forget that I have invited you to stay with us for as long as you like when Ben is in America."

"Bless you, Marcus. You never know. I might come."

They kissed. He got into the back of the car, and Melissa Ryan into the front, her elegant legs wrapped in Robert's car rug. Ben shut the door, then stooped to continue his conversation with her through the open window.

"Emma." It was Robert.

She turned. "Oh, goodbye, Robert."

To her surprise he took off his cap and bent to kiss her. "You'll be all right?"

She was touched. "Yes, of course."

"If you want anything, give me a ring, at Bernstein's."

"What could I want?"

"I don't know. Just a thought. Goodbye, Emma."

They stood, she and Ben, watching until the car had disappeared down the tunnel of trees. After it had gone, neither of them spoke, and then Ben cleared his throat, and said, portentously, as though he were giving a lecture, "What an interesting head that young man has. The narrow skull and the strong facial bones. I should like to see him with a beard. He would make a good saint – or perhaps, a sinner. Do you like him, Emma?"

She shrugged. "I suppose so. I scarcely know him."

He turned to move off, and caught sight of the small gathering of hotel guests, who, setting off for walks, or coming in from golf, or aimlessly snatching at the smallest straw of entertainment, had stayed to witness Melissa's departure. As Ben fixed them with his dark eyes, they became discomfited, turned away and moved on as though they had been caught doing something shameful.

He shook his head in amazement. "I think," he said, "I have had enough of being stared at as though I were a two-headed chimpanzee. Come along, we'll go home."

6

Ben Litton left for America at the end of March, travelling from
Porthkerris to London via British Railways and from London
to New York on a BOAC Boeing. At the last moment Marcus
Bernstein decided to go with him, and the evening papers
carried photographs of their departure, Ben with his white hair
a coxcomb in the breeze, and Marcus almost obliterated by his
black hat. Both looked faintly self-conscious.

It was from Marcus that Emma received the airmail bundle of
American newspapers, carrying in their columns the comments
of every worthwhile art critic in the country. They were unani-
mous in their praise of the whole concept of the Queenstown
Museum of Fine Arts, acclaiming it as a perfect example of
architecture, lighting, and immaculate display. And the Ben
Litton exhibition was on no account to be missed. Never again
would the artist's work be available to the public in its entirety,
and the two or three pre-war portraits, lent by private individuals,
were alone worth a visit, if only to see how a single man could
be painter, psychiatrist and absolving priest at one and the
same time.

''Ben Litton uses his brush as a surgeon's scalpel, first
laying bare the hidden sickness, then treating it with the utmost
compassion.''

The word compassion was used again for his war-time drawings, the shelter groups, the fire-fighters, and a handful of sketches salvaged from the time of the Allied advance in Italy. And of his post-war work they said, "Other painters abstract from nature. Litton abstracts from imagination, and an imagination so lively that it is difficult to believe that these vital paintings were not turned out by a man of half his age."

Emma read these and allowed herself to feel proud. The private view took place on the 3rd of April, and by the tenth there was still no word of Ben's return, but she filled in the days with time-consuming household chores, and eventually moved back to the studio to finish the whitewashing. This took little mental concentration, and her mind wandered aimlessly into the future, indulging in the sort of day dreams that, a month ago, she would never have allowed herself. But now, she truly felt that things had changed. When she had gone to the station to put Ben on to the London train, he had kissed her goodbye – absentmindedly to be sure, as though he had forgotten for the moment who she was, but still, he had kissed her and that surely marked a milestone. And when he did eventually tear himself away from the adulation of the American public and returned to Porthkerris, she saw herself meeting the train, cool and composed, the perfect social secretary. And, maybe the next time he took off for some far-flung, but obviously colourful, corner of the globe, he would take Emma with him, and she would book flights, and see that he caught connections, and keep Marcus informed as to his movements.

And then, a day or two later, there was a letter from Marcus, postmarked London. She opened it hopefully, thinking that it would tell her that Ben was coming back, but, in fact, it was simply to say that Marcus had returned to London alone, and Ben had stayed in Queenstown.

The Ryan Memorial Museum is fascinating, and if I had been able, I should have stayed as well. It embraces all forms of art, has a small theatre and concert hall and a collection of Russian jewellery which has to be seen to be believed. Queenstown itself is charming, full of red brick Georgian houses, set in green lawns and veiled in flowering dogwood ... they all look as though they have been there since the days of William and Mary, but in fact, I saw one in the process of being built, the mature lawn being laid in turves, and the dogwoods planted, fully grown. What it is to have a warm and temperate climate, to be sure.

Redlands (the Ryan homestead) is a great white house with a pillared "porch" where Ben sits in a long chair and gets brought mint juleps by a coloured butler called Henry. Henry comes to work each day in a lilac Chevrolet, and hopes, in the not-too-distant future, to become a lawyer. He is a bright young man and should achieve his ambition. There are also a couple of tennis courts – a paddock (corral) full of spirited horses, and the inevitable swimming-pool. Ben, as you can imagine, neither rides nor plays tennis, but spends long hours, when he isn't adding a little local colour to the retrospective exhibition, floating around the pool on a rubber mattress. I am sorry that he has stayed away from you for so long, but honestly believe that he needs this rest. He has been working hard for the last few years, and a little harmless relaxation will do him no harm. If you are lonely, our invitation still stands. Come and stay with us. We should so love to have you.
Always your loving Marcus.

The whitewashing was finished, the studio floor scrubbed. Ben's drawings had been stacked and stowed in numbered folios. His pens and brushes graded and various tubes of solidified oil paint, used once, and then abandoned, had been discreetly shovelled into the dustbin.

There was nothing left to do.

He had been gone two weeks when the postcard came from Christopher. Emma was in the kitchen of the cottage, making coffee and squeezing orange juice, still wrapped in her dressing-gown and with her hair tied back in a pony tail, when the postman, who was a cheeky young man in an open-necked shirt, put his head round the door and said, "Well, and how are you this morning, my handsome?"

"Splendid, thank you," said Emma, who had been putting up with this camaraderie ever since she returned from Paris.

He flapped a bundle of letters at her. "All for your old man. But . . . here . . . is a postcard for you." He inspected the picture before Emma snatched it from him. "So vulgar those things are; I don't know how decent folks can buy them."

"No, you wouldn't," said Emma rudely, scarcely glancing at the bulging lady in the bikini before turning the card over to see who it was from. The postmark was Brookford.

Emma darling, when are you coming to see me? I can't come and see you, because we're up to the ears in rehearsals for Dead on Time. *Phone number Brookford 678, best about ten in the morning before we start work. Producer nice chap, stage manager bloody, all girls have spots, and not as pretty as you. Love Love Love Christo.*

The nearest phone box was a mile away, so Emma went down the street to the ramshackle grocer's where she bought cigarettes and tins of food and soap flakes, and used the telephone there.

It was an old-fashioned one, in two separate bits, and with a hook that you jiggled to get the operator. She sat on a beer crate and waited while the call was put through and a grey and white cat, fat as a cushion, came and lay exhaustedly across her knee.

The phone was answered at last by a cross-sounding female. "Brookfield Theatre."

"Can I speak to Christopher Ferris?"

"I don't know if he's in yet."

"Could you go and look?"

"Oh, I suppose so. Who shall I say it is?"

"Say Emma."

The cross female departed. Various voices could be heard, chattering. A man in the distance shouted, *"Here I said, you clot, not there."* And then there were footsteps and a voice, and it was Christo.

"Emma."

"You are there. They didn't know if you were in."

"Yes, of course I'm in . . . we're rehearsing in five minutes . . . Did you get my postcard?"

"This morning."

"Did Ben read it?" (He obviously hoped that he had.)

"Ben isn't here. He's in America. I thought you'd know."

"How should I know?"

"It's been in all the papers."

"Actors don't read papers and if they do it's always the *Stage*. But if the old boy's in America, why didn't you let me know and come and stay with me?"

"For a hundred reasons."

"Name two."

"Well, he only meant to go for a week at the most; and I didn't know where you were."

"I told you. Brookford."

"I don't even know where Brookford is."

"Thirty-five minutes from London, trains run every half hour.

Look, do come. Come and stay. I've been moved into a sinister basement flat. It smells of dry rot and old cats, but it's ever so cosy.''

''Christo, I can't. I must be here. Ben'll be home any day now, and . . .''

''Did you tell him about meeting me again?''

''No, I didn't.''

''Why not?''

''The subject never came up.''

''You mean you were scared?''

''I was nothing of the sort. It was simply – irrelevant . . .''

''Nobody's ever called me irrelevant and got away with it. Oh, do come, ducky. My little basement nest needs the touch of a woman's hand. You know, scrubbing and all that jazz.''

''I can't come till Ben's home. Then I'll try.''

''It'll be too late by then. I'll have got it clean. Please. I'll get you a free ticket for the show. Or two tickets and you can bring a friend. Or three tickets and you can bring them all.''

His voice dissolved into amusement. He had always laughed at his own jokes.

''Oh, very funny,'' said Emma, but she was laughing too.

''You're just playing hard to get. You wouldn't stay with me in Paris, and you won't come and keep house in the wilds of Surrey. What have I got to do to win your heart?''

''You won it years ago and you've had it ever since. Truthfully, I'm longing to see you. But I can't come. I simply can't come till Ben gets back.''

Christo said a rude word.

The telephone went pip-pip-pip.

''That's it, then,'' said Christo. ''Let me know when you make up your mind. Goodbye.''

''Goodbye, Christo.'' But he had already hung up. Smiling

foolishly, going back over every word he had said, she put the receiver back on to the hook. The cat on her knee purred momentously, and Emma realised it was about to produce a family at any moment. An old man came into the shop to buy two ounces of plug, and when he had gone Emma picked up the cat and placed her gently on the floor, and felt in her pocket for loose change to pay for the call.

"When are the kittens due?" she asked.

The old woman behind the counter was called Gertie, and wore, indoors and out, an enormous brown beret pulled down over her eyebrows.

"Only time can tell, my dear." She put Emma's money into her till, which was an old tin box, and gave her her change. "Only time can tell."

"Thank you for letting me use your phone."

"It's a pleasure," said Gertie, who always listened, shamelessly, and relayed every word she heard.

In March it had been like midsummer. Now, in May, it was cold as November, and pouring with rain. He had never imagined Porthkerris in the rain; had always pictured it painted in the bright blues of summer, gay with the white wings of gulls and yachts, everything dazzling in a glaring sunlight. But now squalls, borne in on a cutting east wind, were flung against the windows of the hotel, sounding like fistfuls of pebbles. The gusts rattled the casements and then whined away beneath doors, down chimneys, blowing curtains, chilly and inescapable.

It was a Saturday, and Robert, flat on his bed, had been asleep. He looked at his watch and saw that it was five to three, so he reached for a cigarette, and lit it, and lay, watching the leaden sky race across the window, and waiting for the telephone to ring.

It did, at precisely three o'clock. He lifted the receiver.

83

"Three o'clock, sir," said the hall porter.

"Thank you very much."

"Sure you're awake, sir?"

"Yes. I'm awake."

He finished the cigarette, and stubbed it out, and got up, pulling on his white towel robe and heading for the bathroom for a hot shower. He hated sleeping in the afternoon, hated waking with the feeling that his teeth were itching, and that he was on the verge of a splitting headache, but after driving all through the night from London it had been impossible to stay awake. He had had an early lunch, and left word with the porter to call him. But the wind, blown up while he slept, had wakened him first.

He dressed, put on a clean shirt, tied his tie, picked up the jacket of his suit, and then changed his mind, and pulled on a polo-necked sweater instead. He combed his hair, slid his belongings from the top of the dressing-table into his trouser pockets, took a raincoat from the back of the door and went downstairs.

The lounge was thick with the silence of mid-afternoon. Elderly residents snoozed, snoring lightly in dry heated air. Frustrated golfers watched the rain, rattling loose change in the pockets of their tweed knickerbockers, wondering if the weather was going to let up, if there would be time for nine holes before it got dark.

The hall porter took Robert's key and hung it up.

"Going out now, sir?"

"Yes, and perhaps you can help me. I want to get to the Society of Artists Gallery. I believe it's an old chapel, converted. Have you any idea where it is?"

"That's down the old part of the town. Know your way round, do you?"

84

"I know the Sliding Tackle," said Robert, and the hall porter grinned. He liked a man who used pubs as landmarks.

"Well . . . say you're going to the Sliding Tackle, but turn up the street before you get there. Up, away from the harbour. Narrow little road, very steep, and there's a square at the head of it. Gallery's on the other side of the square. You can't miss it. Got great posters up outside . . . not that any living soul can make head nor tail of them . . ."

"Well, we'll have to see. Thank you very much."

"You're welcome." The porter swung the revolving door, and Robert was ejected into the bitter cold. Rain hammered at his unprotected head, he hunched himself into his raincoat, and picked his way across the gravel, trying to avoid the worst of the puddles. Inside, his car smelt damp and musty, an alien smell over the usual one of leather and cigarettes. He switched on the engine and the heater began to hum. A leaf was stuck in the blade of the windscreen wiper, but when he turned it on, the leaf was dislodged and torn from the wet glass by the wind.

He drove down to the town, and it was all deserted, abandoned, the inhabitants in a state of siege from the weather. Only a drenched policeman stood at point duty at the foot of the hill, and an old lady fought with an umbrella. The narrow streets acted as chimneys for the wind, which funnelled up them, cold and ferocious as a torrent of water, and when he came out on to the harbour road, he saw that the tide was full, and the harbour itself grey and choppy, fleeced with white-capped waves.

He found the street the porter had described. It climbed away from the harbour between crowded cottages, the cobbles wet and shining like the scales of a newly-caught fish. It crested the hill, and opened out into a picturesque square, and he saw the old chapel, a solid, gloomy building, quite at odds with the poster at its door.

PORTHKERRIS SOCIETY OF ARTISTS
SPRING EXHIBITION
Admission 5/-

Beneath this was a strange motif in purple – the suggestion of a staring eye, a six-fingered hand. Robert decided that he could see the hall porter's point of view.

He parked the car, and went up the streaming steps, and through the door, and was immediately assailed by the smell of a paraffin stove. He saw that the old chapel had been whitewashed, the walls soared to high private windows, and liberally hung with every sort and size of painting.

Just inside the door, her knees covered with a rug, sat a lady in a felt hat. On one side of her was a wooden table, with catalogues and a bowl for money, on the other was the paraffin heater, at which she was trying to warm a pair of purple-knuckled hands.

"Oh, close the door, close the door," she implored as Robert blew in on a gust of wind. He leaned against the door, shutting it, and feeling in his trouser pocket for two half-crowns. "What a freezing day," she went on, "and this is meant to be summer. You're my first visitor this afternoon. You are a visitor, aren't you? I haven't seen your face around the place."

"No, I haven't been here before."

"We've got a most interesting collection, you'll have a catalogue, of course. Another half-crown, please. But I think you'll agree, well worth it."

"Thank you," said Robert, feebly.

He took the catalogue, decorated with the same purple hand-and-eye motif as the poster outside, and opened it casually, running his eye down the list of artists for the name he wanted. ". . . er . . . any particular artist?" The woman at the desk

86

managed to sound diffident, but she had an inquisitive gleam in her eye.

"No . . . not really."

"Just generally interested, I expect. Are you staying in Porthkerris?"

"Yes . . ." he began to move away from her. "For the moment I am."

He took it slowly, pacing down the long room, feigning interest in every picture. He had found the name, Pat Farnaby. Number 24. The Journey, by Pat Farnaby. He stayed a long time at number 23, then moved on again.

The colour pounced at him. There was a sensation of great height, a dizzying sensation, like vertigo. And yet with it, a sense of elation, as though he were above the clouds, caught, suspended, between the blue and the white.

You must go, Marcus had said. *I want you to form an opinion of your own. You can't remain the man who keeps the books for the rest of your life. Besides, I'd like to see your reaction.*

And this was it. This pure, high note of simple colour.

After a little, he went back to the persistent lady. He was aware that all the time she had been watching him. Now, he thought, she was bright-eyed as a greedy robin, waiting for a bread crumb.

"Is that Pat Farnaby's only exhibit?"

"I'm afraid so. It was all we could persuade him to let us have."

"He lives around here, doesn't he?"

"Oh, yes. Out at Gollan."

"Gollan?"

"That's about six miles away, out on the moor road. It's a farm."

"You mean he's a farmer?"

"Oh, no." She laughed. *Merrily*, thought Robert, as though

she were following the directions in an old-fashioned play. "He lives in the loft over the barn. Here," she drew a scrap of paper towards her, wrote an address. "If you want to see him, I'm sure you'll find him here."

He took the paper. "Thank you very much." He started for the door.

"But don't you want to look at the rest of our exhibition?"

"Another time, perhaps."

"It's so *interesting*." She sounded as though her heart would break if he did not look at some more pictures.

"Yes, I'm sure. But another time." It was at this moment that he thought of Emma Litton. His hand on the doorknob, he turned back. "By the way, if I wanted to find Ben Litton's house . . . is it near here? The house, I mean, not the studio?"

"Well, of course, it's just round the corner. About a hundred yards down the road. It's got a blue gate. You can't miss it. But you do know that Mr Litton's not at home?"

"Yes, I know."

"He's in America."

"Yes, I know that, too."

It was still streaming with rain. He got back into the car, and started the engine, and nosed it forward down a street as narrow as a burrow. At the blue gate he left it, parked, completely filling the road, and went through the gate, and down a flight of steps which led to a flagged courtyard where tubs stood, filled with drowned-looking plants, and a painted wooden seat disintegrating slowly in the damp. The house itself was long and low, single-storied, but the uneven roofs and ill-matched chimney pots indicated that it had once been two small cottages, or even three. The front door was painted blue to match the gate, and had a copper dolphin as a knocker.

Robert knocked. From above a stream of water poured down upon him from a faulty gutter. He stepped back and looked up to see where it came from, and as he did so, the door was opened.

He said, "Good afternoon. Your gutter's leaking."

"Where on *earth* have you sprung from?"

"London. You should get it mended or it'll rust away."

"Have you come all the way from London to tell me that?"

"No, of course I haven't. Can I come in?"

"Of course . . ." She stood back, holding the door open for him. "But you are the most disconcerting man. You keep just turning up, with no notice at all."

"How can we give you notice if you aren't on the telephone? And there wasn't time to write a letter."

"Is it about Ben?"

Robert went into the house, ducking his head beneath the lintel of the door, unbuttoning his wet raincoat.

"No. Should it be?"

"I thought he might be home."

"As far as I know he's still basking in that balmy Virginia sunshine."

"Well, then?"

He turned to face her. It occurred to him then that in an odd way she was unpredictable as the weather itself. Each time he met up with her, she seemed a different person. Today she wore a dress in red and orange stripes, and long black stockings. Her hair had been caught back on the nape of her neck with a tortoise-shell slide, and her fringe had grown. It was too long, it would get into her eyes, give her a squint. As he watched her, she pushed it back, off her face, with the heel of her hand. It was a gesture both defensive and disarming and it made her seem very young.

He took the scrap of paper out of his pocket and handed it across to her. Emma read it aloud.

"Pat Farnaby, Gollan Home Farm." She looked up at him. "But where did you get this?"

"From the female at the Art Gallery."

"Pat Farnaby?"

"Marcus is interested."

"Why didn't he come himself?"

"He wanted a second opinion. Mine."

"Have you formed one?"

"It's difficult to say after seeing only a single painting. I thought I might be able to see some more."

Emma said warningly, "He's a very odd young man."

"I should expect him to be. Do you know where Gollan is?"

"Of course. It belongs to Mr and Mrs Stevens. We used to go out in summer for picnics on the cliffs. But I haven't been since I got back this time."

"Will you come with me now? Show me the way?"

"How do we get there?"

"The car's outside. I drove down from London last night."

"You must be exhausted."

"No, I've had a sleep."

"Where are you staying?"

"At the hotel. Can you come? Now?"

"Of course."

"You'll need a coat."

Emma smiled at him. "If you can spare thirty seconds, I'll get one."

When she had gone, her footsteps clattering away down an uncarpeted passage, Robert lit a cigarette and stood, looking about him, intrigued not only by the oddly-shaped little house, but also because it represented the unfamiliar, domestic side of Ben Litton's stormy personality.

The blue front door had led them straight into the living-room, low ceilinged and darkly beamed. There was a huge window with a view of the sea, its deep sill crowded with indoor plants – geraniums and ivy and a Victorian jug full of pink roses. The floor was flagged with slate and scattered with bright rugs, and there were books and magazines everywhere, and a great deal of blue and white Spanish pottery. In a granite hearth, flush with the floor, a log fire smouldered, flanked by baskets of weathered driftwood, and over this hung the only picture in the room.

His professional eye had noticed this as soon as he came into the house, but now Robert went over to inspect it more closely. It was a large oil of a child on a donkey. She wore a red dress, carried a bunch of white daisies, wore a garland of them on her dark head. The donkey stood knee-deep in the lush grass of summer, and, far beyond, the sea and the sky were suffused by a haze of fine weather. The child's dangling feet were bare, her eyes pale in the brown bloom of her face.

Emma Litton, by her father. Robert wondered when it had been painted.

The wind rose, with a sudden witch's shriek, and flung a torrent of rain at the window. It was an eerie sound and he realised that this could be a lonely place to live, and wondered what Emma found to do on such a day. When she came back, carrying her coat and a pair of gumboots, which she proceeded to pull on, he asked her about this.

"Oh, I clean the house, and I cook things and I go and shop. It all takes quite a long time."

"And this afternoon? What were you doing this afternoon when I knocked on the door?"

Emma tugged at the gumboot. "I was ironing."

"And what about evenings? What do you do in the evenings?"

"I usually go out. I go for walks and things. I watch the gulls and the cormorants. I look at the sunset, pick up driftwood for the fire."

"Alone? Haven't you got any friends?"

"Oh, yes, but the children who lived here when I was little have all grown up and gone away."

It sounded bleak. On an impulse, Robert said, "You could come back to London with me. Helen would love to have you."

"Yes, I know she would, but it's hardly worth it, is it? After all, Ben'll be back any day now. It's only a matter of days."

She began to pull on her coat. It was navy blue and, with her black stockings and gumboots, made her look like a schoolgirl.

"Have you had any word from Ben?" Robert asked.

"From Ben? You must be joking."

"I'm beginning to wish we'd never suggested he went back to America."

"Why?"

"Because it doesn't seem fair on you."

"Oh, heavens, I'm all right." She smiled. "Shall we go?"

The Stevens's farm lay in a grey stretch of moor that swept down to the cliffs. Grey, lichened, sunk like a boulder into the land, it might have been simply another larger outcrop of granite. The lane which led down from the road wound deep between tall stone hedges, crowned with hawthorn and brambles. The car bumped and jolted down the track, crossed a small bridge, came to the first cottages, a flock of white geese, and finally the farmyard, shrill with the voice of a screaming cockerel.

Robert stopped the car and switched off the engine. The wind was dying, the rain seemed to have congealed into a sea-mist, thick as smoke. There were various farm sounds; cows lowing, hens clucking, the distant churning of a tractor.

"Now," said Robert, "how do I find this man?"

"He lives in the loft of that barn . . . you go up the stone steps to his door." The stone steps were already occupied by a number of wet hens, pecking for scraps of grain, and a bored-looking tabby cat. Below them, in the mud of the yard, a huge sow was rootling about. There was a strong smell of manure. Robert sighed. "The things I am expected to do, and all in the name of Art." He opened the door of the car and began to get out. "Do you want to come?"

"I think I'd be more use out of the way."

"I'll try not to be too long."

She watched him pick his way across the sodden farmyard, toe the pig aside, cautiously climb the steps. He knocked on the door, and then, when there was no reply, opened it and stepped inside. The door shut behind him. Almost at once another door opened, in the farmhouse this time, and the farmer's wife emerged, in boots and a raincoat to her ankles, and a black sou'wester. She carried a stout stick and came down the garden path, peering through the rain to see who was in the big green car.

Emma rolled down the window. "Hello, Mrs Stevens. It's me."

"Who?"

"Emma Litton."

Mrs Stevens broke into a cackle of delighted astonishment, slapped her side, put her hand over her heart. "Emma! Well, what a surprise you gave me. I haven't seen you since goodness knows how long. What are you doing here?"

"I came out with a man who wants to see Pat Farnaby. He's up there now."

"Is your father home yet?"

"No, he's still in America."

"On your own, are you?"

"That's right. How's Ernie?" Ernie was Mr Stevens.

"He's lovely, but had to go into town today to see the dentist

93

about his plate. Agony, it gives him, he can scarcely bear to keep it in his mouth. That's why I'm getting the cows in for him . . .''

On an impulse Emma said, ''I'll come with you . . .''

''Too wet for you.''

''I've got boots . . . besides, I'd like the walk.'' She liked Mrs Stevens, too, a woman who remained unquenchably cheerful under all circumstances. They climbed a stile and started out over the sodden fields. ''You've been abroad, haven't you?'' said Mrs Stevens. ''Yes, I thought you had. I never knew you were home. Pity your Daddy had to go off like this. Still, can't be helped, I suppose, him being the sort of man he is . . .''

The interview with Pat Farnaby was a difficult one, to say the least of it. He was an intense young man, very pale and under-nourished, with a shock of carroty hair and a beard to match. His eyes were green and suspicious as a hungry cat's, and he appeared to be very dirty. His abode was also dirty, but this Robert had expected and, accordingly, ignored.

What he had not expected, though, was such antagonism. Pat Farnaby did not like strangers walking in, uninvited and unannounced, when he was working. Robert apologised and explained that he had come on business, whereupon the young man simply asked Robert what he was trying to sell.

Beating down his irritation, Robert tried another tack. With some ceremony, he produced Marcus Bernstein's card. ''Mr Bernstein asked me to come and see you, perhaps to look at your work, find out what your plans are . . .''

''I haven't any plans,'' said the artist. ''I never make plans.'' He treated the card as though it were contaminated and must not be touched, so that Robert was forced to put it down on the corner of a littered table.

"I saw your picture at the Gallery in Porthkerris, but it is only one picture."

"So what?"

Robert cleared his throat. Marcus was infinitely better at dealing with this sort of thing, and Marcus never lost his temper. It took time to cultivate such patience, Robert knew. His own was slipping away, like greasy rope between his fingers. He took a firm grip of it.

"I'd like to see some more of your work."

Pat Farnaby's pale eyes narrowed. "How did you find me?" he asked, sounding like a cornered criminal.

"They gave me your address at the Gallery. Emma Litton came with me to show me the way. Perhaps you know Emma."

"I've seen her around."

They seemed to be getting nowhere. In the silence that followed Robert let his eyes travel over the unsavoury studio. There were only the most sordid signs of human habitation; a bed like a disintegrating nest, a dirty frying pan, some nasty socks soaking in a bucket, an opened tin of beans, the jagged edge of the lid sticking up. But there were also many canvasses, stacked, scattered, propped on chairs, against walls. A potential treasure trove. Anxious beyond belief to inspect them, he dragged his eyes back to meet the cold unwinking stare of the artist.

He said at last, gently, "Mr Farnaby, I haven't all the time in the world."

Put to the test, Pat Farnaby's resistance cracked. He seemed, all at once, unsure of himself. Arrogance and rudeness were his only defences against the whims of a more sophisticated world. He scratched his head, frowned, made a face of resignation, and at last went to lift a random canvas and turn it to face the light.

"There's this," he said uncertainly, and backed away from it to stand by Robert. As he did so, Robert took a new packet of cigarettes from his pocket and handed them across to the young man. In the silence that followed, Pat Farnaby cautiously slit the cellophane wrapper, took out a cigarette and lit it, and then, with the stealthy movements of a man who does not wish to be observed, slid the packet into his own trouser pocket.

An hour later Robert returned to the car. Emma, waiting for him, saw him come down the steps of the barn, pick his way across the farmyard. She leaned across to open the door for him, and as he got in beside her, asked, "How did you get on?"

"I think all right." He sounded cautious, but excited.

"Did he show you his work?"

"Most of it."

"And it's good?"

"I think so. We may be on the verge of something enormously important, but it's all in such an appalling mess that it's hard to be sure. Nothing's framed, there's no sequence or order . . ."

"I was right, wasn't I? He's a real oddball?"

"Crazy," said Robert. He grinned at her. "But a genius."

He turned the car in the yard and headed back up the lane towards the road. He was whistling tunelessly through his teeth and Emma sensed, beneath his excitement, the satisfaction of a job well done.

She said, "You'll want to speak to Marcus now."

"I said I'd telephone right away." He eased his cuff from the face of his watch, checked on the time. "A quarter past six. He said he'd wait in the Gallery till seven and then go home."

"If you like, you can drop me at the crossroads and I'll walk home."

"Now, why should I do that?"

"I haven't got a telephone, and you'll want to hurry back to the hotel."

He smiled. "It's not as urgent as all that. And if it hadn't been for you, I'd probably still be looking for Pat Farnaby. The least I can do is to take you home."

They were on the moor now, high above the sea. The wind had eased off considerably, veering round to the west, and ahead the sky seemed to be opening and breaking up, and there were unexpected scraps of blue, growing larger every moment, and watery fingers of sunlight. Emma said, "It's going to be a lovely evening," and as she spoke was conscious that she did not want Robert to go back to the hotel and leave her to spend it on her own. He had blown, unexpectedly, into the gloomy day, given it shape and purpose, filled with companionship of a shared venture, and now she did not want it to end.

She said, "When are you going back to London?"

"Tomorrow morning. Sunday. Back in the Gallery Monday morning. It's been a full weekend."

So there was only this evening. She imagined him telephoning Marcus from the phone by his bed. Then he would have a bath, perhaps a drink, go down for dinner. On Saturday evenings The Castle Hotel held little dinner dances; there was a band in white mess jackets and a patch of floor cleared for dancing. Deeply influenced by Ben, Emma had been brought up to regard such functions as unbearably genteel and boring, but tonight she felt that it would be fun to let Ben's rigid opinions go to the devil. She yearned for the starched white table-cloths, the last year's hit tunes, the ritual of the wine list, the souped-up glamour of pink-shaded lights.

Beside her Robert spoke unexpectedly, interrupting her train of thought.

"When did your father paint the picture of you on the donkey?"

"Why did you suddenly ask that?"

"I was thinking about it. It's enchanting. You look so solemn and important.'

"That's the way I felt, solemn and important. I was six, and it was the only painting he ever did of me. The donkey was called Mokey. He used to carry us up and down to the beach along with all the picnic baskets and things."

"Have you always lived in the cottage?"

"Not always. Just since Ben married Hester. Before that we used to stay anywhere – in boarding-houses, or with friends. Sometimes we just camped in the studio. It was rather fun. But Harriet said she had no intention of living like a gipsy, so she bought the cottages and converted them."

"She did a good job."

"Yes, she was clever. But Ben has never thought of that house as home. His home is his studio and when he's in Porthkerris, he spends as little time as possible in the cottage. I think its associations with Hester slightly get him down. He's always expecting her to walk in and tell him that he's late for something, or that he's tracking mud on to the floor, or he's putting paint on the sofa cushions . . ."

"The creative instinct seems to thrive in disorder."

Emma laughed. "Do you suppose, that when you and Marcus have made Pat Farnaby rich and famous, he will still want to roost with Mrs Stevens's chickens?"

"That remains to be seen. But if he does come to London, there's no doubt that somebody will have to scrub him down and comb the dust of ages out of that scrofulous beard. Still . . ." He stretched luxuriously, arching his back against the leather seat. "It'll be worth it."

98

They had crested the hill and were now running down the long road that led to Porthkerris. The sea, in the calm evening light, had turned the translucent blue of butterfly wings; the tide was out, and the great bay an arc of newly-washed sand. The rain had left everything sparkling and fresh, and as the moors and the fields fell behind them, and they drove down through the narrow streets, Emma saw windows flung open to the fresh evening air, and caught, from tiny stamp-sized gardens, the heady smells of roses and lilac.

And there were other smells, too. Saturday evening smells, of fish frying and cheap scent. And there were people strolling the pavements in their best clothes, a smattering of early summer visitors, and boys and girls, hand in hand, headed for the cinema and the little cafés that lined the harbour road.

Stopped at the crossroads by the point-duty policeman, Robert observed them.

"What does young love do in Porthkerris on Saturday night, Emma?"

"It depends on the weather."

The policeman waved them on.

"What are we going to do?" asked Robert.

"We?"

"Yes. You and I. Do you want to be taken out for dinner?"

For a mad moment Emma wondered if she had been yearning aloud. "Well . . . I . . . you don't have to feel you have to . . ."

"I don't feel I have to. I want to. I'd like to. Where shall we go? My hotel? Or would you hate that?"

"No . . . of course . . . I wouldn't hate it . . ."

"Perhaps you've got some amusing little Italian place you like better."

"There aren't any amusing little Italian places in Porth-kerris."

"No, I was afraid there wouldn't be. So it'll have to be the palm court and the central heating."

"There's a band too," said Emma, feeling she should warn him. "On Saturday nights. And people dance."

"You make it sound indecent."

"I thought perhaps you disliked that sort of thing. Ben does."

"I don't dislike it at all. Like most things, it can be quite fun if you do it with the right person."

"I never thought of it that way."

Robert laughed and looked again at his watch. "Half past six. I'll take you home, then go back to the hotel and change, and speak to Marcus, and then come back for you. Would half past seven be time enough?"

"I'll give you a drink," said Emma. "There's a bottle of Uncle Remus's Genuine Ole Rye Whisky that Ben was given ten years ago, and it's still not been opened. I've always longed to see what was inside."

But Robert was unenthusiastic. "Perhaps I'd better just make a martini."

At the hotel he collected his key, and three messages with it.

"When did these come?"

"The times are noted, sir. Three forty-five, five o'clock, half past five. A Mr Bernstein, telephoning from London. He says to call him the moment you come in."

"I was going to do that anyway, but thanks."

Frowning a little, for such impatience was foreign to Marcus, Robert went upstairs to his room. The copious telephone calls were disturbing. He wondered if Marcus had heard rumours that some other Gallery was after the young artist. Or perhaps he had had second thoughts about Farnaby's work, and wanted to cancel the whole thing.

In his room, the curtains had been drawn, the bed turned down, the fire turned on. He sat on the bed, and picked up the receiver and gave the number of the Gallery. He took the three telephone messages out of his pocket and put them in a neat row on top of the bedside table. *Mr Bernstein would like you to call him. Mr Bernstein called, will ring later. Mr Bernstein . . .*

"Kent 3778. Bernstein Galleries."

"Marcus . . ."

"Robert, thank God I've got you at last. Did you get my message?"

"Three of them. But I said I would call you about Farnaby."

"This isn't about Farnaby. This is much more important. This is about Ben Litton."

There was a dress, seen in Paris, wildly expensive, coveted, and finally bought. It was black, sleeveless, very plain. "But when will you wear such a dress?" Madame Duprés had asked, and Emma, basking in the luxury of possession, had replied, "Oh, some time. Some special time."

There had never been such an occasion until tonight. Now, with her hair coiled high and pearl earstuds set in her ears, Emma drew the black dress carefully over her head, zipped it up and fastened the tiny belt, and her reflection in the mirror reassured her that all those thousands of francs had been well spent.

When Robert came, she was in the kitchen, struggling with a trayful of ice-cubes for the martinis that he had promised to make. She heard his car, the slam of the door, the gate open and shut and his footsteps as he ran down the steps, and in a panic, she tumbled the ice into a glass dish and went to let him in, and found that the sullen day had turned into a clear and perfect night, jewel-blue and scattered with stars.

In surprise, she said, "What a beautiful night."

101

"Amazing, isn't it? After all that wind and rain Porthkerris is looking like Positano." He came into the house and Emma closed the door behind him. "There's even a moon rising over the sea to complete the illusion. All we need now is a guitar and a tenor singing 'Santa Lucia'."

"Perhaps we'll find one."

He had changed into a dark grey suit, a starched shirt with an impeccable collar and a gleam of white cuff, linked with gold, showing at his wrist. His tawny hair was once more tamed and smoothly brushed, and he brought with him the crisp, lemony smell of aftershave.

"Do you still want to make a martini? I've got everything ready, I was just trying to get the ice . . ." She went back to the kitchen, raising her voice to talk through the open door. "The gin and the martini are on the table and a lemon. Oh, and you'll need a knife to cut the lemon with."

She opened a drawer and found one, pointed and very sharp, and she carried the knife and the bowl of ice back into the living-room. "What a pity Ben isn't here. He adores martinis, only he can never remember the right proportions and he always drowns them with lemon . . ."

Robert made no reply to this. It occurred then to Emma that he had made no effort to make himself at home. He had done nothing about their drinks, he had not even lit himself a cigarette, and this in itself was unusual, for he was normally the most relaxed and composed of men. But now there was a definite constraint about him, and with a sinking heart, Emma wondered if he was already regretting the evening they were to spend together.

She went to put the lemon down beside the empty glasses, told herself she was imagining things, turned to swiftly smile at him. "Now, what else do you need?"

"Not another thing," said Robert, and put his hands into his trouser pockets. *Not the gesture of a man who is about to make a martini.* In the fire a burning log settled and broke, sending up a shower of sparks.

Perhaps it was the telephone call that had upset him. "Did you speak to Marcus?"

"Yes, I did. As a matter of fact, he'd been trying to get me on the telephone most of the afternoon."

"And of course you were out. Was he pleased when you told him about Pat Farnaby?"

"He wasn't calling about Farnaby."

"He wasn't?" Suddenly she was afraid. "Is it bad news?"

"No, of course not, but you may not be very pleased. It's about your father. You see, he called Marcus this morning, from the States. He wanted Marcus to tell you that yesterday, in Queenstown, he and Melissa Ryan were married."

Emma realised that she was still holding the knife, that it was very sharp and that she might cut herself with it, so she set it down, very carefully alongside the lemon . . .

Married. The word conjured up a hysterical image of a wedding; of Ben with a white flower in the button-hole of his sagging corduroy jacket; of Melissa Ryan in her pink wool suit, misted in white veiling and paper confetti; of demented church bells jangling their message out across the verdant Virginia countryside that Emma had never seen. It was like a nightmare.

She realised that Robert Morrow was still talking, his voice even and calm. ". . . Marcus feels that in some obscure way, he is to blame. Because he thought the private view was a good idea, and because he was with them in Queenstown – he saw them together all the time, and he never had the faintest inkling that this was going to happen."

Emma remembered Marcus's description of the beautiful

house, saw Ben caged by Melissa's money, a pacing tiger with all his creative impulses smothered by luxury; and she realised that she had underestimated Melissa Ryan in imagining that Ben would be put off by having to fight for what he wanted. She had not appreciated how much he would want it.

Suddenly, she was angry. "He should never have gone back to America. There was no need. He simply wanted to be left alone and to get on with his painting."

"Emma, nobody made him go."

"It isn't as though the marriage will last. Ben's never stayed faithful to a woman longer than six months, and I can't see Melissa Ryan standing for that."

Robert said mildly, "Perhaps this time it will work, and it will last."

"But you saw them together that day they met. They couldn't keep their eyes off each other. If she had been old and ugly, nothing would have dragged him away from Porthkerris."

"But she wasn't old and ugly. She's very beautiful, and highly intelligent and very rich. And if it hadn't been Melissa Ryan, very soon it would have been somebody else, and what is more . . ." he went on, swiftly, before Emma could interrupt, ". . . you know as well as I do that that is true."

She said bitterly, "But at least we would have had more than a month together."

Hopelessly, Robert shook his head. "Oh, Emma, let him go."

His tone infuriated her. "He's my father. What's wrong in wanting to be with him?"

"He's not a father, any more than he's a husband or a lover or a friend. He's an artist. As that dedicated maniac we went to see this afternoon is an artist. They have no time for our values or standards. Everything, and everybody else, has to take second place."

"*Second* place? I wouldn't mind taking second place, or third, or fourth. But I've always come at the bottom of a long list of priorities. His painting, his love affairs, his perpetual shunting about all over the world; even Marcus, and you. You're all more important to Ben than ever I was."

"Then leave him alone. Think about something else for a change. Chuck all this, leave it behind. Get yourself a job."

"I've done all those things. I've been doing them for the past two years."

"Then come back to London with me tomorrow and stay with Marcus and Helen. It'll get you away from Porthkerris, give you time to get used to the idea of Ben being married again, decide what you want to do next."

"Perhaps I've already decided."

It was there, in the back of her mind. Like watching the revolving stage from the darkened auditorium of a theatre. One set moves out of sight and as it does the new scenery comes slowly on to the stage. A different set. Another room, perhaps. Another view from another window. "But I don't want to come to London."

"And this evening?"

Emma frowned. She had forgotten. "This evening?"

"We're having dinner together."

She felt that she could not bear it. "I really would rather not . . ."

"It'll do you good . . ."

"No it won't. And I've got a headache . . ." It was an excuse, made-up, and it was with astonishment that she realised it was true. A pain that felt like the start of a migraine, with her eyeballs dragged by wires into the back of her head; the thought of food, chicken in gravy, ice-cream, was nauseous. "I couldn't come. I couldn't."

Robert said gently, "It isn't the end of the world," and the old, comforting cliché was somehow more than Emma could take. To her horror, she began to cry. She covered her face with her hands pressing her fingertips into her thudding scalp, trying to stop, knowing that crying would make it worse, that she would be blinded with pain, that she would be sick . . .

She heard him say her name, and in two strides he had covered the space between them, and he put his arms around her, cradling her, letting her cry all over the immaculate grey lapels of his good suit. And Emma did not try to move away, but stayed still, tightly clenched against her own grief, rigid and unresponsive and hating him for what he had done to her.

7

Jane Marshall, her hand curved round a half full tumbler of Scotch-on-the-rocks, said, "... so what happened then?"

"Nothing happened. She didn't want to come out to dinner, and she looked as though she was going to have a bilious attack, so I put her to bed, and gave her a hot drink and an aspirin, and then I went back to the hotel and had dinner on my own. Then, the next morning, the Sunday, I went down to the cottage to say goodbye before I drove back to London. She was up and about, rather pale, but she seemed to be all right."

"Did you try again to make her come back with you?"

"Yes, I did, but she was adamant. So we said goodbye, and I left her. And since then there has been no word."

"But you can surely find out where she is?"

"There is no way of finding out. There's no telephone, never has been. Marcus wrote, of course, but Emma seems to have inherited Ben's built-in aversion to answering letters. There hasn't been another word."

"But this is crazy. In this day and age . . . there must be someone who can tell you . . ."

"There's no one. No one Emma ever talked to. There was no daily woman, coming in to clean, she did it all herself. That was the big reason for going back to Porthkerris in the first place, so that she could keep house for Ben. Of course, after two weeks of frigid silence, Marcus could stand it no longer, and put through a telephone call to the landlord of the Sliding Tackle, which was the pub Ben used to frequent, but Ben had been gone for six weeks, anyway, and Emma never went near the place.''

''Then you'll have to go down to Porthkerris and ask around.''

''Marcus isn't prepared to do that.''

''Why not?''

''For reasons. Emma isn't a child. She's been hurt, and Marcus respects the fact that if she wants to be left alone, he has no right to interfere. He's asked her to come to London and live with Helen and himself . . . anyway until she's found her feet again. He can scarcely do more. And there's another reason, too.''

''I know,'' said Jane. ''It's Helen, isn't it?''

''Yes, it is,'' said Robert, hating to admit it. ''Helen has always resented the hold Ben has over Marcus. There have been times when she would gladly have seen Ben at the bottom of the ocean. But she's accepted it because she had to, because wet-nursing Ben's career is part of Marcus's job, and without Marcus to keep him, more or less on the rails, God knows what would have happened to Ben Litton.''

''And now she doesn't want him to start killing himself over Emma.''

''Precisely.''

Jane rocked her glass, letting the ice clink against its side. She said, ''And you?''

He looked up. ''What about me?''

''Do you feel involved?''

''Why do you ask that?''

''You sound involved.''

"I scarcely know the girl."

"But you're worried about her."

He considered this. "Yes," he said at last. "Yes, I suppose I am. God knows why."

His glass was empty. Jane laid down her own drink, and got up to take his glass and pour him another whisky. From behind him, busy with ice, she said, "Why don't *you* go down to Porthkerris and find out?"

"Because she isn't there."

"She isn't . . . ? You know? But you never told me that."

"After the abortive telephone call to the Sliding Tackle, Marcus got the wind up. He rang the local police, and they found out a few facts and called us back. Cottage closed up, studio closed up, Post Office told to keep all mail until further notice." He reached up to take the fresh drink that Jane handed him over the back of the sofa. "Thanks."

"And her father . . . ? Does he know?"

"Yes, Marcus wrote and told him. But you can't expect Ben to get unduly excited. After all, he's still in the throes of what is virtually a honeymoon, and Emma's been sculling round Europe on her own since she was fourteen. Don't forget, that this is not a normal father-daughter relationship."

Jane sighed. "It most certainly isn't."

Robert grinned at her. She was a comfortingly down-to-earth person and it was for this reason that, on an impulse, he had dropped in this evening for a drink on his way home from work. Usually, the double life he led with Marcus Bernstein, working with him at the Gallery, as well as living in the same house, offered no strain at all. But just now, things were difficult. Robert had come back from a business trip to Paris, to find Marcus on edge, and unable to concentrate for very long on anything but the problem of Emma Litton. After discussing it with him, Robert

109

realised that Marcus blamed himself for what had happened, and refused to be talked out of his guilt. Helen, on the other hand, was unsympathetic, and determined that he should not get himself more deeply involved in the whole sorry business, and for the moment the tensions had got on top of them, and split the ménage at Milton Gardens from top to bottom.

The situation was not improved by the weather. After a cool spring, London had suddenly been caught up in the throes of a veritable heatwave. The early mornings broke in a pearl-like mist which gradually dissolved into day after day of baking sun. Girls went to work in sleeveless dresses, men shed their jackets and sat at their desks in shirt-sleeves. The parks at lunch-time were filled with recumbent picnickers; shops and restaurants sprouted striped awnings, windows were flung open to the smallest breeze, and in the streets, parked cars frizzled and pavements glared, and melted tar stuck to the soles of shoes.

The heat, like some monstrous epidemic, had invaded even the quiet, pond-green recesses of the Bernstein Gallery. All day long there had been an endless stream of visitors and prospective clients, for the trans-Atlantic tourist season had started, and this was apt to be their busiest time. And at the end of it all, Robert, driving home, had found himself longing for a new face, a cool drink, and some conversation that had nothing to do with Artists, be they Renaissance, Impressionist or Pop.

Jane Marshall sprang immediately to mind.

Her little house was in a narrow mews between Sloane Square and Pimlico Road. As he turned the car into the street, and eased down over the cobbles, he gave a double toot on the horn, and she appeared at the open upstairs window, her hands on the sill, her fair hair falling over her face as she leaned out to see who it was.

"Robert! I thought you were still in Paris."

"I was till two days ago. Have you got such a thing as a long, cool, alcoholic drink for an exhausted working man?"

"Of course I have. Hold on. I'll come down and let you in."

Her tiny house had always charmed him. Originally a coachman's cottage, it had a steep, narrow staircase, which led straight up to the first floor. Here there was an open hall-way, a sitting-room, and a kitchen, and upstairs again, in the slope-roofed loft, her bedroom and bathroom. As such it was inadequate enough, but since she had started her interior decorating business, it had become a joke. The sitting-room she had turned into a workroom, but still the bales of fabric, the fringing and the cushions, and the small bits of bric-à-brac she so cleverly picked up, overflowed into every available corner of space, rendering it all as gay and colourful as a patchwork quilt.

She was delighted to see him. She had spent the morning with a tiresome woman who wanted her entire house in St John's Wood done up in cream, which she called "Redecorating in Magnolia." And then there had been a session with a young and rising actress who demanded something startling for her new flat.

"She sat here for hours, showing me pictures of the sort of thing she had in mind. I tried to tell her she should get a bulldozer in, not an interior decorator, but she wouldn't listen. These people never do. Whisky?"

"That," said Robert, collapsing on the sofa in front of the open window, "is the nicest thing anybody has said to me all day."

She poured two drinks, made sure he was supplied with cigarettes and an ash-tray, and then settled herself composedly down to face him. She was a very pretty girl. Her blonde hair was straight and thick, cut in a curve to her chin. Her eyes were green, her nose tip-tilted, her mouth sweet, but implacable. Her broken marriage had left certain scars upon her character and she was not always the most tolerant of people, but there was a directness about her that he found as refreshing as a drink of cold water, and she always looked delicious.

Now he said, "I came here with the express purpose of not talking shop. How did we get on to the subject of Ben Litton anyway?"

"I brought it up. I was intrigued. Every time I saw Helen, she kept dropping maddening hints and then refusing to say more. She feels strongly about this, doesn't she?"

"Only because, in his day, Ben Litton has run poor Marcus ragged."

"Does she know Emma?"

"She hasn't seen her since she went to Switzerland six years ago."

"It's difficult," said Jane, "to be fair about people if you don't know them very well."

"It's sometimes difficult to be fair even if you do. And now . . ." He leaned forward to stub out his cigarette. "Let's drop the subject and make a tacit agreement not to mention it again. Are you doing anything this evening?"

"Not a thing."

"Then why don't we go and find somewhere with a roof garden or a terrace, and have a quiet dinner together?"

"I'd like that," said Jane.

"I'll call Helen and tell her I'm not coming back . . ."

"In that case . . ." She stood up. "I shall go and have a shower and change. I shan't be long."

"There isn't any hurry."

"Make yourself at home . . . get yourself another drink. There are cigarettes here, and an evening paper somewhere if you care to look for it . . ."

112

She went up the stairs. He heard her moving about, high heels tapping on the polished floor. She sang under her breath, slightly out of tune. He put down his glass and went into her living-room, and ran her telephone to earth at last, beneath a bundle of flowered chintzes, and called Helen to say he would not be home for dinner. Then he went back to pour the third drink of the evening, and loosened his tie, and flopped once more on the sofa.

The whisky had revived him slightly, and beneath its clean cold bite, his tiredness had changed from end-of-the-day fatigue to a pleasant lassitude. The paper protruded from beneath a cushion, and he pulled it out, and then saw that it was not the *Evening Standard*, but the *Stage*.

"Jane."

"Hello!"

"I didn't know you took the *Stage*."

"I don't."

"Well it's here."

"Is it?" She didn't sound particularly interested. "Dinah Burnett must have left it behind. You know she's the actress who needs the bulldozer."

He opened it aimlessly. "Wanted One All Round Girl Dancer. Why does she have to be all round? Why can't she be all square?"

"Search me."

He turned to the Repertory page. They were doing Shakespeare at Birmingham, a restoration revival at Manchester, and at Brookford, staging the première of a new play . . .

Brookford.

The name leapt at him from the page like a bullet. Brookford. He sat up, slapped the paper into shape, and read the whole item.

*

113

Brookford Rep's summer season opens this week with the world première of *Daisies on the Grass*, a comedy in three acts by local writer Phyllis Jason. This light but well-knit play stars actress Charmian Vaughan in the lead role of Stella. Other parts are supplementary, but John Rigger, Sophie Lambart and Christopher Ferris all help to bring the mirthful suspense to its climax, and Sara Rutherford is charmingly natural as the bride. Tommy Childers' production is fast and furious, and the set, by scenic artist Brian Dare, evoked a spontaneous applause from the enthusiastic first-night audience.

Christopher Ferris.

He laid the paper carefully down, and reached for a cigarette, and lit it. Christopher Ferris. He had forgotten Christopher.

But now, out of a jumble of memories, he heard Emma's voice again, that first day, when he had given her lunch at Marcello's.

Did you know about Christopher? Quite by chance Christopher and I met up again in Paris. And he came this very morning and saw me off at Le Bourget.

And he remembered – facing her across the table – being suddenly wise, and knowing the reason for her smile and the bloom of her skin and the brightness of her eyes.

And later, in the draughty studio at Porthkerris, the subject of Christopher had, fleetingly, come up again, sandwiched between other more important items of discussion. *He'll be at Brookford by now*, Emma had said. *In the thick of rehearsals.*

He stood up and went to the foot of the stairs.

"Jane."

"Hello!"

"How nearly ready are you?"

"I'm just doing my face."

114

"Where's Brookford?"

"In Surrey."

"How long will it take us to get there?"

"Brookford? Oh, about forty-five, fifty minutes."

He glanced at his watch. "If we leave right away, or as near
as we can . . . we shouldn't be too late."

Jane appeared at the head of the stairs, with a mirror in one
hand and an eyeliner brush in the other.

"Late for what?"

"We're going to the theatre."

"I thought we were going out for dinner."

"Later, perhaps we will. But first we're going to Brookford,
to see a well-knit comedy called *Daisies on the Grass* . . ."

"Have you gone out of your mind?"

". . . by local writer Phyllis Jason."

"You have gone out of your mind."

"I'll explain on the way down. Be a darling and hurry."

As they roared down the M4 Jane said, "You mean that
nobody knows about this young man except you."

"Emma didn't tell Ben, because he'd never liked Christopher
anyway – Helen says he was jealous of the boy."

"And Emma didn't tell Marcus Bernstein."

"I don't think so."

"But she told you."

"Yes, she told me. She told me that very first day. And why
the devil I didn't think of him before I cannot imagine."

"Is she in love with him?"

"I wouldn't know. She's certainly very fond of him."

"Do you think we'll find her at Brookford?"

"If we don't, then I'll bet even money that Christopher Ferris
will know where she is." Jane did not reply. After a little, he
added, his eyes still fixed on the speeding road, "I'm sorry about

115

this. I promised the subject wasn't to be raised again, and here I am whisking you off to the wilds of darkest Surrey.''

"Why," asked Jane, "are you so anxious to find Emma?"

"Because of Marcus. I should like to set Marcus's mind at rest."

"I see."

"Because if Marcus's mind is at rest, then Helen will relax and life will be a great deal more comfortable for all of us."

"Well, that's fair enough . . . Look, I think we should turn off here."

The Brookford Repertory Theatre took some finding. They cruised up and down the High Street, then asked directions from a tired-looking policeman in shirt-sleeves. He sent them a half a mile from the centre of town, and, off a back street, up a cul-de-sac, they found the large brick edifice, looking more like a mission hall than anything else, but for the word THEATRE written above the door in neon letters, deadened by the hot evening light.

Outside, by the pavement, were parked a couple of cars, and alongside them, with their feet in the gutter, sat two small girls playing with a broken perambulator.

There were posters.

WORLD PREMIERE

DAISIES ON THE GRASS

by PHYLLIS JASON

A comedy in Three Acts

Produced by

TOMMY CHILDERS

Jane stood, taking in this inauspicious façade. "So much for the living theatre."

Robert put his hand under her elbow. "Come along now."

116

They went up a flight of stone steps, and into a small foyer, with a cigarette kiosk on one side, and a box office on the other. In the box office a girl sat knitting.

"I'm afraid the show's started," she said, as Robert and Jane appeared on the other side of the glass.

"Yes, we thought it would have. But we'll have a couple of tickets anyway."

"What price?"

"Oh . . . well – stalls."

"That's fifteen shillings. But you'll have to wait till the second act."

"Is there anywhere we could get a drink?"

"The bar's upstairs."

"Thank you very much." He took the tickets and his change. "I expect you know all the people who work here."

"Well, yes . . ."

"Christopher Ferris . . ."

"Oh, is he a friend of yours?"

"Well, a friend of a friend. The thing is, I wondered if he has his sister here . . . at least, she's his step-sister. Emma Litton."

"Emma's working here."

"She's *working* here. In the theatre?"

"That's right. As ASM – Assistant Stage Manager. Our last girl suddenly went off ill with an appendix, and Emma said she'd come and help out. Of course," her voice became professional ". . . Mr Childers usually likes someone in the job who's had a bit of stage training, you know, RADA, or a bit of experience somewhere, so that they double up in small parts. But as she was here, and didn't have anything to do, he let her have the job. Just until the regular girl's better."

"I see. Do you think we'd be able to see her?"

"Well, after the show, yes. But Mr Childers won't have anyone back stage until it's over."

"That's all right. We can wait. Thank you very much."

"Not at all. It's a pleasure."

They went upstairs to a second, larger foyer with a bar in the corner, and sat there, drinking lager and talking to the barman until a light spatter of applause announced the end of the first act. The lights went up, the doors opened, and a small stream of people emerged for refreshment. Jane and Robert waited until the first curtain bell, and then went into the auditorium themselves, buying a couple of programmes on their way, and being shown to their seats by an eager young girl in a nylon overall. Attendance that night was certainly sparse, and Jane and Robert were the only two people sitting in the third row. Jane looked about her with a professional eye.

"I think it was once a mission hall," she decided. "Nobody would have built anything so ugly as a theatre. But I must say, they have done it up quite imaginatively, and the lighting and the colours are good. What a shame they don't get better audiences . . ."

The curtain at last went up on the second act. "The lounge hall of Mrs Edbury's house in Gloucestershire" said the programme note, and there it was, complete with french windows, staircase, settee, table with drinks, table with telephone, low table with magazines (for leading lady to pick up and idly flick through in moments when she did not know what to do with her hands?) and three doors.

"Draughty house," murmured Jane.

"It's better when they shut the french windows."

But the french windows had to be open, for in bounced the *ingénue* (*Sara Rutherford is charmingly natural as the bride*), flung herself on the settee and burst into tears. Jane's profile was alert with delighted disbelief. Robert settled more deeply into his seat.

It was a terrible play. Even if they had seen the first act, and so been able to unravel the tangled skein of the plot, it would still have been a terrible play. It bristled with clichés, with stock characters (there was even a comic charlady), with contrived exits and entrances, and with telephone calls. There were eight of these in the course of the second act alone.

When the curtain came down, Robert said, "Let's go and have another drink. I could do with a double brandy after that."

"I'm not going to move," said Jane. "I'm not going to break the spell. I haven't seen a play like this since I was seven. And the set makes me positively nostalgic. But there's one thing, Robert, that sticks out like a sore thumb."

"What's that?"

"Christopher Ferris is very, very good . . ."

He was, too. When he had shambled on stage, as the vague young university student who was eventually to win the heroine from her stockbroker fiancé, *Daisies on the Grass* showed its first, faint spark of life. His lines were not better than anyone else's, but his timing was impeccable, and he managed to make them funny or sad, or wryly charming. For the part he wore corduroys, a sagging sweater and horn-rimmed spectacles, but even these could not disguise his elegance and his good looks and the natural long-legged grace with which he moved.

". . . and he's not merely very good, he's very attractive," Jane went on. "I can see why his step-sister was so pleased to bump into him again in Paris. I wouldn't mind bumping into him myself."

The third act had the same set, but now it was night. Blue moonlight shone through the open window, and down the stairs came the little bride, carrying a suitcase, tiptoeing, all ready to run away or elope or whatever it was she'd spent the last hour in deciding to do. Robert couldn't remember. He was waiting for Christopher to come back on stage. When he did, Robert simply watched him the entire time, detachedly, absorbed and full of admiration. By now, he had the audience, small as it was, in the palm of his hand. As Robert watched, so they watched. Christopher scratched the back of his head and they laughed. He took off his spectacles to kiss the girl, and they laughed again. He put them back on to say goodbye for ever, and there was silence, and then people began to blow their noses. And when it was all over, and the cast lined up for the curtain call, the applause was long, and real, and it was all for Christopher.

"What do we do now?" asked Jane.

"It's not closing time for another ten minutes. Let's go and find a drink."

They went back to the bar. The barman said, "Well, how did you enjoy the show, sir?"

"Well, I don't know . . . I . . ."

Jane was braver. "We thought it was terrible," she said, but quite politely. "And I've fallen in love with Christopher Ferris."

The barman grinned. "Quite something, isn't he? Pity you had to come tonight, when the audience was so thin on the ground as it were. Mr Childers did hope, Miss Jason being local and all that jazz, that this play would bring them in. But you can't fight a heatwave."

"Do you usually have good houses?" Jane wanted to know.

"They go up and down. Now, last show we did was *Present Laughter* . . . that fairly filled the place up."

"It's a good play," said Robert.

"What part did Christopher Ferris have?" asked Jane.

"Now, let me see. Oh, I know, he was the young playwright.

120

You know, the one that bounces round on the chairs and eats biscuits. Ronald Maule he's called in the play. Oh, very funny, Christopher Ferris was in that part. Brought the house down, he did . . .'' Wiping away at his tumblers, he glanced up at the clock. "I'm afraid I'll have to ask you to drink up, sir . . . closing time . . .''

"Yes, of course. By the way, how do we get back stage? We want to see Emma Litton.''

"You can just go down the auditorium, sir, go through the door at the right of the stage. But watch out for Mr Collins the Stage Manager. He doesn't exactly relish visitors.''

"Thanks,'' said Robert. "And good night.''

They went back into the theatre. The curtains had been drawn back, and the stage was revealed once more, but without footlights the set looked less inspiring than ever. On stage a young boy was struggling with the sofa, trying to heave it to one side, and someone, somewhere, had left a door open, so that the whole theatre was swept with a stuffy draught of used-up air. The programme girl was going round, slapping up the empty seats and collecting empty chocolate boxes and cigarette cartons in a trash can.

"There is nothing,'' said Jane, "so depressing as an empty theatre.''

They started to walk down towards the stage. As they approached, Robert realised that it was not a boy who struggled, single-handed with the heavy sofa, but a girl, dressed in an old blue sweater and jeans.

When he was close enough, he said, "I wonder if you can help me . . . ?''

She turned to look at him, and Robert, with the shock of sheer disbelief, found himself face to face with Emma Litton.

121

8

After a second's gaping silence, Emma stopped trying to move the sofa, and straightened up. He thought that she seemed much taller and thinner, the cold stage light was not flattering, her wrists hung like sticks from her rolled-up sleeves. But the worst thing was her hair. She had cut off her hair, and now her head seemed small and vulnerable, furred like the pelt of an animal.

There was the animal feel of watchfulness about her, too. A scarey look as though she waited for him to make the first move, to say the first word, before she knew which way to jump. He slid his hands into his pockets, in a deliberate attempt to both look and feel casual, and he said, "Hello, Emma."

She gave the ghost of a smile. She said, "This sofa feels as though it's been stuffed with lead and lost its castors in the process."

"Isn't there anyone who can help you?" He came forward to the edge of his side of the stage, so that he was looking up at her. "It looks very heavy."

"Yes, there'll be someone in a moment." She did not seem to know what to do with her hands. She rubbed them on the seat of her jeans as though they were dirty, and then folded her arms. It was a curiously defensive movement, and made her shoulder-bones jut forward beneath the thin cotton of her shirt. "What are you doing here?"

"We came down to see *Daisies on the Grass* . . . We drove down from town. This is Jane Marshall. Jane, this is Emma."

They smiled, nodded at each other, murmured how do you do? Emma turned back to Robert. "Did . . . did you know I was here?"

"No, but I knew Christopher was, and I thought you might be."

"I've been working for a couple of weeks. It gives me something to do."

Robert made no comment on this, and, perhaps disconcerted by his silence, Emma suddenly sat down on the sofa that she was meant to be shifting. Her hands hung listlessly between her knees. After a little, she said, "Did Marcus send you?"

"No. We just came to call. Make sure you're all right . . ."

"I'm all right."

"What time are you finished here . . . ?"

"I'll be about half an hour. I have to clear the stage for rehearsal tomorrow morning. Why?"

"I thought we might have all gone to some hotel or other, for a sandwich and a drink. Jane and I haven't had any dinner . . ."

"Oh, how kind!" She did not sound enthusiastic. "Well . . . the thing is . . . that I usually leave something in the oven at the flat . . . a casserole or something. Johnny and Chris never eat anything otherwise. We'll have to go back or it'll burn."

"Johnny?"

"Johnny Rigger. He was the fiancé. You know, the other man. He lives with Christo . . . and me."

"I see."

There was another silence. Emma, discomfited, struggled with her more hospitable instincts. "I would ask you to come

124

back, if you'd like to, but there's nothing but a few cans of beer . . ."

"We like beer," said Robert promptly.

"And the flat's in a dreadful mess. There never seems to be time to clean it properly. Not now that I'm working, I mean."

"We don't mind. How do we get there?"

"Well . . . have you got a car?"

"Yes. It's outside."

"Yes . . . well. If you go out and wait, Christo and I will join you later. If that's all right. And then we can show you where it is."

"Splendid. How about Johnny?"

"Oh, he'll be along later."

"We'll wait for you."

He took his hands out of his pockets and turned, and he and Jane walked back up the slight slope of the auditorium. As they reached the double doors, and Robert held one half open for Jane to go through, all hell seemed to break loose on stage.

"Where the devil is that Litton girl?" Robert was in time to see Emma scramble off the sofa as though someone had set off a firework, and try once more to move the cumbersome thing. A small man with a black beard shot on stage, looking like the worst-tempered sort of pirate. "Look, ducky, I asked you to move the bloody sofa, not to go to sleep on it. God, I'll be thankful to see that other girl back and you safely out of this place . . ." One either had to go and knock him down, or withdraw. For Emma's sake Robert withdrew.

The door swung shut behind him, but as they crossed the foyer, the voice could still be heard ". . . She's a moron, we all know, but no one could be as crassly stupid as you . . ."

"Charming," said Jane, as they went down the stairs. Robert

did not reply, because, until the white-hot blaze of anger with which he had been suddenly consumed, died down, he was not capable of saying anything. "That must be Mr Collins, the stage manager. Not a very nice man to work for."

They reached the street door, and went down the steps and crossed the pavement and got into the car. It was dark now, a soft, bloomy dusk had descended upon the town, but the heat of the day still lingered, held by the narrow confines of the street, by sunbaked stone and paving. Above them the Theatre sign shone brightly, but as they got into the car, someone from inside the building turned it off. The evening's entertainment was over. Robert reached for his cigarettes, gave Jane one and lit it, and then took one for himself. After a moment he felt a little calmer.

He said, "She's cut off all her hair."

"Has she? What was it like before?"

"Long and silky and dark."

"She doesn't want us to go tonight. You know that, don't you?"

"Yes, I know that. But we must. We don't need to stay long."

"And I hate beer."

"I'm sorry. Perhaps someone will make you some coffee."

". . . It isn't even as though it's a job that requires any sort of brain. The most idiotic creature straight out of RADA could do it more competently than you."

Collins was letting fly, unloading the day's tensions and frustrations in a flood of invective that was directed solely at Emma. He hated her. It had something to do with Christopher; with the fact that her father was both successful and famous. At first, she had tried sticking up for herself, but now she knew better than to try and stem this venomous flood. With Collins,

126

you couldn't win. She simply listened, got on with her work, tried not to let him see how deeply he could upset her.

"... you got this job because I have to have someone to help me ... God help me. You didn't get it because Chris shoved his oar in, and you didn't get it because some fool is willing to pay twenty thousand for a Ben Litton of red spots on a blue background. I've got more sense than that, as by now you have no doubt found out. So don't start thinking you can loll around entertaining your toffee-nosed friends ... and the next time they condescend to visit our humble little show, tell them to bloody well wait till we've finished, will you? Now come on, get that sofa out of the bloody way ..."

It was nearly eleven before at last he let her go, and then she found Christo waiting for her in Tommy Childers' office. The door was open and she heard them talking, and she knocked and put her head in and said, "I'm ready now. I'm sorry I was so long."

Christo stood up. "That's all right." He stubbed out his cigarette. "Good night, Tommy."

" 'Night, Chris."

"Thanks for everything."

"That's OK, old chap ..."

They went downstairs towards the stage door. He put his arm around her as they went. Their warm bodies touched, it was too hot for such contact, but she found it comforting. Outside, in the little alley that led down to the street, he stopped by the dustbins to light another cigarette.

He said, "You were long enough. Collins playing up?"

"He was furious because Robert Morrow's here."

"Robert Morrow?"

"He's in Bernstein's, with Marcus. He's Marcus's brother-in-

127

law. I told you. He came down to see the show . . . He's brought a girl with him.''

Christo stood looking down at her. "To see the show or to see you?"

"I think to see us both.''

"He can't try to take you back. Say you're under age or anything?"

"Of course not."

"Then that's all right."

"Yes, I suppose it is. But, you see, like a fool, I asked them back to the flat. At least, I didn't mean to ask them, but somehow I did, and they're coming. They're waiting for us now, in the car. Oh, Christo, I am sorry.''

He laughed. "*I* don't mind."

"They won't stay long."

"I don't mind if they stay all night. Don't look so tragic." He took her in his arms, and kissed her cheek. She thought that if only the evening, the day, the endless day, could end right here and now, she would be well content. She was afraid of Robert. She was too tired to fence with him, to answer questions, to try and evade those watchful grey eyes. She was too tired to compete with his friend, who was blonde and pretty and almost indecently cool-looking in her sleeveless navy-blue dress. She was too tired to tidy the flat for them, to shovel clothes and scripts and empty glasses out of sight, to open beer cans, and make coffee, and get Christo's dinner out of the oven.

Christo rubbed his chin against her cheek. "What's wrong?" he asked gently.

"Nothing." He did not like her to say she was tired. He was never tired. He did not know what the word meant.

He said, in her ear, "It's been a good day, hasn't it?"

"Yes, of course." She drew away from him. "A good day."

With their arms entwined, they went down the alley towards the street. Robert heard their voices, and got out of the car to meet them. They came towards him, in and out of the patches of light flung by the street lamps. They walked like lovers, Emma trailing a sweater, Christo with a bulky script under one arm and a cigarette between his fingers. When they reached the car, they stopped. "Hello," said Christopher, smiling.

"Christo, this is Robert Morrow, and Miss Marshall . . ."

"Mrs Marshall," Jane corrected sweetly, leaning over the back of the front seat. "Hello, Christopher."

"Sorry we've been so long," said Christo " . . . Emma's only just told me you were here. And she was having her nightly set-to with Collins, so we've all been fairly occupied. I believe you're coming back to have a can of beer, or something. I'm afraid we've got nothing stronger."

"That's OK," said Robert. "If you can tell us the way . . ."

"Of course."

The flat was in the basement of a row of daunting Victorian houses that had once seen better days. They were much gabled, and decorated with fancy brick work and stained windows, but the street itself was dismal, and the curtains of bow-windowed front rooms sagged sadly and were not always very clean. Worn stone steps led down to an area where there were dustbins and one or two dead geraniums in pots, and, as they descended, there was a scream of fury from a frustrated cat, and a black, rat-like form shot up the stairs between their legs. Jane let out a small scream of fright.

"It's all right," said Emma. "It's only a cat."

Christo opened the door, and went ahead, turning on cold overhead lights, for the flat was a furnished one, and not supplied with lamps. Johnny had started making a couple out

129

of Chianti bottles but had got no further than buying adaptors
and a pair of fancy shades. The rooms of the flat had been
sketchily converted, and it was still sadly obvious that their
original intentions had been kitchens, larders, and wash-houses.
An old range had been torn from the wall, and the resultant void
filled with shelves, which no one had ever bothered to paint, and
which acted as a catch-all for books, shoes, scripts, cigarettes,
letters and a pile of old magazines. There was a divan which
had been covered with an orange curtain and piled with thinly-
filled cushions, but remained stubbornly a bed. There were one
or two rickety kitchen chairs and a folding table, and the flagged
floor was sparsely covered by an elderly carpet which had long
since lost all colour and most of its pile. The walls had been
whitewashed, but there were oozing damp stains like maps, and
the corners of a bull-fighting poster, stuck to the bricks, was
already beginning to curl. There was the smell of mice and dry
rot, and, even on this hot summer evening, the very airlessness
was clammy, like the inside of a cave.

Christo dropped his script on a table and went to open the
window which was protected with iron bars, like a prison.

"Let's have some air. We have to keep the place shut up
because of the cats, they get in anywhere. What would you like
to drink? . . . There is beer, if Johnny hasn't drunk it all . . . or
perhaps you'd like coffee. Have we got any coffee, Emma . . . ?"

"There's some instant coffee. I don't get the other sort, because there's nothing to make it in. Do sit down . . . sit on the bed.
Sit anywhere. There are some cigarettes . . ." She found them, a
box of fifty, handed them round, searched for an ash-tray while
Robert lit them. There was no ash-tray, so she went down the
flagged passage to the kitchen for a couple of saucers. The sink
was full of dirty dishes, and for a moment she could not think
when they had used them, when she had last been here, from

130

what back-log of history they dated. Pinned down, remembered, the morning seemed three weeks away. No day had ever lasted for longer. And now, it was past eleven o'clock at night, and still it was not over. Still, the boys had to be given their supper, the kettle boiled for coffee, the can-opener found.

She found two clean saucers and took them back to the others. Christo had put on a record. He could do nothing, not even talk, without perpetual background music. It was Ella Fitzgerald and Cole Porter.

Every time we say good-bye
I die a little.

They were talking about *Daisies on the Grass*. ". . . if you can breathe life into a script like that," Jane was saying to Christopher, ". . . I'm sure you're going to go far." She was laughing. Emma put down the ash-tray, and Jane looked up. "Thank you . . . is there anything I can do?"

"No, nothing. I'll just go and get some glasses. Would you like beer, or would you rather have coffee?"

"Would coffee be too much trouble?"

"No, not at all . . . I'd like coffee too . . ."

Back in the kitchen, she closed the door, so that they would not hear her clattering dishes, and tied on an apron, and put a kettle on to boil. When she lit the gas, it always backfired and frightened her out of her wits. She found a tray and cups and saucers, the tin of coffee, sugar, the cans of beer in a box beneath the sink. There were black beetles on the floor and Johnny had not emptied the trash can. She picked it up to take it out to the dustbin, but as she did so the door behind her opened, and she turned to face Robert Morrow.

He looked at the bucket. "Where are you taking that?"

131

"Nowhere," said Emma, furious at being caught. She turned to sling it back under the sink again, but he caught her arm and took it from her, looking with distaste at the mixture of old tea-leaves and of opened tins, and wet paperbags.

"Where does this go?"

Defeated, Emma told him. "In the dustbin. By the door. Where we came in."

He bore it off, down the passage, looking ridiculous, and Emma went back to the sink, and wished that he had not come. He didn't belong in Brookford; at the theatre; here, in the flat. She didn't want him to be sorry for her. For after all, there was nothing to be sorry about. She was happy, wasn't she? She was with Christo, and that was all that mattered, and how they managed their affairs had nothing whatever to do with Robert.

She prayed that he and his immaculate friend would be gone by the time Johnny Rigger returned.

When he came back with the empty bucket, she was clattering dishes, trying to give the impression that she was being busy. She half-turned over her shoulder and said coolly, "Thank you. I shan't be a moment," hoping that he would take the hint and leave her alone.

But it was no good. He shut the door, put the trash can down on the floor, and taking Emma by the shoulders, turned her round to face him. He wore an unrumpled and cool-looking suit, a blue shirt, and a dark tie, and Emma had the dish-mop in one hand and a plate in the other, and had to make herself look up and meet those probing grey eyes.

She said, "I wish you hadn't come. Why did you come?"

"Marcus has been worried about you." He took the dish-mop and the plate from her and leaned over to tip them back into the cluttered sink. "Perhaps you should have let him know where you were."

"Well, now you can tell him, can't you? And, Robert, I've got a lot to do, and there's just not room for two people in this kitchen . . ."

"Isn't there?" He was smiling. He settled himself on the edge of the table, and now his face was on a level with hers. He said, "You know, this evening, when I first saw you in the theatre I didn't know it was you. Why did you cut your hair?"

He could be very disarming. Emma put up a hand to stroke the stubbly nape of her neck. "When I started working at the theatre, it was such a nuisance. It got in the way, and then it was so hot, and it was always being splashed with paint when I was doing scenery. And there's nowhere here to wash it, and even if I did wash it, it took hours to dry." She hated talking about her hair. She missed it; missed its weight and familiarity and the soothing therapy of brushing it each night. "So one of the girls in the theatre cut it off for me." It had lain on the Green Room carpet like skeins of brown silk and Emma had felt like a murderer.

"Do you like working in the theatre?"

She thought of Collins. "Not much."

"Do you have to . . . ?"

"No, of course not. But Christo's there all day, you see, and there's nothing much to do here, on my own. Brookford's terribly dull. I didn't know such dull places even existed. So when this other girl went ill with appendicitis, Christo fixed it for me to go and help out."

"What will you do when she comes back?"

"I don't know. I haven't thought."

Behind her, the kettle boiled over. Emma turned swiftly to put out the gas, and lift the kettle on to the tray, but Robert said, "Not just yet."

She frowned. "I was going to make coffee."

133

"Coffee can wait. Let's get everything sorted out first."

Emma's face closed up. "There's nothing to sort out."

"Yes, of course there is. And I want to be able to tell Marcus what happened. For instance, how did you get hold of Christopher?"

"I rang him up – early that Sunday morning. I went to the call box and rang him up. They were having a dress rehearsal, so he was at the theatre. You see, he'd already asked me to come to Brookford and be with him, but I couldn't, because of Ben."

"You'd already spoken to him that morning, when I came to say goodbye?"

"Yes."

"And you never told me?"

"No, I didn't tell you. I wanted to start something quite new, a whole new life, without anybody knowing."

"I see. So you rang Christopher . . ."

"Yes, and that night he borrowed Johnny Rigger's car, and he came down to Porthkerris and brought me back here. We closed up the cottage together, and we left the key of the studio at the Sliding Tackle."

"The landlord didn't know where you were."

"I didn't tell him where I was going."

"Marcus phoned him."

"Marcus shouldn't have. Marcus isn't responsible for me any more. I'm not a little girl now."

"What Marcus feels is not simply responsibility, Emma, but a real fondness and you should realise that. Have you heard from Ben?"

"Yes, I had a letter on that Monday morning, before I left Porthkerris. And one from Melissa, too . . . asking me to go out and visit them."

"And did you write back?"

Emma shook her head. "No." She was ashamed of this, and swiftly looked down, to fiddle with a jagged thumbnail.

"Why not?"

She shrugged. "I don't know. I suppose I thought I'd be in the way."

"I should have thought that even being in the way was preferable to this . . ." His gesture embraced the littered kitchen, the whole seedy flat.

It was not the most fortunate of remarks. "What's wrong with it?"

"It's not just this place, it's that crumby theatre, the lunatic with a beard who was yelling at you to move the sofa . . ."

"Well, you told me to get a job."

"Not this kind of a job. You have a good brain, you speak three languages, and you appear to be moderately intelligent. What sort of a job is it pushing furniture around a third class re . . . ?"

"*My real job is being with Christo!*"

After this outburst, there was a terrible silence. A car passed in the street outside. Christopher's voice came up the stone passage, backed by the soft-playing record. A cat started yowling.

Robert spoke at last. "Do you want me to tell your father that?"

Emma blazed once more into the attack. "I supposed that's why you came. Spying for Ben."

"I simply came to find out where you were and how you were."

"Be sure to give him all the ghoulish details. It doesn't matter to us, and he won't take any notice, anyway."

"Emma . . ."

135

"Don't forget, he is no ordinary, run-of-the-mill parent, as you are only too fond of telling me."

"*Emma, will you listen . . . !*"

The last word was scarcely out of his mouth, when the door behind him burst open and a slurred and cheerful voice broke in. "Well, what a nice little chat you two are having!"

Robert wheeled. In the open doorway stood the young man who had played the part of the stuffy stockbroker in *Daisies on the Grass*. Only now he was stuffy no longer, but quite simply very drunk, and to steady himself hung on to the top of the doorway, like a monkey swinging on a trapeze. His legs, buckling slightly, did nothing to dispel this impression.

"Hello, darling," he said to Emma. He let go of the door and weaved into the tiny kitchen, rendering it unbearably crowded. With the palms of his hands flat on the table, he leaned forward to kiss Emma. The kiss was loud and smacking, but did not come within six inches of her face.

"We've got callers," he observed. "And a bloody great car parked outside. It adds great tone to the neighbourhood." His legs buckled again, and for a second his weight was supported solely by his arms. He smiled expansively at Robert. "What's your name?"

"He's called Robert Morrow," said Emma shortly, "and I'll make you some coffee."

"I don't want coffee. I do not want coffee." He raised his fist to the words, and once more his legs let him down. This time Robert caught him, and hauled him upright.

"Thanks, old boy. Very civil of you. Emma, how about a little sustenance? Feed the inner man; you know the routine. I do hope you've asked this nice chap Robert to stay for dinner. There's also a toothsome blonde in the other room, chatting Christopher up to no mean tune. Know anything about her?"

136

Nobody bothered to answer him. Emma turned back to the cooker, took the lid off the kettle and put it on again. Johnny Rigger stared at her back and then at Robert, apparently waiting for life, with all its confusions, to be explained to him.

Robert could not trust himself to speak. He yearned to pick up this shambling drunk by the scruff of his neck and chuck him somewhere; preferably in the dustbin, where he had just dumped the unsavoury contents of the trash can. Then he would come back to deal with Emma in the same way, flinging her into the back of his car, driving her to London, to Porthkerris, to Paris – anywhere, away from this terrible basement, from the theatre, from the depressing suburban town.

He stared at her stubborn back view, willing her to turn round and face up to him. But she did not move, and her thin neck, and her shorn head, and the droop of her shoulders, all of which, he knew, should touch on his sympathy, did nothing but infuriate him.

He said, at last, formally, "This is simply a waste of everybody's time. I think Jane and I should go."

Emma accepted this in silence, but Johnny was full of protests. "Oh, you must stay, old chap. Stay and have something to eat . . ."

But Robert had pushed past him and was already halfway down the flagged passage. He found the other two deep in conversation, and quite unaware of any sort of drama. Christopher was saying, "Yes, it's a wonderful play. And what a part! You can build on to it, yet never overload it, never interfere in any way with production . . ."

(And he remembered bitterly the old crack about actors. "Now, let's talk about *you*, my friend. What did *you* think of my performance?")

"I trust you're not discussing *Daisies on the Grass*."

137

Christopher looked round. "Good God, no! *Present Laughter*. What's Emma doing?"

"Your friend has just arrived back."

"Johnny? Yes, we just saw him tottering by."

"He's drunk."

"He quite often is. We fill him up with black coffee and shovel him into his bed. He's right as rain in the morning. Most unfair, really."

"Is there any particular reason why he should have to be here with you and Emma?"

Christopher raised his eyebrows. "Every reason." His voice was cool. "It's his flat. He got here first. I was second. Emma made a very cosy third."

There was a pause in the conversation. Jane, sensing the worst sort of conflict, broke tactfully in.

"Robert, it is getting late . . ." She picked up her bag and her gloves, and got up off the divan. ". . . Perhaps we should be going."

"But you haven't had your coffee. Or beer, or anything. What is Emma doing?"

"Doing her best to prop up Mr Rigger," Robert told him. "I suggest you go and help her. His legs don't seem to be at their most reliable."

Christopher, shrugging, acknowledged this. He uncurled his length from the low chair in which he had been sitting, and stood up. "Well, if you really feel you have to go . . ."

"I think we should. Thank you for . . ."

The words died out. There was nothing to thank him for. Christopher looked amused and Jane once again came to Robert's rescue.

". . . thank you for your wonderful performance this evening. We won't forget it." She held out her hand. "Goodbye."

138

"Goodbye. And goodbye, Robert."

"Goodbye, Christopher." And then he had to make himself say it. "Look after Emma."

They drove with unlawful speed back to London. On the motorway the needle of the speedometer crept up and up. Eighty, ninety, a hundred . . .

Jane said, "You're going to get into trouble."

"I already am," said Robert shortly.

"Did you have a row with Emma?"

"Yes."

"I thought you were looking a little fraught. What was it about?"

"Snooping. And moralising. And interfering. And trying to make a basically intelligent girl see the smallest glimmer of sense. She looked awful, too. She looked ill."

"She'll be all right."

"Last time I saw her, she was brown as a gipsy, with hair to her waist and a sort of bloom about her, like a delicious ripe fruit." He remembered the pleasure of kissing her goodbye. "Why do people have to do such dreadful things to themselves?"

"I don't know," said Jane. "Perhaps because of Christopher."

"How did you get on with him? I mean, apart from falling in love with him."

She ignored this. "He is clever. He is single-minded. He is ambitious. I think he will go far. But alone."

"You mean, without Emma."

"I'd say that."

Even at one in the morning London was alive with lights and traffic. They turned down into Sloane Street, circled Sloane Square, took the narrow road that led to Jane's mews. Outside her little house, he killed the engine of the Alvis, and it was very quiet. Street lamps shone on to the cobbles, on to the gleaming bonnet of the car, on to Jane's blonde and shining head. Robert was suddenly very tired. He began to reach for a cigarette, but Jane was there first. She put the cigarette into his mouth and lit it for him. In that instant her eyes became large and mysteriously shadowed, and there was a small and beguiling shadow, like a smudge, below the curve of her lower lip.

She snapped out the lighter. He said, ''It's been a bloody awful evening. And I'm sorry.''

''It always makes a change. It was interesting.''

He pulled off his cap and dropped it on to the back seat. ''Do you suppose,'' he said, ''that they're living together?''

''Darling, I wouldn't know.''

''But she's in love with him.''

''I would say so.''

For a little they were silent. Then Robert stretched, flexing himself after the long drive. He said, ''We never got any dinner, did we? I don't know about you, but I'm hungry.''

''If you want, I'll cook you scrambled eggs. And pour you a big cold Scotch-on-the-rocks.''

''You're twisting my arm . . .''

They laughed, quietly. Night time laughter, he thought. Pillow laughter. He put his left hand up and around her neck, slid his fingers up into her hair, and leaned forward to kiss her mouth. She tasted sweet and fresh and cool. Her lips parted, and he threw his cigarette away, and pulled her tightly and closely into his arms.

After a little, he took his mouth from hers. ''What are we waiting for, Jane?''

''One thing.''

He smiled. ''What's that?''

"Me. I don't want to start something that isn't ever going to be finished. I don't want to be hurt again. Even for you, Robert, and God knows how fond I am of you."

He said, "I won't hurt you," and meant it, and kissed the shadow under her mouth.

"And please," she said, "no more Littons."

He kissed her eyes, and the end of her short nose. "It's a promise. No more Littons."

He let her go then, and they got out of the car, and closed the doors as quietly as they had laughed together. And Jane found her key, and Robert took it from her and opened the door, and they went in, and Jane turned on the light, and started up the narrow stairs, and Robert closed the door, gently, behind them.

9

One of the delights of the big old house in Milton Gardens was living there in the summer. At the end of a warm and stuffy June day, and after the frustrations of a snail's-pace, petrol-laden journey back down the Kensington High Street, it was a positive physical pleasure to come in through the front door and slam it with happy finality behind you. The house always felt cool. It smelt of flowers and wax-polish, and in June the chestnut trees were out and so thick with leaves and pink and white blossom that the surrounding terraces of houses were shrouded from sight, sounds of all traffic were muffled, and only the occasional aeroplane, passing overhead, broke the evening calm.

Today was a classic example of this particular relief. There was thunder about, and since morning the temperature had steadily risen as the storm clouds gathered. Beneath this doom-like atmosphere, the city sweltered. By now the parks were dusty and the trampled grass turning brown, and the air about as refreshing as a draught of used bath-water. But here, at home, Helen had the sprinklers working on the lawn, and a gust of sweet, damp air swept through the open door at the end of the hall, and greeted Robert as he came indoors.

He dropped his hat on the hall chair, picked up his letters, called ''Helen?''

143

She wasn't in the kitchen. He went down the hall and out of the door and down the steps to the terrace and found her there, with a tea-tray and a book – unread – and a basket of mending. She wore a sleeveless cotton dress and a faded pair of espadrilles, and the sun had brought freckles out, big as paint spots, across her nose.

He came across the grass towards her, shedding the jacket of his suit.

She said, "You have caught me, doing nothing."

"And very nice too." He slung the jacket over the back of a painted wrought-iron chair, and collapsed beside her. "What a day! Anything left in that teapot?"

"No, but I can make you some more."

"Why don't I?" said Robert automatically, but without notable enthusiasm.

She did not reply to this hypothetical question, simply got up and took the teapot indoors. There was a plate of biscuits, and he took one and began to eat it, pulling his tie loose with the other hand. Beneath the sprinklers the lawn lay thick and green. It needed cutting again. He leaned back and shut his eyes.

It was now six weeks since he had been to Brookford to find Emma Litton, and in all that time there had been no word from her. After some discussion with Marcus and Helen he had written to Ben, telling him that Emma was staying with Christopher Ferris, whom she had re-met in Paris. That she was working in the Repertory Theatre in Brookford. That she was well. He could not, in truth, say more. Surprisingly, Ben had acknowledged this, not directly, to Robert, but as a scribbled footnote to a letter to Marcus. The purpose of the letter itself was purely business, typewritten on the impressive engraved paper of the Ryan Memorial Museum of Fine Arts. The retrospective Litton Exhibition was now over. In every way it had been a resounding success. Now, the new exhibition – a posthumous collection of drawings of a Puerto Rican genius who had lately died in dismal circumstances in a Greenwich Village garret, was well under way, and he and Melissa were taking the opportunity of a trip to Mexico. He intended to start painting again. He did not know when he would be returning to London. He remained, always, Marcus's Ben. And then, under the signature, and in Ben's own indecipherable scrawl:

Had a letter from R. Morrow. Please thank him. Emma always fond of Christopher. Only hope his manners have improved.

Marcus showed this to Robert. "I don't know what you expected," he said, dryly, "but this is what you have got."

So it was over. For the first time Robert found himself in whole-hearted agreement with his sister Helen. The Littons were brilliant, unpredictable and charming. But they refused to conform to any pre-set behaviour pattern and they would not help themselves. So they were impossible.

To his surprise, he found that Emma was easy to forget. He could put her out of his mind as ruthlessly as an old trunkful of junk, relegated to the darkest recesses of some distant, dusty attic. And his life immediately became so full that the void left by her going was, almost at once, filled by more worthwhile pursuits.

At the Gallery, they were furiously busy. His days were a round of prospective clients, foreign visitors, and eager young artists carrying folios which bulged with their unsalubrious paintings. Would Bernstein mount an exhibition for them? Would Bernstein back this flame of new talent? The answer was usually, No, Bernstein's would not, but Marcus was a kindly

145

man, and it was a house rule that no young man was returned to Glasgow or Bristol or Newcastle, or wherever it was he lived, without a good meal in his stomach, and the price of his return fare in the pocket of genuinely work-stained jeans.

Robert found that his vitality leapt to meet these demands, and, running at full speed, his energy could not – or would not – slow down. He could not bear to find himself doing nothing, and deliberately filled his leisure time with extraneous diversions, and a surprising number of them were involved with Jane Marshall.

The fact that their working hours did not always coincide put him off not at all. Sometimes he would call in for a drink at her little house, on the way home from the Gallery, and find her still in an apron, sewing braid on to yards of curtain, or working out the intricacies of a scalloped pelmet on graph paper. Sometimes she was out of town, and then he would fill the evening with furious physical labour, digging the garden or mowing the lawn.

One weekend he and Jane went down to Bosham, where Jane's brother had a small cottage, and kept a catamaran moored out on the choppy waters of the Hard. They sailed all Sunday and there was a stiff breeze and a bright, burning sun, and at the end of the day, sleepy with all the fresh air, they sat in the village pub and drank draught bitter and played shove ha'penny, and drove back to London very late, with the roof of the Alvis down, and wind blowing scraps of cloud across the face of the stars.

Once more Helen started saying, ''I think you should marry her.''

Robert ignored the nudging suspicion that he was behaving badly, and only said, ''Perhaps I will.''

''But when? What are you waiting for?''

He did not answer because he did not know. He only knew that this was not the time to plan; or assess; or to start to analyse the feelings that he had for Jane.

Now, he was disturbed, by Helen, returning with his tea-tray. She set it down, and the iron table grated on the pavings as she pulled it towards him. She said, "Marcus phoned at lunch-time."

Marcus had had to return to Scotland. The whisky-loving Scottish baronet, who had been so anxious to part with his art treasures, was being balked by his son, who would presumably inherit the heirlooms and did not want them sold out of hand. Or, if they were to be sold, he wanted three times as much for them as his thirsty father was prepared to ask. After a great deal of expensive telephoning, Marcus had reluctantly decided that another visit must be paid north of the border. Business must always come before personal comforts and preferences, and if, to lay his hands on those pictures, he had to sleep in damp beds and icy rooms and eat appallingly-cooked food, then he was ready to do so.

"How is he getting on?"

"He was reserved. No doubt speaking from some soaring baronial hall, with the old Laird listening from one end of the room, and the young Laird listening from the other."

"Has he got the pictures?"

"No, but he will. If not all, then some of them . . ." She went away from him, across the grass, to move the sprinkler. "The Raeburn he is determined on," she said, over her shoulder. "He'll go to any price."

Robert poured his tea, and began to read the evening paper. When Helen came back, he handed it to her open at a middle page.

147

"What's this?" she asked.

"That girl. Dinah Burnett . . ."

"Who is she?"

"You should know her face by now. She's a young actress with an efficient publicity agent. Every time you open a paper or a magazine, there's a picture of her perched on a piano, or cuddling a kitten or something equally obnoxious."

Helen made a comic face at the thrusting, sexy photograph, and read the caption aloud.

Dinah Burnett, the red-head who made such an impact on the TV series *Detective*, is in rehearsal now for the new Amos Monihan play *The Glass Door*, her first serious stake in legitimate theatre. "I'm scared," she told our special reporter. "But so very proud to have been chosen for this wonderful play." Miss Burnett is twenty-two and comes from Barnsley.

"I didn't know there was a new Amos Monihan play on the stocks. Who's producing?"

"Mayo Thomas."

"Then she must be good. Extraordinary, what talent can lurk behind really very stupid faces. But why did you suddenly show this to me?"

"No reason, really. Just that Jane's doing up a flat for her. At first it was going to be a pretty modest affair, but as soon as she got this part, she reckoned she'd moved in with the big-time spenders; you know, mirror bathrooms and white mink bedcovers."

"Very nice," said Helen. She tossed the paper back into his lap but he was too hot and lazy to catch it, so it slipped from his knee and fell to the ground. After a little, Helen began, in a

148

desultory fashion, to gather the tea things together. She picked up the tray and started indoors.

"How about dinner?" she asked. "You going to Jane's or are you staying here?"

"I'm going to Jane's."

"That's fine. I'll eat a piece of cheese. It's too hot to cook, anyway."

When she had gone, he lit a cigarette and sat, listening to the pigeons, and watching the shadows lengthen over the grass. The cool and the quiet were like a benediction. The cigarette finished, he got up and went back into the house, and upstairs to his own flat, where he showered and shaved, and changed into jeans and a cool shirt. As he was pouring the first drink of the evening, the telephone rang. He filled the tumbler halfway up with soda, and went to his desk to answer it. It was Jane.

"Robert?"

"Yes."

"Darling, it's me. Look I just wanted to warn you, don't get here till about eight . . ."

"Why, are you entertaining a lover?"

"Wish I were. No, it's Dinah Burnett, she's had a new idea for her bathroom, God rot her soul, and she wants to come along after rehearsals and talk about it."

"For a girl who is so proud about being in the blasted play, her mind does harp on material things, doesn't it?"

"So you've been reading the evening paper. That blurb makes me ill."

"I can't think why she didn't bother to mention that she was doing up a flat, and had chosen well-known interior decorator, twenty-seven-year-old Jane Marshall, 34, 26, 36, to help her. Were you expecting to be taken out for dinner, because I'm not dressed accordingly."

149

"Of course not, it's much too hot. I've got some cold chicken; I thought I'd make a salad."

"And I shall subscribe a frosty bottle of wine."

"Delicious."

"Till eight, then."

"Yes, eight." He was on the point of putting down the receiver when she said again, "Don't come before," and then rang off. Mildly puzzled, he put down the receiver and then decided that he must have imagined a certain urgency in her voice. He went to find ice for his drink.

Deliberately, he was a little late, but even so, when he drew up outside Jane's house, there was a small blue Fiat still parked by her door. He gave his double toot on the horn and got out of the car, carrying the bottle of wine, and almost at once the front door opened and Jane stood there, in a faded pair of pink cotton trousers and a sleeveless top. Her hair fell across her cheek and she looked, for Jane, mildly distraught, making flapping gestures with her hand, and pointing upstairs.

He was amused. He came to kiss her. "What is it?"

She took the bottle of wine from him. "She's still here. She won't go. She won't stop talking. And now you've come, nothing's going to shift her."

"We'll say we're going out, and that we're late already."

"I suppose it's worth a try." They had been talking in whispers. Now she said in clear and social tones, "I wasn't sure if it was you or not. Come along up."

He followed her up the narrow, steep stairs. "Dinah, this is Robert Morrow . . ." Casually she introduced them, before going into the kitchen with the wine. He heard the big fridge door open and shut as she put it away.

Dinah Burnett sat on Jane's big sofa by the open window, with her legs curled up beneath her, looking as though she

150

was expecting a photographer, or an interviewer, or a prospective lover. She was a beautiful girl, ripe and colourful, and it occurred to Robert that no photograph could do her full justice. She had auburn hair and pale green eyes, and skin like an apricot, and was built on proportions that are normally described as "lavish". She wore a short shift dress in a green to match her eyes, and it might have been designed to display as much as possible of her smooth, well-rounded arms and endless legs. Her feet were thrust into wooden sandals, her wrists jangled with gold bracelets and in her ears, gleaming through the profusion of hair, were enormous gold hoop ear-rings. Her teeth were white and even, and her black lashes long and black as soot, and it was hard to believe that she had started life in Barnsley.

"How do you do," said Robert. They shook hands. "I've just been reading all about you in the evening paper."

"Wasn't it a dreadful photograph?" She still had an endearing trace of a Yorkshire accent. "I look like a broken-down barmaid. But still, I suppose it's better than nothing."

She smiled at him, all her feminine charm rising to the bait of a new and attractive man, and Robert, flattered and warmed by her friendliness, settled himself at the other end of the sofa. She went on, "I shouldn't really be here at all, but Jane's doing up this new flat for me, and today I found this American magazine with a fabulous bathroom and I just had to bring it along, after rehearsals, and show it to her."

"How's the play going?"

"Oh, it's most exciting."

"What's it about?"

"Well, it's . . ."

At this juncture Jane reappeared from the kitchen and briskly interrupted. "How about a drink? Dinah, Robert and I are actually going out, but there's just time for a drink before you go.''

"Oh, that's sweet of you. If you're sure. I'd love a glass of beer.''

"How about you, Robert?''

"Sounds very nice, let me get it . . .''

"No, that's all right. I'm up.'' She snapped the top off a beer bottle, and poured a glass expertly, with no head to it. "Dinah, Robert's an art dealer, he works in Bernstein's in Kent Street.''

"Oh, are you really?'' said Miss Burnett, looking wide-eyed and interested, but not very much wiser. "Do you sell pictures and stuff. . . ?''

"Well, yes . . .''

Jane brought Dinah's beer across, pulled up a small table and set the glass down.

"Robert is a very high-powered man,'' she said. "He's always dashing off to Paris or Rome, to pull off enormous deals, aren't you, Robert?'' She went back to her drink tray. "Dinah, you should get him to look out for a picture for the new flat. You need something modern over that fireplace and you never know, it might be an investment. Something to sell when they run out of good parts for you.''

"Don't talk about running out. I've only just started. Besides, wouldn't it be very expensive?''

"Not as expensive as that American bathroom.''

Dinah smiled engagingly. "But, I always feel a bathroom's terribly important.''

Jane had poured two more drinks, now she brought them over, and handed one to Robert. Then settled herself in the chair opposite the sofa, and faced them both across the low table.

"Well, it's your flat, ducky,'' she said.

Her voice was a little acid. Robert said quickly, "You still

152

haven't told me about the new play . . . *The Glass Door*. When are you opening?''

''Wednesday. This Wednesday as ever is. At the Regent Theatre.''

''We must try and get seats, Jane.''

''Yes, of course,'' said Jane.

''The thought of a first night makes me sick with nerves. You see, it's my first shot at the living theatre, as it were, and if it wasn't for Mayo being such a fabulous producer I'd have dropped out weeks ago . . .''

''You still haven't told us what it's about.''

''Well, it's . . . oh, I don't know. It's about this young man, from an ordinary, working-class family. And he writes a book and it's a best seller, and he becomes a sort of celebrity – you know, on television and such. And then he gets mixed up with the film people, and all the time, he's getting richer, and nastier, and he's drinking and having affairs, and generally living it up. And then, of course, in the end, the whole racket falls round his ears like a pack of cards and he finishes up, right where he started, in his mother's house, in the kitchen, with his old typewriter and a blank sheet of paper. It sounds corny, I know, but it's moving and real and the dialogue is out of this world.''

''Do you think it's going to go?''

''I don't see how it can fail. But then I'm prejudiced.''

''What part do you play?''

''Oh, I'm just one of the many girls. But I'm different, because I get pregnant.''

''Charming,'' murmured Jane.

''But it isn't sordid, not a bit,'' Dinah assured her. ''When I first read the script I didn't know whether to laugh or cry. Real life, I suppose.''

153

"Yes." Jane finished her drink, and put down the empty glass and looked at her watch. She said, pointedly, "Robert, I'm going up to change. We mustn't be late. We'll keep everybody waiting." She stood up. "You'll excuse me, Dinah, won't you?"

"Of course I will, and thank you for being so sweet about the bathroom. I'll ring you up and let you know what I've decided."

"Yes, you do that."

When she had gone upstairs, Dinah smiled once more, confidingly, at Robert. "I hope I'm not keeping you. I will go when I've finished my drink, but I live in such a dump just now, it's depressing. And it's so hot, isn't it? I wish it would thunder. It would be so much cooler if only it would thunder."

"It will this evening, I'm sure. Tell me, how did you get this part?"

"Well, Amos Monihan, you know, he wrote the play – he'd seen me on TV in *Detective*, and he rang Mayo Thomas and said he thought I'd be right for the part. So I had an audition. That's all really."

"And who plays the lead? The young man. The writer?"

"This is the gamble. The backers wanted a big name, somebody famous. But Mayo had found this new boy – he'd seen him in some provincial rep, and somehow, he convinced the man with the money to give him a try."

"So you have an unknown in the lead?"

"That's about it," said Dinah. "But, believe me, he's good."

She finished her drink. Upstairs Jane was moving about in her bedroom, going to and fro, opening and shutting drawers. Robert got up to retrieve the empty glass. "Would you like the other half?"

"No, really, I won't. I mustn't keep you any longer . . ."

She stood up, pulling down her dress, and tossing her long hair away from her neck. She called up the stair. "I'm off. Goodbye, Jane!"

"Oh, goodbye." Jane sounded more friendly now that her visitor was actually on her way out.

Dinah started downstairs, and Robert followed her, intending to politely see her off the premises. Over her bright head, he leaned forward to unsnib the latch of Jane's front door. Outside, the mews slumbered in the hot airless evening.

He said, "I'll keep my fingers crossed for Wednesday."

"Bless you."

They went out into the street. He opened the door of the Fiat for her. He said, "What's he called, this young actor?"

Dinah slid into the driving-seat, revealing more leg than was good for anybody's blood pressure.

She said, "Christopher Ferris."

He thought, *So that's why Jane didn't want me to meet you.*

"Christopher Ferris? I know him."

"Do you? How funny."

"At least . . . I knew his sister."

"I don't know anything about his family."

"He's never mentioned her? Emma?"

"Never a word. But then, chaps don't usually talk about their sisters, do they?"

She laughed, and slammed the car door shut, but the window was down, and Robert leaned his elbow on it, like a salesman with a foot in the door.

He said, "I'd like to wish him luck."

"I'll give him a message for you tomorrow."

"Could I ring him up?"

"Well, I suppose you could, but calls aren't exactly welcome when we're working." And then she had a bright idea. "Tell you what, I've got his home number somewhere. I had to ring up for Mayo, once, and leave a message.''

She picked her bag off the other seat, and started to delve. She brought out a script, a purse, a scarf, a bottle of sun oil, a diary. She leafed through the diary. ''Here it is, Flaxman 8881. Do you want me to write it down for you?''

''No. I'll remember.''

''He might be there now . . . I don't know what he does in his spare time.'' She smiled again. ''Fancy you knowing him. It's a small world, isn't it?''

''Yes. It's a small world.''

She started up her engine. ''Well, it's been fun meeting you. Cheerio.''

He stood back. ''Goodbye.''

The little car roared away down the mews, and he watched it go. At the junction at the end of the narrow street it paused for a moment, then shot away, turned left and was gone, the sound of its engine swallowed into the anonymous grumble that was London traffic.

He went back into the house, closed the door, went upstairs. There was no sound from the bedroom.

''Jane.''

She began immediately to move about, as though occupied.

''Jane.''

''What is it?''

''Come here.''

''But I'm not . . .''

''Come down here.''

After a moment, she appeared at the head of the stairs, wrapped in a thin dressing-gown. ''What is it?''

''It's Christopher Ferris,'' said Robert.

156

She stared down at him, her expression closed and suddenly implacable.

"What about him?"

"You knew he was in this play. That he's been in London all this time."

She came down the stairs towards him. When her face was on a level with his, she said coolly, "Yes, I knew."

"But you never told me. Why not?"

"Perhaps because I don't believe in stirring up muddy ponds. Besides, you promised. No more Littons."

"This has nothing to do with that promise."

"Then what are you getting so hot and bothered about? Look, Robert, I think I feel about this business much the same way as your sister Helen. Bernstein's act, in a professional capacity, for Ben Litton, and after that, their commitments to the family should end. I know about Emma and the sort of life she's led and I'm sorry for her. I went to Brookford with you, and I saw that creepy little theatre and that dreadful flat. But she is adult, and, as you said yourself, highly intelligent . . . What if Christopher is in London? That doesn't mean Emma has been abandoned. It's a part of his job, and she'll accept it as such, I'm sure."

"That still doesn't explain why you never told me."

"Perhaps because I knew all along that you'd start running round in circles like a demented sheepdog. Imagining the worst, nagged by responsibility, simply because the wretched girl is Ben Litton's daughter. Robert, you *saw* her. She doesn't want to be helped. And if you try, you'll just be interfering . . ."

He said slowly, "I don't know if you're trying to convince me, or yourself."

"You fool, I'm trying to make you see the truth."

"The truth is that, as far as we know, Emma Litton is alone, living in a damp basement with a paralytic drunk."

"Isn't that what she chose to do?"

She flung the question at him, and then, before he could reply, pushed past him and went to the trolley and began fiddling about with empty glasses and beer-bottle tops in a feeble pretence at tidying up. He watched, with a great sadness, her back view, the smooth bell of hair, the tiny waist, the small, capable hands. She was unrelenting.

He said gently, "Dinah Burnett gave me Christopher's number. Perhaps it would be better if I rang him from here."

"Do whatever you like." She carried the glasses through to the kitchen. Robert picked up her phone and dialled the remembered number. Jane came back to collect up the empty bottles.

"Hello." It was Christopher.

"Christopher, this is Robert Morrow speaking. You remember, I came down to Brookford . . ."

"To see Emma. Yes, of course. How splendid! How did you know where to find me?"

"Dinah Burnett gave me your number. She also told me about *The Glass Door*. Congratulations."

"You can save them till we see what the critics have to say."

"Still, it's a great effort. Look, I was wondering about Emma."

Christopher's voice turned cautious. "Yes?"

Jane had come back from the kitchen and now stood by the window, her arms folded, looking down into the street.

"Where is she?"

"In Brookford."

"In the flat. With your friend?"

"My friend? Oh, Johnny Rigger? No, he left. He came to rehearsals drunk one morning and the producer slung him out. Emma's on her own."

Carefully controlling his temper, Robert said, "You never thought of ringing up Marcus Bernstein or myself and telling us this?"

"Well, I would have, but before I left Brookford, Emma made me promise not to. So, you see, I couldn't." While Robert, in seething silence, tried to accept this excuse, Christopher went on, sounding suddenly much younger and not so sure of himself. "I tell you what I did do, though. I felt a bit of a heel leaving her like that . . . so I wrote to Ben."

"You wrote to *who*?"

"Her father."

"But what the hell could he do? He's in America . . . he's in Mexico . . ."

"I didn't know he was in Mexico, but I wrote to him care of Bernstein's, and put please forward on the envelope. You see, I felt *someone* should know what had happened."

"And Emma? Is she still working in the theatre?"

"She was when I left. You see, there was really no point her coming up to London with me. I rehearse dawn to dusk as it is, and we'd never have seen each other. Besides, if *The Glass Door* folds up after a week, then I'll need my old Brookford job back again. Tommy Childers is very kindly keeping it open for me. So we decided it would be better if Emma stayed down there."

"And if *The Glass Door* runs for two years?"

"I don't know what would happen then. But right now, I'll be honest with you, things are a bit tricky. This house I'm living in – it belongs to my mother. I'm living with my mother. You can see, what with things being the way they are, it is a bit tricky."

"Yes," said Robert. "Yes, I can see . . . as you say, it's tricky."

*

159

He put down the receiver. Jane, not turning from the window, said, "What's so tricky?"

"He's living with Hester, his mother. And she's obviously refusing to let a Litton darken her door. Silly old bitch. And the drunk flatmate has had the sack, so Emma's on her own. And, to ease his conscience, Christopher has written to Ben Litton to tell him what has happened. And I should like to tie the lot of them together with one great big millstone, and consign them all to a bottomless lake."

"I knew this would happen," said Jane. She turned, then, to face him, her arms still rigidly folded, and he saw that she was not only angry, but deeply upset. "It could be good, this thing between us . . . you know that, don't you, as well as I do. And that's why I didn't tell you about Christopher, because I knew, that if you knew, it would be the end of everything."

He wished he could say *It doesn't have to be the end*, but it was impossible.

"In a way, Robert, all this time, you did keep your promise. You never mentioned Emma. But she was never out of the back of your mind."

Now that it was said, and out in the open, he saw that this was true. He said, hopelessly, "Only because in some extraordinary way, I am involved with her."

"If you are involved with her, it's because you want to be. And it's not good enough, Robert. Not for me. I won't settle for second best. I'd rather go without. I hoped I'd made that clear. With me, it has to be all or nothing at all. I can't go through it all again."

He understood. But could only say that he was sorry.

"I think . . . perhaps, you'd better go."

Her arms were still folded, a barrier against him. There was no way to say goodbye. He could not kiss her. He could not

160

lightly say, "It's been fun" in the best traditions of drawing-room comedy. And he could never forgive her for trying to keep him from Emma.

He said, "I'll go now."

"Yes, do that." But as he started downstairs, she remembered something. "You left the wine."

"Forget about the wine," said Robert.

10

The song was over. The lights were dimmed. Charmian as Oberon moved forward for her final speech. The taped Mendelssohn music – for the meagre proportions of the Brookford Rep did not allow space for an orchestra – stole out across the dark cave of the auditorium and evoked for Emma, sitting at the prompt desk – all the distilled magic of a summer night.

> Now until the break of day
> Through this house each fairy stray . . .

It was the end of the first week of *A Midsummer Night's Dream*. The financial fiasco of *Daisies on the Grass* had driven the management to a production of Shakespeare which, although it entailed double the work for everybody, ensured an Arts Council grant and full houses, composed mostly of school children and students.

By now Emma was no longer working for Collins, the stage manager. There was a new ASM, a young girl fresh from drama school, dedicated, tough and seemingly immune to Collins' barbed tongue. She was on-stage now, in the grey velvet tunic and silvered wings of Cobweb, the fairy, for the huge cast of *The*

163

Dream demanded that every member of the company should be called in and given a part.

Because of this, Tommy Childers had asked Emma to come back and lend a hand with the back-stage activities. During the past fortnight she had coped with a number of jobs; helping in the wardrobe, working in the scenery store; typing scripts, and all the time nipping out for sandwiches and cigarettes, and making endless pots of tea.

Tonight, she had been given the job of prompter, and had spent the evening with her eyes glued to the prompt copy, terrified of losing her place, of missing a cue, of letting somebody down. But now, as the play drew to its close, and, knowing the rest of it by heart, she allowed her concentration to relax a little, and indulged in the luxury of watching the stage.

Charmian wore a crown of emerald leaves, a silver tabard and silver tights on her long, slim legs. The audience, caught by the old magic of the words, stayed breathless, spellbound.

Trip away; make no stay;
Meet me all by break of day.

To eke out the cramped wing space on either side of the stage, Tommy Childers had had built a ramp which led down from the stage and into the centre aisle of the auditorium. Now Oberon and Titania, hand-in-hand, and followed by a retinue of fairies, made their exit down this ramp, running, with the draperies flying like exuberant wings, off the lighted stage, and down into the darkness; swift and quiet; up the aisle and out of the double doors at the back with such an airy suddenness that they were gone almost without a sound, without a trace.

And then it was left to Sara Rutherford, playing Puck, as

a tilt-eared teenager, with the stage to herself and a single spotlight.

If we shadows have offended,
Think but this, and all is mended.

She had a little pipe. When she got to ''So good night unto you all,'' she played on it the single thread of notes that was the theme of the Mendelssohn music.

Then, triumphant, ''Give me your hands, if we be friends, and Robin shall restore amends.'' And darkness, and curtain, and applause.

All over. Emma let out a sigh of relief that nothing had gone wrong, shut the prompt copy and sat back in her chair. The cast were surging back on stage for the first curtain call. As he went past her, the boy who played Nick Bottom leant over to whisper,

''Tommy asked me to tell you – there's some chap waiting to see you. He's been sitting in the Green Room for half an hour, but Tommy's put him in his office. Thought it might be a bit more private for you. Better go and see what it's all about.''

''To see me? But who is it?''

But Bottom was already on stage. The curtain swept up, there was a fresh burst of applause, and smiles and bows and curtsies . . .

Emma's first thought was that it was Christo. But if it was Christo, why hadn't he said? She went down the wooden steps and along the cat-walk that led to the landing at the head of the stage door stairs. Ahead, down a short passage, the Green Room door stood ajar, showing a glimpse of sagging velvet sofa, the old playbills framed on the walls. Tommy Childers's office led off this passage. The door was shut.

Behind her, the applause died down, and then rose again for the second curtain call.

She opened the door.

It was a tiny room, scarcely bigger than a cupboard; scarcely big enough to contain the desk, and a couple of chairs and a filing cabinet. He sat behind the desk, in Tommy's chair, behind Tommy's personal and private chaos of scripts and letters and programme proofs and production notes. The wall behind him was thumb-tacked with stage photographs. Someone had made him a cup of tea, but he had not deigned to drink it, and it stood before him, horribly cold, untouched. He wore pearly-grey trousers, a russet corduroy jacket, a dark blue cotton shirt and a chrome yellow tie, loosely tied, so that his top button showed. He was browner than ever, and he looked about ten years younger, and almost indecently attractive.

He was smoking an American king-size cigarette, and an ash-tray full of butts was indicative of the length of time he had been waiting for Emma. When she came through the door, he turned his head to look at her, resting his elbow on the desk, his chin on his thumb. His eyes, through the veil of cigarette smoke, remained dark and shadowed and quite unreadable.

He said, sounding mildly irritated, "What have you been doing?" and Emma was too stunned to do anything but tell him.

"Prompting."

"Well, come along in and shut the door."

She did as she was told. The applause from the auditorium was closed away. She found that her heart was thudding, but whether this was due to shock, or pleasure, or a certain apprehension it was impossible to know. She said at last, feebly, "I thought you were in America."

"I was, this morning. Flew back today. And yesterday . . . at least I suppose it was yesterday, these International date lines

166

and clocks being changed complicate life to an alarming degree . . . I was in Mexico. Yes; yesterday. Acapulco.''

Emma felt for a chair, lowered herself gently on to it before her legs gave way.

''Acapulco?''

''Do you know that the aeroplanes that fly to Acapulco are all painted different colours? And as you go south, the air hostesses do a sort of uniform strip tease. Fascinating.'' He continued to survey her. ''Emma, there's something different about you. That's it, you've cut your hair. What a good idea! Turn around and let me see the back.'' She did so, swivelling her head cautiously, and watching him out of the corner of her eye. ''Much better. Never knew you had such a good shape to your head. Have a cigarette.''

He pushed the packet across the desk. Emma took one, and he lit it for her, leaning forward, cupping the flame with his familiar and beautiful hands. As he shook out the match he said, casually, ''A great many letters have been winging their way across the Atlantic. None of them written by you.''

It was a rebuke. ''No. I know.''

''Difficult to understand. Not that I minded in particular – though I must say, as it was about the first letter I'd ever written you, it would have been pleasant to get a reply. But with Melissa it was different. She wanted you to come out to the States, and be with us, if only for a short visit. You've always been rather good about these things. What happened?''

''I don't know. I suppose I was . . . disappointed because you didn't come home. And the idea of your being married took a bit of time to get used to. And then, by the time I got round to accepting it . . . it had become too late to answer your letters. And every day that passed made it worse; made it more impossible. I never knew that if you did something you weren't particularly

167

proud of . . . it became progressively more difficult to undo it again.'' He did not comment on this. Simply continued to smoke, to watch her. ''You said a great many letters. Who else did you hear from?''

''Well, I heard from Marcus, of course. That was business. And then a rather stilted, formal affair from Robert Morrow. Saying that he'd been here to see some play or other, and had had a drink with you and Christopher. I couldn't gather, however, whether he had come specifically to see the play or to see you.''

''Yes. Well . . .''

''As soon as we realised that you were still alive and apparently occupied and with no intention of visiting us, Melissa and I set off in our coloured aeroplane for Mexico where we stayed with a mad old film star who lives in a house full of parakeets. Then, yesterday, we flew back to Queenstown, and what should I find waiting for me but yet another letter.''

''From Robert?''

''No. From Christopher.''

She could not help it. ''From *Christopher*?''

''He must be an exceptionally talented young man. A London production, so soon, with so little experience. Of course, I always knew that he'd make a flagrant success of his life. Either that or end up in prison . . .''

But even this provocation could not divert her. ''You mean *Christopher*? Wrote to *you*?''

''Said in that tone of voice, it sounds insulting.''

''But why?''

''One can only imagine that he felt mildly responsible.''

''But . . .'' An idea was forming. A suspicion so wonderful that, if it was not true, then it must be scotched immediately. ''But you didn't come home because of that letter? You came home to paint. To go back to Porthkerris and paint again?''

168

"Well, of course, taking the long view, I have. Mexico was inspiring. They have an extraordinary pink that keeps recurring in their buildings, and their pictures, and their very clothes . . ."

"Perhaps you'd had enough of Queenstown, and America," she persisted. "You've never been much good at staying in any one place for more than a couple of months. And, of course, you'll have to see Marcus. And start thinking about a new exhibition."

He stared at her blankly. "Why this catalogue of motives?"

"Well, there has to be some reason."

"I've just told you. I came to see you."

She did not want the cigarette he had given her. She leaned forward and stubbed it out, and then clasped her hands in her lap, the palms pressed tight together, the fingers interlaced. Misinterpreting her silence, Ben looked aggrieved. "I don't think, Emma, that you quite understand the situation. I literally flew in from Mexico, read Christopher's letter, kissed Melissa goodbye and flew out again. Didn't even have time to change my shirt. I then subjected myself to another twelve hours of flying, the tedium broken only by a series of uneatable meals, all of which tasted like plastic. Do you think I endure such tortures simply to talk to Marcus Bernstein about another exhibition?"

"But Ben . . ."

He was, however, well away, and in no mood to be interrupted.

"And, once arrived, do I go to Claridges, where Melissa has thoughtfully cabled in advance and reserved me a room? Do I indulge in a bath, or a drink, or a decent meal? No. I climb into the slowest taxi-cab this side of the Atlantic, and drive, through unspeakable rain, to Brookford" (he said the word as though it were something distasteful), "where, after interminable incorrect directions, I eventually run the repertory theatre to earth.

169

The taxi is at this moment outside, ticking up a monumental fare. And if you don't believe me, you can go and look.''

''I believe you,'' said Emma, quickly.

''And then, when you do deign to appear, all you can talk about is Marcus Bernstein and some hypothetical exhibition. Do you know something? You're an ungrateful brat. A typical example of the modern generation. You don't deserve to have a father.''

She said, ''But I've been alone before. For years I've been alone. In Switzerland and Florence and Paris. You never came to see me then.''

''You didn't need me then,'' said Ben flatly. ''And I knew what you were doing, and who you were with. This time, when I read that letter from Christopher, I knew the first, faint stirrings of concern. Perhaps because Christopher, of all people, would never have written if he hadn't been concerned himself. Why didn't you tell me you'd met him in Paris?''

''I thought you wouldn't be pleased.''

''It depends on what sort of a person he's turned into. Has he changed very much from the small boy who lived with us at Porthkerris?''

''He looks the same . . . but he's tall . . . he's a man now. Single-minded and ambitious and, perhaps, a little self-centred. And with all the charm in the world.'' Talking about him, to Ben, was like having a weight lifted from her shoulders. Emma smiled. She said, ''And I adore him.''

Ben, accepting this, returned the smile. ''You sound like Melissa, talking about Ben Litton. It seems that young Christopher and I have, after all, much in common. It's ironic that we should have wasted so many years in detesting each other. Perhaps I should make his acquaintance again. This time, we might get on a little better.''

"Yes, I think you might."

"Melissa is joining me in a week or two. Coming down to Porthkerris."

"Living at the cottage?" said Emma, unbelieving.

Ben was amused. "Melissa? At the cottage? You must be joking. A suite has already been reserved at The Castle Hotel. I shall lead the life of a goldfish in a bowl, but perhaps, as I get older, the sybaritic existence is beginning to reveal its charms."

"But didn't she mind? Your coming home like that? Kissing her and leaving her without even taking time to change your shirt?"

"Emma, Melissa is a clever woman. She doesn't try to pin a man down or to possess him. She knows that the best way to hold on to someone you love is to . . . very gently . . . let him go. Women take a long time to learn this. Hester never did. How about you?"

"I'm learning," said Emma.

"The extraordinary thing is, I believe you are."

By now, darkness had fallen. This had happened, unheeded, while they talked, the dusk deepening imperceptibly until Ben's face, across the tiny distance that separated them, was simply a blur, his hair a wing of white. There was a lamp on the desk, but neither of them reached out to turn it on. The twilight enclosed them, the shut door kept the rest of the world out. They were the Littons; a family; together.

As they talked, the backstage shell of the theatre had rung with routine sounds. The last curtain call. Voices; Collins swearing at some unfortunate electrician. Hurrying feet, running upstairs to the dressing-rooms, anxious to be away, to be free of costumes and make-up, to catch buses, to go home, to cook food and wash stockings and, perhaps, to make love. Footsteps passed to

171

and fro, in and out of the Green Room, *Darling, have you got a cigarette? Where's Delia? Has anybody seen Delia? There wasn't a phone call for me, was there?*

The sounds thinned out, as in twos and threes they left the theatre. Down the stone stairs, out of the banging door, into the narrow alley. A car started up. Somewhere a man started to whistle.

Behind Emma the door was abruptly opened, and the soft darkness split with an oblong of yellow light.

"Sorry to interrupt you . . ." It was Tommy Childers . . . "Wouldn't you like some illumination?" He snapped on the switch, and Ben and Emma were transfixed, blinking, like a couple of sleepy owls. "I just wanted something off my desk, before I go home."

Emma stood up, pulling her chair out of the way.

"Tommy, did you know this was my father?"

"I wasn't sure," said Tommy, smiling at Ben. "I thought you were in America."

"Everybody thought I was in America. Even my wife did until I said goodbye to her. I hope we haven't inconvenienced you, sitting here for so long in your office."

"Not at all. The only thing is the night-watchman's getting a bit edgy about the stage door. I'll tell him you'll shut it, Emma."

"Yes, of course."

"Well . . . Good night, Mr Litton . . ."

Ben heaved himself to his feet. "I had thought of taking Emma to London with me tonight. You wouldn't have any objections to that?"

"None at all," said Tommy. "She's been working like a slave for the past two weeks. Do her good to have a few days off."

172

Emma said, "I don't know why you ask Tommy, when you haven't even asked me."

"I don't ask you things," Ben said. "I tell you."

Tommy laughed. He said, "In that case, I expect you'll be going to the first night."

Ben remained vague. "First night?"

Dryly, Emma enlightened him. "He means Christopher's private view. On Wednesday."

"So soon? I shall probably be back in Porthkerris by then. We shall have to see."

"You should try and make it," said Tommy. They shook hands. "It's been splendid meeting you. And Emma . . . I'll see you sometime . . ."

"Maybe next week if *The Glass Door* folds up . . ."

"It won't," said Tommy. "If what Chris did to *Daisies on the Grass* is anything to go by, it'll run as long as *The Mousetrap*. Don't forget to shut the door."

He went away, downstairs; they heard his footsteps fade down the alley below the window, out into the street. Emma sighed. She said, "I think we should go. The night-watchman gets traumas if he thinks the place isn't properly locked up. And that taxi driver of yours will either give up hope of ever seeing you again, or else die of old age."

But Ben had once more settled himself into Tommy's chair. "In a moment," he said. "There's just one more thing." He tapped a fresh cigarette from the American packet. "I wanted to ask you about Robert Morrow."

He had the most disconcertingly calm voice. It never changed or varied its inflections so that you were continuously being taken unawares. Every nerve in Emma's body leapt in warning, but she only said, casually enough, "What about him?"

"I always had a . . . strong feeling about that young man."

173

She tried being flippant. "You mean, apart from admiring the shape of his head."

He ignored this. "I asked you once if you liked him, and you said, 'I suppose so. I scarcely know him.'"

"What of it?"

"Do you know him any better now?"

"Well, yes, I suppose I do."

"When he came to Brookford that time, he wasn't simply visiting the theatre, was he? He came to see you."

"He came to find me. That isn't quite the same thing."

"But he took the trouble to find you. I wonder why."

"Perhaps he was prompted by the famous Bernstein sense of responsibility."

"Stop fencing."

"What do you want me to say?"

"I want you to tell me the truth. And to be honest with yourself."

"What makes you think I haven't?"

"Because a light has gone out of your eyes. Because I left you at Porthkerris, blooming and brown as a gipsy. Because of the way you sit, the way you talk, the way you look." He lit the cigarette then, broke the match, and dropped it meticulously into the ash-tray. "Perhaps you forget I've been watching people, dissecting their personalities, painting them, for more years than you've been alive. And it's not Christopher who's made you unhappy. You've as good as told me that yourself."

"Perhaps it was you."

"Rubbish? A father? Angry, maybe. Hurt and resentful. Never heart-broken. Tell me about Robert Morrow. What went wrong?"

The little room was suddenly unbearably stuffy. Emma got up and went to the window, and opened it wide, leaning her elbow on the sill, and breathing in great draughts of cool, rain-washed air.

She said, ''I suppose I never bothered to understand what sort of a person he really was.''

''I don't understand.''

''Well . . . meeting him, for the first time, the way I did. That started everything off on the wrong foot. I never thought of him as a person with a private life, and a private existence, and likes and dislikes . . . and lovers. He was just part of Bernstein's, as Marcus is part of Bernstein's. Simply there to look after us. To arrange exhibitions, and cash cheques and reserve hotel accommodation, and make sure that life, for the Littons, at least, runs on oiled wheels.'' She turned to frown at her father, puzzled by her own revelation. ''How *could* I have been so moronic?''

''You probably inherited it from me. What put an end to this happy illusion?''

''Oh, I don't know. Things. He came down to Porthkerris to look at Pat Farnaby's pictures, and he asked me to go out to Gollan with him, because he didn't know the way. And it was raining, and very stormy, and he had a big thick sweater on, and we laughed about things. I don't know, but it was nice. And we were going to have dinner together, but he . . . well . . . anyway, I had a headache, so I didn't go after all. And then I came to Brookford to be with Christo, and I didn't think about Robert Morrow any more until that evening when he came to the theatre. I was clearing the stage, and suddenly he spoke, just behind me, and I turned round and he was there. And he had this girl with him. She's called Jane Marshall, and she's an interior decorator, or something very talented. She's pretty, and successful, and they seemed so much a couple. Do you know what I mean? Contained and self-sufficient and . . . together. And I felt as

175

though someone had slammed a door in my face and left me out in the cold.''

She turned from the window then, and came back to the desk and sat on it, with her back to her father, and picked up a rubber band and began to play with it, snapping it like a catapult through her fingers.

''And they came back to the flat, for a beer or a coffee or something, and everything was hideous, and Robert and I had a horrible row, and he just walked out without saying goodbye and took Jane Marshall with him. And drove back to London, and, one imagines . . .'' she tried desperately to keep her voice light, ''. . . lived happily ever after. Anyway, I haven't seen him since.''

''Is that why you wouldn't let Christopher tell him that you were on your own?''

''Yes.''

''Is he in love with this girl?''

''Christo thought he was. Christo thought she was gorgeous. He said that if Robert didn't marry her, he ought to have his head examined.''

''And what was the row about?''

Emma could scarcely remember. In retrospect, it jarred as painfully as a gramophone record, played backwards, at full pitch. An exchange of shouted words, meaningless, hurtful, regretted.

''Oh, everything. You. And not answering your letter. And Christo. I think he imagines Christo and I are madly in love, but by the time we'd got round to that I was so angry I didn't bother to disillusion him.''

''Perhaps that was a mistake.''

''Yes, perhaps it was.''

''Do you want to stay here, at Brookford?''

176

"There's nowhere else to go."

"There's Porthkerris."

Emma turned to smile down at him. "With you? At the cottage?"

"Why not?"

"A thousand reasons. Running home to Daddy never solved anything. Besides, you can't run away from the inside of your own head."

He was on his way at last, and the self-delusion and the restlessness of the past six weeks were over. The Alvis – like a home-bound hunter – streamed west, out over the Hammersmith fly-over and on to the M4. Robert settled her permanently in the fast outer lane, and kept her speedometer prudently, carefully down to seventy, for the frustration, at this stage, of being stopped by a police patrol would be almost more than he could bear. As he approached Heathrow Airport, the first rumble of thunder broke the heavy, quiet air, and he stopped in at the first lay-by and put up the hood. He was only just in time. As he moved out into the road again, the sullen evening erupted like a volcano. The wind, with staggering abruptness, swept up from the west, bearing towering black thunderheads before it, and when the rain came it was a positive explosion of water, sheets of it, like a monsoon downpour, against which the windscreen-wipers could scarcely compete. In seconds, the surface of the road was awash, reflecting the livid streaks of forked lightning which split the sky.

It occurred to him that perhaps it would be wise to stop, and wait until the worst of the storm was over, but by now his sense of relief at doing what he had for weeks been subconsciously wanting to do, was stronger than any ideas of caution. So he went on, and the huge cambered curve of the motorway pouted up towards him, and roared beneath his wheels, and was flung away in a wave of water; already a thing of the past; rejected and forgotten, along with his own feeble uncertainties.

He found the theatre closed. By the light of the street lamp, he was able to read the posters. A MIDSUMMER NIGHT'S DREAM. Unlit, deserted, the place looked gloomy as the mission hall it had once been. The door was barred and bolted; all the windows dark.

He got out of the car. It was cooler now, and he reached into the back seat and took out a sweater that had been lying there since the Bosham weekend, and pulled it on over his shirt. He slammed the door shut, and then saw the solitary taxi, waiting at the pavement's edge, the driver slumped over his wheel. He might have been dead.

"Is there anyone in there?"

"Must be, Guv-nor. I'm waiting for a fare."

Robert walked down the pavement, as far as the narrow lane, down which, so long ago, Emma and Christopher had come, walking like lovers, with their arms about each other. On this side of the sombre building a first-floor window blazed with uncurtained light. He went down the shadowed alley, tripped over a dustbin, found an open door. Inside, a flight of stone stairs led upwards, illuminated palely from a light which burned on the first-floor landing. He was assailed by the stale theatre smell of grease-paint, oil-paint, musty velvet. From above came the murmur of voices and he went upstairs, towards it, and found the short passage, and the door marked PRODUCER'S OFFICE, ajar, and edged with bright light.

He pushed the door open and the voices ceased abruptly, and he found himself on the threshold of a tiny, crowded office, looking down into the astonished faces of Ben and Emma Litton.

Emma sat on the desk, with her back to her father, facing

178

Robert. She wore a short dress, cut simply as an overall, and her long legs were bare and brown. The room was so small that as he stood there in the doorway, he was only an arm's length from her. If he wanted he could reach out and touch her. He thought that she had never looked so beautiful.

His relief and pleasure at seeing Emma was so great that the unexpectedness of Ben Litton's appearance became insignificant. Ben himself was equally unsurprised. He simply raised his dark eyebrows and said:

"Well, bless my soul, see who's turned up now."

Robert put his hands in his pockets, and said, "I thought . . ."

Ben held up a hand. "I know. You thought I was in America. Well, I'm not; I'm in Brookford. And the sooner I get out of the place and back to London, the better."

"But when did you . . . ?"

But Ben was stubbing out his cigarette, standing up, ruthlessly interrupting. "You didn't by any chance notice a taxi-cab at the front of the theatre, did you?"

"Yes, I did. The driver looked as though he had become fossilised to the wheel."

"Poor fellow. I must go and put his mind at rest."

"I've got my car," said Robert. "If you like I'll drive you back to London."

"Even better. I can pay the man off." Emma had not moved. Now, Ben edged his way around the desk, and Robert stood aside to let him out of the door.

"By the way, Robert, Emma's coming too. Will you have room for her?"

"But of course." In the doorway, they eyed each other. Then Ben gave a satisfied nod. "Splendid," he said. "I'll wait outside for you both."

*

179

"Did you know he was coming?"

Emma shook her head.

"Did it have anything to do with the letter Christopher wrote to him?"

Emma nodded.

"He flew back, today, from the States, to make sure you were all right?"

Emma nodded again, her eyes shining. "He'd been in Mexico with Melissa. But he came straight here. Even Marcus doesn't know he's in the country. He didn't even go to London. He took a taxi from the airport to Brookford. And he wasn't angry about Christopher, and he says if I want I can go back to Porthkerris with him."

"And are you?"

"Oh, Robert, I can't go on, all my life, making the same mistakes. And it was Hester's mistake, too. We both wanted Ben to conform to our ideas of a nice reliable husband, and a kind domestic father. And it was as realistic as trying to cage a panther. And when you come to think of it, how dull caged panthers are! Besides, Ben isn't my problem any longer. He's Melissa's."

Robert said, "So what price now, coming at the bottom of a long list of priorities?"

Emma made a face at him. "You know, Ben once said that you had a noble head, and that you should grow a beard and then he would paint you. But if I tried to paint you it would be with a great big balloon coming out of your mouth with I TOLD YOU SO written on it."

"I never said that to anyone in the whole of my life. And I certainly didn't come all the way down here tonight to say it."

"What did you come to say?"

"That if I'd known you were on your own, I'd have been here

weeks ago. That if I can get two seats for Christo's first night, I want you to come with me. That I'm sorry about shouting at you, that last time I was here.''

''I shouted too.''

''I hate having rows with you, but in some extraordinary way, being away from you is a thousand times worse. I kept telling myself that it was simply something that was over, and best forgotten. But all the time you were never out of the back of my mind. Jane knew. She told me this evening, she'd known all along.''

''Jane . . . ?''

''I'm ashamed to say I've been running Jane round in demented circles trying to keep myself from squaring up to the horrible truth.''

''But it was because of Jane that I made Christopher promise not to ring you up. I thought . . .''

''And it was because of Christopher that I didn't come back to Brookford.''

''You thought we were having an affair, didn't you?''

''Wasn't that what I was meant to think?''

''But you silly man, Christopher's my brother.''

Robert took her head between his hands, and put his thumbs beneath her chin and turned her face up to his. Just before he kissed her, he said, ''And how the hell was I supposed to know that?''

When they got back to the car, there was no sign of Ben, but he had left a message for them, tucked between the windscreen-wiper and the wind-shield. ''Like a parking ticket,'' said Emma.

It was an unconventional letter, written on a sheet of cartridge paper torn from Ben's sketch book, and headed by two thumbnail sketches – two profiles turned to face each other.

181

There was no mistaking her own determined chin and Robert's formidable nose.

"It's us. It's for both of us. Read it aloud."

Robert did so. "*The cabby seemed morose at the thought of returning to London on his own, so I decided to accompany him. I shall be at Claridges, but would prefer not to be disturbed before noon tomorrow.*"

"But if I'm not to go to Claridges before noon, where am I meant to go?"

"You're meant to come home with me. To Milton Gardens."

"But I haven't any things. I haven't even got a toothbrush."

"I will buy you a toothbrush," said Robert, and kissed her, and then went on reading the letter. "*By then I should have caught up on my sleep and had time to cool the champagne, and will be ready to celebrate anything you may have to tell me.*"

"The wily old brute! He knew, all along."

"*My love, and God bless you both. Ben.*"

After a little while, Emma said, "Is that all?"

"Not quite." He handed her the letter and Emma saw, beneath Ben's signature, a third little drawing. A wing of white hair, a brown face, a pair of dark and cruelly observant eyes.

"Self-portrait," said Robert. "Ben Litton by Ben Litton. It must be unique. One day, we might sell it for thousands of pounds."

My love and God bless you both.

"I shan't ever want to sell it," said Emma.

"Nor I. Come on, my darling, it's time to go home."

THE EMPTY HOUSE

1

It was three o'clock on a Monday afternoon in July, sunny and
warm, the hay-scented air cooled by a sea breeze which blew in
from the north. From the top of the hill, where the road wound
up and over the shoulder of Carn Edvor, the land sloped down
to distant cliffs; farmland, ribboned with yellow gorse, broken
by outcrops of granite, and patchworked into dozens of small
fields. Like a quilt, thought Virginia, and saw the pasture fields
as scraps of green velvet, the greenish gold of new-cut hay as
shining satin, the pinkish gold of standing corn as something
soft and furry, to be stroked and touched.

It was very quiet. But when she closed her eyes the sounds
of the summer afternoon obtruded, singling themselves out, one
by one, for her attention. The humming of the wind, soft in
her ears, stirred the bracken. A car climbed the long hill from
Porthkerris, changed gear, came on up the road. From farther
away came that pleasant summer-sound, the bee-murmur of
combine harvesters. She opened her eyes and counted three, all
minimised by distance to toy-size, scarlet and tiny as the models
that Nicholas pushed around his nursery carpet.

The approaching car appeared over the crest of the hill, driven
very slowly, its occupants, including the driver, staring from

open windows at the marvellous view. Their faces were red with sunburn, spectacles glinted, arms bulged in sleeveless blouses, the car seemed packed with humanity. As it passed the lay-by where Virginia had left her own car, one of the women in the back looked up and saw her watching them from the hillside. For a startling second their eyes met, and then the car had gone, around the next corner and away to Land's End.

Virginia looked at her watch. A quarter past three. She sighed and stood up, dusted grass and bracken fronds from the seat of her white jeans, walked back down the hill to her car. The leather seat was griddle-hot with sunshine. She turned the car and started back towards Porthkerris, her mind filled with random images. Of Nicholas and Cara, incarcerated in the alien London nursery, taken to Kensington Gardens each day by Nanny; to the Zoo and the Costume Museum and suitable films by their grandmother. It would be hot in London, stuffy and airless. She wondered if they had cut Nicholas's hair. She wondered if she should buy him a model combine harvester and send it to him with some suitable, informative, maternal letter.

Today I saw three of these working in the fields at Lanyon, and I thought of you and thought you would like a model so that you could see how it worked.

A letter for Lady Keile to read approvingly aloud because Nicholas, every inch a male, saw no reason in puzzling out his mother's writing if his grandmother was ready and willing to read it aloud to him. She thought of the other letter, the one from her heart.

My darling child, without you and Cara I am without reason,

2

aimless. I drive around in the car because I can think of nothing else to do, and the car takes me to places that I used to know, and I watch and wonder who it is who drives the monster combine, turning out the hay bales, square and strong as neatly tied parcels.

The old farmhouses with their great barns and outbuildings were strung along the five miles of coast like uncut stones on a rugged necklace, so that there was no telling where the fields of Penfolda finished and those of the next farm started. And so distant were the combines that it was impossible to guess at the identity of the men who drove them, or the tiny figures who walked behind, forking the bales into rough stooks to stand and dry in the midsummer sun.

She was not even sure that he still lived here, that he still farmed Penfolda, and yet could not imagine him existing anywhere else in the world. She let her mind's eye, like the lens of some great camera, zoom down on to the busy scene. The figures sprang into focus, huge and clear, and he was there, high at the wheel of the combine harvester, shirt-sleeves rolled back from brown forearms, his hair tousled by the wind. And because there was danger in moving in so close, Virginia swiftly presented him with a wife, pictured her walking across the fields with a basket, flasks of tea, and perhaps a fruit cake to eat, and she wore a pink cotton dress and a blue apron and her long bare legs were brown.

Mrs Eustace Philips. Mr and Mrs Eustace Philips of Penfolda.

The car nosed over the crest of the hill, and the bay and the white beaches and the distant headlands spread out before her, and far below, spilling down to around the blue goblet of the harbour, were the clustered houses and the Norman church tower of Porthkerris.

Wheal House, where the Lingards lived, and with whom
Virginia was staying, lay on the far side of Porthkerris. If she
had been a stranger, new to the district and visiting it for the first
time, she would have followed the main road which led right
down into the town and out the other side, and consequently
become hopelessly ensnared in crawling traffic and hordes of
aimless sightseers who spilled off the narrow pavements, or
stood about at strategic corners, sucking ice-creams, choosing
postcards and gazing in shop windows filled with brass piskies
and pottery mermaids and other horrors considered suitable as
souvenirs.

But, because she was not a stranger, Virginia turned off the
road long before the houses started and took the narrow, high-
hedged lane that wound up and over the hill which stood at the
back of the town. It was the long way home, by no means a
short cut, but eventually emerged out on the main road again,
through a tunnel of wild rhododendrons and not fifty yards from
the main entrance to Wheal House.

There was a white-barred gate and a rough drive that ran
up between hedges of pink-flowered escallonia. The house
was neo-Georgian, pleasingly proportioned, with a pedimented
porch over the front door. The drive swept up between
shaven green lawns and flower-beds heavy with the scent of
wallflowers, and as Virginia parked the car in the shade of
the house, there was a sharp cacophony of barking, and Dora,
Alice Lingard's old spaniel, emerged from the open front door
where she had been lying, for coolness, on the polished floor
of the hall.

Virginia stopped to pat her and speak to her and then went
indoors, taking off her sunglasses because after the bright day
outside, the house seemed pitch dark.

Across the hall the garden doors stood open to the patio, which, facing south and trapping all the sun, was a favourite spot of Alice's in all but really wintry weather. Today, because of the heat, she had unrolled the split cane awnings, and the bright canvas chairs and the low tables, already set out with tea things, were narrowly striped by the shadow patterns which they cast.

On the table in the middle of the hall lay the afternoon's mail. Two letters for Virginia, both with London postmarks. She laid down her handbag and her glasses and picked them up. One from Lady Keile and one from . . . Cara. The italic letters, which she learned at school, were painfully formed, dearly familiar.

Mrs A. Keile,
c/o Mrs Lingard,
Wheal House,
Porthkerris,
Cornwall.

No mistakes, no misspellings. Virginia wondered if she had managed by herself or whether Nanny had had to help. With the letters in her hand she went on across the hall and out to where her hostess sat, reclining gracefully on a long chair, with some sewing in her lap. She was making a cushion cover, stitching silk cord around the edge of the coral velvet square, and the colour lay in her lap like some huge fallen rose petal.

She looked up. "There you are! I was wondering what had happened to you. I thought perhaps you'd got stuck in a traffic jam."

Alice Lingard was a tall, dark woman in her late thirties, her firmly-built figure belied by long and slender arms and legs. She

5

was what Virginia always thought of as a middle-aged friend, not middle-aged in the strictest sense of the word, but belonging to that generation which lay halfway between Virginia and Virginia's mother. She was, in fact, a lifelong family friend, and years ago had been a small bridesmaid at Virginia's mother's wedding.

She herself had married, eighteen years or so ago, Tom Lingard, then a young man on the verge of taking over the small family business of Lingard Sons which specialised in the manufacture of heavy engineering machinery in the nearby town of Fourbourne. Under Tom's chairmanship the firm had expanded and prospered, and after a series of successful take-over bids now controlled interests which spread from Bristol to St Just, and included mining rights, a small shipping business and the sale of agricultural machinery.

They had never had children, but Alice had diverted her natural domestic talents to her house and garden, and over the years had transformed what had once been a fairly unimaginative establishment into an enchanting house and a garden which was constantly being photographed and written about by the Garden Editors of the glossier magazines. Ten years ago, when Virginia and her mother had come to Cornwall to spend Easter with the Lingards, the work had only just started. This time, having not visited Wheal House during the intervening years, Virginia had scarcely recognised the place. Everything had been subtly altered, straight lines curved, outlines and boundaries magically removed. Trees had grown up, casting long shadows on smooth lawns which seemed to spread as far as the eye could see. The old orchard had been transformed into a wild garden tangled with all the sweetest of old-fashioned roses, and where once had drilled rows of runner beans and raspberry canes, now

6

stood magnolias, creamy petalled, and heady-scented azaleas taller than a man could reach.

But, domestically, the patio was Alice's most successful project, neither house nor garden, but with the combined charm of both. Geraniums spilled from terrace pots, and up a trellised wall she had started to train a dark purple-flowered clematis. She had lately decided that she would also grow a vine, and was currently picking the brains of both friends and reference books, to decide on the best way to set about doing this. Her energies appeared to be endless.

Virginia pulled up a chair and dropped into it, surprised to find how hot and tired she felt. She shucked off her sandals and propped up her bare feet on to a handy stool. "I didn't go to Porthkerris."

"You didn't? But I thought you'd gone to the post office."

"I only wanted some stamps. I can buy them another time. There were so many people and so many buses and so much crushed and sweating humanity that I got claustrophobia and never stopped. Just went on driving."

"I can lend you stamps," said Alice. "Let me pour you some tea." She laid down her sewing and sat up to reach for the teapot. Steam rose from the delicate cup, fragrant, refreshing.

"Milk or lemon?"

"Lemon would be delicious."

"So much more refreshing, I think, on a hot day." She handed Virginia the cup and lay back again. "Where did you drive?"

"Um? . . . oh, the other way . . ."

"Land's End?"

"Not so far. I only got as far as Lanyon. I parked the car in a lay-by and climbed the hill for a bit and sat in the bracken and looked at the view."

"So beautiful," said Alice, threading her needle.

"They're cutting hay on the farms."

"Yes, they would be."

"It never changes, does it? Lanyon, I mean. No new houses, no new roads, no shops, no caravan parks." She took a mouthful of scalding hot Lapsang Souchong and then, with care, laid the cup and saucer down on the paved floor beside her chair. "Alice, does Eustace Philips still farm Penfolda?"

Alice stopped sewing, and put up a hand to take off her dark glasses and stare at Virginia. There was a puzzled frown between her dark brows.

"What do you know about Eustace Philips? How do you know him?"

"Alice, your memory is appalling. It was you yourself who took me out there, you and Tom, for an enormous barbecue on the cliffs at Penfolda. There must have been at least thirty people and I don't know who organised it, but we cooked sausages over a fire and drank beer out of a barrel. Oh, surely you remember, and then Mrs Philips gave us tea in her kitchen!"

"Now you remind me, of course I do. It was bitterly cold but quite beautiful and we watched the moon rise from behind Boscovey Head. I do remember. Now, who was it who threw that party? It certainly wasn't Eustace, he was always too busy milking cows. It must have been the Barnets – he was a sculptor and had a studio for a couple of years in Porthkerris before he went back to London. His wife wove baskets or belts or something, terribly folksy, and they had a lot of children who never wore shoes. They were always thinking up the most original parties. It must have been the Barnets . . . How extraordinary! I hadn't thought about them in years. And we all went out to Penfolda." But here her memory let her down.

8

She looked at Virginia blankly. "Or did we? Who went to that party?"

"Mother didn't come. She said it wasn't up her street . . ."

"How right she was."

"But you and I and Tom went."

"Of course. Bundled up in sweaters and socks. I'm not sure I didn't wear a fur coat. But we were talking about Eustace. How old were you, Virginia? Seventeen? Fancy your remembering Eustace Philips after all these years."

"You haven't answered my question. Is he still at Penfolda?"

"As the farm belonged to his father, and *his* father, and as far as I know *his* father before that, do you really think it likely that Eustace would up sticks and depart?"

"I suppose not. It's just that they were cutting hay this afternoon and I wondered if it was he who drove one of the combines. Do you ever see him, Alice?"

"Hardly ever. Not because we don't want to, understand me, but he's a hard-working farmer, and Tom's so busy being a tycoon, that their paths don't often cross. Except sometimes they meet at the hare shoot, or the Boxing Day meet . . . you know the sort of thing."

Virginia picked up her teacup and saucer, and observed, minutely, the rose painted upon its side.

"He's married," she said.

"You say that as though you were stating an irrefutable fact."

"Aren't I?"

"No, you're not. He never married. Heaven knows why. I always thought he was so attractive in a sun-burned, D. H. Lawrence-ish sort of way. There must have been a number of languishing ladies in Lanyon, but he resisted the lot. He must like it that way."

9

Eustace's wife, so swiftly imagined, as swiftly died, a wraith blown to nothing by the cold wind of reality. Instead, Virginia saw the Penfolda kitchen, cheerless and untidy, with the remains of the last meal abandoned on the table, dishes in the sink, an ashtray filled with cigarette stubs.

"Who looks after him?"

"I don't know. His mother died a couple of years ago I believe . . . I don't know what he does. Perhaps he's got a sexy housekeeper, or a domesticated mistress? I really don't know."

And couldn't care less, her tone implied. She had finished sewing on the silk cord, now gave a couple of neat firm stitches and then broke the thread with a little tug. "There, that's done. Isn't it a divine colour? But it's really too hot to sew." She laid it aside. "Oh dear, I suppose I must go and see what we'll have for dinner. What would you say to a delicious fresh lobster?"

"I'd say 'pleased to see you'."

Alice stood up, unfolding her long height to tower over Virginia. "Did you see your letters?"

"Yes, they're here."

Alice stooped to pick up the tray. "I'll leave you," she said, "to read them in peace."

Keeping the best to the last, Virginia opened her mother-in-law's letter first. The envelope was dark blue, lined with navy-blue tissue. The writing-paper was thick, the address blackly embossed at its head.

32 Welton Gardens, S.W.8.

My dear Virginia,

I hope you are enjoying this wonderful weather, quite a heatwave and into the nineties yesterday. I expect you are swimming in Alice's pool, such a joy not having to drive to

*the beach every time you want to swim. The children are both
well and send their love. Nanny takes them into the park every
day and they take their tea with them and eat it there. I took
Cara to Harrods this morning to buy some new dresses, she
is getting so tall and was quite out of her old ones. One is blue
with appliquéd flowers, the other pink with a little smocking.
I think you would approve! Tomorrow they are going to tea
with the Manning-Prestons. Nanny is looking forward to a
good gossip with their Nanny, and Susan is just the right
age for Cara. It would be nice for them to be friends. My
regards to Alice, and let me know when you decide to come
back to London, but we are managing beautifully, and don't
want you to cut short your holiday at all for any reason. You
really were due for one.*

Affectionately,

Dorothea Keile

She read the letter twice, torn by conflicting emotions. Double
meanings sprang at her from between the meticulously-penned,
well-turned sentences. She saw her children in the park, the
baked London grass turned yellow in the heat, trodden and
tired, and fouled by dogs. She saw the white-hot morning sky
high above the roof-tops and the little girl being fitted into
dresses that she would neither like nor want, but would be too
polite to reject. She saw the Manning-Prestons' tall, terraced
house, with the paved garden at the back where Mrs Manning-
Preston held her famous cocktail parties, and where Cara and
Susan would be sent to play while the Nannies talked about
knitting patterns and what a terror Nanny Brigg's little charge
was going to be. And she saw Cara standing silent, petrified
with shyness, and Susan Manning-Preston treating her with

11

contempt because Cara wore spectacles and Susan thought she was a ninny.

And "we are managing beautifully". The statement seemed to Virginia completely ambiguous. Who was "we"? Nanny and the grandmother? Or did it include the children, Virginia's children? Did they let Cara sleep with the old teddy that Nanny swore was unhygienic? Did they remember always to leave the light on so that Nicholas could get himself to the bathroom in the middle of the night? And were they ever left alone, disorganised, dirty, untidy, to play secret, pointless games in small corners of the garden, with perhaps a nut or a leaf, and all the imaginings that were contained within their small, clever, bewildering brains?

She found that her hands were shaking. She was a fool to get into this state. Nanny had looked after the children since they were born, she knew all their idiosyncrasies and nobody could cope with Nicholas's sudden rages better than she.

(But should he have such rages? At six, shouldn't he have grown out of them? What frustration sparks them off?)

And Nanny was gentle with Cara. She made dolls' clothes and knitted scarves and sweaters for the teddies out of left-over bits of wool. And she let Cara wheel her doll's perambulator into the park; over the crossing by the Albert Memorial, they went. (But did she read to Cara, the books that Cara loved? *The Borrowers* and *The Railway Children* and every word of *The Secret Garden*.) Did she love the children, or simply possess them?

These were all familiar questions which, lately, had been raising themselves with ever-increasing frequency within the confines of Virginia's own head. But never answered. Knowing that she was evading a vital issue, she would shelve her own anxiety, always with some excuse to herself. I can't think about it now, I'm too tired. Perhaps in a couple of years when Nicholas goes away to prep school, perhaps then I'll tell my mother-in-law that I don't need Nanny any longer; I'll say to Nanny it's time to go, to find another new baby to look after. And perhaps just now I'm too emotional, I wouldn't be good for the children; they're better with Nanny: after all, she's been looking after children for forty years.

Like a familiar sedative the well-worn excuses came pat, blunting Virginia's uneasy conscience. She put the blue letter back into its expensive envelope and turned, in relief, to the second one. But the relief was short-lived. Cara had borrowed her grandmother's writing-paper, but the sentences this time were neither meticulously penned nor well-turned. The ink was blotched and the lines ran down the side of the paper as though the words were tumbling hopelessly downhill.

Darling Mother,

I hope you are having a good time. I hope it is nise wether. It is hot in London. I have to go and have tea with Susan Maning Preston. I dont no what we will play. Last night Nicholas screemed and Granny had to give him a pil. He went all red. One of my dolls eyes has come out and I cant find it. Please will you rite to me soon and tell me when we are going back to Kirkton.

With love from Cara

P.S. Dont forget to rite.

She folded the letter and put it away. Across the garden, across the lawns, the blue of Alice's swimming-pool glimmered like a jewel. The cooling air was filled with bird-song and the

13

scent of flowers. From inside the house she could hear Alice's voice talking to Mrs Jilkes, the cook, doubtless about the lobster which they were going to eat for dinner.

She felt helpless, totally inadequate. She thought of asking Alice to have the children here, and in the next instant knew that it was impossible. Alice's house was not designed for children, her life did not cater for their inclusion. She would be irritated beyond words by Cara forgetting to change her gumboots, or by Nicholas kicking his football into the treasured flower-borders, or drawing ''pictures'' on the wallpaper. For without Nanny, he would doubtless be impossible because he was always twice as naughty without her to keep an eye on him.

Without Nanny. Those were the operative words. On her own. She had to have them on her own.

And yet the very thought filled her with dread. What would she do with them? Where would they go? Like feelers her thoughts probed around, searching for ideas. A hotel? But hotels here would be filled to the brim with summer visitors and terribly expensive. Besides, Nicholas in a hotel would be as nerve-racking as Nicholas at Wheal House. She thought of hiring a caravan, or camping with them on the beach, like the summer migration of hippies, who lit fires of driftwood and slept curled up on the chilly sand.

Of course, there was always Kirkton. Some time, she would have to go back. But all her instincts shied away from the thought of returning to Scotland, to the house where she had lived with Anthony, the place where her children had been born, the only place they thought of as home. Thinking of Kirkton, she saw tree shadows flickering on pale walls, the cold northern light reflected on the white ceilings, the sound of her own feet going up the uncarpeted, polished stairway. She thought of clear

14

autumn evenings when the first skeins of geese flew over, and the park, in front of the house, sweeping down to the banks of the deep, swift-flowing river . . .

No. Not yet. Cara would have to wait. Later, perhaps, they would go back to Kirkton. Not yet. Behind her a door slammed, and she was jerked back to reality by the arrival of Tom Lingard, back from work. She heard him call Alice, then drop his briefcase on the hall table, and come out to the patio in search of his wife.

"Hello, Virginia." He bent and dropped a kiss on the top of her head. "All alone? Where's Alice?"

"Interviewing a lobster in the kitchen."

"Letters from the children? All well? Well done, that's great . . ." One of Tom's idiosyncrasies was that he never bothered to wait for an answer to any of his questions. Virginia sometimes wondered if this was the secret of his outstanding success. "What have you been doing all day? Lying in the sun? That's the job. How about coming and having a swim with me now? The exercise'll do you good after all this lazing about. We'll get Alice to come too . . ." He went, spring-footed and bursting with energy, back into the house and down the passage towards the kitchen, bellowing for his wife. And Virginia, grateful for directions, stood up and collected her mail and went indoors, obediently, and upstairs to her bedroom to change into a bikini.

2

The solicitors were called Smart, Chirgwin and Williams. At least, those were the names on the brass plate by the door, a plate which had been polished so long and so hard that the letters had lost their sharpness and were quite difficult to read. There was a brass knocker on the door, too, and a brass doorknob, as smooth and shining as the plate, and when Virginia turned the knob and opened the door, she stepped into a narrow hall of polished brown linoleum and shining cream paint and it occurred to her that some hard-working woman was using up an awful lot of elbow grease.

There was a glass window, like an old-fashioned ticket-office with INQUIRIES written over it, and a bell to press. Virginia pressed the bell and the window flew up.

"Yes?"

Startled, Virginia told the face behind the window that she wanted to see Mr Williams.

"Have you got an appointment?"

"Yes. It's Mrs Keile."

"Just a moment, please."

The window slammed down and the face withdrew. Presently a door opened and the face reappeared, along with a well-upholstered body and a pair of legs that went straight down into sturdy lace-up shoes.

"If you'd like to come this way, Mrs Keile."

The building which housed the solicitors' office stood at the top of the hill which led out of Porthkerris, but even so Virginia was taken unawares by the marvellous view which leapt at her as soon as she walked into the room. Mr Williams's desk stood in the middle of the carpet and Mr Williams was, even now, getting to his feet behind it. But, beyond Mr Williams, a great picture window framed, like some lovely painting, the whole jumbled, charming panorama of the old part of the town. Roofs of houses, faded slate and whitewashed chimneys, tumbled without pattern or order down the hill. Here a blue door, there a yellow window; here a window-sill bright with geraniums, a line of washing gay as flags, or the leaves of some unsuspected and normally unseen tree. Beyond the roofs and far below them was the harbour, at full tide and sparkling with sunshine. Boats rocked at anchor and a white sail sped out beyond the shelter of the harbour wall, heading for the ruler line of the horizon where the two blues met. The air was clamorous with the sound of gulls, the sky patterned with their great gliding wings and as Virginia stood there, the church bells from the Norman tower struck up a simple carillon and clock chimes rang out eleven o'clock.

"Good morning," said Mr Williams, and Virginia realised that he had already said this twice. She tore her attention from the view and tried to focus it on him.

"Oh, good morning. I'm Mrs Keile, I . . ." But it was impossible. "How *can* you work in a room with a view like that?"

"That's why I sit with my back to it . . ."

18

"It's breathtaking."

"Yes, and quite unique. We're often asked by artists if they can paint the harbour from this window. You can see the whole structure of the town, and the colours are always different, always beautiful. Except, of course, on a rainy day. Now – " his manner changed abruptly as though anxious to get down to work and to waste no more time " – what can I do for you?" He drew a chair forward for her.

Trying to stop looking out of the window and to concentrate on the matter in hand, Virginia sat down. "Well I've maybe come to quite the wrong person, but you see I can't find an estate agent anywhere in the town. And I looked in the local paper for a house to rent, but there didn't seem to be one. And then I saw your name in the telephone book, and I thought perhaps you might be able to help me."

"Help you find a house?" Mr Williams was young, very dark, his eyes frankly interested in the attractive woman who faced him across his desk.

"Just to rent . . ."

"For how long?"

"A month . . . my children go back to school the first week in September."

"I see. Well, we don't actually *deal* in this sort of thing, but I could ask Miss Leddra if there's anything that she could suggest. But of course this is the high season, and the town is already packed to the gunwales with visitors. Even if you do find something, I'm afraid you'll have to pay a fairly steep rent."

"I don't mind."

"Well, just a moment . . ."

He left her and went out, and Virginia heard him speaking to the woman who had let her in. She got up and went back to the window, and opened it wide and laughed as a furious gull flew crossly off the sill where he had been perching. The wind off the sea was cool and fresh. A pleasure boat packed with passengers started off across the harbour and suddenly Virginia longed to be on board, irresponsible, sun-burned, wearing a hat with KISS ME written on it and screaming with laughter as the first waves sent the boat rocking.

Mr Williams came back. "Can you wait a moment? Miss Leddra's making a few inquiries . . ."

"Yes, of course." She returned to her chair.

"Are you staying in Porthkerris?" Mr Williams asked conversationally.

"Yes. I'm staying with friends. The Lingards up at Wheal House."

His previous manner had been neither off-hand nor familiar, but all at once he was almost deferential.

"Oh yes, of course. What a charming place that is."

"Yes. Alice has made it lovely."

"Have you been there before?"

"Yes. Ten years ago. But I haven't been since."

"Are your children with you?"

"No. They're in London, with their grandmother. But I want to get them down here with me, if I can."

"Is London your home?"

"No. It's just that my mother-in-law lives in London." Mr Williams waited. "My home . . . that is, we live in Scotland."

He looked delighted . . . Virginia could not think why it should delight him that she lived in Scotland. "But how splendid! What part?"

"In Perthshire."

"The most beautiful. My wife and I spent a holiday there

20

last summer. The peace of it all, and the empty roads and the quiet. How could you bear to come away?''

Virginia had opened her mouth to tell him when the discussion was mercifully interrupted by the arrival of Miss Leddra, bearing a sheaf of papers.

''Here it is, Mr Williams. Bosithick. And the letter from Mr Kernow saying that if we could find a tenant for August he'd be willing to rent. But only to a *suitable* tenant, Mr Williams. He's very firm about that point.''

Mr Williams took the papers and smiled at Virginia over the top of them.

''Are you a suitable tenant, Mrs Keile?''

''It depends. On what you're offering me, doesn't it?''

''Well, it's not actually in Porthkerris . . . thank you, Miss Leddra . . . but not too far away . . . out at Lanyon actually . . .''

''Lanyon!''

She must have sounded appalled, for Mr Williams sprang at once to Lanyon's defence. ''But it's a most charming spot, quite the most beautiful bit of coastline left anywhere.''

''I didn't mean that I didn't like it. I was just surprised.''

''Were you? Why?''

He was too sharp, like a beady-eyed bird. ''No reason, really. Tell me about the house.''

He told her. It was an old cottage, neither distinguished nor beautiful, but with a small claim to fame in that a famous writer had once lived and worked there during the nineteen-twenties.

Virginia said, ''Which?''

''I beg your pardon?''

''Which famous writer?''

''Oh, I'm sorry. Aubrey Crane. Didn't you know that he spent some years in this part of the world?''

Virginia did not. But Aubrey Crane had been one of the many authors of whom Virginia's mother did not approve. She remembered her mother's chill expression, lips pursed, whenever his books were mentioned; remembered them being returned swiftly to the library before the young Virginia could get her eyes on them. For some reason this seemed to make the cottage called Bosithick even more desirable. "Go on," said Virginia.

Mr Williams went on. Despite its age Bosithick had been modernised to a certain degree – there was now a bathroom and a lavatory and an electric cooker.

"Who does it belong to?" Virginia asked.

"Mr Kernow is the nephew of the old lady who used to own the house. She left it to him, but he lives in Plymouth so he uses it just for holidays. He and his family intended coming down for the summer, but his wife fell ill and can't make the trip. As we are Mr Kernow's solicitors, he put the matter in our hands, with the instructions that, if we did let the house, it must be to a tenant who can be trusted to take care of it."

"How big is it?"

Mr Williams perused his papers. "Let's see, a kitchen, a sitting-room, a downstairs bathroom, and a hall, and three rooms upstairs."

"Is there a garden?"

"Not really."

"How far is it from the road?"

"About a hundred yards down a farm lane, as far as I can remember."

"And could I have it right away?"

"I can see no objection. But you must see it first."

"Yes, of course . . . when can I see it?"

"Today? Tomorrow?"

22

"Tomorrow morning."

"I'll take you out myself."

"Thank you, Mr Williams." Virginia stood up and made for the door, and he had to make a little rush to get there and open it before she did.

"There's just one thing, Mrs Keile."

"What's that?"

"You haven't asked what the rent is."

She smiled. "No I haven't, have I? Goodbye Mr Williams."

Virginia said nothing to Alice and Tom. She did not want to have to put into words what was, at best, only a vague idea. She did not want to be drawn into an argument, to be persuaded either that the children were best left in London with their grandmother or that Alice could disregard the possible destruction that they might perpetrate at Wheal House and would insist on having them there. When Virginia had found somewhere for them all to live, she would present Alice with what she had done as a *fait accompli*. And then Alice would maybe help her take the biggest hurdle of all, which was to persuade the grandmother to let the children come to Cornwall without Nanny. At the very prospect of this ordeal, Virginia's imagination turned and ran, but there were other and smaller obstacles to be overcome first, and these she was determined to do by herself.

Alice was a perfect hostess. When Virginia told her that she would be out for the morning it never occurred to Alice to quiz her as to what she intended doing. She only said, "Will you be in for lunch?"

"I don't think so . . . Better say not . . ."

"I'll see you at tea-time, then. We'll have a swim together afterwards."

"Heaven," said Virginia. She kissed Alice and went out, got

23

into her car and drove down the hill into Porthkerris. She parked
the car near the station and walked to the solicitors' office to
pick up Mr Williams.

''Mrs Keile, I couldn't be more sorry, but I'm not going to
be able to come out with you this morning to Bosithick. An
old client is coming down from Truro and I must be here to
see her; I do hope you understand! But here are the keys of the
house, and I've drawn a fairly detailed map of how to find it
. . . I don't think you could go wrong. Do you mind going on
your own, or would you like to take Miss Leddra with you?''

Virginia imagined the daunting presence of the formidable
Miss Leddra and assured Mr Williams that she'd manage perfectly on her own. She was given a ring of large keys, each with
a wooden label. Front Door, Coal Shed, Tower Room. ''You'll
need to watch out for the lane,'' Mr Williams told her, as they
went together towards the door. ''It's fairly bumpy and although
there's no room to turn by the gate of Bosithick itself, you can
manage easily if you carry on down the lane; you'll come to an
old farmyard and you can turn the car there. Now, you're sure
you'll be all right . . . I couldn't be more sorry about this, but I'll
be here, of course, waiting to hear what you think of the place.
Oh, and Mrs Keile . . . it's been empty for some months. Try
not to be influenced if it feels a little dingy. Just throw open a
few windows and imagine it with a nice cheerful fire.''

Slightly discouraged by these parting remarks, Virginia went
back to her car. The keys of the unknown house weighed heavy
as lead in her handbag. All at once, she longed for company,
and even considered, for a mad moment, returning to Wheal
House to make a true confession to Alice and persuade her to
come out to Lanyon and lend a little moral support. But that
was ridiculous. It was just a little cottage, to be viewed, and

either rented or rejected. Any fool . . . even Virginia . . . could surely do that.

The weather was still beautiful and the traffic still appalling. She crawled, one of the long queue of cars, down into the depths of town and out the other side. At the top of the hill where the roads forked, the traffic thinned a little and she was able to put on some speed and pass a line of dawdling cars. As she went up and over the moor and the sea dropped and spread beneath her, her spirits rose. The road wound like a grey ribbon through the bracken-covered hillside; to her left towered the great outcrop of Carn Edvor stained purple with heather, and on her right the country swept away down to the sea, the familiar patchwork of fields and farms that she had sat and watched only two days before.

She had been told by Mr Williams to look out for a clump of wind-leaning hawthorns by the side of the road. Beyond this was a steep corner and then the narrow farm track which led down towards the sea. Virginia came upon it and turned the car down into it, no more than a stony lane high-hedged with brambles. She went into bottom gear and edged cautiously downhill, attempting to avoid bumps and potholes and trying not to think about the damage that the prickly gorse bushes were inflicting on the paintwork of her car.

There was no sign of any house, until she turned a steep corner and was instantly upon it. A stone wall, and beyond, a gable and a slated roof. She stopped the car in the lane, reached for her handbag and got out. There was a cool, salty wind blowing in from the sea, and the smell of gorse. She went to open the gate, but the hinges were broken and it had to be lifted before she could edge through. A path of sorts led down towards a flight of stone steps and so to the house, and Virginia saw that it was long and low with gables to the north and the south, and at the north end, looking out over the sea, had been added an extra room with a square tower above it. The tower imparted an oddly sanctified look to the house which Virginia found chilling. There was no garden to speak of, but at the south end a patch of unmown grass blew in the wind and two leaning poles supported what had once been a washing-line.

She went down the steps and along a dank pathway that led along the side of the house towards the front door. This had once been painted dark red and was scarred with splitting sun blisters. Virginia took out the key and put it in the keyhole and turned the doorknob and the key together and the door instantly, silently, swung inwards. She saw a tiny flight of stairs, a worn rug on bare boards, smelled damp and . . . mice? She swallowed nervously. She hated mice, but now that she had come so far there was nothing for it but to go up the two worn steps and tread gingerly over the threshold.

It did not take long to go over the old part of the house, to glance in at the tiny kitchen with its inadequate cooker and stained sink; the sitting-room cluttered with ill-matching chairs. An electric fire sat in the cavern of the huge old fireplace, like a savage animal at the mouth of its lair. There were curtains of flimsy cotton hanging at the windows, fly-blown and dejected, and a dresser packed with cups and plates and dishes in every sort of size and shape and state of dilapidation.

Without hope, Virginia went upstairs. The bedrooms were dim with tiny windows and unsuitable, looming pieces of furniture. She returned to the top of the stairs, and so up another pair of steps, to a closed door. She opened this, and after the gloom of the rest of the house, the blast of bright, northern light by which she was immediately assailed, was dazzling.

Stunned by it, she stepped blindly into an astonishing room; small, completely square, windowed on three walls, it stood high above the sea like the bridge of a ship, with a view of the coastline that must have extended for fifteen miles.

A window seat with a faded cover ran along the north side of this room. There was a scrubbed table, and an old braided rug and in the centre of the floor, like a decorative well-head, the wrought-iron banister of a spiral staircase which led directly down to the room beneath, the ''Hall'' of Mr Williams's prospectus.

Cautiously Virginia descended, to a room dominated by an enormous *art nouveau* fireplace. Off this was the bathroom; and then another door, and she was back where she'd started, in the dark and depressing sitting-room.

It was an extraordinary, a terrible house. It sat around her, waiting for her to make some decision, contemptuous of her faintness of heart. To give herself time, she went back up to the tower room, sat on the window seat and opened her bag to find a cigarette. Her last. She would have to buy some more. She lit it and looked at the bare scrubbed table, and the faded colours of the rug on the floor, and knew that this had been Aubrey Crane's study, the workroom where he had wrestled out the lusty love stories that Virginia had never been encouraged to read. She saw him, bearded and knickerbockered, his conventional appearance belying the passions of his rebellious heart. Perhaps in summertime, he would have flung wide these windows, to catch all the scents and sounds of the countryside, the roar of the sea, the whistle of the wind. But in winter it would be bitterly cold, and he would have to wrap himself in blankets, and write painfully with chilblained fingers mittened in knitted wool . . .

Somewhere in the room a fly droned, blundering against the

27

window-pane. Virginia leaned her forehead on the cool glass of the window and stared sightless at the view and started one of the interminable ding-dong arguments she had been having with herself for years.

I can't come here.

Why not?

I hate it. It's spooky and frightening. It's got a horrible atmosphere.

That's just your imagination.

It's an impossible house. I could never bring the children here. They've never lived in such a place. Anyway, there's nowhere for them to play.

There's the whole world for them to play in. The fields and the cliffs and the sea.

But looking after them . . . the washing and the ironing, and the cooking. And there's no refrigerator, and how would I heat the water?

I thought that all that mattered was getting the children to yourself, away from London.

They're better in London, with Nanny, than living in a house like this.

That wasn't what you thought yesterday.

I can't bring them here. I wouldn't know where to begin. Not on my own like that.

Then what are you going to do?

I don't know. Talk to Alice, perhaps I should have talked to her before now. She hasn't children of her own, but she'll understand. Maybe she'll know about some other little house. She'll understand. She'll help. She has to help.

So much, said her own cool and scathing voice, *for all those strong resolutions.*

28

Angrily, Virginia stubbed out the half-smoked cigarette, ground it under her heel and got up and went downstairs and took out the keys and locked the door behind her. She went back up the path to the gate, stepped through and shut it. The house watched her, the small bedroom windows like derisive eyes. She tore herself from their gaze and got back into the safety of her car. It was a quarter past twelve. She needed cigarettes and she was not expected back at Wheal House for lunch, so, when she had turned the car, and was driving back on to the main road again, she took not the road to Porthkerris, but the other way, and she drove the short mile to Lanyon village, up the narrow main street, and finally came to a halt in the cobbled square that was flanked on one side by the porch of the square-towered church and on the other by a small whitewashed pub called The Mermaid's Arms.

Because of the fine weather, there were tables and chairs set up outside the pub, along with brightly coloured sun-umbrellas and tubs of orange nasturtiums. A man and a woman in holiday clothes sat and drank their beer, their little boy played with a puppy. As Virginia approached, they looked up to smile good morning, and she smiled back and went past them in through the door, instinctively ducking her head beneath the blackened lintel.

Inside it was dark-panelled, low-ceilinged, dimly illuminated by tiny windows veiled in lace curtains; there was a pleasant smell, cool and musty. A few figures, scarcely visible in the gloom, sat along the wall, or around small wobbly tables, and behind the bar, framed by rows of hanging beer-mugs, the barman, in shirt-sleeves and a checkered pullover, was polishing glasses with a dishcloth.

". . . I don't know 'ow it is, William," he was saying

to a customer who sat at the other end of the bar, perched disconsolately on a tall stool, with a long cigarette ash and half a pint of bitter, ". . . but you put the litter bins up and nobody puts nothing into them . . ."

"Ur . . ." said William, nodding in sad agreement and sprinkling cigarette ash into the beer.

"Stuff blows all over the road, and the County Council don't even come and empty them. Ugly old things they are, too, we'd be better without them. Managed all right without them before, we did . . ." He finished polishing the glass, set it down with a thump and turned to attend to Virginia.

"Yes, madam?"

He was very Cornish, in voice, in looks, in colouring. A red and wind-burned face, blue eyes, black hair.

Virginia asked for cigarettes.

"Only got packets of twenty. That all right?" He turned to take them from the shelf and slit the wrapper with a practised thumbnail. "Lovely day, isn't it? On holiday, are you?"

"Yes." It was years since she had been into a pub. In Scotland women were never taken into pubs. She had forgotten the atmosphere, the snug companionship. She said, "Do you have any Coke?"

He looked surprised. "Yes, I've got Coke. Keep it for the children. Want some, do you?"

"Please."

He reached for a bottle, opened it neatly, poured it into a glass and pushed it across the counter towards her.

"I was just saying to William, here, that road to Porthkerris is a disgrace – " Virginia pulled up a stool and settled down to listen. " – All that rubbish lying around. Visitors don't seem to know what to do with their litter. You'd think coming to a

30

lovely part like this they'd have the sense they was born with and take all them old bits of paper home with them, in the car, not leave them lying around on the roadside. They talk about conservation and ecology, but, my God . . .''

He was off on what was obviously his favourite hobby-horse, judging by the well-timed grunts of assent that came from all corners of the room. Virginia lit a cigarette. Outside, in the sunny square, a car drew up, the engine stopped, a door slammed. She heard a man's voice say good morning, and then footsteps came through the doorway and into the bar behind her.

''. . . I wrote to the MP about it, said who was going to get the place cleaned up, he said it was the responsibility of the County Council, but I said . . .'' Over Virginia's head he caught sight of the new customer. '' 'Allo, there! You're a stranger.''

''Still at the litter bins, Joe?''

''You know me, boy, worry a subject to death, like a terrier killing a rat. What'll you have?''

''A pint of bitter.''

Joe turned to draw the beer, and the newcomer moved in to stand between Virginia and lugubrious William, and she had recognised his voice at once, as soon as he spoke, just as she had known his footfall, stepping in over the flagged threshold of The Mermaid's Arms.

She took a mouthful of Coke, laid down the glass. All at once her cigarette tasted bitter; she stubbed it out and turned her head to look at him, and she saw the blue shirt, with the sleeves rolled back from his brown forearms, and the eyes very blue and the short, rough, brown hair cut like a pelt, close to the shape of his head. And because there was nothing else to be done she said, ''Hello, Eustace.''

Startled, his head swung round and his expression was that

31

of a man who had suddenly been hit in the stomach, bemused and incapable. She said, quickly, ''It really is me,'' and his smile came, incredulous, rueful, as though he knew he had been made to look a fool.

''Virginia.''

She said again, stupidly, ''Hello.''

''What in the name of heaven are you doing here?''

She was aware that every ear in the place was waiting for her to reply. She made it very light and casual. ''Buying cigarettes. Having a drink.''

''I didn't mean that. I mean in Cornwall. Here, in Lanyon.''

''I'm on holiday. Staying with the Lingards in Porthkerris.''

''How long have you been here?''

''About a week . . .''

''And what are you doing out here?''

But before she had time to tell him, the barman had pushed Eustace's tankard of beer across the counter, and Eustace was diverted by trying to find the right money in his trouser pocket.

''Old friends, are you?'' asked Joe, looking at Virginia with new interest, and she said, ''Yes, I suppose you could say that.''

''I haven't seen her for ten years,'' Eustace told him, pushing the coins across the counter. He looked at Virginia's glass. ''What are you drinking?''

''Coke.''

''Bring it outside, we may as well sit in the sun.''

She followed him, aware of the unblinking stares which followed them; the insatiable curiosity. Outside in the sunshine he put their glasses down on to a wooden table and they settled, side by side on a bench, with the sun on their heads and their backs against the whitewashed wall of the pub.

''You don't mind being brought out here, do you? Otherwise

we couldn't say a word without it being received and transmitted all over the county within half an hour.''

''I'd rather be outside.''

Half turned towards her, he sat so close that Virginia could see the rough, weather-beaten texture of his skin, the network of tiny lines around his eyes, the first frosting of white in that thick brown hair. She thought, *I'm with him again.*

He said, ''Tell me.''

''Tell you what?''

''What happened to you.'' And then quickly, ''I know you got married.''

''Yes. Almost at once.''

''Well, that would have put paid to the London Season you were dreading so much.''

''Yes, it did.''

''And the coming-out dance.''

''I had a wedding instead.''

''Mrs Anthony Keile. I saw the announcement in the paper.'' Virginia said nothing. ''Where do you live now?''

''In Scotland. There's a house in Scotland . . .''

''And children?''

''Yes. Two. A boy and a girl.''

''How old are they?'' He was really interested, and she remembered how the Cornish loved children, how Mrs Jilkes was for ever going dewy-eyed over some lovely little great-nephew or niece.

''The girl's eight and the boy's six.''

''Are they with you now?''

''No. They're in London. With their grandmother.''

''And your husband? Is he down? What's he doing this morning? Playing golf?''

She stared at him, accepting for the first time the fact that personal tragedy is just that. Personal. Your own existence could fall to pieces but that did not mean that the rest of the world necessarily knew about it, or even bothered. There was no reason for Eustace to know.

She laid her hands on the edge of the table, aligning them as though their arrangement were of the utmost importance. She said, "Anthony's dead." Her hands seemed all at once insubstantial, almost transparent, the wrists too thin, the long almond-shaped nails, painted coral pink, as fragile as petals. She wished suddenly, fervently, that they were not like that, but strong and brown and capable, with dirt engrained, and fingernails worn from gardening and peeling potatoes and scraping carrots. She could feel Eustace's eyes upon her. She could not bear him to be sorry for her.

He said, "What happened?"

"He was killed in a car accident. He was drowned."

"*Drowned?*"

"We have this river, you see, at Kirkton . . . that's where we live in Scotland. The river runs between the house and the road, you have to go over the bridge. And he was coming home and he skidded, or misjudged the turn, and the car went through the wooden railings and into the river. We'd had a lot of rain, a wet month, and the river was in spate and the car went to the bottom. A diver had to go down . . . with a cable. And the police eventually winched it out . . ." Her voice trailed off.

He said gently, "When?"

"Three months ago."

"Not long."

"No. But there was so much to do, so much to see to. I don't know what's happened to the time. And then I caught this bug

– a sort of flu, and I couldn't throw it off, so my mother-in-law said that she'd have the children in London and I came down here to stay with Alice.''

''When are you going away again?''

''I don't know.''

He was silent. After a little he picked up his glass and drained his beer. As he set it down he said, ''Have you got a car here?''

''Yes.'' She pointed. ''The blue Triumph.''

''Then finish that drink and we'll go back to Penfolda.'' Virginia turned her head and stared at him. ''Well, what's so extraordinary about that? It's dinner-time. There are pasties in the oven. Do you want to come back and eat one with me?''

''. . . Yes.''

''Then come. I've got my Land-Rover. You can follow me.''

''All right.''

He stood up. ''Come along, then.''

3

She had been to Penfolda once before, only once, and then in the cool half-light of a spring evening ten years before.

"We've been invited to a party," Alice had announced over lunch that day.

Virginia's mother was immediately intrigued. She was immensely social and with a seventeen-year-old daughter to launch into society one only had to mention a party to capture her attention.

"How very nice! Where? Who with?"

Alice laughed at her. Alice was one of the few people who could laugh at Rowena Parsons and get away with it, but then Alice had known her for years.

"Don't get too excited. It's not really your sort of thing."

"My dear Alice, I don't know what you mean. Explain!"

"Well, it's a couple called Barnet. Amos and Fenella Barnet. You may have heard of him. He's a sculptor, very modern, very *avant-garde*. They've taken one of the old studios in Porthkerris, and they have a great number of rather unconventional children."

Without waiting to hear more Virginia said, "Why don't we

37

go?'' They sounded exactly the sort of people she was always longing to meet.

Mrs Parsons allowed a small frown to show between her beautifully aligned eyebrows. ''Is the party in the studio?'' she inquired, obviously suspecting doctored drinks and doped cigarettes.

''No, it's out at Lanyon at a farm called Penfolda, some sort of a barbecue on the cliffs. A camp fire and fried sausages . . .'' Alice saw that Virginia was longing to go. ''. . . I think it might be rather fun.''

''I think it sounds terrible,'' said Mrs Parsons.

''I didn't think you'd want to come. But Tom and I might go, and we'll take Virginia with us.''

Mrs Parsons turned her cool gaze upon her daughter. ''Do you *want* to go to a barbecue?''

Virginia shrugged. ''It might be fun.'' She had learned, long ago, that it never paid to be too enthusiastic about anything.

''Very well,'' said her mother, helping herself to lemon pudding. ''If it's your idea of an amusing evening and Alice and Tom don't mind taking you along . . . but for heaven's sake wear something warm. It's bound to be freezing. Far too cold, one would have thought, for a picnic.''

She was right. It was cold. A clear turquoise evening with the shoulder of Carn Edvor silhouetted black against the western sky and a chill inland wind to nip the air. Driving up the hill out of Porthkerris, Virginia looked back and saw the lights of the town twinkling far below, the ink-black waters of the harbour brimming with shimmering reflections. Across the bay, from the distant headland, the lighthouse sent its warning signal. A flash. A pause. A flash. A longer pause. Be careful. There's danger.

The evening ahead seemed full of possibilities. Suddenly

excited, Virginia turned and leaned forward, resting her chin on crossed arms on the back of Alice's seat. The unpremeditated gesture was clumsy and spontaneous, a reflection of natural high spirits that were normally battened firmly down under the influence of a domineering mother.

"Alice, where is this place we're going?"

"Penfolda. It's a farm, just this side of Lanyon."

"Who lives there?"

"Mrs Philips. She's a widow. And her son Eustace."

"What does he do?"

"He farms, silly. I told you it was a farm."

"Are they friends of the Barnets?"

"I suppose they must be. A lot of artists live out around this part of the world. Though I've no idea how they could ever have met."

Tom said, "Probably at The Mermaid's."

"What's The Mermaid's?" Virginia asked.

"The Mermaid's Arms, the pub in Lanyon. On a Saturday night all the world and his wife go there for a drink and a get-together."

"Who else will be at the party?"

"Our guess is probably as good as yours."

"Haven't you *any* idea?"

"Well . . ." Alice did her best. ". . . Artists and writers and poets and hippies and drop-outs and farmers and perhaps one or two rather boring and conventional people like us."

Virginia gave her a hug. "You're not boring or conventional. You're super."

"You may not think we're quite so super at the end of the evening. You may hate it, so grit your teeth and reserve your judgement."

Virginia sat back, in the darkness of the car, hugging herself. *I shan't hate it.*

There were headlights like fireflies, coming from all directions, converging on Penfolda. From the road the farmhouse could be seen to be blazing with light. They joined the queue of assorted vehicles which bumped and groaned their way down a narrow, broken lane and eventually were directed into a farmyard which had been turned temporarily into a car park. The air was full of voices and laughter as friends greeted friends, and already a steady trickle of people were making their way over a stone wall and down over the pasture fields towards the cliffs. Some were wrapped in rugs, some carried old-fashioned lanterns, some – Virginia was glad all over again that her mother had not come – a clanking bottle or two.

Someone said, "Tom! What are you doing here?", and Tom and Alice dropped back to wait for their friends, and Virginia went on, loving the feeling of being alone. All about her the soft, dark air smelled of peat and sea-wrack and wood-smoke. The sky was not yet empty of light and the sea was of so dark a blue that it was almost black. She went through a gap in a wall and saw, below her, at the bottom of the field, the golden flames of the fire, already ringed with lanterns and the shapes and shadows of about thirty people. As she came closer, faces sprang suddenly into focus, illuminated in firelight, laughing and talking, everybody knowing everybody. There was a barrel of beer, propped on a wooden stand, from which brimming glasses were being continually filled, and there was the smell of potatoes cooking and burning fat, and somebody had brought a guitar and begun to play and gradually a few people gathered about him and raised uncertain voices in song.

There is a ship
And she sails the sea,
She's loaded deep
As deep can be.
But not as deep
As the love I'm in . . .

A young man, running to pass Virginia, stumbled in the dusk and bumped into her. "Sorry." He grabbed her arm, as much to steady himself as her. He held his lantern high, the light in her face. "Who are you?"

"Virginia."

"Virginia who?"

"Virginia Parsons." He had long hair and a band around his forehead and looked like an Apache.

"I thought it was a new face. Are you on your own?"

"N . . . no. I've come with Alice and Tom . . . but . . ." She looked back. "I've lost them . . . they're coming . . . somewhere . . ."

"I'm Dominic Barnet . . ."

"Oh . . . it's your party . . ."

"No, my father's, really. At least he's paid for the barrel of beer which makes it his party and my mother bought the sausages. Come on . . . let's get something to drink," and he grabbed her arm with an even firmer grip and marched her down into the seething, noisy firelit circle of activity. "Hey, Dad . . . here's someone who hasn't got a drink . . ."

A huge bearded figure, medieval in the strange light, straightened up from the tap of the barrel. "Well, here's one for her," he said, and Virginia found herself holding an enormous mug of beer. "And here's a sausage." The young man whisked one

41

neatly off a passing tray and handed it to her, impaled on a stick. Virginia took that too, and was just about to embark upon some polite social conversation when Dominic saw another familiar face across the circle of firelight, yelled "Mariana!" or some such name, and was away, leaving Virginia once more alone.

She searched in the darkness for the Lingards but could not find them. But everyone else was sitting, so she sat too, with the enormous beer-mug in one hand and the sausage, still too hot to eat, in the other. The firelight scorched her face and the wind was cold on her back and blew her hair all over her face. She took a mouthful of beer. She had never drunk beer before and immediately wanted to sneeze. She did so, enormously, and from behind her an amused voice said, "Bless you."

Virginia recovered from the sneeze and said, "Thank you," and looked up to see who had blessed her, and saw a large young man in corduroys and rubber boots and a massive Norwegian sweater. He was grinning down at her and the firelight turned his brown face to the colour of copper.

She said, "It was the beer that made me sneeze."

He squatted beside her, took the mug gently from her hand and laid it on the ground between them. "You might sneeze again and then you'd spill it all and that would be a waste."

"Yes."

"You have to be a friend of the Barnets."

"Why do you say that?"

"I haven't seen you before."

"No, I'm not. I came with the Lingards."

"Alice and Tom? Are they here?"

"Yes, somewhere."

He sounded so pleased that the Lingards were here that Virginia fully expected him to go, then and there, in search of them, but instead he settled himself more comfortably on the grass beside her, and seemed quite happy to remain silent, simply watching in some amusement, the rest of the party. Virginia ate her sausage, and when she had finished and he still had said nothing, she decided that she would try again.

"Are you a friend of the Barnets?"

"Um . . ." His attention interrupted, he turned to look at her, his eyes a clear and unwinking blue. "Sorry?"

"I wondered if you were a friend of the Barnets, that's all."

He laughed. "I'd better be. These are my fields they're desecrating."

"Then you must be Eustace Philips."

He considered this. "Yes," he said at last. "I suppose I must be."

Soon after that he was called away . . . some of his Guernseys had wandered in from a neighbouring field and a batty girl who had drunk too much wine thought that she was being attacked by a bull and had thrown a pretty fit of hysterics. So Eustace went to put the matter to rights, and Virginia was presently claimed by Alice and Tom, and although she spent the rest of the evening watching out for him, she did not see Eustace Philips again.

The party, however, was a wild and memorable success. Near midnight, with the beer finished, and the bottles going round, and the food all eaten and the fire piled with driftwood until the flames sprang twenty feet high or more, Alice suggested gently that perhaps it might be a good idea if they went home.

"Your mother will be sitting up thinking you've either been raped or fallen into the sea. And Tom's got to be at the office at nine in the morning and it really is getting bitterly cold. What do you say? Have you had enough? Have you had fun?"

"Such fun," said Virginia, reluctant to leave.

But it was time to go. They walked in silence away from the firelight and the noise, up the slopes of the fields towards the farmhouse.

Now, only one light burned from a downstairs window, but a full moon, white as a plate, sailed high in the sky, filling all the night with silver light. As they came over the wall into the farmyard, a door in the house opened, yellow light spilled out over the cobbles, and a voice called out across the darkness, "Tom! Alice! Come and have a cup of tea or coffee – something to warm you up before you go home."

"Hello, Eustace." Tom went towards the house. "We thought you'd gone to bed."

"I'm not staying down on the cliffs till dawn, that's for certain. Would you like a drink?"

"I'd like a whisky," said Tom.

"And I'd like tea," said Alice. "What a good idea! We're frozen. Are you sure it's not too much trouble?"

"My mother's still up, she'd like to see you. She's got the kettle on . . ."

They all went into the house, into a low-ceilinged, panelled hall, with a flagged slate floor covered with bright rugs. The beams of the roof scarcely cleared the top of Eustace Philips's head.

Alice was unbuttoning her coat. "Eustace, have you met Virginia? She's staying with us at Wheal House."

"Yes, of course – we said hello," but he scarcely looked at her. "Come into the kitchen, it's the warmest place in the house. Mother, here are the Lingards. Alice wants a cup of tea. And Tom wants whisky and . . ." He looked down at Virginia. "What do you want?"

"I'd like tea."

44

Alice and Mrs Philips at once busied themselves, Mrs Philips with the teapot and the kettle, and Alice taking cups and saucers down from the shelves of the painted dresser. As they did this they discussed the Barnets' party, laughing about the girl who thought the cow was a bull, and the two men settled themselves at the scrubbed kitchen table with tumblers and a soda siphon and a bottle of Scotch.

Virginia sat too, wedged into the broad window seat at the head of the table and listening to, without actually hearing, the pleasant blur of voices. She found that she was very sleepy, dazed by the warmth and comfort of the Penfolda kitchen after the bitter cold of the outdoors, and slightly fuzzy from the unaccustomed draught beer.

Sunk into the folds of her coat, hands deep in its pockets, she looked about her and decided that never had she been in a room so welcoming, so secure. There were beams in the ceiling, with old iron hooks for smoking hams, and deep window-sills crammed with flowering geraniums. There was a huge stove where the kettle simmered, and a cane chair with a cat curled in its seat, and there was a grain merchant's calendar and curtains of checked cotton and the warm smell of baking bread.

Mrs Philips was small as her son was large, grey-haired, very neat. She looked as though she had never stopped working from the day she was born and would have it no other way, and as she and Alice moved about the kitchen, deft and quick, gossiping gently about the unconventional Barnets, Virginia watched her and wished that she could have had a mother just like that. Calm and good-humoured with a great comforting kitchen and a kettle always on the boil for a cup of tea.

The tea made, the two women finally joined the others around the table. Mrs Philips poured a cup for Virginia and handed it

45

to her, and Virginia sat up, pulling her hands out of her pockets and took it, remembering to say "Thank you."

Mrs Philips laughed. "You're sleepy," she said.

"I know," said Virginia. They were all looking at her, but she stirred her tea and would not look up because she did not want to have to meet that blue and disconcerting gaze.

But eventually it was time to go. With their coats on again, they stood, crowded in the little hallway. The Lingards and Mrs Philips were already at the open front door when Eustace spoke from behind Virginia.

"Goodbye," he said.

"Oh." Confused, she turned. "Goodbye." She began to put out her hand, but perhaps he did not see it, for he did not take it. "Thank you for letting me come."

He looked amused. "It was a pleasure. You'll have to come back again, another time."

And all the way home, she hugged his words close as though they were a marvellous present that he had given her. But she never came back to Penfolda.

Until today, ten years later, and a July afternoon of piercing beauty. Roadside ditches brimmed with ragged robin and bright yellow coltsfoot, the gorse was aflame and the bracken of the cliff-tops lay emerald against a summer sea the colour of hyacinths.

So engrossed had she been in her business of the day, collecting keys, and finding the cottage at Bosithick, and considering such practical questions as cookers and fridges and bedclothes and china, that all the heaven-sent morning had somehow gone unnoticed. But now it was part of what had suddenly happened and Virginia remembered long ago, how the lighthouse had flashed out over the dark sea, and she had been, for no apparent reason, suddenly excited and warm with a marvellous anticipation.

But you're not seventeen any longer. You're a woman, twenty-seven years old and independent, with two children and a car and a house in Scotland. Life doesn't hold those sort of surprises any longer. Everything is different. Nothing ever stays the same.

At the top of the lane which led down to Penfolda was a wooden platform for the milk churns, and the way sloped steep and winding between high stone walls. Hawthorns leaned distorted by the winter winds, and as Virginia followed the back of Eustace's Land-Rover around the corner of the house, two collies appeared, black and white, barking and raising a din that sent the brown Leghorn hens squawking and scuttling for shelter.

Eustace had parked his Land-Rover in the shade of the barn and was already out of it, toeing the dogs gently out of the way. Virginia put her car behind his and got out as well, and the collies instantly made for her, barking and leaping about and trying to put their front paws on her knees and stretching up to lick her face.

"Get down . . . get down, you devils!"

"I don't mind . . ." She fondled their slim heads, their thick coats. "What are their names?"

"Beaker and Ben. That's Beaker and this is Ben . . . shut up, you, boy! They do this every time . . ."

His manner was robust and cheerful as though during the course of the short drive he had decided that this was the best attitude to adopt if the rest of the day was not to become a sort of wake for Anthony Keile. And Virginia, who did not in the least want this to happen, gratefully took her cue from him. The dogs' noisy welcome helped to break the ice, and it was

47

in an entirely natural and easy fashion that they all went up the cobbled path together, and into the house.

She saw the beams, the flagged floor, the rugs. Unchanged.

"I remember this."

There was a smell of hot pasties, mouth-watering. He went in through the kitchen door, leaving Virginia to follow behind, and across to the stove, whisking an oven cloth off a rack as he passed, and crouching to open the oven.

"They aren't burnt, are they?" she asked anxiously. Fragrant smoky smells issued out.

"No, just right."

He closed the oven door and stood up.

She said, "Did you make them?"

"Me? You must be joking."

"Who did?"

"Mrs Thomas, my housekeeper . . . Like a drink, would you?" He went to open a fridge, to take a can of beer from the inside of the door.

"No, thank you."

He smiled. "I haven't got any Coke."

"I don't want a drink."

As they spoke, Virginia looked about her, terrified that anything in this marvellous room should have been altered, that Eustace might have changed something, moved the furniture, painted the walls. But it was just as she remembered. The scrubbed table pulled into the bay of the window, the geraniums on the window-sills, the dresser packed with bright china. After all these years it remained the epitome of everything a proper kitchen should be, the heart of the house.

When they had taken over Kirkton and were doing it up, cellar to attic, she had tried to get a kitchen like the Penfolda one. Somewhere comfortable and warm where the family would congregate, and drink tea and gossip round the scrubbed table.

"Who wants to go into a kitchen?" Anthony had asked, not understanding at all.

"Everybody. A farmhouse kitchen's like a living-room."

"Well, I'm not going to live in any kitchen, I'll tell you that."

And he ordered stainless steel fitments and bright Formica worktops and a black-and-white chequered floor that showed every mark and was the devil to keep clean.

Now Virginia leaned against the table and said with deep satisfaction, "I was afraid it would have changed, but it's just the same."

"Why should it have changed?"

"No reason. I was just afraid. Things do change. Eustace, Alice told me that your mother had died . . . I'm sorry."

"Yes. Two years ago. She had a fall. Got pneumonia." He chucked the empty can neatly into a rubbish bin and turned to survey her, propping his length against the edge of the sink. "And how about your own mother?"

His voice held no expression; she could detect no undertones of sarcasm or dislike.

"She died, Eustace. She became very ill a couple of years after Anthony and I were married. It was dreadful, because she was ill for so long. And it was difficult, because she was in London and I was at Kirkton . . . I couldn't be with her all the time."

"And I suppose you were all the family she had?"

"Yes. That was part of the trouble. I used to visit her as often as I could, but in the end we had to bring her up to Scotland, and eventually she went into a nursing home in Relkirk, and she died there."

"That's bad."

"Yes. And she was so young. It's a funny thing when your mother dies. You never really grow up till that happens." She amended this. "At least, I suppose that's how some people feel. You were grown up long before then."

"I don't know about that," said Eustace. "But I know what you mean."

"Anyway, it was all over years ago. Don't let's talk about miserable things. Tell me about you, and Mrs Thomas. Do you know, Alice Lingard said you'd either have a domesticated mistress or a sexy housekeeper? I can't wait to meet her."

"Well, you'll have to. She's gone to Penzance to see her sister."

"Does she live at Penfolda?"

"She has the cottage at the other end of the house. This used to be three cottages, you know, in the old days, before my grandfather bought the place. Three families lived here and farmed a few acres. Probably had half a dozen cows for milking and sent their sons down the tin mines to keep the wolf from the door."

"Two days ago," said Virginia, "I drove out to Lanyon and sat on the hill, and there were combine harvesters out, and men haymaking. I thought one of them was probably you."

"Probably was."

She said, "I thought you'd be married."

"I'm not."

"I know. Alice Lingard said that you weren't."

After he had finished his beer, he took knives and forks from a drawer and began to lay the table but Virginia stopped him. "It's too nice to be indoors. Couldn't we eat the pasties in the garden?"

Eustace looked amazed, but said, ''All right,'' and found her a basket for the knives and forks and plates and the salt and pepper and glasses, and he eased the piping hot pasties out of the oven on to a great flowered china dish, and they went out of a side door into the sunshine and the untidy little farmhouse garden. The grass needed cutting and the flower-beds were brimming with cheerful cottage flowers, and there was a washing-line, flapping with bright white sheets and pillow-cases.

Eustace had no garden furniture so they sat on the grass, tall with daisies and plantains, with the dishes of their picnic spread about them.

The pasties were enormous, and Virginia had only eaten half of hers, and was defeated by the remainder, by the time that Eustace, propped on an elbow, had consumed the whole length of his.

She said, ''I can't eat any more,'' and gave him the rest of hers, which he took and placidly demolished. He said, through a mouthful of pastry and potato: ''If I weren't so hungry, I'd make you eat it, fatten you up a bit.''

''I don't want to be fat.''

''But you're much too thin. You were always small enough, but now you look as though a puff of wind would blow you away. And you've cut your hair. It used to be long, right down your back, flowing about in the wind.'' He put out a hand and circled her wrist with his thumb and forefinger. ''There's nothing of you.''

''Perhaps it was the flu.''

''I thought you'd be enormous after all these years of eating porridge and herrings and haggis.''

''You mean, that's what people eat in Scotland.''

51

"It's what I've been told." He let go of her wrist and peacefully finished the pasty, and then began to collect the plates and the basket and carry everything indoors. Virginia made movements as though to help, but he told her to stay where she was, so she did this, lying back in the grass and staring at the straight grey roof of the barn, and the seagulls perched there, and the scudding shapes of small, white fine-weather clouds, blown from the sea across the incredibly blue sky.

Eustace returned, carrying cigarettes and green eating apples and a Thermos of tea. Virginia lay where she was, and he tossed her an apple and she caught it, and he sat beside her again, unscrewing the cap of the Thermos.

"Tell me about Scotland."

Virginia turned the apple, cool and smooth, in her hands.

"What shall I tell you?"

"What did your husband do?"

"How do you mean?"

"Didn't he have a job?"

"Not exactly. Not a nine-to-five job. But he'd been left this estate . . ."

"Kirkton?"

". . . Yes, Kirkton . . . by an uncle. A great big house and about a thousand acres of land, and after we'd got the house in order, that seemed to take up most of his time. He grew trees, and farmed in a rather gentlemanly way . . . I mean, he had a grieve – a bailiff you'd call him – who lived in the farmhouse. Mr McGregor. It was he who really did most of the work, but Anthony was always occupied. I mean – " she finished feebly " – he seemed to be able to fill in his days."

Shooting five days a week in the season, fishing and playing golf. Driving north for the stalking, taking off for St Moritz for a couple of months every winter. It was no good trying to explain a man like Anthony Keile to a man like Eustace Philips. They belonged to different worlds.

"And what about Kirkton now?"

"I told you, the grieve looks after it."

"And the house?"

"It's empty. At least, the furniture's all there, but there's nobody living in it."

"Are you going back to this empty house?"

"I suppose so. Some time."

"What about the children?"

"They're in London, with Anthony's mother."

"Why aren't they with you?" asked Eustace, sounding not critical, merely curious, as though he simply wished to know.

"It just seemed a good idea, my coming away on my own. Alice Lingard wrote and asked me to come, and it seemed a good idea, that's all."

"Why didn't you bring the children too?"

"Oh, I don't know . . ." Even to herself her own voice sounded elaborately casual, unconvincing. "Alice doesn't have any children and her house isn't geared for them . . . I mean, everything's rather special and rare and breakable. You know how it is."

"In fact, I don't, but go on."

"Anyway, Lady Keile likes having them with her . . ."

"Lady Keile?"

"Anthony's mother. And Nanny likes going there because she used to work for Lady Keile. She was Anthony's own nanny when he was a little boy."

"But I thought the children were quite big."

"Cara's eight and Nicholas is six."

"But why do they have to have a nanny? Why can't you look after them?"

Over the years Virginia had asked herself that question time without number, and had come up with no sort of an answer, but for Eustace to voice it, unasked, out of the blue, filled her with a perverse resentment.

"What do you mean?"

"Just what I say."

"I do look after them. I mean, I see a lot of them . . ."

"If they've just lost their father, surely the one person they need to be with is their mother, not a grandmother and an old inherited nanny. They'll think everybody's deserting them."

"They won't think anything of the sort."

"If you're so sure, why are you getting so hot under the collar?"

"Because I don't like you interfering, airing your opinions about something you know nothing about."

"I know about you."

"What about me?"

"I know your infinite capacity for being pushed around."

"And who pushes me around?"

"I wouldn't know for sure." She realised with some astonishment that, in a cold way, he was becoming as angry as she. "But at a rough guess I would say your mother-in-law. Perhaps she took over where your own mother left off!"

"Don't you dare to speak about my mother like that."

"But it's true, isn't it?"

"No, it's not true."

"Then get your children down here. It's inhuman leaving them in London for the summer holidays, in weather like this, when they should be running wild by the sea and in the fields.

Take your finger out, ring up your mother-in-law and tell her to put them on a train. And if Alice Lingard doesn't want them at Wheal House, because she's afraid of the ornaments getting broken, then take them to a pub, or rent a cottage . . .''

"That's exactly what I intend doing, and I didn't need you to tell me."

"Then you'd better start looking for one."

"I already have."

He was momentarily silenced, and she thought with satisfaction: That took the wind out of his sails.

But only momentarily. "Have you found anything?"

"I looked at one house this morning but it was impossible."

"Where?"

"Here. In Lanyon." He waited for her to tell him. "It was called Bosithick," she added ungraciously.

"Bosithick!" He appeared delighted. "But that's a marvellous house."

"It's a terrible house."

"Terrible?" He could not believe his ears. "You do mean the cottage up the hill where Aubrey Crane used to live? The one that the Kernows inherited from his old aunt."

"That's the one, and it's creepy and quite impossible."

"What does creepy mean? Haunted?"

"I don't know. Just creepy."

"If it's haunted by the ghost of Aubrey Crane you might have quite an amusing time. My mother remembered him, said he was a dear man. And very fond of children," he added with what seemed to Virginia a classic example of a *non sequitur*.

"I don't care what sort of a man he was, I'm not going to take the house."

"Why not?"

"Because I'm not."

"Give me three good reasons . . ."

Virginia lost her patience. "Oh, for heaven's sake . . ." She made as if to get to her feet, but Eustace, with unexpected speed for such a large man, caught her wrist in his hand and pulled her back on to the grass. She looked angrily into his eyes and saw them cold as blue stones.

"Three good reasons," he said again.

She looked down at his hand on her arm. He made no effort to move it and she said, "There's no fridge."

"I'll lend you a meat-safe. Reason number two."

"I told you. It's got a spooky atmosphere. The children have never lived anywhere like that. They'd be frightened."

"Not unless they're as hen-brained as their mother. Now, number three."

Desperately she tried to think up some good, watertight reason, something that would convince Eustace of her nameless horror of the odd little house on the hill. But all she came out with was a string of petty excuses, each sounding more feeble than the last. "It's too small, and it's dirty, and where would I wash the children's things, and I don't even know if there's an iron for the ironing or a lawn-mower to cut the grass. And there's no garden, just a sort of washing-green place, and inside all the furniture is so depressing and . . ."

He interrupted her. "These aren't reasons, Virginia, and you know they're not. They're just a lot of bloody excuses."

"Bloody excuses for *what*?"

"For not having a show-down with your mother-in-law or the old nanny or possibly both. For making a scene and asserting yourself and bringing your own children up the way you want them to go."

Fury at him caught in her throat, a great lump that rendered her speechless. She felt the blood surge to her cheeks, she began to tremble, but although he must have seen all this, he went calmly on, saying all the terrible things that the voice in the back of her head had been saying for years, but to which she had never had the moral courage to pay any attention.

"I don't think you can give a damn for your children. You don't want to be bothered with them. Someone else has always done the washing and the ironing and you're not going to start now. You're too bloody idle to take them for picnics and read them books and put them to bed. It's really nothing to do with Bosithick. Whatever house you found, you'd be sure to find something wrong with it. Any excuse would do provided you never have to admit to yourself that you can't be bloody bothered to take care of your own children."

Before the last word was out of his mouth, she was on her feet, tearing her arm free of his grip.

"It's not true! It's none of it true! I do want them! I've been wanting them ever since I got here . . .!"

"Then get them here, you little fool . . ." He was on his feet too, and they were shouting at each other across three feet of grass as though it were a desert.

"That's what I'm going to do. That's just exactly what I'm going to do."

"I'll believe that when you do it!"

She turned and fled and was into her car before she remembered her handbag, still lying on the kitchen table. By now in floods of tears, she was out of the car and running into the house to retrieve it before Eustace reached her again. Then back to the car and turning it furiously, dangerously in the narrow confines of the farmyard, then back up the lane, with a roar of the engine and a great spattering of loose gravel from the back wheels.

"Virginia!"

Through tears, through the driving mirror she saw him standing far behind her. She jammed her foot on the accelerator and swung out on to the main road without bothering to wait and see if anything was coming. By good chance there wasn't, but she didn't slow down all the way back to Porthkerris, down into the town and up the other side, parking the car on the double yellow lines outside the solicitors' office and leaving it there while she ran inside.

This time she did not ring the bell, nor wait for Miss Leddra, but went, like the wind, through the outer office to fling open wide the door of Mr Williams's room, where Mr Williams was rudely interrupted in the course of interviewing an autocratic old lady from Truro about the seventh set of alterations to her will.

Both Mr Williams and the old lady, silenced by astonishment, stared, open-mouthed. Mr Williams, recovering first, began to scramble to his feet. "Mrs Keile!" But before he could say another word Virginia had flung the keys of Bosithick on to his desk and said, "I'll take it. I'll take it right away. And as soon's I've got my children, I'm moving in!"

4

Alice said, "I'm sorry, Virginia, but I think you're making the most terrible mistake. What's more, it's a classic mistake and one so many people make when they suddenly find themselves alone in the world. You're acting on impulse, you haven't really thought about this at all . . ."

"I have thought about it."

"But the children are fine, you know they are, settled and happy with Nanny and your mother-in-law. The life they're leading is simply an extension of life at Kirkton, all the things they know and that helps them to feel secure. Their father's dead, and nothing's ever going to be the same for them again. But if there have to be changes, at least let them happen slowly, gradually; let Cara and Nicholas have time to get used to them."

"They're my children."

"But you've never looked after them. You've never had them on your own, except the odd times when Nanny could be persuaded to take a holiday. They'll exhaust you, and honestly, Virginia, at the moment I don't think you're physically capable of doing it. After all, that's why you came here, to recuperate from that loathsome flu, and generally have a little peace and quiet, give yourself time to get over the bad things that have been happening. Don't deprive yourself of that. You're going to need all your resources when you do eventually go back to Kirkton and start picking up the threads and learning to live without Anthony.''

''I'm not going to Kirkton. I'm going to Bosithick. I've already paid the first week's rent.''

Alice's expression stopped being patient and became exasperated.

''But it's so ridiculous! Look, if you feel so strongly about having the children down here, then have them by all means, they can stay here, but for heaven's sake let Nanny come too.''

Only yesterday the idea could have been tempting. But now Virginia never even let herself consider it.

''I've made up my mind.''

''But why didn't you *tell* me? Why didn't you discuss it with me?''

''I don't know. It was just something I had to do on my own.''

''And where *is* Bosithick?''

''It's on the Lanyon road . . . You can't see it from the road, but it's got a sort of tower . . .''

''The place where Aubrey Crane lived? But, Virginia, it's ghastly. There's nothing there but moor and wind and cliffs. You'll be totally isolated!''

Virginia tried to turn it into a joke. ''You'll have to come and see me. Make sure the children and I aren't driving each other slowly insane.''

But Alice did not laugh, and Virginia, seeing her frown and the disapproving set of her mouth, was suddenly, astonishingly reminded of her own mother. It was as though Alice was no longer Virginia's contemporary, her friend, but had swung back a generation and from that lofty height was telling the young Virginia that she was being a fool. But perhaps, after all, this was not so strange. She had known Rowena Parsons long before Virginia was born, and the fact that she had no children of her own to contend with meant that her attitudes and opinions remained rigidly unchanged.

She said at last, "It isn't that I want to interfere, you know that. But I've known you all your life, and I can't stand to one side and watch you do this insane thing."

"What's so insane about having your children on holiday with you?"

"It's not just that, Virginia, and you know it. If you take them away from Lady Keile and Nanny without their approval, which I doubt very much you'll get, there's going to be one devil of a row."

Virginia felt sick at the thought of it. "Yes, I know."

"Nanny will probably take the most terrible umbrage and give in her notice."

"I know . . ."

"Your mother-in-law will do everything she can to stop you."

"I know that too."

Alice stared at her, as though she were staring at a stranger. Then suddenly, she shrugged and laughed, in a hopeless sort of way. "I don't understand. What made you suddenly so determined?"

Virginia had said nothing about her encounter with Eustace Philips and had no intention of doing so.

"Nothing. Nothing in particular."

"It must be the sea air," said Alice. "Extraordinary what it does for people." She picked a fallen newspaper off the floor, began folding it meticulously. "When are you going to London?"

"Tomorrow."

"And Lady Keile?"

"I'll phone her tonight. And Alice, I am sorry. And thank you for being so kind."

"I haven't been kind, I've been critical and disapproving. But somehow, I always think of you as someone young and helpless. I feel responsible for you."

"I'm twenty-seven. And I'm not helpless. And I'm responsible for myself."

Nanny answered the telephone. "Yes?"

"Nanny?"

"Yes."

"It's Mrs Keile."

"Oh, hello! Do you want to speak to Lady Keile?"

"Is she there?"

"Just a moment and I'll get her."

"Nanny."

"Yes."

"How are the children?"

"Oh, they're very well. Having a lovely time. Just gone to bed." (This was slipped in quickly in case Virginia should ask to speak to them.)

"Is it hot?"

"Oh, yes. Lovely. Perfect weather. Hold on and I'll tell Lady Keile you're there."

There were the sounds of Nanny putting down the receiver, her footsteps going across the hall, her distant voice. "Lady Keile!"

Virginia waited. *If I was a woman who was taking to drink I would have one in my hand, right now. A great tall tumbler of dark-coloured whisky.* But she wasn't and her stomach lay heavy with impending doom.

More footsteps, sharp, neat, unmistakable. The receiver was lifted once more.

"Virginia."

"Yes, it's me."

The situation was hideously complicated by the fact that Virginia had never known what to call her mother-in-law. "Call me Mother," she had said kindly, as soon as Virginia and Anthony were married, but somehow this was impossible. And "Lady Keile" was worse. Virginia had compromised by only corresponding by postcard or telegram, and always calling her "you".

"How nice to hear you, dear. How are you feeling?"

"I'm very well . . ."

"And the weather? I believe you're having a heatwave."

"Yes, it's unbelievable. Look . . ."

"How is Alice?"

"She's very well, too . . ."

"And the darling children, they've been swimming today – the Turners have got a delicious pool in their garden, and invited Cara and Nicholas over for the afternoon. What a pity they're in bed; why didn't you call earlier?"

Virginia said, "I've got something to tell you."

"Yes?"

She closed her hand around the receiver until her knuckles ached. "I've been able to find a little cottage, quite near here. It's near the sea, and I thought it would be nice for the children if they came down and we spent the rest of the holidays together."

63

She paused, waiting for comment but there was only silence.

"The thing is, the weather is so beautiful and I feel so guilty enjoying it all on my own . . . and it would be good for them to have some sea air before we all have to go back to Scotland and they have to go back to school."

Lady Keile said, "A cottage? But I thought you were staying with Alice Lingard?"

"Yes, I am. I have been. I'm calling from Wheal House now. But I've taken this cottage."

"I don't understand."

"I want the children to come down and spend the rest of the holidays with me. I'll come up tomorrow in the train to fetch them."

"But what sort of a cottage?"

"Just a cottage. A holiday cottage . . ."

"Well, if that's what you want – " Virginia began to breathe a sigh of relief. " – But it seems hard luck on Nanny. It's not often she gets the chance of being in London and seeing all her own friends." The relief swiftly died. Virginia went back into the attack again.

"Nanny doesn't have to come."

Lady Keile was confused. "I'm sorry, the line's not very clear. I thought you said Nanny didn't have to come."

"She doesn't. I can look after the children. There's not room for her anyway. I mean there isn't a bedroom for her, or a nursery . . . and it's terribly isolated, and she'd hate it."

"You mean you intend taking the children *away* from Nanny?"

"Yes."

"But she'll be most terribly upset."

"Yes, I'm afraid she will, but . . ."

64

"Virginia . . ." Lady Keile's voice was upset, distressed. "Virginia, we can't talk about this over the telephone."

Virginia imagined Nanny on the upstairs landing, listening to the one-sided conversation.

"We don't need to. I'm coming up to London tomorrow. I'll be with you about five o'clock. We can talk about it then."

"I think," said Lady Keile, "that that would be best."

And she rang off.

The next morning Virginia drove to Penzance, left her car in the station park and caught the train to London. It was another hot, cloudless morning and she had not had time to reserve a seat, and, despite the fact that she managed to get hold of a porter and tip him handsomely, he could only find her an empty corner in a carriage that was already uncomfortably full. Her fellow passengers were going home at the end of their annual holidays, grumpy and disconsolate at the thought of returning to work, and resentful at leaving the sea and the beaches on such a perfect day.

There was a family, a father and mother and two children. The baby slept damply in its mother's arms, but as the sun climbed higher into the unwinking sky and the train rattled northwards through the shimmering heat of a midsummer noon, the elder child became more and more fractious, whining, grizzling, never still, and grinding his dirty sandalled feet on to Virginia's every time he wanted to look out of the window. At one point, in order to keep the child quiet, his father bought him an orangeade, but no sooner was the bottle opened than the train lurched and the entire contents went all over the front of Virginia's dress.

The child was promptly slapped by his distracted mother and roared. The baby woke up and added his wails to his brother's. The father said, "Now look what you've done," and gave the child a shake for good measure, and Virginia, trying to mop herself up with face tissues, protested that it didn't matter, it couldn't be helped, it didn't matter at all.

After a good deal of screaming the child subsided into hiccuping sobs. A bottle was produced from somewhere and stuffed into the baby's mouth. It sucked for a bit, and then stopped sucking, struggled into a sitting position and was sick.

And Virginia lit a cigarette and looked firmly out of the window and prayed, "Don't let Cara and Nicholas ever be like that. Don't let them ever be like that on a railway journey, otherwise I shall go stark, staring mad."

London was airless and stuffy, the great cavern of Paddington Station hideous with noise and aimless, hurrying crowds. As soon as she was off the train Virginia, carrying her suitcase, and filthy and crumpled in her stained, sticky dress, walked the length of the platform to the booking-office and, like a secret agent making sure of his escape route, bought tickets and reserved three seats on the Riviera for the following morning. Only then did she return to the taxi rank, wait in the long queue, and finally capture a cab to take her home.

"Thirty-two Melton Gardens, please. Kensington."

"OK. 'Op in."

They went down by Sussex Gardens, across the park. The brown grass was littered with picnicking families, children in scanty clothes, couples entwined beneath the shade of trees. In Brompton Road there were window-boxes bright with flowers, shop windows filled with clothes "For Cruising", the first of the rush-hour crowds was being sucked, a steady stream of humanity, down Knightsbridge Underground.

The cab turned into the network of quiet squares that lay behind Kensington High Street, edged down narrow roads lined

66

with parked cars, and finally turned the corner into Melton Gardens.

"It's the house by the pillar-box."

The taxi stopped. Virginia got out, put her case on the pavement, opened her bag for the fare. The driver said, "Thanks very much," and snapped up his flag, and Virginia picked up her case and turned towards the house and, as she did so, the black-painted door opened and her mother-in-law waited to let her in.

She was tall, slim, immensely good-looking. Even on this breathless day she looked cool and uncrushed, not a wrinkle in her linen dress, not a hair out of place.

Virginia went up the steps towards her.

"How clever of you to know I was here."

"I was looking out of the drawing-room window. I saw the taxi."

Her expression was friendly, smiling, but quite implacable, like the matron of a lunatic asylum come to admit a new patient. They kissed, touching cheeks.

"Did you have a terrible journey?" She closed the door behind them. The cool, pale-coloured hall smelled of beeswax and roses. At the far end steps led down to the glass side door, and beyond it could be seen the garden, the chestnut tree, the children's swing.

"Yes, it was ghastly. I feel filthy and a revolting child spilled orange juice all over me." The house was silent. "Where are the children?"

Lady Keile began to lead the way upstairs to the drawing-room. "They're out with Nanny. I thought perhaps it would be better. They won't be long, not more than half an hour. That should give us time to get this all thrashed out."

Treading behind her, Virginia said nothing. Lady Keile reached the top of the stairs, crossed the small landing and went in through the drawing-room door and Virginia followed her, and, despite her anxiety of mind, was struck, as always, by the timeless beauty of the room, the perfect proportions of the long windows which faced out over the street, open today, the fine net curtains stirring. There were long mirrors, filling the room with reflected light, and these gave back images of highly polished antique furniture, tall cabinets of blue-and-white Meissen plates, and the flowers with which Lady Keile had always surrounded herself.

They faced each other across the pale, fitted carpet. Lady Keile said, "We may as well be comfortable," and lowered herself, straight as a ramrod, into a formal, wide-lapped French chair.

Virginia sat too, on the very edge of the sofa, and tried not to feel like a domestic servant being interviewed for a job. She said, "There really isn't anything to thrash out, you know."

"I thought I must have misunderstood you on the telephone last night."

"No, you didn't misunderstand me. I decided two days ago that I wanted the children with me. I decided it was ridiculous, me being in Cornwall and them in London, specially during the summer holidays. So I went to a solicitor and I found this little house. And I've paid the rent and I've got the keys. I can move in right away."

"Does Alice Lingard know about this?"

"Of course. And she offered to have the children at Wheal House, but by then I'd committed myself and couldn't go back."

"But Virginia, you *surely* can't mean that you want them without Nanny?"

"Yes, I do."

"But you'll never manage."

"I shall have to try."

"What you mean is that you want the children to yourself."

"Yes."

"Are you sure you aren't being a little . . . selfish?"

"*Selfish?*"

"Yes, selfish. You're not thinking of the children, are you? Only yourself."

"Perhaps I am thinking of myself, but I'm thinking of the children too."

"You can't be if you intend taking them away from Nanny."

"Have you spoken to her?"

"I had to, of course. She had to have some idea of what I understood you wanted to do. But I hoped I would be able to change your mind."

"What did she say?"

"She didn't say very much. But I could tell that she was very upset."

"Yes, I'm sure."

"You must think of Nanny, Virginia. Those children are her life. You must consider her."

"With the best will in the world I don't see that she comes into this."

"Of course she comes into it. She comes into everything that we do. Why, she's family, she's been part of the family for years, ever since Anthony was a tiny boy . . . and the way she's looked after those babies of yours, she's devoted herself, given her life to them. And you say she doesn't come into this."

"She wasn't my nanny," said Virginia. "She didn't look

69

after me when I was a little girl. You can't expect me to feel quite the same about her as you do.''

"You really mean to say you feel no sort of loyalty towards her? After letting her bring up your children? After virtually living with her for eight years at Kirkton? I must say you fooled me. I always thought there was a very happy atmosphere between you.''

"If there was a happy atmosphere it was because of me. It was because I gave in to Nanny over every little thing, just to keep the peace. Because if she didn't get her own way, she would go into a sulk that would last for days, and I simply couldn't bear it.''

"I always imagined you were the mistress of your own home.''

"Well, you were wrong. I wasn't. And even if I'd plucked up the courage to have a row with Nanny, and asked her to leave, Anthony would never have heard of it. He thought the sun rose and fell on her head.''

At the mention of her son's name Lady Keile had gone a little pale. Her shoulders were consciously straight, her clasped hands tightened in her lap. She said, icily, "And I suppose now that no longer has to be considered.''

Virginia was instantly repentant. "I didn't mean that. You know I didn't mean that. But I'm left now. I'm on my own. The children are all I have. Perhaps I'm being selfish, but I need them. I need them so badly with me. I've missed them so much since I've been away.''

Outside, across the street, a car drew up, a man began to argue, a woman answered him in anger, her voice shrill with annoyance. As though the noise were more than she could stand, Lady Keile stood up and went over to close the window.

She said, "I shall miss them too."

If we had ever been close, thought Virginia, I could go now and put my arms around her and give her the comfort she is longing for. But it was not possible. Affection had existed between them, and respect. But never love, never familiarity.

"Yes, I'm sure you will. You've been so wonderfully good to them, and to me. And I'm sorry."

Her mother-in-law turned from the window, brisk again, emotion controlled. "I think," she said, making for the bell-pull which hung at the side of the fireplace, "that it would be a good idea if we were to have a cup of tea."

The children returned at half past five. The front door opened and shut and their voices rose from the hall. Virginia laid down her teacup and sat quite still. Lady Keile waited until the footsteps had passed the landing outside the drawing-room door and were on their way upstairs to the nursery. Then she got up and went across the drawing-room and opened the door.

"Cara. Nicholas."

"Hello, Granny."

"There is someone here to see you."

"Who?"

"A lovely surprise. Come and see."

Much later, after the children had gone upstairs for their bath and supper, after Virginia herself had bathed and changed into a clean cool silk dress, and before the gong rang for dinner, she went upstairs to the nursery to see Nanny.

She found her alone, tidying away the children's supper things and straightening the room before she settled to her nightly session with the television.

Not that the room needed straightening, but Nanny could not relax until every cushion was plump and straight on the sofa, every toy put away, and the children's dirty clothes discarded, and clean ones set out for the following morning. She had always been like this, revelling in the orderly pattern of her own rigid routine. And she had always looked the same, a neat spare woman, over sixty now, but with scarcely a trace of grey in her dark hair which she wore drawn back and fastened in a bun. She appeared to be ageless, the type that would continue, unchanging, until she was an old woman when she would suddenly become senile and die.

She looked up as Virginia came into the room, and then hastily away again.

"Hello, Nanny."

"Good evening."

Her manner was frigid. Virginia shut the door and went to sit on the arm of the sofa. There was only one way to deal with Nanny in a mood and that was to jump right in off the deep end. "I'm sorry about this, Nanny."

"I don't know what you mean, I'm sure."

"I mean about my taking the children away. We're going back to Cornwall tomorrow morning. I've got seats on the train." Nanny folded the checked tablecloth, corner to corner into perfect squares. "Lady Keile said she'd spoken to you."

"She certainly mentioned something about some hare-brained scheme . . . but it was hard to believe that my ears weren't playing me tricks."

"Are you cross because I'm taking them, or because you're not coming too?"

"Who's cross? Nobody's cross, I'm sure . . ."

"Then you think it's a good idea?"

"No, that I do not. But what I think doesn't seem to matter any more, one way or the other."

She opened a drawer in the table and laid the cloth away, and shut the drawer with a little slam which instantly betrayed her scarcely-banked rage. But her face remained cool, her mouth primly set.

"You know that what you think matters. You've done so much for the children. You mustn't think I'm not grateful. But they're not babies any longer."

"And what is that meant to convey, if I might ask?"

"Just that I can look after them now."

Nanny turned from the table. For the first time, her eyes met Virginia's. And as they watched each other, Virginia saw the slow, angry flush spread up Nanny's neck, up her face, up to her hairline.

She said, "Are you giving me my notice?"

"No, that's not what I intended at all. But perhaps, now we've started to discuss it, it would be the best thing. For your sake as much as anyone else's. Perhaps it would be better for you."

"And why would it be better for me? All my life I've given to this family, why, I had Anthony to look after from the beginning, and there was no reason why I should come up to Scotland and take care of your babies, I never wanted to go, to leave London, but Lady Keile asked me, and because it was the family, I went, a real sacrifice I made, and this is all the thanks I get . . ."

"Nanny – " Virginia interrupted gently when Nanny paused for a breath " – it would be better for you because of this. For that very reason. Wouldn't it be better to make a clean break, and maybe have a new baby to take care of, a new little family? You know how you always said a nursery wasn't a nursery without a little baby, and Nicholas is six now . . ."

"I never thought I'd live to see the day . . ."

73

"And if you don't want to do that, then why not speak to Lady Keile? You could maybe make some arrangement with her. You get on so well together, and you like being in London, with all your friends . . ."

"I don't need you to give me any suggestions, thank you very much . . . given up the best years of my life . . . bringing up your children . . . never expected any thanks . . . never would have happened if poor Anthony . . . if Anthony had been alive . . ."

It went on and on, and Virginia sat and listened, letting the invective pour over her. She told herself that this was the least she could do. It was over, it was done, and she was free. Nothing else mattered. To wait, politely, for Nanny to finish was no more than a salute of respect, a tribute paid by the victor to the vanquished after a bloodthirsty but honourable battle.

Afterwards, she went to say good night to the children. Nicholas was already asleep, but Cara was still deep in her book. When her mother came into the room, she looked up slowly, dragging her eyes away from the printed page. Virginia sat on the edge of her bed.

"What are you reading now?"

Cara showed her. "It's *The Treasure Seekers*."

"Oh I remember that. Where did you find it?"

"In the nursery bookcase."

Carefully, she marked the place in her book with a cross-stitched marker she had made herself, closed it and put it down on her bedside table. "Have you been talking to Nanny?"

"Yes."

"She's been funny all day."

"Has she, Cara?"

"Is something wrong?"

74

It was hard to be so perceptive, so sensitive to atmosphere when you were only eight years old. Especially when you were shy and not very pretty and had to wear round steel spectacles that made you look like a little owl.

"No, nothing's wrong. Just different. And new."

"What do you mean?"

"Well, I'm going back to Cornwall tomorrow morning in the train, and I'm going to take you and Nicholas with me. Will you like that?"

"You mean . . ." Cara's face lit up. "We're going to stay with Aunt Alice?"

"No, we're going to stay in a house on our own. A funny little house called Bosithick. And we're going to have to do all the housekeeping ourselves and the cooking . . ."

"Isn't Nanny coming?"

"No. Nanny's staying here."

There was a long silence. Virginia said, "Do . . . you mind?"

"No, I don't mind. But I expect she will. That's why she's been so funny."

"It's not easy for Nanny. You and Nicholas have been her babies ever since you were born. But somehow I think you're growing out of Nanny now, like you grow out of coats and dresses . . . You're both old enough to look after yourselves."

"You mean, Nanny's not going to live with us any more?"

"No, she's not."

"Where will she live?"

"She'll maybe go and find another little new baby to take care of. Or she may stay here with Granny."

"She likes being in London," said Cara. "She told me so. She likes it much better than Scotland."

"Well, there you are!"

Cara considered this for a moment. Then she said, "When are we going to Cornwall?"

"I told you. Tomorrow on the train."

"When will we leave?" She liked everything cut and dried.

"About half past nine. We'll get a taxi to the station."

"And when are we going back to Kirkton?"

"I expect when the holidays are over. When you have to go back to school." Cara remained silent. It was impossible to tell what she was thinking. Virginia said, "It's time to go to sleep now . . . we've got a long day tomorrow," and she leaned forward and gently unhooked Cara's spectacles and kissed her good night.

But as she went towards the door, Cara spoke again.

"Mummy."

Virginia turned. "Yes."

"You came."

Virginia frowned, not understanding.

"You came," said Cara again. "I said to write to me, but you came instead."

Virginia remembered the letter from Cara, the catalyst that had started everything off. She smiled. "Yes," she said. "I came. It seemed better." And she went out of the room, and downstairs to endure the ordeal of a silent dinner in the company of Lady Keile.

5

Virginia awoke slowly, to a quite unaccustomed mood of achievement. She felt purposeful and strong, two such alien sensations that it was worth lying for a little, quietly, to savour them. Pillowed in Lady Keile's incomparably comfortable spare bed, lapped in hemstitched linen and cloudy blankets, she watched the early sunshine of another perfect summer morning seep in long strands of gold through the leafy branches of the chestnut tree. The bad things were over, the dreaded hurdles somehow cleared, and in a couple of hours she and the children would be on their way. She told herself that after last night she would never be afraid to tackle anything, no problem was insurmountable, no problem too knotty. She let her imagination move cautiously forward to the weeks ahead, to the pitfalls of coping with Cara and Nicholas single-handed, the discomfort and inconvenience of the little house she had so recklessly rented for them, and still her good spirits remained undismayed. She had turned a corner. From now on everything was going to be different.

It was half past seven. She got up, revelling in the fine weather, the sound of bird-song, the pleasant, distant hum of traffic. She bathed and dressed and packed and stripped her bed and went downstairs.

Nanny and the children always had breakfast in the nursery and Lady Keile had hers on a tray in her bedroom, but this was a perfectly ordered household and Virginia found that coffee had been set out for her on the dining-room hotplate, and a single place laid at the head of the polished table.

She drank two cups of scalding black coffee and ate toast and marmalade. Then she took the key from the table to the hall and let herself out of the front door into the quiet morning streets and walked down to the small old-fashioned grocer's patronised by Lady Keile. There she laid in sufficient provisions to start them off when they eventually got back to Bosithick. Bread and butter and bacon and eggs and coffee and cocoa, and baked beans (which she knew Nicholas adored, but Nanny had never approved of) and tomato soup and chocolate biscuits. Milk and vegetables they would have to find when they got down there, meat and fish could come later. She paid for all this, and the grocer packed it for her in a stout cardboard carton and she walked back to Melton Gardens with her weighty load carried before her in both arms.

She found the children and Lady Keile downstairs; no sign of Nanny. But the small suitcases, doubtless perfectly packed, were lined up in the hall, and Virginia dumped the carton of groceries down beside them.

''Hello, Mummy!''

''Hello.'' She kissed them both. They were clean and tidy, ready for their journey, Cara in a blue cotton dress and Nicholas in shorts and a striped shirt, his dark hair lately flattened by a hairbrush. ''What have you been doing?'' he wanted to know.

''I've been buying some groceries. We probably won't have time to go shopping when we get to Penzance; it would be terrible if we didn't have anything to eat.''

"I didn't know till this morning when Cara told me. I didn't know till I woke up that we were going in the train."

"I'm sorry. You were asleep last night when I came in to tell you and I didn't want to disturb you."

"I wish you had. I didn't know until *breakfast.*" He was very resentful.

Smiling at him, Virginia looked up at her mother-in-law. Lady Keile was drawn and pale. Otherwise she looked, as always, perfectly groomed, quite in charge of the situation. Virginia wondered if she had slept at all.

"You should telephone for a taxi," said Lady Keile. "You don't want to risk missing the train. It's always best to be on the early side. There's a number by the telephone."

Wishing that she had thought of this herself Virginia went to do as she was told. The clock in the hall struck a quarter past nine. In ten minutes' time the taxi was there and they were ready to leave.

"But we have to say goodbye to Nanny!" said Cara.

Virginia said, "Yes, of course. Where is Nanny?"

"She's in the nursery." Cara started for the stairs, but Virginia said, "No."

Cara turned and stared, shocked by the unaccustomed tone of her mother's voice.

"But we *have* to say goodbye."

"Of course. Nanny will come down and see you off. I'll go up now and tell her we're just on our way. You get everything together."

She found Nanny determinedly occupied in some entirely unnecessary task.

"Nanny, we're just going."

"Oh, yes."

''The children want to say goodbye.''

Silence.

Last night Virginia had been sorry for her, had, in a funny way, respected her. But now all she wanted to do was take Nanny by her shoulders and shake her till her stupid head fell off. ''Nanny, this is ridiculous. You can't let it end this way. Come downstairs and say goodbye to them.''

It was the first direct order she had ever given to Nanny. The first, she thought, and the last. Like Cara, Nanny was obviously shaken. For a moment she stalled, her mouth worked, she seemed to be trying to think up some excuse. Virginia caught her eye and held it. Nanny tried to stare her out, but was defeated, her eyes slid away. It was the final triumph.

''Very well, madam,'' said Nanny and followed Virginia back down to the hall, where the children rushed at her in the most gratifying way, hugged her and kissed her as though she were the only person in the world they loved, and then, with this demonstration of affection safely over, ran down the steps and across the pavement and into the waiting taxi.

''Goodbye,'' said Virginia to her mother-in-law. There was nothing more to be said. They kissed once more, leaning cheeks, kissing the air. ''And goodbye, Nanny.'' But Nanny was already on her way up to the nursery again, fumbling for her handkerchief and blowing her nose. Only her legs were visible, treading upstairs, and the next moment she had reached the turn of the landing and disappeared.

She need have had no fear about her children's behaviour. The novelty of the train journey did not excite, but silenced them. They had not often been taken on holiday, and never to the seaside, and when they travelled to London to stay with

80

their grandmother had been bundled into the night train already dressed in their pyjamas and had slept the journey away.

Now, they stared from the window at the racing countryside as though they had neither of them ever seen fields or farms or cows or towns before. After a little, when the charm of this wore off, Nicholas opened the present Virginia had bought for him at Paddington and smiled with satisfaction when he saw the little red tractor.

He said, "It's like the Kirkton one. Mr McGregor had a Massey Ferguson just like this." He spun the wheels and made tractor noises in the back of his throat, running the toy up and down the prickly British Rail upholstery.

But Cara did not even open her comic. It lay folded on her lap, and she continued to stare out of the window, her bulging forehead leaning against the glass, her eyes intent behind her spectacles, missing nothing.

At half past twelve they went for lunch and this was another adventure, lurching down the corridor, rushing through the scary connections before the carriages came apart. The dining-car they found enthralling, the tables and the little lights, the indulgent waiter and the grown-upness of being handed a menu.

"And what would madam like?" the waiter asked, and Cara went pink with embarrassed giggles when she realised that he was speaking to her, and had to be helped to order tomato soup and fried fish, and to decide the world-shaking problem of whether she would eat a white ice-cream or a pink.

Watching their faces Virginia thought: Because it's new and exciting to them, it's new and exciting for me. The most trivial, ordinary occurrences will become special because I shall see them through Cara's eyes. And if Nicholas asks me questions that I can't answer, I shall have to go and look them up and

I shall become informed and knowledgeable and a brilliant conversationalist.

The idea was funny. She laughed suddenly, and Cara stared and then laughed back, not knowing what the joke was, but delighted to be sharing it with her mother.

"When did you first come on this train down to Cornwall?" Cara asked.

"When I was seventeen. Ten years ago."

"Didn't you come when you were a little girl my age?"

"No, I didn't. I used to go to an aunt in Sussex."

Now, it was afternoon and they had the compartment to themselves. Nicholas, charmed by the adventure of the corridor, had elected to stay out there, and could be seen straddle-legged, trying to adjust his small weight to the rocking of the train.

"Tell me."

"What? About Sussex?"

"No. About coming to Cornwall."

"Well, we just came. My mother and I, to stay with Alice and Tom Lingard. I'd just left school, and Alice wrote to invite us, and my mother thought it would be nice to have a holiday."

"Was it a summer holiday?"

"No. It was Easter. Springtime. All the daffodils were out and the railway cuttings were thick with primroses."

"Was it hot?"

"Not really. But sunny, and much warmer than Scotland. In Scotland we never really have a proper spring, do we? One day it's winter and the next day all the leaves are out on the trees and it's summertime. At least that's the way it's always seemed to me. In Cornwall the spring is quite a long season . . . that's

82

why they're able to grow all the lovely flowers and send them
to Covent Garden to be sold.''

''Did you swim?''

''No. The sea would have been icy.''

''But in Aunt Alice's pool?''

''She didn't have a pool in those days.''

''Will we swim in Aunt Alice's pool?''

''Sure to.''

''Will we swim in the sea?''

''Yes, we'll find a lovely beach and swim there.''

''I . . . I'm not very good at swimming.''

''It's easier in the sea than in ordinary water. The salt helps
you to float.''

''But don't the waves splash into your face?''

''A little. But that's part of the fun.''

Cara considered this. She did not like getting her face wet.
Without her spectacles things became blurred and she couldn't
swim with her spectacles on.

''What else did you do?''

''Oh, we used to go out in the car, and go shopping. And if it
was warm we used to sit in the garden, and Alice used to have
friends to tea, and people for dinner. And sometimes I used to
go for walks. There are lovely walks there. Up to the hill behind
the house, or down into Porthkerris. The streets are all steep
and narrow, so narrow you could scarcely get a car down them.
And there were lots of little stray cats, and the harbour, with
fishing boats and old men sitting around enjoying the sunshine.
And sometimes the tide was in and all the boats were bobbing
about in the deep blue water, and sometimes it was out, and
there'd be nothing but gold sand, and all the boats would be
leaning on their sides.''

"Didn't they fall over?"

"I don't think so."

"Why?"

"I haven't any idea," said Virginia.

There had been a special day, an April day of wind and sunshine. On that day the tide was high, Virginia could remember the salt smell of it, mixed with the evocative sea-going smells of tar and fresh paint.

Within the shelter of the quay the water swelled smooth and glassy, clear and deep. But beyond the harbour it was rough, the dark ocean flecked with white horses and, out across the bay, the great seas creamed against the rocks at the foot of the lighthouse, sending up spouts of white spray almost as high as the lighthouse itself.

It was a week since the night of the barbecue at Lanyon, and for once Virginia was on her own. Alice had driven to Penzance to attend some committee meeting, Tom Lingard was in Plymouth, Mrs Jilkes, the cook, had her afternoon off and had departed, in a considerable hat to visit her cousin's wife, and Mrs Parsons was keeping her weekly appointment with the hairdresser.

"You'll have to amuse yourself," she told Virginia over lunch.

"I'll be all right."

"What will you do?"

"I don't know. Something."

In the empty house, with the empty afternoon lying, like a gift, before her, she had considered a number of possibilities. But the marvellous day was too beautiful to be wasted, and she had gone out and started walking, and her feet had taken her down the narrow path that led to the cliffs, and then along the cliff path, and down to the white sickle of the beach. In the summer this would be crowded with coloured tents and ice-cream stalls and noisy holidaymakers with beach balls and umbrellas, but in April the visitors had not started to arrive, and the sand lay clean, washed by the winter storms, and her footsteps left a line of prints, neat and precise as little stitches.

At the far end, a lane leaned uphill and she was soon lost in a maze of narrow streets that wound between ancient, sun-bleached houses. She came upon flights of stone steps and unsuspected alleys and followed them down until all at once she turned a corner out at the very edge of the harbour. In a dazzle of sunshine she saw the bright-painted boats, the peacock-green water. Gulls screamed and wheeled overhead, their great wings like white sails against the blue, and everywhere there was activity and bustle, a regular spring-cleaning going on. Shop-fronts were being whitewashed, windows polished, ropes coiled, decks scrubbed, nets mended.

At the edge of the quay a hopeful vendor had set up his ice-cream barrow, shiny white, and lettered seductively "Fred Hoskings, Cornish Ice-cream, The Best Home-made" and Virginia suddenly longed for one, and wished she had brought some money. To sit in the sunshine on such a day and lick an ice-cream seemed, all at once, the height of luxury. The more she thought about it the more desirable it seemed, and she even went through all her pockets in the hope of finding some forgotten coin, but there was nothing there. Not so much as a halfpenny.

She sat on a bollard and gazed disconsolately down on to the deck of a fishing boat where a young boy in a salt-stained smock was brewing up tea on a spirit lamp. She was trying not to think about the ice-cream when, like the answer to a prayer, a voice spoke from behind her.

"Hello."

Virginia looked around over her shoulder, pushing her long dark hair out of her face, and saw him standing there, braced against the wind, with a package under his arm, and wearing a blue polo-necked sweater that made him look like a sailor.

She stood up. "Hello."

"I thought it was you," said Eustace Philips, "but I couldn't be sure. What are you doing here?"

"Nothing. I mean, I just came for a walk, and I stopped to look at the boats."

"It's a lovely day."

"Yes."

His blue eyes gleamed, amused. "Where's Alice Lingard?"

"She's gone to Penzance . . . she's on a committee . . ."

"So you're all alone?"

"Yes." She was wearing worn blue sneakers, blue jeans and a white cable-stitch sweater, and felt miserably convinced that her naiveté was painfully obvious not only in her clothes but her lack of smalltalk as well.

She looked at his package. "What are *you* doing here?"

"I came in to pick up a new rick cover. The wind last night blew the old one to ribbons."

"I expect you're going back now."

"Not immediately. How about you?"

"I'm not doing anything. Just exploring, I suppose."

"Don't you know the town?"

"I've never got this far before."

"Come along then, I'll show you the rest of it."

They began to walk back along the quay, in no hurry, their

slow paces matched. He caught sight of the ice-cream barrow and stopped to talk.

"Hello, Fred."

The ice-cream man, resplendent in a white starched coat like a cricket umpire, turned and saw him. A smile spread across features browned and wizened as a walnut.

"'Allo, Eustace. 'Ow are you?''

"Fine. How's yourself?"

"Oh, keeping not too bad. Don't often see you down 'ere. 'Ow are things out at Lanyon?''

"All right. Working hard." Eustace ducked his head at the barrow. "You're early out. There's nobody here yet to buy ice-creams."

"Oh well, early bird catches the worm I always say."

Eustace looked at Virginia. "Do you want an ice-cream?''

She could not think of any person who had offered her, so instantly, exactly what she wanted most.

"I'd love one, but I haven't any money."

Eustace grinned. "The biggest you've got," he said to Fred, and reached his hand into the back pocket of his trousers.

He took her the length of the wharf, up cobbled streets at whose existence she had never even guessed, through small, surprising squares, where the houses had yellow doors and window-boxes, past little courtyards filled with washing-lines and flights of stone steps where the cats lay and sunned themselves and attended to their ablutions. They came out at last on to a northern beach which lay with its face to the wind, and the long combers rolled in jade green with the sun behind them, and the air was misted with blown spume.

"When I was a boy," Eustace told her, raising his voice above the wind, "I used to come here with a surf-board. A little

87

wooden one my uncle made me, with a face painted on the curve. But now they have these Malibu surf-boards, made of fibreglass they are and they surf all year round, winter and summer.''

''Isn't it cold?''

''They wear wet suits.''

They came to a sea wall, curved against the wind with a wooden bench built into its angle and here Eustace, apparently deciding that they had walked far enough, settled himself, his back to the wall and his face to the sun and his long legs stretched in front of him.

Virginia, consuming the last of the mammoth ice-cream, sat beside him. He watched her, and when she had demolished the final mouthful and was wiping her fingers on the knees of her jeans he said, ''Did you enjoy it?''

His face was serious but his eyes laughed at her. She didn't mind. ''It was delicious. The best. You should have had one too.''

''I'm too big and too old to go walking round the streets licking an ice-cream.''

''I shall never be too big or too old.''

''How old are you?''

''Seventeen, nearly eighteen.''

''Have you left school?''

''Yes, last summer.''

''What are you doing now?''

''Nothing.''

''Are you going to university?''

She was flattered that he should imagine she was so clever. ''Goodness, no.''

''What are you going to do, then?''

Virginia wished that he had not asked.

''Well, eventually, I suppose, next winter I'll learn how to cook or do shorthand and typing or something gruesome like that. But you see my mother has this bee in her bonnet about being in London for the summer and going to all the parties and meeting all the right people and generally having a social whirl.''

''I believe,'' said Eustace, ''it's called 'Doing the Season'.''

His tone of voice made it very clear that he thought as little of the idea as she did.

''Oh, don't. It gives me the shivers.''

''It's hard to believe, in this day and age, that anybody bothers any more.''

''I know, it's fantastic. But they do. And my mother's one of them. She's already met some of the other mothers and had ghastly tea parties with them. She's even booked a date for a dance, but I'm going to try my hardest to talk her out of that one. Can you think of anything worse than having a coming-out dance?''

''No, I can't, but then I'm not a sweet seventeen-year-old.'' Virginia made a face at him. ''If you feel so strongly about it why don't you dig in your toes, tell your mother you'd rather have the price of a return ticket to Australia or something?''

''I already have. At least I've tried. But you don't know my mother. She never listens to anything I say, she just says that it's so *important* to meet all the right people, and be asked to all the right parties and be seen in all the right places.''

''You could try getting your father on your side.''

''I haven't got a father. At least I never see him; they were divorced when I was a baby.''

''I see.'' He added, without much heart: ''Well, cheer up – who knows – you might enjoy it.''

''I shall hate every moment of it.''

"How do you know?"

"Because I'm useless at parties, and I get tongue-tied with strangers, and I can never think of anything to say to young men."

"You're thinking of plenty to say to me," Eustace pointed out.

"But you're different."

"How am I different?"

"Well, you're older. I mean you're not young." Eustace began to laugh and Virginia was embarrassed. "I mean you're not really young, like twenty-one or twenty-two." He was still laughing. She frowned. "How old *are* you?"

"Twenty-eight," he told her. "Twenty-nine next birthday."

"You are lucky. I wish I was twenty-eight."

"If you were," said Eustace, "you probably wouldn't be here now."

All at once it turned dark and cold. Virginia shivered, and looked up and saw that the sun had disappeared behind a large grey cloud, the vanguard of a bank of dirty weather which was blowing in from the west.

"That's it," said Eustace. "We've had the best of the day. It'll be raining by this evening." He looked at his watch. "It's nearly four o'clock, time I made for home. How are you getting back?"

"Walking, I suppose."

"Do you want a ride?"

"Have you got a car?"

"I've got a Land-Rover, parked round by the church."

"Won't I be taking you out of your way?"

"No. I can go back to Lanyon over the moor."

"Well, if you're certain . . ."

Driving back to Wheal House, Virginia fell silent. But it was

90

a natural, companionable silence, comfortable as an old shoe, and had nothing to do with being shy or unable to think of anything to say. She could not remember when she had felt so at ease with a person – and certainly never with a man whom she had known such a short time. The Land-Rover was an old one, the seats worn and dusty and there were stray scraps of straw lying about the floor and a faint smell of farmyard manure. Virginia did not find this in the least offensive – rather, she liked it because it was part of Penfolda. She realised that she wanted, above all things, to go back there. To see the farm and the fields in daylight, to inspect the stock and be shown around, perhaps to be allowed to see the rest of the farmhouse and be asked to tea in that enviable kitchen. To be accepted.

They came up the hill out of the town, where the houses of the old residential area had all been turned into hotels, with gardens bulldozed into car parks, and glassed-in porches. There were sun-rooms and palm trees, dismal against the grey sky, and municipal flower-beds planted with straight rows of daffodils.

High above the sea, the road levelled out. Eustace changed into top gear and said, "When are you going back to London?"

"I don't know. In about a week."

"Do you want to come out to Penfolda again?"

This was the second time that day that he had offered her what she craved most. She wondered if he were psychic.

"Yes, I'd love to."

"My mother was very taken with you. Not often she sees a new face. It would be nice for her if you'd come and have a cup of tea with her."

"I'd like to come."

"How would you get out to Lanyon?" asked Eustace, his eyes on the road ahead.

''I could borrow Alice's car. I'm sure if I asked her she'd let me borrow it. I'd be very careful.''

''Can you drive?''

''Of course. Otherwise I wouldn't borrow the car.'' She smiled at him. Not because it was meant to be a joke, but because all at once she felt so good.

''Well, I'll tell you,'' said Eustace in his deliberate way. ''I'll have a word with my mother, find out which day suits her best, give you a ring on the telephone. How would that be?''

She imagined waiting for the call, having it come, hearing his voice over the wire. She almost hugged herself with pleasure.

''It would be all right.''

''What's the number?''

''Porthkerris three two five.''

''I'll remember that.''

They had reached home. He turned into the white gates of Wheal House and roared up the drive between the hedges of escallonia.

''There you are!'' He stopped with a great jerk of brakes and a splattering of gravel. ''Home safely, just in time for tea.''

''Thank you so much.''

He leaned on the wheel, smiling at her. ''That's all right.''

''I mean, for everything. The ice-cream and everything.''

''You're welcome.'' He reached across and opened the door for her. Virginia jumped down on to the gravel, and as she did so, the front door opened and Mrs Parsons emerged, wearing a little suit of raspberry-red wool, and a white silk shirt, tied like a stock at the neck.

''Virginia!''

Virginia swung around. Her mother came across the gravel towards them, immaculate as always, but her hair, short and dark, blew casually in the wind and had obviously not been attended to that afternoon.

"Mother!"

"Where have you been?" The smile was friendly and interested.

"I thought you were at the hairdresser."

"The girl who usually does me is in bed with a cold. They offered me another girl of course, but, as she's the one who usually spends her days sweeping hair off the floor, I declined with thanks." Still smiling, she looked beyond Virginia to where Eustace waited. "And who is your friend?"

"Oh. It's Eustace Philips . . ."

But now Eustace had decided to get out of the car. He jumped down on to the gravel and came around the front of the Land-Rover to be introduced. And, hating herself, Virginia saw him through her mother's eyes: the wide powerful shoulders beneath the sailor's sweater, the sun-burned face, the strong, calloused hands.

Mrs Parsons came forward graciously. "How do you do."

"Hello," said Eustace, meeting her eyes with an unblinking blue gaze. Her hand was halfway out to shake his, but Eustace either didn't see this or chose to ignore it. Mrs Parsons's hand dropped back to her side. Her manner became, subtly, a fraction more cool.

"Where did Virginia meet *you*?" The question was harmless, even playful.

Eustace leaned against the Land-Rover and crossed his arms. "I live out at Lanyon; farm Penfolda . . ."

"Oh, of course, the barbecue. Yes, I heard all about it. And how nice that you met up again today."

"By chance," said Eustace, firmly.

"But that makes it even nicer!" She smiled. "We're just going to have tea, Mr Philips. Won't you join us?"

Eustace shook his head. His eyes never left her face. "I've got seventy cows waiting to be milked. I'd better be getting back . . ."

"Oh, of course. I wouldn't want to keep you from your work." Her tone was that of the lady of the house dismissing the gardener, but she continued to smile.

"I wouldn't let you," said Eustace, and went to get back into the car.

"Goodbye, Virginia."

"Oh. Goodbye," said Virginia faintly. "And thank you for bringing me home."

"I'll ring you up some time."

"Yes, do that."

He gave a final salute with his head, then started the engine, put the Land-Rover into gear, and without a backward glance, shot away, down the drive and out of sight, leaving Virginia and her mother standing, staring after him, in a cloud of dust.

"Well!" said Mrs Parsons, laughing, but obviously nettled.

Virginia said nothing. There did not seem to be anything to say.

"What a very basic young man! I must say, staying down here, one does meet all types. What's he going to ring you up about?"

The tone of her voice implied that Eustace Philips was something of a joke, a joke that she and Virginia shared.

"He thought perhaps I might go out to Lanyon and have tea with his mother."

"Isn't that marvellous? Pure *Cold Comfort Farm*." It began, very lightly, to rain. Mrs Parsons glanced at the lowering sky and shivered. "What are we doing, standing out here in the wind? Come along, tea's waiting . . ."

Virginia thought nothing of the shiver, but the next morning her mother complained of feeling unwell, she had a cold, she said, an upset stomach, she would stay indoors. As the weather was horrible nobody questioned this, and Alice laid and lit a cheerful fire in the drawing-room, and by this Mrs Parsons reclined on the sofa, a light mohair rug over her knees.

"I shall be perfectly all right," she told Virginia, "and you and Alice must just go off and not bother about me at all."

"What do you mean, we must just go off! Where is there to go off to?"

"To Falmouth. To lunch at Pendrane." Virginia stared blankly. "Oh, darling, don't look so gormless, Mrs Menheniot asked us ages ago. She wanted to show us the garden."

"Nobody ever told me," said Virginia, who did not want to go. It would take all day to get to Falmouth and back again and have lunch and see the boring garden. She wanted to stay here and sit by the telephone and wait for Eustace to ring.

"Well, I'm telling you now. You'll have to change. You can't go out for lunch dressed in jeans. Why not wear that pretty blue shirt I bought for you? Or the tartan kilt? I'm sure Mrs Menheniot would be amused by your kilt."

If she had been any other sort of a mother Virginia would have asked her to listen for the telephone, to take a message. But her mother did not like Eustace. She thought him ill-mannered and uncouth, and her smiling reference to *Cold Comfort Farm* had put the official stamp of disapproval upon him. Since his departure his name had not been mentioned, and although, during dinner last night, Virginia had tried more than once to tell Alice and Tom about her chance encounter, her mother

95

had always firmly overridden the conversation, interrupting if necessary, and steering it into more suitable channels. While she changed, Virginia debated what to do.

Eventually, dressed in the kilt and a canary yellow sweater, with her dark hair brushed clean and shining, she went along to the kitchen to find Mrs Jilkes. Mrs Jilkes was a new friend. One wet afternoon she had taught Virginia to make scones, at the same time regaling her with a great deal of gratuitous information concerning the health and longevity of Mrs Jilkes's numerous relations.

'' 'Allo, Virginia.''

She was rolling pastry. Virginia took a scrap and began, absently, to eat it.

''Now, don't go eating that! You'll fill yourself up, won't have no room for your lunch.''

''I wish I didn't have to go. Mrs Jilkes, if a phone call comes through for me, would you take a message?''

Mrs Jilkes looked coy, rolling her eyes. ''Expecting a phone call are you? Some young man, is it?''

Virginia blushed. ''Well, all right, yes. But you will listen, won't you?''

''Don't you worry, my love. Now, there's Mrs Lingard calling . . . time you was off. And I'll keep an eye on your mother, and give her a little lunch on a tray.''

They did not return home until half past five. Alice went at once to the drawing-room, to inquire for Rowena Parsons's health, and to tell her all that they had done and seen. Virginia had made for the stairs, but the instant the drawing-room door was safely closed, turned and sprinted down the kitchen passage.

''Mrs Jilkes!''

"Back again, are you?"

"Was there a phone call?"

"Yes, two or three, but your mother answered them."

"Mother?"

"Yes, she had the phone switched through to the drawing-room. You'll have to ask her if there are any messages."

Virginia went out of the kitchen, and back down the passage, across the hall and into the drawing-room. Across Alice Lingard's head, her eyes met and held her mother's cool gaze. Then Mrs Parsons smiled.

"Darling! I've been hearing all about it. Was it fun?"

"It was all right." She waited, giving her mother the chance to tell her that the telephone call had come through.

"All right? No more? I believe Mrs Menheniot's nephew was there?"

". . . Yes."

Already the image of the chinless young man was so blurred that she could scarcely remember his face. Perhaps Eustace would ring tomorrow. He couldn't have phoned today. Virginia knew her mother. Knew that, however much she disapproved, Mrs Parsons would be meticulous about such social obligations as passing on telephone messages. Mothers were like that. They had to be. Because if they didn't live by the code of behaviour which they preached, then they lost all right to their children's trust. And without trust there could be no affection. And without affection, nothing.

The next day it rained. All morning, Virginia sat by the fire in the hall, pretending to read a book, and flying to answer the telephone each time it rang. It was never for her; it was never Eustace.

After lunch her mother asked her to go down to the chemist

in Porthkerris to pick up a prescription. Virginia said she didn't want to go.

"... It's pouring with rain."

"A little rain won't hurt you. Besides, the exercise will do you good. You've been sitting indoors all day, reading that silly book."

"It's not a silly book . . ."

"Well, anyway, reading. Put on some Wellingtons and a raincoat and you won't even notice the rain . . ."

It was no good arguing. Virginia made a resigned face and went to find her raincoat. Trudging down the road towards the town, the pavements dank and grey between the dripping trees, she tried to face up to the unthinkable possibility that Eustace was never going to ring her.

He had said that he would, certainly, but it all seemed to depend on what his mother said, when she would be free, when Virginia would be able to borrow the car and drive herself out to Lanyon.

Perhaps Mrs Philips had changed her mind. Perhaps she had said, "Oh Eustace, I haven't got time for tea parties . . . what were you thinking of, saying she could come out here?"

Perhaps, having met Virginia's mother, Eustace had changed his own mind about Virginia. They said that if you wanted to know what sort of a wife a girl was going to turn into, you looked at her mother. Perhaps Eustace had looked and decided that he did not like what he saw. She remembered the challenge in his unblinking blue eyes, and that final bitter exchange.

I wouldn't want to keep you from your work.

I wouldn't let you.

Perhaps he had forgotten to telephone. Perhaps he had had second thoughts. Or perhaps – and this was chilling – Virginia had misconstrued his friendliness, unburdened all her problems, and so aroused his sympathy. Perhaps that was all it was. That he was sorry for her.

But he said he would telephone. He said he would.

She collected the prescription and started home once more. It was still raining. Across the street from the chemist stood a call-box. It was empty. It would all be so simple. It wouldn't take a moment to look up his number, to dial. She had her purse in her pocket, with coins to pay for the call. *It's Virginia*, she would say, and make a joke of it, teasing him. *I thought you were going to ring me up!*

She almost crossed the road. At the edge of the pavement she hesitated, trying to pluck up the courage to take the initiative in a situation which was beyond her.

She imagined the conversation.

"Eustace?"

"Yes."

"This is Virginia."

"Virginia?"

"Virginia Parsons."

"Oh, yes. Virginia Parsons. What do you want?"

But at this point her courage turned on its heels and fled, and Virginia never crossed the road to the telephone box, but carried on up the hill with the rain in her face and her mother's pills deep in the pocket of her waterproof coat.

As she came in through the front door of Wheal House she heard the telephone ringing, but by the time she had got her Wellingtons off the ringing had stopped, and by the time she burst into the drawing-room, her mother was just putting down the receiver.

She raised her eyebrows at her breathless daughter.

"Whatever's wrong?"

"I . . . I thought it might be for me."

"No. A wrong number. Did you get my pills, darling?"

"Yes," said Virginia dully.

"Sweet of you. And the walk has done you good. I can tell. Your cheeks are quite pink again."

The next day Mrs Parsons announced out of the blue that they must return to London. Alice was astonished. "But, Rowena, I thought you were going to stay at least another week."

"Darling, we'd love to, but you know, we do have a very busy summer to put in, and a lot of arrangements and organisation to be seen to. I don't think we can sit here enjoying ourselves for another week. Much as I would adore to."

"Well, anyway, stay over the weekend."

Yes, stay over the weekend, Virginia prayed. *Please, please, please stay over the weekend.*

But it wasn't any use. "Oh, adore to, but we must go . . . Friday at the latest I'm afraid. I'll have to see about booking seats on the train."

"Well, it seems a shame, but if you really mean it . . ."

"Yes, darling, I really do mean it."

Let him remember. Let him phone. There wouldn't be time to go out to Penfolda but at least I could say goodbye, I'd know that he'd meant it . . . perhaps I could say I'd write to him, perhaps I could give him my address.

"Darling, I wish you'd get on with your packing. Don't leave anything behind, it would be such a bore for poor Alice to have to parcel it up. Have you put your raincoat in?"

This evening. He'll ring this evening. He'll say, I am sorry but I've been away; I've been so busy I haven't had a moment; I've been ill.

"Virginia! Come and write your name in the visitors' book! There, under mine. Oh, Alice, my dear, what a wonderful holiday you've given us. Sheer delight. We've both adored it, haven't we, Virginia? Can't bear to go."

They went. Alice drove them to the station, saw them into their first-class carriage, the corner seats reserved, the porter being deferential because of Mrs Parsons's expensive luggage.

"You'll come again soon," said Alice as Virginia leaned out of the window to kiss her.

"Yes."

"We've loved having you . . ."

It was the last chance. *Tell Eustace I had to go. Tell him goodbye for me.* The whistle shrilled, the train began to move. *Ring him up when you get back.*

"Goodbye, Virginia."

Send him my love. Tell him I love him.

By Truro her misery had become so obvious with sniffs and sobs and brimming tears that her mother could ignore them no longer.

"Oh, darling." She put down her newspaper. "Whatever is the matter?"

"Nothing . . ." Virginia stood at the window swollen-faced, unseeing.

"But it has to be something." She put out a hand and rested it, gently, on Virginia's knee. "Was it that young man?"

"Which young man?"

"The young man in the Land-Rover, Eustace Philips? Did you break your heart over him?" Virginia, weeping, could make no reply. Her mother went on, reassuring, gentle. "I wouldn't be too unhappy. It's probably the first time you've been hurt by a man, but I assure you it won't be the last. They're selfish creatures, you know.''

''Eustace wasn't like that.''

''Wasn't he?''

''He was kind. He was the only man I've ever really liked.'' She blew her nose lustily and gazed at her mother. ''You didn't like him, did you?''

Mrs Parsons was momentarily taken aback by such unusual directness. ''Well . . . let's say I've never been very fond of his type.''

''You mean, you didn't like him being a farmer?''

''I never said that.''

''No, but that's what you mean. You only like chinless weeds like Mrs Menheniot's nephew.''

''I never met Mrs Menheniot's nephew.''

''No. But you would have liked him.''

Mrs Parsons did not reply to this at once. But after a little she said, ''Forget him, Virginia. Every girl has to have one unhappy love affair before she finally meets the right man and settles down and gets married. And this summer's going to be such fun for us both. It would be a pity to spoil it, yearning for something that probably never even existed.''

''Yes,'' said Virginia and wiped her eyes and put her sodden handkerchief away in her pocket.

''That's a good girl. Now, no more tears.'' And, satisfied that she had poured oil on troubled waters, Mrs Parsons sat back in her seat and picked up the newspaper again. But presently, disquieted, disturbed by something, she lowered the paper and saw that Virginia was watching her, unblinking, an expression in her dark eyes that her mother had never seen before.

''What is it?''

102

Virginia said, "He said he'd phone. He promised he'd telephone me."

"Well?"

"Did he? You didn't like him, I know. Did you take the call and never tell me?"

Her mother never hesitated. "Darling! What an accusation. Of course not. You surely didn't think. . . ?"

"No," said Virginia dully as the last flicker of hope died. "No, I never thought." And she turned to lean her forehead against the smeared glass of the train window, and the rocketing countryside, together with everything else that had happened, streamed away, for ever, into the past.

That was April. In May Virginia met up again with an old schoolfriend, who invited her down to the country for the weekend.

"It's my birthday, darling, too super, Mummy says I can ask anyone I like, you'll probably have to sleep in the attic, but you won't mind, will you? We're such a madly disorganised family."

Virginia, taking all this with a pinch of salt, accepted the invitation. "How do I get there?"

"Well, you *could* catch a train, and someone *could* meet you, but that's so dreadfully boring. I tell you what, my cousin's probably coming, he's got a car, he'll maybe give me a lift. I'll speak to him and see if he's got room for you. You'll probably have to squeeze in with the luggage or sit on the gear lever, but anything's better than fighting the crowds at Waterloo . . ."

Rather surprisingly, she duly arranged this. The car was a dark blue Mercedes coupé, and once Virginia's luggage had been crammed into the over-loaded boot, she was invited to squash herself into the front seat, between the girlfriend and the cousin. The cousin was tall and fair, with long legs and a grey suit and hair that curled in ducks' tails from beneath the brim of his forward-tilted brown trilby hat.

His name was Anthony Keile.

6

Travel-worn and tired, and with all the problems of Bosithick still to be faced, Virginia got out of the train at Penzance, took a lungful of cool sea air, and was thankful to be back. The tide was low, the air strong with the smell of seaweed. Across the bay, St Michael's Mount stood gold in the evening sun, and the wet sands were streaked with blue, where small streams and shallow pools of sea-water gave back the colour of the sky.

Miraculously, here was a porter. As they followed him and his barrow out of the station Nicholas said, "Is this where we're going to stay?"

"No, we've got to drive over to Lanyon."

"How are we going to drive?"

"I told you, I left my car here."

"How do you know it hasn't been stolen?"

"Because I can see it, waiting for us."

It took some time to pack all their belongings into the boot of the Triumph. But in the end it was all piled in, crowned by the cardboard crate of groceries, and Virginia tipped the porter and they got in, all three of them in the front seat, with Cara in the middle, and the door on Nicholas's side firmly locked.

She had put down the hood and then tied a scarf around her head, but the wind blew Cara's hair forward all over her face.

"How long will it take us to get there?"

"Not long, about half an hour."

"What does the house look like?"

"Why don't you wait and see?"

At the top of the hill she stopped the car, and they looked back to see the view, the lovely curve of Mount's Bay, still and blue, enclosed in the warmth of the day that was over. And all about them were little fields, and ditches blue with wild scabious, and they went on and dropped into a miniature valley filled with ancient oak trees, and a stream ran beneath a bridge, and there was an old mill and a village, and then the road twined up on to the moor again, and all at once the straight bright horizon of the Atlantic lay before them, glittering to the westward in a dazzle of sun.

"I thought the sea was behind us," said Nicholas. "Is that another sea?"

"I suppose it is."

"Is that our sea? Is that the one we're going to use?"

"I expect so."

"Is there a beach?"

"I haven't had time to look. There are certainly a lot of steep cliffs."

"I want a beach. With sand. I want you to buy me a bucket and spade."

"All in good time," said Virginia. "How about taking things one at a time?"

"I want to buy a bucket and spade *tomorrow*."

They joined the main road and turned east, running parallel

to the coast. They left Lanyon village behind them and the road which led to Penfolda, and they climbed the hill and came to the clump of leaning hawthorns which marked the turning to Bosithick.

"Here we are!"

"But there's no house."

"You'll see."

Bumped and jarred, the car and its occupants lurched down the lane. From beneath them came sinister banging sounds, the great gorse bushes closed in at either side, and Cara, anxious for their provisions, reached back a hand to hang on to the grocery carton. They swung around the last corner with a final lurch, ran up on to the grass bank at a frightening angle, and stopped with a jerk. Virginia put on the handbrake, turned off the engine. And the children sat in the car and stared at the house.

In Penzance there had been no wind, the air was milky and breathlessly warm. Here, there was a faint whining, a coolness. The broken washing-line stirred in the breeze and the long grass on the top of the stone hedge lay flattened like a fur coat, stroked by a hand.

And there was something else. Something was wrong. For a moment Virginia stared, trying to think what it was. And then Cara told her. "There's smoke in the chimney," said Cara.

Virginia shivered, a frisson of unease, like a trickle of cold water, ran down her spine. It was as though they had caught the house unawares, they had not been expected by the nameless, unimagined beings who normally occupied it.

Cara felt her disquiet. "Is anything wrong?"

"No, of course not." She sounded more robust than she felt. "I was just surprised. Let's go and investigate."

They got out of the car, leaving the cases and groceries behind. Virginia manhandled the gate open and stood aside for the children to go through while she felt in her bag for the ring of keys.

They went ahead of her, Nicholas running, to investigate what lay around the far corner of the house, but Cara trod cautiously as though trespassing, avoiding an old rag, a broken flower-pot, her hands held fastidiously, anxious not to be asked to touch anything.

Together, they opened the front door. As it swung inwards Cara said, "Do you suppose it's gipsies?"

"What's gipsies?"

"Who've lit the fire."

"Let's look . . ." The smell of mice and damp had gone. Instead the house felt fresh and warm, and when they stepped into the living-room they found it bright with firelight. The whole aspect of the house was changed by this, it was sullen and depressing no longer . . . on the contrary, quite cheerful. The hideous electric fire had somehow been disposed of, and a tall rush basket stood by the hearth, piled with a good supply of logs.

What with the fire and the last of the afternoon sun filtering in through the west window, the room was very warm. Virginia went to open a window, and saw, through the open kitchen door, the bowl set on the table, piled with brown eggs, the white enamel milk pan. She went into the kitchen and stood in the middle of the floor and stared. Someone had been in and cleaned the place up, the sink was shining and the curtains laundered.

Cara stole in behind her, still cautious. "It's like fairies," she said.

"It's not fairies," said Virginia, smiling. "It's Alice."

"Aunt Alice Lingard?"

"Yes, isn't she a dear? She pretended to be so disapproving about us coming to Bosithick and then she goes and does a thing like this. But that's just like Alice. She's very kind. We'll have to go tomorrow and thank her. I'd ring up, only we haven't got a telephone."

"I hate the telephone anyway. And I want to go and see her. I want to see the swimming-pool."

"If you take your bathing-suit you can have a swim."

Cara stood staring up at her mother. Virginia thought she was still thinking about swimming and was surprised when she said, "How did she get in?"

"Who?"

"Aunt Alice. We've got the keys."

"Oh. Well. I expect she got a spare key from Mr Williams. Something like that. Now what are we going to do first?"

Nicholas appeared at the door. "I'm going to look all over the house and then I want some tea. I'm starving!"

"Take Cara with you."

"I want to stay with *you*."

"No." Virginia gave her a gentle push. "You go and tell me what you think of the rest of the house. Tell me if you don't think it the funniest house you've ever seen in your life. And I'll put the kettle on and we'll boil some eggs, and after that we'll bring all the stuff in from the car and see about unpacking and making the beds."

"Aren't the beds even made?"

"No, we've got to do it all. We're really on our own now."

Somehow, by the end of the evening they had managed to attain a semblance of order, but finding the switch for the hot-water tank and the cupboard where the sheets were kept, and trying to decide who was going to sleep in which bed, all took a very long time. For supper Nicholas wanted baked beans on toast, but they couldn't find a toaster and the grill on the cooker was fiercely temperamental, so he had baked beans on bread instead.

"We need washing-up stuff and a mop, and tea and coffee . . ." Virginia searched for a piece of paper and a pencil and started, frantically, to make a list.

Cara chimed in, ". . . And soap for the bathroom and stuff to clean the bath with, because it's got a *horrid* dirty mark."

"And a bucket and spade," said Nicholas.

"And we'll have to get a fridge," said Cara. "We haven't got anywhere to keep our food and it'll all grow a blue beard if we let it just lie about."

Virginia said, "Perhaps we could borrow a meat-safe," and then remembered who had offered to lend her one, and frowned down at her shopping list and hastily changed the subject.

When the little water tank finally heated up, they had baths in the gimcrack bathroom, Nicholas and Cara going in together, and then Virginia swiftly before the water went cold. In dressing-gowns, by firelight, they made cocoa . . .

"There isn't even a television."

"Or a wireless."

"Or a clock," said Nicholas cheerfully.

Virginia smiled and looked at her watch. "If you really want to know, it's ten past nine."

"Ten past nine! We should be in bed ages ago."

"It doesn't matter," she told them.

"Doesn't *matter*? Nanny would be furious!"

110

Virginia leaned back in her chair, stretched out her legs and wriggled her bare toes at the heat of the fire.

"I know," she said.

After they were in bed, after she had kissed them, and left the door open on the landing and showed them how the light worked, she left them, and went down the narrow passage and up the two steps that led to the Tower Room.

It was cold. She sat by the window and looked out across the still, shadowed fields, and saw that the peaceful sea had turned pearly in the dusk, and the sky in the afterglow of sunset was streaked in long scarves of coral. Clouds were gathered in the west. They lay, piled beyond the horizon, threaded with shafts of gold and pink light, but gradually even these last shreds of light filtered away, and the clouds turned black, and in the east a little new moon, like an eyelash, floated up into the sky.

One by one lights started to twinkle out across the soft darkness, along the whole length of the coast, from farmhouses, and cottages and barns. Here, a window burned square and yellow. There a light bobbed across a rick yard. A pair of headlights tunnelled up a lane, and headed out on to the main road towards Lanyon, and Virginia wondered if it was Eustace Philips, making for Lanyon and The Mermaid's Arms, and she wondered if he would come and see how they were getting along, or whether he would be taciturn and sulky and wait for Virginia to produce some sort of an olive branch. She told herself that it would be worth doing even this, if it were only for the satisfaction of seeing his face when he realised how well she and Cara and Nicholas were managing for themselves.

But next day it was different.

In the night the wind had got up, and the dark clouds

111

which last evening had lain banked on the horizon, were blown inland, bringing with them a dark and drenching rain. The sound of gutters trickling and dripping, the rattle of raindrops against the glass of the window-pane were the sounds which woke Virginia up. Her bedroom was so gloomy that she had to turn on the lamp before she could read her watch. Eight o'clock.

She got out of bed and went and shut the window. The floorboards beneath her feet were quite wet. The rain curtained everything, and she could see no more than a few yards. It was like being in a ship, marooned in a sea of rain. She hoped the children would not wake up for hours.

She dressed in trousers and her thickest jersey and went downstairs and found that the rain had come down the chimney and effectively put out the fire, and the room felt damp and chilly. There were matches, but no firelighters; wood, but no kindling. She pulled on a raincoat and went out into the rain and across to the sagging garden shed, and found a hatchet, blunt with age and misuse. On the stone front doorstep, and at considerable personal danger to herself, she chopped a log into kindling, then took some paper which had been wrapped in with their groceries, and kindled a little fire. The sticks snapped and crackled, the smoke, after one or two surly billows into the room, ran sweetly up the chimney. She piled on logs and left the fire to burn.

Cara appeared when she was cooking breakfast.

"Mummy!"

"Hello, my love." She bent to kiss her. Cara wore sky blue shorts, a yellow tee shirt, an inadequate little cardigan. "Are you warm enough?"

"No," said Cara. Her fine, straight hair was bunched into a

slide, her spectacles were crooked. Virginia straightened them. "Go and put on some more clothes, then. Breakfast isn't ready yet."

"But there isn't anything else. In my suitcase, I mean. Nanny didn't pack anything else."

"I don't believe it!" They gazed at each other. "You mean no jeans or raincoats or gumboots."

Cara shook her head. "I suppose she thought it was going to be hot."

"Yes, I suppose she did," said Virginia mildly, mentally cursing Nanny. "But you'd have thought she knew enough about packing to put a raincoat in."

"Well, we've sort of got raincoats, but not proper ones."

She looked so worried that Virginia smiled. "Don't worry."

"What shall we do?"

"We'll have to go and buy you both some clothes."

"Today?"

"Why not? We can't do anything else in weather like this."

"How about seeing Aunt Alice and swimming in her pool?"

"We'll keep that for a finer day. She won't mind. She'll understand."

They drove through the downpour to Penzance. At the top of the hill the mist was thick and grey, swirling in the wind, parting momentarily to allow a glimpse of the road ahead, and then closing in once more so that Virginia could scarcely see the end of the car bonnet.

Penzance was awash with rain, traffic and disconsolate holidaymakers, prevented by the weather from their usual daily ploy of sitting on the promenade or the beach. They clogged the pavements, stood in shop doorways, aimlessly surged round the counters of shops, looking for something to buy. Behind the steamy windows of cafés and ice-cream shops they could be seen, packed in at little tables, slowly sipping, licking, munching; spinning it out, making it last, so as to postpone the inevitable moment when they had to go out into the rain again.

Virginia drove around for ten minutes before she found a place to leave the car. In the rain they searched the choked streets until they came to a shop where fishermen's oilskins were for sale, and huge thigh-length rubber boots and lanterns and rope, and they went in and she bought jeans for Cara and Nicholas, and dark blue Guernseys, and black oilskins and sou'westers which obliterated the children like candle-snuffers. The children put on the new oilskins and the sou'westers, then and there, but the rest of the clothes were tied up in a brown paper parcel. Virginia took the parcel and paid the bill, and with the children, stiff as robots in their new coats, blinded by the brims of the hats, she went out into the street again.

It still poured. "Let's go home now," said Cara.

"Well, while we're here, we may as well get some fish or some meat or a chicken. And we haven't any potatoes or carrots or peas. There may be a supermarket."

"I want a bucket and spade," said Nicholas.

Virginia pretended not to hear. They found the supermarket, and joined the herd-like crowds, queuing and choosing, waiting and paying, packing the parcels into carriers, lugging them out of the shop.

The gutters gurgled, water streamed from drainpipes.

"Cara, can you really carry that?"

"Yes . . ." said Cara, dragged down to one side by the weight of the carrier.

"Give half of it to Nicholas."

114

"I want a bucket and spade," said Nicholas.

But Virginia had run out of money. She was about to tell him that he would have to wait until the next shopping expedition, but he turned up his face under the brim of the sou'wester, and his mouth was mutinous, but his eyes huge and beginning to fill with tears. "I want a bucket and spade."

"Well, we'll buy you one. But first I'll have to find a bank and cash a cheque and get more money."

The tears, as if by magic, vanished. "I saw a bank!"

They found the bank, filled with queuing customers.

The children made their way to a leather bench and sat, exhausted, like two little old people, their chins sunk into their chests, and their legs stuck out in front of them, regardless of whom they might trip up. Virginia waited in a queue, then produced her bank card and wrote her cheque.

"On holiday?" asked the young cashier. Virginia wondered how he could still be good-tempered at the end of such a morning.

"Yes."

"It'll clear up by tomorrow, you'll see."

"I hope so."

The red bucket and the blue spade were their final purchases. Laden, they walked the long way back to the car, and for some reason it was all uphill. Nicholas, banging the bucket with the spade as though it were a drum, trailed behind. More than once Virginia had to turn and wait for him, exhort him to get a move on. Finally, she lost her patience. "Oh, Nicholas, *do* hurry," and a passing woman heard the suppressed irritation in her voice, and glanced back, her face full of disapproval at such a disagreeable and short-tempered mother.

And that was after only one morning.

It still rained. They came at last to the car, and loaded the boot with parcels, and pulled off their dripping raincoats and stuffed them into the boot, and then scrambled into the car and slammed the door, thankful beyond words to be at last sitting down and out of the rain.

"Now," said Nicholas, still banging the bucket with the spade, "do you know what I want?"

Virginia looked at her watch. It was nearly one o'clock. "Something to eat?" she guessed.

What I would like would be to go back to Wheal House and know that Mrs Jilkes had lunch ready and waiting, and there would be a cheerful fire in the drawing-room, and lots of new magazines and newspapers and nothing to do for the rest of the afternoon except read them.

"Yes, that. But something else as well."

"I don't know."

"You've got to guess. I'll give you three guesses."

"Well." She thought. "You want to go to the loo?"

"No. At least not yet."

"You want . . . a drink of water?"

"No."

"Give in."

"I want to go to a beach this afternoon and dig. With my new bucket and spade."

The young man in the bank proved to be quite correct in his weather forecast. That evening, the wind swung around to the north, and the shredded clouds were sent bowling away, over the moors. At first small patches of sky appeared, and then these grew larger and brighter and at last the evening sun broke through, to set, triumphantly, in a welter of glorious pinks and reds.

"Red Sky At Night, Shepherd's Delight," said Cara as they went to bed. "That means it's going to be a lovely day tomorrow."

It was.

"I want to go to the beach today and dig with my bucket and spade," said Nicholas.

"You will," Virginia told him firmly. "But first we have to go and see Aunt Alice Lingard, otherwise she'll think we're the rudest, most ungrateful people she's ever known."

"Why?" said Nicholas.

"Because she got the house all ready for us and we haven't even said thank you . . . finish up your egg, Nicholas, it's getting all cold."

"I wish I could have cornflakes."

"We'll buy cornflakes," said Virginia, and Cara got the pencil and the shopping list and they wrote Cornflakes underneath Steel Wool, Peanut Butter and Caster Sugar, Splits, Jellies, Soap Powder and Cheese. Virginia had never done so much shopping in her life.

She sent them off to play while she did the breakfast dishes and went upstairs to make the beds. The children's room was awash with clothes. Virginia had always imagined they were neat and tidy, but realised now that it had simply been Nanny, who moved along behind them, picking up and putting away everything that they dropped. She gathered up the clothes, not knowing if they were dirty or clean, took a sock from the top of the chest of drawers, and carefully did not touch a crumpled paper bag with two sticky sweets in the corner.

There was also a big pigskin folder of photographs. This belonged to Cara, and had been packed by Nanny, with what

117

intention Virginia could only guess. One side of the folder was taken up with a selection of small photographs, many of which had been taken by Cara herself, and arranged with more affection than artistry. The front of the house, rather crooked; the dogs, the farm men on the tractor; an aerial view of Kirkton, and a picture postcard or two. On the other side was an impressive studio portrait of Anthony, a head and shoulders, all lighting and angles, so that his hair looked white-blond, and his jaw very square and determined. The photographer's impression was of a strong man, but Virginia knew the narrowed eyes, and the weak, handsome mouth. And she saw the striped collar of the Turnbull and Asser shirt, the discreetly patterned silk of the Italian tie, and she remembered how clothes had mattered to Anthony; just as his car was important, and the furnishings of his house and his manner of living. Virginia had always imagined that these were subsidiary considerations, and took their shape from the character of the individual. But with Anthony Keile it was the other way round, and he had invariably given the highest priority to the smallest details, as though realising that they were the props behind his image, and without them his inadequate personality would crumble.

Carrying the armful of clothes, she went downstairs and washed them in the tiny sink. When she took these outside to peg them crookedly on to the knotted clothes-line, she found only Nicholas, alone, playing with his red tractor and a few pebbles and bits of grass. He wore his new navy-blue Guernsey and was already scarlet in the face with heat, but Virginia knew better than to suggest that it might be a good idea if he took the sweater off.

"What are you playing?"

"Nothing much."

118

"Is the grass straw?"

"Sort of."

Virginia pegged out the last pair of pants. "Where's Cara?"

"She's inside."

"Reading, I expect," said Virginia and went in to find her. But Cara was not reading; she was in the Tower Room, sitting by the window staring sightlessly out across the fields to the sea. When Virginia appeared at the door, she turned her head slowly, bemused, unrecognising.

"Cara . . ."

Her eyes behind the spectacles came into focus. She smiled. "Hello. Is it time to go . . .?"

"I'm ready when you are." She sat beside Cara. "What are you doing? Thinking, or looking at the view?"

"Both, really."

"What were you thinking about?"

"I was really wondering how long we were going to stay here . . ."

"Oh – I suppose about a month. I've taken it for a month."

"But we'll have to go back to Scotland, won't we? We'll have to go back to Kirkton."

"Yes, we'll have to go back. There's your school for one thing." She waited. "Don't you want to go?"

"Isn't Nanny coming with us?"

"I shouldn't think so."

"It'll be funny, won't it, Kirkton, without Daddy or Nanny? It's so big for just the three of us. I think that's why I like this house. It's just the right size."

"I thought perhaps you wouldn't like it."

"I love it. And I love this room. I've never seen a room like it, with the stairs going down in the middle of the floor and all the windows and the sky.'' She was obviously not bothered by spooky sensations. ''Why isn't there any furniture, though?''

''I think it was built as a study, a workroom. There was a man who lived here, about fifty years ago. He wrote books and he was very famous.''

''What did he look like?''

''I don't know. I suppose he had a beard, and perhaps he was rather untidy and forgot to do up his sock suspenders, and buttoned his suit all wrong. Writers are often very absent-minded.''

''What was his name?''

''Aubrey Crane.''

''I'm sure he was nice,'' said Cara, ''to have made such a pretty room. You can just sit and see everything that happens.''

''Yes,'' said Virginia, and together they gazed out at the patchwork fields, where peaceful cows grazed, and the grass was emerald green after the rain, and stone walls and leaning gateposts were tangled with brambles which, in just a month or two, would be sweet and heavy with black fruit. Away to the west a tractor hummed. She turned her head, pressing her forehead against the window and saw the patch of scarlet, bright as a pillar-box, and the man sitting up behind the wheel, wearing a shirt as blue as the sky.

''Who's that?'' asked Cara.

''That's Eustace Philips.''

''Do you know him?''

''Yes. He farms Penfolda.''

''Are these all his fields?''

''I expect so.''

''When did you know him?''

''A long time ago.''

120

"Does he know you're here?"

"Yes, I think so."

"I expect he'll come for a drink or something."

Virginia smiled. "Yes, perhaps he will. Now come and comb your hair and get ready. We're going to see Alice Lingard."

"Shall I put in my bathing things? Can we swim in her pool?"

"That's a good idea."

"I wish we had a swimming-pool."

"What, here? There wouldn't be room in the garden."

"No, not here. At Kirkton."

"Well, we could," said Virginia, without thinking. "If you really wanted one. But do let's go, otherwise it'll be lunchtime, and we shall have done nothing but sit here and talk."

But when they got to Wheal House, they found only Mrs Jilkes at home. Virginia had rung the bell but only as a formality, immediately opening the door and stepping into the hall with the children at her heels. She waited for the dog to start barking, for Alice's voice to say "Who is it?" and Alice to appear through the drawing-room door. But she was met only by silence, broken by the slow ticking of the grandfather clock which stood by the fireplace.

"Alice?"

Somewhere a door opened and shut. And then Mrs Jilkes came up the kitchen passage, like a ship in full sail with her starched white apron. "Who is it?" She sounded quite cross until she saw Virginia standing there with the children beside her.

Then she smiled. "Oh, Mrs Keile, you did surprise me, I couldn't think who you were, standing there. And these are your children. My, aren't they lovely? Aren't you lovely?" she inquired conversationally of Cara, who had never been asked such a question before. She wondered if she would say "no"

121

because she knew that she wasn't lovely, but she was too shy to say anything. She simply stared at Mrs Jilkes.

"Cara, isn't it? And Nicholas. Brought your swimming things, too, I can see. Going to go and have a dip in the pond?" She turned back to Virginia. "Mrs Lingard's not here."

"Oh dear."

"Been away she has, ever since you went. Mr Lingard had to go to some big dinner in London, so Mrs Lingard suddenly decided she'd go too. Said she hadn't been up for a bit. She'll be home this evening, though."

Virginia worked this out. "You mean, she's been away since Thursday?"

"Thursday afternoon she went."

"But . . . Bosithick . . . A fire had been lighted when we got there, and it was all clean and there were eggs and milk waiting for us . . . I thought it was Mrs Lingard."

Mrs Jilkes looked coy.

"No. But I'll tell you who it was, though."

"Who was it?"

"It was Eustace Philips."

"*Eustace?*"

"Well, don't sound so shocked, it's not as though he's done anything wrong."

"But how do you know it was Eustace?"

"Because he telephoned me," Mrs Jilkes said, importantly. "Least, he telephoned Mrs Lingard, but her being in London I spoke to him instead. And he said was anybody doing anything about you coming back to Bosithick with those children, and I said I didn't know, and told him Mrs Lingard was away, and he said, 'Well, never mind, I'll look after it,' and that was it. Make a good job, did he?"

122

"You mean he came in and did all that *house-cleaning*?"

"Oh no. Eustace wouldn't know one end of a duster from the other. That would have been Mrs Thomas. She'd scrub the flags off the floor if you'd give her half a chance."

Cara put her hand into Virginia's. "Is that the man on the tractor we saw this morning?"

"Yes," said Virginia, distracted.

"But won't he think we're terribly rude? We haven't said thank you."

"No, I know. We'll have to go this afternoon. When we get back, we'll go down to Penfolda and explain."

Nicholas was furious. "But you said I could dig on the beach with my bucket and spade!"

Mrs Jilkes knew a rebellious voice when she heard one. She stooped towards Nicholas, hands on her knees, her face close to his, her voice seductive.

"Why don't you go and have a lovely swim? And when you come out you and your Mummy and your sister can come and eat shepherd's pie, in the kitchen with Mrs Jilkes . . ."

"Oh, but Mrs Jilkes . . ."

"*No*." Mrs Jilkes shook her head at Virginia's interruption. "It's no trouble. All waiting to be eaten it is. And I was just beginning to think that the house was somehow empty, and me rattling around in it like a pea in a drum." She beamed at Cara. "You'd like to do that, wouldn't you, my lovely?"

She was so kind that Cara's icy shyness thawed. She said, "Yes, please."

That warm Sunday afternoon they walked across the fields to Penfolda, across the stubble fields where, only a week ago, Virginia had watched the harvesters at work; across the grassy meadows, going from field to field by stiles made of granite

123

steps laid across the open ditches. As they approached the farm, they saw the Dutch barns, the gates, the concrete cattle court, the milking parlours. Cautiously opening and shutting the gates behind them they crossed the court and came out in the old cobbled farmyard. There was the sound of scrubbing, wet bristles on stone, and Virginia went to an open door of what looked like stables, with loose-boxes, and found a man, who was not Eustace, cleaning the place out. He wore a faded navy-blue beret on the back of his curly grey head, and old-fashioned dungarees with braces.

He saw her and stopped sweeping. Virginia said, "I'm sorry, I'm looking for Mr Philips . . ."

"'E's around somewhere . . . up at the back of the house . . ."

"We'll see if we can find him."

They went through a gate, and along a path that led between the farmhouse and the tangled little garden where she and Eustace had shared the pasty. A tabby cat sat on the doorstep in a warm patch of sun. Cara squatted to pet it and Virginia knocked on the door. There were footsteps and the door opened, and a little round woman stood there, cosy as an armchair, upholstered in a black dress and loose-covered with a print apron. From behind her, from the kitchen, came a good smell, the memory of a hearty Sunday dinner.

"Yes?"

"I'm Virginia Keile . . . from Bosithick . . ."

"Oh yes . . ."

A smile creased the rosy face, pushing up her cheeks into two little bunches.

"You must be Mrs Thomas."

"That's right . . . and these your children, are they?"

"Yes. Cara and Nicholas. We feel so bad because we never came down to thank you. For cleaning the house I mean, and leaving the eggs and the milk and the firewood and everything.''

"Oh, that wasn't me. I just cleaned the place up a bit, opened a few windows. It was Eustace who got the logs there, took up a load on the back of the tractor . . . left the milk and the eggs at the same time. We thought you wouldn't have had time to do much before you went to London . . . dismal it is coming home to a dirty house; couldn't let you do that.''

"We'd have come before, but we thought it was Mrs Lingard . . .''

"Want to see Eustace, do you? He's up in the vegetable garden at the back, digging me a bucket of potatoes.'' She smiled down at Cara. "Do you like the little pussy cat?''

"Yes, she's sweet.''

"She's got kittens in the barn. Do you want to go and see them?''

"Will she mind?''

"She won't mind. Come along, Mrs Thomas will show you where to find them.''

She made for the barn, with the children at her heels; not a backward glance did they spare for their mother, so intent were they on seeing the kittens. Left alone, Virginia went up the garden path, through a wicket gate, arched in ivy. Eustace's blue shirt could be glimpsed beyond the pea-vines, and she made her way towards this and found him forking up a drill of potatoes. Round and white and smooth as sea pebbles, they were, caked in earth the same colour and consistency as rich, dark chocolate cake.

"Eustace.''

He looked over his shoulder and saw her. She waited for him

to smile, but he did not. She wondered if he had taken offence. He straightened up, leaning on the handle of the spade.

"Hello," he said, as though it were a surprise to see her there.

"I've come to say thank you. And I'm sorry."

He shifted the spade from one hand to another. "What have you got to be sorry for?"

"I didn't realise it was you who'd brought the wood and lit the fire and everything. I thought it was Alice Lingard. That's why we haven't been down before."

"Oh, that," said Eustace and she wondered if there was something else she should be sorry about.

"It was terribly kind. The milk and the eggs and everything. It just made all the difference." She stopped, terrified of sounding insincere. "But how did you get into the house?"

Eustace drove the prongs of the fork into the ground, and started towards her. "There's a key here. When my mother was first married, she used to go over sometimes, do a bit of work for old Mr Crane. His wife was ailing, my mother used to clean the place up. He gave her a key to hang on the dresser and it's been there ever since."

He reached her side, and stood, looking down at her, then he suddenly smiled, his blue eyes crinkled with amusement and she knew that her fears were unjustified, and that he bore no grudge. He said, "So you decided to take the house after all."

Ruefully, Virginia said, "Yes."

"I felt badly, saying those things, and you so upset about everything. I lost my temper, but I shouldn't have."

"You were right. It was all I needed to make me make up my own mind."

"That's why I brought up the logs and stuff . . . I thought it was the least I could do. You'll be wanting more milk . . ."

126

"Could you let us have it every day?"

"If someone comes and fetches it."

"I could, or one of the children. I hadn't realised, but over the fields and the stiles it's no distance at all."

They had begun to walk back towards the gate.

"Are your children here?"

"They've gone with Mrs Thomas to see some kittens."

Eustace laughed. "They'll fall in love with them, so be warned. That little tabby got caught by a Siamese up the road, and you've never seen such pretty kittens." He opened the gate for Virginia to go through. "Blue eyes they've got and . . ."

He stopped, watching over her head as Cara and Nicholas came, slowly, carefully, out of the barn, their cupped hands held cradled to their chests, their heads bent in adoration. "What did I tell you?" said Eustace and shut the gate behind them.

The children came up the slope of the lawn, ankle deep, knee deep, in plantains and great white daisies. And all at once Virginia saw them with fresh eyes, with Eustace's eyes, as though she were seeing them for the first time. The fair head and the dark, the blue eyes and the brown. And the sun blinked on to Cara's spectacles so that they flashed like the headlights of a little car, and their new jeans, bought too big, slipped down over their hips and Nicholas's shirt-tail hung out over his firm, round little bottom.

A love-like pain caught at Virginia's throat, unshed tears prickled at the back of her eyes. They were so defenceless, so vulnerable, and for some reason it mattered so much that they should make a good impression on Eustace.

Nicholas caught sight of her. "Look what we've got, Mummy; Mrs Thomas said that we could bring them out."

"Yes," said Cara, "and they're tiny and they've got their

eyes . . .'' She saw Eustace, behind her mother, and stopped dead, where she was' standing, her face closed up, her eyes watching him from behind her glasses.

But Nicholas came on . . . ''Look, Mummy you've got to look. It's all furry and it's got tiny claws. But I don't know if it's a boy or girl. Mrs Thomas says she can't tell.'' He looked up and saw Eustace and smiled engagingly into his face. ''They've stopped sucking their mother, Mrs Thomas says, she was getting too thin, and she's put a little saucer of milk out for them, and they lap and their tongues are tiny,'' he told Eustace.

Eustace put out a long brown finger and scratched the top of the kitten's head. Virginia said, ''Nicholas, this is Mr Philips, you're meant to say how do you do.''

''How do you do. Mrs Thomas said that if we wanted one we could have one but we had to ask you, but you wouldn't mind, would you, Mummy? It's so little and it could sleep on my bed and I'd look after it.''

Virginia found herself coming out with all the classic arguments produced by the parents of children, in the same situation as herself. *Too young to be taken from its mother yet. Still needs her to keep him warm. Only at Bosithick for the holidays, and think how he'd hate the train journey back to Scotland.*

Eustace had put down the bucket of potatoes and now went over to where Cara stood, clutching her kitten. Virginia, in agony for her, saw Eustace squat to Cara's height, loosen her fingers gently with his own. ''You don't want to hold him too tight, otherwise he won't be able to breathe.''

''I'm frightened of dropping him.''

''You won't drop him. He wants to look out and see what's happening in the world. He's never seen sun as bright as that.'' He smiled at the kitten, at Cara. After a little, slowly, she smiled back, and you forgot the ugly spectacles and the bumpy forehead and the straight hair, and saw only the marvellous sweetness of her expression.

After a little he sent them to put the kittens back, and telling Virginia to stay outside in the sunshine, went into the house with the potatoes for Mrs Thomas, only to emerge a moment or so later with a packet of cigarettes and a bar of chocolate. They lay where they had lain before, in the long grass, and were joined there by the children.

He gave them the chocolate but talked to them like adults. What have you been doing? What did you do yesterday in all that rain? Have you been swimming yet?

They told him, voices chiming against each other, Cara, her shyness over, as eager to impart information as Nicholas.

"We bought raincoats, and we got *drenched*. And Mummy had to go to the bank to get more money, and Nicholas got a bucket and spade."

"But I haven't been to the beach to dig yet!"

"And we swam this morning at Mrs Lingard's. We swam in her pool. But we haven't swum in the sea yet."

Eustace raised his eyebrows. "You haven't swum in the sea and you haven't been to a beach? That's all wrong!"

"Mummy says there hasn't been time . . ."

"But she promised me," Nicholas, reminded of his grievance, became indignant. "She said today I could dig with the spade, but I've not been near one grain of sand."

Virginia began to laugh at him, and he became, naturally, angrier than ever. "Well, it's true, and it's what I want more than anything."

"Well," said Eustace, "if you want it more than anything, what are we doing sitting around here talking our heads off!"

Nicholas stared at Eustace, his eyes narrowed suspiciously. "You mean go to the beach?"

"Why not?"

"Now?" Nicholas could not believe his ears.

"Is there anything else you'd rather do?"

"No. Nothing. Nothing else." He sprang to his feet. "Where shall we go? Shall we go to Porthkerris?"

"No, we don't want to go there – nasty crowded place. We'll go to our own private beach, the one that nobody knows about, that belongs to Penfolda and Bosithick."

Virginia was astonished. "I didn't know we had one. I thought there was nothing but cliffs."

By now Eustace was also on his feet. "I'll show you . . . come along, we'll take the Land-Rover."

"My bucket and spade's at our house."

"We'll pick them up on the way."

"And our swimming things," said Cara.

"Those too."

He went into the house to fetch his own things, shouted a message to Mrs Thomas, led the way through the gate and back across the farmyard. He whistled and the dogs, barking, came rushing around the side of the barn, knowing that the whistle meant a walk, smells, rabbits, maybe a swim. Everybody, including the dogs, clambered into the Land-Rover, and Cara, her shyness now quite forgotten, screamed with delight, as they lurched out of the cobbled farmyard, and went bumping and bouncing up the lane towards the main road.

"Is it far?" she asked Eustace.

"No distance at all."

"What's the beach called?"

"Jack Carley's cove. And it's not a place for babies, only

for big children who can look after themselves and climb down the cliff.''

They assured him hastily that they came into this category and Virginia watched Nicholas's face, and saw the joyful satisfaction upon it at being indulged, at last, in the one thing he had been wanting to do for a whole day. And what was more, doing it instantly. Not told maybe, or tomorrow, or to wait or to be patient. And she knew exactly how he felt for long ago Eustace had done the very same, performed the same miracle for the young Virginia; had bought her the ice-cream she had been yearning for, and then, out of the blue, asked her to come back to Penfolda.

7

They left the Land-Rover in the deserted farmyard below
Bosithick and started to walk down towards the sea. At first,
crossing the fields, they went in a bunch, four abreast, Eustace
taking Nicholas by the hand because he was inclined to lag. But
then the fields gave way to brambles and bracken and they fell
into single file with Eustace leading the way; over crumbling
stone walls and across a stream, where rushes grew shoulder
high to a small person. Then over another wall, and the path
disappeared beneath a jungle of green bracken. Through this
they pushed their way, gorse bushes pressing in at either side.
The ground all at once slid steeply away from beneath their
feet, and the path zig-zagged down through the undergrowth,
down to the very lip of the curving cliff. And beyond, space.
Blue air. Soaring, screaming gulls, and the distant creaming
of the sea.

At this point the coast seemed to fling itself out into a jagged
headland, composed of great granite outcrops. Between these
the turf was smooth and very green, stained with patches of
purple-belled heather, and the path wound down between these
outcrops and as they followed its convolutions, a little cove,
sheltered and enclosed, gradually revealed itself, far below. The

133

sea was deep and still, purple over the rocks and jade green over the sand. The beach was tiny, and backed by the remains of an old sea wall. Beyond this the land sloped up to the green wedge of the cliff, down which trickled, in a series of small waterfalls, a fresh-water stream. And above the sea wall, tucked snug against the foot of the cliff, stood the remains of a cottage; derelict, windows broken, slates torn from the roof.

They stood in a row, the four of them, buffeted by the gentle wind, looking down. It was a disturbing sensation. Virginia wondered if the children might suffer from vertigo, but neither of them seemed in the least disturbed by the dizzy emptiness of the great height.

"There's a house," said Cara.

"That was where Jack Carley lived."

"Where does he live now?"

"With the angels, I reckon."

"Did you know him?"

"Yes, I knew him. He was an old man when I was a boy. Didn't like people coming down here. Not any old people. Had a great barking dog and he used to chase them away."

"But he let you come?"

"Oh, yes, he let me come." He grinned down at Nicholas. "Do you want me to carry you, or can you manage?"

Nicholas peered out and over. The path trickled down the face of the cliff and so out of sight. Nicholas remained undismayed.

"No. I don't want to be carried, thank you. But I'd like it better if you went first."

In fact, the dogs went first, unafraid, sure-footed as goats. The humans followed at a more prudent speed, but Virginia found that the path was not as dangerous as it appeared. After the dry spell the ground was hard and firm underfoot, and in steep places, steps had been cut, shored up with driftwood or fashioned roughly out of cement.

Much sooner than she had expected they were all safely down. Above them, the cliff loomed, dark and cold in the shadow, but when they jumped down on to the beach they came out of the shade and into the sunshine, and the sand was warm, and there was the smell of tar from the little house, and no sound but the gulls and the creaming sea, and the splash of the stream.

There was an air of unreality about the little cove, as though they had somehow strayed out of time and space. The air was still, the sun burning hot, the sand white and the green water clear as glass. The children stripped off their clothes, and took Nicholas's new bucket and spade and went at once to the water's edge, where they began to dig a sandcastle, moated and turreted with bucket-shaped towers.

"If the tide comes in it'll wash the whole castle away," said Cara.

"No, it won't, because we're going to make a great huge moat and then the water will go into that."

"If the tide comes in higher than the castle, it's going to wash it away. Like King Canute."

Nicholas considered this. "Well, it won't for ages."

It was the sort of day that they would remember for the rest of their lives. Virginia imagined them, middle-aged, reminiscing, nostalgic.

There was a little cove and a ruined cottage and not another soul but us. And there were two dogs and we had to climb down a suicidal path.

Who took us?

Eustace Philips.

135

But who was he?

I can't remember . . . he must have been a farmer, some sort of a neighbour.

And they would argue over details.

There was a stream.

No, it was a waterfall.

There was a stream running down the middle of the beach. I can remember it quite clearly. And we dammed it with a sandbank.

But there was a waterfall too. And I had a new spade.

When the tide was high, they all swam, and the water was clear and salty and green and very cold. Virginia had forgotten her cap and her dark hair lay sleek to her head, and her shadow moved across the pebbled sea-bed like some strange new variety of fish. Holding Cara, she floated, drifting between the sea and the sky, with her eyes dazzled by water and sunshine; and the air was cleft with screaming gulls, and always the gentle murmur of breaking waves.

She became very cold. The children showed no signs of chill, however, so she left them with Eustace, and came out of the water, and went to sit on the dry sand, above the high-water mark.

She sat on the sand because they had brought no rug, no super-sized bath-towels. And no comb or lipstick, or biscuits or knitting, and no Thermos of tea, and no extra cardigan. And no plum cake or chocolate biscuits, and no money for the donkey rides or the man with the ice-cream.

She was joined at last by Cara, teeth chattering. Virginia wrapped her in a towel and began gently to dry her. "You'll soon be swimming at this rate."

Cara said, "What time is it?"

Her mother squinted up at the sun. "I suppose, nearly five
. . . I don't know."

"We haven't had tea yet."

"No, nor we have. And I don't suppose we will either."

"Not have any *tea*?"

"It doesn't matter for once. We'll have supper later on."

Cara made a face, but raised no objections. Nicholas, however, was vociferous in his complaints when he realised that
Virginia had brought nothing for him to eat.

"But I'm hungry."

"I'm sorry."

"Nanny always had shivery bites and you haven't got
anything."

"I know. I forgot. We were in such a hurry and I never
thought of biscuits."

"Well, what am I going to eat?"

Eustace caught the tail end of this conversation as he came,
dripping, up the beach. "What's this?" He stopped to pick
up a towel.

"I'm very hungry and Mummy hasn't brought anything to
eat."

"Too bad," said Eustace unsympathetically.

Nicholas sent him a long, measured look, and turned away,
headed in a sulky silence back to his digging, but Eustace caught
him by an arm and pulled him gently back and held him against
his knees, rubbing at him absently with the towel, rather as
though he were fondling one of the dogs.

Virginia said, placatingly, "Anyway, we'll have to go soon,
I expect."

"Why?" asked Eustace.

"I thought you had all those cows to milk."

"Bert's doing them."

"Bert?"

"He was at Penfolda today, cleaning out the loose-boxes."

"Oh, yes."

"He used to work for my father, he's retired now, but he comes along every alternate Sunday, gives me a hand. He likes to do it, and Mrs Thomas feeds him a good dinner, and it means I have a few hours to myself."

Nicholas became irritated by the pointless small talk. He reared around in Eustace's hands, turned up a furious face towards him. "I am *hungry*."

"So am I," said Cara, wistful if not so vehement.

"Well, listen," said Eustace.

They listened. And heard, over the sound of the sea and the gulls, another sound. The soft drumming of an engine, putt-putt-putt, all the time coming closer.

"What is it?"

"You watch and see."

The sound grew louder. Presently around the point they saw approaching a small open boat, white with a blue stripe, riding the waves with a scud of white spray. A stocky figure stood at its stern. Putt-putt, it swung round into the shelter of the cove, and the engine idled down to a steady throb . . .

They all stared. "There you are!" said Eustace, smug as a conjuror who has brought off a difficult trick.

"Who is it?" asked Virginia.

"That's Tommy Bassett from Porthkerris. Come to pick up his lobster pots."

"But he won't have any biscuits," said Nicholas, who would never be diverted from the matter in hand.

"No. But he might have something else. Shall I go and see?"

138

"All right." But they sounded doubtful.

He put Nicholas aside and went back down the sand and into the sea, diving through the eye of a peacock-coloured wave, and swimming, with a strong and steady crawl, far out to where the boat bobbed. The lobster pots were already being hauled aboard. The fisherman emptied one and dropped it back, and then saw Eustace coming, and stood, watching.

"Hello there, boy!" His voice carried across the water.

They saw Eustace catch the gunwales with his hands, hang there for a moment, and then with a heave pull himself clean out of the water and into the rocking boat.

"What a long way to swim," said Cara.

Nicholas said, "I hope he isn't going to bring back a lobster."

"Why not?"

"Lobsters have got claws."

In the boat, some discussion seemed to be taking place. But at last Eustace stood up, and they saw that he was carrying some sort of bundle. He let himself overboard and started back, swimming more slowly this time, hampered as he was by his mysterious burden. This proved to be, of all things, a string shopping-bag, but it contained, wet and dripping, a dozen gleaming mackerel.

Nicholas opened his mouth to say, "I don't like fish," but caught Eustace's eye, and closed his mouth and said nothing instead.

"I thought he might have a few," Eustace told them. "He usually puts a line out when he's coming out to the pots." He smiled down at Cara. "Ever eaten mackerel, have you?"

"I don't think so. But," said Cara, "fancy giving you the string bag." To her, this seemed far more amazing than the gift of the mackerel. "Doesn't he want it back again?"

"He didn't say he did."

"Shall we have to take them back to Bosithick?"

"What would we do that for? . . . No, we cook them here
. . . come on, you can come and help."

And he collected six or seven big stones, round and smooth,
and built them into a ring, and he took matches, and a scrap of
an old cigarette packet, and some chips of driftwood and straw,
and he kindled a fire and sent the children off to find more
wood and soon they had a regular bonfire going. And when the
wood ash was deep and grey and burned red when you blew
on it, he laid the fish there, in a row, and there was a sizzling
and a spitting and presently a most delicious smell.

"But we haven't got knives and forks," said Cara.

"Fingers were made before forks."

"But it'll be hot."

She and Nicholas squatted by the fireside, hair on end, naked
except for their bathing pants and a coating of sand. They looked
like savages, and perfectly content.

Cara watched Eustace's clever hands. "Have you done this
before?"

"What, whittled a stick?"

"No, had a fire, and cooked fish."

"Many times. This is the only way to cook mackerel, and
eat it, fresh out of the sea."

"Did you use to do this when you were a boy?"

"Yes."

"Was the old man alive then? Jack Carley."

"Yes. He used to come out and sit on the beach and join in
the party. Bring a bottle of rum with him and a smelly old pipe
and sit there and tell us yarns so hair-raising we could never be
quite sure if they were true."

140

"What sort of yarns?"

"Oh, adventures . . . he'd been all over the world, done everything. Been a cook on a tanker, a lumberjack, built roads and railways, worked in the mines. He was a tin miner, see. A tinner. Went off to Chile, worked there for five years or more, came home a rich man, but all his money was gone within the twelve months, and he was off again."

"But he came back."

"Yes, he came back. Back to Jack Carley's cove." Cara shivered. "You cold?"

"Nanny calls it a ghost going over your grave."

"Put on a sweater then, and that'll keep the ghosts away, and then it'll be time to eat our tea."

And seeing him with her children, Virginia thought of Anthony who had missed so much because he had never wanted to have anything to do with them. If Cara had been pretty, perhaps he would have paid attention to her . . . Cara who longed for attention and love and thought her father the most wonderful being in the world. But she was plain and shy and wore spectacles, and he never endeavoured to hide the fact that he was ashamed of her. And Nicholas . . . with Nicholas it might have been different. When he was old enough, Anthony would have taught him to shoot and play golf and fish, they would have become friends and gone about together. But now Anthony was dead, and none of this would happen and she felt sorry because they would never now remember swimming with him, they would never crouch with him round a camp fire, listening to his stories and watching his clever hands whittle wooden skewers to be used instead of forks.

The sun slipped down out of the sky, shone directly in upon them, and the sea was turned to a liquid dazzle. It would soon be

141

evening and then it would be dark. And Jack Carley had lived here, just as Aubrey Crane had lived at Bosithick. You didn't see them. You didn't hear them. But you knew that they were still around.

It was disturbing, this awareness of the past, but somehow elemental, and so not really frightening. And it was not possible to live in this part of the world as a nervous or a timid person, for, beneath the beauty it was a savage land, and danger lurked everywhere. In the sea, deep and treacherous, with its undertows and unsuspected currents. In the cliffs and caves, so swiftly cut off and submerged by racing tides. Even the quiet fields down which they had walked this afternoon concealed unthought-of horrors; abandoned mine workings, deep pits and shafts, black as wells, lay hidden beneath the bracken. And scraps of fur and feather, and little bleached bones bore witness to the foxes who built their lairs in earthy hollows under the gorse.

And after nightfall the owl set up his predatory hooting, and the badger emerged to tunnel and scavenge. Not for him the thrill of the hunt. He was just as content to push the lid off a dustbin in the middle of the night, causing such a clatter as to waken the farmer's wife in a cold sweat of fright.

"Mummy. It's cooked." Cara's voice broke across her thoughts. She looked up and saw Cara holding a stick aloft, a fragment of fish impaled dangerously upon its point. "Come and get it *quickly* before it falls off!" Her voice was agonised, and Virginia got to her feet, dusting the sand off the seat of her bathing-suit, and went down to join in the picnic.

In the afterglow of the setting sun, with the offshore wind cool on their faces, they climbed slowly home. After the swim the children were sleepy and silent. Nicholas was not too proud to accept a piggy-back from Eustace, and Virginia carried the wet

142

bathing things and towels in the string bag which had been used for the mackerel, and helped Cara along with the other hand. They were all sandy, salty, tousled, weary, and the path was steep and the climb, up through the bracken and the treacherous undergrowth, exhausting. But at last they reached the fields at the top, and after that the going was easy. Behind them the sea, luminous in the half-light, reflected all the colours of the sky, and ahead was Bosithick, cradled in the curve of the hill, with the road behind it flickering, every now and then, with the searchlight glare of a passing car.

Some of Eustace's cows had strayed through a gap in the hedge into the top field. In the dusk they loomed, brown and white, and made pleasant munching sounds, raising their heads to watch as the small procession walked by.

Nicholas said, leaning forward to speak into Eustace's ear, "Are you going to come back with us?"

He smiled. "Time I was getting home."

"We would like you to stay for supper."

"You've had your supper," Eustace told him.

"I thought that was tea."

"Don't tell me you've got room for more food."

Nicholas yawned. "No, maybe not."

Virginia said, "I'll make you cocoa, and you can drink it in bed."

"Yes," said Nicholas. "But it would be nice if Eustace would come and talk to us while we had our baths . . ."

Cara chimed in. "Yes, and then Mummy could get our cocoa ready, and you could talk to us."

"I'll do more than that," said Eustace. "I'll scrub the sand off your backs."

They giggled in a high-pitched fashion as though this were

143

very funny, and as soon as they were indoors raced for the bathroom to fight over the taps. Ominous splashing sounds came from beyond the door, and Eustace, rolling up his sleeves, moved in to break it up. Virginia heard him saying, "Quiet now, you'll sink the ship if you don't watch out."

Leaving him to it, she carried the fishy string bag out to the kitchen and emptied the bathing things and the sand-encrusted towels into the sink, and rinsed them out and wrung them, and carried them out into the dark garden, and, by feel, found the clothes-line and pegged them out, leaving them to billow and flap like ghosts in the darkness.

Back in the kitchen, she poured milk into a saucepan, put it on to heat, stood watching it, leaning against the cooker, yawning a little. She put up a hand to her eyes, and found that her face was rough with sand, so she took the little mirror out of her handbag, and a comb, and propped the mirror on one of the shelves of the dresser and tried to do something about her hair, but it was stiff and dry with salt, and full of sand. She thought that if there had been a shower, she would have washed it, but the idea of putting it under a tap was somehow all too difficult, too complicated. In the inadequate light her reflection gazed back at her from the round mirror, and there were freckles across the bridge of her nose, but her eyes were shadowed, dark as two holes in her face.

The milk rose in the pan. She made the two mugs of cocoa, put them on a tray, started upstairs with them. She saw that the bathroom was empty, a trail of damp towels and footprints led upstairs. She heard voices and came along the passage, and their bedroom door stood open.

They were inside and they did not see her. She stood and watched them. Eustace sat, with his back to her, on Cara's bed,

144

and the children were perched on Nicholas's bed. All three heads together, Eustace was being given a guided tour of Cara's photographs.

"And this is Daddy. The big one here. He's terribly good-looking, don't you think? . . ." This was Cara, as chatty now as she could be with someone with whom she was completely at ease. "And this is our house in Scotland, that's my bedroom, and that's Nicholas's bedroom, and that's the nursery up at the top . . ."

"That's my bedroom!"

"I said it was that bedroom, silly. And this is Nanny's room, and that's Mummy's room, but you can't see the rooms at the back because they're round at the back. And this is an aerial view . . ."

"A man took it in an aeroplane . . ."

"And that's all the park and the river. And that's the walled garden."

"And that's Mr McGregor on his tractor, and that's Bob and that's Fergie."

Eustace was beginning to lose the thread. ". . . Hold on now, who are Bob and Fergie?"

"Well, Bob helps Mr McGregor and Fergie helps the gardener. Fergie plays the bagpipes and do you know who taught him? His uncle. And do you know what his uncle is called? Muncle." Nicholas triumphantly produced the answer.

Eustace said, "Uncle Muncle."

"And this is Daddy skiing at St Moritz, and that's all of us at a grouse shoot – at least, we went to the picnic bit, we didn't go up the hill. And that's the bit of the river where we sometimes swim, but it's not always very safe, and the stones hurt your feet. But Mummy says we can have a swimming-pool, she says when we go back to Kirkton, we can have a swimming-pool, just like Aunt Alice Lingard's . . .''

''And that's Daddy's car, it's a great big Jaguar. It's a . . .'' Nicholas faltered. ''It was a great big Jaguar.'' He finished bravely, ''Green.''

Virginia said, ''Here's your cocoa.''

''Oh Mummy, we were showing Eustace all the photographs of Kirkton . . .''

''Yes, I heard.''

''That was very nice,'' said Eustace. ''Now I know all about Scotland.''

He stood up, as though to get out of Virginia's way, and went to put the photograph frame back on to the chest of drawers.

The children climbed into bed. ''You'll have to come and see us. You'll have to come and stay. Won't he, Mummy? He can sleep in the spare room, can't he?''

''Maybe,'' said Virginia. ''But Eustace is a busy man.''

''That's it,'' said Eustace. ''Busy. Always got plenty to do. Well . . .'' He moved towards the open door. ''I'll say good night.''

''Oh, good night, Eustace. And thank you for taking us to that lovely place.''

''Don't dream about Jack Carley.''

''Even if I do I shan't be frightened.''

''That's the way. Good night, Nicholas.''

''Good night. I'll see you in the morning.''

Virginia said to him, ''Don't go. I'll be down in a moment.''

He said, ''I'll wait downstairs.''

The cocoa was duly consumed, between yawns. Their eyes drooped. At last they lay down and Virginia kissed them good night. But when she kissed Nicholas he did a surprising thing.

Most undemonstrative of children, he put his arms around her neck and held her cheek down against his own.

She said, gently, "What is it?"

"It was a nice place, wasn't it?"

"You mean the little beach?"

"No. The house where Eustace lives."

"Penfolda."

"Will we go back?"

"Sure to."

"I loved that little kitten."

"I know you did."

"Eustace is downstairs."

"Yes."

"I shall hear you talking." His voice was filled with satisfaction. "I shall hear you go talk, talk, talk."

"Will that be cosy?"

"I think so," said Nicholas.

They were near to sleep, but still she stayed with them, moving quickly about the room, picking up stray clothes and folding them and putting them, neat as Nanny, across the seats of the two rickety cane chairs. This done, she went to close the window a little, for the night air was growing chill, to draw the skimpy curtains. The room, by the meagre light of the bedside lamp was all at once enclosed, safe, soft with shadows, the only sound the ticking of Cara's clock and the breathing of the children.

She was filled, in that moment, with love. For her children; for this strange little house; for the man, downstairs, who waited for her. And aware, too, of a marvellous sense of completion, of rightness. It will be the first time, she thought, that Eustace and I have been alone, with all the time in the world. Just the

147

two of us. She would light the fire for company and draw the curtains and make him a jug of coffee. If they wished, they could talk all night. They could be together.

Cara and Nicholas were sleeping. She turned off the light and went downstairs to unexpected and surprising darkness. For an incredulous moment she thought that Eustace had changed his mind and already gone, but then she saw that he stood by the window, smoking, watching the very last of the light fade from the sky. A little of this light was reflected upon his face, but when he heard her footstep he turned, and she could see no expression on his face, only shadows.

She said, "I thought you'd gone."

"No. I'm still here."

The darkness disturbed her. She reached for the lamp on the table and switched it on. Yellow light was thrown, like a pool, between them. She waited for him to speak, but when he said nothing, simply stood there, smoking, she began to fill the silence with words.

"I . . . I don't know about supper. Do you want something to eat? I don't even know what time it is."

"I'm all right."

"I could make you some coffee . . ."

"You haven't got a can of beer?"

She made a helpless gesture. "I haven't, Eustace. I'm sorry. I never bought any. I never drink it." That sounded priggish, as though she disapproved of beer. "I mean, I just don't like the taste." She smiled, trying to turn it into a joke.

"It doesn't matter."

The smile collapsed. Virginia swallowed. "Are you sure you wouldn't like coffee?"

"No, thank you." He began to look about for somewhere to

148

stub out his cigarette. She found him a saucer and put it on the table, and he demolished the stub as though he had a personal, vicious grudge against it.

"I must go."

"But . . ."

He turned towards her, waiting for her to finish. She lost her nerve. "Yes. It's been a good day. It was kind of you to give up your day for us and show us the cove and . . . everything." Her voice sounded high-pitched and formal as though she were opening a sale of work. "The children loved it."

"They're good children."

"Yes. I . . ."

"When are you going back to Scotland?"

The abruptness of the question, the coldness of his voice, were shocking. She was suddenly cold, a shiver of apprehension trickling down her spine like a stream of icy water.

"I . . . I'm not sure." She took hold of the back of one of the wooden chairs, leaning against it as if for support. "Why do you ask?"

"You're going to go back."

It was a statement, not a question. Faced with it, Virginia's natural diffidence leapt to the worst conclusion. Eustace expected her to go, even wanted her to go. She heard herself telling him, with marvellous lightness, "Well, some time, of course. After all, it's my home. The children's home."

"I hadn't realised until this evening that it was such a considerable property . . ."

"Oh, you mean, Cara's photographs . . ."

"But then, you have plenty of people to help you run it."

"I don't run it, Eustace."

"Then you should. Learn something about farming. You'd be

surprised how much there is to it. You should take an interest, start up something new. An Aberdeen Angus herd. Did your husband ever think of doing that? You can sell a good bull at the Perth sales for sixty, seventy thousand pounds.''

It was like a conversation in a nightmare, mad and pointless. She said, ''Can you?'' but her mouth was dry and the words scarcely made any sound at all.

''Of course. And who knows, one day you may have built up something really great to hand on to that boy of yours.''

''Yes.''

He said again, ''I must go.'' The trace of a smile crossed his features. ''It was a good day.''

But Virginia remembered a better one, that other day she had spent with Eustace, the spring afternoon of sun and wind when he had bought her an ice-cream and finally driven her home. And he had promised to telephone her, and then forgotten, or perhaps he had changed his mind. She realised that she had been waiting, all afternoon, for him to tell her what really happened. She had been expecting him to bring up the subject, perhaps as a story for the children to share, or as a scrap of harmless nostalgia to be remembered, over the years, by two old friends. But he had said nothing. And now she would never know.

''Yes.'' She let go of the chair and straightened up, folding her arms across her chest as though she were trying to stay warm. ''A special day. The kind that people never forget.''

He moved towards her, around the edge of the table, and Virginia turned away from him and went to open the door. Cool air, smelling sweet and damp, flooded in from a night arched in a sapphire sky, bright with stars. Out of the darkness a curlew sent up its long mournful cry.

He was beside her. ''Good night, Virginia.''

"Good night, Eustace."

And then he was going down the steps, away from her, over the wall and down the field towards the old farmyard where he had left his car. The dusk swallowed him. She closed the door and locked it and went back to the kitchen and took the children's cocoa mugs and washed them, slowly and carefully. She heard his Land-Rover go grinding up past the gate, up the lane towards the main road, heard the sound of the engine die away into the quiet night, but she never looked up from what she was doing. When the mugs were dry, the tea towel folded and there was nothing more to do, she found that she was exhausted. She turned off the lights and went slowly upstairs and undressed and climbed into bed. Her body lay slack, but the inside of her head behaved as though she had been living on black coffee for a week.

He doesn't love you.

I never thought he did.

But you were beginning to think so. After today.

Then I was wrong. We have no future together. He made that very clear.

What did you imagine was going to happen?

I imagined that he would be able to talk about what happened ten years ago.

Nothing happened. And why should he remember?

Because I did. Because Eustace was the most important person, the most important thing that ever happened to me.

You didn't remember. You married Anthony Keile.

They were married in London, in July; Virginia in a cream satin dress with a six-foot train and a veil that had belonged to Lady Keile's grandmother, and Anthony in a grey frock-coat and an immaculately cut pair of sponge-bag trousers. They emerged from St Michael's, Chester Square, with bells jangling, sun shining, and a small retinue of beribboned bridesmaids, extorting *oohs* and *aahs* of admiration from the thin crowd of inquisitive women who had realised that there was a wedding going on, and hung about to see what turned up when the doors were opened.

The excitement, the champagne, the pleasures of being loved and congratulated and kissed kept Virginia going until it was time to go upstairs and change. Her mother was there, ubiquitous, efficient, to unzip the clinging satin and unpin the borrowed tiara and the filmy veil.

"Oh, my dear, it all went off so beautifully, and you really did look enchanting, even though perhaps I shouldn't say anything so conceited about my own child . . . Darling, you're shivering, you're surely not cold?"

"No. I'm not cold."

"Change your shoes, then, and I'll help you on with your dress."

It was rose pink, with a tiny petalled hat to match, a charming useless ensemble that she would never wear again. She imagined coming back from her honeymoon, still wearing paper silk and pink petals, a little crushed by now, and going brown at the edges. (But of course they couldn't go brown, they weren't real, they were pretence petals . . .)

"And your suitcase is in the boot of Anthony's car, such a good idea taking a taxi round to the flat and picking the car up there, then you have none of this terrible horse-play with kippers and old shoes."

A roar, a galloping of feet, came from the passage outside the bedroom. Anthony's voice was raised in a comic sound like a hunting horn. ''There! He sounds as though he's ready.'' She kissed Virginia briskly. ''Have a good time, my darling.''

The door burst open, and Anthony stood there, wearing the suit that he had chosen to go away in, and with a large sunhat on the top of his head. He was considerably drunk.

''Here she is! We're off to the South of France, my love, which is why I am wearing this hat.''

Mrs Parsons, laughing indulgently, removed it, smoothed his hair with her long fingers, straightened his tie. She might have been the bride, not Virginia, who stood and watched this little ceremony with a face that held no expression whatsoever. Anthony held out a hand to her. ''Come on,'' he said. ''Time we went.''

The hired car, awash in confetti, took them back to the Parsons' flat, where Anthony's car was waiting for them. The plan had been that they should get straight into his car and drive to the airport, but Virginia had a latch-key in her purse, and instead, they let themselves in and went into the kitchen, and she tied an apron around the pink silk dress, and Anthony sat on the table and watched while she brewed him up a jug of black coffee.

For their honeymoon they had been lent a villa in Antibes. By their second day Anthony had met an old friend; by the end of the first week, he knew everyone in the place. Virginia told herself that this was what she had expected, was what she wanted. Anthony's gregarious instincts were part of his charm, and one of the things that had attracted her to him in the first place. Besides, after one day it became very obvious that they were going to find it hard to think of things to say to each other. Conversation at meals was inclined to be distinctly sticky. She realised then, that they had never been alone together before now.

There was a couple, called Janey and Hugh Rouse; he was a writer and they had rented a house at Cap Ferrat. Janey was older than Virginia and Virginia liked her, and found her easy to talk to. Once, sitting on the terrace at the Rouses' house, waiting for the men to come up from the rocks, Janey had said, "How long have you known Anthony, honey?" She had lived, as a child, in the States, and although she did not speak with an American accent, her speech was spattered with words and phrases which instantly gave her origins away.

"Not very long. I met him in May."

"Love at first sight, hm?"

"I don't know. I suppose so."

"How old are you?"

"Eighteen."

"That's awfully young to settle down. Not that I can see that Anthony settling down too much for a few years yet."

"He'll have to," Virginia told her. "You see, we're going to live in Scotland. Anthony's been left this estate, Kirkton . . . it used to belong to an uncle who was a bachelor. And we're going to go and live there."

"You mean, you think Anthony will spend all his time tramping around in a tweed suit with mud on his boots?"

"Not exactly. But I can't believe that living in Scotland is going to be quite the same as living in London."

"It won't," said Janey, who had been there. "But don't expect the simple life, or you'll be disappointed."

But Virginia did expect the simple life. She had never seen Kirkton, never been to Scotland for that matter, but she had once spent an Easter holiday with a schoolfriend who lived in Northumberland and somehow she imagined that Scotland would be rather like that, and that Kirkton would be a low-ceilinged, rambling, stone farmhouse, with flagged floors, and worn Turkey carpets, and a dining-room with a great log fire and hunting prints on the walls.

Instead, she was presented with a tall, square, elegantly proportioned Adam house, with sash windows full of reflected sunshine, and a flight of stone stairs which led, from the carriage sweep, up to the front door.

Beyond the gravel was grass, and then a ha-ha wall, and then the park, landscaped with giant beeches, sloping down to the distant silver curve of the river.

Overwhelmed, silent, Virginia had followed Anthony up the steps and through the door. The house was empty, old-fashioned and unfurnished. Between them they were going to do it up. To Virginia the task seemed daunting, but when she said as much Anthony overrode her.

"We'll get Philip Sayer on to it, he's this interior decorator my mother got to do the house in London for her. Otherwise we'll make the most ghastly mistakes and the place will be a mess."

Virginia privately thought she preferred her own ghastly mistakes to somebody else's impeccable taste – it was more homely; but she said nothing.

"And this is the drawing-room, and then the library beyond. And the dining-room, and there are kitchens and stuff downstairs."

The room soared and echoed; the icy prisms of crystal chandeliers glinted, descending from ornately decorated ceilings. There was panelling and marvellous cornices over the tall windows. There was dust and a distinct feeling of chill.

They mounted to the first floor up a curved stairway, airy and elegant, and their steps echoed on the polished treads and through the empty house. Upstairs, there were bedrooms,

155

each with its own bathroom, dressing-rooms, linen rooms, housemaid's cupboards, even a boudoir.

"What would I do with a boudoir?" Virginia wanted to know.

"You can come and boud in it, and if you don't know what that means, it's French for sulk. Oh, come on, take that horrified expression off your face and look as though you're enjoying yourself."

"It's just so big."

"You talk as though it were Buckingham Palace."

"I've never been in such a big house. I certainly never thought I would live in one."

"Well, you're going to, so you'd better get used to it."

Eventually they were outside again, standing by the car, staring up at the elegant front elevation, regularly spaced with windows. Virginia put her hands deep in the pockets of her coat and said, "Where's the garden?"

"What do you mean?"

"I mean flower-beds and stuff. Flowers. You know. A garden."

But the garden was a half-mile away, enclosed by a wall. They drove there and went inside and found a gardener and rows of fruit and vegetables like soldiers, waiting to be picked off.

"This is the garden," said Anthony.

"Oh," said Virginia.

"What's that meant to mean?"

"Nothing. Just oh."

The interior decorator duly arrived. Hard on his heels came vans and lorries, builders, plasterers, painters, men with carpets, men with curtains, men in pantechnicons which spilled out furniture like cornucopias, endlessly, as though they would never run out.

156

Virginia let it all happen. "Yes," she would say, agreeing to whatever shade of velvet Philip Sayer was suggesting. Or "Yes" when he thought of Victorian brass bedsteads in the spare room, and thick white crochet bedcovers. "Terribly Osborne, my dear, you know, Victorian Country Life."

The only time that she had raised her voice with an independent idea was over the kitchen. She wanted it like the one she remembered, the marvellous room at Penfolda with its air of stability, the suggestion in the air of good things cooking, the cat in the chair and the geraniums crowded on the window-sill.

"A farmhouse kitchen! That's what I want. A farmhouse kitchen's like a living-room."

"Well, I'm not going to live in any kitchen, I'll tell you that."

And she had let Anthony have his way because, after all, it was not her house, and it was not her money which paid for the stainless steel sinks, and the black-and-white floor and the patent self-cleaning cooking unit with eye-level grill, and a spit for broiling chickens.

It was finished and Virginia was pregnant.

"How marvellous for Nanny!" said Lady Keile.

"Why?"

"Well, darling, she's in London, doing temporary work, but she's longing, but longing for a new baby. Of course she won't be all that keen on leaving London, but she's bound to make friends, you know what this nannies' network's like, better than the English Speaking Union I always say. And that top floor is *meant* to be a nursery, you can tell by the gate at the top of the stairs, and the bars on the windows. Gorgeously sunny. I think pale blue, don't you? For carpets, I mean, and then French chintz curtains . . ."

Virginia tried to stand up for herself. To say, *No. I will look after my own baby.* But she was so sick carrying Cara, so weak and unwell, that by the time she once again felt strong enough to cope with the situation and stand on her own two feet, the nursery had been decorated and Nanny was there, established, rigid, immovable.

I'll let her stay. Just until the baby's born and I'm on my feet again. She can stay for a month or two, and then I'll tell her that she can go back to London because I want to look after my baby for myself.

But by then, there were further complications. Virginia's mother, in London, complained of pains and tiredness; she thought she was losing weight. Virginia at once went south to see her, and after that, her loyalties were torn between her baby in Scotland and her mother in London. Travelling up and down in the train it became very clear that it would be madness to get rid of Nanny until Mrs Parsons had recovered. But of course, she didn't recover and, by the time the whole ghastly nightmare was over, Nicholas had arrived and, with two babies in the nursery, Nanny was dug in for good.

At Kirkton they were surrounded, within a radius of ten miles or so, by a number of entertaining neighbours. Young couples with time and money to spare, some with young children like the Keiles's, all with interests which matched Anthony's.

For appearances' sake, he put in a certain amount of time on the farm, talking to McGregor, the grieve, finding out what McGregor thought should be done, and then telling McGregor to do it. The rest of the day was his own, and he used it to the full, doing exactly what he wanted. Scotland is a country geared to the pleasures of menfolk, and there was always shooting to be got, grouse in the summer, and partridges and pheasants in the autumn and winter. There were rivers to be fished and golf courses and a social life which was even gayer than the one he had left behind in London.

Virginia did not fish or play golf and Anthony would not have invited her to join him even if she had wanted to. He preferred the company of his men friends, and she was expected to be present only when they had been invited specifically as a couple. To a dinner or a dance, or perhaps to lunch before a point-to-point, when she would go through agonies trying to decide what to put on, and inevitably turn up in what everybody had been wearing last year.

She was still shy. And she didn't drink so there seemed no artificial way of getting over this terrible defect. The men, Anthony's friends, obviously thought her a bore. And their wives, though kind and friendly, terrified her with their private jokes and their incomprehensible references to places and persons and events known only to them. They were like a lot of girls who had all been to the same school.

Once, driving home after a dinner party, they quarrelled. Virginia had not meant to quarrel but she was tired and unhappy, and Anthony was more than a little drunk. He always seemed to drink too much at parties, almost as though it were a social grace that was expected of him. This evening it made him aggressive and bad-tempered.

"Well, did you enjoy yourself?"

"Not particularly."

"You certainly didn't look as though you did."

"I was tired."

"You're always tired. And yet you never seem to do a thing."

"Perhaps that's why I'm tired."

"And what does that mean?"

"Oh, nothing."

159

"It has to mean something."

"All right, it means that I get bored and lonely."

"That's not my fault."

"Isn't it? You're never there . . . sometimes you're not in the house all day. You have lunch at the club in Relkirk . . . I never see you."

"OK. Me and about a hundred other chaps. What do you suppose their wives do? Sit and mope?"

"I've wondered what they do with their time. You tell me."

"Well, they get around, that's what. They see each other, take the children to Pony Club meets, play bridge; I suppose, garden."

"I can't play bridge," said Virginia, "and the children don't want to ride ponies, and I would garden only there isn't a garden at Kirkton, just a four-walled prison for flowers, and a bad-tempered gardener who won't let me so much as cut a bunch of gladioli without asking him first."

"Oh, for heaven's sake . . ."

She said, "I watch other people. Ordinary couples, sometimes on Saturdays in Relkirk. Doing the shopping together in the rain or the sunshine, and children with them, sucking ice-creams, and they put all the parcels into shabby little cars and drive home, and they look so happy and cosy, all together."

"Oh, God. You can't want that."

"I want not to be lonely."

"Loneliness is a state of mind. Only you can do anything about that."

"Weren't you ever lonely, Anthony?"

"No."

"Then you didn't marry me for company. And you didn't marry me for my startling conversation."

"No." Coldly agreeing, his profile was stony.

"Then why?"

"You were pretty. You had a certain fawn-like charm. You were very charming. My mother thought you were very charming. She thought your mother was very charming. She thought the whole bloody arrangement was charming."

"But you didn't marry me because your mother told you to."

"No. But you see, I had to marry somebody, and you turned up at such a singularly opportune time."

"I don't understand."

He did not reply to this. For a little he drove in silence, perhaps prompted by some shred of decency not to tell her the truth, now or ever. But Virginia, having come so far, made the mistake of pressing him. "Anthony, I don't understand," and he lost his temper and told her.

"Because I was left Kirkton on condition that I was married when I took it over. Uncle Arthur thought I would never settle down, would break the place up if I moved in as a bachelor . . . I don't know what he thought, but he was determined that if I lived at Kirkton I'd do it as a family man."

"So that's why!"

Anthony frowned. "Are you hurt?"

"I don't think so. Should I be?"

He fumbled for her hand with his own . . . the car swerved slightly as his fingers closed over hers. He said, "It's all right. It may be no better, but it's certainly no worse than other marriages. Sometimes it's a good thing to be frank and clear the air. It's better to know where we both stand."

She said, "Do you ever regret it? Marrying me, I mean."

"No. I don't regret it. I'm just sorry that it had to happen when we were both so young."

161

One day she found herself in the house alone. Quite alone. It was Saturday, and afternoon. Mr McGregor, the grieve, had gone to Relkirk, taking Mrs McGregor with him. Anthony was playing golf, and Nanny and the children were out for a walk. An empty house and nothing to do. No washing to be done, no cake to be baked, no ironing, no garden to weed. Virginia walked through it, going from room to room, as though she were a stranger who had paid to see around, and her footsteps echoed on the polished staircase, and there was the tick of the clock, and everywhere order, neatness. This was what Anthony loved. This was what he had created. This was why he had married her. She ended up in the hall, opened the front door and went down the steps on to the gravel, thinking that she would maybe spy Nanny and the children in the distance; she would go to meet them, run and snatch Cara up in her arms, hug her and hold her, if only to prove that she really existed, that she was not a dream-child that Virginia had conceived, like some frustrated spinster, out of her own imagination.

But there was no sign of Nanny and, after a little, she went back up the steps and so indoors again, because there did not seem to be anywhere else to go.

There was a pretty girl, called Liz, married to a young lawyer. He worked in Edinburgh, but they lived only a mile or two from Kirkton, in an old, converted Presbyterian manse, with a wild garden, that was filled with daffodils in the spring, and a paddock for the ponies.

She had young children, dogs, a cat, and a parrot in a cage, but – perhaps because she missed her husband who was in Edinburgh all week, or perhaps because she was simply a girl who enjoyed people – her house was always full. Other mothers' children lolloped about on the ponies, crowded the dining-room table at tea-time, played rounders on the lawn. If she didn't have whole families staying with her, then she had whole families for the day, feeding them on huge roasts of beef, and steak-and-kidney pies, marvellous old-fashioned puddings, and home-made ice-creams. Her drinks cupboard, which must have taken a frightening beating from the hordes who passed through her hospitable doorway, was always open, always at hand for any guest in need of a little liquid refreshment.

"Help yourself," she would call through the open door, while she knocked up a three-course dinner for ten unexpected guests. "There's ice in the fridge if the ice-bucket's empty."

Anthony, naturally enough, adored her, flirted cheerfully and openly with her, put on a great show of jealousy when the weekends came around and her husband was home.

"Get that bloody man out of the house," he would tell Liz, and she would go into gales of delighted laughter, as would everybody else who was listening. Virginia smiled, and over their heads met the eye of Liz's husband. He was a quiet young man, and though he stood there, with a glass in his hand, smiling, it was almost impossible to tell what he was thinking.

"You'll have to watch out for that husband of yours," one of the other wives said to Virginia. But she only said, "I have been, for years," and changed the subject, or turned to speak to somebody else.

One Tuesday, Anthony called her from the club in Relkirk. "Virginia. Look, I've got embroiled in a poker game, God knows when I'll be home. But don't wait, I'll get a bite to eat here. See you later."

"All right. Don't lose too much money."

"I shall win," he told her. "I shall buy you a mink coat."

"That's just what I need."

He arrived home, after midnight, stumbling up the stairs. She heard him moving about in his dressing-room, dropping things, opening and shutting drawers, swearing at some cuff-link or button.

After a little, she heard him getting into bed, and the light beyond the open door went out, and there was only darkness. And she wondered if he had chosen to sleep in his dressing-room out of consideration to Virginia, or whether there was some other, more sinister reason.

She soon knew. The society in which they moved, the narrow clique, was too small for secrets. "Virginia darling, I told you to watch out for that naughty man of yours."

"What's he done now?"

"You are marvellous, the way you never get ruffled. You obviously know all about it."

"All about what?"

"Darling, the intimate dinner party that he had with Liz."

". . . Oh, yes, of course. Last Tuesday."

"He is an old devil. I suppose he thought none of us would find out. But then Midge and Johnny Gray suddenly decided on the spur of the moment to go up to the Strathtorrie Arms for dinner, you know, there's a new manager now, and it's all frightfully dark and chic and you can get a very good dinner. Anyway, off they went, and of course there were Anthony and Liz, all snugged up in a corner. And you knew all the time!"

"Yes."

"And you don't mind?"

"No."

That was the terrible thing. She didn't mind. She was apathetic, bored by Anthony and the outrageous schoolboy charm that had, as far as Virginia was concerned, long since worn itself to shreds. And this was not the first affair. It had happened before and it would doubtless happen again, but still, it was daunting to look down the years ahead and see herself tied for ever to this tedious Peter Pan. A man so unperceptive that he could gaily embark on a clandestine involvement, and yet conduct the whole affair on what was virtually his own front doorstep.

She thought about divorce, but knew that she would never divorce Anthony, not simply because of the children, but because she was Virginia, and she could no more embark, voluntarily, upon such a course than she could have flown to the moon.

She was not happy, but what would be the good of broadcasting her failure, her disillusion, to the rest of the world? Anthony did not love her, had never loved her. But then she had never loved him. If he had married Virginia to get his hands on Kirkton, then she had married Anthony on the rebound, in an emotional state of extreme unhappiness, and in a desperate bid to avoid the London Season that her mother had planned for her, culminating in the final nightmare of a coming-out dance.

She was not happy, but, to all intents and purposes, she had everything. A lovely house, a handsome husband, and the children. The children were worth everything. For them she would shore up her crumbling marriage, and for them she would create a world of security that they would never know again.

Anthony had been with Liz that night he was killed. He had called in at the Old Manse for a drink on his way back from Relkirk and was invited to stay for supper.

He rang Virginia.

"Liz has got the Cannons staying. She wants me to eat here and make up a four for bridge. I'll be home some time. Don't wait up."

Liz's cupboard with the whisky bottle stood open, as always. And as always Anthony helped himself liberally and with a generous hand. It was two o'clock before he started home, a black and starless night of pouring rain. It had been raining for days and the river was in spate. Afterwards the police came with tape measures and bits of chalk, and they measured the skid marks, and hung over the broken rail of the bridge and stared down into the muddy, swirling waters. And Virginia stood with them, in the drenching rain, and watched the divers go down, and there was a kindly sergeant who kept urging her to go back to the house, but she wouldn't go because, for some reason, she had to be there, because he had been her husband and the father of her children.

And she remembered what he had said, that night he told her about Kirkton. *I'm just sorry that it had to happen when we were both so young.*

8

The quiet night moved slowly past, the seconds, the minutes, the hours, measured by the ticking of Virginia's wristwatch which she had put on the table by her bed. Now, she reached out for it and saw that it was nearly three o'clock in the morning. She got out of bed, wrapped herself in the quilt and went to sit on the floor by the open window. It was the hour before dawn, dark and very still. She could hear, a mile or more away, the gentle movement, like breathing, of the sea. She could hear the soft shufflings and munchings of the Guernseys, grazing two or three fields distant; she could hear rustlings and whisperings and creepings from hedgerow and burrow, and the hooting of a night owl.

She found that she was devilled by the memory of Liz. Liz had come to Anthony's funeral wearing a face of grief and guilt so naked that instinctively one had turned away from it, not wanting to witness such pain. Soon afterwards her husband had taken her to the South of France for a holiday and Virginia had not seen her again.

But now she knew that she must go back to Scotland and soon, if it was only to square things up with Liz. To convince Liz that no blame could ever be laid at her door, to make – as far as was humanly possible – friends with her again. She thought of returning to Kirkton and this time her imagination did not turn and run but took the journey quietly and without horror. Off the road it went, and down over the bridge and the river, and up the drive between the lush meadows of the park. It came to the curving sweep in front of the house, and went up the steps and in through the front door, and now there was no longer the old familiar sensation of loneliness, of being trapped. But simply a sadness that the lives of the people who had lived in this beautiful house had achieved no lasting cohesion, but had unravelled like a length of badly spun yarn, and finally shredded away.

She would sell the house. Somewhere, some time, her subconscious had made the decision and now presented it to her conscious mind as a *fait accompli*. How much this phenomenon had to do with Eustace, Virginia could not at the moment comprehend. Later on, no doubt, it would all work itself out. For now the relief was enormous, like the shedding of a load carried too long, and she felt grateful, as though another person had stepped in and made the decision for her.

She would sell Kirkton. Buy another house, a little house . . . somewhere. Again, later on, it would all work itself out. She would make a new home, new friends, create a garden, buy a puppy, a kitten, a canary in a cage. Find schools for the children, fill the holidays with pleasures she had previously been too diffident to attempt. She would learn to ski; they would go on skiing holidays together. She would build kites and mend bicycles, let Cara read all the books she ever wanted, and go to Nicholas's sports days wearing the right sort of hat, and achieve marvellous things like winning the egg-and-spoon race.

And it would happen because she would make it happen. There was no more Eustace, no more dreams, but other good things were constant. Like pride, and resolution, and the children. The children. And she smiled, knowing that, like the arrow on the compass forever pointing north, whatever she did and however she behaved, she was always left, facing squarely in their direction.

She was beginning to be cold. The first lightening of dawn was beginning to creep up into the sky. She got up off the floor, took a sleeping-pill and a glass of water and climbed back into bed. When she opened her eyes again the sun, high in the sky, was shining full in her face, and from downstairs came a terrible racket, a banging at the front door and a voice calling her name.

''Virginia! It's me. Alice! Wake up, or are you all dead?''

Dazed with shock and sleep, Virginia stumbled out of bed, across the floor, and hung out of the window. ''Alice! Stop making such a din. The children are asleep.''

Alice, foreshortened, turned up an astonished face. Her voice dropped to an exaggerated stage-whisper. ''I'd begun to think you'd all passed out. It's past ten. Come down and let me in!''

Yawning, incapable, Virginia groped for her dressing-gown, pushed her feet into slippers and went downstairs, pausing at the open door of the children's room on the way. To her surprise they were still asleep, undisturbed by Alice's shouting. She thought, we must have been late last night. We must have been much later than I realised.

She unlocked the door, to let in a flood of sunshine and Alice. Alice wore a crisp blue linen dress, a silk scarf over her head. As usual she was bright-skinned, clear-eyed, maddeningly awake.

''Do you usually wake up at this hour?''

''No, but – '' Virginia swallowed a yawn '' – I couldn't get to sleep last night. Eventually I took a pill. It must have knocked me out.''

"And the children?"

"I didn't give them a pill, but they're still asleep. We were late, we were out all day." She yawned again, forced her eyes open. "How about some coffee?"

Alice looked amused. "You certainly look as though you'll need some. I tell you what. I'll make it, you go and get yourself woken up, and put some clothes on. It's no good talking to you when you're in this state." She laid her handbag on the table in a purposeful way. "I must say, this really isn't too bad a little house, is it? And here's the kitchen. A little poky, perhaps, but perfectly adequate . . ."

Virginia ran a bath, got into it and washed her hair. Afterwards, she went upstairs, wrapped in a towel, and took clean clothes from the drawer, and a cotton dress, as yet unworn, from the wardrobe. She pushed her feet into sandals, combed her sleek wet hair into place, and feeling clean and strangely hungry, went back downstairs to Alice.

She found her thoroughly organised, the kettle on the gas, the jug ready with the coffee, mugs laid out on the table.

"Oh, there you are . . . we're just about ready . . . I thought we'd have proper coffee; I get so fed up with this wishy-washy stuff, don't you?"

Virginia sat on the edge of the table. "When did you get back from London?"

"Last night."

"How was it? Did you have fun?"

"Yes, but I didn't come here to talk about London."

"In that case, what brought you here at ten o'clock on a Monday morning?"

"Curiosity," said Alice. "Sheer, undiluted curiosity."

"About me?"

"About Eustace Philips!"

Virginia said, "I don't understand."

"Mrs Jilkes told me. I was scarcely in through the front door when I was hearing all about it. She said that Eustace had telephoned her while I was away to ask if anybody was getting Bosithick ready for you and the children. And she said I was in London, and he said not to bother, he'd see to it."

"Yes, that's right . . . and he did too . . ."

"But Virginia . . . You talked about Eustace, but you never told me that you'd met him again."

"Didn't I?" Virginia frowned. "No, I didn't, did I?"

"But when did you meet him?"

"That day I came out to see the cottage. Do you remember? I said I wouldn't be back for lunch. And I went to the pub in Lanyon to buy cigarettes and I met him there."

"But why didn't you say anything about it? Was there any particular reason that you didn't want me to know?"

"No." She tried to remember. "But I suppose I just didn't want to talk about him." She smiled. "It wasn't as though it had been such a friendly reunion. In fact, we had the most terrible row . . ."

"But did you *mean* to meet him again?"

"No. It just happened."

"And he remembered you? After all this time? But he'd only ever seen you that once at the barbecue."

"No," said Virginia. "I did see him again."

"*When?*"

"About a week after the barbecue. I met him in Porthkerris. We spent the afternoon together and he drove me back to Wheal House. You didn't see him because you were out that day. But my mother was there. She knew about it."

171

"But why was it all kept such a secret?"

"It wasn't a secret, Alice. It was just that my mother didn't like Eustace. I must say, he didn't make much of an effort to impress her, and he was rude and the Land-Rover was covered with bits of straw and mud and manure . . . not my mother's cup of tea at all. She treated the whole incident as though it were a sort of joke, but I knew that he had made her angry, and that she didn't like him."

"But you could have talked to me about him. After all, it was I who introduced you to Eustace."

"I tried, but every time I started, my mother somehow broke into the conversation or changed the subject or interrupted in some way. And . . . you mustn't forget this, Alice . . . you were her friend, not mine. I was just the little girl, out of the nursery. I never imagined for a moment that you'd take my side against hers."

"Was it a question of taking sides?"

"It would have been. You know what a snob she was."

"Oh, yes, of course, but it was harmless."

"No, Alice, it wasn't harmless. It was terribly dangerous. It affected everything she did. It deformed her."

"Virginia!" Alice was shocked.

"That's why we suddenly went back to London. You see, she knew, she guessed right away, that I was in love with Eustace."

The kettle boiled. Alice lifted it, and filled the coffee jug, and the kitchen was suffused with a delicious fresh smell. Alice drew a spoon gently across the surface of the coffee.

"And were you?" she asked at last. "In love with Eustace?"

"Of course I was. Wouldn't you have been at seventeen?"

"But you married Anthony Keile."

172

"Yes."

"Did you love him?"

"I . . . I married him."

"Were you happy?"

"I was lonely . . ."

"But, Virginia, I always thought . . . I mean, your mother always said . . . I thought you were so happy," Alice finished, hopeless with confusion.

"No. But it wasn't all Anthony's fault. It was my fault, too."

"Did Lady Keile know this?"

"No." Nor did she know the circumstances of Anthony's death. Nor did she know about Liz. Nor was she ever going to. "Why should she know? She used to come and stay with us, but never for more than a week at a time. It wasn't difficult to foster the illusion of an idyllically happy marriage. It was the least we could do for her . . ."

"I'm surprised Nanny never said anything."

"Nanny never saw anything she didn't want to see. And to her, Anthony was perfection."

"It can't have been easy."

"No, but like I said, it wasn't all Anthony's fault."

"And Eustace?"

"Alice, I was seventeen; a little girl, waiting for someone to come and buy her an ice-cream."

"But not now . . ." said Alice.

"No. Now I'm twenty-seven and the mother of two children. And I'm not waiting for ice-creams any longer."

"You mean, he has nothing to give you."

"And he needs nothing from me. He's self-sufficient. He has his own life. He has Penfolda."

"Have you discussed this with him?"

173

"Oh, Alice . . ."

"You obviously haven't. So how can you be so certain?"

"Because all those years ago, he said he'd phone me. He said that he wanted me to come out to Penfolda for tea or something, to meet his mother again. And I was going to borrow your car and drive myself out here. But you see, he never telephoned. I waited, but he never telephoned. And before there was time to find out why, or do anything about it, I'd been whisked back to London by my mother."

Alice said, "And how do you *know* he never telephoned?" She was beginning to sound impatient.

"Because he never did."

"Perhaps your mother took the call."

"I asked her. And she said there'd never been any telephone call."

"But, Virginia, she was perfectly capable of taking a call and never telling you about it. Specially if she didn't like the young man. Surely you realised that."

Her voice was brisk and practical. Virginia stared, scarcely able to believe her ears. That Alice should say such things about Rowena Parsons – Alice of all people, her mother's oldest friend. Alice, coming out with a dark truth that Virginia had never had the courage to find out for herself. She remembered her mother's face, smiling across the railway carriage, the laughing protest. *Darling! What an accusation. Of course not. You surely didn't think* . . .

And Virginia had believed her. She said at last, helplessly, "I thought she was telling me the truth. I didn't think she was capable of lying."

"Let's say she was a determined person. And you were her only child. She always had great ambitions for you."

174

"You knew this. You knew this about her and yet she was still your friend."

"Friends aren't people you particularly like for any special reason. You just like people because they're your friends."

"But if she was lying, then Eustace must have thought that I didn't want to see him again. All these years he's been thinking I simply let him down."

"But he wrote you a letter," said Alice.

"A *letter*?"

"Oh, Virginia, don't be so dense. That letter that came for you. The day before you went back to London." Virginia continued to stare blankly. "I know there was a letter. It came by the afternoon post, and it was on the table in the hall and I thought 'How nice' because you didn't get many letters. And then I went off to do something or other and when I came back the letter had gone. I presumed you'd taken it."

A letter. Virginia saw the letter. Imagined the envelope as white, the writing very black, addressed to her. Miss Virginia Parsons. Lying unattended and vulnerable upon that round table that still stood in the centre of the hall at Wheal House. She saw her mother come out of the drawing-room, perhaps on her way upstairs, pause to inspect the afternoon's mail. She was wearing the raspberry-red suit with the white silk shirt, and when she put out her hand to pick up the letter, her nails were painted the same raspberry-red, and her heavy gold charm bracelet made a jingling sound, like bells.

She saw her frown at the writing, the black masculine writing, inspect the postmark, hesitate for perhaps a second, and then slip the envelope into the pocket of her jacket and carry on with what she was doing, unperturbed, as though nothing had happened.

175

She said, "Alice, I never got that letter."

"But it was there!"

"Don't you see? Mother must have taken it. Destroyed it. She would, you know. She would say, 'It's all for Virginia's sake. For Virginia's own good.' "

Illusions were gone for ever, the veil torn away. She could look back with a cool, objective regard and see her mother the way she had really been, not merely snobbish and determined, but devious too. In some odd way, this was a relief. It had taken some effort, all these years, to sustain the legend of an irreproachable parent, even though Virginia had been deceiving nobody but herself. Now, remembered, she seemed much more human.

Alice was looking upset, as though already regretting any mention of the letter.

"Perhaps it wasn't from Eustace."

"It was."

"How do you know?"

"Because if it had been from anyone else, then she would have given it back to me, with some excuse or other about opening it by mistake."

"But we don't know what was in the letter."

Virginia got off the table. "No. But I'm going to find out. Now. Will you stay here till the children wake up? Will you tell them I shan't be long?"

"But where are you going?"

"To see Eustace, of course," said Virginia, from the door.

"But you haven't drunk your coffee. I made you coffee and you haven't even drunk it. And what are you going to say to him? And how are you going to explain?"

But Virginia had already gone. Alice was speaking to an

176

empty room, an open, swinging door. With an exclamation of exasperation, she put down her coffee-cup and went to the door as though to call Virginia back, but Virginia was already out of earshot, running like a child through the tall summer grass, across the fields in the direction of Penfolda.

She took the field path because it would have taken too long to get into the car and turn it and drive back along the main road. And time was too precious to be wasted. They had already lost ten years, and there was not another moment to spare.

She was running, through a joyous morning of honey-scents and white daisies and tall grass that whipped at her bare legs. The sea was a dark, purplish blue, striped with ribbons of turquoise, and the horizon was blurred in a haze that promised great heat. She was running, long-legged, taking the steps of the stiles two at a time, and the ditches of the stubble fields brimmed with red poppies and the air was filled with the petals of yellow gorse flowers, blown to confusion, like confetti, by the sea-wind.

She came across the last field, and Penfolda lay ahead of her, the house and the long barns, and the little garden, wall-enclosed from the wind. She went over the last stile that led into the vegetable garden, and down the path and through the gate, and she saw that the cat and her half-Siamese kittens lay in the sun on the doorstep, and the front door stood open and she went indoors and called Eustace, and the house was dark after the brightness of the day outside.

"Who's that?"

It was Mrs Thomas, carrying a duster, peering over the banister.

"It's me. Virginia. Virginia Keile. I'm looking for Eustace."

"He's just coming in from milking . . ."

"Oh, thank you." Without bothering to wait and explain, she

went back out of doors, and started across the lawn, making for the cattle court and the milking parlour. But at that moment he appeared, coming through the gate that opened into the far side of the garden. He was in shirt-sleeves, aproned, wearing rubber boots and carrying a polished aluminium pail of milk. Virginia stopped dead. He closed the latch of the gate behind him and looked up and saw her.

She had meant to be very sensible. To say, calmly and quietly, "I want to ask you about the letter you wrote me." But it didn't happen like that at all. For everything was said in that long moment, while they stood and looked at each other, and then Eustace set down his bucket and started towards her, and she ran down the slope of the grass and into his arms, and she was laughing, her face pressed into the front of his shirt, and he was saying, "It's all right. It's all right," just as though she were crying, not laughing. And Virginia said, "I love you," and then she burst into tears.

He said, "Of course I telephoned. Three or four times. But you were never there. It was always your mother and each time I felt more of a fool and each time she said that she'd tell you I'd called and that you'd ring me back. And I thought maybe you'd changed your mind. I thought perhaps you'd decided you had better things to do than come and have tea with someone like me and my old mother. I thought maybe your mother had talked you round. She didn't lose any love on me, not from the first moment she set eyes on me. But you knew that, didn't you?"

"Yes, I knew. And I wondered. Once, I nearly rang you up. I thought perhaps you'd forgotten . . . and then I lost my nerve. And then, out of the blue, my mother said we had to go back to London and after that, there wasn't any time. And in the train, I asked her, straight out, if you'd ever called and she said never. And I believed her. That was the terrible thing, I always believed her. I should have known. It was my fault, I should have known. Oh, Eustace, why was I such a ninny?''

They had come indoors, ostensibly to find a clean handkerchief for Virginia, and for no particular reason had stayed there, ending up, inevitably, in the kitchen, sitting at the scrubbed table, with the air filled with the smell of baking saffron bread, and the only sound to disturb them the slow ticking of the old-fashioned pendulum clock.

''You weren't a ninny,'' said Eustace. ''You were seventeen. That was another of the things that bothered me. It would have been easy to persuade you, push you around, before you'd even had time to grow up and make up your own mind about things. That's what I said in the letter. When you never rang me back, I thought maybe you'd got cold feet. So I said that if you wanted to wait a couple of years, I'd be ready to wait too, see how we felt about things then.'' He grinned, ruefully. ''It took some writing, I can tell you. I'd never said such things to a girl before, nor have since.''

''And you thought I'd never even bothered to reply?''

''I didn't know what to think . . . And then, the next thing, I saw in the paper that you were getting married.''

''Eustace, if I'd got the letter, I wouldn't have gone back to London. I'd have refused.''

''You couldn't refuse, you were under age.''

''I'd have had hysterics, then. A nervous breakdown. Made the most ghastly scenes. Made myself ill.''

''You'd still have gone.''

She knew that he was right. ''But I'd have known you were there, waiting. And I would never have married Anthony. I

179

would never have gone to Scotland. I would never have wasted all these years.''

Eustace raised his eyebrows. ''Wasted? They weren't wasted. What about Cara and Nicholas?''

Virginia's eyes stung with sudden tears. She said, ''Now it's all too complicated.''

He put his arms around her, kissed the tears away, pushed her hair back off her face. He said, ''Things happen the way they're meant to. There's a pattern and a shape to everything. You look back and see it all. Nothing happens without a reason. Nothing is impossible, like meeting again, walking into The Mermaid's Arms and seeing you sitting there, just as though you'd never been away. Like a miracle.''

''You didn't behave as though it were a miracle. In no time at all you were bawling at me.''

''I was scared of getting hurt a second time. I was scared that I'd been mistaken about you, that all the things that were so important to your mother had become important to you, too.''

''I told you. They were never important.''

He took her hand in his. ''After the picnic yesterday, I thought it was going to be all right. After being with you and Cara and Nicholas, and swimming and cooking the fish, and you all seeming to enjoy it so much, I thought then, coming up the cliff, that it was like being back where we started. And I thought I would be able to talk about that time, when you went back to London and I was left not knowing what had happened, and we never saw each other again. I thought we could have talked about it, perhaps made a new beginning.''

''But I was thinking the same, you stupid man, and all you did was to tell me to go back to Scotland and learn how to be a farmer. I want to be a farmer's wife, but I don't want to be a

180

farmer. And I wouldn't know one end of an Aberdeen Angus herd from the other."

Eustace grinned again, faintly sheepish. "I told you, it was those photographs of Cara's. We'd seemed so close all day, and all at once I realised that we weren't close, we belonged to different worlds. We always have done, Virginia. A place like Kirkton and a little farm like Penfolda, well, you just don't talk about them in the same breath. And suddenly it seemed insane to imagine that I could ask you to leave all that, give it all up, just for the sake of being with me. Because that's all I've got to offer."

"And that's what I want. That's all I've ever wanted. Kirkton was Anthony's house. Without him to keep it going, it has no life at all. Anyway, I'm going to sell it. I decided last night. I shall have to go back, of course, break the news to everybody, put the whole thing in the lawyer's hands . . ."

"Have you thought about the children?"

"I never stop thinking about them. And they'll understand."

"It's their home."

"Penfolda's going to be their home." She smiled at the thought, and Eustace took her shoulders between his big hands and leaned forward to kiss her open, smiling mouth. "A new home and a new father," she finished when she had got her breath back.

But Eustace did not seem to be listening to her. "Talk of the devil," he said.

And Virginia heard the children, coming across the garden, talking, their voices high-pitched.

"Look, there are the kittens. Look, they're in the sun, and they haven't drunk their milk."

"Oh, leave them, Nicholas. They're having a sleep."

"This one isn't sleeping. It's got its eyes open. Look. Its eyes are open."

"I wonder where Mummy is? Mummy!"

"In here," called Eustace.

"Mummy, Aunt Alice Lingard wants to know if you're ever coming home again." Cara appeared at the kitchen door, her spectacles crooked, her hair hanging out of its slide. "She gave us some bacon and eggs, but we've been waiting and waiting and she says Mrs Jilkes will think that she's been in a car accident, and died . . ."

"Yes," said Nicholas, appearing, hard on her heels, with a kitten spread-eagled by pin-like claws across the front of his sweater. "And we didn't wake up till ten past ten when Aunt Alice came up to see us, and we very nearly didn't have any breakfast at all, we very nearly just waited until lunch-time . . . but I was . . . so hungry . . ."

His voice trailed away. He had realised that nobody was talking but him. His mother and Eustace were simply sitting, watching him, and Cara was staring at her mother as though she had never seen her before. Nicholas was disconcerted. "Well, what's wrong? Why isn't anybody talking?"

"We're waiting for you to stop," said Virginia.

"Why?"

Virginia looked at Eustace. Eustace leaned forward to draw Cara towards him. Very gently, seriously, he set her spectacles straight. Then Nicholas saw that he was smiling.

"We've got something to tell you," said Eustace.